THE COMPLETE
ALIENS™
COLLECTION
LIVING NIGHTMARES

ALIENS: PHALANX
by Scott Sigler

ALIENS: INFILTRATOR
by Weston Ochse

ALIENS: VASQUEZ
by V. Castro

THE COMPLETE ALIEN™ LIBRARY FROM TITAN BOOKS

THE COMPLETE
ALIENS™
COLLECTION
LIVING NIGHTMARES

ALIENS: PHALANX
by Scott Sigler

ALIENS: INFILTRATOR
by Weston Ochse

ALIENS: VASQUEZ
by V. Castro

TITAN BOOKS

THE COMPLETE ALIENS COLLECTION: LIVING NIGHTMARES

Print edition ISBN: 9781803366609
E-book edition ISBN: 9781803366616

Published by Titan Books
A division of Titan Publishing Group Ltd
144 Southwark Street, London SE1 0UP
www.titanbooks.com

First edition: November 2024
10 9 8 7 6 5 4 3 2 1

A CIP catalogue record for this title is available from the British Library.

Printed and bound by CPI Group (UK) Ltd,
Croydon CR0 4YY.

CONTENTS

BOOK ONE

PHALANX

A PLEA FROM ME, THE AUTHOR, TO YOU, THE READER— *NO SPOILERS*

We live in an interconnected world. Everything you put online—from a blog post, to reviews on Amazon and Goodreads, to a YouTube comment, to a simple Tweet—is instantly visible to other readers interested in the same kind of books you are. I have worked hard to craft a compelling story with what I hope are some unexpected twists. If you choose to discuss ALIENS: PHALANX online, please be courteous to your fellow readers and avoid mentioning these surprises.

Those of us who love reading know there is only one chance to enjoy a book for the first time. Those of us who adore the ALIENS franchise get precious few moments to discover new elements of this enduring universe. Whether you love or hate this book, I encourage you to tell people how you feel about it, but please consider the enjoyment of others. Avoid posting spoilers, and let people experience this story for themselves.

Thank you.

Scott
@scottsigler

To Myke Cole, whose book LEGION VS. PHALANX *was instrumental in the writing of this story. Thank you for answering my constant barrage of questions about ranks, spears and shields, thank you for your friendship, and thank you for your service to the United States of America.*

Dinashin River

iseth

Lake
Mip

Takanta

Vinden

Rhimbis River

A T A E G I N A

1

Stillness is strength.

The black demon came closer.

Ahiliyah stayed strong.

She breathed slow, steady, deep. The way Aiko had taught her.

Ahiliyah moved nothing, save for eyelids; she even blinked slowly, making no motion that might draw the beast's attention.

Her gloved hand gripped the handle of her knife, the kind called *little friend*. Not a loose grip, where the knife might fall and make noise. Not a tight grip, either, where her hand might tire, start to shake, make her breathe faster.

The demon's rigid belly stayed low to the ground, its four backsticks reaching up to the noonday sun. Its tail—a black spine as long as its body, ending in a vicious blade of bone—twitched behind it. A long, thin arm reached out, spindly hand silently resting on a rock. The big body moved forward, a silent shadow.

The demon stopped, still as the mountain itself.

Black lips curled back. Sunlight gleamed off metallic teeth. The jaws slowly opened; the toothtongue extended. It, too, opened—the demon let out a low, barely audible hiss. It angled its long black head left, then right.

It was hunting. If it found her, she would die.

Had it seen her? Had it seen Brandun or Creen? Ahiliyah didn't know where her crewmates had hidden. She dared not move her head, even a inch. If the demon spotted big Brandun or little Creen, there was nothing she could do for the boys.

If the demon saw them, they had their own little friends.

She'd observed the black beasts dozens of times, usually from a great distance. This was only the fourth time she'd been this close, close enough to count teeth.

The first time, she'd been lucky—her crewmates had survived.

The second time, Heyran Bouchard had died.

The third time, Admar Polous had been carried off.

The demon started moving again, stop-starting its way across the fallen, bleached trunks of alkan trees, through the thick, crimson leaves of the caminus bushes, over the rain-streaked, moss-spotted grey boulders and jagged piles of broken stone.

She silently wished for the beast to move faster, to rise up on two legs the way they sometimes had when she saw them from far away, in the night when there were no clouds to block the glow of the Three Sisters. But this one, moving in daylight… so rare.

That was how it almost got them. They hadn't been expecting it. She couldn't say that Brandun and Creen had grown careless, but she *could* say they hadn't been as careful as they should have been. Brandun had stepped on a stick, broken it, a noise so loud it echoed lightly off the mountainside. He and Creen had kept walking. They'd stopped only because Ahiliyah ordered them to follow Aiko's rules: hide, listen, wait.

Brandun and Creen had both groaned. Creen complained that he'd been walking for days, he didn't want to wait. It was daytime, and the demons rarely came out during the day. Brandun complained too, which he only did when Creen was around.

As the crew leader, Ahiliyah had pulled rank, threatened them with punishment if they disobeyed. They'd listened. Because of that, hopefully, they might survive.

Of the three, one had to make it back.

The demon crawled, stopped, crawled some more. Death, silent and sure. Not coming directly at her, but moving in her direction. They looked different in daylight. It wasn't shiny, like getum bugs were, but sunlight did gleam from various areas. At night, the demons merged with the dark, were nearly invisible against a rock face or in the trees and bushes. In the day, though, they were far easier to spot.

For three years, with her first run coming at dawn on her sixteenth birthday, Ahiliyah Cooper had done her duty, making the long walks between the holds, always in daylight. While those hikes frightened her—frightened everyone with even an ounce of smarts—it was the long hours between sunset and sunrise that brought true terror.

Because the demons mostly came at night.

The black beast stopped again, sinuous left arm paused in mid-reach. The long head slowly turned her way. No eyes on that curved surface, but... was it looking at her?

A light breeze blew in, carrying its scent to her, strangely similar to the richness of damp moss peeled back from a wet rock. She could smell it—could it smell her? Two days since she'd last bathed, hiking and sweating during every minute of sunlight, sleeping in her unwashed clothes. She *stank*.

If the breeze changed, if it smelled her, would she die?

Ahiliyah realized she was clutching the knife handle too hard. She forced herself to relax, settling into that perfect balance between *too strong* and *too loose*. In that moment, the knife truly was her little friend.

If the demon came for her, would she have the will to use the blade?

In Heyran's moment of truth, he'd done what Aiko had trained him to do. When the demon had come for him, Heyran drove the point of his little friend deep into the right side of his own neck, just below his jaw. He'd sliced outward, away from his body, worsening the cut.

Then, as now, Ahiliyah had been hiding. Hiding and watching. She'd seen Heyran's blood spray across the demon's horrid black head. In death, Heyran had helped his people by depriving the demons of one more crawling black spot of evil.

Heyran Bouchard had been strong—Admar Polous had not.

Admar ignored his training. Instead of using his little friend, he'd drawn his spearhead from its back-scabbard and tried to fight. She didn't know if Admar had landed a blow or not. If he had, the spearhead hadn't slowed the beast in the slightest. Black talons sliced through hidey suit, clothing and skin. Admar had screamed, just once, then the demon had carried him away, never to be seen again.

Would it soon be Ahiliyah's moment of truth? If this demon came for her, would she be strong like Heyran, or weak like Admar?

It was only ten steps away now.

Moving, looking, hunting.

Eight steps.

Her breath came slightly faster, perceptibly shallower—fear, taking control.

Silence is strength.

Ahiliyah forced herself still. All the training she had endured to learn how to control her breathing—Aiko screaming at her, beating her, drilling the mantras into her head—preparing her for a moment just like this.

Her breathing slowed, deepened, even as the demon crawled closer.

Six steps.

The beast hesitated, lowered the hand to the ground. Its head angled left, then right.

Had it heard her breathing? Was that what it had been homing in on?

Aiko wasn't her only teacher—there was also Sinesh.

Sinesh Bishor never hit her, but his lessons were just as exhausting.

When death comes, see the beauty in life.

How many times had Sinesh told her that? How many times had he told her stories of his days in the shield line, of standing face to face with men who were trying to kill him, so close they could touch, so close they could kiss?

See the beauty. Ahiliyah did as Sinesh had taught. She widened her vision, took in all before her. The tans and grays of the mountain's endless stone. The bleached tans of old logs. The deep crimson of the caminus bushes. The brownish-yellow moss. The pale green-white pokey plants that had managed to find a patch of soil. The blue sky. The mountain's rich fragrance.

She felt… calm. Death was a few steps away, one sniff or one cough or one whimper away, and she felt at peace. It took another step toward her—her time had come.

In her mind, she walked through her training: lift her little friend, turn the blade, stab *hard*, not at her neck, but *through* it, then pull the blade out while pushing it forward. There would be pain—pain that would not last long.

Another step. The mouth opened again…

The rustle of distant trees. A breeze pushed her hidey suit netting up against her face.

The demon's head slowly turned. The beast stayed motionless for a long moment, then scurried away, faster than the shadow of a flying bird.

The breeze blew harder. Ahiliyah closed her eyes, listened to that glorious sound. Had the sound of blowing trees and bushes and grass saved her?

She counted as Aiko had trained her to do, breathing steadily, concentrating on the numbers. When her count reached two thousand, she finally allowed herself to move. Little friend held in her gloved hand, Ahiliyah stepped out from the bush.

Wind caressed the mountain, rustling through the bushes, making the pokey plants bend. A rattlewing launched from a tree, fluttered noisily through the air and flapped off into the distance.

As if that flight had been a signal to the world, the sounds of the mountain animals returned. The high-pitched chirps of getum bugs. The piercing *vin-DEEE, vin-DEEE* of a vindeedee, hidden somewhere in a clump of pokey plants. The deep *goon-goon-gaaaahn* of a nearby humped gish that was probably hunting the vindeedee. The throaty *voot-voot-VERT* of a vootervert, once again happily digging away at a burrow.

The creatures always knew when a demon was about—their silence was as deafening as any alarm. When they again let loose with their music, the demon was almost assuredly gone.

Almost assuredly.

Relief flooded through Ahiliyah—she might live to see another day. Glancing up, she saw that the sun had moved farther in the sky. How long had she stayed hidden? Two hours? Perhaps a little bit more. Ahiliyah slowly turned her head, searching the mountain face, the bushes, the trees… she couldn't see Brandun or Creen.

She made the sound of a vootervert. From higher up the slope came an answering *voot-voot-VERT*, as did one from a bush a few yards away.

"Come out," she said.

Brandun stood first. He'd been higher up the slope, his hidey suit thick with fresh moss and threaded with dead sticks that helped break up his outline. He was only fifteen. He should have had another year in the hold, but he was so big the council had started him early. Already six feet tall, weighing over a hundred bricks, if his growth spurt continued his size would soon make him a liability on runs.

The bigger you are, the easier it is for the demons to see you.

"I thought you were dead," he said softly. "I almost peed myself."

This was his second run. He'd made his first with her as well; on that run they'd seen a demon, but only from a great distance.

He came closer to her, until his wide shoulders blocked out the sun. Ahiliyah didn't know if he stood so near because he was afraid, and took comfort by her, or because he just didn't understand the concept of personal space. So big, and only *fifteen*—someday, he might be the biggest person in Lemeth Hold.

"The world went quiet," he said. "Does that always happen when a demon comes?"

"Yes, but don't count on it. Sometimes they hide. They can stay still for a long time, long enough that the animals forget they are there and start making noise again. That's why you have to use everything— your ears, your eyes, even your nose. Did you smell it? A smell like rock when you peel moss away?"

Brandun shook his head. "No, I didn't smell it."

"I can sure smell you, you giant stinky fuck." Creen Dinashin stepped out from the bush. He was a head shorter than Ahiliyah, just as Ahiliyah was a head shorter than Brandun. Creen's hidey suit was so stuffed with caminus leaves he couldn't put his arms all the way down. So many leaves threaded into his gloves she couldn't make out his fingers. He looked like a walking crimson teddy bear. He flipped his face netting up on top of his head, revealing his ever-present sneer and his blazing orange-yellow eyes.

Creen's nose wrinkled with a theatrical sniff. "I smell shit. You shit yourself, Brandun?"

"I did not," Brandun said. "But I wish the demon had taken you, so I wouldn't have to listen to your mouth anymore."

"Fuck off." Creen glanced to the sky. "We lost time. I don't want to sleep outside for another fucking night. I want to be home with a big, hot mug of tea. The wind's getting stronger, Liyah—can we double-time it? We can use our torches, we might make it back before nightfall."

This was his third run, yet still he hadn't learned. As smart as Creen was—smarter than anyone Ahiliyah had ever met—he liked to cut corners, try to take shortcuts.

"Wind is a double-edged blade," she said. "They can't hear us, but we can't hear them. And torches? Do you *want* the demons to find us?"

Creen patted the sides of his hidey suit. "We're *required* to carry three torches on every run, plus matches—why do we have them if we never use them?"

"They're for emergencies, you know that," Ahiliyah said. "We're *not* making it back tonight. With the wind blowing, be sure you're looking all around you, not just straight ahead, got it?"

Both boys nodded.

"Good," she said. "Now, come look at this." She moved to where the demon had been, knelt next to a half-footprint left in the dirt. "I've been learning how to track them."

Creen blinked, shook his head. "You've been working on *what*?"

"How to track them," Liyah said.

Creen reached into his hidey suit, drew his little friend, held the blade point near his throat.

"I should just kill myself now and save time, because my crew leader is *fucking insane*. We want to stay the hell away from them. Why would we want to *track* them?"

Sometimes, she hated Creen Dinashin with all that she was.

"So we can know our enemy," Ahiliyah said. "That's why."

Brandun knelt, touched the footprint. "Because, someday, we'll hunt them instead of them hunting us."

Creen slowly pretended to slice his own throat. "We all know I'm smarter than both of you, but you don't need to find ways to make it so glaringly obvious. Can we go now?"

Ahiliyah walked back to the bush that had hidden her from the demon. She retrieved her heavy, overstuffed backpack. That was part of the training—once you find a place to hide, drop your pack. That way, if a demon took a runner, one of the runner's crewmates could make sure that the letters, medicine, and other precious cargo might still make it home.

"Get your packs," she said. "Let's get as far as we can before dark."

2

Never the same route twice.

One of the running mantras. Ahiliyah followed it religiously. She'd learned it from Aiko, who'd learned it from Colson Yinnish, who'd learned it from Olliana Ming.

Demons tended to avoid dense underbrush, loose stones, anything that might make noise to alert their prey. But no one knew if they could identify foot-worn trails through those same areas. No one knew if they could track people. No one knew if they might quietly follow a runner, hoping to discover a hold. Because of these things, runners needed to reconnoiter a new route every single time they traveled from hold to hold, including the trips home.

Home. After a grueling, nine-day run, with the sun nearing the horizon, Ahiliyah and her crew finally saw the familiar slopes of Lemeth Mountain. They'd be safely inside before daylight vanished, but they couldn't rush things now, because, here, demons weren't the only danger.

Traps of all kinds lined the winding climb to the ridge, to the entrance of Lemeth Hold. Traps that would kill demons, raiders, war parties and—unfortunately—runners. Subtle markers showed the only safe route up: dead trees with intentionally broken branches pointing inward toward the path; bushes with crimson leaves partially stripped on one side; broken rocks with the less-weathered, lighter part facing in.

The winding approach was thirty feet wide in most places, offering enough space that runners didn't have to follow the same path every time. Ahiliyah, Brandun and Creen worked their way up, choosing the firm, print-less surface of rocks or boulders whenever possible.

Long ago—well before the Rising, even—Lemeth Hold had been part of King Paul's Crown of War, a series of fortresses carved into the mountains themselves. In those fortresses, so the story went, King Paul the Unifier had garrisoned troops, troops ready to march down the mountainsides and attack any lowland cities that might rebel against his rule. When King Paul died, the fortresses had been largely abandoned. They'd lain unused for a century.

Without maintenance, Lemeth's outer wall had become little more than a ruin. Huge stones had come loose and tumbled down the slope, leaving gaps that made the wall look like the rotted brown teeth of someone suffering from weakling disease.

There were places where the wall still stood, secretly maintained in a way that ensured it didn't *look* maintained. Vertical slots lined the stone every five yards. Long ago, those slots allowed archers to launch death down upon advancing troops. Now, though, the slits were useless—demons were so fast they were hard to hit, and a single bolt barely slowed them down.

Above the old wall ran a thick stone lid, once meant as protection against showers of rain, or of arrows. Much of that lid had long-since collapsed, either because of natural forces or through the efforts of the hold's stone-masons, to help make the place look even more abandoned.

"About fucking time," Creen said. "This pack is killing me."

Ahiliyah could sympathize. Beneath her hidey suit, her shoulders were rubbed raw; nine days with the heavy pack had taken their toll.

"I'm glad to be home," Brandun said. "So glad."

His pack was much larger and heavier than Ahiliyah's or Creen's, yet the big boy didn't complain, didn't lose focus. He remained cautious and alert; Ahiliyah could see it in his actions, hear it in his voice. That was good. This close to the end of a run, some people got careless. If Brandun kept up his discipline, he might survive long enough to become a slash.

If he reached that mark, his running days would end. For most boys, five runs completed their obligation. That was how it would work for Brandun, certainly; as big as he was, the warriors couldn't wait to get their hands on him. There was even a rumor he was already being considered for the Hold Guard, the protectors and enforcers of Margrave Aulus Darby.

Five and done for most boys—but girls had to do ten.

From the age of sixteen to the age of thirty, women were obligated to serve the hold as runners. There were only three ways to get out of that duty: death, complete ten runs and become a double-slash, or get knocked up.

Those with child, or those who had given birth in the last six months, were exempt from runs. Because of that, most of the girls who got pregnant *stayed* pregnant, as often as they could, until they reached their thirtieth birthday.

"I don't feel so good," Creen said.

Ahiliyah shook her head. "I told you to go easy."

"But we never get berries below," he said, groaning in discomfort. "I can't wait to get inside and squat on a real toilet. I'm so fucking sick of wiping my ass with bush leaves."

Ahiliyah heard Creen's anger and frustration. The constant fear of a run caused some runners to become quiet, trembling things, scared of every shadow. With other people—people like Creen—that fear manifested in a slow-burning rage.

Admar had been like that. Admar died on his third run.

Halfway up the approach, they reached the signaling point. Ahiliyah stopped there, stared up at the steep incline. Dozens of traps lined the ruined wall. Boulders, blocks and piles of rocks were precariously held in place by linchpin stones; kick the wrong branch, step on the wrong stone, use the wrong root to pull yourself up, and death would tumble down far faster than you—or even a demon— could move out of the way.

If the demons finally came calling to Lemeth Hold, many of them would be smashed flat.

"Creen," Ahiliyah said, "call up."

Creen made the vindeedee's high-pitched call. Brandun's voice was already too deep to make the sound. Ahiliyah could make it, but Creen was better. It was impossible to tell the difference between his call and the real thing.

Moments later, an answering, higher-pitched vindeedee call, followed by the low croak of a humped gish—*goon-goon-GAAAAAN*. Ahiliyah reached through her hidey suit netting into her thigh pocket, felt for and found the preserved gish throat-box with its tanned air-bladder. She blew into the throat-box. The bladder filled with air. She slowly squeezed it, matching the rhythm—*goon-goon-GAAAAAN*.

Up on the ridge, a tiny, hidey-suited head peeked over the old wall. The voice of a little girl called out, a practiced whisper-shout that would not carry, would not echo across the mountain.

"Ahiliyah?"

The lovely sound of a familiar voice—the sound of home.

"It's me, Susannah," Ahiliyah said. "Brandun and Creen are with me."

"Okay! Come up!"

A wall watcher's job was boring, yet critically important. Always alone, watchers often stayed on the stone deck for days at a time, waiting for runners to return. Only the wall watcher on duty could call for the hold's heavy door to be opened. In theory, that prevented raiders from capturing runners, then using the runners to gain access to the hold.

Ahiliyah and her crew ascended the final thirty feet, where the incline grew so steep they had to climb on all fours. Going up that slope, her backpack somehow felt lighter. It wasn't light, not at all—it was more than half her weight—but soon she would be free of it. At least until the next run.

She was almost home—almost *safe*.

A snorfling sound, followed by the rattle of dirt skittering across rock. Ahiliyah held up a fist; the boys stopped instantly. Probably just a vootervert, but this close to home she wasn't taking any chances.

The snorfle again—she turned her head, trying to locate the source of the sound. There, at the base of the wall, a white paw flinging dirt out of a hole.

"Dammit," she said. "We have to kill it."

Creen shot her a dirty look. "It's just a vootervert. It's not hurting anything."

Did he have to fight her on everything?

"Where there's one vootervert, there will be a dozen," Ahiliyah said. "They can set off traps that take months to make. This is part of our job."

"Fuck our *job*," Creen said. "Nobody asked me if I wanted this job."

Brandun reached to his back, gripped the handle of his spearhead, thinking.

"I'll do it," he said. He sounded sad.

Ahiliyah nodded. "Go ahead. Use your spear—vooterverts are strong, and they kick."

It didn't matter if he was upset about it, as long as he did it. This kill would protect the hold, and would provide around twenty bricks' worth of meat—a rare thing indeed.

Like all runners, Brandun wore his spearhead scabbard on his back. If a runner needed to move fast, one could drop the pack to shed weight, yet not lose one's weapon. He shrugged off his pack, set it down quietly. From the bulky leather holster lashed to it, he drew both of his tapered, yard-long halfstaffs, along with the the metal coupler, and set them all at his feet. He then removed the heavy butt-spike and stuck the metal point in the ground. He jammed one end of a halfstaff into the butt-spike's socket, twisted the wood hard to make sure he had a tight fit. He then put the coupler onto the halfstaff's open end, twisted it, put the other halfstaff into the coupler, twisted that as well.

Finally, Brandun reached to his back and drew his two-foot-long spearhead free with the soft whisper of bronze against leather. He slid the halfstaff's tapered end into the spearhead's hollow handle, twisted until his gloved hands shook.

He spun the assembled, six-foot-long weapon once, gave it a hard shake, then stalked toward the vootervert hole.

"Figures he'd kill it," Creen said under his breath. "The wannabe warrior."

Brandun moved so smoothly, so silently, that he reminded Ahiliyah of a demon. She shivered, imagining Brandun sneaking up on *her*, to bury that spear in *her* back. As attuned as she was to the sounds of the surface, she doubted she would hear him coming.

The vootervert kept kicking dirt out of its hole, unaware of the threat.

Brandun reached the hole. He raised the spear, crouched low. He waited.

After a few minutes of kicking dirt, the vootervert finally turned around and poked its long, narrow head out of the hole, perhaps to look for threats, perhaps to sniff for more of its kind.

Brandun drove the spearhead through the animal's neck. One strike, one kill—the vootervert didn't even have time to let out a squeal of pain.

"Sometimes," Creen said quietly, "Brandun scares the living fuck out of me."

Brandun hauled the limp animal out of its hole. The vootervert was almost as big as Creen. Filthy yellow fur, thick with dark dirt. Long nose with a pinkish snout, which was the most delicious part of the animal. Big paws with four long, brown claws that fit together like the scoop of a single shovel. Someone would make scrapers or jewelry out of those.

Liyah reached into an inner pocket of her hidey suit, pulled out a coil of twine. Brandun set the dead animal on his backpack.

"I'll tie it down," Ahiliyah said.

Brandun started disassembling his spear and putting the parts back in the holster.

Creen waved his hand in front of his nose. "Wow, that animal *stinks*."

Ahiliyah sniffed. "Um… I think that's mostly us, Creen."

He sniffed his armpit. "Ugh. Too many days away from the river, eh, Brandun?"

When the bigger boy didn't answer, Creen leaned closer. Ahiliyah saw Creen's smile, a smile that always seemed to precede an insult or a snotty comment.

"Hey, Dumbdun," Creen said, "are you *crying*?"

Ahiliyah glanced at Brandun. Sure enough, tear trails lined the big teen's cheeks.

Creen laughed. "You're so *sensitive*, Dumbdun! Crying over a stinky chunk of meat? What a big, tough warrior you'll make."

Ahiliyah stood, stepped close to Creen.

"You wouldn't go near that animal," she said, her voice low and cold. "Say one more thing to Brandun, and next reservist training you get to spar with me."

Creen's smile vanished. "I'll shut up."

Ahiliyah patted him on the shoulder. "See? I knew you were smart."

Everyone in the hold between the ages of ten and fifty had to train as a reservist every month. Those who could hold a shield and spear practiced phalanx tactics, those who could not trained with longbow, crossbow, or sling. As a senior runner, Ahiliyah could make junior runners put in additional work—which included hand-to-hand combat training.

Creen did *not* enjoy hand-to-hand combat training.

Brandun shrugged on his heavy pack. The vootervert's stubby tail flopped back and forth with his every movement.

"Let's get inside," Ahiliyah said.

They each fastened a rope to their backpacks. Tying the other end around their waists, they carefully scaled the wall, using the edges of the old stone blocks as foot- and handholds. As far as overall strength went, Creen was by far the weakest of the three, but when it came to climbing he moved with the speed and grace of a hookarm closing in on trapped prey—he was up and over before Ahiliyah and Brandun had reached halfway.

Ahiliyah was slightly faster than Brandun. Exhausted, breathing hard, she slid over the top, under the overhanging lip, and dropped down lightly to the flat stone deck on the other side. Creen was already pulling hard on his rope, hauling his heavy backpack up the wall. Ahiliyah did the same—the sooner this was done, the sooner she'd be safe inside.

"I knew you'd make it," Susannah said. "I knew it!"

Aliyah smiled at the gangly fifteen-year-old girl. Susannah had yet to fill out. All knees and elbows, she beamed with unabashed hero worship.

Susannah laughed and pinched her nose. "Oh, my goodness, you guys need a bath. Everyone will be so happy to see you back—the flu outbreak got worse while you were gone."

Worse? Ahiliyah's heart sank. The powder she and the others had brought from Keflan Hold would save lives, but with more people infected, would it be enough?

"Let me help," Susannah said. She grabbed Ahiliyah's rope and pulled.

Creen hauled his pack over the wall. He glared at Susannah.

"Why didn't you help me?"

"Because no one likes you," Susannah said.

Brandun dropped down to the deck. Without a word, he started hauling up his pack. His reached the top at the same time as Ahiliyah's did.

"I'm in runner training now," Susannah said as she set the pack at Ahiliyah's feet. "Someday I'm going to be just like you. And I'm *fast*! Faster than most of the boys, even."

When Ahiliyah had been that young, she'd said almost the same words to Danielle Sanyan. Ahiliyah had been the wall watcher when Danielle went out for her slash-plus-two run. Ahiliyah had been the wall watcher when Danielle had returned, had hauled Danielle's pack up the wall just as Susannah had done. Ahiliyah had also been the wall watcher when Danielle had left for her slash-plus-three run.

Danielle had never returned.

Ahiliyah chased the thought away. She reached into a side pocket of her hidey suit, pulled out a stick of millasis wrapped in a grass leaf—she offered it to Susannah.

The girl's eyes lit up. "Thank you, Liyah! Thank you!"

Susannah unwrapped the grass. The translucent brown candy had snapped in half.

"Sorry it's broken," Ahiliyah said.

"Don't care!" Susannah shoved a piece into her mouth, smiled wide. "It's so good!"

"If you're done stuffing your little mouth," Creen said, "can you signal for them to open the fucking door? Do you think I want to stand here and watch you *eat*?"

Susannah's smile faded. She looked down, spoke around the candy. "I already signaled them."

Ahiliyah turned to Creen. "Do you always have to be such a jerk?"

He glared back. "I don't have time for children's games."

Creen was sixteen—only a year older than Susannah.

Ahiliyah heard the telltale grinding of heavy stone. To her left, the deck ended at a wall of blocks, each bigger than a man. The center block slowly slid backward. Most of the time the big block opened or closed without a problem. Sometimes, though, the men moving the tons of rock would lose control.

Sometimes people got hurt. Sometimes people died. That was the price of an entrance that could not be opened from the outside.

To the right, spaced out along the abandoned deck, were two ancient, traditional doors, the kind that, once upon a time, had swung inward. The first was only partially visible, forever sealed when the thick roof lip above it had collapsed. The second door not only went nowhere, it was rigged as a trap—whoever opened it would be instantly crushed beneath a ton of falling rock.

The big block stopped sliding backward into the thick wall, started sliding sideways. In that dark space, the pinkish light of a glowjar, then the face of Cadence Barrow. The older woman blinked against the light of early evening, even though the stone roof kept the deck in permanent shadow. Her hair and her skin were the pale white of those who never saw the sun.

"Brandun." Her smile seemed to split her face with deep lines that ran from the corners of her eyes to the bony point of her jaw. "I was so worried."

"Hi, Mom," Brandun said. He stepped to Cadence, hugged her. He was already much taller than she was, and outweighed her by five or six bricks.

"For *fuck's sake*," Creen said. "Can we please *fucking get inside* and deliver this shit?"

Brandun turned and glared. In that instant, Ahiliyah saw the man he was becoming—he would be a giant, one not constrained by the fears and anxieties of an inexperienced teenage boy.

"Just because your parents are dead doesn't mean you can be mean to mine," Brandun said.

Creen fumed. He'd been very small when his parents had died of forgetter's syndrome. He didn't like to be reminded that he was an orphan.

"Leave Creen be, Brandun," Cadence said. "He's obviously tired."

Being kind to Creen only made things worse. "I'm nicer underground. You know, that place where demons can't get us? And I know Ahiliyah wants to steal off to the armory with Tolio and touch uglies, so why are we still up here jabbering?"

Ahiliyah flushed with embarrassment. "Fine. Let's go. Susannah, want to come with?"

"I can't," she said. "Aiko was due back yesterday from Vinden. Gotta wait for her."

Vinden was a safer run than the Dakatera/Keflan/Lemeth route Ahiliyah and the boys had just run, but it still had its share of danger. Aiko was the most experienced runner in Lemeth, having continued serving long after her obligation had been fulfilled. One day overdue wasn't great, but where Aiko was concerned, it was probably nothing to worry about.

"Liyah, come on," Brandun said. "The Margrave will be expecting us."

Ahiliyah stepped into the opening. She waited a moment for her eyes to adjust to the dim light of the glowpipes—she'd escaped injury for nine days on the surface and wasn't about to slip and fall on the stone steps—then started down. As she did, she heard Brandun, Cadence and Creen following her, and the grinding of stone as men slid the stone block back into place.

3

It was a hero's welcome.

Lemethians packed into the stone corridor, all trying to get near her, Brandun and Creen, trying to see the trio for themselves, as if the word that they had survived might somehow be a lie. People cheered. They hugged her, kissed her, threw so many pink flowers at her the petals caught in her hidey suit, hung in her hair, stuck to the filthy sweat coating her face. The sweet-smelling flowers were always part of the coming-home ritual, helping to mask the stench of people who had spent days hiking hundreds of miles, never changing their clothes or even taking them off—on a run, constant camouflage was of the utmost importance.

The flowers weren't *really* pink, they just looked that way in the reddish light of the glowpipes that ran along the corridor's arched ceiling. The glass tubes channeled the river's luminous water all through the hold. In pure sunlight, the imbid flowers blazed white as snow.

Bodies and faces pushed in all around her. The women dressed simply, in plain shifts of different colors, because Lemeth Hold was too hot to wear much else. They used jewelry to create their individual style, with vootervert-claw hair pins and combs, necklaces of copper, bronze and iron, copper nose-rings, the occasional gleaming bit of bloodglass shining from a leather bracelet or a metal necklace. The men wore pants, but no shoes. Most didn't wear shirts. A gleam of sweat always seemed to glisten from arms tattooed with heavy black lines.

Hands patted her shoulder, tousled her hair, pulled her in for hugs. People she had known all her life smiled and laughed and praised her. They shouted questions, asking about loved ones, about life in the other holds. Ahiliyah answered what questions she could.

"You brave dear," said old lady Yuzuki, her wrinkled face split by a smile. She kissed the dirty, smelly, unwashed skin of Ahiliyah's forehead. "Do you have a message from Cireno?"

"He told me to make sure I tell you he loves you," Ahiliyah said. "And that the gloves you made will help him with the iron powder harvest."

Instant tears in Yuzuki's eyes. Those words were more powerful than food, than medicine, than drugs. The old woman hadn't heard from her son in months. The last set of runners sent to Dakatera hadn't made it. All three had been lost. This time, though, with lives on the line, the Council had sent Ahiliyah.

People hugged her, kissed her, threw so many imbid flowers at her that they coated the stone floor. So many *questions,* shouted by people desperate for information.

"*Did you see Usko?*"

"*Did Fabinin get my letter?*"

"*Is gramma Danise still alive?*"

After the endless quiet of the surface, the shouts and laughter and questions and screams of joy felt overwhelming. Ahiliyah knew her people meant no harm, but she didn't like how they packed so close, and she couldn't help but feel anxious at how *loud* they were.

People, everywhere. Adults, teenagers like her, but also the elderly, and children and babies. So *many* children. Some standing by themselves, with wet noses and wide eyes. Some weaving between the legs of the adults, chasing each other in a game of *demon gonna get ya*. Some carried in the arms of mothers who were three, four, even five years younger than Ahiliyah. Some holding the hands of women Ahiliyah's age or older.

The adults were loud; the children were deafening. Their excited shouts bounced off the walls. Their laughter filled the air. Their playful shrieks sounded far too close to the hunting noises demons made in the night.

Ahiliyah pushed her way through the crowd, trying to be nice, trying to understand that everyone was excited by her return. Still they shouted questions at her—so many questions.

"Did those Keflanian bastards give us the medicine?"

"How much do they have? Are they really hoarding it?"

"I hope you kids steered clear of those Dakaterans and their messed-up religion."

Sounded like her people's distrust of other holds hadn't ebbed during her run. Maybe the medicine she brought would help that. Maybe not. Ahiliyah couldn't control that.

The crowd quieted, parted. What had seemed like an impenetrable mass made way for three men—three *large* men—dressed in the sleeveless white shirts of the Margrave's personal guard. Rinik Brennus, with his droopy eye and big nose, blond-haired Shalim Aniketos, who thought he was god's gift to women, and—worst of the three—Drasko Lamech. Brennus and Shalim wore spearhead scabbards at their hips, not on their backs like runners did.

Drasko didn't carry a blade. He didn't need one—the often-used wooden billy club sticking out of his leather belt was threat enough.

"Welcome home, runners." Drasko had a voice like a tumbling boulder.

"Thank you," Ahiliyah said. "It was a close thing."

Dark-haired Drasko wasn't tall—he was the same height as Ahiliyah—but he was wide, easily more than twice her weight. Scars lined his exposed arms, scars earned fighting the Southerners, Islanders and various raiders.

Without taking his eyes off Ahiliyah, Drasko held his hand back to the younger and taller Shalim, who gave him a cloth sack. Drasko opened the sack, held it out.

"If you brought back capertine powder, let's have it."

Ahiliyah glanced back at Brandun, but the boy had already slid off his pack and opened it—he was so eager to impress these men.

"We usually take capertine powder to the hospital," Ahiliyah said. "We'd be happy to drop it off there. No need to bother yourself with it."

Drasko smiled, showing the missing teeth he'd lost in one of his many fights.

"Margrave's orders, my girl. People might try to bribe you with a gift of this or that. After another successful run, we wouldn't want you beset with temptation, would we?"

Susannah had said more people were ill. An understatement, apparently—things were so bad that Drasko had come to make sure people didn't try to take the capertine powder out of turn.

Brandun dumped several tied-off cloth bags into Drasko's sack. Drasko smiled at Brandon—Ahiliyah could almost *feel* the pride radiating off the boy.

"Well done, young man," Drasko said. "Little Liyah here says your return was a close thing, but I know you would have protected her, right?"

"More like she protected me." Brandun held his arms shoulder-width apart, palms facing each other. "She was *this close* to one, and she didn't flinch!"

A murmur rolled through the packed corridor.

Drasko gave the bag a little shake. "Creen, Liyah, hurry it up. I've got better things to do."

Ahiliyah shrugged off her backpack and opened it up. She dumped her six bags into the sack. Creen did the same.

Drasko looked into the bag, then at Ahiliyah. "That's it?"

She nodded.

"You're *sure*?"

As insulting as that was, she nodded again. Drasko wasn't known for a sense of humor, or an ability to put up with backtalk. Not even Creen said something smart.

"Excellent job, young Brandun," Drasko said. "I'll be on the sand tomorrow morning at first sounding. Will you join me?"

Brandun's eyes went wide. "Yes *sir*! I'll be there!"

Drasko slung the bag over his shoulder. He and his two goons walked back up the corridor, the crowd again parting for them, closing in behind them as if to block Ahiliyah's way.

Creen looked at Brandun, and smiled.

"*Sir*," Creen said in a high-pitched voice. "*I'll be there to lick the sweat off your balls, sir!*"

Brandun's smile vanished. He said nothing, just walked down the corridor. He barely had to push to make room—people got out of his way almost as fast as they had for Drasko.

Creen cupped a hand to his mouth. "*Your ball sweat is so tasty, SIR!*"

Ahiliyah cuffed the smaller boy in the ear.

He flinched, held his ear, sneered at her. "Don't be such a jerk, Liyah!"

"Better I hit you than he does," she said. "I swear, Creen, someday soon that mouth of yours is going to get your ass kicked."

He glanced around, saw people staring at him, or making a point of *not* staring at him.

"Right," he said in a low voice. "Like I haven't got my ass kicked before."

His words brought instant guilt; was she bullying him like so many others had? Maybe, but getting hit by people her size was one thing—Brandun was already big enough that his punches could cause real damage. There was a difference between getting hurt, and getting *hurt*.

Creen smiled wide and turned away from her.

"My lovely Lemethians," he said, playing to the crowd, "kindly let us through. The Margrave desires an audience with us!"

Just like that, the awkward moment passed. The crowd parted just enough to let him through. Liyah followed him. On the surface, she always took the lead. In the safety of the hold, she didn't mind bringing up the rear.

A flower hit her in the eye; she winced reactively, but it didn't hurt. She laughed, wiping at the eye and continuing on after Creen. She found it ironic that her people used imbid flowers for celebrations like this. She and Brandun and Creen had carried half their body weight in those flowers to trade with the people of Dakatera and Keflan.

Those holds had tried for decades to cultivate their own imbid flowers, but had failed. Just as the capertine mold—which when dried and ground up produced the life-saving capertine powder—grew only in Keflan, imbid mushroom grew nowhere but Lemeth. Imbid soup countered weakling disease. In Dakatera and Keflan, imbid flowers were priceless; in Lemeth, they were so common they could be wasted at will, trampled underfoot and forgotten until someone swept them up and dumped them in the river.

Ahead of her, Ahiliyah heard Brandun laughing. He had forgotten about Creen's mocking insult and was enjoying the attention, reveling in the moment. The people of Lemeth lavished him with praise and affection. More, she noticed, then she got, and she'd been the senior runner. But Brandun was a boy, and a tall, strong boy at that—people reacted to him differently than they reacted to her.

Such was the way of things.

Even Creen laughed a little, a rare sound if she'd ever heard one.

He deserved to be happy. So did she, and Brandun as well. They had returned, packs stuffed to breaking not only with the capertine powder and candy from Keflan, but also with sizzle spice, paper and iron powder from Dakatera, along with correspondence from both holds. After months with no contact, grandfathers and grandmothers, fathers and mothers, aunts, uncles, brothers, sisters and friends could finally see the words of their loved ones. The celebration would go long into the night.

She and Creen endured the back-pats and well wishes. They caught up to Brandun just as he entered the Community Chamber. The Lemethians who hadn't mobbed them in the corridors were waiting there, cheering loudly for their successful run. Some people were at the wooden tables spread across the stone floor. Others were seated on the four rows of stone steps that ran the circumference of the round room.

Ahiliyah followed Brandun and Creen out of the Community Chamber and onto the walkway that ran along the training pit. The wooden bleachers on either side of the pit were empty, but the pit itself was not. Down in the the wide, oblong, sand-filled space, she saw warriors practicing at the combat stations.

Will Pankour and Grian Yinnish stood in the archery range, practicing with the crossbows that fired heavy bolts the size of Ahiliyah's forearm. Kadri Nemensalter and his brother Farid were working as a team, Kadri holding a spearman's round shield, Farid behind him with a warrior spear, which was three yards long instead of the two-yard-long runner's version. Kadri moved and turned, Farid staying behind him, jabbing the spear at an imaginary demon.

When men had fought other men, the shield had been an important part of war. Men didn't fight men anymore. Not that often, anyway. Shields were a holdover from the past. They were big, bulky, awkward, and—against a demon—all but useless. Ahiliyah would rather put her faith in a hidey suit any day.

The warriors, though, did not share her opinion. Old ways died hard.

Brandun stopped suddenly—Creen bumped into him, Ahiliyah bumped into Creen.

"Brandun, you clod," Creen said. "What the shit?"

Brandun stared toward the back of the pit—Ahiliyah saw what he was looking at and understood why he'd stopped short.

Near the far wall, a demon stalked three warriors.

Leonitos Lamech and Masozi Dafydd each had a shield and a three-pronged spear known as a *demon fork*. They were crouched, shields just below their eyes, demon forks held in their right hands, points and shaft above the shield, both aimed at a man dressed in the stiff shell of a dead demon, complete with the long, gleaming head. Behind Leonitos and Masozi stood Andan Gisilfred, aiming a crossbow between their shields.

"It's not *real*, you dolt," Creen said.

Of course it wasn't. They'd all seen the suit a hundred times, a thousand times. It was part of their runner training. Until this run, however, Brandun had only seen real demons from a great distance. Seeing one up close had affected him, impacted his reaction to something as simple as a man in a costume. Ahiliyah couldn't blame Brandun—an encounter like they'd had the day before changed a person.

"Probably Benji Johnson in the demon suit," Brandun said. "He's the only one that tall. Sometimes they put me in it, when I'm not out running."

Ahiliyah bit back instant jealousy. Brandun was only fifteen, four years younger than her. He got to train with the warriors—she did not. Because warriors didn't take women.

"You'd look good in that demon's suit," Creen said.

Brandun grinned. "Thanks!"

"I mean," Creen said, "anything that covers up your ugly face is good, right?"

One look at Brandun—face red, head hung—and Ahiliyah's jealousy vanished. He was just a kid. He didn't make the decisions in the hold.

"Don't let Creen bother you," she said to him. "You're better-looking than that midget."

Creen huffed. "Yeah, right."

In the pit, the "demon" rushed at Leonitos, who extended his shield to meet the charge. The demon crashed into it, stumbled back. Leonitos stabbed with his demon fork—the point jabbed into the demon's chest. The demon toppled backward, big hands and feet flailing about.

"The point is blunted," Brandun said. "But that still hurts."

Andan raised his crossbow and fired. Even from up on the deck, Ahiliyah could see the bolt's padded end—which struck the demon right between the legs. The demon cried out, rolled to his side and tucked into the fetal position, long black hands clutching at its crotch. The narrow black head tumbled away, revealing Benji's curly red hair and tightly squinted eyes.

Creen laughed so hard he hung over the rail.

"*Ouch*," Brandun said. "Got him where it counts."

The warriors were also laughing. They lowered their shields, gathered around Benji.

"If only the demons had balls," Andan said, leaning on his crossbow, "we'd be fine."

"Andan, you marksman," Leonitos said. "Only a gifted sharpshooter could hit such a tiny target!"

Renewed laughter. Benji lifted one hand—a hand in a gnarled demon-skin glove—and extended his middle, talon-tipped finger.

Creen couldn't stop laughing. He leaned over the wooden rail, slapping the flat surface with his palm. That drew the warriors' attention. They looked up at the runners and cheered, thrusting their weapons into the air or clacking them loudly against their shields. Ahiliyah felt a rush of pride. Next to the Margrave, warriors were the most revered people in Lemeth.

"Hail, Brandun," Farid said. "Did you kill a demon?"

Ahiliyah's jealousy burned hot again.

"No, warrior." Brandun shook his head. "I did not."

"Because he killed *two*," Grian said. "Isn't that right, Brandun?"

Brandun's face turned red. He laughed, uncomfortable with the attention—but also pleased by it. And why shouldn't he be?

Because he wasn't the crew leader. Because he did nothing but manage not to piss himself. Ahiliyah shook off the thought. Brandun had done nothing wrong. He wasn't bragging, or making up stories about his run. Her problem was not with him.

"We didn't kill any," Creen called down, "but we stood strong while one hunted us."

The warriors nodded politely. They paid little attention to Creen—he was small and weak. He would never become a warrior. He was smarter than all of them combined, she knew, but these men respected strength, not intelligence.

"Come on," Ahiliyah said to Brandun and Creen. "We have to see the Margrave."

The mention wiped the smile from Brandun's face.

Ahiliyah continued on past the training pit, and down the corridor that led to the hold's administration section. Even before she could bathe, before she could remove the stinking hidey suit, she had to report to the men who ruled Lemeth.

4

Outside the Margrave's Chamber, Ahiliyah, Brandun, and Creen sat on a bench below a map of Ataegina painted on the stone wall. They'd taken off their hidey suits, rolled them up into tight bundles that they'd strapped to their backpacks. It felt good to be out of the cumbersome collection of netting and vegetation. They still wore the same shirts and pants they'd worn underneath, though—the fabric had absorbed eight days' worth of sweat, dirt and body odor.

Sitting there in the still air, waiting to be called in, Ahiliyah was acutely aware of how much they all stank.

"I really wish they'd let you two bathe first," she said.

Creen huffed. "As if you smell like flowers and cake."

The door to the Margrave's Chamber opened. Thesil Akana, the Margrave's assistant, stepped out, carrying a tray with three steaming mugs of caminus tea.

"Thesil," Creen said, taking a mug, "I could kiss you."

Brandun and Ahiliyah took a mug.

"Thank you, Thesil," she said.

He said nothing, just tucked the tray, went back into the chamber and shut the door.

Thesil had been in the same grade as Ahiliyah. He'd been such a funny kid, always laughing and smiling. On his fifth and final run, demons had taken *both* of his crewmates. He didn't smile anymore.

"I miss tea more than I miss bathing," Creen said. "Even this crappy stuff. People don't know how to filter out the bitterness like I do. Drives me crazy to have to smell caminus leaves the whole time we're running and not be able to start one little fucking fire, you know?"

Ahiliyah did know. On runs, Creen complained about the lack of tea.

They sat in silence, sipping the hot tea. In moments, she started to feel the little kick that caminus tea always brought.

Brandun cleared his throat. He often did that when he was looking for the right words.

"For God's sake, Dumbdun," Creen said, "just spit it out."

Brandun thought for a moment, then turned to Ahiliyah.

"That demon," he said, his voice low, "do you think it was Vanessa?"

Ahiliyah didn't want to think about that demon at all, but it was a good question. Vanessa had been in Mari Jolla's crew. On a run two weeks ago, a demon had caught Vanessa and carried her off.

"I don't know," Ahiliyah said. "I hope not. And if you see Mari, Brandun, do *not* mention that to her, all right? Mari took her loss really hard."

Creen rubbed his face. "You idiots—people do not turn into demons."

Brandun leaned away from Creen, as if Creen had suddenly become toxic.

"Don't blaspheme," Brandun said. "Everyone knows that magic—"

"There is no such thing as magic," Creen said. "That's bullshit the preachers tell us because they don't know what happens and they won't *admit* they don't know. It's impossible for a person to become a demon. Isn't that right, Liyah?"

Ahiliyah leaned away from Creen, realized she was doing it, stopped herself.

"I don't know," she said. "I mean… that's what the legends say."

Creen crossed his arms. "Right. The Demon Mother uses *magic spiders*, whatever the hell a *spider* is, to turn people into demons. It makes no sense. No one's ever even seen a spider."

Brandun's mouth hung open. He was very religious, which Creen knew full well.

"No more talk of spiders," Ahiliyah said. "Or Vanessa. That's an order."

Creen made a farting sound with his lips, leaned against the wall. He sipped his tea, tried to look like the boredest boy in all the land.

"That demon," Brandun said. "It was right on top of you. How did you stay so *calm*?"

The encounter had really got to him, more than she'd thought.

"I stayed calm because I want to live," Ahiliyah said. "Silence is strength."

She expected Creen to say something else dismissive, or demeaning, or insulting, as he usually did when she cited the training mantras, but for once he did not.

"Silence is strength," he said.

"Which means," Brandun said, "that Creen is the weakest person alive."

Ahiliyah laughed. Eyebrows raised, Creen sat up and looked up at Brandun, who was trying to hold back a laugh of his own.

"The walking boulder can get in a dig once in a while," Creen said. He leaned back against the wall. "I couldn't have stayed still like you did, Liyah. I'd have run."

"Then you'd have been taken," Ahiliyah said. "Aiko says they can sense vibrations in the ground when they're close. Running actually brings them *to* you, so your best bet is to stay still."

Creen stared into his mug. "I don't want to run again. Fuck, I wish I could get knocked up."

She wondered if he'd feel that way if he actually had a uterus.

Ahiliyah stood and stretched, trying to loosen muscles tight and sore from eight days on the run. She looked up at the painted map. The island of Ataegina, surrounded by the blue of an ocean that she'd never seen. Further in, bumpy dark green lines with blue rivers that represented the coast and the plains, the green turning lighter and mingling with brown as the inland hills grew higher in elevation. Those hills led to the many mountain peaks that surrounded Lake Lanee and Lake Mip.

Those lakes had been volcanoes once, like Black Smoke Mountain. That's what Creen said, anyway. He was an endless source of useless information. The map showed the names of old towns and cities. The one called Hellan had supposedly held fifteen thousand people. Swarmore, *twenty* thousand.

And Tinsella, so big she could still make out the tree-covered ruins when she visited her friend Panda at the signaling station atop Lemeth Mountain, had held *fifty thousand people.*

Unimaginable.

Colorful marks signified the mountain holds that had once been King Paul's Crown of War. Keflan, Dakatera and Lemeth around Lake Lanee. Takanta, southeast of Lake Mip. Vinden, near the southeast coast. Jantal on the west coast, and south of it, the lost holds of Hibernia and Pendaran. On the southern coast, the place of nightmares—Black Smoke Mountain, home of the Demon Mother.

Somewhere off the map lay the lands of the Northerners. No one on Ataegina had ever seen those lands. No one living, anyway. It had been a long time since the Northerners had landed an invading army. Not that long ago, they'd been a constant threat to the coast and the plains, but there wasn't anything left there worth fighting for, at least nothing that was worth the risk of facing demons.

That didn't stop the raiders from Manroon Island, though—they still came, one or two boats at a time, roaming the countryside looking for people to kill. As far as Ahiliyah knew, they mostly left with nothing but fruit. Was fruit worth crossing the ocean and risking your life? Maybe. God knew that she had risked her life five times now just to bring goods back to Lemeth.

The chamber door opened. Thesil stepped out. "Ahiliyah, the Council will see you now."

He took Ahiliyah's mug. She entered the chamber. Brandun and Creen would wait on the bench in case of the rare chance the Margrave or a councilman wanted to hear from someone other than the crew leader.

The Margrave's Chamber wasn't the biggest room in the hold, but it was the most brightly lit. Glowpipes ran in parallel lines across the arched stone ceiling, and along the walls as well. The builders had wanted to make sure there was ample light for the room's main feature: the table model of Ataegina.

The table sat in the center of the room. Nine feet square, the table's edges were the blue of the ocean, made from an old material—no one even knew what it was anymore, let alone how to manufacture it. Metal markers stuck up from the raised peaks, marking the still-active holds. The most prominent marker was reserved for Lemeth, of course. Not surprising considering how proud her people were of their home.

Around the table sat the Council, the five men who controlled every aspect of life in Lemeth Hold. At least in theory. In practice, the man at the head of the table, Aulus Darby, the Margrave of Lemeth, ran everything.

He wore his robes of office, purple with white trim at the cuffs and collars. He was in his sixties, but his back was still straight and he was taller than almost everyone in Lemeth Hold. Glowlight made his white beard and thinning white hair gleam a light pink.

Aulus had been the Margrave since before Ahiliyah was born. He was a good man, a fair man, but a man not to be trifled with.

Ahiliyah hadn't spent much time in the Margrave's Chamber. She came only before a run—to receive orders and plot out her course on the table model—and after a run, to report to the Council. In those limited times, though, she'd learned that while the four council members occasionally offered suggestions, their primary duty was to agree with the Margrave.

"An excellent run," Councilman Tinat said. "We are grateful for your service."

Not much more than thirty, Tinat was the youngest council member. He was also the most famous warrior in Lemeth—he'd killed *two* demons, as evidenced by the pair of toothtongues hanging from his copper chain necklace. Tinat liked to fill the hollow toothtongues with river water each morning, making them glow from the inside, making the clear teeth sparkle with the colors of gemstones. The glow faded as the day went on, but at that moment it remained bright enough to reflect off his graying beard. A mug of tea sat on the table's edge in front of him.

"A full trade with Dakatera and Keflan," he said. "You delivered correspondence, returned with the same, you obtained everything you were instructed to obtain, and all three runners made it home." He smiled at her, put his left fist against his sternum. "Ahiliyah Cooper, I salute you."

She flushed. Tinat was a hero, a legend. He still trained with the warriors when he could, and had the thick frame to show for it. Five misshapen scars dotted the left side of his face, marks left from the burning blood of one of his demon kills. Most of the girls thought it made him look hideous, but not Ahiliyah. To her, the scars showed Tinat's bravery—in Lemeth, only three people still alive had survived an encounter with a demon.

Only *two* had killed one.

"The girl obtained *almost* everything," Councilman Balden said, his attention fixed on the letters Ahiliyah had brought back. "You were told to get one hundred doses of capertine powder from Keflan. You brought back eighty. Our people *need* that medicine. Don't you know this?"

He had a mug in front of him, too, but Ahiliyah could smell the rivergrass booze in it. With Balden's head angled down to read, she couldn't see his eyes past his bushy gray eyebrows. Thin and frail, he was the type of man Creen would grow to be if Creen survived more runs.

"That was all they would give me, Councilman," Ahiliyah said. "Glynnis flu has broken out there, as well. The Margrave of Keflan assured me his people are working hard to increase production. They will have more for us soon."

"The *liars*," Balden said. "They have plenty to spare. They want us to suffer, to die."

As if he had any idea of what it was like to do a run nowadays, what it was like to stand face to face with the Margrave of Keflan or the Dakateran Margravine. Balden hadn't run in forty years. How easy it was for him to sit here, safe in the hold, and think he could do better.

"It's that evil religion of theirs," he said. "It's corrupted them beyond belief."

To Balden, all religions—save for the right and proper faith practiced in Lemeth, as defined by Preacher Ramirus—were "evil."

"I believe they traded all they could spare," Ahiliyah said.

Councilman Poller sighed. "Sometimes I think we need to stop sending mere children to trade." He was so fat his neck jiggled when he spoke. "I think the people of Keflan might be more honest about their capertine stockpile if our warriors were to show up on their doorstep."

A grumble of agreement from Balden.

Councilman Jung nodded, the lines of the glowpipes reflecting from his lumpy bald head.

"Without our flowers, the people of Keflan would all waste away from weakling disease," he said. "You would think they'd realize that and stop pretending they can't pay."

These men hadn't seen the people of Keflan, how sickly and malnourished they'd looked.

"They have their own outbreak of Glynnis flu, as I told you," Ahiliyah said. "They are suffering. And a lot of their people are coming down with forgetter's syndrome."

That sparked interested from the Council. Interest, and a pathetic, instant *eagerness*.

"Surely the Margrave of Keflan didn't tell you that," Jung said. "That would make him seem weak. What makes you think they're suffering from forgetter's?"

Ahiliyah suddenly regretted saying anything. How naïve of her to think the councilmen might feel bad for the Keflanians.

"I saw people lying in the corridors," Ahiliyah said. "People here have had forgetter's—I know what it looks like. And people were quietly asking me if we had any plinton fruit to trade."

Without plinton fruit, forgetter's syndrome progressed unchecked. Simple confusion was the initial symptom, victims wondering where they left this or that, being unable to remember names and details. As it got worse, people became lazy. They often just lay in a bed, on a floor, wherever they could find. Forgetter's victims didn't look sick, but they didn't *work*—after murder and rape, there was no worse sin in the world than not contributing.

"Dakatera exports plinton," Jung said. "Are they not trading it with Keflan for capertine?"

The people of Dakatera had seemed healthy enough.

"I don't think they're suffering from the flu," Ahiliyah said. "At least not much."

Tinat rapped his knuckles on the table. "Which means the Dakaterans have stockpiled plenty of capertine powder. The bastards are trying to drive up the price of plinton fruit."

Ahiliyah stood quietly. Sometimes her council reports devolved into these kinds of discussions, what the councilmen called *economics*. Balden tossed the letter onto the table. It landed half on the blue of the ocean, half on the green of the flatlands.

"Speaking of Dakatera, this letter is from one of their councilmen. Correction—" he waved a hand dismissively "—council*woman*. Such a thing exists there, it seems. *She* seems to think we're charging too much for imbid flowers. If this complaining continues, something must be done. Really, Ahiliyah, you could have done better in managing this nonsense."

The Margrave stood; the councilmen stilled.

"Councilmen, you are focusing on the wrong things," he said. "Before us stands Ahiliyah Cooper, who just completed her *fifth* run, and did so with no deaths or injuries under her leadership. You all seem to forget that we can sit here safe and warm in the hold, while it is she and her fellow young runners who face danger up on the surface."

Ahiliyah could barely breathe. The Margrave not only complimented her, he was echoing her own thoughts.

"Only Tinat has it right," the Margrave said. "We all need to follow his fine example and salute our new slash, not chastise her or blame her for decisions made by the leaders of Dakatera and Lemeth. Ahiliyah Cooper—" he smiled, placed his fist on his sternum "—I salute you."

Was this really happening? The Margrave was saluting *her*?

His smile faded. "I said, *we need to salute her.*"

Balden was first on his feet. He put his left fist on his sternum. "The Margrave is right, of course. Ahiliyah, I salute you for your service."

Poller and Jung stood, put their fists on their chests.

"We salute you," they said in unison.

Aulus smiled. "That's better. Ahiliyah, I thank you for your brave work and your report. Well done. Oh… how did Brandun do?"

Brandun was a good person, Ahiliyah liked him, but his as-yet unearned prominence bothered her. He hadn't led the run… *she* had. He wouldn't have to do ten runs… *she* would.

"Brandun Barrow did well," she said. It was the truth, after all.

The Margrave nodded. "Thank you, Ahiliyah. Anything else you would like to add?"

That question always marked the end of her report. She was supposed to say *no, Margrave,* then the council would move on to discussing when her crew would run again.

She hesitated. For this brief moment, she had their attention. She had to say something.

"The demons are moving in the daylight," she said. "I think they might be trying to figure out how to catch us on runs."

Balden rolled his eyes, whatever respect he'd just given her instantly and visibly gone.

"This nonsense again?" He shook his head. "This girl makes five runs and suddenly she knows all there is to know about the demons."

"It's different now," Ahiliyah said.

The Margrave dismissed her comment with a wave. "Demons have been seen in daylight before, Ahiliyah. You are not the first runner to experience this."

As if he knew anything about running. The rumor was that the Margrave had *never* done a run—not a real one, anyway—because his father, the Margrave before him, had made sure his son wasn't exposed to danger. Even if Aulus had done a run, it had been forty years ago, maybe even *fifty*. What did he know of the dangers up on the surface?

She had to explain the significance. The Margrave had much to do down here, she knew. How could he understand the problem if she didn't explain it to him? She was a slash now, after all, among the most experienced runners in the hold.

"Margrave, on my first two runs I didn't see any demons in the daylight. My third, I saw one. On each of my last two runs, I saw demons *twice* in the daylight. I think that—"

"Enough," the Margrave said. "You have told me your concern."

"But Margrave, I—"

"*Enough,*" he said. He put his hands on the table's edge, leaned forward like a giant towering over the miniature mountain range. "Were you talking back to me, Ahiliyah? To *me*?"

The council stared at her with a mixture of scowls and disbelief. She had overstepped her bounds and she knew it.

The Margrave sat. "Do not think that we are not proud of your service, but decisions are made at the *top*, not the bottom. You young runners always think you've discovered something that the rest of us are too old and blind to see. Is that what you think, Ahiliyah?"

That was exactly what she thought. "No, Margrave."

He smiled at her. Even though he'd just put her in her place, his smile made her feel good. He'd snapped at her, yes, but he *believed* in her, which was more than she could say of the other councilmen. Save for Tinat, of course.

"Superb," the Margrave said. "Councilman Balden, the correspondence from Dakatera—what does it say they are in need of, trade-wise?"

Balden looked at the letter. "The usual. They always need more of our rope, and they want more imbid flowers—at a lower price, which I mentioned earlier."

The Margrave frowned. "Do you think I need to be told things twice?"

A chill fell over the room.

Balden stared at the table, his head down, his bushy brows hiding his eyes.

"No, Margrave," he said quietly. "My mistake."

Aulus nodded. "Now, if you're finished calling me stupid, what else does Dakatera need?"

The paper in Balden's shaking hand rattled audibly.

"Hotspice from Takanta," he said. "Red fabric from Vinden, and salt from Biseth."

Councilman Poller raised a finger. "Leith Malmsteen's crew came back from Biseth yesterday, carrying a full load of salt."

The Margrave stood again, put his hands on the table, leaned over the table's mountain range. His eyes traced the peaks and valleys. He pointed at the peak labeled *Dakatera*.

"They need salt," he said. "We run half of ours there, trade it for plinton fruit. We'll demand a high exchange rate, and we'll get it." He pointed from Dakatera to Keflan. "Our runners continue on, trade the plinton fruit for capertine powder. If the Keflanians are as desperate as Ahiliyah says, we'll again get a favorable exchange rate. All three holds benefit."

The Margrave looked around the table, seeing if anyone opposed. He found only nods.

"A sound strategy," Councilman Tinat said. "Who do we send on the run?"

His words brought a tightness to Ahiliyah's belly. They wouldn't send her crew out again, not this soon. Would they?

"Tinat," the Margrave said, "what is the status of the available crews?"

As the newest councilman, Tinat was responsible for the runners.

"Aiko Laster's crew is on a run to Takanta and Vinden," Tinat said. "Jeanna Bouchard's crew is doing the dangerous run through the valley to Jantal." He lowered his head. "Brenda Dafydd's crew left for Jantal two weeks ago. All three are presumed lost."

Aulus placed his fist against his sternum, bowed his head. "We will continue to pray for their safe return." He looked up again. "What about Fabian Acosta?"

"Julie Hammal and Britt Denisander were in his crew," Tinat said. "Julie is six months along, Britt announced her pregnancy just last week. Fabian is waiting for Bruce Pindall and Susannah Albrecht to finish training."

Susannah, the girl on the deck who had welcomed them home. She was too young, too skinny, too… too *sweet*. No way was Susannah ready. Ahiliyah's hands curled into fists—they were going to make her and Brandun and Creen run again, she could feel it.

"Mari Jolla's crew is still here," Ahiliyah said. "Right? I know she lost Vanessa, but Tobias Penn is a good replacement. And she still has Lucas Kim, he's solid."

The room fell silent. Had she said something wrong?

Tinat cleared his throat. "I'm afraid Lucas and Tobias also need a new crew leader."

Had Mari come down with Glynnis flu? While Ahiliyah felt bad for her—no one liked to spend days feverish and vomiting—she still had to do her duty.

"We brought back eighty doses of capertine powder," she said. "Runners always get priority. Mari should be fine in a day or two."

More uncomfortable silence.

Tinat sighed. "Mari's crew was ordered to make the long run to Vinden. She refused."

Ahiliyah felt like she'd been punched in the gut. "She must have had a good reason."

"She's not hurt, or sick," Tinat said. "Mari told me that she will run no more."

Goosebumps washed over Ahiliyah's skin. The silence of the room told her Mari had already been sentenced for her crime.

"Let me talk to her," Ahiliyah said. "I can make her change her mind."

All eyes turned to the Margrave.

"Several people have," he said. "Still she refuses. You know what this means."

Everyone in Lemeth knew.

"Margrave, please," Ahiliyah said. "Mari only has two more runs to go. Let me try."

Aulus tugged absently at his beard. "You may speak with her tonight, in her cell. If she runs, she's forgiven, but she must complete two additional runs beyond her current obligation."

A sinking feeling. Mari had completed eight runs. Now to fulfill her obligation, instead of two more, she would have to complete *four*. Ahiliyah wanted to argue, but everyone knew the cost of refusing a run—a penalty of only two additional runs was more than generous.

"Thank you, Margrave," Ahiliyah said.

He sighed, spread his hands. "Even if Lucas agrees, I will not trust him on such an important run. Do you understand how badly we need this medicine from Keflan?"

She understood just fine—the warriors would not go, the other crews were either already on the surface or were waiting for inexperienced trainees. With Aiko gone, Ahiliyah was the best runner in Lemeth. Everyone knew it. Without the powder, dozens would die. Maybe hundreds.

The burden fell on *her*. On her, Creen and Brandun.

"Yes, Margrave. I understand."

"I'm sorry to do this so soon after your return," he said. "Ahiliyah, you and your crew will leave tomorrow at first light."

She closed her eyes. There hadn't even been a chance to bathe, and he was already asking her to risk her life again. She held back a scream of frustration.

"My team needs rest," Ahiliyah said. "A few days, at least."

Poller shook his head, made a disgusted, clucking sound.

"*Rest*." Balden spat the word like a curse. "People are *sick*, and you want to take a nap?"

Tinat slapped the table. "You make it sound so easy, Balden. Why don't you volunteer?"

Balden huffed. "I have more important duties here, Tinat. You should mind your words."

"If I don't," Tinat said, smiling, "will you be the one to teach me a lesson?"

Balden huffed again, but refused to meet the younger, bigger man's gleaming eyes.

"Enough," the Margrave said. "Ahiliyah, I either send you and your team, or I send Acosta and his trainees. We cannot wait. We've already lost two Lemethians to the flu."

Ahiliyah thought of skinny Susannah making the two-day trek to Dakatera, then another two-day trek to Keflan, then back again. Eight days round-trip, *if* there was no demon sighting. Susannah wouldn't last eight days—she wouldn't last eight *hours*.

All the adults in the Lemeth, the warriors, the councilmen, the tradesmyn... none of them would go. Why? Because they had already fulfilled their "obligation." Because of *tradition*. Even with lives at risk, the Council sent only the young to the surface, to run, to hide... to die.

How had their culture wound up like this?

"I can give you one day of rest," the Margrave said. "You leave the day after tomorrow. But I won't order you, Ahiliyah. It is your choice—will it be your crew, or must I send Acosta?

On the mountainside, Acosta made more noise than two mating vindeedees. He had only made the safer run to Biseth. A run to Dakatera and Keflan, with demons hunting in the daylight? He would die. His team would die. And many of the people sick with the flu would die when his crew didn't return with the medicine.

If Ahiliyah had been in charge, she would have ordered some of the men in this very room to make the run. Maybe Balden. *Especially* Balden.

But she wasn't in charge.

For the good of her people, there was only one choice to make. Creen and Brandun were under her leadership—they had no choice at all. If she went, they went with her.

How would they take the news?

"We'll do it," she said. "Day after tomorrow, we will go."

The Margrave nodded, solemnly, his half-smile communicating so much: pride at her bravery, sadness at what she had to endure. He knew. He *understood*. That helped. Not much, perhaps, but it did help.

"We will move your return ceremony to tomorrow," the Margrave said. "Tomorrow is also phalanx reserve training. Your crew may skip that training, to get additional rest."

Miss her chance with shield and spear? Her chance to prove to the warriors that she belonged in their ranks? No way.

"I'll still train, if that's all right," Ahiliyah said. "I'm sure Brandun will as well."

Creen would not, which went without saying.

The Margrave smiled the smile that made Ahiliyah think of her father, made her miss him even more than she already did.

"Of course you want to train, Liyah," the Margrave said. "By all means, do so. I will see you tomorrow at your return ceremony. You are dismissed."

The two boys sitting on the bench stared at her, one with shock, the other with rage.

"The day after tomorrow?" Brandun leaned back against the wall. "So soon?"

"This is *bullshit*," Creen said. "I'm going to give the Margrave a good talking-to."

Creen stepped to the chamber door. Ahiliyah reached for him—too late. He grabbed the door handle, then Brandun wrapped his arms around Creen's chest, effortlessly lifted him.

Creen's little feet kicked uselessly. "You big stupid fuck, *let me go!*"

Ahiliyah pressed her hand hard over Creen's mouth, got a kick in the thigh for her troubles.

"Creen, shut up," she said, leaning close. "You barge in there and they'll send you to lockup. Is that what you want?"

The boy stiffened. Glaring at her with all the hate in the world, he shook his head.

Ahiliyah let him go. Brandun gently set Creen back on his feet.

Creen crossed his arms over his chest. "I'm *not* going on this run."

His words scared her. He was probably just venting, but what if he turned out like Mari?

"You're going," Ahiliyah said. "We need more medicine."

Brandun nodded slowly. "Liyah's right, Creen, we gotta. My mom has the cough. I heard all the medicine we brought back will be used on people who are way more sick than she is."

"I'm sorry about your mom," Creen said. "But me being *dead* isn't going to keep her alive. I'm serious—I'm not going on this run."

With that, the boy grabbed his pack and stormed down the hallway.

Brandun and Ahiliyah watched him go.

"You gotta talk to him," Brandun said. "I don't want to see him get in trouble."

Get in trouble. Well, that was one way to put it.

"Creen will be all right," she said, although she wasn't sure if she believed that. "I'll stop by and see your mother later, okay?"

Brandun smiled a tired but sweet smile. "Wanna come see her now? I'll carry your pack."

She was fairly sure he was developing a crush on her. That happened a lot between younger crew members and older crew leaders.

"No, thanks, I want to stop by the hospital and see how bad things really are. Then I'm going to see General Bishor and I have plans with Tolio tonight."

Brandun's smile faded slightly, most likely from the subtle reminder that Liyah had a boyfriend, then it was back.

"Oh," he said. He perked up. "Wargames with the spider? Could I play sometime?"

"Not if you call him that name you can't."

She hadn't meant the words to sound like a sharp rebuke, but that was how they came out.

Brandun sagged. "Sorry. I didn't mean it like that."

She knew he hadn't. He just repeated the mean things other people said. Which, in its own way, was even worse.

Ahiliyah put her hand on his shoulder. "I'll see you at the return ceremony tomorrow, all right?" Her tone of voice told him he was forgiven.

Brandun smiled again. "Yeah, all right. Thanks, Liyah. Don't forget about mom, okay?"

He grabbed his pack and ran down the hall, somehow finding a new source of energy when he should have none left at all. Despite his size, he rarely got tired. Another reason he would be a warrior and she would not.

Ahiliyah picked up her own backpack, then stared at the map on the wall. Five more runs, then she would be free of her obligation—but did she *want* to be free of it?

She didn't know. She didn't know a lot of things.

Ahiliyah shouldered the pack, took a moment to find a spot where the skin of her shoulders wasn't rubbed raw, then left the Margrave's Chamber behind.

5

The people who'd come to welcome her crew home were mostly gone from the stone corridors, all probably back at work, toiling away to keep the hold alive. The few people she passed by smiled at her, thanked her for her service, but no one stopped her.

If she hadn't known the hospital's location by heart, she could have just followed the sound of the vomiting. She set her backpack down outside the hospital's arched entrance, then stepped inside. Twenty-two beds—all full. The outbreak had, indeed, gotten worse. Everyone here would probably soon recover, thanks to the capertine powder that she, Brandun, and Creen had brought back.

One of the hospital's pipes had a leak. Glowing water trickled down the dark stone wall, casting odd shadows across the room. All glowpipes steadily filled with gunk. If they weren't cleaned out every few weeks, increasing water pressure could crack the glass. Judging by the ridges of that same gunk building up on the wall, this leak had sprung days ago. Someone should have fixed it already, which probably meant that many in the maintenance crew were sick.

Ahiliyah knew most of these patients by sight. Steffan Andersson, the first boy she'd kissed, coughing wetly, his thick body laid low. Her friend Lola Yinnish lay on her side, violently throwing up into a wooden bucket. Old Man Sarkozy was on his back, moaning, his wrinkled face sheened with sweat. All three of the Baines boys—Jermaine, Bharat and Andrey—laid up, covered in sweat, their skin red from fever. Their mother, Tameika, was pulling double-shifts in one of the mushroom farms, trying to make up for her sons' lack of productivity.

Doctor Talbot and Doctor Fran moved from bed to bed. They both looked like they hadn't slept since Ahiliyah had left on her run eight days earlier.

Talbot's assistant—Chloe Jakobsen—trailed him, carrying a wooden tray that held a pitcher of water and a stack of small ceramic cups. Talbot stopped at a bed. Ahiliyah couldn't make out the woman tucked beneath the covers, shivering madly. Talbot poured water into one of the brown cups on Chloe's tray, then gently lifted the patient up enough so that she could drink. Ahiliyah saw who it was—old Rose Porter, one of the weavers. Talbot helped Rose drink the entire cup, then he laid her back down on the bed.

The look on Talbot's face told Ahiliyah all she needed to know; Rose would live. The medicine had arrived in time. Ahiliyah felt a rush of pride in a job well done. The run had been hard and terrifying, but it had saved lives—probably everyone in this room, and many more. Maybe Ahiliyah couldn't be a warrior like she'd always dreamed of being, but she was good at running, and her runs *mattered*.

Was that enough?

No, but it was definitely something good. If it was all she could get out of this life, she would keep doing it until she could run no more, or until the demons finally brought her down.

Time to see Sinesh, then get some sleep. Ahiliyah started to turn away when Talbot saw her. The doctor put the cup back on the tray, then hurried over.

"Liyah," Talbot said, then pulled her in for a hug. "You are an angel, my girl. An *angel*."

She hugged him back. He was a good man, a hard worker who contributed to the hold every single day.

He held her at arm's length, smiling. He was so wrinkled he reminded Ahiliyah of bark stripped from a tree and left to dry in bleached-out, bone-hard strips. Dark circles under his eyes, a nose red from sneezing and wiping, skin paler than normal.

"Doc, you look like hell."

"I *feel* like hell. Or at least I did until the capertine powder arrived."

Ahiliyah glanced past him into the hospital. "Are they all going to make it?"

"I don't know," Talbot said. "The powder you brought will save most of them, but they aren't the only ones. We don't have enough beds. We've ordered some people to stay in their rooms. To be honest, we need an additional delivery of powder, and we need it soon. Otherwise, we could lose more than the two we already lost."

Ahiliyah's heart sank. "What is our population now?"

"Three thousand, four hundred and twelve," Talbot said. "And no births while you were gone. The number is accurate."

When she'd been younger, Lemeth had held over five thousand people. The hold was dying. All of Ataegina was dying.

"Who passed?"

"Letar Haines," Talbot said. "And Olliana Ming."

Ahiliyah closed her eyes, felt the rush of sadness that came with the news. Some thirty or forty years ago, Olliana had been Lemeth's senior runner—the most experienced runner in the hold, the person responsible for training all new runners. Olliana had made sixteen runs before she'd stopped. She'd then joined the sewage crew, where she'd worked her fingers to the bone every day, looking forward to when she could put that burden down and join the hold's other old ladies as a weaver. Olliana would have spent her remaining years chatting and chewing on Lisa's root while she made rope, twine, and wove netting.

Glynnis flu had ended that dream.

Ahiliyah would always remember Olliana's snake pies, the way she liked to roast kittle bugs with sweetspice and hand them out, still warm, to the children of the hold.

"It was her time," Talbot said. "She was sixty-two, you know."

Older than most people in the hold.

"Letar seemed so strong," Ahiliyah said. "What was he, thirty?"

"Twenty-nine. If he'd said something sooner, he might have survived. He waited too long." Talbot leaned closer to Ahiliyah, his eyes searching her up and down. "You don't look so great yourself. You look a little red."

He put his hand against her forehead.

"Hey," Ahiliyah said, "you need to ask permission to touch me."

"Oh, do shut up. Any aches and pains?"

"Just the usual. I've been on a run for eight days."

He pressed his fingers against her neck. She winced as pain radiated from somewhere inside her throat.

"You're sick," Talbot said. "You need a dose of what you brought back for everyone else."

"I'm fine. I just need some sleep."

"Funny, that's exactly what Letar told me. Three days later, a blood clot hit his heart. Now he's dead. Chloe, get over here."

Chloe rushed over, tray in hand. "Hi, Liyah. Sorry I wasn't there to welcome you back."

Ahiliyah reached out, touched her shoulder. "I don't mind. I can see you've been busy."

The capertine powder was already in the cup. Talbot poured in some water; the powder dissolved, turning the water blue. He held the cup in front of her.

Ahiliyah glanced at the hospital beds. "They need it more than I do. You just told me there isn't enough to go around."

"Which means someone has to make a run," Talbot said. "Considering what's on the line, I assume the Council will send our best."

He already knew. No one could have told him—she'd come here straight from the Margrave's Chamber. Maybe no one *had* to tell him. Talbot was good at figuring things out.

She took the cup, drank. Capertine powder tasted like farts.

"Ugh," she said, setting the cup on the tray. "What's that stuff do, anyway?"

"It kills the bacteria that make you sick. And it dissolves the blood clots formed by the bacteria wastes."

"You mean... I have tiny bug poop in me?"

He laughed as he lifted her left eyelid, leaned in close to look.

Ahiliyah stood there, letting him prod and poke her. She worked her tongue against the roof of her mouth, trying to scrape away the horrid taste.

"Doctor Talbot, what's a blood clot?"

He grabbed her wrist—gently but firmly—and raised it up so they could both see a long, scabbed-over scratch on her forearm.

"When you got this, it bled, right?"

Ahiliyah nodded. "A little bit, yeah."

"When the bleeding slowed, tell me what that blood looked like."

"It kind of got… *thicker*, I guess." She shrugged. "It just stopped."

"*Thicker* is a good word for it. That was your blood *clotting*. That's one of the symptoms of Glynnis flu, except the *clots*"—he made a fist—"form *inside* your body. They get stuck in your veins, which is what causes the aches. If a clot reaches your heart"—he opened the fist quickly, fingers splayed—"*pow*, there goes your heart, and you're one dead runner. Now, are you happy I made you take your medicine?"

Ahiliyah frowned at him. She didn't like the idea of anyone "making" her do anything. But still, an exploding heart?

"Thank you, Doctor Talbot."

Talbot tousled her hair, just as he'd done to her when she'd been a child.

"Get some rest," he said, then walked back to his patients. Chloe followed close behind.

Rest. She was bone-tired. Looking at the sick people made her more so. If she and her crew didn't complete the next run to Dakatera, then Keflan, and back, the death toll would quickly rise higher. She would not let that happen. She'd find a way to return safely, to keep Creen and Brandun alive, to save as many of her people as possible.

There was still much to do. She wanted to see him. He could make her forget all about the demons, the surface, the running, the danger… for a little while, at least.

But before she saw Tolio, before her slash ceremony, before she tried to talk some sense into Mari Jolla, Ahiliyah needed to deliver her present to the General.

6

Finally bathed, dressed in sandals and a clean, white, short-sleeved nawton-fiber shift, Ahiliyah descended the long, narrow stairway. Her footsteps echoed off the stone walls until the river's growing roar drowned them out.

She loved this walk. No matter how much water pumped through the glowpipes, the pale reddish light couldn't compare to the blazing glory of sunshine up on the surface. The river, though, came close.

Two little girls—Miriam and Debbany—trailed behind her, begging for candy.

Miriam tugged on her sleeve. "*Please*, Ahiliyah! Just one more! I'll eat slow, I promise!"

"That's what you promised the last time," Ahiliyah said. "I'm sorry, girls, but I only have a little bit of candy left, and it's for the netmakers."

The girls groaned as if the world were ending and their lives were so, *so* unfair. Ahiliyah laughed—she had acted the same way when she'd been their age and a runner had come back from Keflan.

"Wait," Debbany said, "the netmakers? Does that mean you're visiting the spider?"

Such a horrible nickname. Ahiliyah felt her anger rise, but she held it in check—these were just little kids, they didn't understand.

"That's *mean*," she said. "You shouldn't call people that."

Miriam sneered. "We don't call *people* that, just him. He's all ugly and scary."

Ahiliyah stopped walking. She turned; the girls froze in place, looked up at her.

"General Bishor isn't *scary*," she said. "He's a good person. Have you ever talked to him?"

Miriam reached out, held Debbany's hand.

"We haven't talked to him but we've *seen* him," Miriam said. "I... sometimes I have dreams that he's coming to get me. He's *awful*, Liyah. You shouldn't be friends with him."

Such horrible little girls. Who did they think they were? Sinesh was a hero. The girls were afraid of *him*? Maybe they needed a real scare.

Ahiliyah knelt down so she was eye to eye with them.

"A spider," she said in a sweet voice. "Do you girls know what a *spider* really is?"

Miriam and Debbany exchanged a glance.

"Yeah," Miriam said. "In Black Smoke Mountain, the Demon Mother uses spiders to magic you into a demon."

Debbany nodded. "Then you're damned. Preacher Ramirus told us. Everyone knows."

Ahiliyah smiled an evil smile. She couldn't help it. She raised her right hand, palm toward the girls. She curled her fingers in like claws, then wiggled them, trying to make them look like the legendary creature.

"You're *almost* right, girls. What Preacher Ramirus didn't tell you was the spiders aren't only in Black Smoke Mountain."

Ahiliyah wiggled her fingers faster. The girls' eyes widened. They clung to each other, watched her hand.

"Where... where..." Debbany licked her dry lips. "Where else are they?"

"They're *everywhere*," Ahiliyah said. "They hide in the shadows, listening for little kids who say mean things, who call people mean names. When the spiders hear that? They wait until those kids go to sleep. Then in the night, the spiders come and wrap themselves around your face, and they magic the bad kids away to Black Smoke Mountain. So unless you want to turn into a demon, unless you want to be *damned*, maybe don't talk about people behind their backs."

Ahiliyah's hand shot out—her fingers wrapped around Debbany's face.

Miriam and Debbany screamed so loud it made Ahiliyah wince. Debbany slapped Ahiliyah's hand away, and the two girls sprinted up the stone stairs.

Ahiliyah watched them go, satisfied they'd got the scare they deserved.

That satisfaction quickly faded, replaced by guilt. Had she just terrified two little girls who didn't know any better?

"Wow, Liyah," she said to herself. "You're a real example to others, huh?"

Well, maybe next time they'd think twice before they called people names.

Would the girls grow up someday and learn to look past Sinesh's disfigurement, to see the person inside? Maybe. Ahiliyah had. But she was one of the few. Most people didn't want to go anywhere near "the spider."

Ahiliyah continued down the stairway, loving how the narrow walls amplified the river's roar. She reached the bottom and stepped out onto the walkway, stared out at the Bitigan River—her favorite part of Lemeth Hold.

The wide, rushing river filled the long cavern with white light. Very little pink tint here: that only happened with the small quantities flowing through the glowpipes. Ahiliyah took in a deep, slow breath, felt her body relax as she watched water rage across jutting boulders.

Two wood-and-rope footbridges stretched above the water to the far shore. One led to the fishing platform, where people threw out weighted nets. Divers also worked from that platform, tightly fastening ropes around their waists so they could enter the glowing water and not be swept away and lost forever. Below the surface, they searched for limpets, harvested rivergrass that had grown long enough for the toxins to leech out of it, or collected fibrous nawton plants.

The other footbridge led to a cliff face that had long ago been leveled and turned into a broad, tiled plaza. On that plaza, old women spent their days tearing nawton roots into long strands, braiding those strands into twine, then weaving that twine into netting. Like everyone in Lemeth, these women worked constantly, but it was an honored job reserved for those who had managed to reach old age. For every hundred girls born to the hold, perhaps ten lived long enough to earn their spot on that plaza.

Long, thick, fluffy streaks of white lined the cavern walls—imbid flowers, which grew from thin creepers that branched off a thick, winding central stem. Nothing summed up the dismal state of Ataegina like these life-saving flowers. Here, they grew all year round, so plentiful most of them went to waste, yet in other holds, people died from weakling disease because it was so dangerous to carry the flowers—to carry *anything*—from one place to another.

Ahiliyah walked across the second bridge, river mist wetting her hair and skin. She stopped in the middle to take in the view. So much *power* rushing past far, beneath her feet. The current steadily turned the tall water wheel mounted on the river wall. The wheel pumped the water into the glowpipes that ran through the corridors, rooms, and tunnels, illuminating Lemeth Hold. Without that wheel, without that water, life would be dark indeed.

Stalactites hung down from the cavern ceiling above, their dim yellow glow lighting up the ever-present river mist. Furgles crawled on and among the stalactites. Furgles were easy to catch, and easy to cook—just boil them until their shells split. She'd eaten more of those animals than she could count, and was glad she'd brought back spice from Dakatera. Furgles had no taste—without spice, eating them was like chewing water.

Ahiliyah saw a great bat flying upstream, toward her. Its four long wings seemed to flap in slow motion. The creature skimmed the river's glowing surface, probably looking for a crelfish. Suddenly, it flapped hard and shot straight up toward the ceiling. Wings spread, it came to a hovering stop between two long stalactites. The bat's legs reached out—long talons sank into a furgle. The furgle let out a croak of distress, barely audible over the river's steady roar, but it was already too late. The great bat dropped like a rock and flew fast upstream, skimming the water. As it flew, it pushed the furgle beneath the surface. If talon punctures hadn't already killed the animal, it would quickly drown.

A hundred yards downstream, cavern and river banked to the right, out of sight. The great bat followed that bend, and was gone.

Ahiliyah didn't feel bad for the furgle. The animal was destined to die, either by bat, by person, or when it grew too old and weak to cling to the stalactites. On Ataegina, death was never far away.

Such a beautiful place, this chamber. She loved it here almost as much as she loved it up on the surface. The river glowed like a living, moving jewel, and yet it was nothing compared to the spectacle of a sunrise.

Sometimes she and Tolio would sit together on this bridge, their feet dangling over the side. He would bring fresh-baked bread and they would sit in silence, the river's roar the only conversation they needed. Thinking of him brought back the fact that she only had a day before she had to leave again—in the little time she had, sitting in silence wasn't what she wanted to do with him, and she knew that wasn't what he wanted to do with her.

Ahiliyah continued across the bridge to the plaza. There, two dozen old women sat in a steaming hot spring, working with the long, wet nawton fibers that soaked along with them. They smiled at her. So much joy on those wrinkled faces—probably because they were constantly high from chewing on Lisa's root all day. The root helped them forget the pain of their ancient bodies.

"Hello, everyone," Ahiliyah said as she passed out her last sticks of candy. The women smiled their toothless smiles, their eyes beamed with love. Most runners brought them nothing. Ahiliyah always tried to find some treat for her elders.

She wondered what the women talked about all day as they braided rope and twine, wove fishing nets and made hidey suits. If she survived her next five runs, maybe she would live long enough to find out.

But she didn't *want* to give up running. When she became a double-slash, maybe she would just keep going. Sometimes people did that. Tristan Garza, from Dakatera Hold, had supposedly made *thirty* runs. What were the odds of surviving that many trips across the surface? Ahiliyah had made only five, yet on those runs she had seen four people die or be carried away to Black Smoke Mountain.

Every time she went to the surface, she knew it might be her last.

She said goodbye to the ladies and walked across the damp stone to see Sinesh. He was alone. He was always alone.

"Hello, General."

With his one good eye, the scarred old man looked up at her.

"*General*," he said, his tone mocking. "Why don't you call me *spider* like the others do? I am no longer a general."

"You are to me. You had great victories."

The old man laughed, a harsh rasp gurgled out by what was left of his throat.

"I won a few skirmishes, then lost the greatest battle the world has ever seen. Sit and be still while I finish this net."

In a way, Sinesh's skinny, scarred body did resemble a three-limbed version of the skeletal, eight-limbed spiders. The ones in the ancient drawings, anyway—no one alive had ever seen a real spider. That didn't mean Ahiliyah doubted their existence. Spiders turned people into demons, and she'd seen *plenty* of demons.

Still, it was a horrible thing to call someone so brave, so important.

Ahiliyah sat and watched him work. With his withered, three-fingered right hand, Sinesh wrapped twine around his left foot, pinning the leading edge between his big toe and index toe. Ragged, parallel scars ran down that leg from when the demon had raked him.

His right leg was the least-damaged part of his body, carrying only a few scars. His chest and the right side of his face were nothing *but* scars. He had only patches of hair left, the rest his scalp twisted into gnarled flesh.

He had no right eye, just a hollow socket hooded with wrinkled, drooping skin. Demon blood had eaten away half of his upper lip. His teeth—the few that were left—were visible through that hole. So much damage, yet still Sinesh still did his part for the hold.

He'd learned to use his right foot like another hand. The leg bent sharply at the knee, his foot up by his chest. Right foot and right hand combined to weave twine, to tie permanent knots, to craft nets, hammocks, hidey suits, anything that required skill and finesse.

His skinny arm and leg pulled, looped, tied, wrapped. Before her eyes, the webbing took shape. He performed these actions automatically, without thinking, as repetitive and easy to him as breathing was to her.

"I made it back," Ahiliyah said.

He nodded. "Obviously."

"You promised that if I did, you'd tell me the story again."

Sinesh paused in mid-weave. "The horrors that happened to me could happen to you, child. Why do you wish to hear the same story over and over again?"

Ahiliyah wondered what it would be like to see the world with only one eye.

"Because it helps keep me sharp."

Sinesh paused, then continued weaving. "As you wish."

Ahiliyah closed her eyes and listened to his scratchy voice tell a story she already knew so well that she could picture every moment in her mind as if she had lived it herself.

Sinesh and his three surviving men had almost made it home.

They were only half a kilometer away when the demon surprised them. It drove its tailspike through Christuno's shoulder, a blow that cracked bone and splattered blood across the rocks. Terrified, the other two men forgot their training. They dropped their heavy crossbows and ran. Sinesh did not run—he fought to save Christuno from being carried away.

Sinesh thrust his demon fork, impaling the beast. Had the two men stayed, one could have also used his fork, helping to pin the demon, while the other hit it with crossbow bolts.

Sinesh fought on, alone.

The black beast was too powerful for him. It swung an arm down, snapping the demon fork's staff, then reached out, long black fingers grabbing Sinesh's right hand. The demon yanked, trying to pull Sinesh in, but the pull was so strong it ripped off two of the man's fingers.

Broken shaft still in his left hand, Sinesh stumbled back, blood spilling down.

The demon screeched. It dropped to all fours, gathered, and sprang.

Sinesh fell to his back, planted the shaft's butt against the rock. The falling demon impaled itself on the broken end. Sinesh used the beast's momentum to carry it over him, planted his boot soles on the gnarled body to help it along. Sinesh rolled backward and kicked out hard—the demon sailed five yards, crashed into a boulder so hard two of its backsticks broke off.

The beast righted itself. Burning blood poured from its wounds, sizzling against rock, melting dirt into tiny, smoking puddles. The demon clawed at the smoking, broken spear shaft still embedded in its chest.

Sinesh saw his only chance—a dropped crossbow, still cocked, long shaft waiting to fly. He ran for the weapon. The demon rushed him. Sinesh dove, grabbed the big crossbow, and rolled to his back. Before he could shoot the beast landed on him, pinning him to the ground.

Claws raked down the man's leg.

The demon's head came close, so close Sinesh smelled its putrid breath, so close the creature's hateful hiss was the only sound in the world. Thick saliva dripped in wiggling strands. Black lips wrinkled back, the jaws opened, and inside that mouth Sinesh saw the toothtongue sliding forward, opening to strike.

One-handed, Sinesh hauled the crossbow butt to his shoulder, angled it up and pulled the trigger.

The long bolt drove through the extended toothtongue and into the demon's long black head. The bolt's point punched the other side, an eruption of black chitin, thick yellow flesh, and splashing green blood. The beast shuddered, then collapsed, trapping Sinesh beneath. Burning blood flowed onto his left arm, his chest, his face.

As his nose filled with the acrid scent of his own bubbling flesh, Sinesh began to scream.

Horribly wounded, Christuno stumbled over, pushed the dead beast off. Sinesh's left arm smoldered and sizzled, a mess of wet-pink and yellow-red, the acid eating through skin and muscle, scoring bone.

His own blood draining away, Christuno fought to save Sinesh just as Sinesh had fought to save him. Christuno dug his fingers into Sinesh's eye socket, scooped out acid and melted eye, flung the mess away.

Christuno drew his little friend, used the small blade to cut away the bubbling spots of Sinesh's skin and muscle. There wasn't time for precision or care, only time to slice and throw. Christuno's blood flowed, as did Sinesh's, puddles of wet red mingling on the stone and dirt.

When the last smoking patches of Sinesh had been carved away, Christuno bandaged himself as best he could, trying to stem his bleeding long enough to haul Sinesh back to the hold. Sinesh had risked everything to save Christuno who, in turn, risked everything to save Sinesh.

Against the odds, both men survived.

Sinesh was never the same, of course. Crippled, a withered husk of a man, he recovered as much as one can recover from such catastrophic injuries.

Christuno fared slightly better. His wounds healed, although his arm never worked properly again. Eventually, he married. His wife bore him a son. That son grew up, married, and had a daughter.

A daughter named *Ahiliyah.*

Sinesh had sacrificed his future to save Christuno Cooper. If he had not, Ahiliyah would have never been born.

"Ahiliyah?"

She twitched, realized that Sinesh was talking to her.

"Yes?"

"You have something for me," Sinesh said. "I hope you do."

"Oh, yes." She'd almost forgotten.

She looked behind her, to make sure the old women weren't watching, then across the river, to make sure no one else was, either. From her pocket, she pulled out the last of her gifts—a small pouch of crushed red moss.

"Set it in the twine coil," Sinesh said.

Ahiliyah did, glad no one could see the bag inside the coil. Red moss was forbidden. Too much of it, even a few grains too much, could kill. Almost any amount left people nearly comatose for hours at a time. In tiny doses, though, it could mask pain.

Pain, the only thing Sinesh possessed in abundance.

"Tell me of the run," he said, and began weaving again.

She told him, taking care to review every detail. Even with that focus, though, Sinesh asked questions that revealed to her things she'd glossed over or forgotten. He seemed to be able to crawl inside her mind, to experience the run as she had. When she finished, he paused his work, a strand of twine running from his foot to his hand.

"You've seen them in daylight," he said. "Three times now."

Ahiliyah nodded. "I think it is a pattern. I think they are changing."

Sinesh stared off. "Then we will all die." He started weaving again.

His response surprised her. "What do you mean? We can fight."

"You told the Margrave, and he ignored you. Correct?"

Ahiliyah said nothing.

"As long as that man is in charge, nothing will happen," Sinesh said. "If the demons change and we do not, we are finished. They killed thousands. There are no people left in the lowlands. The demons have no choice but to hunt us in the mountains. The holds can't stay hidden forever, Ahiliyah. It is only a matter of time before Lemeth falls."

Sinesh was the smartest, wisest person she knew. How could he think there was no hope?

He paused. His stare made her wonder if she'd done something wrong.

"If we are to survive, someone must lead," he said. "The Margrave will not. I have tried to convince him otherwise. So have many others—people who are now dead. If we are to survive, someone must take over."

"We can vote him out."

The old man laughed his raspy laugh. "Vote him out? After *five* runs, can you still be that naïve? The next vote isn't for another year, and no matter how many votes are cast for his opposition, he will win. He controls the warriors, Ahiliyah. He who controls the warriors counts the votes. You are old enough to figure out the rest."

Had the Margrave cheated? That seemed impossible, and yet…

The elections were held every four years. Aulus Darby had won every election he'd entered. Just as his father had before him.

Their family had ruled Lemeth for thirty-six years.

"We have to do something," Ahiliyah said.

"We?" Sinesh shook his head. "I am too old and too weak to play such games. If the demons come or if they do not, I will die anyway. And if you, my little fool, try to do anything, then you will die sooner than I."

He stopped weaving. There was enough there now that Ahiliyah recognized what he was making—a hidey suit for a young runner, one even smaller than Creen.

Sinesh reached into the coil of twine, opened the bag of red moss. He licked his fingertip, stuck it in the bag, then touched the clinging red powder to his tongue.

"Enough talk about doom and gloom," he said. "You would like to hear one of my stories, perhaps, from when I was not the crippled man you see before you? Shall I tell you again of how I led Lemeth to victory over the Bisethians in the Battle of Bigsby's Pass?"

She loved his war stories, loved the way he told them. So much detail, from arms and armor to tactics, weather conditions, terrain, right down to the food the soldiers ate, the conditions they endured before the battle. Sinesh remembered all of it.

Simply listening to him, though, wouldn't chase the dark thoughts from her mind. She needed to be active. She needed to *learn* from him.

"I'd rather play out the Battle of Hollow Hill, if that's all right."

Hollow Hill was where Sinesh had led his two hectons—two hundred soldiers—to victory against a force more than twice as large. The battle had turned the tide against the Northerners, resulted in them fleeing to the ocean and abandoning their invasion of Ataegina.

Sinesh nodded. "Get the pieces."

Ahiliyah stood and walked to a large coil of rope. Inside, out of sight, was a wooden box. She set the box down next to Sinesh. She opened the box, and started setting out the pieces—limpet shells, each with a thin, pointed stick glued to it. Each shell represented ten warriors. Some shells were painted yellow, some blue.

She pushed fifty yellow shells toward Sinesh. The old man smiled.

"You wish for me to be the Northerners? To have the superior force?"

"Superior *numbers*," Ahiliyah said. "There is no equal to a Lemethian spearman."

Sinesh nodded. "True. But are you sure you want to play the Lemethians in this scenario? I won't make the same mistakes my opponents made that day."

Ahiliyah counted out twenty blue shells, arranged them on the flat stones in front of her.

"I'm sure," she said. "I like the challenge… but *no cheating* this time, all right?"

Sinesh lined up some of his pieces into a block consisting of three rows of ten. The glued sticks pointed forward—a representation of the spears of a phalanx.

"Girl, how many times must I tell you? In war, if—"

"*If you aren't trying to cheat, you don't really want to win,*" Ahiliyah said. "I know, I know. Just set up the pieces, old man."

7

Tolio arched his back. Ahiliyah gripped his shoulders, fingertips digging into his muscles. In the fading light of the glowjar, she watched his face, watched his eyes scrunch tight.

Pleasure washed over her, shook her, *owned* her, wiped out all other thoughts. For one instant, there was nothing but her and him. For one sweet moment, she was whole.

Tolio fell to her side, his chest heaving.

"My god, you're good at that," he said. He wiped sweat from his forehead.

He was good at it, too. He wasn't her first lover, but he was the best she'd had by far. Tolio didn't need to be told what to do, yet when she did ask for something in particular, he listened. Those two things combined drove her insane with lust. Add his handsome face to that mix, and perhaps it was a good thing she had to do runs after all, or she would want to spend all of her time getting sweaty with him.

He took in a big breath, held it, let it out slow. "I love you, Liyah."

Tolio said that a lot. She never said it back. She *liked* him, liked being with him, but she wasn't sure if that was love or not.

Like many young Lemethians, Ahiliyah and Tolio had stolen away to the armory to be together. They were a little old for the armory, truth be told—it was a place for teenagers discovering themselves, mostly—but she preferred it.

Tolio's room was too close to his parents' room. She preferred to meet him in the armory because she could leave when she wanted to.

She'd had him over to her room twice—the second time, he'd insisted on talking about their "future" together, and when she'd asked him to leave, he refused. She'd had to leave her own room to get away from the conversation.

She sighed, reveling in how her body felt. So relaxed. So at peace.

Weapons and armor packed the expansive, dark chamber. Rows upon rows of old spears, demon forks, shelves filled with bronze chestplates, shields and helmets … the place seemed to go on and on. All part of King Paul's once-great army, all part of his constant threat to anyone who dared rise up against him.

"Hungry?" Tolio propped himself on one elbow, picked up a cupcake from a wooden tray next to the bed roll, held it toward her.

The cupcake smelled so good. She took it; it was still warm. Tolio had made them for her, even put icing on them—white, topped with four black lines crossed by a slash. She bit into it, reveling in the sweetness. Sex made everything better, even food.

At least for a little while.

"I said *I love you*, Liyah. Do you love me?"

The scent of the cupcake hit her again, but this time it smelled… sour. It made her queasy. Maybe Brandun killing the vootervert bothered her more than she thought. Or, more likely, Tolio's constant pressure made her sick to her stomach.

She handed him the cupcake; she didn't want anymore. Maybe later. She chewed, swallowed, annoyed that she couldn't even have five minutes to herself to enjoy the treat.

"I don't have time in my life for that now," she said. "I have to focus on my runs."

She hoped he would leave it alone. He did not.

"Life is short," Tolio said. "And damn shorter for runners. You shouldn't go out anymore."

"I have five more runs to make."

He stroked her hair. "Not if you're pregnant."

This again?

"You know how I feel about that," she said. "I asked you not to mention it. Didn't I?"

"I'm a grown man. I don't answer to you."

Which was why she never wanted to get pregnant by him. He didn't understand how things *should* be. In Lemeth, women answered to men, but when love was real, both partners answered to each other. A few people in Lemeth understood that. Brandun's parents—Cadence and Aaron, before Aaron died—had understood it, treated each other like equals, but that was rare with men and women.

Not for the first time, Ahiliyah wished she was attracted to girls. Britt Malmsteen and Theora Denisander had been together for years. They didn't treat each other poorly. One didn't rule over the other.

But Ahiliyah wasn't attracted to girls. She liked boys. Boys like Tolio.

"You don't answer to me and I don't answer to you, either," she said. "Understand?"

She stared into his eyes, stared hard, thinking he might look away, like Creen or Brandun did when she lectured them. Tolio didn't look away, though. The four lines and a slash tattooed on his right shoulder were evidence to his five runs—after staring down demons, maybe it was hard to be intimidated by anyone, especially a woman so much smaller than he was.

"I understand," he said. "But I just… I mean… don't you ever think about your mother?"

He sounded open and honest. He wasn't trying to control her anymore, wasn't trying to lead her—he was asking a genuine question. He wanted to know how she felt. When he spoke to her like this, she could talk to him for hours and hours.

And yet, his question roiled up long-suppressed pain. "I think about her all the time."

Which wasn't true anymore, hadn't been true for a while. Lately, she thought about her mother—and her father—less and less. Which made her feel guilty as hell.

"If she'd had another baby, she might still be alive," Tolio said. "She died running. Do you want to end up like her?"

"You're an idiot. Of course I don't."

"You're running the same route that got her killed. Lemeth to Dakatera to Keflan."

Ahiliyah had been the firstborn. After her, a brother who had died as an infant. The death had hit Ahiliyah's mother hard. She couldn't bring herself to have another child. She'd returned to running. Ahiliyah had been six when her mother had gone out on a run and never come back.

"It's *because* she could have stopped and she didn't that I want to keep going," Ahiliyah said. "I need to finish my obligation. For her. For my father."

Her father had been a warrior. He'd died when she was ten, in a raid against Biseth. Both of her parents had given everything in service of Lemeth Hold. If she died in service, just as they had, that was the will of God.

Ahiliyah rolled out her neck, tried to let her annoyance go.

"Look," she said, "I appreciate that you want a family, but I don't want a baby."

He smiled. "You will. All the mothers say that about you, that someday you'll change."

And just like that, Ahiliyah's annoyance returned, stronger than it had been before.

"Aiko didn't change," she said. "She doesn't have a baby. She doesn't want one."

Tolio laughed. "You want to be like that dried-up old bitch?"

"Aiko Laster is on her twenty-third run," Ahiliyah said. "*Twenty-third*. She's a hero."

Tolio fell back on the bed roll. "Hero? Maybe she's survived a long time, sure, but she's going to die out there. It's inevitable. Same for you, Liyah—if you don't stop running, sooner or later the demons are going to get you."

How could he so casually dismiss Aiko's accomplishments, disrespect her choices?

Maybe it was time to find someone else to fuck.

"So say you get me pregs," she said. "I pop out a baby like almost every other woman in this damn place, then six months after I give birth I'm back on the surface. I still have to do my ten runs, you know."

His fingertips caressed her hip. "Not if you get pregnant again."

And again. And again. Until she turned thirty. That was how most women did it in Lemeth—have a baby, get another in their belly as soon as possible. Repeat often enough, survive until thirty, and your obligation is fulfilled.

She was more than a breeding machine. She didn't know *what* she was yet, not really, but her life had to be more than just making babies and taking care of them. The women who wanted that life? Good for them. The hold needed mothers, needed babies.

That life was not for her. Why couldn't she become a warrior? She knew danger. She was willing to fight. She was as good with a spear as any man.

Ahiliyah shifted to the side, started to slide off the bed roll.

Tolio grabbed her wrist. "Stay." He grinned. "I'm ready again."

He meant it playfully, enticingly. It came across like neither.

"Let me go." She heard the coldness in her own words.

Tolio's grin faded. He didn't release her. "Think about your future. I won't wait forever."

She hadn't even been back for a full day and night, and already he was putting this pressure on her. Had he completely forgotten what it was like to survive a run?

"Tolio, if you don't let me go, I will break your thumb."

Tolio laughed; it sounded forced. He was bigger than her, and stronger, but there was a vast difference between the monthly phalanx training required of everyone in Lemeth and an active runner's grueling regimen. Add in that he'd spent the last three years in the bakery with his family—all the sweets a boy could eat—and he wasn't as skinny as he'd once been.

On the other hand, Ahiliyah's body was lean. Lean and *hard*. Could she *beat* Tolio in a fight? Maybe not. But win or lose, they both knew she could hurt him.

He eased his grip, making it soft, sensual.

"Sorry I grabbed you," he said. "I didn't mean it like you took it."

Unlike the tough-guy laugh, his apology was genuine. She felt bad for threatening him.

"I'm sorry, too," she said.

Ahiliyah slid off the bed roll. This time, he let her go. As he watched, she slid her shift back on. She tilted her head toward the cupcakes. There were five left.

"Can I still take these?"

"Of course," he said. "Bring the tray back to me later, all right?"

There was longing in those words, and trepidation. He knew he'd made a mistake.

Her mood shifted yet again. She felt bad for Tolio. He'd made it clear he wanted to be with her, for good. Tolio was acting the way boys in love were supposed to act.

She was the one who wasn't following the unwritten rules.

Ahiliyah knelt on the bed roll, leaned in and kissed him.

"Of course I'll bring it back," she said.

He smiled, relieved. "Good," He caressed her cheek. "Hey, my dad said he would like to cook us dinner. He wants to make seagrass casserole."

William Minsala was one of the nicest people in the hold. Considering that he'd lost two children on runs, his optimism was legendary.

"I love seagrass casserole," she said.

"That's why he wants to make it. Tomorrow night?"

"I can't tomorrow," Ahiliyah said. "I have to make another run the next morning."

"*Already?* But you just got back!"

"More people are sick. The Margrave wants medicine right away."

Tolio scowled, glanced away. "The Margrave should send someone else. It's not fair. You just did a run." He rubbed at his face. "No wonder you were in such a hurry to get me into bed."

His sadness… it was sweet. His hurt dug at her.

"We'll do dinner with your dad as soon as I get back."

Tolio looked at her, his eyes like ice. "*If* you get back."

She couldn't seem to win with him. Didn't he understand this run would save lives? The Margrave wanted her because she was the best at the Lemeth/Dakatera/Keflan route. The *best*.

Tolio fell to his back, stared up at the stone ceiling. "Good luck."

Ahiliyah took the cupcakes and left. She walked past racks of shields, armor and weapons. From the shadows and dark areas came the sounds of young people in love—soft conversations, quiet laughs, and, occasionally, the stifled sounds of passion.

She had to set the cupcakes down to open the heavy wooden armory door. Hinges creaked as she did, and the sounds of lovers fell silent—most of them, probably, worried about a parent or an angry brother storming in, looking for a son, a daughter, a sister.

Cupcakes in hand, Ahiliyah turned right and continued down the corridor. The armory door swung shut on its own, closed with a rattle of wood and metal.

She didn't have to walk far. The lockup was only forty yards further down the corridor. Not much else on this side of the hold. Past the lockup there were only a few small rooms. The Windens lived in that area, as did Mags Yinnish and her family, and the Baines family as well.

The lockup's arched entrance was almost identical to that of the hospital's, save for the lockup's floor-to-ceiling iron bars and the heavy iron gate. That gate, as usual, was open.

Ahiliyah walked through. Only one guard on duty: Galen Yates. He smiled wide.

"Liyah, welcome back. I would have been there to greet you, but—" he spread his hands to show the two desks of the entrance area "—duty calls."

Galen was a good man. He'd completed *six* runs, volunteering for a critical extra run to fetch medicine from Biseth a few years back. Taller than Brandun, even skinnier than Creen, Galen was stronger than he looked—in phalanx training, the shield never seemed to tire him.

"Too bad for you," she said. "I smelled *wonderful*."

Galen laughed. "I'm sure you did." His eyes flicked to the tray of cupcakes. "Speaking of things that smell wonderful…"

She gave him a cupcake.

"You are a goddess," he said. "Did Tolio make these?"

Ahiliyah nodded, even though she suspected Tolio's father had done the actual work.

Galen bit down, chewed, closed his eyes in pleasure. "I was told to expect you. You didn't have to bribe me."

"I notice you didn't tell me that *before* I gave you the cupcake."

He laughed, not caring that his mouth was full of half-chewed confection. Galen was like that—he was himself, and didn't give a damn about what other people thought of him.

"Go on in," he said. "Don't expect much from her, though."

"Anyone else in the cells?"

"Just your cousin Jane," Galen said. "Same-old, same-old."

Ahiliyah thought of asking what Jane had done, but there was no point—by mushroom wine, by red moss or by something else, Jane Xi had been intoxicated in public. Again.

"Thanks," Ahiliyah said.

Galen eyed the cupcake tray. "Any chance I can have another?"

"They're for Mari."

The tall man sighed. "Fair enough. Good luck. And remember—this is *her* choice, it's got nothing to do with you. Okay?"

Galen's one extra run meant his opinion carried more weight than those of most men.

Ahiliyah walked past the desks into the corridor that held the hold's ten iron-barred cells.

Eight cells were empty. Halfway down on the right lay Jane Xi. Ahiliyah's second cousin on her mother's side, the woman was only a few years older than Ahiliyah. Ahiliyah remembered playing with her when they were children. Jane had completed her five runs, but three of those runs had involved close calls with demons. On two of those runs, Jane's crewmates had died horribly. The losses had affected her. Sometimes, with runners, that happened. There was nothing to be done for it but hope the person eventually got over the trauma.

Ahiliyah paused at Jane's cell, thought about saying something, but Jane was passed out on the wooden cot, face hidden by her red hair. From the smell, Ahiliyah knew her cousin had shit herself. Jane was in lockup more often than not. A wasted life—it was all just so sad.

Ahiliyah reached through the bars and set one cupcake on the floor. Maybe Jane would have it when she woke up.

In the last cell on the left, Mari was sitting on the edge of her bed, staring into nothing.

"Hi," Ahiliyah said. "I brought you a treat."

Mari slowly turned her head. Dark circles under her eyes, magnified by her pale skin.

"Don't bother," she said. "I'm not going out there again."

Those eyes—haunted eyes, eyes that had seen too much. Part of Ahiliyah felt for her, because Ahiliyah had seen the living nightmares up close, and part of her hated Mari for trying to get out of her duty to the hold.

"That's stupid," Ahiliyah said. "You only have two… I mean, four runs to go."

Mari smiled a hopeless smile. "I was only punished two additional runs? How nice."

"Cupcakes," Ahiliyah said, holding up the tray. "They're amazing. Want one?"

Mari stared blankly at the treats. She shook her head. "Not hungry."

Ahiliyah set the tray down. She put a cupcake on the floor through the cell bars, then stood.

"Mari, they're going to kill you."

Mari shrugged. "Yeah."

Ahiliyah had known this woman all her life. While not die-hard friends, they'd grown up together, shared in the joys and sadness of hold life. Mari had talked about raising a family, following in her parents' footsteps and becoming a diver.

"You always wanted a kid," Ahiliyah said. "Isn't that worth keeping on?"

Mari stared at the floor. "I won't bring a new life into this world of death."

Ahiliyah thought of a hundred things to say, a dozen reasons why Mari should make those last four runs, but knew none of them would have an impact—there was nothing to be done.

"I'm so sorry." Ahiliyah knelt, put the last two cupcakes on the floor inside the cell, then left. Jane was still passed out—now her cell smelled like she'd pissed herself as well.

Best to put both women out of her mind. It seemed the demons could take lives even from a distance. Mari and Jane had both given up. Ahiliyah would not.

She would *never* give up.

8

Ahiliyah stepped onto the training pit sand. Many people hated phalanx reserve exercises. Not her. She loved all of it. And she'd been trying to get stronger—perhaps today would be the day she could finally show she belonged in the warriors.

She milled around with the other forty-seven Lemethians who had reported for this training session. Takwan and Tameika Baines had come, despite their three sons still lying in hospital beds. Mags Yinnish and Cruden Poller had put their wine-making and glass-blowing duties, respectively, on hold, or perhaps apprentices were doing the never-ending work. Master fisherman Callow Winden and all of his junior workers were there; there would be no fish tonight. Ahiliyah saw Lucas Kim and Tobias Penn, the runners from Mari's crew. Would one of them become a crew leader, or would Aiko and Tinat give the promotion to someone else?

Everyone wore spearhead scabbards on their hips, had shaft holsters slung across their backs—they'd use the longer warrior spears, which were heavier and more awkward than the runner spear she favored. Ahiliyah eyed the big stack of heavy shields. In her quest to join the warriors, the shield was her nemesis.

In Lemeth, if you could walk, you trained. That included even those who would be basically worthless in a fight. If war came with another hold, the Margrave—as had his father before him—wanted to make sure Lemeth could field as many reservists as possible. While Ahiliyah had never been in a battle, she'd studied enough to know that war often came down to superior training and superior numbers. The phalanx had not worked against the demons, but if Takanta or Vinden should ever march on Lemeth, the Lemethians would be ready.

Phalanx training happened in two-hour shifts. There wasn't enough room in the pit sands for everyone to show up at once. Ahiliyah was in the fourth session of the day. There would be three sessions more before the day was out.

Will Pankour stood at attention, waiting to call the training session to order. Ahiliyah hoped it was his first session of the day—the warrior got mean when he got tired.

"Liyah! Liyah!"

Ahiliyah turned to see her friend Panda running toward her. *Waddling* might have been a better word for his labored movement. In a place where no one knew for sure when the next meal might come, he somehow weighed almost twice as much as any other person his same height.

"Hi, Panda." She gave him a big hug. "I haven't seen you in ages."

He pointed upward. "A signalmyn apprentice's job is never done."

Panda was the apprentice to Daneton Sander, Lemeth's master signalmyn. The two spent weeks at a time in a small room near the top of Lemeth Mountain.

"The last two times I've visited you he's been asleep," Ahiliyah said. "You're going to be the master soon."

His face flushed red, but he smiled. "Someday, I hope."

Panda was nineteen, the same age she was. He'd probably be named master signalmyn in a year or so, the youngest in the history of Lemeth.

There was something different about Panda. When he'd trained to be a runner, when Aiko had practically starved him in an effort to get him in shape, the best they managed was to make him stop gaining—but the boy had never really *lost* weight. Even without a pack that weighed ten bricks or more, Panda could barely climb a foothill, let alone manage fifty-mile hikes or scale a mountainside. Any run he went on would not only end in his death, but also, most likely, the death of his crewmates. On Aiko's recommendation, the Council excused Panda from his obligation.

Fortunately for Panda, he was as smart as he was fat. Maybe not as smart as Creen, but intelligent enough to understand the math, maps and code needed to be a signalmyn.

Not as smart as Creen...

A thought struck her—if Panda became the master, he would need an apprentice.

"Has Creen Dinashin ever come up to the signaling station?"

Panda's nose wrinkled. "He's an asshole, Liyah. No one likes him."

Creen was an asshole, true, but he was in her crew—it was her duty to look out for him. When he finished his mandatory five runs, if he didn't have a job that was critical to the hold, the Council might make him do more.

"I think he'd love to see what you do," she said. "Can I bring him up to visit?"

Panda shook his head. "No way. He always calls me fat."

"You *are* fat."

"Yeah, but that doesn't mean people have to be *mean* about it." He glanced at Will, then back. "If you'll help me get through the training today, though, you can bring him up."

"Done," she said.

Panda's chubby face broke into a wide smile. "Thank you. You know I'm no good at this."

She squeezed his shoulder. "I know. I'll help. We'll get through it together."

"Ranks of twelve," Will called out in his booming voice. "Assemble your weapon."

Before Panda could protest, Ahiliyah pulled him into the front rank. The reservists lined up in four lines of twelve. People unslung their holsters and got to work. Panda drew his spearhead from its scabbard. Ahiliyah slapped his leg to get his attention.

"Put your blade away," she said quietly. "Shaft first, remember?"

Panda nodded, slid the spearhead back into his scabbard, clumsily unslung his holster.

Ahiliyah assembled her own weapon. Butt-spike, then halfstaff, then coupler, then halfstaff. She took a knee, angled the assembled shaft over her thigh, drew her spearhead from its scabbard. She slid the spearhead's hollow handle over the halfstaff's tapered end, grunted as she twisted it tight.

She stood, butt-spike in the sand, spear tip pointed straight up. Ahiliyah was pleased to see she was the first one finished.

"You're all taking too long," Will called out. "The enemy is marching on us. *Move it!*"

Panda hadn't even put the coupler on yet. Ahiliyah handed him her spear, finished assembling his weapon, then switched back just as the rest of the trainees were standing, their spears at their sides.

"Thanks," Panda said. "I need to work on that."

"Yeah, you do," Ahiliyah said. "It's not an optional skill."

Will slowly walked in front of the first rank.

"What you do here today, you will do when the fighting is real," he said. "You are not an invidual, you are a unit. If you fail, the man on your left or right will die. If he fails, you will die. Remember our motto—the strength of the phalanx is the spearman."

"*And the strength of the spearman is the phalanx*," Ahiliyah yelled in unison with the others. The call and response marked the true beginning of the training.

Will positioned himself on the formation's left side. "Front rank, *lower!*"

Ahiliyah held her spear shaft not at the coupling—the weapon's mid-point—but halfway between that and the butt-spike. When she lowered her spear parallel to the ground, the heavy butt-spike balanced out the weight of the rest of the shaft and the bronze spearhead. She held the spear easily, but at almost two bricks in weight, she knew it would soon feel much heavier.

On her right, Panda lowered his spear.

Will bellowed: "Second rank, *lower!*"

The second rank did as ordered, their spears leveled between the people in the front rank. Whoever was behind Ahiliyah missed, brought the staff down on the back of her head.

"*Hey!*" Pain blossomed, but she managed to keep her spear in position.

"Sorry, Liyah," said Martin Yates from behind her. He was in his twenties, a big man, yet still as uncoordinated as a teenager in a first growth spurt. His spear dropped down on her right.

Twenty-four spears now pointed forward, parallel and deadly. Ahiliyah pushed away the pain, reveling in the moment. Even with reservists, it made for a fearsome sight: a hedgerow of shafts, metal blades reflecting the glowpipe light.

"March and turn," Will said. "Takwan Baines, call out the steps."

Takwan did as he was told. The phalanx marched forward.

The spears weren't all parallel to the ground—some angled slightly up, some slightly down. The steps weren't in unison, either; each of Takwan's counts was joined by a muffled *thump* instead of the sharp report that came when the well-trained warriors did this same drill. When the reservists reached the training pit wall, Takwan called out the turn. Ahiliyah and the others in the front two ranks raised their spears to vertical. Everyone turned to their right and faced back the way they had come, reversing the formation. The front two ranks lowered their spears—Ahiliyah and Panda were now in the rear rank, spears pointed up. Were people in the ranks ahead of them to fall in battle, or lose a spear, Ahiliyah and Panda would step up to take their place.

"*March*," Takwan called out.

Panda grunted with effort. "I can't hold this much longer."

"We only just started," Ahiliyah whispered. "Come on, Panda, toughen up."

They hadn't even got to shield practice yet. How could the boy be so *weak*?

Will drilled them for the next twenty minutes, marching, doing full turns, half-turns, and practicing one-handed spear thrusts. Ahiliyah's right arm began to burn. By the time Will called for everyone to set down their spears and fetch shields, she was sweating and breathing hard. At least she was better off than Panda—the boy was already shaking and looked like he might pass out.

The shields… would she fail again?

She pulled one from the rack, instantly feeling the weight—at five bricks or so, the bronze-covered wooden shield was one-quarter her body weight. She slid her left arm through the leather strap bolted to the shield's concave side.

So *heavy*. She could do it this time. She *could*.

She moved to her position, held her spear in her right hand.

"Reservists," Will called out, "shields *up!*"

Ahiliyah lifted her shield. The lines weren't quite as neat as before. Even though most of the women and several of the men struggled to control both sword and spear, the phalanx now looked unstoppable, a moving wall of bronze with rows of deadly blades reaching far in front.

Will drilled them. They marched. They turned. They thrust. Over and over again.

After another twenty minutes, Ahiliyah's left arm began to shake. Her muscles burned. She struggled to keep the heavy shield up and in front of her. She fared better than Panda, who stumbled on a turn, the edge of his shield digging into the sand.

Will was there in an instant. "Panda! You miserable *maggot*! You just let the people on either side of you *die!* Pick up that shield!"

Panda did, his eyes wide with fear, his face red with shame. Will screamed at him a few moments more, until the thump of another dropped shield echoed off the stone walls. Will moved off to scream at that person, then barked more orders—the drills continued.

Ahiliyah struggled on, sweat pouring, but she knew she wouldn't make it. Warriors had to hold shields up and in position for at least an hour—thirty-five minutes into drills, the weight became too much. Her shield drooped once, twice, then, eventually, it hung down, throwing off her balance. She fell to the sand, found herself looking at Tameika, who had taken a knee.

"Don't know… why we gotta do this." Tameika's face sheened with sweat. Her chest heaving, she shook her head. "We all know… how this drill turns out."

Will raised his fist. "Phalanx, *halt!*"

Some people fell to one knee, unable to keep the shield up any longer. Those that remained standing, shields still in position, were almost all men.

"Those of you who stumbled or dropped your shield, get a bow," Will said. "We will now practice combined phalanx and missile support."

Tameika got to her feet. "About fucking time." She dragged her shield to the rack.

Ahiliyah felt humiliated. She'd lasted longer than the rest who had failed, but she had failed nonetheless. As she had in many previous training sessions, she came to a frustrating and inevitable conclusion— she just wasn't big enough.

Women couldn't join the warriors, but did her gender even matter? The shield was a quarter her weight—if she couldn't carry it properly for an hour or more, she couldn't be a warrior. It was that simple.

"Liyah, you did well," Will said. "Now, go get a bow."

Fighting back tears, her arms shaking, Liyah carried her shield to the stack.

9

From being humiliated to being honored—what a difference a few hours could make.

Bathed, dressed in a formal, sleeveless white shift, Ahiliyah sat on the Community Chamber's stone steps, quietly watching the silent ceremony along with over a thousand people. Some two thousand more were still hard at work fixing crumbling corridors, working the mushroom farms, preparing food, repairing pipes… the labor needed to keep the hold alive went on and on and on.

Even the Margrave and the councilmen had come to the Community Chamber. No one spoke. Everyone watched the somber proceedings. That was the way of things.

Brandun and Creen lay on their backs, on cloth-draped tables positioned before the steps. Both boys were naked to their waists, wearing only nawton-fiber pants. No shoes.

Standing next to each table, a doctor and a child. Doctor Talbot for Brandun, Doctor Monique for Creen. Miriam—one of the girls who had begged for candy—assisted Doctor Talbot. Ahiliyah didn't know the boy assisting Doctor Monique. A Nemensalter, by the looks of his big jaw. Each assistant held a ceramic pot of black ink in one hand, a tan cloth in the other.

The doctors worked slowly, methodically, each dipping a wood-handled metal stylus into the ink, placing the ink-wet stylus tip against the runner's chest, then using a ceremonial stone dowel to tap the wooden handle.

Dip… tap-tap-tap-tap-tap.

They raised their styluses. Miriam and the Nemensalter boy wiped away ink and blood.

Dip… tap-tap-tap-tap-tap. Wipe.

Dip… tap-tap-tap-tap-tap. Wipe.

A heavy black line steadily formed on each boy's left breast. Brandun already had one line; this was his second. Creen was getting his third.

When the doctors finished, Brandun and Creen rose without a word. Tears in Creen's eyes. That was understandable—the tattoos hurt, Ahiliyah knew from experience.

Even Brandun had cried a little on his first line. That had been three months ago. He wasn't crying now. His face had a hard set to it. He'd changed so much since being assigned to Ahiliyah's crew, just six months earlier. He'd grown two inches in that time, added ten bricks in weight—all muscle. He was closer to the man he would become than the boy he no longer was.

Without a sound, Brandun and Creen took their seats in the first row: Brandun on Ahiliyah's right, Creen on her left. Normally, they would have been tattooed together.

But not this time.

Ahiliyah stood, walked to the table.

Monique moved to the stone seats and sat. The Nemensalter boy pulled the fabric off the table, meticulously folded it as everyone watched, then sat next to Monique.

Ahiliyah still wore her simple nawton-fiber shift. She could not expose her breast in public, like the boys could. Women were tattooed on the right shoulder. Ahiliyah already had four parallel lines there. Each one marked a terrifying trek across the surface. This one, though—this one was a true badge of honor.

She lay on the table, stared up at the arched ceiling above. She heard the clack of wood on ceramic as Doctor Talbot dipped his stylus into the pot.

The voice of Aulus Darby broke the silence: "Miriam, sit. I will assist Doctor Talbot."

Ahiliyah's eyes widened. She forced herself to remain still, not to sit up and see if this was really happening. The Margrave himself would be part of her ceremony?

He leaned over her, smiling yet serious.

"Your bravery means everything, Ahiliyah. The warriors are our muscle, the workers our bones, the Council our beating heart, and the runners are our blood. We recognize your commitment to the hold. I salute your first five runs, and I salute your next five."

Her chest tingled and pulsed. The Margrave, recognizing her in front of *everyone*.

The cold stylus pressed against her shoulder, sending goosebumps up and down her skin. Ahiliyah closed her eyes and prepared for the now-familiar pain of the tattoo. Her fifth—her *slash*.

Tap-tap-tap-tap-tap.

10

Many had come to the tattoo ceremony, and many had continued to work.

Everyone came to the execution. People packed into the stands above the training pit, so much so that the wooden bleachers creaked in complaint. Children climbed support poles. Men and women alike sat on the edge of the pit, feet dangling over the side, arms and heads leaning on the lower rail.

A tattoo ceremony was a celebration of life. An execution, a reminder that death comes to all—some sooner than others. Ahiliyah should have watched the event alongside Brandun and Creen, but she wanted to be alone. She was afraid seeing Mari might make her cry; she did not want the boys to know she could be so weak.

Down in the pit, the warriors stood in ranks against the stone walls: bronze shields on their left arms, fully assembled spears in their right hands—spearheads pointed high, spear butts resting against the sand. The round shields were all the same: painted blue, with a yellow sun rising above the distinctive brown outline of Lemeth Mountain. While the paint was new, the metal beneath them was often gouged and battered.

The warriors' armor consisted of helmets, chestplates, shin and foot guards, all made of bronze. The helmets' riveted-on faceplates had one horizontal line to see through, and a vertical line that made it easier to breathe. The lines—both too thin for a spearpoint to slide through—formed a distinctive "T" shape. Like the shields, most of the armor was scratched and dented. Some of that damage had been incurred in the past few years, fighting off raiders, but the majority of it had come decades ago—possibly *centuries* ago—during the wars against the Northerners, or between the cities of Ataegina.

Everyone, warriors and spectators alike, watched the wooden doors set into the pit's back wall. Ahiliyah watched as well, hoping—even *praying*—she would never have to come to an event like this for one of her own crew.

The wooden doors opened; Margrave Darby stepped out, Drasko Lamech at his side, dressed in the same armor as the warriors lining the walls. They strode to the center of the sandy pit. The Margrave tilted his head back, and spoke with the commanding tone Ahiliyah had come to know, love and trust.

"People of Lemeth Hold, this is a sad moment."

His words caressed the stone walls and ceiling, came back even sweeter and louder. The man knew how to control his voice better than most warriors could control their spears.

"Everyone must contribute," he said. "That is our way. We find work for all, no matter age, strength, physical deformity or mental inability. The hardest job—running—falls to our youth, for all must prove their worth to the hold if the hold is to feed them, clothe them, protect them, give them a warm, safe place to raise families, to grow old."

The Margrave pointed to the stands, slowly sweeping his finger from left to right.

"Many of you have done your part. Those of you who are too young, someday you will bravely do your part as well. Is this not our way?"

The crowd responded in practiced unison: "*It is our way.*"

He lowered his arm. "When someone will *not* work, when someone will *not* contribute, we cannot sit idly by and let them do *nothing*. We cannot banish these freeloaders from the hold, for that was tried many times in the past. The banished always tried to get back in. They make noise. They cry, they scream, they beg… they draw the demons. Noise is the enemy."

"*Silence is strength*," the crowd chanted.

Aulus nodded, slowly turned in place as he looked up at the packed mass of people.

"Silence is strength," he said. "To preserve the silence, to preserve our way of life, when a runner will *not* run, we all know the penalty."

The crowd's volume and intensity sent a chill over Ahiliyah's skin.

"*The penalty is death*."

Aulus turned toward the open doors. Rinik Brennus and Shalim Aniketos, in full armor, entered, each holding an arm of the gagged Mari Jolla. Her hands were lashed behind her back, her ankles tied together with a short rope. She did not fight. She didn't even walk— Rinik and Shalim dragged her. Mari's bare feet left two long, parallel lines in the sand.

Ahiliyah wanted to run to her, to try one more time, to say *if you're going to die, die on the surface while doing your duty!* But there was no point. Mari knew the price of cowardice.

In a world plagued with demons, no one got a pass.

Rinik and Shalim dragged Mari before the Margrave. She hung between them, knees bent, completely defeated.

"You have failed in your duty to the hold," the Margrave said. "You have failed your people. You will leech from us no more. Captain of the Guard, carry out the sentence."

Aulus stepped aside.

Drasko dropped into a fighting position, shield in front of him, spear pointed over the top, tip aimed at Mari.

Something about the gleaming spearpoint, perhaps, made what was about to happen finally hit home. She screamed behind her gag, jerked her shoulders, tried to break free. Even if she hadn't been tied, she couldn't have come close to overpowering Rinik and Shalim.

"For the people of Lemeth," Drasko said. "For our survival."

He stepped forward and thrust the spearhead into Mari's chest— the crack of her sternum echoed through the pit.

Mari Jolla's scream stopped forever.

She hung there for a moment, arms held by the two guards. Drasko pulled the spear free. Rinik and Shalim let go. Mari fell to her side. Her blood spilled onto the sand.

Aulus walked to the doors, Drasko at his side, Rinik and Shalim falling in behind them. They wouldn't move the body—Mari would lie there for a few hours, a symbol of the price of cowardice. Workers would gather her up, carry her corpse to the river and throw it in, to be unceremoniously swept downstream with the fish guts, the garbage, and the human waste that was carried away by the strong current.

The crowd dispersed.

Ahiliyah stayed. She was still watching when Mari's small movements stopped. Still watching when her stare lost focus, when it became the endless stare of the dead.

Ahiliyah stood there, saying nothing, thinking nothing. Maybe she stood there for a few minutes, maybe for a few hours. She wasn't sure. She stayed until workers came to gather up the corpse. Only then did she become aware that she wasn't the only one watching…

Creen, high up in the bleachers. Sitting. Staring.

Brandun, on the edge of the pit, his feet hanging over the side, head resting on the rail.

Lucas Kim, Mari's crewmate, sitting in the bleacher's first row. Had he made one run with Mari, or was it two? Lucas had trained with her, bled with her, risked his life with her, and now she was gone, dead at the hands of her own people.

Fabian Acosta, sitting with his arms around the shoulders of Susannah Albrecht and Bruce Pindall, his new team members— two *children*. Susannah and Bruce were still in training. Had they seen an execution before? Probably. Everyone in the hold had, but Ahiliyah knew from personal experience that this one felt different for them. Now that they were close to making their own runs, the execution was something that could happen to them, it was now *real*.

There was no avoiding it. Everyone had to contribute. It was the way of things.

"How ridiculous."

Ahiliyah jumped at the voice on her right, slid to her left, felt a splinter dig into her left thigh—Aiko Laster, sitting right next to her. Aiko had managed to not only sneak up on Ahiliyah, but sit down next to her without making a sound. The woman's shaved head glistened beneath the glowpipe's gleam.

"You scared me," Ahiliyah said. She slid her shift up; buried in the back of her left thigh, a thick splinter. Blood oozed up around it. She saw the splinter's dark outline beneath her skin.

"If you stop paying attention to your surroundings, you deserve to be scared," Aiko said. "Turn toward me, I'll pull it out."

Oh, this was going to hurt. Ahiliyah turned her hips, letting Aiko at the splinter.

"You're acting like a child," Aiko said. "It's only pain."

It's only pain. A mantra not just of the runners and the warriors, but everyone in Lemeth.

Aiko pinched the end of the splinter. With her other hand, she pressed down on Ahiliyah's thigh. A fast pull, a stabbing sensation, and it was out—a shard of wood at least two inches long, a sheen of blood on one end. Aiko tossed it away.

"Sit," she said.

Ahiliyah sat. When Aiko Laster told you to do something, you did it.

The older woman stared down into the training pit. She seemed to be looking at the blood spot where Mari's life had spilled out onto the sand. Aiko wore a sleeveless shift—she wanted everyone to see her tattoos. Four lines and a slash, repeated four times down her left arm. Two parallel lines below the last completed group, soon to be joined by a third.

"Welcome back," Ahiliyah said. "Did Jenna and Tomas make it?"

No emotion on Aiko's face, only the stone-hard expression of a woman who'd just completed her twenty-third run. With her gaunt features, shaved head and taut, skinny body, Aiko sometimes reminded Ahiliyah of the demons.

"They did," Aiko said. "I reported to the Margrave right before he had Mari murdered."

Murdered? Ahiliyah glanced around, wondered if anyone else was close enough to hear.

"Mari refused to run," Ahiliyah said. "I tried to talk to her, but... well, she wouldn't run."

Aiko's head turned toward Ahiliyah, the gray of her eyes like chips of broken rock.

"And for that, Mari deserved to die?"

Was this a test of some kind? Aiko was always about tests, always trying to trick you, to make you think, trying to tie anything and everything to survival up on the surface. Ahiliyah felt trapped between the law of her hold and the question of her lead trainer.

"I... I don't know," Ahiliyah said.

Well, *that* was definitive. She felt like an idiot.

Aiko stared for an uncomfortable moment, then again looked out at the bloody sand.

"The Council told me about the run to Dakatera and Keflan," she said. "They asked if my crew would go instead of yours, because this run is so important."

Ahiliyah felt a surge of hope—maybe she wouldn't have to go back out so soon after all.

"I told them to send you," Aiko said.

Hope crashed to the ground, turned to guilt—why should she wish that Aiko's crew go on no rest instead of *her* crew going on no rest—then to anger.

"But... you're better," Ahiliyah said. "Your crew is better."

Aiko scratched at a scar atop her thigh. "You need the experience. I'm not going to run forever, Liyah. Our hold needs to know that someone beside me that can be counted on for a critical run. It's your turn to carry the weight. Can you do it?"

Ahiliyah blinked, searched for words that were slow in coming. "I... I'll do my best."

"Your best?" Aiko's eyes narrowed. "If you fail, how many do you think will die?"

Ahiliyah shook her head. "I'm not a doctor, I wouldn't know."

"*Guess,*" Aiko said, the one syllable loud enough to echo back from the arched ceiling.

Liyah realized, suddenly, that everyone else had left—she was alone with Aiko.

"Uh... well a lot of people are sick... maybe—" she felt a churning in her belly as she thought of what she knew, what she'd seen "—maybe fifty?"

Fifty people, dead if she and her crew didn't make it back. Ahiliyah's pulse began to race.

"Try a hundred," Aiko said. "At least. Old people mostly. Children. Babies." She again fixed Ahiliyah with those unforgiving slate eyes. "Get the medicine. Don't screw this up. And remember to *always* be aware of your surroundings—if I can sneak up on you in the safety of the hold, you won't know a demon is stalking you until it's too late."

Aiko stood and walked up the bleacher steps, somehow silent on the creaky old wood.

Ahiliyah sat there for a moment, alone, trying to control her breathing. More pressure than ever before. A hundred dead. At least. Old people. Kids. *Babies*. Mari's blood was still wet on the sand. It was all too much, too soon.

Ahiliyah left the training pit behind. She set out to find Tolio and try to forget—at least for a little while—just how fucked up her life had become.

11

"I don't know why you're making *me* do this," Creen said. "Dumbdun could carry these fucking buckets with one muscly pinky."

Ahiliyah wondered if anything could stop Creen's mouth from running.

"Brandun did phalanx training," she said. "You did not. So shut up and climb."

"All this to see that big fat lazy fuck?"

"Panda isn't lazy. And back off, he's my friend. You need to see how things work up there, Creen. It might be the job for you."

He huffed. "Fuck that. I'm too smart for it."

Ahiliyah carefully watched her steps. A glowjar hung from her neck, but its light had almost faded. Creen's glowjar was already out—in an effort to lug less up the stairs, the little shit probably hadn't completely filled it.

"Just don't be mean to Panda," she said. "All right?"

"No promises."

Here she was trying to do something good for Creen, and he was already getting on her nerves. Did he realize that if he didn't get an important job, they would probably make him do more than the mandatory five runs? Probably not—Creen thought he knew everything. He didn't belong on the surface. He was destined for something else. She didn't know what, but she felt in her bones that, someday, as annoying and rude as Creen was, he would do something amazing for the hold.

"My legs are tired," he said. "So are my arms."

So were Ahiliyah's. Her legs were screaming, in fact. She knew she was in amazing shape—one had to be to survive on the surface—but carrying two bricks worth of water up three hundred steps? That tired one out in a hurry.

"Just keep climbing," she said.

"So many damn steps. How can someone be *fat* when they have to walk this many steps?"

Maybe he'd do something amazing. The more he whined, the less sure she was.

"Creen, do you ever stop complaining?"

"I prefer the term *bravely stating the obvious*."

Anyone who climbed to the signal station had to bring two buckets with them—one full of water, one full of candles and food. Two full buckets up, two empty buckets down. That gave the signalmyn water to drink, and to flush their waste down shit-shafts that led straight to the river.

"Hey," Creen said, "we must be close—I can smell his stink."

So could Ahiliyah, although today, at least, the stink wasn't Panda's. He'd obviously bathed in the river before yesterday's training. Had to be Daneton, then, or perhaps the stench of unwashed human bodies had seeped into the stone walls. There was no way to pump water all the way up to the signal peak—considering that signalmyn stayed in their perch for weeks at a time, hand-washing only did so much.

Ahiliyah thought her legs might give out on her, but a flickering light up above told her she was close. She fought her way up the last few steps, into the candle-lit signalmyn quarters, a small stone room that stank beyond belief.

"So gross," Creen said.

Clothes scattered everywhere. A wicker basket full of food waste. Two beds—one empty, one filled by an old, snoring Daneton Sander, who had been a signalmyn longer than Aulus had been the Margrave.

Creen set his buckets down. He bent at the waist, hands on his knees, breathing heavily. He jutted his chin toward the sleeping Daneton.

"We should wake him up. Dump some of this water on him. That would be hysterical."

Ahiliyah glared. "Do it and I'll kill you."

Creen rolled his eyes, but he made no move toward Daneton. Ahiliyah hefted her water bucket again, dumped the contents into the water trough carved into the stone wall.

"It's so strange to see this much water just... sit there," she said. "It doesn't glow at all."

Creen poured his bucket into the trough. "The bacteria that make the light need food and oxygen, just like we do. Without it, the bacteria die. We could make an agitator, I bet." He stared into the water. "Yeah, I think it could work, especially if we made the trough bigger."

An agitator? What he was talking about? When Creen spoke like that, about things that Ahiliyah didn't really understand, he sounded like a different person. No whine to his voice, no arrogance... just a sense of wonder. When he talked about inventions and science, he sounded like someone else entirely—a person Ahiliyah might like to spend time with.

"I'll tell you what would be funny," Creen said. "If I peed in their trough, and they didn't know and they drank it."

Or maybe she already spent far too much time with him as it was.

"Let's see Panda," she said.

If he wasn't in this room, he was out on the observation deck. At the back of the small room, opposite the stairs, was a sliding stone door. It had been built back in King Paul's day.

Creen grabbed the metal handle and started to lean back, to slide the door open.

"Wait," Ahiliyah said.

"You *really* think there's a demon outside? Come on, Liyah, this gets so old."

The boy needed to learn lessons, lessons he should have already internalized after his three runs. If he didn't yet understand that one *always* had to be on guard, that lack of focus could put him in danger—and put her and Brandun in danger as well.

She stepped close to him. She was two inches taller than he was. He looked up at her, trying to pretend he wasn't intimidated.

"I've seen people carried off, Creen. Have you?"

He tried to roll his eyes yet again—Ahiliyah grabbed his chin, forced him to look at her. They were so close their noses almost touched. Creen's eyes flared with anger, but he didn't push her hand away. As much of a jerk as he was, he knew her experience had kept him alive.

More important, he knew she could kick his ass.

She made a claw of her hand, put her fingertips on his chest, slowly dragged them down his shirt. "Sometimes, before they take you, demons cut you with their talons." She raised her hand, thumb pressed up against flat fingers, a beak pointed at Creen's face. "Sometimes, they use their toothtongues to bite you, knock you silly." She jabbed her hand foreward—her fingers and thumb tapped Creen hard on the forehead.

He slapped at her hand, but she was too quick and had already pulled it away.

"I've watched two people carried off to Black Smoke Mountain," she said. "When your crewmates get caught, you can't help them. You can't. I never saw them again. Once you hear a crewmate *beg* for you to save them, and keep begging until their voice fades away for good, you can't *un*-hear it. It gets in your dreams. It stays there."

No glare on his face now, no anger… just fear he couldn't quite hide.

"So," Ahiliyah said, smiling, "do I want to make sure there's not a demon outside? You bet your tiny dick I do. If you ignore the rules, it won't just be you who gets carried off. It will be Brandun.

It will be *me*." She stepped back. "Now, kind sir, would you mind following protocol?"

Creen rubbed at his face. "You can be one intense bitch. Anyone ever tell you that?"

"Only the people who piss me off."

"Which I need to stop doing." He'd lost the attitude. It would come back. It always did.

Creen looked to the right of the door, found what he knew would be hanging there: a wooden mallet. He lifted it off its hook, gently tapped on the stone door: *tap-tap*, pause, *tap-tap*.

A few seconds later came the answer from the other side: *tap-tap*, pause, *tap-tap*, pause, *tap-tap*. That simple code meant that all was clear on the other side of the door.

Creen hung the mallet on the hook. "See? Told you there was nothing to worry about."

He gripped the handle and leaned back. Ahiliyah helped him. Together, they slid open the heavy door. Bright sunlight made her squint. Cold air rushed in, chilling the sweat she'd built up climbing the stairs.

Panda leaned in, smiling, his face red from the cold, a little snot under his nose.

"Liyah! So good to see you!" He looked at Creen, frowned. "You brought your friend."

"Don't worry," Creen said. "I'm not friendly at all."

He'd gone right back to being a jerk. Of course he had.

"Come on, Creen," she said. "Step outside and see what Panda gets to look at every day." She grabbed Creen's wrist, pulled him through the opening and onto the observation deck before he could say anything else.

They stood atop Lemeth Mountain. Perhaps this space had been a natural plateau, or maybe King Paul's men had leveled it. Whatever had brought it into being, there was no other place like it.

Creen slowly turned in place, taking it all in. "This is… this is fucking *amazing*."

Ahiliyah couldn't argue with that.

The mountains stretched out to the east and the south. Somewhere farther than the eye could see, those ranges reconnected, forming a rough circle around Lake Lanee. Near the shore, she could easily make out the tree-thick ruins of Tinsella. How *huge* it had been. To the southwest, Lemeth Mountain angled down to green slopes and lush plains that ran to the edge of Lake Mip. A century ago and more, those plains had held several towns, the smallest of which had been significantly larger than Lemeth Hold.

That was before the Rising, before the demons came.

Ahiliyah had heard the stories, how the beasts had rushed up the river valleys, swept through the plains, killing the warriors and villagers who tried to stop them, dragging survivors to Black Smoke Mountain. Those who survived those horrible years fled to the empty mountain holds, which had been abandoned after King Paul had been assassinated.

Ahiliyah pointed down. "See that grouping of trees there? That's the ruins of Tinsella."

Creen leaned out slightly, squinted. "No shit?"

"No shit," Panda said. "That big gap in the mountains is Bigsby's Pass. From the pass to the lake, people grew food, so much food people couldn't eat it all and some of it rotted. No one went hungry."

Creen huffed. "Just another made-up story. Don't believe everything you hear, Fatty."

Ahiliyah had been down there once, with Aiko. Some fruit trees remained, but gone were the things that the very old people called *wheat*, *potatoes*, *strawberries* and more.

Supposedly, there had even been a fruit called a *pumpkin*. Olliana used to tell kids about pumpkins, although few believed that there was a giant, hard orange fruit bigger than their heads. Ahiliyah believed, though—who could make up such a thing?

"I brought Creen up here to see your mirrors," Ahiliyah said. "He needs to understand how we communicate with the other holds."

Panda nodded. "I'm happy to help."

Maybe Panda wasn't cut out for running, but he took his job very seriously—in that, he was just as good a citizen of Lemeth as anyone else.

He glanced up at the sun, then at a straight staff sticking up from a stone hole.

"Sun shadow reads fifteen hours," he said. "You're just in time for us to talk to Dakatera."

Panda walked to a contraption set up at the plateau's edge. A wooden tripod, legs scratched, chipped and dented from many years of use. Atop the tripod, a metal U-bracket holding a square of four horizontal metal slats, each about two inches tall. From the base of the U-bracket jutted a metal arm that held a smaller, round mirror.

He moved the mirror, then angled it up. Doing so cast a reflection of light on the horizontal metal slats. He looked through a small tube, squinting tightly.

"Nice face," Creen said. "Looks like you're trying to squeeze out a fart. Do you fart a lot? I only ask because your room smells like ten farts merged together into an immortal superfart."

Panda keep squinting, kept making slight adjustments.

"If I do get gas," he said, "you're so tiny I bet I can hold you down and fart on your head."

Creen bristled. "Just fucking try it, fatso."

Ahiliyah whacked Creen on the arm.

"If you're going to make fun of people," she said, "you should be able to handle it when they make fun of you."

Creen's face burned red.

"This device is called a *sun-signaler*," Panda said. He stood, pointed northwest. "Dakatera is signaling. See?"

From a peak in the west, Ahiliyah saw a point of light, pulsing rhythmically.

Panda again leaned closer to the device. He flicked a lever on the side of the metal square. Doing so made the horizontal slats open and close.

"He's answering Dakatera," Ahiliyah said. "They send flashes, Panda reads them, then—"

"Yeah, I got it," Creen said. "The obvious doesn't need an explanation."

God, why did he have to be such a jerk?

Creen stepped closer to the sun signaler. "The flashes are a language?"

"Exactly," Panda said. From a pocket, he pulled out a small notebook and a stick of charcoal wrapped in nawton fiber. "The language is called *Morse Code*."

"*Morse*," Creen said. "What's a *Morse*?"

Panda made marks in the book, shrugged. "Someone from history, maybe."

Creen watched the flashes from the distant mountaintop. "I wonder if we could use flashes like this on runs. Hand signals only work when we can see each other. A system like this could let us communicate over greater distances."

A thought Liyah had had before. "Up here is one thing. On a run is another. We don't know if the flashes might attract the demons to us."

Creen bit his lip, thinking. "Yeah, I suppose. Maybe I can figure out a way to do an experiment, see if they react to it. Hey, fatso, show me this code."

Panda sighed. He flipped to the back of his notebook, handed Creen a small sheet of paper. Creen took it, studied it.

"The dots are short flashes," Panda said. "The dashes are longer flashes. You combine them to signify letters, and—"

Creen offered him the paper back. "I've got it."

Panda blinked. "You've got what, exactly?"

"The code," Creen said. "I memorized it."

Panda took the paper. He looked at it as if to make sure he'd given Creen the right one.

"There are twenty-six symbols here," Panda said. "You just memorized Morse Code?"

Creen looked to the flashes coming from Dakatera Mountain.

"We… need… silk… from… Tak," he said "Obviously *Tak* is short for *Takanta*, so they don't have to signal as many characters. Right?"

Panda glanced at Ahiliyah. "This is a joke, right? He already knew Morse Code?"

Sometimes, Creen's brain amazed her.

"If he says he didn't know it, he didn't," she said. "Creen, what do you think of signaling? I thought this might be a good job for you. After your fifth run is done."

Creen sighed heavily and rolled his eyes; Liyah cringed inside.

"Um, maybe I'll find a job that requires *brains*," he said. "Any idiot can count flashes of light. Stay up here in my own stink for weeks at a time? No thanks."

Panda glared.

Ahiliyah wanted to punch Creen. He was so... damn... *rude*.

"Creen, let's go," she said. "Panda has work to do, and it's a long way back down."

12

Forty-four... forty-five... forty-six...

In the silence and privacy of her room, Ahiliyah focused on the push-ups, making sure her back stayed straight, letting her sternum touch the stone floor before extending her arms again.

Forty-seven... forty-eight...

Some runners could do a hundred push-ups, but not if they used the same form she used: slow and steady, five seconds for each decline, five seconds for each extension.

Fifty.

She hopped to her feet, grabbed her runner's spear from where she'd leaned it against the wall. She worked through her forms—*crouch, step, thrust, step back, crouch, step, thrust.* She spun the spear, turned, went the other way, grateful for the space her room provided.

A knock on her door.

Ahiliyah ignored it, kept going through her forms.

"Ahiliyah, open up."

She stopped. Had that been the Margrave's voice? She stood, rushed to the door, opened it. Margrave Aulus Darby stood there, Drasko behind him.

"Hello," the Margrave said.

Ahiliyah stared, stunned. Had she done something wrong?

Images of Mari, dying on the sand, flashed through her thoughts.

The Margrave smiled. "Now is when a polite young person would invite me in."

"Yes... yes, of course. Please come in." She stood aside. The Margrave entered. Drasko turned his back to the door frame, took up a position to block anyone else who might want to enter.

"Shut the door, please," the Margrave said.

Ahiliyah did.

It hit her, suddenly, how messy her room was.

As a runner, she was in the minority in that she had a room all to herself. She'd been told that, back in King Paul's day, rooms this size had been meant for a file leader, a soldier who commanded nine other men in the phalanx.

Nowadays only runners, councilmen, and the Margrave had individual rooms. Everyone else packed into the available spaces—husbands, wives, and children all in one room, or four warriors. Groups of orphans packed in ten at a time, five or six single people lumped together, and so on. There were only so many rooms to go around. With more than three thousand people living in a space originally meant for about thirteen hundred, space was always at a premium.

She had a pile of dirty clothes in one corner. In another corner, her laundered hidey suit was latched up on a net repair table. On her bed, sheets rumpled into a fabric mountain. A sink with running water—another luxury—and a shelf chiseled into the wall, holding her personal treasures and mementos of her runs: her mother's bloodglass necklace; her father's ceremonial dagger; three so-bad-they-were-cute wood carvings that Tolio had done himself; a pair of dolls dressed in the yellow and red clothing of the Dakaterans; a small pyramid carved from Bisethian salt; a hand-carved, green toy bow modeled after the famous longbows of Takanta.

"As well as you run your crew," the Margrave said, "I would have assumed your room would be more organized."

"Yes, Margrave. I'm sorry for the mess."

He dismissed her apology with a wave. "May I sit?"

She grabbed the mountain of sheets and blankets, shoved them onto the floor.

"Please," she said, gesturing to the bed.

The Margrave sat. Fortunately, he didn't ask her if she wanted to sit next to him, so she stood there, sweating slightly from the push-ups.

"Ahiliyah, you know the importance of tomorrow's run, yes?"

She nodded.

"There's a reason we insist your crew makes it," he said. "Aiko feels—and I agree—that you can not only perform *this* duty, you can take on even more. Are you ready for more?"

She was. *So* ready for more. "I am, Margrave."

"What do you want, Ahiliyah? What do you want out of life?"

She couldn't believe he was here, alone, asking her directly. Should she say she was happy doing her duty as a runner? Perhaps that's what she was supposed to say, but an opportunity like this was unheard of—she had to speak her mind.

"I want to be a warrior."

The Margrave stroked his beard. "You know that is not possible. Women can't serve in the warriors. You simply aren't big enough to properly use a shield and spear."

"If I command, I don't have to carry a shield."

The words had rushed out before she'd even thought of them. She realized how ridiculous they sounded—she was nineteen, a woman, and had no military experience. She waited for the Margrave to laugh at her. He did not.

"Every warrior starts in the ranks," he said. "How can you expect men to follow you into battle if you don't know what it's like to fight in the front row?"

"Using a spear is one thing. Knowing where to put the people *using* the spears is another."

She was bordering on insolence, but she couldn't stop herself—she might never have a chance like this again.

"I will not tell you that view is wrong," the Margrave said. He stared off, nodded to himself, "But change takes time. I will think on this, I promise. "

Ahiliyah felt more frustrated than she would have if it hadn't come up at all. To keep such desires internalized was one thing—to voice them and have them rejected was another.

"For now, though, Liyah, there must be something else you want. Perhaps you wish to start a family? I could see to it that you are assigned a job that is less physically demanding, so you would have more time to spend with your children. Ginger Patrice is looking for a smart apprentice to take over for her as vintner in a few years. Wouldn't that be nice?"

Make mushroom wine and crank out babies? Was that what he thought she was good for? The Margrave's words stirred anger, but Ahiliyah pushed that anger down—most women in Lemeth *did* want to have children. He was making her an offer that many women would have loved, but Ahiliyah wasn't like most women. She never had been.

"Margrave… I don't think I want children."

He regarded her for a moment. Kindness in his eyes, not judgment.

"Perhaps you will change your mind when you complete your ten runs."

Ahiliyah thought of Mari, choosing death over running. She thought of her cousin, Jane, who spent her days swimming at the bottom of a wine flask. If Ahiliyah kept running, would she wind up like either of them? Would her next encounter with a demon be her last?

No. She was destined for more. She knew it.

"Maybe I will," she said. "Maybe I'd rather keep running. No one *likes* running, but I know how important it is. If I can't serve in the warriors, I may keep at it after my ten is complete."

"If you do, I know who the senior runner will be when Aiko retires." He leaned closer. "Or when I retire her. She is almost forty, you know."

Ahiliyah hadn't known that. Aiko kept to herself. Forty? She was in such amazing shape, but *forty*? How much longer could she keep going up there?

Ahiliyah Cooper, senior runner… it wasn't the warriors, but it was a position of honor, a position of great importance.

"I think I'd like that," she said.

The Margrave smiled. He had such a kind smile.

"Superb," he said. "Now I must ask something of you, Liyah. Your intelligence has not escaped my notice. You leave for Dakatera tomorrow. I need you to study that hold."

Something about his tone made her nervous. "Study it? What do you mean?"

"Memorize the approach, where you see traps," he said. "When you return, I want you to be able to sketch their wall for me, tell me where their main door is, how many men guard it. When you go inside, remember where any warriors are. And, most important, *count* all the warriors you see—I need to know that most of all."

There was only one reason to need to know all of that, but that reason simply could not be.

"May I ask why, Margrave?"

His eyes narrowed, and for a moment she knew he was going to say something like *that is not your concern*, but he did not. His expression softened.

"I could lie to you or dismiss your question, Liyah, but I will not. I believe the Margravine wants Lemeth Hold for herself. I believe she wants to make war on us."

"*War?*" That made no sense. "But they're barely surviving as it is. We all are. The demons are everywhere. Why would they go to war with us?"

"Because of their religion. There is no explaining it in logical terms. Have you not seen how they dress? Have you not seen their strange rituals?"

She glanced at the red and yellow dolls on her stone shelf. She'd got them in Dakatera, trading them for some rope.

"They don't dress like us," she said. "But that doesn't mean—"

"They are *zealots*. Preacher Ramirus fears they will not rest until they have converted everyone to their blasphemous ways, or killed those who refuse. Demons or no demons, the Dakaterans want to rule Ataegina. Trust me when I tell you this, Ahiliyah—their hostile intentions are certain."

Ahiliyah had been to Dakatera three times. The people there were doing better than the Keflanians, but not much—malnutrition and disease seemed more visible than hostile intentions.

But knowing the business of other holds wasn't her job. That fell to the council. As much as she despised most of the men in that body, they knew about politics and economics. If the Margrave thought the

Dakaterans were prepping for war, he must know something she did not.

She could not second-guess her hold's leadership. She had seen with her own eyes what happened when runners did not believe in the training and the mantras. Rules and structure existed for a reason.

"I will get you the information."

"Superb," the Margrave said. "You've talked to the Margravine before?"

Ahiliyah nodded. "She insists on her people weighing our goods while she's present."

"I'm sending you to make a three-way deal, one that will undercut her pricing of plinton fruit to Keflan. She will not be happy about this, but if you stay the course, Ahiliyah, the Margravine will go along with it. Her hold needs the salt we can trade. We've learned that she has lost two runner crews that were sent directly to Biseth. Our shipment of salt is all she can get—we must press our advantage now. Do you understand?"

Like Lemeth, Dakatera's crews consisted of three runners. Unlike Lemeth, Dakatera's runners were volunteers. Six brave people gone, just like that.

"I understand, Margrave."

"Superb. Be warned, Ahiliyah—once the Margravine senses what we are doing with the plinton fruit, she will try to take advantage of you. At all times, you must be wary of her conniving ways. Can you protect us against her? Can you perform these duties for your hold?"

"I will do my best."

He smiled. "That is all we can ask. I know that your best will be exceptional indeed."

A flush of pride. The Margrave was again singling her out. Not Brandun—*her*.

He stood. "Most of the hold is unaware of the threat of the Dakaterans. If war happens, our primary trade route to Keflan will be cut off. That is why it is critical you complete this run and bring back as much capertine powder as you can get, so we can not only cure the sick we have, but also lay in a supply for the future." He put his hand on her shoulder. "I know you can do this."

With that, Aulus Darby left her room, closing the door behind him.

Ahiliyah tried to process what had just happened. War? Between *people*? Could that really happen? Could people be so stupid they fought against each other when the demons had already killed so many, were *still* killing?

The Dakaterans were... different. *Weird*, even—but she'd never thought of them as warmongers. Maybe she'd missed those signs. Maybe she needed to pay more attention, not just to Dakatera, but to every hold she ran to.

Ahiliyah would not let the Margrave down.

13

Cold wind caressed the mountainside. Summer was coming to a close, and fall wouldn't last long. In a way, Ahiliyah was glad her sixth run had come before winter set in. In winter, snow and ice made finding new routes across the mountain far more dangerous, and the only warm place to sleep was bundled up in a vootervert burrow.

"Creen, call out," she said. "Dakatera's signal sound is—"

"The charmed rat, I know." He rolled his eyes. "Not like I was here a few days ago, right?"

Brandun nudged him. "Quit complaining and just do it."

Creen had a gift for animal sounds. Whether it be the humped gish, the vindeedee or the charmed rat, his calls were indistinguishable from the real thing.

Creen cupped his hands to his mouth, sounded out the charmed rats' low *whaNA-whaNA* .

When an answering call came down from the broken wall, it brought with it relief from long-held tension. It had taken two days to reach Dakatera. They'd seen no sign of demons, but Ahiliyah couldn't shake the sensation that the monsters were out there, in blazing daylight, searching... *hunting*.

"Let's get inside," Brandun said. "I got a bad feeling."

Creen laughed quietly. "So big and yet so superstitious. Did you bring a lucky gish foot to ward away the evil spirits, Dumbdun?"

"Superstitious?" Brandun shook his head. "Demons *are* evil spirits, Creen. You know this. Preacher Ramirus says that evil magic is everywhere."

"Ramirus?" Creen shook his head. "You're listening to that twat? The demons aren't evil spirits, they're just *animals*. We don't know enough about them is all. I swear, you'd think someone your size would have a big brain, but apparently not."

Brandun's shoulders slumped. He seemed to shrink in on himself. He was twice Creen's size, yet sometimes Creen's words delivered blows more powerful than Brandun's fists ever could.

"*Just animals* wiped out our civilization," Ahiliyah said. Creen didn't have to be so mean—she felt compelled to defend Brandun. "Is that what you're saying? *Just animals*?"

Creen tilted his head at Brandun. "Don't tell me you're as dumb as he is. Don't tell me you believe in God and all that religion garbage."

She stared at him, not knowing what to say. Of course she believed in God—everyone did. This wasn't the time to argue, though; they needed to get inside. And she knew she couldn't win an argument against Creen, so why bother?

"Let's go," Ahiliyah said, shrugging off the insult. "Follow my path, and follow it *carefully*. Dakatera's traps don't care if you're a demon or a person, they'll—"

"—*kill you just the same*," Creen said, finishing her words for her. "Did I not just mention that we were here a few days ago?"

He was maddening. Just maddening.

"I'll take lead," she said. "Creen, you bring up the rear. Brandun covers our tail often enough, it's your turn for a while."

Ahiliyah started up the approach, her eyes scanning for traps. She saw a deadfall, silently pointed it out, then remembered the Margrave's request—she needed to memorize the defenses.

As if runners didn't already have enough to worry about.

Ahiliyah and her crew unpacked their backpacks, carefully arranging the cloth-wrapped, fist-sized parcels into rows on the map table. Ten in each row, eleven rows; the salt that runners from Biseth had brought to Lemeth.

The table was identical to the one in the Margrave's Chamber, showing rising mountain peaks, the lakes, the ocean, and the locations of the surviving holds. Five people sat around it, a council similar to Lemeth's, but with one key difference—two "councilmen" were women.

One of the women—Margravine Herriet Lumos—stood.

"Bring in the scales," she said. "Weigh ten random parcels."

The Margravine was the most impressive woman Ahiliyah had ever met. Grey hair, wrinkled skin, she looked like she was old enough to join the weavers in Lemeth Hold, although she seemed far sharper than those root-chewing old ladies. Like most Dakateran women, the Margravine wore a high-collared yellow dress that hung to the floor, with long sleeves that ended in fingerless gloves. That was the way of things here: Dakaterans showed as little skin as possible. Women all wore yellow, men all wore red. To Ahiliyah, these traditions seemed silly and repressive. Here, the light shift she wore back home would be considered sacrilegious.

Each hold had its own way of doing things.

The Dakaterans had their own military style as well. Many of their warriors carried crossbows slung over their backs. They wore metal helmets, painted red, but their white chest and shoulder armor was made of some type of stiff, heavy fabric. Where Lemethian shields were round and solid metal, Dakateran shields were rectangular, made of thick wood painted red on one half and yellow on the other. And there were so *many* warriors—from what Ahiliyah had seen, they had twice as many as Lemeth. The Margrave would not be happy about that.

The chamber doors opened. Two attendants—both men, wearing long-sleeved red shirts, red pants and red shoes—rolled in a cart holding an ancient scale from before King Paul's time. Two square silver trays, one hanging from each arm of a lever mounted atop an ornate pedestal. Small metal weights nestled in wooden rows along the side.

Creen stared at the scale as if it were magic. His eyes flicked about madly, taking in every detail. Lemeth Hold didn't possess anything as delicate, or as accurate.

The Margravine sat back down in her high-backed chair. It was the same yellow as her dress—exactly the same. A pretty color, but Ahiliyah imagined she'd go mad if she had to look at the same color every single day.

"Welcome back, Ahiliyah Cooper. You were here so recently," the Margravine said. "You took a rather large shipment of paper and sizzle spice with you. I can't imagine you need more of either so quickly, so what are you looking for in return this time?"

The woman was suspicious, just as Aulus had warned.

"Plinton fruit," Ahiliyah said.

The Margravine frowned. "Which you plan to take to Keflan, no doubt. If you do that, you're interfering with the trade rates between Keflan and Dakatera."

Interfering? Is that what she called keeping medicine from the sick people who needed it?

"I wouldn't know anything about that, Margravine," Ahiliyah said. "I've brought the goods I was told to bring, and I hope to get the goods I was told to get."

The woman let out a sound that was half hiss, half clearing of her throat. Ahiliyah couldn't help but notice that her councilmyn winced at that noise, as if they had heard it before and knew it accompanied bad things.

"Funny," the Margravine said, "you don't *look* as stupid as you're pretending to be. Perhaps more of your people are sick with Glynnis than you let on the last time you were here."

Did the Margravine think she was lying?

"It's a disease," Ahiliyah said. "It spread."

The Margravine waited for more. Ahiliyah said nothing. Sinesh had taught her long ago that people used silence as a negotiating trick, trying to make the other person uncomfortable so that they would be the first to make an offer.

Silence is strength.

Ahiliyah waited.

Finally, a smile ticked the right corner of the Margravine's mouth. "It *spread*, she tells us. Diseases do have a tendency to do that." She turned to her attendant. "Weights?"

"Each parcel weighs one-point-six bricks," an attendant said. "There are slight variations, but within acceptable tolerances."

The Margravine drummed her fingers on the tabletop. She again stared at Ahiliyah.

"I can't believe Aulus sent you out again, so soon after your last run. It's as if he doesn't care about your safety."

Insulting the Margrave? Was this part of the manipulation effort he'd warned her against?

"Margrave Darby cares deeply about his people." Ahiliyah tried to mask the pride in her voice, but knew she'd failed. Why shouldn't she be proud? Lemeth was far from perfect, but it was home.

The Margravine stared. Was she trying to use silence again? Perhaps to get Ahiliyah to offer up information. Or… was it more than that? The Margravine's silence didn't feel like a game. It felt more like she was silent because she was thinking, analyzing.

"Ahiliyah, you will stay," the Margravine said. "Everyone else, out."

The councilmyn's wooden chairs squeaked against the stone floor. Ahiliyah watched them stand and head for the door.

"You boys as well," the Margravine said, pointing first to Brandun, then to Creen. "Out."

Creen and Brandun exchanged a glance.

"Uh, we'll stay," Creen said. "One of our running tenets is *always stay together*. So, you know, we kind of have to."

Brandun nodded. "We'll stay."

Ahiliyah felt a rush of pride—her crewmates were trying to protect her. Even Creen.

The Margravine stood. "Young men, get out before I have you *thrown* out."

Ahiliyah turned to them. "Guys, it's okay."

The boys exchanged another glance.

"We'll be right outside," Creen said.

Brandun nodded. "Yeah. Right outside. Come on, Creen."

They left the room. Some unseen person shut the door.

Ahiliyah suddenly felt very much alone. She was alone with the Dakateran Margravine, a woman that radiated a calm aura of power, of danger. In that, she was like Aulus Darby. In that, they were both a little like the demons.

"Ahiliyah, do you like Lemeth?"

"Yes, Margravine. I like it very much."

"You have how many more runs ahead of you after this one? Four? That's so dangerous."

As if Ahiliyah needed to be reminded of the danger. "Four to finish my obligation. But I may continue on after that."

The Margravine moved around the corner of the table, came closer. She sat on the table's edge, close to Ahiliyah.

"*Obligation,*" the Margravine said, folding her hands in front of her. "We don't have that here. Our runners *choose* to risk their lives for their hold."

Ahiliyah didn't know what to say. "Yes, Margravine," was all she could manage.

The older woman glanced to the door. "Those boys are loyal to you. For now, at least. Do you think they will be loyal when their obligations are completed? Or will they treat you like breeding stock, like the rest of Lemethian men treat Lemethian women?"

Ahiliyah's face grew hot. "That's not true."

"Isn't it?" The Margravine smiled. "Well, I don't live there, so you'd know better."

The older woman's fingers drummed on the tabletop. Ahiliyah suddenly wished she'd fought for her crew to stay with her.

"You must be a good leader," the Margravine said. "Do you think so?"

"I … I try."

"If Lemethian boys are defending you, you certainly are."

The Margravine squinted, stared hard. Ahiliyah felt like she was standing on one side of a giant scale, and the Margravine was slowly adding weights to the other side.

"We've lost runners, Ahiliyah. Far more than normal. Something out there has changed. We need to change with it. I want to make you an offer. I want you to move here, to Dakatera. I want you to train our runners."

Ahiliyah looked down, no longer able to meet the Margravine's eyes.

"Be your senior runner, you mean?"

"No, our *trainer*," the Margravine said. "You teach our volunteers how to survive the way you have survived. You stay down here—you never have to run again."

Safety. But to have it, she had to leave everything she knew. Her friends. Would Tolio come with her? To move to another hold. Such an overwhelming thought.

"I... I'll consider your offer, Margravine. But..."

"But what?"

"The Margrave said he will make me the senior runner of Lemeth," Ahiliyah said. "After Aiko Laster retires. I could stay home and train."

The Margravine's squint deepened. Ahiliyah felt another invisible weight placed on the imaginary scale.

"Senior runner," the Margravine said. "Something tells me that's not really what you want. What do you *really* want, Ahiliyah?"

Could this woman see right through her? Ahiliyah didn't know why she was telling this woman *anything*. Had not the Margrave warned her? And yet, women and men were different—could this powerful woman better understand what Ahiliyah wanted out of life?

"I want to be a warrior," Ahiliyah said in a whisper.

The older woman raised an eyebrow. "A warrior? That's all?"

She hadn't laughed. "I... want to be a general. Like you. To command troops in battle."

The silence again. More stressful this time, with no one else in the room.

"We have women warriors in Dakatera," the Margravine said. "And Anette Tasker is the Takantan general. Did you know a woman commands the Takantan military?"

Ahiliyah hadn't known that. She wondered why she hadn't heard it before.

"It doesn't matter." The Margravine dismissed the thought with a wave. "You can't be a warrior in Lemeth, let alone a general. That fool Aulus would never allow it."

This judgmental woman had no right to speak poorly of the Margrave.

"The Margrave said he would consider it. He said change takes time."

"Ah, is that what he told you? Aulus has been in charge for how long now?" She tapped her temple, pretending to think. "He's on his fifth term. *Twenty-one years.* How old are you?"

Ahiliyah fought back anger. "Is this some tactic so you get a better deal for the salt?"

The Margravine's face clouded over, and for a moment Ahiliyah understood why the councilmyn had left the room so quickly—that expression radiated power and danger. Then, the woman smiled a half-smile, and the tension was gone.

"Fair enough, Ahiliyah Cooper. Being a bitch comes with the job. I just so hate to see talent like yours wasted. Consider my offer. I know people normally only move from one hold to another for love. I couldn't help but notice that you are not married yet. I asked you how old you were—you didn't answer me. Are you eighteen?"

"Nineteen."

The Margravine shook her head, as if it were somehow a sin to be nineteen and unmarried.

"It's my choice," Ahiliyah said.

"Of course it is. Is there someone you plan to marry back in Lemeth?"

Ahiliyah thought of Tolio, of his constant pressure to start a family.

"I'm... honestly, I'm not sure."

Why had she said that? It was none of this woman's business. The Margravine's silence hadn't moved Ahiliyah to speak, but her questions apparently did.

"Love," the Margravine said. "You could tell your people back home that you met someone here, that you fell in love. That would eventually wind up being the truth. There are many fine young men here." She raised an eyebrow. "And young women as well."

Ahiliyah couldn't deny it might be nice to see different faces, perhaps kiss different lips. She'd grown up with all the Lemethian boys her age. Most had married years earlier, at fifteen, sixteen or seventeen, as was custom. Many of the married ones still wanted to sleep with her, in secret, but that wasn't her way. It never would be.

Maybe it would be nice to come to Dakatera, where everyone would be new to her and she'd be new to everyone. She could become a different person here. She'd be a trainer. A trainer of *volunteers*.

And she could stop running.

But was this really any different from what Tolio offered? An end to running. A way to stay inside—to stay *safe*—for the rest of her life.

She didn't want to be safe. She didn't *want* to stop running.

"I'm happy where I am, Margravine."

The older woman forced a tight-lipped smile. "Somehow I doubt that. But we make our own choices in life, do we not? The offer will remain open to you. If you change your mind, all you have to do is come back. Come *home*, to Dakatera."

The Margravine returned to her seat.

"I'll grant you your trade request for the plinton fruit," she said. "You can make your trade with Keflan. Good day, Ahiliyah. As I told you, things have changed around here—I hope you have better luck than our runners have had."

14

From somewhere deep in the darkness came a man's scream. The sound faded, then stopped. Had the man run away, or had he been *caught*?

Behind a fallen log, under the cover of a sparse caminus bush, Ahiliyah huddled with Creen. They stayed very still.

"We have to turn back," he whispered. "The demons are out here. They're hunting."

Ahiliyah wanted nothing more than to leave, to work her way back to the safety of Lemeth, but that wasn't an option. They'd reached the approach to Keflan—they had to get inside.

"We can't," she said. "We have to get that medicine."

Creen leaned so close to her, his whisper seemed like a shout.

"If we die, how does that help the hold? We go back, wait until things die down."

From their right, the sound of something crawling across the dirt. Ahiliyah froze, listening, analyzing—she recognized Brandun's quiet breathing a moment before he slid next to her, on her left.

"I heard you, Creen," he said. "My mother is sick. We're going in there and getting the medicine. That is that."

He wasn't supposed to give orders—that was Ahiliyah's role. But at the moment, she didn't care who kept them moving, as long as they kept moving forward.

She rose up enough to look over the log. They were so close. The sloping approach was right in front of them. Fifty, maybe sixty yards up, the cloud-dampened light of the Three Sisters played off the broken wall of Keflan Hold.

Another distant scream—a girl's, this time—tore at the night.

And from another direction, a different kind of scream.

"That was a fucking demon," Creen said. "If we can't leave, we have to *wait*. We can't go up now, they're out there."

Ahiliyah fought to control her fear. She'd thought they could make it here before sunset—she'd been wrong.

Brandun reached behind Ahiliyah and put his hand on the back of Creen's neck; whether it was a grip of comfort and support, or one of threat, Ahiliyah couldn't tell.

"I know you're afraid," Brandun whispered, "but every moment we wait is another moment my mother gets worse. If you want to run, then run. Ahiliyah and I are going in."

Ahiliyah couldn't let Creen leave—she needed him to carry as much medicine as he could.

"The traps," Creen said. "It's dangerous for us to go now anyway. We *have* to wait. I saw vooterver burrows a few yards back. We can hide in those and wait for morning."

He wasn't wrong. Moving up that slope in the darkness brought with it the risk of serious injury, even death. But if they hid, if they waited for the sun to rise, that was another six or seven hours' delay in getting the capertine powder back to Lemeth—in that time, how many would die?

"This is my third time here," Ahiliyah said. "Just follow me, stay quiet, and we'll be fine. You're coming with us, Creen, so get your head around it. This is our duty."

He sniffed, tried to choke back sudden sobs. "I don't want to die. I'm so fucking scared."

Brandun patted Creen on the back. "I'm scared, too. I'm scared shitless."

There was something unique about Brandun. Other boys aspiring to be warriors were all swagger and fake bravado. They never wanted to admit they were afraid. Brandun not only admitted it, he did so openly, without jokes or artifice.

He was scared, and he was going anyway. So was Ahiliyah.

"Creen," she said. "Call out."

His face snapped toward her. "*Call out*? Are you out of your fucking mind?"

She felt the darkness closing in around her, and in it, long claws, sharp teeth, and vicious toothtongues.

"We have to let the watcher know we're coming up," she said.

Creen shook his head. "I'm not calling out shit, and neither are you guys. What is wrong with your heads? The demons are *out there*, they are *hunting*. Let's get the fuck out of here!"

"My mother is sick," Brandun said. "We are going up there. You're coming with us."

Malice in his voice—Creen didn't seem to hear it. He sneered, his face a mask of arrogance.

"What good does it do our people if *we* die first, Dumbdun? Huh?"

"My mother—"

"*Your mother will live*," Creen said. "And you know the rules—better to make it back late than not at all. Why don't you pull your head out of your ass, Dumbdun, you—"

The bigger boy grabbed Creen by the throat, smashed him flat against the ground.

"I've *had it* with you calling me dumb!"

"Brandun, *stop*!" Ahiliyah grabbed his shoulder, tried to pull him away—his body didn't move. He didn't even seem to know she was there.

Creen gagged and choked. His face turned red. He clawed at Brandun's hand, trying to grab a finger, to grab anything—but he wasn't strong enough.

Brandun was killing him.

Ahiliyah threw herself on Brandun's back.

"Let him go!"

She'd never realized how strong Brandun was—just a boy, but solid as a rock. He reached back with his free hand, grabbed Ahiliyah by her hair and yanked her off. She fell hard, dirt and rock knocking the wind from her lungs.

Stunned, she saw Creen reach to his belt. She tried to say *no*—she didn't have the air.

The boy drew his little friend, drove the blade through the forearm of the hand that was choking him. Brandun cried out, fell back to his butt, stared, dumbfounded, at the knife handle sticking out of his arm, at the blood already staining his shirtsleeve, gleaming in the moonslight.

Ahiliyah stared, too, hoping she'd imagined it, hoping that the boys hadn't actually been *shouting* so loud their voices echoed back from the hold wall.

Brandon blinked, looked at Creen.

"You stabbed me?"

Creen coughed, his hands clutching his throat. He rolled to his side, got to one knee. He stared at Brandun, wide-eyed and terrified.

In the strange bit of silence that followed, Ahiliyah heard a patter of liquid hitting dirt—Brandun's blood, spilling down.

Demons smell blood.

She forced herself up, grabbed his wounded arm.

"Creen stabbed me," Brandun said, quietly, calmly, as if he were a schoolboy tattling on a naughty classmate.

"Hold still," Ahiliyah said. She grabbed his wrist, held his arm steady, examined the thin knife jammed through Brandun's bleeding arm. With her free hand, she reached into a hidey-suit pocket, pulled out a bandage. "Creen, help me."

"Fuck… him," the smaller boy said, forcing out the words.

Ahiliyah turned and snarled, her own quiet anger matching Brandun's violent outburst.

"Give me your fucking bandage unless you want to die."

Creen struggled to his feet, dug in his hidey suit.

Ahiliyah focused on the knife. "Brandun, I have to pull this out."

He stared at the handle, didn't seem to know she was there.

"Brandun!"

His eyes snapped to hers. She saw the fear in them, the confusion.

"We have to get inside," she said, keeping her voice quiet and calm. "The demons had to have heard us. They're coming. I'm going to pull the blade out, then we're going to wrap your wound as tight as we can, then we move. Do you understand?"

Brandun nodded, now looking every bit as stupid as Creen's nickname insinuated.

"Hold still," Ahiliyah said, "and *do not scream*."

She grabbed the handle of Creen's little friend. With one strong yank, she slid the blade free from Brandun's arm, dropped the knife to the dirt.

Brandun hissed in a breath and his face wrinkled into a sheet of pain, but he did not cry out. She wrapped her bandage over his blood-soaked sleeve as tightly as she could, tied it off.

Creen knelt next to her, his breathing labored, raspy. He wrapped his bandage around hers, which was already soaking through with blood, then tied it off neatly and efficiently.

She took Brandun's free hand and placed it on the bandages. "Keep up the pressure."

Brandun nodded.

Creen stood in a crouch, searching the darkness. "I don't see anything."

"You won't," Ahiliyah said. "Not until they're on you. We move fast but steady, we stay as quiet as we can. Brandun, follow me. Creen, bring up the rear. Do *not* move ahead of us. Got it?"

Creen nodded. She saw the trails of tears on his cheeks.

"Follow me."

She started up the approach at a jog, eyes searching for linchpin rocks, trip-strings or deadfall covers. The darkness was a thick blanket cloaking the bushes and trees and logs, hiding death in its shadowy folds.

They were halfway up the steep slope when a screech echoed through the night.

Brandon stopped. Wounded arm held tight to his chest, he looked around, searching for the danger that sounded far too close.

"Oh, God," he said. "The demons are coming."

Creen slid off his backpack. "Lose your bags, we need to sprint for it."

"Put that back on," Ahiliyah said. "We need it. *Keep moving*."

Creen did as he was told.

Ahiliyah continued up the approach. On the ridge, faint moonslight lit up the ruined battlements of Keflan Hold—a broken-down, ancient wall, stone overhang cracked and collapsed in many places. It was only a hundred feet or so up the slope.

They were so close.

Another demon screech—did that sound closer than the first one?

"Stay close," she said.

Ahiliyah ran up the steep slope. No time for caution now—she had to trust her memory more than her eyes. In seconds, her legs began to burn.

That boulder… was the safe zone to its left, or its right? Left. Had to be left. She angled that way—something gripped her shoulder. Her body froze, her thoughts flooded with images of a demon tail driving toward her back before she realized the hand was Brandun's.

"Wrong way." He pointed to a branch, barely visible in the darkness. "Linchpin."

The clouds broke enough for the light of the moons to shine through. She saw it—a log with many long branches spreading out in all directions. The top of the log was wedged beneath a moss-covered boulder, which itself held in place a dozen larger boulders. If she had hit one of those branches, the log would have given way to the weight above it. She and her crew would have died, or been trapped and forced to wait for the demons.

"That way," Brandun said, pointing up the slope.

Ahiliyah didn't question him—she ran. They followed.

The three runners reached the battlements, which themselves were laced with deadly traps. Behind them, yet another demon screech—no doubt this time, it *was* closer.

Ahiliyah looked at Brandun. "Which way?"

He stared at the battlements, looked left, then right. "I don't know."

Creen pushed past. Shaking, he stared at the broken wall, pointed to a section on the right.

"Not there," he said. "See the chip marks on that bottom block? It's a linchpin, we touch it and that whole area collapses on us." He pointed farther to the right. "See?"

Ahiliyah squinted through the darkness. There, where he was pointing, a section of the wall had collapsed, revealing sheer stone behind it. Sticking out from the pile of rocks, she saw a foot—a foot as black as night, as gnarled as a tree root. The deadfall had killed a demon.

She saw something else in that pile of rock, something pale and pink… a human hand?

"Here," Creen said.

Ahiliyah turned and saw him on hands and knees at the base of the wall.

"Less moss here, and it's worn smooth," he said.

He climbed, fast, fear driving him, hands and booted feet tapping, reaching, searching for the safe way up.

Ahiliyah thumped Brandun's back. "Go. I'll follow."

He shook his head. "If I fall, you go with me. You go first."

Could he climb at all with his wounded arm?

Another screech, then another, made up her mind for her.

Terror clawed at her, tried to control her, but she would not let it. *Twice* she'd been face to face with demons, and she hadn't given in to the fear. She would not do so now.

She caught up to Creen, watched his every handhold and foothold, mimicked his every movement. He quickly reached the top. She followed him onto the deck, then they both leaned against the wall and reached down to grab Brandun, who was struggling to get over with only one hand working. Together, she and Creen hauled him onto the deck.

"Thank you," Brandun said, his voice trembling. "Thank you."

They helped him stand. Together, the three of them looked over the wall, back down the slope—they all saw it at the same time.

A demon, cutting through the darkness, coming up the slope far faster than any of them could ever hope to run. Thin black arms stretching out, thin black legs pushing hard. Moonslight gleamed off the long head, made its hideous teeth sparkle like tiny jewels.

"Creen, find a way to get the door open!" Ahiliyah shoved him toward the end of the deck—the door would be there, somewhere in the pitch-black beneath the stone overhang.

She should have helped him, but she couldn't look away from the demon rushing toward them. It reached the boulder that had almost marked her death. It started left, then went right.

The beast's gnarled body cracked against dried branches.

The log spun, only slightly, but it was enough; the deadfall gave way. Boulders crashed down with the sound of rolling thunder. The demon turned to flee; a smaller boulder smashed down on its foot. The beast screeched, fell to the ground. It tried to pull free—a boulder bigger than Brandun crashed down on it so hard that burning blood shot out in long jets.

Then, nothing. It was dead.

"Holy shit," Brandun said. "Holy shit."

But the nightmare wasn't over. In the moonlight, down on the path, she saw two more demons sprinting up the slope. She ducked down, pulling Brandun with her.

"Come on," Creen shouted, "it's open!"

Ahiliyah and Brandun crawled toward his voice, staying beneath the top of the wall. In the almost total darkness beneath the overhang, she saw the patch of absolute black that marked the entryway. Creen was there, waiting for them.

"It was already open," he said, his whisper edging toward hysteria. "Just sitting here, *open*. Where's the wall watcher? Anyone see the watcher?"

The wall watcher had to be inside somewhere.

"Get inside," Ahiliyah said.

They crawled into the darkness. No glowlight. No light at all. She couldn't see her hand in front of her face. The stairs down were close, she knew, but she couldn't spot them.

The sound of rattling rocks echoed up from beyond the ruined wall.

"If we run down the stairs in the darkness, we'll kill ourselves," Creen said. "We have to get the door shut. I can't fucking see anything in here!"

"Brandun, help him," Ahiliyah said, shrugging off her pack. She pulled her spear staves from their holster, started screwing the staves together. She reached to draw her spearhead from its scabbard when Brandun grabbed her wrist.

"I'm a better fighter than you," he said.

"Not wounded, you aren't." Ahiliyah yanked her arm free. "Help Creen with the door!"

Ahiliyah twisted the spearhead onto the staff, looked back out toward the deck. The dimmest bit of moonlight showed her the space between the stone lip and the old wall.

"Here's the lever," she heard Creen say. "Come on, *close it*!"

"I'm trying," Brandun said, his words barely audible grunts.

Ahiliyah held her spear in both hands. She squatted into a fighting position. She knew she couldn't win, but if she could hold off a demon long enough for Brandun and Creen to shut the door, they might still complete the mission.

In that ever-so-faint light that turned the battlement into a soup of black and dark grey, she saw movement—a skeletal black hand reaching up and over the wall.

The sound of grinding stone made her jump—to her left, a slab of stone as thick as her arm was long started to slide toward her.

Hands grabbed her, yanked her into the darkness. She fell on her butt, dropped her spear.

Out on the deck, a demon crawled over the battlement. Its long head turned toward her.

With a heavy thud, the stone door slid shut in front of her, blocking out all light.

15

Ahiliyah sat there on her ass, chest heaving. She fought to control her breathing, to make as little noise as possible.

"I can't see *dick*." In the darkness, Creen's panicked voice seemed to come from everywhere and nowhere at once. "We need light."

"Not yet," Ahiliyah said, her voice a harsh whisper. "And keep your voice down."

Something smelled funny, like a broken sewage pipe, but with other scents mixed in—like millasis candy, but more powerful. From somehere below, down the stairwell, she heard the regular sound of water splashing on stone.

"I can reach the glowpipes," Brandun whispered. "They feel solid. They must be broken farther down."

A scratching sound almost made her scream. Talons on rock— demons outside the door.

Could they get through the thick stone?

Or… were monsters just like them already here, *inside*? No one had been on watch. When glowpipes broke, fixing them was a high priority. One break in the system could lead to entire sections of a hold falling into total darkness.

How long had the pipes here been broken?

The scratching grew louder.

"Liyah," Creen whispered, "*do something*."

He was about to lose it, she could hear it in his voice.

"Both of you, stay still," she said.

Ahiliyah felt for her spear, found it. In the close confines, in the dark, she could hurt one of the others with it. She quickly broke it down, sliding the spearhead into its scabbard, putting the staves in their container. She slid her backpack on, tied it tight.

"Reach out to me," she whispered.

She stretched both arms out into the total darkness, fighting the fear that a demon was about to bite. She managed not to flinch when she felt Brandun's big hand, then she felt Creen's.

"Stay quiet," she whispered. Did the scratching grow louder when she did?

She placed Brandun's hand on the small of her back, a silent signal that he needed to follow her, to not let go, something they'd all trained doing back in Lemeth Hold. She felt his fingers lock into her webbing. She then took Creen's trembling hand, awkwardly fumbled around both boys to put it on the small of Brandun's back.

Ahiliyah shuffled forward, feeling with the toe of her boot for the stairway. She hit it, lifted that foot, set it down lightly on the step below, making sure her whole foot was there before putting her weight on it.

Into the darkness they went, one slow step at a time.

One step down, the slight pull of Brandun catching up. Step after step after step. Thirty steps down, the stairwell turned to the right.

The scratching sound faded.

The water sound grew louder.

The stink was getting worse. She heard Creen choke off a cough. Brandun did the same. She'd never smelled anything quite so awful. She wanted to run away from it, but could not—*down* was the only way they could go.

She wanted to light a torch so badly, but if demons were close they would come so fast. They could be *right in front of her* for all she knew, lips curled, waiting for her, ready to sweep her in like a pouncing hookarm when she got close.

Creen wasn't the only one on the edge of panic. The darkness seemed to press into her temples and fill her brain.

She stepped down; her boot slid on something wet.

Please let that be spent glowpipe water, oh God, please…

She gently felt with her toe, looking for a dry spot—her boot pressed against something solid and soft.

Something squishy.

A light double-tug on her hidey suit—Brandun wanted to know why she'd stopped.

Ahiliyah couldn't stay in the dark anymore. She reached into her hidey suit, pulled out a match and a piece of kindling wrapped in oiled cloth. The match came alive on the third strike, blinding her for an instant. She lit the torch, paused for a moment to revel in the smell of the burning cloth and wood, a smell that chased away the sweet stink.

Her eyes adjusted, and she saw the squishy thing.

A bloated corpse, swelling skin stretching at shirt and pants. And on the next step down, another. A man and a woman? Too swollen to tell for sure.

"Oh, God," Brandun said. "Oh, *God*."

The awful stink hadn't changed, yet now it seemed so much *more*, filling her nose and lungs and face.

The one she'd stepped on had a fist-size hole through the left temple and eye. The other one's head was twisted at a strange angle.

Her torchlight played off the corpses, and off the stairs. Rust-colored stains on the stone. Rust-colored, but not wet—this blood was dry.

"Let's go," Creen said. "I don't want to be here with those things."

Those things. Dead people.

"Liyah," Brandun said, "we have to keep moving."

She knew he was right, but she couldn't take her eyes off the bodies. They'd died long enough ago for their blood to dry, long enough for them to begin swelling with rot.

Her fear made the torch shake.

"They were in here," she whispered. "The demons. Maybe they still are."

She couldn't go back up—the demons were still out there, still waiting, still *scratching*. She couldn't continue down, because if the demons had got in, if they were still here, *down* was where they would be.

Her body shuddered so hard she almost dropped the torch. She willed herself to stop shaking—her body ignored her.

She felt Brandun's hand on her arm, sliding up to her hand to take the torch.

"Get behind me," he whispered. "It's okay. I'll take point now."

Part of her wanted to argue with him; it was her responsibility to lead. Another part of her wanted to thank him, over and over again, because she'd hit a limit she hadn't known existed. They were all screwed, but letting big Brandun go first might allow her to go on.

She moved behind him. She felt Creen's hands, helping her, positioning her between the two of them. No attitude from Creen now, no fighting, no insults—the three of them were in this together. Together, they would live, or they would die.

Brandun stepped around the bodies and started down. Ahiliyah followed him. Creen followed her.

"One more flight," she whispered. "Two at most. Then we'll be in the main corridor."

When they reached the next landing and turned the corner, Ahiliyah saw light—a glowpipe, bright on one side of a jagged break, dark on the other, water pouring down to the stone, coursing into narrow gutters on either side of the steps to vanish into drains carved into the stone. Keflan's water had a bluish tint, different from Lemeth's faint red hue.

Brandun tapped the torch out against the wall. He started down. Liyah followed, stopped suddenly as the overpowering stench of death made her stomach rebel. She swallowed hard, managed to stop herself from vomiting.

They descended the last flight, fighting against the stench of death. From there, the hold spread out in a fashion similar to Lemeth's layout: wide stone corridors and smaller tunnels, rooms and ceilings, living quarters and common rooms. The light was dimmer than she remembered, but anything was better than the total blackness of the stairs.

Three more corpses—two people and a demon. A pair of crossbow bolts jutted up from the twisted black body.

"They got one of the fuckers," Creen said.

A crossbow lay on the stone floor, wood etched where burning blood had scored it.

"And the fucker got them," Brandun said.

Creen moved toward the demon's corpse.

"Don't touch it," Ahiliyah whispered. "It will burn you."

Creen paused. "It's too old. Whatever makes the blood burn has burned out."

He knelt next to the bodies, started poking at the demon corpse.

"Oh, God," Brandun said. "That *smell*."

He turned away, threw up into the gutter that lined the base of the wall. The smell of his vomit was just enough to push Ahiliyah over the edge; she threw up on her boots.

Wiping her mouth with her sleeve, she looked to Creen, expecting to see him throw up as well, but he seemed unfazed.

"The demon looks… deflated," he said. He coughed, gagged, held a fist to his mouth, but didn't throw up. "This one looks different than the ones we've seen on the surface, or the suit back in the training pit. Come look."

Ahiliyah glanced at Brandun. He shook his head—he wasn't going near the thing. She was the leader, though, and if she could get any information that might help keep her people alive, she had to push past her own fears.

Kneeling down next to Creen, she stared at the nightmare.

She never seen a demon this close up, living or dead. Gnarled ridges ran the length of the long head. The ones she'd seen on the surface had smooth heads. So did the training suit. The teeth looked the same, though—hard bits of metal that gleamed in the torchlight.

Creen poked at the corpse. "The hard parts are like armor. But they have soft parts, too. I didn't know that from looking at them at a distance."

Ahiliyah stood, looked up and down the corridor. The light let her see demons, but it would also let the demons see her. Hidey suit camouflage was worthless down here.

"We need to find their capertine powder," she said, "then we're getting out of here."

16

The trip down terrified her. An entire hold, empty, as hollow and lifeless as a getum bug shell. Behind every corner, in every shadow, in every room, there might be a demon. Each step brought with it the promise of death, yet she kept moving—the lives of her people depended on it.

The layout of Keflan was similar enough to that of Lemeth that Ahiliyah knew roughly where to go. Some areas were lit, the glowpipes working as designed, and other areas were pitch-black. They moved quickly, quietly, sticking to the main corridors and stairs down, using torches only when absolutely necessary. They saw no one, heard nothing.

Several rooms had been barricaded with furniture, furniture now broken and splashed with human blood. After looking in the second barricaded room and finding only rotting bodies, Ahiliyah decided not to look in any more. It was just too much, and they needed to move fast.

Four levels down, they found the mold farm. The large room was dark, the corridor's glowlight reaching only a few feet into the entrance.

Ahiliyah lit a torch. The light barely dented the darkness in front of her, let alone chase away the chamber's deep, heavy shadows. Rows of tables stretched off into the blackness. Trays of dirt lined each table, filled with clumpy, bluish mold clusters in various stages of growth.

"Good," Brandun said. "Let's fill our packs and get the hell out of here."

He knew so little.

"The mold itself is no good," Ahiliyah said. "It gets processed and ground down into capertine powder. We have to find where the powder is stored."

How much powder had the Keflanians made since she'd been here ten days earlier? Would it be enough to help all the sick people back in Lemeth? She lifted her torch higher, as if that might somehow light up more of the long cavern.

The glowpipes... from what she could see, none appeared to be broken.

"Creen, find the water valve," she said. "Maybe they shut it off."

Capertine mold, like the mushrooms that grew in Lemeth, grew best in the dark. The Lemeth mushroom farms were often left without light.

"Found it," Creen said.

The familiar *chonk* of a valve lever being pulled down. Then, the sound of water running through pipes. To her right, up near the ceiling, she saw the first faint glow.

"At least *something's* working," Brandun said. The glow flowed through the pipes, down to the chamber's far wall, then back again, looping through the glass tubes. It reached the door behind her, doubled back yet again, and then halfway down the room, water gushed out of a crack, spilled down and splashed against an unmoving, bloated man lying atop a table. In seconds, his corpse glowed like a ghastly lantern.

Brandun pointed to the gushing crack. "The gardener must have seen a demon come in. I bet he threw something at the pipe, broke it so he could hide in the darkness."

"That was stupid," Creen said. "Half the room would still be lit up, like it is now."

Brandun nodded. "Maybe it's hard to think straight when one of those things comes for you. I hope we never find out for ourselves."

Creen grunted in agreement.

The glowpipes lit up the right half of the chamber, casting a dim glow on the left-hand side. At least they could see the whole room now. Dark alcoves lined both walls.

A demon could be hiding in any of them. In *all* of them.

Ahiliyah took a deep breath, trying to remember Sinesh's training. If she let fear take her now, she would run and never, ever come back.

"Find the processing station," she said.

She glanced over her shoulder, toward the chamber's open entry arch. The corridor beyond glowed brightly, or at least brighter than the half-lit, spacious room.

"Creen, watch the entryway," Ahiliyah said. "If you see anything coming, shut off the valve and hide. Brandun, search the right side, I'll search the left."

Both the boys were terrified, but they obeyed. They wanted to finish the job and get the hell out of there, just like she did.

There were no glowpipes in the alcoves—the inky darkness inside the arched entrances seemed to radiate evil, danger... death. She stepped into the first one, letting her torch lead the way—empty. Nothing in the second one, either. Would a demon be waiting in the third?

Ahiliyah began to tremble. She breathed deep; slow in, slow out. No time for fear.

She stepped into the fourth alcove. Her flickering torch lit up stacks of empty trays speckled with clumps of dirt.

The fifth alcove stank like shit. She stepped in, saw stuffed canvas bags stacked against the side and back walls. They looked like the sandbags her people stacked along the river during flooding season. The bags weren't filled with sand, though—they were fertilizer. The room reeked, but she'd take the stench of human feces over the scent of death any day.

"I think I found it," Brandun called out.

Ahiliyah winced at his volume. How did he not understand the danger they were in?

She crossed the chamber, weaving between the tables of mold clusters, giving the splashing pipe and its lantern-corpse a wide berth. Brandun stood next to an alcove entryway. Ahiliyah slipped past him, her torch leading the way. Wooden racks lined each wall. On them, small, stuffed burlap bags, stacked in orderly rows.

For the people of Lemeth, this was life itself.

"There's so much of it," Brandun said. "They told us they'd given us all they could spare, that they needed the rest for their own sick people. Did they make all this extra in the few days we've been away?"

Of course they hadn't. They'd had a large supply all along. The Margrave had been right—Keflan *had* been holding out. They'd lied, claimed a shortage so they could dictate a better price.

Why were people such *assholes*?

"We need to bring all of it," Ahiliyah said.

Brandun picked up one bag, tossed it up and down in his hand.

"That'll be tough," he said. "These weigh about half a brick each." He glanced at Ahiliyah's backpack. "If you take out everything, I think we can fit thirty-five to forty of these in your pack. That's *nineteen* bricks' worth, Liyah. How much do you weigh?"

The thought of carrying that much made her heart sink. "I weigh twenty-seven bricks."

"More than half your body weight." Brandun said. "On a three-day hike. Four days, more like it, considering how much you'd be weighed down. You should carry thirteen, at the most."

They didn't have four days. They *had* to make it in three, even if they had to move at night.

Ahiliyah counted up the bags sitting on the shelves. "There's one hundred and twenty-five bags. I'm taking forty.'

"Forty?" Brandun shook his head. "Liyah, you can't—"

"*We don't have a choice.* Creen is smaller than me. I need him to carry thirty-one. That means you need to carry the rest. Can you do it?"

Brandun's eyebrows rose. He looked at the racks.

"I weigh thirty-four bricks," he said. "You want me to carry fifty-two bags, a weight of twenty-six bricks." He winced. "I'm strong, I know, but come on. Carry that much for *four days*? Through the mountains? We have to climb and descend along the way."

She put her hand on his arm.

"We'll make it in three days. Not four. Whatever you can't carry, I have to take."

He looked at her with a pained expression. Carrying that much weight might kill him. She knew it, and so did he.

"Brandun, yes or no—can you do it?"

He nodded slowly.

She slid off her backpack, handed it to him. "Start packing."

Scowling, he took her bag and got to work.

Ahiliyah headed back to the chamber's entrance, once again aware of the sound of water splashing down on rotting flesh and stone. She passed an alcove with a circular wooden press inside. That had to be the grinder—there was one like it Lemeth. The next alcove held long strings of mold clusters hanging down from the ceiling. Still drying? Could someone come back and grind those? Maybe, but the fact was that no one in Lemeth knew how to properly process capertine mold, and there was no one left in Keflan to show them.

Creen was crouched low, just inside the entrance, his little helper clutched in a shaking hand. He stared around the wall's edge, out into the corridor. He looked so small.

"We found it," she whispered. "You see anything? Any movement?"

He shook his head. "I might have heard something. Maybe it was a person. I don't know."

A person? The hold had seemed empty. Could someone still be alive down here? Could she take the chance to try and help a Keflanian if that meant risking a safe return of the medicine?

Ahiliyah tugged lightly at Creen's hidey suit. She led him to the alcove where Brandun was tying off the top of her backpack. His overstuffed pack sat at his feet.

"Creen," Ahiliyah said, "give him your pack."

Creen did so, then watched, blank-faced, as Brandun shoved bag after bag inside. Brandun tied off the pack, handed it to Creen. Brandun let go, the backpack yanked Creen's arms down, hit the floor with an audible *whump*.

Creen shook his head. "I can't carry this. It's too heavy."

"You'll carry it," Ahiliyah said. "We don't have a choice."

"You don't seem to understand what the word *choice* actually means, Liyah," Creen said. "We do have a choice. We can *choose* not to weigh ourselves down so bad that we can't fucking make it home. We can choose to live."

"People are sick," Brandun said.

Creen sneered. "Really? People are sick? Really? You big duh…" His voice trailed off, his eyes flicked to Brandun's big hands. "Sorry. I'm losing it. Sorry."

"It's fine," Brandun said. "It's okay, let's just get home."

Creen turned to Ahiliyah. "All three of us are so burdened down I doubt we'll make it back. We need probably *half* of this to help the people who are sick right now."

"And what about the people who get sick next?" she said. "Take a look around. The Keflanians are *gone*. They're either dead or they've been carried off to Black Smoke Mountain. There's no one here to make more medicine. The demons killed this place—they're out there, hunting. That means this might be the last medicine there is. We have to take *all* of it."

"Even if we do take it all, it's going to run out eventually." No arrogance in Creen's voice, no insult, just a low monotone of dread. "What happens to us then?"

People get sick and they die.

Was that the accurate answer to his question? Maybe, but figuring that out wasn't her duty—it was the Council's.

She lifted her backpack, cringing at the thought of carrying that much weight through the mountains. She tried to put it on, staggered a step as she did. Brandun had to help her. Ahiliyah tied her chest straps, wondering if it was her imagination that her legs were already starting to burn.

Favoring his injured arm, Brandun slid into the straps of his backpack, showing far more grace than Ahiliyah had. The bigger boy fastened his straps, tied them tight.

The two of them then stared at Creen. He stared back, anger written across his face.

"I fucking hate you guys," he said, then, with a grunt, he picked up his backpack and struggled into it. He tried to tie his chest straps, almost fell backward. Brandun steadied him while Ahiliyah tied off the straps. She finished, patted Creen's chest, took a step back.

The backpack looked bigger than Creen was. "This is gonna suck." He shrugged his shoulders, testing out the weight. "What now? Can we get out of here?"

They had the medicine. That noise Creen had heard… a survivor, a demon, nothing at all? The choice to run or try and help was hers and hers alone—she wanted to be sick all over again.

"We leave," she said. "If we find survivors along the way, we help them, but we need to get home as fast as possible."

They would not look for survivors. All three of them understood the magnitude of her decision. They might be abandoning human beings to a lonely, brutal death. Or worse.

"We should head back to the deck," Creen said. "We follow the same way we came in. I'm sure the demons have left by now."

Ahiliyah remembered the sickening sound of talons scratching on the rock. She imagined the demons sitting just outside the door, crouched, waiting…

"If we open that door and they're still there, we're dead," she said.

Brandun bent at the knees, popped up, adjusting the weight of his pack.

"Keflan has a river, just like Lemeth," he said. "We could try floating out?"

She hadn't seen the river here. If its current was as violent as the Bitigan River's back home, she didn't like their chances. The medicine bags were waxed and waterproofed against rain, but would they hold up while soaking in a roaring river for an hour or more?

"Oh, shit," Creen said. His face looked ashen. "Keflan has a signaling station."

Ahiliyah sagged, thinking of all those stairs.

Brandun looked from Creen to her. "What's a signaling station go to do with it?"

"It's our way out," Ahiliyah said. "We go up to the station, climb down the mountain."

Brandun blinked. "Keflan Mountain is higher than Lemeth. The climb down could kill us."

"It's our only choice," she said. "If we don't make it back, our people will die. Your mother will die."

Brandun paused a moment, then nodded. He knew what was at stake. He accepted the responsibility, the coming pain.

Creen glanced down. He started to shake again. "I'm not made for this kind of thing."

"I'll help you," Brandun said. He gripped the smaller boy's shoulder. "We can do this."

Tears in his eyes, Creen looked up at Brandun. "I'm sorry I stabbed you."

"I choked you first." Brandun shrugged. "I would have stabbed me, too."

Ahiliyah hoped the boys would remain unified for the coming ordeal.

"We need to find the signal station stairs," she said. "Let's go."

17

Her legs *screamed*. She was only halfway up, and that was *if* the Keflan steps were identical to Lemeth's.

What if there were more?

"I need a rest." Creen bent at the waist, hands on his knees. "Come on, we have to stop."

Their heavy breaths sounded far too loud in the tight stairwell. If there were demons above them, there was no way they wouldn't hear. Ahiliyah leaned against the wall, trying to draw in as much air as she could.

"Move," Brandun said, his voice a harsh whisper. "Both of you."

Creen glared at him. "Fuck you."

Brandun reached out, sank the fingers of his good hand into Creen's hidey-suit webbing. Brandun continued up the stairs, pulling Creen along.

"*Asshole*," Creen hissed, stumbling up the steps. "This is fucking *stone*, you're going to make me fall and hurt myself!"

"Then don't fall," Brandun said. "You'll keep your balance better if you move on your own, right?" He stopped long enough for Creen to get his balance back. The smaller boy stared at the bigger one with such *hate*.

They were at each other's throats again. Ahiliyah didn't have the energy to get between them.

"Fuck you, Brandun," Creen said, then he started up again, one heavy step after another.

Brandun's chest heaved, but he stood straight and tall. He glared at Ahiliyah.

"Move," he said. "Or do I have to drag you as well?"

She stared at Brandun with as much hate as Creen had… if not more.

"I've never liked you," she said.

He smiled, wiped sweat from his face, then gestured up the stone stairs.

"After you, oh great leader."

Ahiliyah pushed off the wall, tried to ignore the fact that her legs wobbled with each step. She continued up the stairs.

The signal station looked eerily similar to the one in Lemeth Hold, save for a lack of clothes tossed carelessly about. The sun signaler— wood tripod legs folded together—leaned against a corner.

No one home. No demons, no rotting bodies. She could still smell the dead—she feared that stench had sunk into her hidey suit, her backpack.

The sliding stone door that led to the outside was shut and sealed. Beyond that door, Ahiliyah and the others would begin a dangerous, grueling, desperate trip back home.

"Take a break," she said, untying her backpack and sliding out of it. "We need to stop sweating before we go outside, it's going to be cold out there."

Creen didn't bother taking his off, he just lay down in one of the room's two beds. Brandun slid out of his pack, walked to the sliding door, put his ear against the stone.

On a table, Ahiliyah saw buckets similar to the ones she and Creen had carried to the Lemeth signaling station a few days before. Inside, some stale bread, a few broken bits of mushroom, some dried rivergrass, half a fish sausage. Broken bits of food had spilled on the table, even on the floor. The buckets looked like someone had grabbed what they could before rushing out.

"We need to eat," she said, and started dividing up the food.

Creen pinched his nose. "I can't get the stink of the dead out of my face. I don't think I could hold down any food."

Ahiliyah shoved crumbly bread and a chunk of the mushroom into his hands. "This is a brownie shroom, it will help settle your stomach."

She took a bite of bread, another of the fish sausage. Ahiliyah hated fish sausage, but she needed the little bit of protein. She chewed as she joined Brandun at the stone door.

"Hear anything?"

He pressed his hands to the stone slab, as if he might feel vibrations in addition to hearing them.

"Nothing," he said. "Wind. Sounds pretty strong, but no sound of a demon that I can tell."

Which only meant that if there was one out there—one or more—they were sitting still, waiting.

Ahiliyah held out the sausage and bread. Brandun took the food. She gave the boys a few minutes to eat.

"Drink water from their cistern," she said. "Then fill up your canteens."

Even the thought of that little bit of extra weight made her want to scream. Her legs *hurt*.

"Creen, take off your pack," she said. "You'll open the door. Brandun, assemble your spear. I'll be ready with a net. Once we know the way is clear, we'll put the packs on and start down."

Brandun screwed his spear together. Ahiliyah pulled a net free from the webbing of her overstuffed backpack, spread her hands, stretching the net wider. Her heart kicked. The net wouldn't hold a demon for long, but hopefully long enough for Brandun to strike before it ripped free or its burning blood ate through the twine.

Brandun spun his spear—six feet long from butt-spike to spearpoint—and pointed it toward the door. He bent his knees, bounced lightly in place, maybe trying to loosen up his legs.

"Sooner started," he said, "sooner done."

Ahiliyah saw fear on his face. Despite it, Brandun was willing to be first in line. Only fifteen years old—was he naturally brave, or was this a result of his early warrior training?

Creen unbolted the door, winced as the mechanism made a metallic squeal. Everyone waited, listening for sounds from outside. There were none but the wind.

He gripped the handle and leaned back, little arms pulling, shaking legs pumping.

Ahiliyah held her breath.

The door slid open.

The night wind rattled papers, scattered crumbs of food. A few flakes of snow whipped around. *Cold* seeped in as well, instantly chilling her sweat-damp clothes.

The three of them waited—no demon.

Legs still bent, Brandun stepped forward, rear foot touching front, front leg stretching out, never crossing his feet.

Already shivering, Ahiliyah walked out behind him onto the small plateau. The cloud cover had broken. The Three Sisters gleamed down, showing the wide expanse of Lake Lanee. She looked northwest, across the water. The night was so clear that in the distance, silhouetted against the cloudy, star-speckled horizon, she saw the familiar outline of Lemeth Mountain.

So far away…

"Get out your climbing gear," she said. She wanted to whisper, but she had to speak with volume to be heard over the wind that whipped at her hair and the bush leaves in her hidey suit.

Brandun stepped to the edge of the plateau, leaned out, looked down. "Climbing at night is suicide. Can we wait until morning? Go at first light?"

"Fuck that," Creen said. "Demons could still be in the hold, they could be coming up for us right now. We have to get the hell out of here."

Creen was right. If even one demon came up those stairs, there was nowhere to run. Climbing at night was extremely dangerous, true, but Ahiliyah liked her chances on the rock face better than her chances in this dead-end room.

"Get your packs," she said. "We're going."

Creen was the best climber by far. He led the way down. Any child of Lemeth grew up climbing; scaling rock was second nature to them all, but not in high wind, and not in blowing snow. Ahiliyah guessed their chances of making it down alive at somewhere below fifty percent.

Normally nighttime meant hiding time. Maybe that rule didn't apply any more. This high up, there wasn't enough vegetation to hide behind. With the demons moving in the daylight, when the sun rose Ahiliyah and her team would be utterly exposed on the mountainside, visible and unprotected—there was no point in waiting until morning.

They moved down in stages, tying long ropes to their packs and lowering them to a boulder or crack in the rock below. If they made it to the foothills, they'd have to carry the heavy packs, but for now they let gravity do the work. Their hidey suits were heavy, too, but she and the others didn't dare take those off. If the demons did come their way, the suits might be their only chance at survival.

The trio stayed close enough together that they could communicate with hand signals. No words were spoken. Their ears filled with the sound of the wind that drove snow against mountain walls, that roared off cliff faces, that chilled their sweating bodies.

It took them an hour—a freezing, bitter hour—to descend far enough that they left the snow behind. The vegetation was far from lush, but at least there were enough caminus bushes to provide cover.

Creen was the first to see movement.

He pointed to his eyes, pointed down and east, then tapped his right shoulder: the *hide* signal.

Ahiliyah scanned her surroundings, then moved toward a single caminus bush voluminous enough to hide her. Only when she was behind it, with a split boulder behind her, did she look for the threat. In the moonslight, perhaps a quarter-mile north and a few hundred yards down, she saw three demons moving in single file.

She sank down between rock face and crimson leaves. Slowly, methodically, she used her little friend to cut fresh branches from the bush. These she wove into her webbing, never taking her eyes off the black beasts.

The boys were nowhere to be seen. Good. She hoped they were well hidden. If they weren't, she couldn't help them.

The demons angled closer. The wind and cold didn't bother them— they moved across the rocks with ease. She'd seen two demons working together before, moving through the night, but never three—how many more might be hunting?

Ahiliyah breathed slowly. In her mind she became part of the bush, rooted to the ground, bending with the wind. Eventually, the demons angled away, and vanished from sight. She wanted to wait, give the killers more time to move on, but there wasn't time. She stood, gave the hand signal telling her crew to get ready to move on.

Another hour of climbing brought them to the foothills just as the sun broke above the mountains to the east. No more lowering the packs—from here they would have to be carried.

She'd never felt so drained.

Creen waved at her. He flashed the hand signals for *rest* and *hide*. Brandun, bent over at the waist with his hands on his knees, nodded in agreement.

They wanted to stop for a while.

So did Ahiliyah. But what she wanted and what had to be done were two different things. She made hand signals of her own: *pack up, move out,* and *on me.*

Ignoring their stares, she coiled her ropes and stashed her climbing gear. When she finished, she tried to slide into her backpack, but it was too heavy for her to manage on her own. Brandun had to help her put it on.

Days of hiking to go, yet every muscle already begged for her to stop.

Brandun leaned in close. "We can rest at Dakatera."

Dakatera's walls and warmth beckoned, but was that the right choice? Dakatera Hold was two days away, along a route frequented by runners. She'd seen a handful of bodies in Keflan—not the thousands there would have been had most of its people been killed there. The demons had carried many off to Black Smoke Mountain, but *thousands*?

Ahiliyah had no doubt that survivors would have fled toward Dakatera. On her way to Keflan, she and her crew hadn't seen any of those survivors heading north, but they'd *heard* them, heard their screams in the night.

She waved Creen closer. The crew huddled together, their eyes constantly flicking left and right, looking for danger.

"Survivors would have headed north, to Dakatera," she said. "The demons would have followed them. We need to go east, all the way around Lake Lanee."

If they made good time, that route would also take four days to reach Lemeth, but the going would be much harder, much less traveled. Her team was already burned out, and she was asking for more of them than any leader should ask of anyone.

Yet it had to be done.

Creen stared at her with pure venom. Brandun stared, too, the fatigue written on his face.

"We don't know that route," Creen said. "You want us to go four days with no break?"

Brandun nodded; he understood. "Liyah's right. We can't risk going through Dakatera."

"We *need* to go through Dakatera," Creen said. "Just one night in that hold, just one night of real sleep."

Brandun's face hardened. "Time for you to grow the fuck up and be a man."

He walked east.

Creen's face wrinkled with fear, with worry.

"Please, Liyah—you're in charge. Tell him to come back. *Please*."

She should have been furious with Creen for being so weak, so cowardly, but she wasn't. She just felt bad for him.

"You can do it," she said. "I believe in you."

With that, she started after Brandun.

It took only seconds for Creen to follow.

She forced them to walk all day long, deciding that they were all better off putting as much distance as they could between themselves and Keflan. Just past noon, they saw another trio of demons—moving in blazing daylight—but the beasts were far enough away that she and her team easily hid, savoring thirty minutes of rest.

Twice they had to break out climbing gear to get across steep ridges. Going down with the overstuffed packs had been hard, but nothing compared to going *up*. The packs slowed them significantly. When they had to ascend sheer cliff faces, Creen had to climb up, loop a rope around a rock, then she and Brandun had to pull, raising the pack until Creen could grab it and tie it off.

By dusk, they were so cold and weak they were beginning to stumble. She had to slow their pace to avoid a fall or slip that might result in a twisted ankle, or even a broken leg.

Just after sunset, things got even worse—it began to rain.

She pushed them as long as she could. Hidey suits and packs alike were waxed, able to resist the water, but only for so long. Once it started to soak in, the additional weight was too much to bear.

Near the bottom of a ravine, they found a network of abandoned vootervert burrows. A godsend, as they were the best places to hide, and the animals instinctively dug holes that stayed dry even in the worst storms. Ahiliyah chose three that were close to each other, but far enough apart that if one of her team was taken, the other two would likely be left alone.

They layered their nets with sticks, twigs, rotting leaves and even bits of stone—the same material that coated the sides of the ravine—then draped the camouflage over the burrows. The good news: the dens also blocked most of the wind. The bad news: their suits and underclothes were all soaked through, and there would be no warmth that night.

Ahiliyah stood in the rain, watched both of the boys crawl into their dens. She checked their netting, adjusting a stick here, a bit of moss there. In the darkness, the camouflage was perfect—the vootervert holes had simply ceased to exist.

Finally, she crawled into her own hole. She lowered her netting, embraced the darkness. Shivering madly, she gave in to her fatigue.

A few hours of sleep would make everything better.

18

Ahiliyah came awake with no movement, with no sound. Her body felt stiff, but she did not stretch, did not yawn. She simply opened her eyes. Even as she woke, her training taught her to be still—*silence is strength*.

That training, that discipline, it saved her life.

Through the netting she'd spread over the hole she'd dug, she saw it. A demon.

Close enough to reach out and touch.

The urge to scream came and went, as did the instinct to run, for to do either was to die.

It crouched next to her, back legs folded, talon-tipped hands flat against the ravine's muddy, sloping sides. It was listening.

No… it was *feeling*. Feeling for the vibrations of something moving across the ground.

Ahiliyah took in a slow breath, as slow as she could manage, her mouth open wide. It had to know she was there. It *had* to. It was less than an arm's length away.

Kill herself. She had to. She could not be taken, *would* not be taken. If she reached for her little friend, could she draw the blade and drive it into her neck before the beast crawled in after her, before the toothtongue shot out and *broke* her?

Breathe in, breathe out, calm, slow, steady. Enough wind out there to mask this tiniest of sounds. If she didn't move, it wouldn't feel her.

But… what about her heartbeat?

She was on her back. Her heart…could the demon feel that rhythm in the ground?

Morning light gleamed from his smooth head. The skull was almost translucent. Could she see *through* it, or was that the play of light and shadows?

The faint odor of moss peeled back from a rock.

She smelled of wet twine and wet caminus leaves—enough to hide her own scent? The cold of her clothes and hidey suit sank into her, reached her bones, made her body start to shiver.

The long head turned, angled right, toward her.

Ahiliyah fought against her shivering, willed her body to *stop*, to *be still*.

It knew she was close. It was looking for her, listening for her, feeling for her.

Her body shivered again.

The demon's left claw slid slightly, moving across the dirt and rock toward her.

She again controlled her shivering, battling against her own body.

The creature stood as still as she was. They were two animals trying to outwait each other.

The demon opened its mouth, let out a low, long hiss.

Ahiliyah felt the deep cold throughout her very being, knew she could hold on no longer, that her next shiver would be her last.

A rattle of a rock rolling down the ravine face. A tiny sound, one she wouldn't have noticed if she hadn't been trapped in the utter silence of survival. The demon's blank face snapped left, pointing somewhere down the ravine.

Another rattle, another stone tumbling down the ravine's side, clattering against rock.

The demon shot forward, out of her sight.

A boy's scream—*Creen.*

Footsteps running past her, *human* footsteps, big feet moving swiftly—*Brandun.*

In a frozen instant, Ahiliyah knew everything was lost. Creen would die, Brandun would die trying to save Creen—and hundreds of Lemethians would die without the capertine they carried. If she lay there and did not move, if she just *breathed*, she might survive, she might get at least some of the medicine home.

All she had to do was lie still.

Creen screamed again.

Her crew… her *friends*.

Before she knew what she was doing, Ahiliyah was up, fingers sliding through the net that had hidden her, ripping it free, bringing it with her as she scrambled out of the burrow and sprinted toward the sound of Creen's cries.

She saw Brandun's wide back as he rushed forward, feet splashing ravine mud, his full spear assembled and in hand, and beyond him, a hissing demon reaching into the vootervert hole that hid Creen.

Brandun drove his spear into the demon's back. The impact knocked the monster to one hip, made it screech in pain, a piercing cry that seemed to fill the ravine. Brandun leaned on the spear, trying to drive it in further, trying to pin the beast to the ground.

Burning blood squirted out in wiggling bursts.

The demon twisted, bent, angled its long head toward Brandun—its hissing mouth opened, the toothtongue lashed out. Brandun ducked left as the small teeth clacked on empty air.

From inside the burrow, Creen screamed in agony.

"Get it off! It burns!"

The demon's black arm whipped down, snapping the wooden spear staff. The beast scrambled to its feet just as Ahiliyah threw her net—a perfect, spinning throw that spanned it wide just as it landed on the reaching monster. Twine tangled in the talons, hooked on the backsticks. The demon clawed frantically, trying to cut the slack, fibrous threads.

"It burns it burns it burns!"

Brandun spun his spear, held it with both hands. He drove off his back foot in a perfect lunge, jamming the pointed metal spear butt into the demon's shoulder—black shell cracked.

Burning blood shot out.

Brandun cried out, spun away, left hand holding his right wrist, his right hand smoking, sizzling, bubbling.

The monster fought madly at the net. Its feet tangled and it fell. Talons cut, teeth bit—twine snapped and tore, the net started to come apart. In seconds, the demon would be free.

A bitter cold wind blew with the force of a hurricane, but it wasn't real, it wasn't on the surface. Ahiliyah felt this wind *inside* of her.

Fear vanished—anger remained.

A weapon... she needed a weapon. There it was, to her right, half-embedded in the muddy ravine wall—a jagged chunk of rock, as long as her forearm.

The demon squealed and hissed.

Net strings snapped.

Creen screamed.

Brandun whimpered.

Ahiliyah's fingers slid into dirt and mud. On the first pull, she wrenched the jagged rock free. Feeling the weight, she turned to face the monster.

The demon ripped the net in two, casting part of it aside, fighting at the other half still hooked between hands and back spikes.

Two strides took Ahiliyah past Brandun—the third brought her to the demon.

As Ahiliyah raised the stone above her head, the demon's long head turned toward her—black lips curled back from jagged teeth, lethal jaws opened. With all that she was, with every ounce of strength in her being, Ahiliyah Cooper drove the rock downward.

The sharp stone point punched into the top of the demon's smooth head, penetrated the hard shell with a satisfying *crunch*. The skull seemed to fold in on itself, blank face still pointed up at her, curved back end angling up and away.

She felt her hands burning. She didn't care.

"I'll kill you," she said, her voice a throat-ripping roar of rage that sounded strange to her own ears. "I will kill *all* of you."

The demon hissed and screeched at the same time. The mouth opened wider—inside, Ahiliyah saw the toothtongue flex, jut forward, but not far enough to get beyond the curled black lips. The rock's point must have pinned it, or broken it. The demon sagged, fell to its side, broken head thumping against the ravine wall, blood spilling out onto the dirt and rock.

It last sound was a hiss so soft it sounded like distant music.

Ahiliyah smelled her own burning flesh.

She looked at her hands. Wisps of smoke rose up from her hidey suit, from the caminus leaves, from her skin beneath. The crimson leaves… spots of grey on them, puffy and powdery. Not quite ash but… something else.

Creen's cries of pain brought her back. She turned to him, still mostly hidden in the burrow beneath his camouflage net. Ahiliyah drew her little friend. Leaves rattled as she sliced at the twine. Spots of powdery grey where the demon's blood had splashed against flat crimson.

Beneath the net, Creen lay flat and shaking, his hands held in front of him like clutching claws, his eyes wide with terror. Curls of smoke rose up from his hidey suit—a great gout of demon blood had splashed his chest. Tiny yellow-red spots on his face where his skin bubbled.

"*Help me,*" he said. "*It burns!*"

Ahiliyah glanced back at Brandun; he was sitting on his butt, staring at the thin smoke rising up from his hidey-suit-covered hand.

She turned back to Creen. Visions of her grandfather, slicing away Sinesh's ruined flesh.

Ahiliyah hauled Creen out of the burrow. She pulled at the chest of his suit, used her little friend to slice through the strands. If the acid had burned through to his chest and belly, he was as good as dead. She had to cut away any bubbling flesh before it was too late.

The stench of scorched leaves and cooking skin filled her nose and mouth, sank deep into her lungs. Creen panicked, started to fight her, to claw at her.

She elbowed him in the mouth.

He sagged back, stunned.

Ahiliyah cut his suit down the middle, from his collar to his navel. She sheathed the blade, then yanked his suit apart, exposing the undershirt beneath.

She stared, confused, at a dozen small holes burned through the shirt. The way his hidey-suit had been smoking... how could there only be a few small holes?

Ahiliyah slid the shirt up Creen's chest. A dozen yellow-red dots on his skin, some still bubbling slightly, but they were minor—none big enough to threaten his life. She'd expected to see hideous wounds, sizzling muscle, even exposed bone.

A low moan from Brandun.

Ahiliyah turned, saw him still sitting there, still staring at his hand. *The bush leaves...*

She ripped free handfuls of bush leaves from the legs of Creen's hidey suit. She stumbled to Brandun, dropped the leaves at his muddy knees, then sliced at the netting covering his hand.

"Liyah," he said, his voice a thin, distant thing, "Liyah, I—

"Shut up." She exposed his hand—much worse than Creen's chest, Brandun's skin bubbled, dripping rivulets of yellow-red to splash into the mud. Ahiliyah grabbed the handfuls of leaves and pressed them hard against his injured hand.

He came back to his senses in an instant, shoved her away so hard she fell onto Creen.

Brandun looked at her with unhidden fury, with pure hate... then that expression faded. He looked at his hand. It still smoked. Half the skin had been eaten away.

But the bubbling had stopped.

Brandun stared at it, then at Ahiliyah, his mouth open.

"How—" he glanced at his hand, then back to her "—how did you stop the burning?"

How? She didn't know. There wasn't time to figure it out. She had seen the demons working in packs—she had to get her crew out of there.

Ahiliyah sheathed her little friend. She grabbed Creen, shook him.

"Creen, *get up*."

He blinked slowly, perhaps not really seeing her. There wasn't time for this—Ahiliyah slapped him. He blinked faster. She slapped him again, harder.

Creen shoved at her, tried to sit up. "Fucking *stop it*, you psycho bitch!"

She leaned in, covered his mouth with her hand.

"Be quiet," she said. "Get your pack on, we're moving out."

Ahiliyah pulled her hand from his mouth, kept it close in case he shouted again.

Tears formed in his eyes. "I'm wounded, I can't carry—"

She drew her hand back, threatening to slap him again.

Creen winced, pushed away from her. "I'm moving, all right? I'm moving."

She rushed to Brandun's side. "Can you walk?"

Still staring at his mangled hand, he nodded.

"Get your pack," Ahiliyah said. "There could be more of them."

Without a word, he stood on wobbling legs, jogged to his hiding spot, his burned hand held close to his chest. She started toward her own burrow, to get her own pack, but something stopped her. She turned to look at the demon.

Head caved in… yellowish blood spreading across the ravine bottom, sending up tendrils of acrid smoke. It was *dead*.

Ahiliyah walked to the unmoving beast. She stared down at it. Had this been someone she'd known? Vanessa Peters? A runner from another hold?

This close, looking at the dead body… no, no it couldn't be a person. The legends were wrong—Creen was right. She didn't know how she knew it, but she *knew*.

She put her foot on the broken head. She reached down—careful that her backpack didn't send her tumbling to the side—and gripped the rock still sticking out of the demon's head. She yanked; it came free with a squelch.

A rock. Not a magic weapon. Not a blessed blade. Just a normal, everyday rock. She set it down, carefully, so as not to make more vibrations in the ground. She drew her little friend.

Foot still on the demon's head, that dark feeling of rage swirling in her chest and belly, Ahiliyah reached into the demon's mouth. She grabbed the toothtongue and pulled. It resisted. With her other hand, she slid in her blade, angled it as far back as she could.

She cut, back and forth, slicing like a saw.

The toothtongue resisted. Cutting through the hard skin was like trying to punch through fergle shell. Instead of sawing, she started jabbing, driving the blade tip through the toothtongue—she heard and felt the shell give way with a satisfying crunch. With the shell broken, the knife sliced away at what lay beneath. Smoke and stink rose up—Ahiliyah realized the demon blood was melting her blade.

She yanked, felt something unseen give, but only partway. She leaned harder on the head, her foot pushing the broken skull into the mud, and she yanked again—she stumbled backward, the severed toothtongue in her grip.

Demon blood spilled on the leaves of her glove. She stared, stunned, knowing the burning would begin, knowing her skin would bubble. She felt the heat rise, instant and fast.

And then, nothing.

Coming to her senses, she wiped her gloves against the ravine's dirt wall. She stared through the leaves that had turned from crimson to grey ash, stared through the strands, examined areas of exposed skin—red welts rising up, painful, demanding.

But no smoke. No bubbling flesh. What was happening?

She realized anew what she was held in that hand—a toothtongue. She had killed a demon.

From somewhere in the mountains, a demon's screech echoed off stone.

Ahiliyah shook the toothtongue, splashing out the last of the burning blood. She pulled leaves from her suit, packed them into the pocket where she usually carried candy, then shoved her trophy in after them.

One last look at the dead demon. It was the first one she'd killed—it would not be the last.

Creen was waiting. Brandun had his pack on, had hers leaning against his leg. With his uninjured hand, he helped her into it. She tied it tight, and they headed for home.

19

They spent the next two days marching in silence. Creen didn't say a word, a strange development, but Ahiliyah thought she understood. She didn't talk much, either, and on a run Brandun never started a conversation. Although, the big boy seemed gloomier than normal; perhaps the close call with death and the constant pain from his burns had got to him. Regardless, all three of them kept their focus on taking one step at a time, at making sure they got home—both to deliver the critical medicine, and to report on their strange discovery.

Hiking through the mountains, Lake Lanee to their left, they made good time. They saw no more demons. Ahiliyah drove her crew as hard as she dared, even considered marching through the night, but the weight of the packs made periodic rest imperative. They fell into their normal pattern, pushing hard through the day, sleeping at night.

Had demons learned that runners liked to hide in vootervert burrows? Maybe that was how the six Dakateran runners had been lost, so she avoided the burrows, opting instead for sleeping in thick patches of caminus bush. That made for frigid nights, but the beasts were too big to slip through the cover unheard—shivering from the cold was better than hiding in a hole, wondering when black hands would reach in to drag you out.

As sun set on the third day, they were only four or five hours from Lemeth. She thought about pushing through the night to reach home, but decided against it. Creen stumbled more than he walked. Ahiliyah fared little better—her legs either ached so badly she nearly cried, or they felt numb. Brandun, injuries and all, seemed tireless.

They found a caminus bush patch that ran right up to an overhanging ledge of stone, giving the crew shelter from a light drizzle and protecting them from one side. They'd no sooner cleared out a small area in the center and strung nets threaded with caminus leaves than Creen crawled under his net and curled up into a fetal ball.

Despite her own utter exhaustion, Ahiliyah could not sleep. Neither, apparently, could Brandun. He sat down next to her. He pulled off his hidey suit glove, kept looking at his wounded hand. Even in the moonslight, she saw the dark blood spots on his bandages.

"Can you move your fingers?"

He wiggled them, then made a fist. "Well enough, I suppose."

"Does it hurt?"

He nodded. "Feels like it's on fire. Has since we killed it."

Ahiliyah reached to her neck, pulled loose a biting getum bug. "That was two days ago. You haven't complained once."

"It's only pain," Brandun said. "It won't stop me."

Ahiliyah thought of Letar Haines, not telling anyone how sick he was, staying at his job until he was beyond help. That was the Lemethian way—work hard, don't stop, don't complain.

"It's all right if it hurts, you know," she said. "You can tell me."

He shrugged. "If talking about pain won't make it go away, why talk about it?"

Brandun wiggled his fingers once more, then slid his hand back into the glove.

Ahiliyah reached into a suit pocket, pulled out the toothtongue, examined it. Had it been soft before? Flexible? She wasn't sure. It had all happened so fast. Now it was a rigid thing, stiff as a board, far lighter than it looked.

A trophy. The greatest prize her people knew.

"You should be a warrior," Brandun said. "I know you want to be one."

She snapped a look at him, hating him for teasing. He wouldn't look at her. Instead, he stared straight at the ground.

"That's ridiculous," Ahiliyah said. "Who told you I wanted to be a warrior?"

"I'm dumb about most things, Liya, but not *all* things."

Blank-faced Brandun. Quiet Brandun. Creen called him stupid more often than not, but could a stupid person see through her so well?

"Well, I don't want to move to Dakatera or Takanta," she said. "So there's no point in me wanting to be a warrior, right?"

"You killed a demon." He couldn't hide his mood, which seemed darker than the night. "Only three people alive in Lemeth have done that. You're one of them."

Sinesh, Tinat… and her.

Ahiliyah turned the toothtongue in her hands, feeling its ridges, the strange squarish shape. So *light*—strange to think these tiny teeth could punch through human skin and bone.

"Lemethian women can't be warriors. Those are the rules."

Brandun shrugged. "Then change the rules. You killed a demon."

He made it sound so easy. He had no idea. He was fifteen—when he was older, he'd better understand how Lemeth worked.

You killed a demon.

But… had she? At first she'd thought this trophy was a symbol of her bravery. Now, holding it, she realized it was a symbol of cowardice. She wasn't the brave one—*Brandun* was. If he hadn't attacked the demon, she knew in her heart that she would have stayed in her burrow, cowering. She would have let Creen die.

That's what the mantras and Aiko's training dictated: a hidden runner stays hidden, even if another runner is in danger. That was why they traveled in threes, in the hopes that at least one would make it back. Ahiliyah been taught to stay quiet—that *silence is strength*—for so long she'd accepted it as fact. She wouldn't have helped Creen. Leave it to a fifteen-year-old to show more bravery than she ever dreamed possible.

Ahiliyah held the toothtongue out to him. "Take it. Creen would be dead if not for you."

Brandun's thick head turned, slowly. He looked at the offered trophy, but didn't take it.

"You killed it, Liyah," He sounded… angry? "You're the fucking hero. Not me."

Hero. She finally understood his mood. He was bitter that she'd delivered the final blow? He could see through her, but they'd spent enough time together that she could do the same—when she actually cared enough to try.

She felt her face flush hot, felt shame overwhelm her. She glanced at Creen, who slept, unmoving, beneath his leaf-lined net.

"I wouldn't have moved," she said, her voice a hollow shell. "I wouldn't have saved him."

Brandun shrugged. "That is what Aiko trained you to do, is it not?"

"That's what I trained *you* to do, too. But you didn't hide. You were brave. You *fought*."

He huffed. "Which was pretty stupid, right? A real *dumbdun* move."

He was trying to be modest about it now? How infuriating.

Ahiliyah tossed the toothtongue into his lap. "Take it. If it wasn't for you, Creen would be dead. Take it. That's an order."

Brandun picked it up, looked at it. A sliver of moonslight gleamed from the teeth, tiny parallel reflections winking in the night. He set the toothtongue in his lap, reached into his hidey suit, drew his little friend. With the tip, he punched holes in the sides of the toothtongue, near the ragged base where Liyah had cut it free of the beast.

"*The run is more important than the runner*," he said. "You taught me that. Right?"

She said nothing.

From another pocket, Brandun drew a bit of twine. He slid one end through the holes he'd just made, his wounded hand making the movement awkward. He tied the two ends together.

"You said I was brave for trying to save Creen," he said. "Then you saved me. So what does that make you?"

Again, she said nothing. It was bad enough that this fifteen-year-old *boy* had shown more courage than she ever could, and now he had to rub it in?

Brandun held up the necklace. The toothtongue swung slightly on the end of the string.

"I know I'm not smart like Creen," he said. "But I'm good with the spear and shield. Real good. In training drills, I can already beat everyone except Drasko and Leonitos. Tinat says I'll be able to beat them soon. I know I'm strong for my size, faster than most, but I win because I put in more practice time than anyone else. I work harder than anyone else. Do you know why I do that?"

She shook her head. The toothtongue swung out, then back, almost hypnotic in its rhythm.

"Because I want to be a hero for our people," he said. "Ever since I can remember, that's all I've ever wanted to be. I want people to write poems about me. Things are so bad right now… we *need* heroes. When my chance came to be one, I failed. You did not."

His words held her, made her feel like he was talking about someone else—but he wasn't. Brandun clumsily hung the toothtongue necklace around Ahiliyah's neck.

"You saved my life," he said. "You killed a demon. You didn't hit it from a distance with crossbow bolts, then wait for it to die, like Tinat did—you smashed its head in with a fucking rock. No one has *ever* done that before. Someday they'll write poems about you. Not me… you."

She lifted the toothtongue, looked at it. Black and gnarled, yes, but the regular pattern of ridges down its length spoke to a certain beauty of order. The teeth gleamed like jewels.

A toothtongue. *Hers.* She wouldn't have thought it possible, yet here it was.

"Thank you," she said.

Brandun shrugged. He looked at his gloved hand, wiggled his fingers. He winced.

Ahiliyah reached into a pocket, felt for and found the twisted, thumbnail-sized knot of Lisa's root. She offered it to Brandun.

"For the pain," she said.

He stiffened. "I can handle it."

God, but he was stubborn. "For your breath, then, because it smells like vootervert ass."

At any other time, he would have laughed. Boys loved such humor. Now, though, it seemed as if laughing were a thing he didn't remember how to do.

He took the root, popped it into his mouth, and chewed.

They sat in silence for a moment. He again looked at his hand—his eyes were already dilated, black as demonskin.

"Liyah, how come no one told us that the bush leaves stopped the burning?"

The same question she'd thought about for the last two days. "I guess they didn't know."

That answer seemed obvious, but also impossible. Crews had been running for over sixty years, since shortly after the Rising when people fled to the abandoned mountain holds. Maybe warriors didn't march out to battle demons anymore, but in Sinesh's time, they had. How could thousands of people, battling nonstop against a deadly enemy, not discover that one of the most plentiful plants in the mountains could help that fight?

Maybe because warriors didn't cover themselves in caminus leaves—only runners did. And maybe because no runner had survived contact with a demon before.

"This changes things," she said. "Maybe the leaves are a weapon against the demons."

Brandun's head fell forward. He jerked it up, tried to open his eyes wide, but could not—the root was already taking effect.

"It's not a *weapon*," he said, slurring his words slightly. "It's only good if we live long enough to fix our wounds in the first place. Good thing there was only one of them. If the three we saw near Keflan attacked as a team, all the bush leaves in the world wouldn't help."

Ahiliyah thought of Brandun's perfect spear thrust, then the follow-up blow with the butt-spike. The demon had fought on despite wounds that would have killed any human.

Brandun crawled to his netting, stretched tight between the bushes. He slid under it, his boots sticking out slightly. He stopped moving, already asleep.

Ahiliyah crawled to him, gently pushed his feet underneath so they could not be seen.

"Sleep well," she whispered, then crawled beneath her own net. Would death come for them in the dark, just as it had two nights ago?

Ahiliyah touched her trophy. Her fingertips explored the toothtongue's ridges. Feeling it, holding it… it made her feel better, made her realize, truly realize, that demons *could* be killed.

She'd killed one. Could she kill more?

Brandun was right—the leaves weren't a weapon. And that was what Ahiliyah's people needed, what *all* people of Ataegina needed: a new weapon.

When she returned to Lemeth, she was going to find one.

20

Everything felt different.

The same Lemeth corridors, many of the same people packed in tightly, there to welcome a crew of runners who had finally returned home.

But this time, no loud cheers. No flowers. No shouted questions. Just *stares*.

As Ahiliyah walked past, the people of Lemeth Hold couldn't look away from her toothtongue necklace.

"Nice fucking welcome," Creen said. "What's the matter, you people never seen a demon-killer before?"

It was the first time he'd spoken a word since he'd been attacked. No one answered.

People had seen demon-killers, of course—but there hadn't been a new one in years.

Callow Winden stepped out from the crowd that packed against the wall, blocked Ahiliyah's path with his burly fisherman's body. He'd finished his five runs. His sons Abrams and Duvall—teenagers both due to soon start running—stood close by, watching.

"Everyone thought you were dead," Callow said. "Dakatera signaled with news that Keflan Hold had fallen. Dakatera took in hundreds of refugees. The refugees said they were hunted all the way there. The death toll is in the hundreds."

Ahiliyah felt Brandun's big hand on her shoulder.

"You were right to take us the long way," he said.

Ahiliyah had thought everyone was quiet because they were shocked by her toothtongue necklace. Maybe they were, but that wasn't the main reason for this cold welcome—the Lemethians were *scared*.

Farther down the hall, big bodies pushed through the crowd. Rinik Brennus and Shalim Aniketos, flanking Doctor Talbot. The doctor came forward, threw his arms around Ahiliyah.

"Liyah! We thought you were gone."

She hugged him back. "We made it—and we brought medicine."

He stepped back. "How much?"

Ahiliyah shrugged off the heavy backpack, set it at the doctor's feet. Brandun and Creen did the same. Without the constant weight, she suddenly felt like she could float away.

Talbot stared at the three overstuffed packs. "Those are *full*? Of capertine powder?"

"You bet your sweaty balls they are," Creen said. "Get to work, Doc."

Talbot opened up the top of Liyah's pack, stared inside. "It's a miracle." He looked up to Rinik and Aniketos. "Bring the rest."

Neither guardsman argued. They each took a pack. Ahiliyah felt an odd sense of satisfaction when Rinik stumbled shouldering the same pack Brandun had carried for four days.

"The Council wants to see you," Rinik said. "All of you. Right now."

He and Aniketos followed Talbot down the corridor.

The crowd remained frozen for a moment, then the people found their voices—the questions came like an avalanche. Ahiliyah's pride in her achievement shattered under desperate questions about loved ones who had lived in Keflan, about the demon attack, if Lemeth was in danger... if all of Ataegina was about to fall.

People pushed closer to her, surrounded her from all sides. She wasn't used to that kind of crowding—she turned left, then right, looking for a way out.

For an instant, a dark, horrifying instant, the packed crowed turned pitch-black, their words became hisses, and their mouths filled with metallic teeth.

"Back the *fuck* up!" Creen pushed in and shoved a man twice his size. He kicked another man in the shin. The man yelped, hopped on one foot than reached for Creen—Brandun stepped between them.

"Don't touch him," Brandun said.

The man—who was a man again, not a demon, and Ahiliyah knew it was Armando Sanyan—took a limping step back. Armando was bigger than Brandun, but the teenager's body language left no doubt who would fight harder.

Yuzuki Xavi pushed through the crowd. "Brandun, your ma is sick. She's in the hospital."

Brandun strode through the crowd, roughly pushing past anyone who didn't get out of his way fast enough. Ahiliyah started after him— Creen grabbed her wrist.

"The Council," he said. "We'll check in with Brandun after."

They rushed through the crowd, following in Brandun's wake, ignoring all the questions thrown at their backs.

21

They walked past the training pit.

There were only four warriors down on the sand: Will Pankour, Leonitos Lamech, Farid Nemensalter, and Andan Gisilfred. Four warriors, and one "demon"— Ahiliyah assumed it was the tall Benji Johnson, once again wearing the black skin.

The four men—and the demon, perhaps—stared up at Ahiliyah.

She knew they were staring at her toothtongue.

Will and Leonitos looked as if they were watching a ghost stroll along the walkway, as if they couldn't believe what they saw. Farid pressed his fist to his sternum. He smiled at her, a strange, small smile. It was an expression she'd rarely seen on a warrior's face, at least when looking at her—an expression of respect.

Andan showed neither respect nor disbelief. He glared at her. He looked… jealous.

Ahiliyah and Creen headed for the Margrave's Chamber, leaving the training pit behind.

When she'd first come to council meetings as one of Aiko's new runners, the councilmen had acted as if Ahiliyah were beneath them, like she was a nuisance rather than an asset to the hold. That had improved slightly when she completed her first run as a team leader, improved even more when she became a slash, but it was nothing compared to how they looked at her now.

Now that she wore a toothtongue.

Ahiliyah stood at the table's edge, Creen a step behind her and a step to her left. The Council wanted Brandun there as well. Ahiliyah had told them he'd gone to see his mother. They'd sent Thesil Akana to fetch him.

"We got within a few kilometers of home last night," Ahiliyah said, finishing her report. "We didn't want to take a chance that they might be hunting us in the dark, so we camped, then came first thing this morning. We gave Doctor Talbot the medicine, then came right here."

She didn't like most of the councilmen, but knew they were all smart men. It was clear they understood that things had changed. They tried to hide their fear, but she saw it plain as day.

"Keflan will recover," Councilman Jung said. "I have faith in God. When this dies down, God will see fit to bring the surviving Keflanians back to their hold."

When this *dies down*? She wanted to ask if he really understood what had happened, but this wasn't the time to show disrespect—either intentional or accidental.

"You killed a demon," Councilman Tinat said. He absently played with the two toothtongues hanging from his neck, still faintly glowing from river water. "That makes you part of a very"—he glanced at Poller, Balden and Jung—"*very* special group."

Special indeed. Her, Tinat and Sinesh, the only living demon-killers.

"The information from Dakatera is spotty," Councilman Poller said. "Their signaled reports have been somewhat conflicting. They say they have taken in five hundred Keflanian refugees, and they think another two hundred may have fled to Jantal. Keflan's last census report put the hold's population at thirteen hundred. That means some six hundred people were killed or are still on the surface, hiding."

"Or were taken to Black Smoke Mountain," Ahiliyah said. "We didn't see that many bodies in Keflan Hold, but we didn't explore it, either. We found the mold farm, got the capertine powder, and left as fast as we could."

Thirteen hundred people. More than a third of Lemeth's population, dead or forced to flee from their homes. Keflan was—or had been—

the smallest hold on Ataegina. If the demons got inside one of the bigger holds, the horror would be far worse.

"Our brothers and sisters perished," the Margrave said. He shook his head. "A tragic loss."

"Tragic," Poller said.

Balden nodded. "Tragic indeed."

Had it been just a few days earlier that Poller and Balden had accused Keflan of holding out, of unfair bartering? They'd been right. Keflan *had* been lying about their stockpiles of capertine powder. If not for her crew's run, more Lemethians would have *died* because of that lie.

How could people be that selfish? How could they think their own needs and wants were more important than the very *lives* of others?

Councilman Poller cleared his throat. "There is one other thing the Dakaterans signaled—they say they don't have enough food. They are asking us to take some refugees."

The Margrave raised an eyebrow. "How many is *some*?"

"Half," Poller said.

Jung gasped. "Two hundred and fifty? Impossible! We can barely feed our own people as it is!"

Tinat leaned forward on the table. "Councilman Jung, Dakatera can't shoulder the entire burden alone. How are they going to feed the refugees? Where are they going to put them?"

Jung threw a hand in the air, as if to bat away the statement. "Then Dakatera can send them elsewhere. Those blasphemers in Biseth have more than enough room."

Tinat stood, reached out to the model of Ataegina. He tapped the flag of Dakatera, then Lemeth, then Biseth.

"Lemeth is on the way to Biseth," he said. "The Keflanians lost their home, saw their loved ones murdered. You can't expect them all to make the journey directly from Dakatera to Biseth."

"That's better than bringing them here," Balden said. "Because we certainly can't feed them. Besides, if we let them in here, who's to say they'll leave at all?"

Tinat's face flushed red. "You bunch of sniveling, selfish—"

"*Enough,*" the Margrave said. "We will take the status of the refugees into consideration. It is not a decision to be made this second."

Tinat seemed to want to argue, seemed to think the better of it. He sat down.

"Now, Ahiliyah," the Margrave said, "did you see anything else?"

"We did." She glanced at the mountain range on the table, her eye drawn to where Tinat had tapped his fingertip. "We found out that... that..."

Keflan. Where it sat on the map... closest to Black Smoke Mountain. Where the Demon Mother supposedly lived.

It wasn't a straight-line path, but the ridge of the mountains led from the tall peak of Black Smoke Mountain, to Keflan, to Dakatera...

... to Lemeth.

"Ahiliyah?"

She came back to the moment. The councilmen were staring at her, waiting.

"Um... sorry, I got distracted."

The Margrave nodded. "You have been through much, runner. Tell us what you found."

Keflan, then Dakatera, then Lemeth. Her stomach churned. She felt panicky, an echo of what she'd felt when she woke up with a demon just on the other side of her netting.

"The caminus leaves," she said. "They stopped the burning blood from burning."

Councilman Jung huffed. "That's ridiculous. Have you been eating red moss?"

"It's true," Creen said. He stepped forward, stood shoulder to shoulder with Ahiliyah. He pointed to the small holes in his shirt. "See these?" He lifted the shirt, showing his wounds. "When Brandun stabbed the demon, burning blood splattered all over me. My hidey suit was covered in caminus leaves. If it hadn't been, the blood would have burned right through."

Jung and the others still seemed doubtful. They traded glances.

Tinat stood again. "Those wounds are small, so it must have been a small splatter of blood." He reached up, absently, held his toothtongues. "Is that right, Creen? A small amount hit you? And from a distance?"

"The demon was as close to me as Ahiliyah is right now." Creen lowered his shirt, hiding his wounds, but the holes in the fabric were impossible to miss. "Demon blood poured down on me. I *smelled* my own skin cooking, I…"

He started to shake.

Ahiliyah put her arm around his shoulder. She saw Tinat, his fingertips tracing the scars on his face.

Creen looked down at the floor. He began to cry.

"Fuck this," he said, wiping at his eyes with the backs of his hands. "Fuck all of this."

Tinat pressed his fist against his chest. "There is no shame in crying." He looked like he might cry himself. "Not after what you went through. You are braver than most men in this hold." His eyes caught Ahiliyah's. "Excuse me, most *people*."

The scarred councilman's expression hardened. He leaned forward, fists pressing against the map table, his burning gaze fixing on the other men in turn, even on the Margrave.

"None of you know what it's like to face a demon," he said. "I do. Ahiliyah Cooper does. Creen Dinashin does. If he says he's alive because of the leaves, then I believe him. We must study this. We must find out why this happens."

Jung dismissed the thought with a wave. "They are children and they got lucky." He glanced at Ahiliyah. "Not to diminish the fact that you killed one, that is to be lauded, but to think that *caminus leaves* somehow counteract the burning blood? Those leaves are *everywhere*. How could we not have known this before?"

"Perhaps someone *did* know," Tinat said. "Perhaps someone saw this during the Rising, but didn't survive long enough to share it. Four hundred thousand people died in those two years, Jung. We lost more knowledge than we will ever understand."

The Margrave laced his fingers together, bowed his head, either praying or pretending to pray. The room waited for him to speak.

"I agree, this needs to be studied." He looked up. "But considering how many people are sick right now, our doctors will be very busy for some time to come. And we have to deal with Dakatera's request to help with refugees. The study of the leaves must wait."

"It can't wait," Creen said, still fighting his sobs, wiping snot from his nose. "I can do it."

Jung regarded Creen as if he were a gish that had suddenly started reciting poetry.

"He's a *boy*," the councilman said. "What can he know—?"

The Margrave held up a hand, cutting Jung off. Aulus Darby stared at Creen. The boy didn't look away. He wiped away the last of his tears, then puffed up his chest, jutted out his burn-dotted chin and stared right back.

"I know I'm young, Margrave, but I would be lying if I said I'm not the smartest person in the hold—and lying is a sin."

All around the table, eyebrows rose.

"Smartest person in the hold," the Margrave said, a grin playing at the corners of his mouth. "Smarter than *me*?"

Ahiliyah cringed at the question. She expected Creen to backpedal, to make some fawning excuse, but—as usual—the boy surprised her.

"Yes. Even you." Not a hint of hesitation or doubt in Creen's voice.

"So arrogant," Balden said, frowning. "You dare to insinuate that you have more wisdom than our Margrave?"

Creen glared at Balden. "*Wisdom* and *intelligence* are not the same thing, Councilman. I would think someone in your position would be—pardon the timing of this expression—fucking *smart* enough to know the difference."

The councilmen laughed. All but Balden, who was so angry he literally bit his lip to stop himself from saying something else.

Tinat slapped the table, smiled wide. "This boy is *bold*. If only he were big enough to be a warrior, we can always use courage like this. Margrave, why not let him try?"

"Creen is an experienced runner," Balden said, raising a finger in objection. "With Keflan destroyed, we will need our runners to go further and more frequently than before. We need our runners to be *running*, now more than ever."

The Margrave nodded.

"That is a good point," he said. "However, we do not have anyone else who would have the intelligence and the available time to study the leaves. Let's not be coy—we all know the boy is smart." He smiled at Creen, warmth in his eyes. "Young man, you will have your chance to prove you're as brilliant as you claim, but only if your crew leader allows it. You may be smarter than me, but I've enough *wisdom* not to break up a good team if doing so will cause problems."

Creen turned to Ahiliyah, a desperate look on his burn-spotted face. The boy had come so close to dying, or to being carried away to Black Smoke Mountain. He'd made four runs. He'd done his part. She couldn't bring herself to make him do one more.

"Creen should study the leaves," Ahiliyah said. "I will miss him on runs, but the hold needs him in a different way now."

Creen smiled. A genuine, heartfelt smile. It made him look like a different person.

"Very well," the Margrave said. "Creen, can you make a list of what you might need?"

"A demon," Creen said instantly. "I need a demon."

Tinat slapped the table again, roared with laughter. "These are dark times, but this boy's sense of humor is a wonderful reprieve."

Tinat thought Creen was joking.

Ahiliyah knew better.

22

People packed into the training pit bleachers. More people even than when Mari had been executed. The Margrave had called for the assembly—he would tell the people what happened in Keflan, and what Lemeth was going to do in response.

Liyah wove through crowd, looking for her crew. She hadn't seen Brandun since they'd got back the day before. She'd heard Cadence was recovering, though—the capertine powder they'd brought back had saved her life.

She saw Creen sitting at the rail, his feet dangling over the training pit wall. He had his hand pressed down on the empty space to his right; he glared at anyone who tried to sit there.

"Hey, Smartest Man In The Hold," she said. "That seat taken?"

He glanced up, pulled his hand away. "Saved it for you."

"Thanks." She sat, appreciative of the front-row view. "Make space for Brandun, too."

"Oh, he's too *important* to sit with the likes of us."

Creen pointed across the pit. Brandun sat in the bleachers with the warriors, fresh, clean bandages on his hand. He was almost as big as most of the warriors, even bigger than a few. The older men laughed with him, thumped him on the back, treated him like he was one of their own.

Ahiliyah felt a stab of jealousy.

"Forget him," Creen said quietly. "*You* should be the next warrior, like you want."

Ahiliyah's head snapped toward Creen. "Did Brandun tell you that?"

"He didn't tell me anything. He doesn't need to. It's obvious."

She stared at the side of his face, at the small burn scabs that would soon become scars.

"What you do mean, *it's obvious*?"

Finally, he looked at her. "You and Sinesh play those miniature war games all the time. When you're in phalanx training, you try so hard, like it's the real thing. I see the way you look at the warriors when they're in the pit. And I saw the way you looked at Brandun just now."

She stared at him, dumbfounded. Creen knew her this well? She'd told her deepest desire only to Brandun and the Margrave. She hadn't even told Tolio. Her boyfriend had no idea, yet Creen knew without her saying a word.

The pit doors opened, saving Ahiliyah any need to respond. The Margrave walked across the sand, his purple robes flaring, Rinik Brennus and Drasko at his sides. The three men stopped in the middle of the pit.

The crowed hushed.

"You've all heard the rumors floating through our corridors," the Margrave said, his voice booming off the stone walls and arched ceiling. "Here is the truth— Keflan Hold has fallen."

The large room remained eerily still. The Margrave slowly turned in place, letting everyone see his face. He looked sad, but not afraid.

"This is a tragedy," he said. "Hundreds of our brothers and sisters are dead, or have been lost to the demons. Why did this happen? We can only guess. Perhaps they forgot the need to stay hidden. Perhaps they forgot the need to stay quiet. Perhaps too many of them wandered into the valley to collect fruit, forgetting the trials that God has put before us."

Creen leaned close, whispered. "The fuck is he talking about? They were hiding, like us."

Ahiliyah shushed him.

"Perhaps," the Margrave said, "they stopped listening to their leaders, to the very people who kept them safe. Perhaps it was their strange religion, an affront to God's clear instructions. Perhaps it was all of these things."

He blamed the Keflanians? That didn't make sense. Demons didn't pick and choose, they killed whoever they saw.

The Margrave paused. He looked down at the sand. He stayed still for a few moments. The audience barely breathed. Finally, he looked up, started turning in a circle again.

"Yes, this is a tragedy, but it is also a lesson. We *must* stay hidden. We *must* obey the rules of the hold. We *must* follow the teachings of God. If we do not, if *any* of us do not, then we might well wind up like Hibernia. Like Pendaran... like Keflan."

He gestured toward the pit doors. Preacher Tumalo Ramirus stepped out, his black robes dragging on the sand. He strode forward, stood shoulder to shoulder with the Margrave.

"Let us pray," Tumalo said.

He dropped to one knee. So did the Margrave. A rustle from the crowd as people bowed their heads. Ahiliyah glanced at Creen—he stared straight ahead, a fierce look on his face.

She elbowed him, whispered: "Bow your head."

He kept his head high. "He's using this to increase his control. Unfuckinbelievable."

"These are trying times," Tumalo said, his voice resonating through the chamber. "God is testing us. The people of Keflan failed that test, which brought down God's wrath."

Tumalo also blamed the people of Keflan? If the preacher had seen the bodies—bloated and rotted and ripped part—he would know that no God would bring such a thing upon anyone.

"We must obey our rules," Tumalo said. He gestured to the Margrave. "We must do what God asks of us. If we are to be delivered from evil, we must—we *must*—listen to our leaders."

The Margrave rose first. He put a hand on Tumalo's shoulder; the preacher stood. Together, the two men walked out of the training pit.

People stood and started filtering out of the room. Ahiliyah listened to snippets of hushed conversation. Some sounded like Creen, expressing disbelief at what they'd just seen. Some were *angry* at it. Others, many others, talked about how the Margrave knew best.

All of the voices, though, had one thing in common—they sounded *afraid*.

Ahiliyah leaned close to Creen, whispered so only he could hear. "You said the Margrave is using this to increase his control? What did you mean?"

He looked at her, his face wrinkling as if she'd spoken the dumbest words of all time.

"For someone so sharp," he said, "you can be *so* blind. I'm sure you'll see soon enough."

Creen was wrong. Maybe the Margrave shouldn't have blamed the Keflanians for what happened, but that didn't mean he'd turn tragedy into a power grab. Aulus was better than that.

Creen pulled himself up. "I'm gonna go take a shit."

He joined the crowd exiting the training pit. Ahiliyah stayed where she was, thinking about what she'd just heard, thinking about Keflan. An entire hold, *gone*. Yes, it had happened to Hibernia and Pendaran, but those holds had fallen before she'd been born.

To see it happen in her own lifetime... it felt unreal.

Ahiliyah heard the laughter of the warriors. They were filtering into the tunnel that led back into the hold. She looked for Brandun, didn't see him among them.

Then she looked across the pit again—there he was, sitting in the same place. Sitting alone. Alone, and staring down into the training pit sands.

She wondered what he was thinking.

23

The weavers looked up expectantly.

"I'm sorry, ladies," Ahiliyah said. "I didn't bring any candy this time."

She thought they would be disappointed, but they smiled at her, with love and appreciation.

"Next time, dear," Maybeth Dafydd said. "We know you tried. And thank you for killing one of those rotten bastards."

Wrinkled, grey-haired heads nodded.

They knew about the fall of Keflan, yet their disposition hadn't changed. Maybe they were so old they didn't care anymore. Or maybe they were just high.

Ahiliyah noticed that Lulu Bouchard wasn't with the netmakers. Was that because she'd taken sick with Glynnis flu? Or was it because she was sick to the soul—Lulu's daughter and three grandchildren had been in Keflan. Maybe they were in Dakatera. Maybe they were dead. Maybe they'd been carried off to Black Smoke Mountain and fed to the Demon Mother.

Ahiliyah continued on her way. General Sinesh Bishor was in his usual place, sitting by the edge of the plateau, which dropped off to the roiling water thirty feet below. A large coil of twine lay next to him. His two feet and one hand were a blur, weaving the twine into netting.

What would he say when he saw her trophy? He would be proud of her, she knew. Would he beam and smile? Or would he try to be stoic, act like he wasn't impressed? He was like that sometimes, for reasons she could not fathom.

Ahiliyah—a *girl*—had killed a demon.

She had joined the rarest of groups; in this way, she was more like Sinesh than ever before.

"You have something for me?" Sinesh spoke without looking away from his weaving. The river light cast small shadows on his thick scars, making them stand out even more.

Ahiliyah had visited a slaughterhouse, had brought back critical medicine, had killed a demon, and yet still she felt guilty—red moss powder was the one thing that helped Sinesh, and she hadn't been able to bring it back for him.

She sat in front of the twine coil. "I'm sorry. I brought nothing this time."

He stopped weaving, stared out across the river. "That is unfortunate. The pain is… well, it is only pain. Forgive me for asking for it, Liyah. Even an old man can be selfish at times. I am told you brought back enough medicine to cure all of our people."

"Yes, General," she said. "Enough for now, at least."

He kept weaving. *Pull, stretch, wind, tie.* The motions were rhythmic, hypnotic. She watched him for a while.

"Tell me of your run," he said finally.

She told him everything she'd told the Margrave, and more. The bodies. The stench. The killing of the demon, the effects of the caminus leaves. She told him about the fear she'd felt… it was as if she were vomiting some deep-seated evil that had taken root inside her. When she finished, she saw that he had stopped weaving, that he was looking at her.

"You were very brave, Liyah. Most people would not have gone in."

He began weaving again, his hand and feet working together with the steady efficiency of the waterwheel.

Pull, stretch, wind, tie. Over and over again.

"They're coming for us," she said quietly.

Sinesh nodded. "I know."

Pull, stretch, wind, tie.

He didn't seem bothered in the least.

"Everyone is very upset," Ahiliyah said.

"I am not everyone."

He kept weaving. What had been hypnotic moments ago now infuriated her.

"Sinesh, do you understand what I mean when I say Keflan Hold has been wiped out?"

"Burning blood took my arm and my eye," the old man said. "It did not leak into my brain. Just because something is new to you does not mean it is new to me. Pendaran and Hibernia fell, not so long ago. Do you cry for those people?"

Pull, stretch, wind, tie.

"No," Ahiliyah said. "They were gone before I was born."

"If we are lucky, a child born today might think the same thing of Keflan."

"What do you mean, *if we're lucky*?"

He stopped weaving, stared at her.

"You say the demons are coming for us, Liyah. They have already come. We are the last people. It is only a matter of time until we are gone, and the evil inherits Ataegina."

His words angered her. "We lost one hold. Just *one*."

He lifted a foot, curled in his smallest two toes, leaving the bigger three extended out.

"We've lost *three*," he said. "The others will fall eventually. *Lemeth* will fall eventually. It is best if you understand the realities of life."

"What is wrong with you? You act like we should just accept that they'll kill us all."

Sinesh shrugged, went back to weaving. "The interesting thing about the truth is that it doesn't matter if you accept it or not—it remains true."

Pull, stretch, wind, tie.

She reached out, grabbed the twine, yanked it off his foot and out of his hand. She picked up the entire coil, launched it over the edge of the plateau—it slapped against the water below.

"We have to *fight*, you twisted old man! *We have to fight!*"

"Why bother? We lose every battle."

"Brandun and Creen and I didn't," she said. "We killed a demon."

"Which marks the first time in history that humans have killed a demon and suffered no casualties. With my own eyes I saw a single demon kill *five* warriors before it was brought down, and when we finally killed it, its splashing blood took out yet another warrior. You were lucky."

A kill ratio of six to one. Sinesh was right—she, Brandun and Creen had been lucky. If a second demon had been there, they would all be dead. Knowing that, though, didn't chase away her fury. Her face felt as hot as if it had been splashed with burning blood.

"You used to command thousands in battle," Ahiliyah said. "You've told me all your old stories a hundred times. You fought then, why don't you want us to fight now?"

Sinesh looked up at her, nonplussed. "I have no more twine to weave. Shall we play?"

With one foot, he gestured to the case with the wargaming pieces.

Her anger remained for a moment, then flowed out of her. He was just an old man. A crippled old man. He couldn't fight. Why be mad at him? He hadn't made any of this.

"No," she said. "I have to figure out what we're going to do."

He pointed his big toe at the case. "Humor me. Or dive in and retrieve my twine."

Ahiliyah glanced over the edge to the rushing water below. She shouldn't have thrown his twine—it was valuable. This wasn't the time for games, but an hour or so wouldn't hurt.

She brought the case over, opened it. She took out the yellow pieces, set the shell-spearmen in front of her into tight ranks.

"Get more," Sinesh said. "Use all of the yellow pieces as your infantry. Take fifty blue, use them as your archers."

"What scenario are we playing?"

"Any scenario you like. Set them up as you wish."

"Terrain?"

"Let's say the plains. Solid footing, no significant elevation advantage."

She laid out all the yellow shells. When she finished, she had seven yellow blocks set up, each with four rows of ten shells. Four blocks side by side on her front line, one on each end angled back at forty-five degrees, and one behind the front lines. She arranged her archers in a two-deep rank in front of her yellow blocks.

Sinesh studied her arrangement. "You don't want to put your men in a single phalanx?"

"I like this better," Ahiliyah said. "It's more mobile. I can use the reserves to flank you, or to take advantage of a weakness in your lines."

"Where did you learn this? Have you been playing with others? With Creen, perhaps?"

Ahiliyah felt offended, but at least Sinesh hadn't asked if it had been Brandun's idea.

"It's been brewing in the back of my head since the last time we played," she said.

Sinesh stared at her formation. Had she done something wrong?

"This tactic that comes naturally to you took decades of war for others to discover," he said. "In the time when men fought men and tactics *worked* of course. But we are not in the time of men fighting men. You say you want to fight the demons, Ahiliyah—do you mean it?"

It was as if he suddenly didn't know who she was.

"I do," she said. "I told you I do."

He stared at her, until she began to feel uncomfortable. The river's roar seemed too loud.

"In the back of my cabinet is another drawer," Sinesh said. "Open it."

Ahiliyah had never noticed that drawer. She looked at the back of the box—sure enough, there it was. She opened it. Inside lay hundreds of shells—shells painted *black*.

The black of the demons.

"Take the pieces out," Sinesh said.

Ahiliyah did as she was told. Sinesh used his feet to spread the black shells in a wide arc facing her position. So many. Just looking at all the black shells made her skin crawl.

"Why haven't you shown me these pieces before?"

"There was no point. If I could not think of a way to beat the demons, who could?" He tilted his scarred head. "But perhaps you can, Liyah. You have a mind for this. Maybe the inventiveness of youth can find a strategy missed by the wisdom of age. Would you like to hear the rules for these pieces?"

Without looking up from the shells, Ahiliyah nodded.

"The black pieces move six times faster than normal pieces," Sinesh said. "Once the battle is engaged, you cannot outrun them. The black pieces are much stronger. They use claws, teeth and tail. Their weapons do not dull, nor do they *melt* when they strike, as yours do. The only advantages you have are ranged weapons—bows, crossbows and thrown spears—and spear length, as a spear is longer than their arms or their tails. However, when a black piece dies in hand-to-hand combat, by sword, spear, or—" he smiled his twisted smile "—by smashing their head in with a rock, they damage any yellow pieces around them."

So many variables. Ahiliyah tried to process them, even as Sinesh explained how to use the modified numbers in game play. The differences were stark, and overwhelming. But she had one change of her own.

"I also have a new rule. The leaves of the caminus bush stop the burning blood. Can we work that in?"

Sinesh thought for a moment. "How would that be used in an actual battle?"

Ahiliyah stared at the pieces. Leaves reduced the effect of the burning blood, but didn't eliminate it—and leaves would do nothing against claws, teeth or tailspikes.

"Hidey suits for everyone," she said. "And on the shields as well. And helmets. I will cover my soldiers in leaves."

Sinesh nodded, explained how he'd modify the effects of burning blood.

Ahiliyah suddenly felt so… *excited*. This wasn't just a game—this was preparation to fight the demons. She didn't know how it would come into play, but deep down, she felt it would.

"The demons will attack in a great rush," Sinesh said. "This, too, I have seen with my own eyes." He arranged the black pieces in a scattered wave a good distance from her pieces. "They begin their attack. What would you do first?"

"I'd open up with missile fire, obviously."

"Say you have your ranged weapon of choice," Sinesh said. "Bows, spears or crossbows?"

"Crossbows." She knew full well that the lighter shafts of a drawn bow were all but useless against the demons. "I'll try to get two salvos off before they close, then have my crossbowmen move to the back."

"Two rounds would be a challenge, would you agree?"

Ahiliyah closed her eyes. She thought of all the times she'd seen the demons sprinting across the mountainside, how fast they moved.

"I agree. That would be a challenge."

"Let's assume no one panics, your crossbowmen stand firm, you do get off two full salvos. That will never happen on the field, but we will use it here. And let's be generous and say that twenty-five percent of your shots stop a demon."

That was *too* generous. Ahiliyah knew all the stories—both the ones Sinesh had told her and the ones she'd read in the history books. Only with a rare head-shot could one bolt take down a demon. In almost every story, the beasts absorbed two, three, even four heavy crossbow bolts and still kept coming.

With his toes, Sinesh picked up black pieces and moved them to the side, out of the game. Her yellow and blue pieces now outnumbered the active black pieces more than six to one.

He moved the rest of his pieces up to her front blocks. As he did, she moved her blue-shell archers behind her phalanxes.

"You've had your successful salvos," Sinesh said. "Now, you tell me what happens next."

She looked at her ranks, imagined the demon horde rushing in, lurching forward, their jaws wide, their gleaming teeth bared, their tailspikes arched and ready to deliver killing blows.

"Our spears would get some," she said.

"They are heavy beasts. Many spear shafts would snap. Spearheads begin to melt. Demon blood splashes onto your men, burning them, causing panic, making your ranks lose cohesiveness."

She shook her head. "Not with the bush leaves… and we can wrap the shields with nets, stuff those nets with leaves. The shields would catch most of the burning blood."

"For how long? How much blood can these leaves absorb?"

She didn't know. *Absorb* wasn't the right word, but that didn't matter—Sinesh had a point. He removed more black pieces, pushed the remaining ones into her ranks, making her ranks slide back, distort slightly.

"Your turn," he said.

He wasn't even checking the actual game results. He was leaving it up to her to remove the number of shells she thought was reasonable. She felt a sinking feeling—Sinesh only acted like this when he already knew what the outcome would be.

She removed two dozen yellow pieces. Maybe she wasn't being fully honest, but her lines looked like they could hold.

"Less than generous," Sinesh said. "But I accept your limited losses. The battle has been joined. Some of your spears are broken, or damaged, and now comes the problem—that close to your front, demons can *leap*."

He began to pick up black shells, drop them in the midst of her ranks. Some of those demons would die on the spearheads of her back ranks, but demons were heavy—they would break spears, fall upon the rear ranks, raining burning blood all the way. Others might leap into the gaps created. Once past her massed spearpoints, she envisioned the remaining demons lashing out in all directions, tearing her warriors to pieces.

Men would break. Men would run. Her phalanx would collapse.

"You lose," Sinesh said.

There had to be a way to change that outcome…

"The demons will come to me," she said. "I could prepare the ground with more spears, three or four for each man, lying on the ground next to them."

"Interesting. Would your warriors have time to pick up those spears? And if they did have time, would not the demons already be inside the spears' killing zone? Your troops might as well be waving broomsticks from side to side for all the good they would do."

He was right. *If* she had that many warriors, and *if* they had multiple spears, and *if* they were able to choose the terrain and the place of battle, even then the multiple spears would be useless.

"We have only looked at a frontal assault," Sinesh said. "The demons are never so polite. They *swarm*." His toes pushed a handful of demons around her left flank, and a handful around her right.

"They spread out, they come from all directions. You will be dealing with a frontal assault and, simultaneously, the beasts outflanking you, far faster than you can adjust."

She didn't bother moving her reserve unit. If she broke it in two, moved each half to one side, they wouldn't arrive in time to help. Even if they did, they wouldn't be in proper formation. The demons would quickly tear through those men, hit the rest of her forces from behind.

Sinesh wasn't tricking her. He wasn't cheating. He was showing her things she already knew but hadn't put together yet.

"Let's go again," she said.

Ahiliyah tried another strategy, taking away a block and making more reserves that could react to the demon's fast flanking tendency. That seemed to work for a moment, but as her front lines broke she didn't have reserves to move in to fill the gaps.

She tried leaving half her forces in reserve—her front ranks were instantly overwhelmed.

Doubling the archers? That helped, but she knew Sinesh was taking far more damage than real archers could ever hope to land. Three times the archers? She actually won that battle, but lost three-quarters of her force.

By the fourth play-through, it became clear that on open ground, even if her warriors had perfect accuracy, perfect discipline, *and* a huge numerical advantage, the best she could hope for was to hold the field and lose the majority of her troops. If a second battle occurred, she would stand no chance at all.

Ahiliyah had seen enough demons in real life to know they were too fast, too strong, too durable, and too deadly—there was no way to win.

"We have to lure them into one of the mountain passes," she said. "We force them to come straight in, so they can't flank us."

Sinesh nodded. "I am sure we could, as they attack on sight, but what are you forgetting?"

She stared at the pieces, realized what she'd missed. "They can climb. Very fast."

From a distance, she had seen them scale a cliff face almost as fast as she could sprint across open ground. Putting troops in any kind of walled chasm would actually *help* the demons, give them a way to climb high and dive straight into her ranks from above.

"You can't beat them in the mountains," Sinesh said. "You see this. You can't beat them on the plains, not unless you outnumber them at least fifteen to one. While I concede that you may have a chance to choose the terrain—if you can move that many men without drawing a horde—the terrain doesn't matter."

"But the bush leaves—"

"Bush leaves don't stop teeth. They don't stop tailspikes. They don't stop claws. The leaves can't stem the flow of blood from a man's slashed throat, or stuff his intestines back into his belly. The demons will drive their tailspikes over the top of your shields, or they will rip the shields away, and your men will die. Even if your bush leaves *completely* counter the burning blood, the demons are too strong and too fast."

Sinesh sighed, looked longingly at the pieces.

"You are gifted, Liyah, but you have no strategies I have not already considered, or that I did not try in the Rising. Forgive an old man for being foolish, for allowing himself to hope."

Had she really thought the leaves would make a difference? She'd been so excited at the thought they had something to use against the demons, but in the end it might help runners once in a great while—that was it. And only if the runners were attacked by a single demon. And only if the runners got *lucky*.

The leaves were not the weapon that would bring salvation to her people.

Her eyes traced the pieces, tried to find a formation that would work. How could she stop the demons from pouring around the flanks? She couldn't. Unless...

"A circle!" She pointed to the pieces. "A phalanx with the ends touching! It can't be flanked. Ranks in the middle point spears high, the demons *can't* jump into our formation."

She started to move the pieces, but quickly saw there was no point. So they couldn't be flanked—so what? The demons were too strong. Eventually, they would get past the spearheads, reach the shields, then fight until they died.

"I've considered circles," Sinesh said. "And squares to protect crossbowmen. And luring the beasts toward a cave large enough to put a phalanx at the mouth... everything. No matter the terrain or formation, they are too tenacious. A rare blow through the head can kill them instantly, but most of them fight on, even when they are mortally wounded. With their strength, their toughness, their resilience, once they reach our lines, it is already over. A phalanx can maintain cohesion for a few minutes—I have seen this with my own eyes—but nothing stops the demons, and eventually, they win."

She realized that the paint on the black pieces was scratched, chipped, as if from long use.

Ahiliyah looked at Sinesh. Sitting there, gnarled and wrinkled, his withered limbs tucked in against his body, he really did look like the spiders from the old drawings.

"How long have you been looking for a way to beat them?".

Sinesh stared at the pieces. Ahiliyah sensed the despair inside him.

"I have been looking since the Rising," he said. "The demons rose in the year 252. Maybe a thousand people died that year. The next year, thirty-five thousand. The legions tried to fight, but the demons were unstoppable. Savage. Merciless. We thought we knew what war was, but—" he shrugged "—we knew nothing."

He looked off over the plateau's edge, seemed to be listening to the river's roar.

"The third year of the Rising was the worst," he said. "Everything fell apart. No one knows how many people died. Some said it was a hundred thousand. Not just from the demons, although many died at their black hand, but also from starvation and disease. Another hundred thousand tried to sail across the ocean. Perhaps they drowned. Perhaps they landed and the Northerners killed them. We will never know, since they took all the ships. No one knows how to build ships anymore. People have tried, but if you stay in one place on the shores for too long, you know what happens."

He reached out a foot, picked up a black piece, turned it in his toes.

"I used these very pieces, Liyah, to come up with a strategy to beat the demons. I was the one who convinced the holds to unite their forces. I was the one who convinced them to let me lead those troops to Black Smoke Mountain. We were five thousand strong. Experienced warriors. Well-armed. Righteous. Willing to face any danger to rid our world of the beasts."

His foot began to tremble. His toes turned white—Ahiliyah jerked in surprise when the black shell shattered. A piece dug into the bottom of his big toe. A single rivulet of blood slowly curled down his foot.

"I was thirty-one years old. I knew I was hand-picked by God. I knew it. I marched five thousand men onto the Boiling Plains. When the demons came, all of my plans, all of my strategies, they collapsed. We held discipline for all of ten minutes. Perhaps fifteen. Then, we broke. When it was done, only five *hundred* men made it back."

He flicked his foot, tossing away the bits of black-painted shell, along with a drop of blood.

"I have spent the last sixty years trying to think of a way to beat them. The truth is that there isn't one. I wanted you to play out the game, Liyah, because I thought… I thought… ah, what does it matter? You need to understand that—in the end, we will be wiped out. Enjoy your life while you can. Be *happy* while you can. Now, put the pieces away and go fetch me another coil of twine. I have work to do."

Ahiliyah stood. She gave the pieces one last look, then turned and walked away. Distantly she heard Sinesh calling after her, telling her to clean up the pieces, but his words didn't fully register. It was as if he were speaking to a person who no longer existed.

Ahiliyah felt numb. Every ounce of her, cold and numb.

Her bed.

Sleep.

That was all she wanted.

24

Nothing mattered.

The end of the world. Ahiliyah would die. So would Creen. Brandun. Tolio. Aiko. The Margrave. Sinesh. Susannah, Brandun's mom, Tolio's parents, the warriors, the craftsmyn, the weavers…

Everyone.

She lay in her bed, on her back, staring up at the stone ceiling. She'd closed her glowpipe valve to only one-quarter open, enough to give her room a bare minimum of light. The mug of caminus tea on her bedside table was growing cold.

Nothing mattered.

Sixty-seven years ago, nearly half a million people had lived on Ataegina. That number had dropped to below thirty thousand.

Humanity was being wiped out. For good. *Forever.*

Maybe Sinesh was right. Maybe she should learn how to enjoy herself. Stop training all the time. Stop worrying about not becoming a warrior, or Tolio wanting a family, or about the next run. What difference did any of it make? None at all. She would die. She would be forgotten. Everyone would be forgotten.

The demons would rule the land.

Fun. That was what she needed. Maybe get drunk. Maybe get laid. Hell, why not both?

A scratching sound.

Liyah rolled to one elbow, looked through the dimness to the door of her room. Had Tolio somehow read her mind? Had he sensed that she needed his body, needed him to help her forget everything, if only for a few precious moments?

"Come in, lover," she said. "It's open."

The scratching grew louder. What kind of a game was he playing?

"Knock it off," Ahiliyah said. "Get your ass in here already."

The door began to rattle. Rattle *hard*.

What the fuck was Tolio…

Ahiliyah smelled wet rocks. Moss. When had she smelled that before?

Up on the surface.

Fear ripped through her, turned her guts to liquid.

The door smashed inward, split down the middle, the two halves cracking off the walls, smashing glowpipe glass. Glowing water sprayed everywhere.

In the dim light gleaming on the wet floor, she saw it…

… a demon, coming toward her.

Ahiliyah couldn't move, she was tangled in her blankets, as trapped as if they were a net. Black jaws opened, showing silvery teeth. They opened wider.

Cold, black hands grabbed her face.

A hateful hiss—the toothtongue shot out.

Ahiliyah screamed. She tried to move, the blankets trapped her. She felt the demon's hands on her shoulders, squeezing, shaking her.

"Liyah! Wake up, it's all right!"

Tolio's voice.

"It's all right," he said. "You had a nightmare." His face seemed to float in the darkness, barely illuminated by a glowjar on the floor beside the bed roll.

A dream. Just a dream.

She threw her arms around him, held him tighter than she'd ever held him before.

"Take it easy," he said. He kissed her hair, held her close. "You're safe."

Safe? There was no such thing.

Ahiliyah let him go, looked around. In the faint light, she could make out a rack of spears, the curve of a chestplate... she was in the armory. She'd found Tolio, brought him here, to their special place where they could be together.

"Liyah, are you all right?" He rubbed her shoulders.

She looked at him, wondered how he would die. Talons ripping into his guts? Jaws tearing out his throat in a spray of blood? A toothtongue punching through his skull?

Or perhaps he would not die at all, at least not right away. Maybe he'd be carried off to Black Smoke Mountain, where a spider would turn him into a mindless, murdering demon.

The thought made her sick to her stomach.

"Liyah, I love you."

And she loved him. She knew it now. She *felt* it.

But she loved others as well—Brandun and Creen. Not in the same way she loved Tolio, of course, but after what she'd been through with the boys, her love for them ran far deeper.

"I have to go." She slid off the bed roll, found her dress in the darkness. She expected to hear Tolio's usual, mewling *do you love me?* This time, though, he surprised her.

"I can't imagine how bad it must have been, fighting that demon," Tolio said quietly. "But if you ever want to talk about it, I'm here for you."

Ahiliyah pulled on her shift, yanked at it so hard she heard fabric rip. *Now* Tolio had figured out how to be a good boyfriend. *Now?*

"Liyah, is there anything I can do?" Such sweetness in his voice. For once he was worried more about *her* than he was about *him*, or the life he wanted for both of them. His concern—his genuine concern—cut through the sudden anger she didn't understand.

No... she did understand it. She was angry at the demons.

It wasn't just the killings. Because of the beasts, people starved. People couldn't get simple, life-saving medicine. Family members could never see each other again. Cultures were cut off from each other, breeding hate and distrust.

Demons had destroyed her world. They could not be defeated, could not be stopped.

That was the cause of her anger—they wanted to take away everything she had.

Ahiliyah knelt on the bed roll, kissed the top of Tolio's head.

"There's nothing you can do right now," she said, "but thank you for asking."

She stood, and strode out of the armory.

By the time she realized she'd left her sandals, she didn't care.

25

Ahiliyah walked through the corridors of Lemeth Hold.

A sprawling place, but with a population far greater than it was designed to house—people were everywhere. In the common areas, they sat and talked. They ate. They drank. In rooms with open doors, families and friends gathered, happy to have a moment away from work. In the factories and the farms they toiled away, everyone doing their part for the good of the hold.

All of these people, hurting in one way or another. Walking on broken legs and toes, working with broken arms and fingers. Not enough food. Not enough medicine. In Lemeth, people worked until they could work no more.

They worked until they died.

Had it been like that for the people of Keflan? Probably.

Was Ahiliyah any different? Would she keep running, like Aiko? Aiko and her crew were on a run to Jantal—would this be the trip where Aiko's luck ran out? Would Aiko vanish, like those Dakateran runners had, like Ahiliyah's mother had?

Aaliyah continued on, running her fingertips along familiar stone walls, returning the nods and smiles of those who nodded and smiled at her. These people had either known her her entire life, or she had known them all of theirs.

Would they end up like the people of Keflan? Their bodies torn apart, bloated, stinking… *rotting*? She thought of Yuzuki, of Maybeth Dafydd and Lula Poller, of Mags Yinnish and Susannah Albrecht, of Tameika Baines and her sons, of Panda, of Crag Halden, of William Minsala.

Everyone she knew was at risk. Why wouldn't the council do something? What if Keflan wasn't an isolated incident? What if that hold hadn't fallen because of their *strange religion*, or because they'd committed some *affront to God?*

What if…

A thought stabbed through Ahiliyah, so sharp and fast it almost made her whimper.

The demons had cleared out the lowlands decades ago. The coasts as well. They had hunted runners in the mountains. What if the demons had finally figured out those runners had to come from somewhere *in* the mountains?

What if the demons had been specifically *looking* for the Keflan Hold?

She thought of the map of Ataegina. Hibernia and Pendaran, closest to Black Smoke Mountain. Those holds had been lost years ago. The next closest? Keflan.

The closest after that? Dakatera... then Lemeth.

If Dakatera fell...

She had to do something.

Sinesh said there was no point in fighting. He'd shown her that a phalanx couldn't beat the demons. He'd *lived* it, watch thousands of warriors die while under his command.

So it was pointless. All of it.

Ahiliyah felt that anger in her chest again, a tiny coal slowly heating up. All was lost? She refused to accept that.

If Dakatera fell, Lemeth would be next. So why were the holds so distrustful of each other? They *needed* each other. The warriors of each hold were a little different, brought different strengths and weaknesses.

The Dakaterans took pride in their combination of phalanx and crossbow. Bisethians supposedly didn't fight other than to defend their hold, but their spearmen were more heavily armored and could be a centerpiece of a combined line. The Takantans—with their *female* general—supposedly had the best archers, more warriors than anyone else, and they were far enough away from Black Smoke Mountain that the rumor was they trained *outside*, practicing formations, practicing charges. The Jantalians, the Vindenians... surely they had warriors, too, surely they had people trained with the spear, just as Lemeth did.

She thought of Sinesh's board, but with hundreds more pieces, representing *thousands* more warriors. If they were all covered in caminus leaves, could they defeat the demons then?

Could they march on Black Smoke Mountain itself?

Could they kill the Demon Mother?

Sinesh had failed trying to do exactly that.

And the holds had grown even further apart in the years since. Differences in religions, philosophies, military tactics... all of it caused conflicts. Holds were now more likely to go to war against one another than to unite against the common enemy—it was far easier to kill another human than to kill a demon.

But the holds had united once. They could again, they just needed a *reason*. Something that would stop a unified legion from being slaughtered, that would stop history from repeating itself.

A new weapon, a new strategy... whatever it was Ahiliyah was going to find that reason.

She closed her eyes. She stopped walking, rested her forehead against the corridor wall, felt the coolness of the carved stone against her skin. She was a part of this place. This place was a part of her. No matter what she had to do, she would save it.

She would find a way, or she would die trying.

26

Ahiliyah shuffled out onto the training pit sand. She felt so drained. Nightmares had kept her from getting any sleep. She glanced at the stack of shields, dreading the next two hours—phalanx reserve training seemed simultaneously pointless, and the most important thing she could be doing.

Pointless because fighting the demons head-on just didn't work. *Important* because there was something about the formation and strategy that she'd missed, that Sinesh had missed, that *everyone* had missed. If she could find that thing, she could give hope to her people.

Tameika Baines was here again, this time with her sons Bharat and Andrey, who had fully recovered from their bouts of Glynnis flu. They—along with Doctor Monique, Barton Mason, Panda and a dozen more—were loosening up, shaft holsters on their backs, waiting for Andan Gisilfred to start the training session.

Ahiliyah saw Panda shuffling over. She cringed inside. He would ask for her help, and even though she didn't want to help him, she would.

Who was going to help *her*? Didn't she deserve it?

"Liyah, is it true? Did you... did you really kill a demon?"

This was probably the first time he'd left the signaling station since the last session.

"*We* killed it," she said. "My crew and I."

"Was it scary?"

Ahiliyah couldn't help but laugh. "Yes. Of course it was. It almost took Creen away."

"That's amazing," Panda said. "They're going to write a poem about you someday."

She thought of Brandun's desire to be a warrior so famous that poets celebrated him. That might happen for Brandun—he would soon enter the warriors ranks.

Ahiliyah knew that could never happen for her.

"Line up," Andan called out. "Four ranks of twelve. You all…"

His voice trailed off as everyone looked up to the stands, to the entrance that led to the main corridor. People were shouting—a lot of people.

Doctor Talbot rushed through the opening, followed by a line of people. Ahiliyah instantly recognized the clothes many of them wore—Keflanians.

Talbot leaned over the railing. "Clear the pit! We need the space for refugees. *Hundreds* of them!"

Ahiliyah and the other reservists helped Andan and Talbot arrange the refugees into rows on the training pit sand. Many of the refugees were injured, mostly with broken bones, sprains, scratches… the kind of damage sustained from slipping or falling in the mountains, bashing up against rocks, tearing skin on logs or branches or bushes. Had they run all the way, pushing themselves well past the point of exhaustion? There were more than a few wounds obviously caused by demon claws or burning blood, but those wounds looked several days old.

Talbot moved from wounded person to wounded person, figuring out who needed to be treated first. Lemethians ripped up their own shirts to make bandages. Ahiliyah and Panda busied themselves bringing water.

The refugees were oddly quiet. It was kind of spooky. Perhaps fifty were lined up on the sand, with more coming down, when the Margrave's roaring voice made everyone freeze.

"What in the *hell* is going on here?"

He was up on the walkway, his hands holding the rail in a white-knuckle grip.

"Refugees from Keflan," Talbot called up to him. "They told me the Margravine sent them, that Dakatera couldn't feed them all."

"And *we* can?" The Margrave slapped the rail. "*Who let them in here?*"

The question confused Ahiliyah—what did it matter who let them in?

"I don't know," Talbot said. "I don't have time for this now, I have to help these people. Send someone for Doctor Monique, and for all of our assistants."

Talbot turned his back on the Margrave, rushed to the nearest refugee.

Red-faced, the Margrave strode down the walkway and back into the main corridor.

Ahiliyah carried her water bucket to a Keflanian woman who had a bloody wound on her forehead. With a shaking hand, the woman took the water ladle and drank greedily.

"Thank you," she said, putting the ladle back in the bucket.

"Were there demons?" Liyah gestured to the other refugees. "There's so many of you."

"Not as many as there were. They *hunted* us."

A bolt of fear shot through Ahiliyah, and she suddenly understood the Margrave's rage. If the demons had followed the refugees here…

"They hunted you, when? When you came here?"

The woman stared at a wall, perhaps not really seeing anything.

"We were fleeing from Keflan to Dakatera," she said, her voice dropping to a hush. "They hunted us, killed *hundreds*, dragged hundreds more away. The only reason I'm here is because I was faster than some of the others. If there had been more demons, they'd have gotten us all."

Liyah didn't know what to do, so she hugged the woman. The woman stiffened, then relaxed. She started to sob, rested her head against Liyah's shoulder.

More commotion up on the catwalk—Drasko leaned over the rail.

"All Lemethians *out*," the big warrior yelled. "Except for Talbot. Out, *now*!"

Leave? But there were so many people…

"I need help," Talbot shouted back. "Can't you see these people need help?"

Ahiliyah saw movement through the open training pit doors. Warriors poured in, Leonitos, Masozi, Benji, Farid, Kadri and…

… and *Brandun*?

Drasko cupped his hands to his mouth. "All refugees, stay in the training pit. Do not try to leave or you will be dealt with. Food is coming. All Lemethians, get out and spread the word—only warriors and doctors allowed in the training pit until further notice. Those that defy the Margrave's order will be taken to lockup. Now *get out*."

Some of the reservists left immediately, some tried to keep helping the refugees.

"Warriors," Drasko said, "remove those who are hard of hearing."

The warriors started grabbing the people who were trying to help the refugees, pushed them toward the door. Some Lemethians pushed back—those people were knocked to the ground, shoved toward the door, even *kicked* until they got up and ran.

Lemethian warriors beating Lemethians? What the hell was happening?

Ahiliyah saw Brandun grab Panda, give him a light shove toward the door. Panda waddled across the sand, his hands up and his head down. Brandun turned to look for someone else to bully—his eyes met Ahiliyah's.

He looked away, embarrassed. Then, he clenched his jaw and strode toward her.

"Liyah, I'm sorry about this, but you've got to go, the Margrave says so."

"Oh, does he? What are you going to do, Brandun? Throw me out yourself, or have one of your new friends do it for you?"

He winced, and she saw the conflict in him. He glanced up at Drasko, then back to her.

"Just go, please," he said quietly. "I'll catch up with you in Creen's lab."

Did she even want to *see* him later? What the hell was he doing?

"Demon Killer," Drasko called down, "please leave. Our respect for you won't last if you disrespect us."

Ahiliyah realized she was the last non-warrior left. She glared daggers at Brandun, then walked out of the training pit, leaving him, the refugees, Doctor Talbot, and the warriors behind.

27

The factory area lay far below river level.

Ahiliyah imagined this had been done intentionally, long ago, because of the danger of fire. With the glassworks, the bakery, the forge and the brewery all using hot ovens of one kind or another, the constant hazard of a spreading fire was countered with large pipes and large valves positioned atop the wide stone steps—in case of fire, flood the area with water.

Sure, that would result in ruined bread, beer and wine, but it was better than corridors filled with choking, lethal smoke. And everyone who worked in the factory level had been trained how to tread water, then calmly work their way to stone escape tunnels built into the ceilings of the arched corridors.

In the factory area, everyone could swim. Everyone except Creen.

Ahiliyah hadn't seen him since their report in the Margrave's Chamber. She was embarrassed to realize she hadn't really thought much about him until Brandun mentioned his name. She'd had much on her mind, and she hadn't missed his rude jokes and caustic attitude.

Forgetting about him had been a mistake. She needed a weapon, and Creen was the only person working with something new—the caminus leaves. Well, maybe the leaves weren't a *weapon*, exactly, but they would be part of her plan when she went to war against the beasts.

Despite the oppressive heat, the craftsmyn were usually happy in their job—day in and day out, they directly contributed to the hold's survival. As with the rest of Lemeth Hold, however, a dark mood had taken over the factory level. She could feel it even before she talked to anyone.

Ahiliyah's first stop was the forge. The room was almost as big as the training pit, but the massive oven took up over half the space, while bins of coal and metal ingots filled up the rest.

Crag Halden, the master metalsmith, had once explained to her how the forge worked, from the fire to the complex chimney system that took the smoke away and merged it with the steam coming off the hot springs. They couldn't just vent the smoke on its own, as it might draw the demons—as with everything else in hold life, staying hidden was the most important thing.

Crag was filing away on the edge of a bronze spearhead. The oven's fire lit up the soot-spotted brown shirt he wore over his massive arms and shoulders. He saw her enter, placed his left fist over his sternum.

"Demon Killer," he said. "I am sorry I missed your slash ceremony, but…" He gestured to the oven in a way that said *the work here is never done.*

"I understand," Ahiliyah said. "What would we be without your work, Master Crag?"

"Someone would take over for me." He shrugged. "Everyone must do their part. I heard you were there when the refugees came in yesterday."

Ahiliyah nodded. "I was in phalanx reserve training."

"Did they look dangerous? Like they wanted to hurt us?"

The question was as confusing as it was ridiculous—as if one of those hungry, frightened people could possibly hurt the burly metalsmith.

"Hurt us? What do you mean?"

"Well, they lost their hold, so obviously they want ours, right? They're already eating our food, getting help from our doctors. What about our sick and wounded? People are hungry as it is, even without a hundred and sixty new mouths to feed."

Ahiliyah wondered if some evil spirit had possessed Crag. This wasn't like him at all.

"They don't want to hurt us," she said. "They lost hundreds of their own people."

"People can pretend to be a lot of things. You should watch out for them. They're not *us*."

She'd known this man all her life. When times had been far leaner, she'd seen him give his meager share of food to children who would have otherwise gone hungry.

"Crag, where are you getting all of this? Who told you the Keflanians want our hold?"

"Preacher Ramirus did," Crag said. "He came by, told us to be careful, that if we see strangers, take them back to the warriors at the training pit. I don't like this any more than you do, Liyah, but you know we're already low on food. We've got to look out for our own people first. You know what it's like when everyone is hungry."

Ahiliyah did know what that was like. Even at her hungriest, she would have never acted like Crag was acting now. At least, she hoped she wouldn't.

"I'm looking for Creen's lab," she said.

Crag sighed. "Oh. *Him.* He's been asking me to make him needles and scalpels and all kinds of things. If you don't mind me saying so, he's a real pain in the ass."

At least some things remained the same.

"Where is he?"

"Down one level, past the bakery, there's a staircase," Crag said. "You familiar with it?"

The bakery, where Tolio worked. She knew that place well enough.

"Yes, I know it."

"Take the staircase down two more levels, to the very bottom. You'll find Creen there."

Ahiliyah cringed. The further down you went, the hotter it got. Combine that with Creen's fear of water, and she knew he would be pleasant company indeed.

"Thank you," Ahiliyah said.

Crag again put his hand on his sternum. "And thank *you*, Demon Killer."

She left, upset and confused. It was Crag, good old Crag, and yet, the man she thought she'd known wouldn't have looked at the refugees like they were a threat. And the way he'd spoken to her—Crag had never *dis*respected her, but now his voice carried reverence.

A toothtongue necklace was a powerful thing, it seemed.

Ahiliyah headed down to the next level, hurried past the entrance to the bakery. She hadn't seen Tolio since her nightmare in the armory. She was embarrassed by that, and she didn't want to have another conversation about love and kids and all that shit. There wasn't time to worry about matters of the heart—if she didn't find a way to defeat the demons, love wouldn't matter.

Ahiliyah passed by more of the craftsmyn who contributed to the hold by doing the hot, smelly work that had to be done. Brandun's uncle Solomon Barrow, who turned the ore brought up from the mines into the metal ingots that Crag and his apprentices fashioned into shields, spear parts, demon forks, nails and screws, crossbow arms, utensils, door hinges, barrel hoops and more. Cruden Poller, who used a big oven to turn sand into ceramics for dishes, glass for glowpipes, and the mirrors needed by the signalmyn. William Minsala—Tolio's father—who ran the bakery, turning mushroom flour, rivergrass and fish bones into various kinds of bread. Barton Mason shaping stone for repairing corridors, doorways and ceilings, Mags Yinnish brewing beer, Ginger Patrice making wine, Journay Barrow making shoes... so many people down here contributed to the hold.

The lowest level of the factory area was almost as hot as Crag's oven. By the time Ahiliyah found Creen's lab, she was sweating buckets. She would need a dip in the river after this. For all the time she spent on the surface, sweating and filthy and stinking, she liked to stay as clean as possible when in the hold. His lab was literally the last room on the corridor—beyond it, nothing but the solid stone of Lemeth Mountain.

"Hello, Creen. I've come for a visit."

He was bent over a large, beat-up wooden table in the center of the room, looking into a contraption with several small, round pieces of glass mounted on a central metal staff. It looked like the circles of glass could swing to the side, or line up one over the other. It reminded Ahiliyah of Panda's sun-signaler.

"Fuck off and die," Creen said without looking up.

"Love you, too."

The room was even hotter than the corridor—so much that she could feel the hot, damp air, deep in her lungs. The stone ceiling gleamed with wetness, even dripped down in a few places from little mineral stalactites to make small, regular *plunks* against the floor.

His tables looked old, as if they'd been dug out of some storeroom after decades of disuse. The wood was dented and gouged, warped, splintering in places. Atop the central table were four vertical glass pipes, each about as long and wide as her forearm. Ceramic mugs dotted the table—leftovers from Creen's tea-drinking habit, no doubt.

Next to the table, two pieces of flat white quartz on easels. The slabs were ground smooth, marked with words and numbers written in charcoal. Hanging from each easel, a string with a stick of charcoal, and a rag that was already so black from wiping away his notes that she had no idea what its original color might have been.

And *everywhere*, bush leaves. Stacks of caminus branches, some freshly cut with bright red leaves, others that had been there for a few days, the red faded to light brown, the edges turning crisp. A wicker basket filled with leaves. A hip-high mortar and pestle, filled with red paste. There were even three clay pots with small bushes planted in them.

"I like how you set up those pipes," she said, pointing to the glass cylinders on the table. "Or, *half*-pipes, since they have a butt."

He looked up from his circles of glass. "A *butt*? Seriously?"

"Do you want me to call it an *ass*?"

He rolled his eyes—eyes with dark rings around them, showing his lack of sleep.

"*An ass*. Honestly, Liyah, could you be any more immature?"

She laughed, delighted at his unexpectedly demure behavior.

"Oh, I see—when it's science, we don't talk nonstop about pooping, farting, and peeing?"

"For your information, Demon Killer, these *tubes with a butt* are called *beakers*. Mags Yinnish gave them to me. She said she uses them to check beer quality."

In less than a week, Creen had made this old, mildewy, too-hot room his own. Ahiliyah saw a hammock strung in the corner, which meant Creen rarely left. He slept where he worked—just like Panda. Ahiliyah would have to tell Panda the next time she was up there. The chubby boy would get a kick out of it.

Against the far wall, she noticed a third easel holding a slab of white quartz. On it, Creen had drawn a bush leaf. She walked closer, examined it. There was little use for art in the hold, but that's what this was—art. Such *detail*. It looked almost real, like she had shrunk to a tenth her size and was looking at the real thing.

"Creen… this is amazing. It's beautiful."

He squinted at her, suspicious.

"I'm not messing with you," Ahiliyah said. "I didn't know you were so good at art."

Creen looked at the drawing. "Neither did I. I've never drawn anything before."

Ahiliyah sighed. Another of Creen's gifts? And yet the boy constantly had a chip on his shoulder, constantly felt inferior to those around him. She wondered if he would ever understand how truly talented he was.

"I've been down here for days," he said. "Is it true about the refugees?"

His voice had turned soft, quiet. Maybe it was the thought of the terror they'd felt in Keflan that stilled him.

"I was in the training pit when they brought them in," Ahiliyah said.

"How many were there?"

"A hundred and sixty. That's the number that's floating around, anyway. It's not like we can go in and count. The Margrave won't let anyone in to see them, except for the doctors."

Creen swallowed, then bent to look through his lenses. "Yeah, that's what I heard. Can you imagine fleeing Keflan when the demons attacked, then reaching Dakatera only to be forced to march here?"

Forced. Ahiliyah hadn't thought of it that way at first, but of course that was what the Margravine had done to those poor people.

"Maybe she had her reasons," Ahiliyah said. "Maybe Dakatera didn't have enough food."

He adjusted one of the lenses. "While you were with the refugees, did you ask them how demons got into their hold?"

"No. I didn't have time. The Margrave showed up right away. He was pissed someone had let the refugees in. He sent Drasko and the warriors to clear everyone out. Has… has Brandun been down here to see you?"

"Him, come to see me?" Creen laughed, as if the question was beyond stupid. "No. Why?"

"Because he was with the warriors when they kicked all of us out of the training pit."

Creen stood, stared at her. "Dumbdun was with the warriors? Like, *helping* them?"

Ahiliyah nodded. "He even roughed up Panda a little."

She was exaggerating, maybe, but she still couldn't believe Brandun had been a part of that debacle.

"So he's a warrior now," Creen said. "He's not in our crew anymore?"

A question she needed to get answered. "I don't know."

She didn't want to think about Brandun. She didn't want to think about Preacher Ramirus, and she didn't want to think about the refugees.

"Your drawing is so detailed," she said. "What are the little lines running through the leaf?"

"Veins. Fluid gets pumped through them, like blood does with us."

Plants had blood? *Fascinating.* "And what are these little spots?"

"Holes," Creen said. "Tiny holes. They're only on the bottom side."

"What are they for?"

"I don't know. Yet."

Ahiliyah plucked a leaf from one of the planted bushes. She squinted, looked closely at the underside. Sure enough, there were tiny spots there, spaced out evenly in a regular pattern.

"That's amazing," she said. "I've handled bush leaves *thousands* of times, and I never noticed those. How did you see them?"

He pointed to the contraption atop the table. "With this. Cruden Poller gave it to me. Doctor Talbot has one like it, but he said he couldn't part with it. Come look."

She stood next to him. The device had five glass circles. Two were swung to the side, three stacked over a piece of gray slate. On that slate, an upside-down bush leaf.

"Look through here," Creen said, pointing to the top piece of glass, a circle no bigger than Ahiliyah's thumbnail. She did as he instructed; what she saw stunned her.

"Is this the bottom of a leaf?"

"Give the girl a ribbon for brains."

"Go eat a fart," she said, but she didn't look up from the glass. How amazing—the same type of leaf she'd seen and touched more times than she could count, but now it looked... *magical*. Like an entirely different world. Veins branched in all directions, like tiny creeks feeding larger streams feeding rivers. And the unified red color wasn't unified at all, but rather splotches and patterns of light and dark red, even some yellows and oranges.

"I've never seen anything like this."

"Me neither," Creen said. "Not until a few days ago. Oh, I need to borrow something."

She stood. "Really? The boy who told me to *fuck off and die* wants to borrow something?"

"Do you want me to figure out what the leaves do to demon blood, or not?"

He looked exhausted, yet still had that angry edge. His burning-blood pockmarks had healed somewhat. Now they were tight little scabs. Some were almost gone, flaking at the edges, while others still seemed fresh, even open and wet.

"You need to stop picking at those burns, Creen."

"And you need to mind your own fucking business."

He closed his eyes, rubbed at them. For such a foul-mouthed boy, he could look so adorable when he did that.

The poor kid... working so hard, doing his part, so tired...

Ahiliyah put her hand on his shoulder.

He screamed, smacked her arm away and tried to backpedal so fast he fell hard on his ass. Eyes wide and panicked, he pushed backward, heels scuffing against the stone floor. He stared at her, but he wasn't seeing *her*.

"Creen, it's all right! Calm down."

He backed into an easel, sent the white quartz tumbling. Ahiliyah reached for it, but it was too late—the sheet hit the ground, broke into a dozen pieces that scattered across the floor.

Creen huddled against the wall, shaking. He was staring at nothing. She knelt next to him, chunks of quartz digging into her knees. She didn't touch him.

"Creen, it's all right." she said in a soft voice. "It's Liyah. You're safe."

His eyes snapped to her. His lips curled back in a pre-scream, then he froze, blinked madly.

"Liyah?"

He grabbed her fast, hugged her so tight. She hugged him back.

"I've got you," she said. "You're safe."

Quietly, the boy started to cry.

She held him and waited.

This wasn't the first time she'd seen a runner lose it. A demon had been *right on top* of Creen, had tried to take him away. Of course that would haunt him.

Creen let her go, stood. "Sorry." He wiped at his nose and eyes.

Ahiliyah stood, brushed quartz dust from her dress. "No apology necessary." She knew he was hopelessly embarrassed. Creen tried so hard to act tough, like the danger didn't get to him. She had to let him know he wasn't alone.

"I've been having nightmares," she said.

He looked at her, water still in his eyes. "Really?"

"Yeah. I keep dreaming they're in the hold. They get me in my room."

Creen sniffed. "I dream about them, too. I haven't slept for shit since we got back." He glanced off. "Sometimes when people touch me, I... I think it's *them*."

Her heart broke for him.

"Then I'm sorry I touched you. Especially when you had your eyes closed."

He drew in a big breath, then closed one nostril and shot a glob of snot onto the floor.

"My head is so fucked up," he whispered. "I can't go out there again, Liyah. I can't."

She thought of Mari, of all the runners who had refused their obligation over the years. Maybe Brandun was done running, but Creen wasn't—not unless his work here produced something truly significant. He had two more runs to make, at least—if he refused, the Council would order his death.

If that happened, she didn't think she could bear it. She didn't want to think about it.

"You said you wanted to borrow something from me?"

Creen wiped his eyes again, cleared his other nostril—good God, that boy was gross—then he shook himself, as if ridding himself of the unfortunate moment.

"Right." He finally met her eyes, flashed his best grin. "Can I borrow your toothtongue?"

Her hand flew to it, as if he'd tried to snatch it away. The trophy brought her respect, respect from people who'd never really given her a second thought. It was already *part* of her.

"I need it," Creen said. "For my experiments."

"Are you sure you need it?"

His eyes narrowed. "If you can get Councilman Tinat to part with one of his, then no, I don't need yours. You want to ask him for me?"

She thought of asking Tinat for one of his toothtongues. The idea made her stomach churn—even when he was being nice, Tinat was an imposing man.

"I can't keep going without it," Creen said. "Please?"

Ahiliyah sighed. "Can you bring it to me as soon as you're done with it?"

"So hard to part with it, I see." The mischief had returned to his eyes. "Already getting used to being *special*?"

"That's not it."

But that was it. That was *exactly* it.

She handed him the necklace. Creen glanced at the entryway. Seeing no one, he grabbed a small bronze box from a shelf under the table. He put the toothtongue inside, shut the lid tight.

"I'll take good care of it, Liyah. I promise."

Creen set the box on the table. He seemed suddenly nervous… uncomfortable.

"After you and Brandun killed the demon… I guess I didn't say *thank you*. You guys were supposed to let it take me. I should be dead. Or worse. I guess what I'm saying is… I owe you."

She knew how hard it had to be for him to say that.

"You'd have done the same thing for me."

Creen's face flushed red. He knew that wasn't true. So did Ahiliyah. It didn't matter.

"You'll be a demon-killer," she said. "You'll kill more than anyone ever has."

He glanced at her, suspicious. "How, exactly, will I do that?"

"That's what you're here for, right?" She gestured to the room, the bushes, the branches, the beakers on the table. "With your fancy lenses and your beaker-asses?"

He sighed. "You need to temper your expectations. The leaves don't *kill* the fucking beasts. I mean, I wish they did, I'll keep working on this, but… "

It wasn't just the nightmares, or the flashbacks—stress was eating him up from the inside. He knew the stakes. If he didn't produce something of use here, he would be forced back to the surface. He would run again. Or, he would refuse, and for that, he would be executed.

She had a strong feeling he would choose the latter.

"You'll figure something out," she said.

"No one has *figured out* anything for fifty years," he said. "Demons just keep killing us."

"You're not *no one*. There's never been anyone like you. You can do this. I *know* it."

He stared at her, his disbelief slowly giving way to acceptance.

"That means a lot," he said. He shrugged. "At least, as much as it *can* mean from someone half as smart as me."

And just like that, the old Creen was back.

She tapped the bronze box holding her toothtongue. "Work on this first, okay?"

He nodded. "Want some tea?"

What she wanted to do was get out of that sweltering room, but he needed her.

"Sure, I'd love some."

He plucked fresh bush leaves and dropped them into one of the beakers. There was a cistern on the wall, with shelves built above it that held a few ceramic mugs. With a bucket, he scooped water from the cistern, poured it into the beaker. Most people liked tea with water fresh from the river, still glowing, but Creen said it added a bitterness he didn't like. Sliding a burner tray under the beaker, he carefully set in a chunk of coal. He used a sparker to light a twig, held the burning end to the coal until the black chunk started to glow. As it burned, he fetched two mugs from the shelf.

When the beaker water boiled, Ahiliyah and Creen watched the flame, the bubbles, the leaves churning inside the beaker. They were comfortable enough in each other's presence that they didn't have to talk.

When the cube burned out, crumbled and broke apart, Creen put a metal grate atop the beaker, then tipped the glass. Only then did Ahiliyah see that the beaker was mounted on a pivot. Creen filled the mugs with steaming tea, slid one of them across the table to Ahiliyah.

"You served me first," she said, blowing away steam. "Wow, you must really like me."

He made a *pshhhh* sound. "Woman, go fetch me some bread."

She laughed. With anyone else, that joke would have been an insult, but Creen had long ago accepted her leadership and proficiency. There were plenty of people in the hold who didn't think women and men were equal, but for all of Creen's faults, he wasn't one of them.

Her first sip was a delight. "It's so good. How do you get out the bitterness of river water?"

"I filter it through crushed limestone."

Crushed limestone? Where did he come up with such ideas?

He drank deep, lowered the mug. "We're all gonna die. You know that, right?"

"You should hang out with Sinesh. You two could have a nice, morbid conversation."

Creen affected a shiver. "Spend time with the Spider? No thanks." He saw her glare. "Oh, sorry about that." He drained his mug, set it with the other empties atop the table.

"It's like a mug graveyard," Ahiliyah said. "You going to clean those up?"

He glanced at the mugs, shrugged. "I've got more important things to do. Take yours with you, if you like. I've got work to do. And by *I've got work to do*, I mean *get the fuck out*."

Needy one moment, a demanding ass the next. Such a piece of work, he was.

"A pleasure as always," Ahiliyah said.

She walked to the entryway, expecting to hear another of Creen's insults. When she didn't hear one, she stopped, looked back into the room. He held her toothtongue necklace by its string. His eyes were wide, excited—no trace of sleeplessness now. Was that from the tea's kick, or from something else?

He set the toothtongue on the table. From the rack of small tools, he pulled out tweezers and a small pair of pliers. Ahiliyah saw him whisper something, then he bent close to the toothtongue. She couldn't make out exactly what he'd said, but it looked like the words *more than anyone else*.

He'd already forgotten she was there, probably forgotten she'd been there at all. Ahiliyah hoped the boy could find something. Find *anything*. Because if he could not, he—and Sinesh—might turn out to be right after all.

28

Ahiliyah walked quickly through the crowded corridor, part of the crowd heading for the stairs that led down from the deck. She carried a bag of fresh imbid flowers. Word had spread quickly—Aiko Laster's crew had returned from Jantal.

When Ahiliyah and her crew had returned from Keflan, there had been no imbid flowers to welcome them back. People had thought she, Brandun and Creen were dead, true, and they'd been understandably frightened and upset about the fall of Keflan. But even though things were bad—*so* bad—that didn't mean runners shouldn't be celebrated upon their return. Ahiliyah would shower Aiko, Jenna and Tomas with flowers, let them know that they were appreciated, that at least one Lemethian respected them risking their lives

"Hey, Liyah, hold on."

Brandun, coming up behind her. She stopped, turned so quickly he almost tumbled into her.

"Oh, sorry," he said, taking a step back. "I need to talk to you."

"Really? Because I've been to Creen's lab three times. He says you haven't been by once. Isn't that where you said you'd catch up with us?"

He blinked, looking every bit the *Dumbdun* that Creen called him. "Are you mad at me?"

She crossed her arms. "Mad? Why would I be? Because we haven't heard a word from you in *days*? Because you haven't come to see us? Because you're busy with your new friends?"

Venom in her voice, but she couldn't help it. If he wasn't officially a warrior already, he soon would be one. She was hurt at being so quickly forgotten.

"I've been doing my part for the hold," he said. "The warriors needed my help."

"Doing your part?" She leaned in close. "Keeping refugees locked up in the pit is *doing your part*?

He leaned back slightly. "I'm doing what the Margrave told me to do. Isn't that what we're supposed to do? Isn't that what *you* do?"

Her anger flared anew, not just at Brandun, but also at the Margrave. How could the Margrave order those people to be held like prisoners? She would never have thought him capable of such callousness.

"I'd do the *right* thing." She knew full well she wasn't being honest, that she would have obeyed the Margrave, but she said it anyway, unable to stop herself.

For the first time ever, she saw anger flare across his face—anger at *her*.

"You're jealous," he said, just as quietly as she'd spoken to him. He pointed at her chest. "You wanted to be a warrior and you're mad because I got it first."

He got it first? Did he not get that she couldn't become a warrior at all?

People passed them by, heading to welcome Aiko home. She and Brandun were like a rock in the river, standing close and whispering while the others flowed around them like water.

"You're an asshole, Brandun," Ahiliyah said. She sounded petty and bitter, she could hear it in her own words. And yet, her weak words hurt him.

"I'm serving the hold," he said. "You're not the person I thought you were."

He was going to put this on her? "You ungrateful shit. You'd be dead if it wasn't for me."

His lip curled—she'd never seen him truly angry before.

"You think I'm too stupid to know that, Liyah? Well, guess what—I'm *not* stupid. Drasko says I'm going to be the best warrior the hold has ever seen. The others say the same thing. What do you think of that?"

"I think you don't need a brain to be a warrior, which makes it the one job you *can* be good at, *Dumbdun.*"

His lip curl relaxed. He looked at her as if she had betrayed him. She'd gone too far, instantly hated herself for her lack of control.

"Brandun, I didn't mean that."

"Save it," he said. "You and I are done. You don't talk to me, I don't talk to you. Remember how you wanted to know how the demons got into Keflan Hold? Well, I asked some of the refugees, when the other warriors weren't looking. The refugees said the demons just showed up in the corridors, they don't know how. Demons started killing people, taking others away. The survivors were the ones who just ran. You wanted to know, I found out what I could for you. Now leave me alone."

He'd sought her out to give her information she'd *asked* for, and this was how she'd treated him? If he wasn't on her crew anymore, she couldn't let their friendship end like that.

"Listen," she said, "I got mad there, and—"

"*Clear the way! Get the doctor!*"

Everyone stopped walking. A hush fell over the crowd. People pressed themselves to the walls, Ahiliyah and Brandun did the same.

Was Aiko hurt? Or Jenna or Thomas?

Down the corridor, through the parting crowd, Ahiliyah saw tall Will Pankour, carrying someone in a hidey suit bristling with caminus leaves. He came closer, and Ahiliyah saw he was carrying Aiko Laster.

"Oh, God," Brandun said. "Look at her."

Her left arm was a stump, severed at the elbow, a mess of torn flesh and broken bone. Dirt, pebbles and bits of dry grass stuck to the wound, like seasoning spread on raw meat. Strands of her hidey suit dangled, as did ragged strands of muscle and sinew. She stared out with half-lidded eyes. Dried blood on her face, wet blood visible from a deep cut in her lower lip.

Doctor Talbot pushed past Ahiliyah and Brandun, reached Will and Aiko. Talbot lifted one of Aiko's eyelids, hurriedly felt at her neck for her pulse.

Ahiliyah couldn't stop herself. She rushed to them, stood next to Talbot.

"Aiko, it's Liyah. What happened?"

Aiko's dazed eyes blinked, came into focus for a moment.

"Jantal has fallen," she said. "The demons... everyone is dead."

A woman shoved her way through the crowd—Carmen Ball.

"My daughter," Carmen said. "Where is Jenna? Where is my daughter?"

Aiko blinked slowly. "Dead. Both of them. My crew is dead."

Carmen's wail filled the corridor. The woman fell to her knees, slumped to her side.

"We have to get her to the hospital," Talbot said. "Brandun, clear a path!"

Brandun gave Ahiliyah a look she would not soon forget—the look of a born killer giving a final warning.

"We're *done*," he said. "You leave me be."

He strode down the corridor—people plastered themselves against the wall to get out of his way. Ahiliyah had never seen Brandun seems so *big*, so *intimidating*. Will Pankour followed, Talbot at his side, examining Aiko even as they walked.

In seconds, they were gone, leaving a shocked crowd, silent save for the soul-wrenching wails of Carmen Ball.

29

Ahiliyah knew what Tinat was going to say before he even opened his mouth. One look at his somber expression communicated more than words ever could. And yet, the words had to be spoken.

"Aiko Laster died in the night," Tinat said. "Doctor Talbot couldn't save her."

The Margrave's Chamber felt still, suffocating. Ahiliyah didn't want to be there. By the looks of things, neither did the councilmen, or the Margrave.

As soon as she'd been summoned here, she'd known her hero was gone. Hell, she'd known when she'd seen her missing arm, how pale her skin had been, her glassy stare.

"Such a loss," the Margrave said. "She will be sorely missed."

Councilman Jung nodded in a way that was more *time to get down to business* then *yes, I agree it's a devastating loss*.

"Sad, without doubt," Jung said. "But she said that Jantal had fallen. Did she give us information on that? Details?"

Tinat leaned back in his chair. He looked… defeated. Ahiliyah had never seen him look that way.

"Nothing," he said. "Doctor Talbot was with her until the end. I visited her bedside as well, trying to get something out of her, but she was delirious. She didn't give any details."

Jung huffed and sat back, crossed his arms. He was *annoyed*?

"She fought to get back here," Ahiliyah said. "Demons took her arm, killed her crew, and she *fought* to get back here and make sure we knew Jantal had fallen. So you uncross your arms, you piece of shit, and you show Aiko Laster some *god-damned respect*."

The men stared at her, wide-eyed. Ahiliyah had crossed a line. She didn't care. Could *any* of these people have done what Aiko had done?

Jung uncrossed his arms.

"Liyah, that is unacceptable," the Margrave said, his voice soft but stern. "Apologize."

Ahiliyah wanted to kick Jung in the throat, but she knew she'd snapped.

"I'm sorry, Councilman Jung. Aiko was… she meant a lot to me."

"To all of us," the Margrave said. "But she is gone, and we remain. Liyah, I am naming you senior runner."

Only yesterday, that honor would have felt so fulfilling, an accomplishment second only to the impossibility of being named a warrior. Now, though, it felt hollow. If having Aiko back meant Ahiliyah would accomplish nothing, she would have chosen nothing.

"You will make the next run to Takanta," Tinat said. "Three days from now. We have new hidey suits to trade with them. In return, we're getting a shipment of hotspice."

Ahiliyah stared at him, dumbfounded. "Hotspice? You're worried about that now? Jantal just fell. Keflan fell. Dakatera is next, then us."

Councilman Poller sighed. "You see? I told you this would go to her head."

"We need to *do* something," Ahiliyah said, struggling to control her rage.

Balden wagged a finger at her, as if she was a naughty five-year-old.

"Hotspice preserves meat," he said. "We need to lay in as large a store as possible in case the demons take Takanta as well."

Was she hearing him right?

"Wait… you are planning for Takanta to fall as well? What about fighting back?"

The Margrave spread his hands. "Fight back with what? Has Creen finally come up with something? What is the latest on his work?"

Ahiliyah felt torn in multiple directions. She wanted to fight, but the Margrave was right—fight with what?

"He's figured out how to dry and crush the leaves into a fine powder," she said. "He calls it a *concentrate*. He says it should work faster and better on burning blood."

Poller leaned forward. "He can crumple leaves. Amazing. But no *weapon*. Correct?"

She nodded.

"There you are," Poller said. "Enough of this, Margrave. The boy is shirking his obligation, and right now we need every runner to do their part."

They were going to shut Creen down. She couldn't let that happen.

"Margrave," she said, "he needs more time, he—"

The Margrave held up a hand, silencing her. "Creen is needed as a runner. When you make your run to Takanta, he will go with you. Tinat? Who will be the third in her crew?"

The third? But that was… oh, no…

"Susannah Albrecht," Tinat said. "She needs to do her first run with our lead trainer, and Brandun is needed elsewhere."

There it was. After only three runs, Brandun never had to run again. Ahiliyah *hated* him.

"Do the hold proud, Liyah," the Margrave said. "Dismissed."

30

Ahiliyah held out her hand. "Give it back to me. It's over."

Creen stared at the ground. Without looking at her, he opened the bronze box, pulled out her toothtongue and handed it to her.

"I need more time, Liyah." Creen said. "I'll find something. I will."

She smiled a supporting smile, even though he wasn't looking at her. What *could* he find? There was only so much about a bush leaf that he could study.

"No harm in you keeping at it until the run to Takanta," she said. "Want some tea?"

He grunted once, a sound she assumed was a *yes*. She brought his limestone-filtered water bucket to the table, poured the water into the beaker. She reached for the box with the coal cubes, then glanced at the shelf—no mugs there. They were scattered across the table, sitting in corners, resting on every flat surface *other* than the shelf where clean mugs were supposed to go.

"Creen, have you just been reusing the mugs without washing them?"

He walked to a wooden chair, sat heavily. He ignored her.

Ahiliyah set the water bucket back in its place and started gathering up the mugs, placing them on the cistern. While he kept working, she could wash the mugs for him, one small act of kindness and support in the midst of what felt like impending doom.

She quickly ran out of space at the cistern and had to stack the mugs on top of each other. They were nasty, speckled inside with bits of bush leaf, some smears of whitish paste where the leftover tea had evaporated, and rough, sandpaper-like patches where the paste had fully dried.

She turned back to the table for a fourth load of mugs when she stopped cold.

The mugs … the paste.

Slowly, Ahiliyah turned back to the cistern. With a trembling hand, she picked up a mug, stared into it. A few bits of dried-out caminus leaves stuck to the bottom, but so, too, was a crust of powder. It reminded her of something… something important.

Ahiliyah reached in one finger, scraped her fingernail against the bottom, feeling the *chit-chit-chit* of the dust coming loose. She held the finger up to her face. An image flared in her mind, a memory of a victory snatched from the demon-jaws of defeat.

"Creen, come look at this."

"I'm busy sitting here awash in misery."

"Come here, *now*."

He stood, came over to join her.

She held the finger up so he could see. "What does this look like?"

"It looks like a fingernail."

"*On* the fingernail, smart-ass."

He squinted, leaned closer. "Powder. And a little bit of paste. Why, exactly, should I care about the scrapings from the bottom of a day-old mug of tea?"

"When demon blood touches bush leaves, that grey powder forms, right?"

"As I am intimately aware," Creen said. "What's that got to do with tea?"

He was the smartest person she knew, possibly that she would ever know, but he didn't see the connection. She did. That thrilled her. Maybe he would shoot her idea down, but she had a feeling he would not.

"Demon blood turned to ash on the leaves," she said. "Ash kind of like this powder."

Creen squinted more. "Kind of, yes, but it's not the same. The powder and paste on your fingernail is white, the ash was grey. I'm kind of busy, Liyah, can you get to the point?"

"What if this white stuff is what turns burning blood to ash?"

"It's probably the other way around," Creen said. "Something in the blood turns something in the leaf to ash. But for argument's sake, let's say the powder or the paste contains the active ingredient. Again— what is your point?"

"Blood hit the leaf and made ash. If the *active ingredient*, as you call it, is in this powder"—she moved her finger closer to him, so it was only fractions of an inch from his face— "what happens if we put this powder *inside* a demon?"

Creen laughed. "*Inside* of one!" He bent at the waist, left hand on left knee, the other held up, palm out. "Oh, that's good, Liyah. That's *good!*" He stood, wiped away tears. "And how, exactly, do we get the powder inside a demon? Maybe sprinkled on a cupcake baked by Tolio?"

Ahiliyah knew she was on to something, something *big*, so his arrogance didn't bother her.

"No cupcakes," she said. "How do we get it inside of them? With something pointy."

Creen laughed again, but the laugh slowly faded.

"Something… pointy." He blinked, eyes still wet. "You mean… like a spear. Or a crossbow bolt."

Ahiliyah nodded.

Creen stood there for a moment. Breathing. Blinking. "Holy shit-balls, Liyah." He held out his hand. "Gimme back the toothtongue."

A pang of loss—she should have known that was coming. She removed the necklace, handed it to him. With his free hand, he took the mug out of her hand, then walked to his worktable. She knew him well enough to know that he'd already forgotten she was there.

Was there anything to her idea? Anything at all? If so, Creen was the one to find out.

Ahiliyah left him in the lab.

31

Ahiliyah had needed a new weapon—Creen had found one.

"The bush jizz makes demon blood clot," Creen said, slapping his wooden pointer into an open palm. "We stick the big fuckers with an arrow coated in said jizz, then it's bye-bye demon."

The Margrave and the councilmen exchanged glances, frowns of disapproval.

"Creen," the Margrave said, "it's bad enough that we came down to this sweltering room, as Liyah asked, so could you kindly watch your language?"

"Ah, fuck," Creen said, genuinely embarrassed. "I forgot, Margrave. Sorry."

The Margrave sighed, nodded, apparently happy to take what he could get from the boy.

Ahiliyah could have had Creen do the presentation in the Margrave's Chamber, but she wanted the men to experience just a few moments of what Creen went through every day down here. The Margrave, Poller, Balden, and Jung were sweating like mad. She'd always wondered if they wore anything under their bulky, official robes—now she knew they did not, otherwise they would have surely taken them off to ease the heat. Only Tinat had thought ahead; his robe hung over his forearm. He sweated, too, but not as much thanks to his thinner undershirt.

Doctor Talbot had come as well, on the Margrave's orders. Talbot had visited the factory levels enough to expect the heat and humidity. He wore only shorts and sandals. Sweat coated his saggy body, gleamed off his grey chest hair.

"You say this substance clots demon blood," Talbot said. "Have you seen this happen?"

Creen licked his lips, hesitated. "Not exactly. There was dried residue in Ahiliyah's toothtongue. I was able to observe the residue's reaction to the jizz. I'm one hundred percent confident that my caminus leaf extraction is a lethal poison to the demons. But as I told the council when I started this process, I need a demon so I can run experiments on it."

"Ridiculous," Jung said. "This is a waste of time. We can't bring you a demon."

Ahiliyah moved to stand shoulder to shoulder with Creen.

"We don't need to bring him one," she said. "We just need to *find* one. I can track them. Give me a party of warriors. We'll track a demon, hunt it, shoot it with poisoned bolts, and we'll prove Creen right."

The gathered men said nothing. Not even Tinat.

Ahiliyah didn't understand. She thought they'd be elated at a chance to fight back.

On the quartz slabs, Creen had drawn beautiful, detailed pictures of caminus leaves. He'd also drawn his process for extracting the white paste, and drawn the "crystallization process," as he called it, that he believed happened when burning blood touched caminus leaves.

"This is untested," Poller said, wiping sweat from the fat rolls of his neck. "Can we risk sending warriors to the surface at this critical time?"

His words were like a wind made of stupid. How could they not see the opportunity?

"Of course it's *untested*," Ahiliyah said. "No one has thought of it before. We have to risk the warriors, now, before we lose another hold. If the weapon works, we can gather the holds and march on Black Smoke Mountain. We can kill the Demon Mother and take our world back."

The men stared at her.

"You want us to *attack*," Councilman Jung said. "Attack Black Smoke Mountain?"

Ahiliyah nodded. "We have to, while we still have enough numbers to take them on. If we don't, they'll pick us off one hold at a time."

"Sinesh tried attacking Black Smoke Mountain," Jung said. "Look what happened—five thousand warriors, dead."

Ahiliyah pointed to Creen's drawings. "General Bishor didn't have *that*. We can do this. We can fight. We can win."

The Margrave walked to the slates. He looked the drawings up and down.

"This *bush-jizz*, it… " he turned to Creen. "Can you please call it something less crass?"

Creen ran to the easel. He used his sleeve to erase the words "bush-jizz" and replaced them with the word "goop."

"Much better," Aulus said. "This *goop*, is it difficult to make?"

Creen shook his head. "Easier than whacking off, Margrave. You grind the leaves into mush, add water, and boil for fifteen minutes. We let that cool, strain out all the chunks, add in some starch, boil it again until it becomes jizz… I mean… *goop*. It takes about six hours to make a full barrel. We just need bush leaves, and lots of them."

The Margrave stared at the drawings. Did he understand them, Ahiliyah wondered?

"This goop," he said, "how much is needed to kill a demon?"

Creen shrugged. "I'm not sure. We don't know anything about demon innards."

"If it works the way he thinks it does," Talbot said, "it might not take much to disable or kill the demons. There's no way of knowing."

"I've talked to Tolio Minsala about this," Ahiliyah said. "He says they have enough spare kettles in the bakery to produce as much goop as we want."

The Margrave turned back to the councilmen. "I see no reason not to move forward and make a few barrels. We can keep them in the armory. Runners can carry vials of it. Wouldn't that be wise, Councilman Tinat?"

Tinat sat up straighter. "I agree, Margrave. Very wise."

"Good," the Margrave said. "That's settled. Well done, Creen. I think you've earned the right to stay down here a little while longer, see what else you can come up with."

The boy beamed. Ahiliyah was so happy for him.

"This will change everything, Margrave, you'll see," she said. "Who can I take with me to hunt a demon? Will Pankour is a good choice, and Andan Gisilfred is the best shot in the hold."

The Margrave gave Ahiliyah a stern look. "We can't risk our warriors right now."

"But… we have a weapon," she said.

Poller raised a finger. "You don't have a *weapon*. Not yet. Not until it's tested."

The other councilmen nodded, all but Tinat.

"You'll have the Minsalas make barrels of goop," she said, "but you won't *use* it?"

The Margrave frowned, glanced at Tinat. Tinat caught the signal— he cleared his throat, moved his robe from one arm to the other.

"I think the Margrave means for runners to carry the goop," he said. "If they are attacked by a demon, they use the goop, and that will be the test. Since the runners are already in danger by the very nature of their job, we might get our test without risking irreplaceable warriors."

The Margrave nodded.

They wanted to *wait*? What was wrong with them?

"Fine," Ahiliyah said. "Keep your precious warriors. I'll go test it myself. Tonight. I'll track one and shoot it. You'll see. You'll all see."

Again the Margrave glanced at Tinat. Again Tinat looked uncomfortable, but he did the Margrave's bidding.

"We can't risk you, either," Tinat said. "You're our senior runner, Liyah. Our most important runs fall to you. Your job is to avoid demons, not go out and look for them."

She couldn't believe her ears. "Do you all want to just wait until they come for us? Until *everyone* is wiped out?" She looked at Tinat. "You know I can do this. Tell them."

He glanced away, refused to meet her gaze.

"Coward," she said. Then to all of them, "You *cowards*."

She saw anger flare up in the Margrave's eyes.

"For *thirty-six years*, my family has protected Lemeth Hold," he said. "In that time, Hibernia has fallen. And Pendaran. And Keflan. And now, Jantal. Four holds, gone. *Thousands* dead. Yet here we are, safe, and you think I'd let you try and *find* a demon, possibly lead others of its kind back here?"

Ahiliyah felt her temper take off at a sprint. "You think we're safe. I bet that's what they thought in Keflan and Jantal. Maybe they had their heads up their asses, just like you do!"

The Margrave's face flushed red. His nostrils flared.

Fear fluttered in Ahiliyah's stomach. She'd gone too far, *way* too far.

"You *will not* hunt demons," the Margrave said, his voice tight, controlled. He stepped closer to her, coming in slow like a creeping demon searching for prey, only he knew exactly where she was. "You've served this hold well, Ahiliyah Cooper. For that, I will forgive your insult. I will *not* forgive you a second time."

He turned on one heel and strode out of the lab, his purple robe flowing out behind him. The other councilmen followed him out, each with a stern, disappointed glare at Ahiliyah—all except for Tinat, who would not look her in the eye as he left.

Talbot crossed his arms and shook his head. "Liyah, your mouth will be the death of you. Do you want Drasko to pay you a visit and drag you to lockup? Because that's what happens to people who piss off the Margrave. You're not a child anymore—figure out how life actually works before it's too late."

With that, he left.

Creen let out a long-held breath. "That was fucking *heavy*. But hey, at least when our runners are facing a horrifying death, they'll be able to fight back with a completely untested weapon. Gosh, our leadership really gets it, don't you think?"

The councilmen and the Margrave didn't understand. Maybe Talbot didn't either. Did Creen? Did he *really* understand what his discovery meant?

"I won't stop," Ahiliyah said. "They won't help me. Will you?"

Creen's jaw muscles twitched. "Can *helping you* involve me staying safe down here, sweating my tiny balls off?"

She shook her head.

"Fuck." Creen started to shake. He reached out, held the table's edge to steady himself. "I don't know if I'll be any good to you out there. Take Brandun with you. He wants to be a hero, not me."

She thought of her argument with Brandun in the corridor, before

Aiko's return.

"He's a warrior now," she said. "He won't help us. I need you, Creen. Lemeth needs you. The entire human race needs you."

He was so small, so fragile. He *shook*. It was too much to ask of him, she knew, but if she was going to risk her life, she would not feel bad about asking others to do the same.

"I made you a present." He held out his hand. "Give me your toothtongue."

"Doesn't a *present* mean that *you* give something to *me*?"

He waggled his fingers: *gimme*. She sighed, lifted the toothtongue necklace and handed it over. He lifted his bronze box out from under the table. From inside, he removed a small glass vial. It took some effort, but he jammed the vial into the hollow toothtongue, then offered the necklace back to her.

"I appreciate the effort," Ahiliyah said, "but I'm not like Tinat. I don't need mine to sparkle."

He gave the necklace a shake. "I know you better than that. Open the vial."

She took the toothtongue, saw that vial had a cork. She pulled out the cork. What filled the vial wasn't water. She dipped in a finger—it came out glistening with goop.

"Oh, Creen," she said, smiling, "you shouldn't have."

"Just what every girl needs. A vial full of bush-jizz."

"So romantic. Tolio will be jealous." She put the cork back in, put the necklace over her head. She held on to the toothtongue. She'd grown accustomed to the feel of it, the texture. "This either means we're engaged, or you're going to help me kill one."

"You're not my type, if that's a clue." He was quiet for a moment. "If my poison doesn't work, if they get us, I don't think I can use my little friend. Don't let them carry me away. Understand?"

She did. "If it comes to that, I'll take care of us both."

He stared at her, measuring her words, then nodded. "All right. I'm in."

32

It wasn't the time for tea.

Ahiliyah swallowed, feeling the rivergrass booze burn its way down her throat. It didn't burn as bad as her second drink, which hadn't burned as bad as the first.

Creen held out his hand. "You going to keep that to yourself?"

They'd chosen his swelteringly hot lab as their prep area. Even though she could shut the door to her room, people visited her there. No one came down here unless they were asked to come. No one wanted to deal with the heat—or with Creen's mouth.

Ahiliyah passed him her mug. He drank too fast—predictably— and coughed, spraying some of the booze across the room. Water beaded in the corners of his tightly scrunched eyes.

"Smoother than a baby's ass," he said, his eyes still scrunched tight.

"You drink baby ass?"

Creen opened his eyes, coughed again. "Good point. I need to find another analogy."

Tolio had given her the bottle. He was still trying to be there for her, still didn't know how to do that. She'd thought of asking him to go with her and Creen, but in the end knew he would try to stop her—he loved her too much to see the value of risking one life to save thousands.

Creen offered her the mug.

"You drink that one," she said. "I'll get another."

She looked for a clean mug, wasn't surprised she didn't find any. It didn't matter—the booze was strong enough to sterilize anything left in one of Creen's nasty mugs. She grabbed one off the table, filled it with the booze.

Creen coughed. "Smooth as a demon fart."

Well, that was a little better, at least.

"Let's get to work," she said.

He joined her at the table. They'd cleared the surface of mugs, lenses and tools. On it now were coiled ropes, bandages, nets, torches, matches, a vial of "bush-jizz," knives, bags of caminus leaf powder, dried food, and the things that might mean the difference between life and death—a heavy crossbow, bolts, and extra spearheads taken from the armory.

"You know none of this shit will matter," Creen said. "We're gonna die."

"I see you have total confidence in your own brilliance."

He raised his eyebrows, nodded. "If only it was just the jizz. Or are you forgetting the part where one of us actually has to *hit* a demon with the crossbow?"

No. She hadn't forgotten. She clinked her mug against Creen's.

"Let's get to work," she said.

They started checking and double-checking everything they would need. They sharpened blades. They drank. They checked ropes, hidey suits and gloves. They drank. They made sure the bandages were tightly wrapped and the torches would stay dry. They drank.

"This is bullshit," Creen said. "Warriors are the ones who train with bows and crossbows and spears. What the flying fuck is wrong with the Council? What good are the warriors if they aren't used to, you know, actually *defend* us?"

She didn't have an answer for him. Only a few weeks ago, she'd all but worshipped the ground that Aulus Darby walked upon. He was *the Margrave*, he was the selfless protector.

How had she been so naïve?

Aulus didn't want to fight. He wanted to hide. He would ignore the obvious until the obvious came to tear Lemeth Hold to pieces. He wasn't a *leader*, he was a *controller*, subtly using the warriors to keep him in power.

Creen wobbled slightly, eyed his half-full mug. "If I drink any more, I'll probably puke." He drained the mug in one pull, burped one cheek-puffing burp, then glanced to the room's entryway. "Well tickle my balls and take me to church—look who decided to join us."

Brandun stood in the entrance. He wore a warrior's sleeveless white shirt. White, streaked with red. A scratch across the bridge of his nose, sweating blood. Three angry, parallel scratches on the left side of his cheek. Not from demons—from human fingernails.

"Can I come in?"

Creen shrugged. "Does a warrior need to ask permission?"

Brandun stood there, staring down. Something was wrong.

"Come in," Liyah said. "Sit."

Brandun walked to the table, sat heavily on a stool. He stared out at nothing. What had happened? Any thought of their fight was instantly forgotten—her friend was hurting. She'd never seen him like this.

"Brandun," she said softly, "you're bleeding."

He touched the scratch on his nose. He stared at the blood on his fingertips.

The blood on his tunic… Ahiliyah realized it wasn't his.

"Get him a drink," she said.

Creen grabbed a dirty mug, filled it with rivergrass booze. He offered the mug to Brandun, who took it, drank it all in one pull. A slight twitch of his lip was the only indication of the booze's horrible taste.

"Tell us what happened," Ahiliyah said. "Whose blood is this?"

Brandun took another sip, draining the mug.

"There were more refugees," he said quietly. "From Jantal, this time. The Margrave sent the warriors out to… to tell them we couldn't take them, that they needed to go Biseth. The refugees wouldn't leave. They were in bad shape, Liyah. Exhausted, thirsty, hungry, wounded. We should have helped them. They wouldn't leave. They tried to push past us, to get in. One of them cut Will Pankour. When that happened, Drasko ordered us to… to…"

Brandun stared out. He'd always had such light in his eyes, but no more. His blank stare scared her almost as bad as a demon would.

"We hurt them. And… and worse." Finally, he looked at her. She saw only the tears in his eyes. "I didn't think it would be like that. I didn't think warriors did things like that."

He leaned into her, put his head against her shoulder, his weight making her take a step back to keep from stumbling. She didn't know what to do, so she held him.

"It will be all right," she said.

Ahiliyah felt his head shake. "It won't. Not ever again."

She tilted her head at Brandun's mug. Creen quickly refilled it.

"I don't know what happened out there, Brandun," Ahiliyah said, "but whatever it was, it wasn't you. It wasn't the real you. Do you want another drink?"

He sat up straight, wiped his eyes with the backs of his hands. He took the mug, drained it in one pull. He stared at the empty mug.

"I heard that the Margrave told you that you couldn't hunt demons," he said. "Is that true?"

Ahiliyah nodded.

"But you're going to anyway." Brandun looked at her, red eyes burning. "Right?"

She didn't know what to say. Here he was, wearing a warrior tunic stained with blood, because he'd been doing the Margrave's work.

"Of course we're not hunting demons," Creen said, slurring his words. "I mean, we do is what Margrave tells us to do is. So you can take that message back to his and tell him Ahiliyah and I are good little workers. The *besss* workers, the *bess*."

Brandun glanced over his shoulder, looked at Creen, who smiled a wide, drunken smile.

"You got him to go," Brandun said, nodding. "He's always been braver than he knows."

Creen's smile faded. He blinked slowly, stared at Brandun.

Brandun held his mug out to Ahiliyah. She grabbed the bottle, drained the last of it into his mug. He drank that down as well.

"If we hide away, the demons will kill us." He hung his head. "Or we'll kill each other."

He sat there, shattered, and the last of her resolve drained away.

"Yes, we're going hunting," she said. "We're going out to test Creen's goop. We're going to kill a demon, then bring it back here to show everyone. We're going to demand the Margrave use the new weapon to go to war against the demons."

Brandun was quiet for a moment. Finally, he looked up, looked at her. So much fear in those eyes, but also shame—and pure, blazing anger.

"Say you get your demon," he said. "And the Margrave still won't go to war? What then?"

The words of Sinesh flashed in her thoughts: *If we are to survive, someone must lead.*

The Margrave was powerful. He controlled Drasko and the other warriors. But if he stood by and refused to act while holds fell, if he refused to fight while there was still a chance, then leaving him in charge might doom more than just Lemeth Hold—it might doom all of humanity.

"If we catch a demon, and he won't fight—" Ahiliyah breathed in sharp, aware her next words could lead to her blood spilling out on the training pit sand "—then we take him out."

Creen's jaw dropped. "Hold on, I muss be drank... you juss say what I thought you say?"

Brandun stood. He towered over them both.

"She did." He put his fist on his sternum. "And if you'll both still have me, I want in."

He was saluting her. Saluting them both.

"Brandun, you need to be sure," Ahiliyah said. "Creen and I won't be missed, but you're with the warriors, they'll know you're gone."

He didn't move his fist. "I will serve my hold. If the warriors won't do that, I will cast my lot with someone who will. Will you have me?"

The flood of relief shocked her. She blinked away tears.

"Yes," she said. "We'll do it together. Creen? What do you say?"

He opened his mouth to speak, then bent over, hands on his knees.

"Yeahokay," he said, then vomited onto the stone floor.

Brandun nodded. "Heartfelt, Creen. Very heartfelt. There's a problem, Liyah—the Margrave gave orders that except for scheduled runners, no one is allowed to enter or leave the hold. Drasko has two warriors stationed at the stairs to the deck. If we're going to go out hunting, how are we going get past them?"

Aaliyah smiled. "I've already taken care of that part. And Creen, clean up your puke. We've got work to do."

33

Ahiliyah was first up the long flights of stairs. When she entered the signalmyn's quarters, Panda was there, sitting at the table. He pressed a finger to his lips, pointed to Daneton Sander, asleep on his bed.

Ahiliyah quietly dumped her bucket of water into the cistern carved into the wall. Creen came next, silently set a bucket of bread on the table in front of Panda. Brandun came up last. He'd lagged behind from carrying an overstuffed pack nearly as big as he was.

Panda saw him, blanched, scooted backward so fast his chair tipped, dumping him onto the stone floor.

Ahiliyah quickly moved over to him.

"It's all right," she whispered. "Brandun's with us, not the Margrave."

Panda shook his head, hard. "I didn't tell anyone, I swear!" His voice bordered on a shout. "And I didn't see anything!"

Brandun shrugged off his backpack and shot across the room with the speed of a demon. He covered Panda's mouth, so hard his fingers made a white line on the boy's fat cheeks.

Panda froze—his nostrils flaring, his eyes wide with terror.

Daneton grumbled, and moved. Everyone fell silent. The old man snorted, rolled over, and began snoring.

"Panda," Ahiliyah whispered, "will you be quiet?"

His mouth still covered, his eyes still fixed on Brandun, he nodded. Brandun removed his hand; his fingers left fading white marks on Panda's pink skin.

"Is this a trick?" Panda looked at Ahiliyah, then at Brandun, then back again. "Because if it is, I'm loyal to the Margrave. I swear it."

"I'm with Ahiliyah," Brandun whispered. "I'm helping her kill a demon. This isn't a trick."

Panda rubbed at his mouth, stared at Brandun with wide eyes.

Ahiliyah sighed. "Panda, he knows you agreed to let us out. If it's a trick, it's already too late—he'll tell the Margrave you were in on our little scheme whether you help us or not. So let us out and hope for the best, all right?"

Panda didn't take his eyes off Brandun, but he nodded.

"It's cold out," Panda said. "Really cold. I hope you came prepared."

Brandun opened his bulky bag, passed out the hidey suits and warm clothes stuffed inside.

Ahiliyah slid her warm long pants on under her shift. Long-sleeve shirt and warm socks came next. Then her winter boots. She buckled on her spear-tip scabbard and winter coat, slid into her hidey suit, made sure the spear tip handle stuck out cleanly and was easy to grab. She notched her shaft holster into her backpack netting, then put on the backpack. Finally, she donned her heavy hat, pulled the hidey-suit hood up over her head, lowered the mask.

Creen and Brandun finished dressing.

The three of them looked very fat… they looked a bit like Panda.

Panda gripped the door handle. "Good luck. I hope I see you again."

Creen held up a hand. "Wait a second. When you saw Brandun, you said you *didn't tell anyone*. You didn't tell anyone what?"

Panda again looked at Brandun. "Do you know?"

"Know what?" Brandun glanced at Ahiliyah. "I don't know what he's talking about. Honest."

Panda was afraid of Brandun, that was obvious, but he was more afraid of someone else, someone he thought Brandun represented.

"Tell us," Ahiliyah said. "We're risking our lives. What do we need to know?"

Panda breathed in, perhaps wondering what he should do. Ahiliyah saw him straighten up, as if he'd found some internal resolve.

"Dakatera stopped signaling," he said.

Ahiliyah's heart sank. Brandun closed his eyes, leaned against the wall.

"The last signal I received was yesterday morning," Panda said. "They missed their afternoon signal, and this morning's, as well."

The thought of another hold falling…

"That doesn't mean the demons got in," Creen said. "Their signaler might be broken, right?"

Panda shook his head. "They have *two* signalers, the main and a backup. I've been talking to them for years—they have *never* missed a scheduled session. Not until yesterday."

Keflan, Jantal, Dakatera… Lemeth was next.

"We have to tell the Council," Ahiliyah said.

Creen snorted. "Why do you think Panda is afraid, Liyah? He already told them."

"I went down myself," Panda said quietly. "Yesterday. I told them." He hesitated.

Ahiliyah touched his arm. "What did they say?"

"Poller said Dakatera called the wrath of God upon themselves for their evil religion." Panda held the sides of his head, as if talking about this might make his head explode. "Jung said they were probably careless, that they were openly gathering food from the valley."

The same things they'd say when Keflan fell. Were they in denial, or were they ignoring this deadly pattern for some reason she couldn't understand?

"The Margrave," Ahiliyah said, clinging to a shred of hope that he was the man she'd once thought he was, a good man, one who did the right thing. "What did the Margrave say?"

Panda closed his eyes, moved his hands to his ears. He started to rock back and forth.

"The Margrave ordered me not to tell anyone, said it would cause a panic. He said if I spoke a word of it, to anyone, even Daneton, I'd be thrown in lockup, or… or I could wind up like Mari."

The Council had threatened his life. Ahiliyah had been right to keep her plan secret from everyone, even Tolio. Lemeth Hold was too small, word could spread too fast.

She could trust no one—no one who wasn't in this room.

"The Margrave told me to keep a lookout for refugees, so he could get the warriors out in time to stop them—" Panda finally opened his eyes, looked at Brandun "—like they stopped the refugees from Jantal."

Brandun turned away suddenly, stared down at the floor, the wall, anywhere but at Panda.

"We should be taking the refugees in," Creen said. "They're going to die out there, either from demons or winter or starvation. Why won't he let more in?"

Panda finally looked away from Brandun's back. He was still afraid, but now there was an air of anger to his words, a trace of disgust.

"The Margrave thinks demons will follow the refugees," Panda said. "He thinks that if we take in any more, we'll all die."

Creen glanced at Brandun, then back to Panda.

"When you first saw Brandun, you said *you hadn't told anyone*," Creen said. "You also said *you didn't see anything*. What didn't you see, Panda?"

Panda said nothing. He stared at Brandun's back.

Ahiliyah thought of Brandun's white tunic, streaked with blood…

"It doesn't matter what he saw," she said. "We need to go."

Creen gestured to Brandun. "But he was—"

"It *doesn't matter*," Ahiliyah snapped. "If we don't prove the goop works to kill demons, the Margrave won't let anyone in, and all those people could die. Panda, open the door."

Panda gripped the handle and leaned back, sliding the door open. Winter's angry hand reached in and slapped everyone. Despite her thick clothes, Ahiliyah shivered—it was going to be a brutal climb down.

"Creen, lead the way," Ahiliyah said.

The boy stared at Brandun for a moment, then shouldered his pack and stepped out onto the observation deck.

"Brandun," Ahiliyah said. "Move it."

Never taking his eyes off the floor, Brandun did as he was told.

Ahiliyah followed.

Ahiliyah stood at the edge of a shallow crevasse that ran through Bigsby's Pass, looking down one end, then the other. To make this work, to stay alive, she had to choose the perfect terrain. Winter winds cut through the crevasse, made the mountain's bushes and trees rattle. No snow yet, but it wouldn't be long.

"This is crazy," Creen said. "And I mean this is *we ate the wrong mushrooms and ran naked through the common room, dipping our balls in the stew and then naming our cocks Claudius the Great* crazy. Are we really doing this?"

Ahiliyah glanced behind her. Brandun was sharpening spear blades, while Creen sat there, staring off into nothing. Leaf-packed hidey suits obscured their dimensions.

"Well," Ahiliyah said, "for starters, I don't have a—"

"You don't have a cock." Creen nodded. "You get what I mean. This is crazy."

Brandun tested the blade's edge with his thumb. "If what we've been doing as a people all these years is *sane*, look where it got us."

Creen grinned. "That sounded pretty smart. For a Dumbdun, I mean."

"I do my best," Brandun said, then went back to sharpening.

Creen tried to hide behind his jokes. He trembled—Ahiliyah suspected it wasn't from the cold. He was trying hard to face his fears, to be brave, but lives were on the line.

"I need to know you can do this, Creen," she said. "If you can't, you can either go back, or find a place to hide and we'll get you when it's over."

To his credit, he didn't answer right away. Brandun stopped sharpening, lowered the spear blade, and waited patiently.

"Trust me, I don't want to be out here," Creen said. "The demons almost got me. If I don't help with this, sooner or later they will get me. Do I want to hide? Yeah. More than anything. Keflan showed me there is no place to hide. I'm sticking with you both."

Brandun reached out a gloved hand, squeezed Creen's shoulder. The two boys argued more often than not, but not now. Their lives depended on each other.

"You're braver than all the warriors," Brandun said. "Not one of them would do what you're willing to do."

Creen reached up, put his gloved hand over Brandun's. "Just don't miss, all right?"

Brandun nodded, went back to sharpening.

Ahiliyah again examined the crevasse. Only about fifteen feet deep at its deepest. Hopefully that would be deep enough. It hadn't rained in a while, otherwise it would have been flowing fast with mountain runoff.

It wasn't perfect. She didn't have time for *perfect*.

"Let's get ready," she said. "We've got to move some rocks."

The sun crawled toward the horizon, turning the sky orange and yellow. Ahiliyah had chosen the time carefully—late enough to be sure demons were out hunting, yet early enough that she could see them coming in the dwindling daylight. She, Brandun and Creen had made the afternoon count, quietly doing the work needed to set the trap.

Not even five miles from Lemeth Mountain, she had found demon tracks. A day old, at most, maybe even more recent than that. She had to hope the beast that made them was close enough for her plan to work.

Was she really going to do this?

Ahiliyah would be first. She was faster than Creen. Brandun was faster than both of them, but he was the best shot.

She crawled across the cold ground, across rocks and dirt, wanting to make sure she was in the right spot before any demons spotted her. While the crevasse had steep sides, she'd found a spot where runoff had carved a sloping approach down into it.

What happened next was a gamble. Bigsby's Pass ran northwest from Lake Mip to the northeast shore of Lake Lanee. If the demons came from the Lake Mip side, this might work. If they came from the Lake Lanee side, she was screwed.

Ahiliyah felt for her little friend. Her hand wrapped around the cool wooden handle. It wasn't just for herself. Not anymore. Creen's goop in the scabbard, coating the blade. If it came down to it, she would try to stab the thing, giving up her own life to test the poison, to hopefully give life to thousands of others.

She reached the runoff that angled down into the crevasse. It was time.

Ahiliyah breathed in deep through her nose, taking in the scents of the mountains—the smell of dirt, of damp rock, of trees and—of course—the caminus bushes. If this went wrong, she wanted to treasure this moment, because it might be her last. Such beauty here. What other sights did Ataegina hold? She would never know, not unless this worked.

She stood, picked up a round rock. Another big breath, a moment to fight the urge to abandon this idiocy, to run and hide, then she knelt and banged the rock against a boulder: once, twice, a third time.

Ahiliyah stared southeast through the pass. Mountains rose up on either side. No movement. She watched. She waited.

Decades ago, Sinesh had won a key battle somewhere around here, phalanx versus phalanx, men fighting, screaming, bleeding, dying. Even before the Rising, life on Ataegina had been about death.

Ahiliyah banged the rock again. On the third hit, it split down the middle, half of it tumbling from her hand. She picked up the fallen half, stood, looked—

—and saw it.

A black shape in the distance, moving toward her, faster than any person could ever run.

Ahiliyah rushed down the runoff channel, her feet kicking up clumps of dirt and rock that tumbled down alongside her.

She came around a bend in the crevasse, heard the beast racing along behind her, big feet and clawed hands crunching across dirt and gravel. Its hissing grew louder. Weathered stone walls rose up on either side— there was no escape, nothing to do but keep running, keep praying. One wrong step on a loose bit of rock or a soft spot of wet dirt could be her death.

Up ahead, a sharp bend to the right, her only chance at survival. Did she have enough of a lead? Ahiliyah sprinted harder, putting everything she had into her rush for life. She reached the bend, was going so fast she had to lean right to make the turn—her shoulder scraped against the rough wall, making her stumble. She waved her hands, trying to get control. For just a moment, she saw Creen, fifty yards further down the crevasse, standing right in the middle, then Ahiliyah skidded to a stop and dove into the oval of stones she and the others had set up hours earlier. She curled up and wedged herself in, feeling rock against her knees, her feet, her back, her head. She reached up, yanked the stick- and leaf-lined webbing over herself and the edge of the rock ring.

She shut her eyes, held her breath. She heard the demon skid to a stop—had it seen her?

"Hey, fuckface!" Creen's voice echoed off the crevasse walls. "Come and get me!"

Ahiliyah heard big feet dig in and gravel skitter as the demon rushed after the boy, heard Creen cry out in surprise even though he'd known exactly what was coming.

She counted to five before she lifted the netting just enough to look out. Down the walled crevasse, she saw the demon's long black tail swishing as the beast closed in on a fleeing Creen. Ahiliyah shoved the netting aside, was up and after the demon, moving as quietly as she could.

Creen stopped at a pile of stones thicker and taller than hers had been, a pile built into a spot where rushing water had carved out an undercut in the crevasse wall. His thin body squeezed into a slot barely big enough for him—his hidey suit caught on a rock.

The demon closed in, a blur of black trailed by a cloud of dust.

Creen's foot stuck out, wiggled as he tried to free himself. The monster reached for him just as the foot vanished into the hastily built mini-fortress.

Up on the edge of the crevasse, Ahiliyah saw Brandun rise from his hiding spot, looking more like a moving bush than a human being—a moving bush holding a crossbow.

The demon screeched as it pulled at the rocks that were hiding Creen. Rocks that Ahiliyah and Brandun and Creen had been forced to lift together were thrown aside. Beneath them, Creen screamed, a high-pitched siren of terror.

Brandun stood tall. What was he waiting for?

"Shoot," Ahiliyah whispered. "*Shoot.*"

The demon flung head-sized rocks aside as if they were dried chunks of wood. Stone smashed into the far wall, spun off to thud against the dirt.

"*Liyah, help me! Help me, please!*"

Ahiliyah felt the rage flow through her. She drew her little friend, started toward the monster, when the metallic thrum of a crossbow string stopped her.

The crossbow bolt punched into the demon's back, just below the backsticks, just left of the spine. The monster turned sharply, long head searching for its attacker.

Brandun put the crossbow stirrup on the ground, put his foot through it, grabbed the string with both hands and yanked it back, locking it into the latch.

The demon rushed away from Creen's pile of stones. Spindly legs carried it to the gulley wall and up it went, long arms fast and reaching.

Brandun scooped up the crossbow. As the demon rushed toward him, he tried to nock a new bolt—it tipped off the side, fell to the ground.

Ahiliyah's feet carried her forward, knowing it was already too late, knowing that she couldn't rescue him, that she would die along with him, knowing she should have stayed in the hold, that she should have never tried this idiotic stunt.

Brandun reached down for the dropped bolt; the demon's skeletal hand reached up over the edge of the gulley, grabbed Brandun's wrist.

The crossbow tumbled away as Brandun was yanked out into open air. He fell hard, bringing his arms up to shield his face just as he slammed into the dirt and stones.

The demon sprang off the rock wall, a picture of violent grace. Arms and legs both bent as it landed, absorbed the fall. The curved tail rose high.

Brandun rolled onto his back; blood streamed down his forehead, sheeting his face.

Creen kept screaming.

Crossbow bolt still jutting from its back, the demon crawled toward Brandun.

Ahiliyah shifted her little friend to her left hand. With her right, she drew her spearhead.

She didn't speak—she *roared*, bellowing a guttural cry that tore at the flesh of her throat.

The demon spun in place, crouched low. Black lips wrinkled back from metal teeth, teeth that opened to let out a low hiss.

"*Come on*," Ahiliyah screamed. "*Come on and get me, you fuck!*"

The beast crawled toward her, long black tail coiled and quivering.

Ahiliyah lowered into a fighting stance, wishing she'd taken the time to assemble her spear. Too late for that. Ten yards away, crawling toward her. Teeth and claws and tail… she didn't stand a chance. She would die here, in the dirt and the cold.

Ten yards away, death crawled toward her.

Run… just run, it will get Brandun…

Eight yards…

Creen, screaming… Brandun, weakly calling for help…

Six yards…

What are you doing? RUN!

The mouth opened, the toothtongue slid out.

Ahiliyah felt an icy tingle blossom in her chest. The feeling spread, washed through her body. Fear thinned, faded. In its place, something far more powerful, far more pure.

Hate.

She flipped the little friend in her left hand, held it tight to her palm with three fingers and a thumb as she used her pointer finger to lift her face net, flip it over her head. The demon hissed. Ahiliyah hooked her finger around the chain of her necklace, then pulled, lifting the toothtongue free of her hidey suit. She raised it, showed the dangling trophy to the beast.

"You see this?" She tugged on the necklace, making the toothtongue dance. "I killed your friend, I'm going to kill you, then I'm going to kill every single fucking one of your kind."

The demon reached out, came closer, just four yards away…

Ahiliyah let the necklace drop. She flipped her knife again, crouched, held both blades toward the beast. The hate inside her, so *powerful*. She would try to stab with the spearhead, make it go for that, then she'd lunge with the little friend. Maybe the goop worked, maybe the crossbow bolt just hadn't delivered enough.

She would die. If Brandun and Creen lived, it was worth it.

"Come on," Ahiliyah said through clenched teeth. "Come and get it."

The demon scurried forward, stopped only three feet away. Ahiliyah flinched at the sudden movement, felt her back hit the jagged stone wall—the beast had maneuvered her so she could only go left or right, where it would instantly catch her.

It didn't matter—this was the end, and she would do Lemeth Hold proud. She crouched low, her heart threatening to launch itself out of her chest.

The demon leaned forward, stretched out a hand... the long-fingered hand was *trembling*.

The beast leaned back, weight on its bent legs. It held the trembling hand up in front of its long head. The demon twitched sharply, as if stabbed by some invisible spear. The curled tail began to thrash spasmodically. Its body began to shake. Black jaws opened and closed, opened and closed, a rapid *clack-clack-clack* of metallic teeth that echoed off the crevasse walls.

A sharp, short screech, then the demon lurched away from her, scurrying backward. It tripped over Brandun, fell on its backsticks and quivering tail. The monster rolled to its side, arms thrashing at nothing, long legs kicking out in random directions.

Ahiliyah forgot her pain, her terror. She sheathed her spearhead as she ran to Brandun, grabbed him under his armpits and dragged him clear of the lurching beast.

"Liyah," he said. "What's... what's happening?"

Her heel caught a rock and she fell backward, falling to her ass just as the demon had. She scrambled to her knees, saw her little friend. She snatched it up, squatted next to Brandun, the blade tip pointed at the demon.

Creen's hidey-suit-covered head popped up from the ruined pile of rocks.

"It's dying," he said. He sounded different, and not just because he'd screamed himself hoarse. He sounded like a person who had endured something that would change him forever.

The demon jerked, rolled from its left side to its right. The toothtongue shot out and clamped down on empty air. The beast's back arched, its arms reaching out toward nothing.

"I hope it hurts," Creen said. "That's your blood coagulating, you piece of shit. That's chunks of ash clogging in whatever passes for your heart."

The demon's arms dropped, limp. Its chest rose and fell.

Creen stood, carefully stepped over the pile of rocks.

"Don't," Liyah said. "Don't go near it."

Creen ignored her, stepped past her. The boy who had been begging for his life now stood in front of the beast that had been trying to kill him.

With one foot, Creen reached out, kicked the demon's leg—there was no reaction. The demon twitched slightly—*almost* dead, but not quite.

Creen fumbled at his hidey suit; Ahiliyah couldn't see what he was doing.

"Before you die, I got something for you," the boy said. "Enjoy."

A stream of piss rained down on the demon, splashing off the long, round head to splatter on dirt and rocks.

34

Darkness fell. There was no time to hide until morning, they had to get back as fast as possible, no matter what the risks of moving at night.

They'd stayed at the kill site only long enough for Ahiliyah to stitch up the cuts on Brandon's face and arms. She used all the thread she had, and most of Brandun's as well. The stitches looked terrible, but Brandun didn't seem to mind—he sat there, still as could be, trying to deal with the dull pain in his head.

While she had stitched and bandaged his wounds, Creen had used his spearhead to make small, careful cuts to drain what was left of the demon's blood onto the crevasse floor. There was enough left to turn the dirt into a smoking, stinking, bubbling mess that would soon cool to form bloodglass. After draining the corpse, Creen had used his half-melted blade to saw off the demon's head. He'd emptied out his backpack—the demon's dead face poked out the top.

They marched single file, with Liyah in the lead and Creen bringing up the rear. They weren't far from home. They knew this terrain well and made good time. Bigsby's Pass behind them, they started up the foothills of Lemeth Mountain. Against the backdrop of a cloudless, starry sky, the Three Sisters high above it, Ahiliyah saw the peak of her mountain home.

"Hey, Creen," Brandun whispered, his words slowed by his pain, "you smell like piss."

Ahiliyah heard Creen stifling a laugh.

"Yeah," he said, "I should have thought about that before whizzing on the thing."

All three of them had come close to death—they had survived. Ahiliyah could barely contain her feelings of satisfaction, of elation. Now they had *hope*. Everyone did.

From far up ahead, a faint noise. She raised a fist—Brandun and Creen stopped behind her.

Ahiliyah slowly turned her head, searching for the sound. It came again. Distant, faint, but regular. Was that... *people?*

"Marching," Brandun whispered. "Unorganized, but sounds like a lot of people."

His ears were better than hers. In seconds, she heard what he'd heard, the soft, steady tread of hundreds of feet. It was close, coming from the northwest, just around the next foothill.

Too much noise—it might draw the demons.

Ahiliyah waved her hand forward and moved toward the sound, knowing her crewmates would follow. She heard the soft sound of a spearhead being drawn from a scabbard.

She reached the crest of the foothill, stopped, stared down. There, in the light of the Three Sisters, only a few hundred yards from the final approach of Lemeth Hold, was a column of people working their way up the rocky slope. *Hundreds* of them—most dressed in red or yellow.

"Dakaterans," Ahiliyah said. "Refugees."

Brandun stepped forward, stood shoulder to shoulder with her.

"The Margrave won't let them in," he said. "We have to help them. Drop your packs, they'll slow us down. Liyah, assemble your spear."

She did as he asked. Standing side by side, their hands moved in a blur of well-practiced motions.

"Oh, shit," Creen said. "The refugees aren't alone."

He pointed southwest. There, far away, racing along the shore of Lake Lanee, Ahiliyah saw the light of the Three Sisters gleaming off the heads of a horde of demons.

"Fifty, at least," Creen said, his voice wavering. "Hard to tell from this far."

Brandun finished assembling his spear. "How long until they reach the refugees?"

Ahiliyah finished hers. She stood, fought down her rising anxiety, forced herself to look, to think.

"Fifteen minutes. Maybe less."

"Creen, get to the wall and drop ropes," Brandun said. "Keep the head with you—the hold has to know your poison works. Liyah, you and I are helping the refugees."

Creen grabbed ropes from all three packs, then dug in his pack for the jar of poison. He handed it to Ahiliyah, who shoved it inside her hidey suit. She felt its cold through the belly of her shirt.

"If we don't make it, show people the head," she said. "Tell *everyone* what you did before you tell *anyone* in the Council. Scream it if you have to."

Creen yanked his little friend scabbard out of his suit, pressed it into Ahiliyah's hand.

"You can count on me," he said. "I'm good at being loud. Please don't get killed. That goes for both of you."

With that, he sprinted toward the approach to the hold, while Liyah sprinted after Brandun.

The refugees saw them coming; five warriors in dirty, blood-streaked white cloth armor spread out, three with spears and battered wooden shields painted yellow and red, two behind them with crossbows. Brandun waved his free hand over his head, signaling to them.

"Demons are coming, fast," he said. "Keep moving, come on."

The warriors craned their heads to look back, quietly urged the others to move faster.

"They've been after us the whole way," one of the warriors said. "They keep grabbing our people and taking them away. We have to get inside."

Someone stepped out of from the crowd of red and yellow—it was the Margravine.

Ahiliyah flipped her face netting back, rushed to her.

"Margravine, we'll guide you up the approach."

"Will you?" The old woman shook her head. "Your *leader* sent a signal we got before we were attacked, told us Lemeth Hold would take no more refugees. I hope you can do something about that, otherwise—" she gestured to the long line of exhausted, shivering, bedraggled people "—we're all as good as dead."

Ahiliyah would not let that happen. "We'll get you in, I promise. Come on."

She took the Margravine by the elbow, urged her toward the approach. All around, people bordered on panic. Men and women looked over their shoulders, stumbled on loose rocks and dirt. Some carried babies. Some dragged exhausted children stumbling along. Ahiliyah saw few old people in the column—if the elderly had escaped, they hadn't made it here.

"Fall in behind us," Brandun said. "Liyah, take the left."

She did, and Brandun took the right. Together, they set the outer boundaries for where the refugees could walk. That helped the column of shuffling, sniffling, scared people move quickly.

Behind them came the distant screech of a demon.

Time was running out.

They reached the base of the ruined wall. Ropes dropped down, one, two, three. Some people sent their children up the ropes, other people began climbing the wall, fumbling their way for footholds and handholds in the moonlight. The Dakateran warriors stayed at the base, helping people up.

Ahiliyah looked down the approach—the first demons were almost to the base. Some must have been faster than others, causing the pack to stretch out.

"We fought them all the way," the Margravine said, "but for every one we kill, they got ten of ours. It's hopeless."

As a tight pack, there was no chance to beat the demons, but they'd thinned into a long line. Killing the first few would come at a cost, but it would buy time.

Ahiliyah again felt that coldness blossom in her chest. Everything seemed… calm. She felt the hate rise up, and she did nothing to stop it.

"It's not hopeless," she said. "Tell your men to do exactly what I say."

The Margravine looked at her, tired, wrinkled eyes narrowing with doubt.

Liyah pulled out her toothtongue necklace, held it up. "I know how to kill them."

"I hope so," the Margravine said softly, then she waved at her warriors. "Get over here! Do whatever this woman tells you to do."

More ropes came flying down from above. People scrambled up. Even with the ropes, Ahiliyah saw that she couldn't save everyone. She had to get the warriors to higher ground—the longer they lived, the more people would survive.

"Get up the wall," Ahiliyah said. "Now, use the ropes."

The warriors glanced backward at the oncoming demons, then at their people. They saw what Ahiliyah saw, that not everyone would make it up in time. They wanted to stay and fight to the last—these were *real* soldiers, not the polished shields that bossed people around Lemeth.

"*Climb!*" Ahiliyah grabbed a warrior, pushed him toward a rope. "Help the Margravine!"

That got them moving. The five warriors slung shields and bows. They helped tie a rope under the Margravine's arms, then climbed along with her as someone above pulled her up.

A demon screamed. She took one last look back down the approach, saw a demon impaled on the spikes of a tree-branch trap, saw a second demon rushing past. The second demon caught the last refugee in the column. A reach, a grab, a stifled scream, and the demon took off in the other direction, a doomed woman in its black hands.

Ahiliyah scrambled up the wall, the memory of all her climbs guiding her hands and feet to the safe spots. In seconds, she climbed over the top and into the darkness below the overhang. She looked back in time to see a demon trigger one of the traps just as it grabbed a terrified man—a boulder smashed down, crushing them both. Burning blood squirted out, sprayed across a little boy who had either become separated from his parents or had made the journey alone. His high-pitched scream ate at the night. He fell to his back, kicking and thrashing, moonslight reflecting off the blood of his melting face.

More demons closed in.

Ahiliyah glanced right, to the door that led to the stairs down—the door wasn't open. Creen was slapping his hands on the stone, screaming as refugees packed in around him.

"Creen, get the damn door open!"

"*I'm trying*," he shouted back. "People inside are just getting to it now!"

Brandun and other refugees were pulling at the ropes, hauling up the last of those that would make it. The screams of those that would not tore at Ahiliyah's heart.

The Margravine's men gathered around her. She had to trust Creen would get the door open. She reached into her suit, pulled out Creen's jar and held it so the warriors could see it.

"This is demon poison. Hold out crossbow bolts and spear blades."

The men obeyed. She talked quickly as she dipped her fingers into the jar and slathered the bronze weapons with the goop.

"This kills them, but not right away. If they get on the deck, stick them once and try to keep them at a distance until it works. Archers, take out the front runners."

She glanced at the door—through the mass of yellow- and red-clad people, she could see it was open. Creen, Brandun and the Margravine stood there, waving people in a few at a time, trying to keep them calm and avoid a stampede down the stone steps.

The *thrum* of a crossbow brought Ahiliyah back to the task at hand. She saw the bolt sail through the air, land just wide of the leading demon. A second bolt buried itself in the beast's shoulder—it kept coming.

Behind it, several demons carrying people away, and two dozen or more rushing in—the pack had arrived.

Ahiliyah glanced at the opening—half the people were still working their way inside.

"Keep firing," she said. "Spearmen, wait for me here."

She sprinted along the deck, away from the opening, careful to give a linchpin stone a wide berth. One step on that stone would drop the whole overhang down on her head. Twenty yards from the door, she stopped—she was directly above one of the traps built into the wall below. She stood tall, waved both arms above her head.

"Come and get me, you cocksuckers!"

The wounded demon and one other continued on toward the archers, but the three right behind them angled her way. So fast, so deadly... death itself, black as night, coming to take her.

Ahiliyah ducked down. Out of sight behind the wall, she quickly crawled back to the spearmen. There were only about twenty people left at the stone door, filtering in two at a time. As she reached the spearmen, a demon scurried over the wall—two spearmen impaled it, then both shoved forward, flinging the dying beast out into the open air to crash to the rocks below.

"Lock shields," Ahiliyah said. "On me, backward to the door, crossbowmen behind us."

The three spearmen overlapped their shields instantly, as if they had trained with Ahiliyah all their lives. They leveled their spears over the top—smoke rose from two of the blades.

On the deck where she'd waved, a cloud of dust puffed up from below, catching the moonlight. Two demons crawled through that dust and over the wall—the trap had only got one of the three.

"*Liyah*," Brandun bellowed from behind her, "*move!*"

Ahiliyah tugged at the red tunics of the spearmen.

"Back steady," she said. "Come on, move!"

The spearmen shuffled backward. The two demons on the deck rushed in. One hit the linchpin stone—the overhang collapsed like the flat grey hand of a giant, smashing them flat. Burning blood sprayed out. The spearmen and Ahiliyah ducked reactively—burning blood sprayed against the shields and over the top of them, catching one of the crossbowmen behind her. The man screamed, dropped his cocked crossbow. Ahiliyah reached for it, realized she couldn't operate it and hold the jar of goop. She kicked the weapon aside so it wouldn't trip the spearmen.

"Keep moving," she said. "Back, back, come on."

Demons crested the wall and dropped onto the deck, started crawling toward the warriors and their smoking shields. One of the spearmen cried out, shook his shield off his arm, let it clang to the stone. One glance in the darkness told Ahiliyah why—demon blood had eaten through the metal. The other two spearmen closed ranks.

They were almost to the door when black hands reached in from the overhang, grabbed the screaming crossbowman and yanked him clean off his feet. In an instant, the crossbowman was gone, hauled up above the overhang, out of sight.

A hand on her shoulder, then Brandun's voice: "*Get in here!*"

She rushed through the door. Inside, she found both Creen and the Margravine urging people down the packed stairs, yelling for them to make space for the warriors. Ahiliyah saw Lemethian men at the door's edge, waiting for the order to slam it shut.

She looked back outside, as the remaining Dakateran bowman rushed in. The spearmen turned to move in, and when they did a demon shot forward, hissing, claws reaching and mouth open—Brandun drove his spear deep into its throat. Burning blood sprayed out, splashing against a spearman's leg. He screamed, fell on his chest, his body half in and half out of the door.

Ahiliyah and Creen grabbed him, hauled him in.

Brandun snatched up the man's smoking spear. "Close it, now!"

As the door slid, Ahiliyah saw more of the beasts—dozens of them—pouring over the wall like boiling black pudding.

The stone door slammed shut.

Ahiliyah dropped to her knees. She heard the pounding footsteps of refugees running down the stone steps, the heavy breaths of the Dakateran warriors, of Brandun and Creen and the Margravine, the screaming of the wounded spearman and the sizzling of his flesh.

Creen grabbed the jar of goop out of her hand.

"Brandun, hold him," he said, then dug two fingers into the jar.

Brandun all but sat on the struggling, screaming man.

Creen smeared the goop on the sizzling, smoking wound. The burning blood instantly foamed, turned to grey ash. The man stopped screaming. Blinking rapidly, he looked at Creen, then fell to his back.

The Margravine snatched the jar from Creen's hands.

"What is this?" She held it up to Ahiliyah. "It stops burning blood? You *kept* it from us?"

"And the poison," the last archer said through heavy breaths. "I took one down with a single bolt, Margravine. I hit him twenty yards out. By the time it reached the wall, it fell dead. I wouldn't have believed it if I hadn't seen it with my own eyes."

Fury danced in the Margravine's eyes. "You have a *weapon* against the beasts, and you didn't tell us. How long have you known?"

Ahiliyah tried to count the days, wondered if it was wise to say anything right then.

"Two weeks," Creen said. "We've known for two weeks. Don't blame Liyah. Want to know why you weren't told? Ask the Margrave."

The Margravine's fury faded. From her face, at least—it still burned brightly in her eyes.

"Oh, I will ask the bastard," she said. "You bet I will."

Brandun leaned in, whispered fiercely. "Be quiet! Can't you hear them out there?"

In the silence that followed, they all heard it— claws scratching against the rock door.

"They're looking for a way in," the Margravine whispered. "Let's get our wounded to the hospital. Ahiliyah, you lead the way."

The hate was gone. So was the cold feeling, and the focus. Now she only felt tired, drained of all energy. Ahiliyah pushed herself to her feet, and—quietly—led the others down the stairs.

35

The hospital whirred with activity. Ahiliyah stood just inside the entrance. The Margravine held her elbow, quietly commanding her to stay put.

Two Dakateran warriors flanked them; both were exhausted, spotted with raw sores brought on by tiny drops of burning blood, the same blood that had scored their helmets, eaten through small spots on the red and yellow shields they'd rested against the wall. They'd broken down their spears; their fingers flexed on the handles of their sheathed spearheads. They glanced around nervously, as if they expected demons to tear through the walls.

The men had quietly thanked Ahiliyah for what she'd done, and introduced themselves—Greg Lindeman and Nicholas Malmsteen. Nicholas was a distant cousin of Britt Malmsteen. Small world.

The Dakateran warrior wounded up on the deck—Ahiliyah didn't know his name—lay face-down on a hospital bed, chewing madly on Lisa's root, grimacing as Doctor Talbot bandaged his horrid wounds.

The warrior wasn't the only casualty. Lemethians helped crying, moaning Dakaterans into the hospital, put them on beds at the direction of Doctor Monique. Most wounds were from burning blood. A few refugees had torn clothes soaked with blood, the result of claws or tails or teeth. There were other injuries as well, incurred during the long, cold march from Dakatera or from the mad climb up Lemeth's old walls.

"I'm sorry your people died out there," Ahiliyah said. "I wish I'd got to you sooner."

The Margravine turned to face her. Ahiliyah stared into the woman's riveting blue eyes.

"You owe no apology," the Margravine said. "The evil beasts *hunted* us, like we were animals. If not for you and the other one… what is the big boy's name?"

"Brandun."

"If not for you and Brandun, there would be *no* survivors. Up on the deck, I watched you take command. You have a brilliant mind."

Ahiliyah glanced at the wounded people, thought of the screaming Dakaterans carried off by demons, thought of the warrior who had been snatched right off the deck.

"But I lost so many."

"That's what happens in war," the Margravine said. She smiled sadly. "When you lead people into battle, don't think of the ones you lost." She gestured to the beds, now full of crying, tired, bleeding Dakaterans. "Think of the ones you *saved*."

Shouts came from down the corridor—the booming voice of the Margrave.

The Margravine stiffened, stood straight. Ahiliyah saw the look in her eyes, recognized an emotion now familiar and powerful. In her eyes, Ahiliyah saw pure hate.

Aulus Darby stormed into the hospital, flanked by Drasko Lamech, Rinik Brennus, and Shalim Aniketos. Rinik and Shalim each held a runner-length spear, while Drasko carried only his billy club.

The Margrave saw the Margravine, strode toward her. The two Dakateran warriors bristled at the sight of Drasko and the others, started forward to intercept, but a flick of the Margravine's hand stopped them.

Drasko pointed at the Dakateran warriors. "Put those weapons *down*."

"Do no such thing," the Margravine said.

Aulus strode up to her as if the two Dakateran warriors weren't even worth his notice.

"*Herriet*," he said, growling out the word. "You and your people need to leave."

She sneered. "The demons attacked Dakatera. Drove us out. There may be more of us nearby, hiding until daylight—come morning, you will let them in. My people need shelter."

"There is no shelter for you here," Aulus said. "We've already got refugees from Keflan, and we can't even feed them. At first light, you will take your people to Biseth."

The hospital had been buzzing with the moans of the wounded and injured, the calls of the doctors, the scurrying of assistants and other Lemethians who scrambled to help in any way they could. Now, all were silent—everyone watched the two leaders square off.

"You *will* help us," the Margravine said, staring up defiantly at the taller man. "What are you going to do, Aulus? Force us to leave while your people stand by and watch?"

The Margrave thumped his fist against his chest. "These people do what *I tell* them to do. Lemeth Hold is *mine*, Herriet. If you push me further, you'll be lucky to leave here alive."

Ahiliyah couldn't believe what she was hearing. He would cast out these wounded, exhausted people? He was threatening the Margravine's life?

"Luck?" The Margravine pointed her finger in the Margrave's face. "We wouldn't have needed *luck* if you'd told us about the demon poison! You selfish bastard—where is your humanity? You're just as much a monster as the demons are."

The Margrave's face flushed red. "Drasko, put this bitch in lockup."

Drasko stepped forward, reached for the Margravine.

Her warriors reached for their spearheads. Greg Lindeman's blade barely cleared its scabbard before Rinik Brennus thrust his spear—the blade drove deep into Greg's neck.

Blood sprayed, hitting the Margrave and the Margravine.

People screamed, Talbot shouted *stop*—the sounds seemed distant, seemed to come from some other place, some other time.

Nicholas Malmsteen's blade flashed, slicing a deep gash across Rinik's cheek. Rinik cried out, dropped his weapons, his hands flying to his bloody face. Nicholas stepped forward to plunge his blade into Rinik's chest, but Drasko's club cracked down on Nicholas's forearm; Ahiliyah heard bones *crack*. The spearhead fell free, bronze clattering against stone. Drasko twisted his hips, whipped his club in a blurring backhand that caught Nicholas in the forehead. Nicholas fell backward like a rock, unconscious before his back hit the floor.

A moment of utter stillness, then Talbot rushed to Greg, tried to stem the flow of blood pouring out of the Dakateran's neck. Greg's mouth opened and closed—Ahiliyah had seen enough death to know there was nothing Talbot could do to save the man.

Drasko turned on Rinik. "You idiot! Why did you stab him?"

Rinik pressed his blood-sheeted hand against his blood-sheeted cheek.

"They drew first," he said. "We had to protect the—"

Drasko's club smashed Rinik's mouth, sending a tooth skittering across the floor. Rinik wobbled, fell to his knees. Drasko whipped the club down again, the wood cracking against Rinik's head. Rinik sagged, fell to his side.

Drasko raised the club to strike a third time—but before he could, Talbot shoved him hard enough to make the big man stumble.

"Get *out*," the doctor screamed. "You fucking *animals*! Get out of my hospital!"

Talbot knelt next to Rinik, fingers probing the man's wound as if Rinik was just another patient, as if he hadn't just killed a man, as if Drasko wasn't standing right there.

The shock of the sudden fight held a moment more, then broke.

"You murdering bastards," the Margravine said. "My man survived the demons, he fought to keep his people alive, and in the safety of your hold, you murdered him."

The Margrave no longer looked confident. He looked like a man who had lost control. Red blood splattered across his white beard. He glanced at Talbot and Rinik, at the unconscious Nicholas, at Greg, who had stopped moving, who stared up at the ceiling with dead eyes.

"We must control the Dakaterans," he said. "Drasko... take the Margravine to lockup."

Drasko grabbed the Margravine by the hair, yanked the old woman toward the door. Her feet caught; she fell hard on her knees. She cried out, curled into a shaking ball.

"Leave her *alone*," Ahiliyah said. "What's wrong with everyone? The demons are right outside and we're killing each other!"

The Margrave slowly turned his head. He stared at Ahiliyah. As he did, he seemed to gather strength, become his old self again.

"And take our *senior runner* to lockup as well," he said. "She let them in."

Drasko let go of the Margravine's hair, took one step toward Ahiliyah, the club held out in front of him. Embedded in the bloody wood, she saw a bit of white—one of Rinik's broken teeth.

"You've got weapons stashed in your hidey suit, Liyah," Drasko said. "Take them all out. Nice and slow. If you conveniently forget any, I promise I will make you hurt."

Ahiliyah had just witnessed the man's speed, seen how hard he could hit. Drasko weighed more than twice what she did. No one moved to help her. If she tried anything, it would be *her* teeth flying across the room.

One man on the floor, dead. Another knocked out cold. Another bleeding all over the place. She'd survived a wave of demons only to face this?

The world had gone mad.

She slowly reached to her back, drew her spearhead from its scabbard and dropped it on the floor. She reached into her netting, did the same with her little friend.

Drasko raised an eyebrow. "Nothing else stashed in that hidey suit?"

"Just the normal stuff I need for a run," Ahiliyah said. "No weapons."

Drasko pointed his bloody halfstaff at the Margravine. "Help her up."

Ahiliyah stepped to the Margravine, took her gently by the shoulders. The Margravine stood on wobbly legs, leaned heavily on Ahiliyah— she had never seemed so *old*.

"Murderers," the old woman said. "Are you going to murder me as well?"

The Margrave scowled. "You were told not to come here, yet you did, and the evil came with you. Murder you? You may have murdered this entire hold. I'll see you put in lockup myself. You as well, runner." He pointed at the unconscious Nicholas. "Shalim, tie him up, then bring him to lockup. Drasko, if they disobey, kill them."

Drasko pointed his club toward the entryway. "Move it, Liyah. You know the way."

Ahiliyah didn't know what had just happened, didn't know what to do, but she knew that if she didn't move, Drasko wouldn't hesitate to obey the Margrave's orders.

"Come on, Margravine," she said. "I'll help you."

Ahiliyah helped the woman out of the hospital and into the corridor.

36

"Everyone clear the way," Drasko called out. "The Margrave is coming through."

Lemethians pressed against the corridor walls, peered out from doorways. Word had quickly spread about the demons attacking, almost getting inside. Ahiliyah could *feel* their fear.

"Don't be a fool, Aulus," the Margravine said. "Stand and *fight*, before it's too late."

Ahiliyah felt a hard poke in the back—Drasko prodding her with the billy club.

"Keep moving," he said. "Both of you."

Ahiliyah half-supported, half-pulled the woman along.

"Not much further," Ahiliyah said. "The armory is up ahead, the lockup is just after that."

On the ceiling, the glowpipe lights flickered.

"Stop," Drasko said.

Ahiliyah and the Margravine did.

Drasko's glance flicked between the glowpipes and Ahiliyah. She supposed she should have been flattered—she was unarmed, yet the toughest man in the hold still considered her a threat. *Demon Killer*, he called her. For all the good that did her now.

"Keep moving," the Margrave said. "I want this woman behind bars."

The glowpipes again gleamed bright.

Before Drasko could poke her again, Ahiliyah urged the Margravine along.

They left the residential rooms behind, entered the long corridor that led to the armory and the lockup.

The glowpipes dimmed again—dimmed to almost nothing, to only a film of water coating the glass that gave off almost no light at all. That, too, faded, and all went black.

"This is how it started in Dakatera." The Margravine's voice, eerily disembodied in the absolute darkness. "They take out the pipes. They don't need light."

From far back in the residential section, the haunting echo of a woman's scream. Goosebumps rippled across Ahiliyah's skin. So dark—she could see *nothing*.

"I have a torch," she said. "Hold on."

She reached into her hidey suit pockets, hoping Drasko wouldn't think she was trying to find a hidden weapon and smash her over the head for it. Even in the absolute darkness, the corridor was so small he could grab her and hit her in an instant.

"Hurry up," the Margrave said.

Ahiliyah heard the fear in his voice. She felt that same fear—had the lords of the night found a way in? Through the darkness, another distant scream echoed through the corridor. A man's scream this time, and the faint hint of shouts… of calls for help.

Ahiliyah struck a match against the floor. The flame flared up, briefly blinding. She held her torch over it, watched the dry wood catch fire, bringing light back to the corridor.

In the flickering torch's glow, the Margravine smiled.

"Now you will see what it's like, Aulus," she said. "You'll watch your people die."

Aulus Darby stepped past Drasko, grabbed the Margravine and threw her hard against the corridor wall. The old woman grunted on impact, crumpled into a yellow pile.

"This is *your* fault, you stupid bitch!" He leaned over her, the torchlight playing off his wrinkled face and blood-streaked beard. "They followed you here!"

He stepped back, kicked her in the ribs. The Margravine cried out and tucked into a ball.

Ahiliyah dropped the torch, threw herself down, covered the older woman with her own body. She closed her eyes and waited for the next kick.

It never landed—the echoing, soul-shriveling screech of a demon froze everyone in place.

In the silence that followed, the torch's soft crackle seemed impossibly loud.

"They're inside," the Margrave whispered. "How could they get inside?"

Drasko took him by the arm. "Margrave, we need to move."

From the corridor's darkness came a new sound… the sound of falling rock?

Aulus reached down, yanked at the netting of Ahiliyah's hidey suit.

"Liyah, your Margrave needs your service," he said, his words coming far faster than normal. "We may have to get to the surface, you know the surface better than anyone."

Now he wanted her help? "You'll get no assistance from me."

The Margrave grabbed her wrist, yanked her to her feet. "I *said*, your *Margrave* needs your *service*! Leave that old bitch where she lies, she will buy us time!"

Ahiliyah yanked her arm free, stepped forward and smashed her fist into the Margrave's nose, rocking his head back. Blood gushed, reflecting like molten metal in the torchlight.

Her head exploded with pain. She fell in a heap on the corridor floor. A hand grabbed her hair, yanked her head back—she stared up into the too-close face of Drasko Lamech.

"Kill her," the Margrave said, his words nasal, muted. "Kill that little cunt."

Drasko let her go, stepped back. "No, you were right, we need her. I haven't been on the surface in ten years, and you've *never* been up there."

The Margrave snarled. Fluttering torchlight reflected off the whites of his too-wide eyes, played off the white of his blood-streaked beard. He looked like a madman.

"I am your Margrave, you *will do what I say*. I gave you an order. She *hit* me. Kill her!"

If it had been any other time, any other place, Ahiliyah might have laughed—Drasko could break Aulus Darby in half with one hand, yet the big warrior shrank at the older man's words.

Ahiliyah's head throbbed. She felt a trickle of blood rolling down the back of her neck, realized that Drasko had hit her with his billy club.

She heard a muffled noise, distant, barely audible over the torch's crackle. A scraping sound, intermittent, coming in fast bursts, then nothing at all. She'd heard something like it before...

"We'll find another runner," Aulus said. He pointed at Ahiliyah. "*Kill her*, Drasko. *Now!*"

Drasko shrank further. His hand flexed on the billy club's handle. He looked at her from under his eyebrows, and she knew he would obey the Margrave's order.

"I'm sorry, Liyah," he said. "I'm sorry."

If Ahiliyah was to die at the hands of this spineless, mewling worm, then she would make him earn it. She bent into a fighting stance and raised her fists.

"Don't call me Liyah, you coward—call me *Demon Killer*."

The Margrave's scream of pain made them both jump.

Aulus Darby fell to the floor, his hands clutching at the back of his right knee. He cried out in agony, rolled to his side.

The Margravine slowly stood, that mad smile wide on her wrinkled face. Her dress, torn and bloody. Her dry hair, wild and tangled.

In her hand, a little friend—the blood on the blade gleamed in the torchlight.

"Should have had your thug search me, Aulus." She knelt next to the Margrave, examined him the way a cook might examine a gulping fish. "I sliced your hamstring. I'd kill you, but I'd like to know you died at their hands. Maybe you'll buy us time. Who is the bitch, now, eh?"

The leader of Lemeth Hold clutched at his knee, his hands red with blood.

Back down the corridor, not even five yards away, the ceiling collapsed, filling the corridor with tumbling stones and spilling dirt. Ahiliyah squinted her eyes against billowing dust, saw something fall through and land hard on the rubble-strewn floor.

Something *black*.

Ahiliyah saw her torch on the floor, flickering flame lighting up the floating dust. She snatched it up, held it toward the black thing. It was a demon, yes, but different from the ones she'd seen on the surface. Thin, lethal, but … *small*, only a bit bigger than she was. The long black head looked thin, pointy. No backsticks. The tail was a squat black stub.

The beast slowly rose to all fours. Arched back, narrow hips and shoulders. Its hands—no, its *paws*—were larger and thicker than any Ahiliyah had seen before, and the talons looked less like claws and more like a shovel blade sliced lengthwise into four parts.

One of the claws was missing from its left paw; burning blood oozed out onto the tunnel floor, not just from that wound but from a dozen cuts and tears on both hands.

"God help us," the Margravine whispered.

Ahiliyah final realized what she was looking at—a demonic vootervert. In that instant, she understood how the beasts had got into Keflan, into Jantal, into Dakatera. And, now, into Lemeth.

They had *dug* their way in.

The hunchbacked demon opened its metal-toothed mouth. A toothtongue slipped out, tasted the air. It squealed a squeal that Aaliyah had never heard before.

"Margravine, come to me, slowly," Liyah whispered. "We are leaving."

Aulus coughed from the dust. He was still on the floor, between the vootervert demon and Ahiliyah. He saw the beast, rolled to his hands and knees, tried to stand. He could not.

"Liyah, help me," he said, far too loud. He reached toward Drasko. *"Help me!"*

Drasko stayed motionless, billy club in his hand.

The Margravine backed toward Ahiliyah. Drasko did the same.

The vootervert demon squealed again, louder this time. From the hole above it came an answering, deep hiss—that sound Ahiliyah recognized.

"Come on," she whispered. "Faster!"

Drasko and the Margravine reached her. Ahiliyah wanted to run, but found she couldn't make herself move. No matter what the Margrave had done, did he deserve this?

From the hole in the corridor ceiling above him, a black, spiny tail curled out, a sharp black tailspike reflecting the torchlight.

The Margravine pulled at Ahiliyah's arm. "Come, girl—we have to *run*."

From the hole, long black legs stretched down. With a shivering, echoing hiss, a demon—the kind she had seen dozens of times, the kind she'd smashed with a jagged rock, the kind she'd trapped in the crevasse, the kind she'd fought on the deck—dropped down to the floor.

The vootervert demon looked up at it, let out a soft squeal that sounded almost… loving.

The Margrave rolled to his back, looked up, and saw his death.

"No… not *me*," he said, in a voice that was far, far too quiet for someone's last words.

The demon snatched him, tucked him in one sinewy arm, then leapt up into the ragged ceiling hole. In an instant, the demon—and the Margrave—were gone.

Aulus Darby didn't even scream.

The vootervert demon turned, started digging mindlessly at the wall, its entire body contracting and convulsing with the effort. Another shovel-claw snapped off as rocks tore free. Burning blood sizzled on stone and dirt.

Whatever force had held Ahiliyah in place, that force vanished.

"Come on," she said. "We're going to the armory."

She turned and ran, leaving the monster to dig in the darkness. She only made it twenty or thirty yards before she realized the Margravine couldn't keep up. Ahiliyah stopped, fished another torch out of her suit and lit it while she waited.

Drasko ran ahead of the Margravine, then ran back to her. He scooped the old woman into his arms. Even with her weight, he was almost as fast as Ahiliyah. He caught up, and together they jogged down the hall.

"The beasts can *dig*," Drasko said. "We need to get out of here, not go to the armory."

"There are weapons and poison in the armory," Ahiliyah said. "Just keep moving!"

At least the poison would give them a fighting chance. After she had it? She had no idea what to do next—hopefully someone else could figure that out.

37

When they reached the armory, Ahiliyah saw men rushing into the room— the Windens, Callow and his sons Abrams and Duvall. They entered, then Solomon Barrow, the foundryman, leaned out, torch in hand, looked up and down the hall. He saw Ahiliyah, waved her forward.

"Come on, girl!"

She rushed in; Drasko—still carrying the Margravine—came in right behind. Solomon again leaned out the door, quickly looked up and down the corridor, then slammed the wooden door shut.

At least fifty people stood in the armory, a dozen of them holding torches that filled the air with the smell of smoke. Some people held weapons, and more than a few—including Councilman Poller—held bronze shields. Leonitos Lamech, a warrior, wore full armor.

Word had spread about Creen's goop. An open barrel stood a few yards inside the door. Poison paste gleamed wetly from spearheads, demon forks, knives and arrowheads.

Everyone, including Leonitos, looked terrified, unsure of what to do next.

Martin Yates, the man who had accidentally bonked Liyah in the head in phalanx reserve training, stepped out from the crowd. He looked like he might shit himself at any moment.

"The demons are in the hold," Martin said. "Councilman Poller, what do we do?"

Everyone looked to Poller. It was his moment to lead—a moment he did not seize.

"I don't know," he said quietly. "I don't know."

Callow Winden's chest heaved, more with panic than fatigue. "Drasko, where's the Margrave? He'll get us out of here, he'll lead us!"

The Margravine whispered something in Drasko's ear. He gently set her on her feet.

"I am Herriet Lumos, Margravine of Dakatera Hold," she said. "Your Margrave is dead. Demons are running wild through the hold. Together, we will figure out a way to save as many people as we can and escape this place. Does anyone doubt my authority to lead?"

People exchanged glances. No one contradicted her, not even Poller. The Margravine's air of command really left no choice—especially not with Drasko standing right behind her.

"Good," the Margravine said. "Ahiliyah, we'll start with you—what do you suggest?"

She took a step back. The Margravine wanted *her* to decide?

"I'm just a runner," Aaliyah said.

"*Senior* runner," Drasko said. "And a demon-killer."

That made her qualified? She'd done well up on the surface, yes, but that was *up there*, in the open spaces, not *down here* in the tight corridors.

"Our choice is obvious," Callow Winden said. "We stay here, with the weapons.'

His son Abrams grabbed his arm. "Dad, our people are *dying*. We have to fight!"

"The demons will slaughter us if we leave," Leonitos said. "They're too fast, too strong."

People began to shout, to argue. The Margravine held up a hand, a simple gesture that, somehow, instantly silenced everyone.

"Liyah, this is your home," she said. "You have more experience against the demons than anyone here. *Think*. You can come up with something, I know it."

She looked around the armory. Racks and racks of armor and weapons… spears and bows and crossbows… barrels full of arrows and bolts… demon forks and armor… chestplates, helmets and shields… three more sealed barrels of Creen's goop.

The demon-vert. Had it dug randomly, or had the sound of the Margrave's yelling drawn it? Maybe both—the creature had likely burrowed into the mountain, stopping to listen, dug some more, repeated the process until it heard something and moved toward it.

"Stay as quiet as you can," she said. "Vootervert demons dug holes, letting the monsters in. We can't hide here, they'll find us eventually. We need to fight, to drive the demons out. We have Creen's goop, and…"

The goop. It made clots in the demons' burning blood.

Clots.

Ahiliyah glanced at the armory door, envisioning the corridor beyond. The confined, narrow corridor, not all that different from a vein or an artery. Just wide enough for three overlapping shields.

She thought of her wargames with Sinesh, how the demons' speed always allowed them to outflank any phalanx. But in the narrow corridors, there *were* no flanks.

Clots… they could clot the corridor, block access from in front and behind.

Ahiliyah knew what needed to be done.

She reached into her hidey suit, pulled out her toothtongue, let it drop against her chest.

"We will form two shield walls, back to back." Her words poured out, sounded strange to her, as if she was someone else listening to an other-Liyah speak. "Each wall will have two ranks each of three shields, with spearmen behind to stab through the gaps. Our most vulnerable will stay between the walls, keep coating weapons and shields with Creen's goop. Those holding shields, stay behind them, *do not look around them*—you must protect yourself from demon tails. Once we're in the corridor, we will make as much noise as we can, draw the demons to us."

"Draw them to us?" Poller blanched. "Are you mad? How will that help us escape?"

Moments earlier. Ahiliyah had thought someone else should figure out what to do. Now, looking at Poller, she realized *she* was the one. These people needed someone to take command.

"We're not going to *escape*, Councilman—we're going to drive the beasts from our home."

All around her, faces blank with disbelief, with fear and confusion, but also faces hard with anger, with determination.

Solomon Barrow smiled and nodded. "Fucking hell. Liyah's right. Let's kill the bastards."

More nods. These people were afraid—Ahiliyah was, too, no denying that—but now they had a simple objective. They could take control of the situation, take control of their fate.

"This is ridiculous," Poller said. "We're not taking orders from this Dakateran blasphemer and this, this *girl*. I've changed my mind. I'm a Councilman, and I'm taking charge. We *stay*, right here, we stay and defend this room and wait for help."

The Margravine glanced at Drasko, tilted her head toward Poller.

Drasko's fingers flexed on his bloody billy club. "Councilman, you're going to want to shut the fuck up and do what you're told. The demon-killer says fight, so we fight. Understand?"

Ahiliyah realized how quickly power had changed hands. Aulus was gone. Drasko had quickly aligned himself with the person he thought would wind up in charge—Herriet Lumos.

Poller stared at Drasko, then at the billy club. He looked around, just as Ahiliyah had done in the hospital, hoping someone would help him—no one did.

"Enough talk," Ahiliyah said. "Open another barrel, quickly. Everyone, cover yourself in goop. It's time to fight."

Ahiliyah worked the goop into her hair, smeared it on her skin, rubbed it into her clothes, quietly giving orders as she did. She arranged people by skill, size and strength, placing Poller at the center-front of one shield wall, Martin Yates at the center-front of the other. Some people would hold shields, some spears, some bows. Those that could do none of those things would carry arrows, extra spears and barrels of Creen's goop.

People worked together to coat themselves in the goop. They grabbed shields, quickly donned chestplates and helmets, piled weapons on the floor. She told them to use runner spears—in the tight corridors, the longer warrior spears would be far less maneuverable.

A demonic screech sounded from just outside the door, freezing everyone. An instant later, the wooden door rattled violently.

Ahiliyah pointed her spear as she called out orders. "Wall one, left, wall two, right!"

Terrified people rushed to their assigned positions. Reservist training came into play—the two walls formed with little confusion. Each wall had three ranks; three overlapped shields in front, their bearers crouched down; a second rank behind, their shields just above those in front; and a third rank with goop-smeared spears and demon forks pointing out through the gaps.

The door hammered again, a booming drum of death, then the thick wood split down the middle. Through the crack, Ahiliyah saw a writhing blackness and flashes of metal teeth reflected the light of the armory's torches.

"Shield walls, move closer," Ahiliyah said. "Angle in from the sides of the door, don't leave space for it to get through! Archers, with me, fire only when I command. Margravine and the other non-fighters, get behind the archers."

The two shield walls touched, forming a V. When the demon came through, there was nowhere for it to go. Ahiliyah stood behind the point of that V. Behind her and to her sides, the creak of bowstrings being drawn.

Gnarled black fingers reached through the crack, grabbed the wood and yanked, ripping away fat, splintering chunks.

"Archers, *loose!*"

Bowstrings thrummed. Two arrows stuck in the wooden door, and two went through—a squeal of pain answered. The black hands vanished for a moment, then reached in again, furiously ripped free huge chunks of wood. The shield walls wavered. Poller, in the front-center spot on the left wall, stood, his skin white as an imbid flower.

"Front ranks," Liyah screamed. *"Hold your positions!"*

Poller squatted down—bronze clanged as the shields slammed back into place.

A black body rammed through the ravaged door. The demon rushed, a blur of claws and glittering teeth. It slammed into Poller's shield—the beast bounced off even as Poller rocked back. The Councilman screamed in terror, but he leaned forward, holding his place in the line.

The demon coiled to spring again—spears impaled it, punching into belly and head and shoulder. A demon fork plunged deep in the black chest. The beast screeched and writhed, batted at the fork. The spears withdrew and drove in again. Burning blood splashed, filling the air with an acrid stench that overpowered the smell of torch smoke.

A second demon rushed through the door, angled right, slammed into the shield wall. Its claws raked across bronze. Spears jabbed out, puncturing the hard black shell. The demon grabbed the center shield, yanked it away, pulled it right off Martin Yates's arm—the black tail whipped in, the tailspike punched into Martin's chest.

"Fill the gap," Liyah called out. *"Now!"*

Someone from the second row stepped over Martin to take his place. Drasko leaned out from the back row, jammed his spear forward—the blade slid into the left side of the demon's head, crunched out the right. The beast stiffened, then fell, quivering.

The first demon stumbled backward, leaving a trail of burning blood sizzling on the floor. It reached the doorway and fell back, arms sticking up stiff and twitching. Blood loss, poison or both... it was dying.

"Hold your positions," Ahiliyah said.

Her people did as she said. She heard their heavy breathing. Some cried. Some muttered prayers. Someone said Martin was dead.

Ahiliyah smelled the beast now, that scent of wet rocks and moss combined with the acrid stink of burning blood.

She waited. No more demons entered.

A hand, gentle on her back.

"It's not enough," the Margravine whispered. "Look at them, Liyah—they need *more*."

Ahiliyah glanced around, saw that the Margravine was right. The cobbled-together unit had won this tiny battle, yet they focused more on Martin Yates then they did on the demon that Drasko had put down, or on the beast still twitching in the doorway—none of them would go near it. Despite the victory, Ahiliyah could tell, somehow, that these people would not yet follow her into the corridors, would not yet go on the offensive with her.

"Show them," the Margravine said. "Show them that you are the one."

Ahiliyah pushed past the shields. People stared at her as if she were mad. She stood over the twitching demon. Even in its death throes, it tried to reach out for her.

She raised her spear, drove the thick butt-spike down through the demon's curved head. A splash of burning blood hit her goop-smeared leg, sizzled into grey ash. She wiggled the spear, trying to scramble the beast's brains—if it had brains there at all.

It stiffened, and finally fell limp.

She turned her back to the door, faced her people, let them see her naked rage. Maybe another demon would grab her from behind, but she didn't care—this was the moment where she would *make* her people follow her into war.

Ahiliyah Cooper had never felt so alive.

"Do not cry for Martin Yates," she said. "He died protecting his hold, against the demons that have tried to destroy our world."

She pointed down at the demon she'd finished off, at its broken black head, at the greenish meat inside the hole and the burning blood sizzling up from the stone floor beneath it. Her people stared at the dead creature. Ahiliyah saw their faces change, saw the courage build, saw them hunger to—at long last—fight back.

"They *can* be killed," she said. "The demons are bigger, faster, stronger, but we are *smarter*. We fight as *one*. Are you ready to take back your hold?"

The shout came back, powerful, instant, undeniable. Even Poller roared in agreement. These people were no longer impotent, left to the mercy of fate.

The Margravine grinned her mad grin.

"Poller," Ahiliyah said, "your wall leads, form up ten yards down the corridor. Archers and non-fighters behind them, with me. Wall two, form up behind us, facing the other way. Don't let even one of them past your shields. Let's go!"

People scrambled into the corridor, their reservist training keeping them orderly and efficient. Ahiliyah could *feel* the difference in these people. Yes, they were afraid, but they had reached their limit and would hide no more.

In the corridor, her clot formed—shield walls on either side, spearmen and archers in the middle. Torches mounted on poles stuck out through the shields, offering shaky light, but it was better than facing the beasts in the dark. Shields touched the wall on the right, and on the left, reached up almost to the ceiling. There was no way around, no way under, no way over.

Ahiliyah found herself standing next to the Margravine. The woman held a small torch in one hand, a quiver of crossbow bolts in the other.

"Kill the bastards, Ahiliyah," she said. "Kill them all."

Ahiliyah nodded. "Drasko! March us forward."

The former enforcer for the Margrave—now, apparently, the enforcer for the Margravine—barked out a cadence, *left, left, left-right-left*. The wall moved forward, a thick, bronze plug sliding through the corridor.

Demons thrashed against the front wall. In the jittering torchlight, glimpses of black talons raking against shields, peeling paint and scratching bronze. The shield bearers had learned from Martin's death—they tucked in tight behind the metal discs, held on with all their strength, leaned forward with all their weight, the weight of those behind them helping anchor them against the savage onslaught. Spears thrust out and back, points sliding through the small gaps, punching into black-armored bodies.

Burning blood flowed, sizzling against stone as it ran to the gutters on either side. Screeches and grunts filled the air, reverberated off the walls and ceiling. Ahiliyah heard frustration in the beasts' screams— claws, teeth and tails rarely found a soft target.

Councilman Poller cried out, stumbled back, blood flowing from his left shoulder—he did not let go of his shield.

Ahiliyah shoved Duvall Winden forward.

"Duvall, *fill the gap!*"

The teenager roared in rage and fear as he ducked behind his shield and stepped into the center of the wall. Ahiliyah grabbed Ruslan Porter, who was in the last rank, shoved him into Duvall's former position an instant before two more demons slammed against the shield wall.

Poller snarled, tore his robe to expose the wound. "Someone tie this off!"

The Margravine moved to him, her small body jostled by bodies in front and behind. She used her little friend to cut strips from her own dress. She put the blade between her teeth to free both hands, wrapped the strips around Poller's wound and tied them tight.

"*Poller,*" Ahiliyah said, bracing herself against the jostling bodies, "can you fight?"

He winced as another knot cinched down, then smiled a madman's smile. "It's only pain, General." He hefted his shield and leaned forward, adding his weight to the wall.

The demon screeches thinned, suddenly, then stopped.

"Clear behind," Leonitos called out.

"Front as well," Drasko answered. "Ahiliyah?"

She reached out, thumped Drasko on the back. "Move us forward. Fresh torches!"

People lashed torches to spear shafts, lit them, slid them forward to light the way.

The wall wavered for a moment as people stepped around and over the broken bodies of demons. The monsters bore many wounds, but the finishing damage was always the same—black heads smashed to pulp by heavy butt-spikes.

Men dropped spears that had melted to slag, called for replacements. Weapon-bearers slathered goop on fresh blades, handed them up. Archers nocked new arrows, crossbowmyn cranked back crossbow strings.

How many demons had they killed? Eleven? Twelve? Two more

Lemethians had died, but the clot strategy was working. They were *winning*.

"Light ahead," Drasko called out. "It's the common room, demons are trying to get in!"

Ahiliyah leaned forward, peered between the shields. Up ahead, she saw two black beasts ripping at wooden furniture stacked in an entryway. Spears thrust through the furniture, jabbing the demons, keeping them at bay more than killing them.

A spearman leaned out, fearless and snarling, thrusting his spear— it was Brandun.

"Archers," she said, "loose!"

Poisoned arrows and bolts flew down the corridor; some bounced off hard black skin, some punched through. The beasts turned to face the new threat.

Whatever the cost, Ahiliyah would save her friend,

"Wall one, *move forward. Kill them all!*"

Two hundred people, including Brandun and Creen, had barricaded themselves in the common room. They fought to stay alive, using a handful of spears and clubs made from broken furniture. At least a dozen people lay dead, their bodies torn to pieces by demon claws, teeth and tails.

The shield wall hit the demons hard, pinned them against the barricades. The beasts had nowhere to maneuver. In seconds, they were all down, their evil lives ended by butt-spikes driven through their black skulls.

The common-room survivors added numbers, and with those numbers Ahiliyah quickly turned the tide of battle. She formed new shield walls, sent them with Brandun back to the armory for more weapons, more demon poison. She kept Creen and the Margravine at her side.

Her strategy spread like wildfire. Throughout the hold, shields slowly moved through the corridors, rescuing people who had barricaded themselves in their rooms. Small battles raged. People died, but so, too, did demons—far more demons than people.

At some point, Ahiliyah couldn't say when, she couldn't say why, the surviving demons fled Lemeth hold. They crawled into the holes they had dug to get in, and were gone, leaving death in their wake.

No one cheered.

"There are dozens of holes," the Margravine said. "This hold is not safe. The glowpipes are broken, and the torches won't last long. We'll soon be in the dark if we stay here."

"The river won't be dark," Creen said. "We can get everyone down there."

The river… *Sinesh*.

"Get everyone to the river," Ahiliyah said. "I'm going there now."

Poller grabbed her arm. "I'm going with you, Liyah. Wall one, to the river!"

Shields rattled as people formed up in front of her. They were all exhausted, all wounded, and all ready to keep going.

"I'm with you, Liyah," Creen said. "Lead the way."

She glanced at the Margravine, for some reason feeling the need to get the woman's approval. The Margravine nodded.

"Councilman Poller," Ahiliyah said, "let's go get our people. Move them out."

38

Ahiliyah stared down at what was left of General Sinesh Bishor.

"I'm so sorry, Liyah," Creen said.

The hold had been ripped apart. The dead and missing were still being counted, yet Creen was with her. He understood what Sinesh had meant to her.

A demon had driven a toothtongue through the old man's face, out the back of his head. If not for his withered body, missing arm and mass of scars, he would have been unrecognizable.

"They didn't take him," she said. "Why not?"

Creen glanced back to the spot where the weavers sat all day, every day, chewing Lisa's root and reminiscing about their good old days.

Half of the women were gone—the other half were dead, brutalized by the monsters.

"They take people to Black Smoke Mountain so the Demon Mother can turn them into new demons," he said. "Maybe they don't take people they sense won't survive the journey, or the process of being converted."

Ahiliyah couldn't look away from Sinesh's body. He'd gone to war against the demons and paid a horrible price. A life of constant pain. Spurned by the very people he'd fought for. Treated like a joke, his legacy of victory and service dismissed.

A curl of rope lay next to his body. Burning blood had eaten through it, leaving blackened ends. Had Sinesh fought to the end? Maybe, with no other weapons at hand, he'd tried to strangle the very beast that killed him. The scorched rope showed one thing—Sinesh had drawn blood.

No suicide for him.

"Liyah, the Margravine is calling you," Creen said.

"But his body… "

"Someone will take care of it," Creen said. "The smart thing to do is put the bodies in the foundry oven. They'll start rotting soon, which will only add to our problems when we rebuild."

Ahiliyah looked up at the cavern roof, at the hole there. Far below it, a vootervert-demon that had fallen to its death, black body smashing on the rocks at the river's edge. Demons had entered here, and in at least two other places in the hold.

"We're not rebuilding," she said.

Creen's face wrinkled in confusion. "We're not?"

Ahiliyah stepped around Sinesh's body, picked up his small box of wargaming miniatures. She headed back toward the footbridge. Creen said something, asked a question maybe, but his words didn't register. She crossed the bridge, trying not to think of all the days spent wargaming with Sinesh, listening to his stories, learning from him. If not for him, she would have never been born. Now he was gone.

Gone, because of *them*.

The survivors of Lemeth crowded the river's plateau. Two thousand, maybe more, covering every surface. Men, women, children, old and young. Mostly Lemethians, but also many Keflan refugees and Dakateran survivors. She heard the moans of the wounded, and the wails of those who had lost loved ones. Men and women with spears and shields—the same moving shield walls that had fought off the beasts—clustered near the stairway, tending to their wounds, drinking water from bottles, ready to fight if the demons poured down the stairs.

The Margravine waved her over.

Ahiliyah walked through the crowd of frightened, exhausted people. When she passed by, they stopped talking, stopped crying. People she'd known all her life reached out to touch her. Their hard expressions wordlessly told her they knew they were alive because of her.

Near the walkway's edge, twelve demon corpses lay in a neat row. Ahiliyah had ordered it. She wanted everyone to see that the demons could be killed.

The Margravine stood in a small circle with other important people: stonesmiths, glassmiths, and head craftsmyn; Councilman Kanya Poller, still sweaty, bloody, slathered in caminus goop; Preacher Ramirus, who looked unharmed; Panda; Councilman Tinat, a bloody bandage around his head, a third toothtongue added to his necklace.

Drasko stood behind the Margravine, just as he'd once stood behind the Margrave. Perhaps some objected to her taking charge, but if so they were too tired—or too intimidated—to argue.

All of them, including the Margravine, held spears.

Councilman Jung and Balden were nowhere to be seen. They were dead, or carried off.

"We're deciding what to do next," the Margravine said. "We can't make that decision without you, Liyah."

Ahiliyah set the box down. "Has anyone seen Brandun?"

No one answered.

"Let us begin," the Margravine said. "Who here is the head glassmith?"

Cruden Poller stepped forward. "I am, Margravine."

He resembled his cousin, Councilman Kanya Poller, or he had before the day's fighting began. Kanya was as fat as ever, but he stood taller, seemed... *dangerous*. Kanya almost looked like a different person.

"We have to repair the hold and get ready for the next attack," the Margravine said. "The hold is in the dark. How long to fix the broken pipes?"

Cruden sighed, shook his head. "Half of my workers are dead or gone. I'd have to train help, and glassmaking ain't something you can learn overnight. There's so many busted pipes. I'd have to start getting water flowing to the factory area, obviously, then if you wanted the main areas lit—common room, training pit, the bigger rooms—that's four days. Maybe three."

"We can stay by the river until then," the Margravine said.

Solomon Barrow took a step forward, his blacksmith's hammer in his hand, the thick iron head scarred with deep lines caused by burning blood.

"The foundry forge makes its own light," he said. "Most of my people survived. We'll work nonstop, make whatever tools Cruden needs and that Barton Mason needs to fill the holes."

"Barton Mason?" The Margravine glanced around. "What does he do? Is he here?"

Nicole Mason stepped forward. Her eyes were red and swollen from tears.

"The demons took him," she said. "He was the master stone-mason, but now I guess I am."

The Margravine bowed. "I am sorry for your loss. Have you looked at the hole near the armory? Can it be repaired?"

Nicole sniffed, wiped her nose with the back of her hand. "That one and the one in Tamara Jacobson's quarters. If I get all the help I need, I can fill those holes in two days, maybe three. The beasts dug though solid rock. We'll have to cut new stone to fill the holes. It won't be easy."

Ahiliyah pointed to the hole in the cavern ceiling. "How long to fix that one?"

"We'd have to build scaffolding to reach it," Nicole said. "At least four days for that, maybe five. Then we'd have to haul rock up the scaffolding, cement it in place. If we worked day and night, two weeks."

"We won't have that long," the Margravine said. "They came in waves. The first wave was like what we just endured, a few dozen demons. At the time, we didn't know they'd dug their way in. When the beasts appeared in the corridors and smashed the glowpipes, everyone fled to the surface. Up there, we tried to organize, to figure out how to go back in and kill them. A few hours later, the second wave hit. We think the first wave were some kind of large scouting force— they found us, then went back to Black Smoke Mountain to get more."

The woman shivered once, the memory of that horror gripping her.

Brandun pushed through the crowd, entered the circle. His eyes were swollen and red, tears still trickling from them. He shook with anger.

Ahiliyah stepped to him, took his arm. "What happened?"

"I found my mother," Brandun said. "She's dead."

With so many deaths, one more shouldn't have hit hard, but it did. Ahiliyah had known that woman well. It hurt that she was gone, but hurt far more to see the anguish on Brandun's face.

"I'm so sorry," Ahiliyah said.

Brandun sniffed, moved to the spot in the circle where Ahiliyah had just stood. He turned, faced in, left space for her. She understood in an instant—he wanted to stand behind her the same way Drasko stood behind the Margravine.

Ahilyah took her place, feeling strangely comforted that Brandun had her back.

"The second wave of demons," Tinat said, "how many?"

The Margravine shrugged. "I couldn't say. Two hundred? Three hundred? My people ran in all directions. I ran, too. I gathered up as many as I could, and we marched here."

"And brought the demons with you," Preacher Ramirus said. "The blood of our dead stains your hands. Because of *you*, our Margrave is gone. God will punish you."

Suspicious eyes shifted toward the Margravine.

Ahiliyah had had enough. "Ramirus, God doesn't give a fuck about any of this."

"Why are you even speaking?" The preacher glared at her. "You're just a runner."

Ahiliyah curled one finger inward. "Come find out what I am, you worthless shit."

Ramirus took a step toward her. Only one, because the moment he did, Brandun, Councilman Tinat, Councilman Poller and Drasko all took a step toward him.

"We're alive because of her," Brandun said. "And you all know it."

Ramirus glanced at the men, then he took a step back.

"Ahiliyah Cooper is not *just a runner* anymore," the Margravine said. "For the first time in history, humans battled demons, and won. Without her, a thousand more would be dead, the rest of us scattered, hunted as we marched to Biseth and begged to be let in. As of this moment, Ahiliyah Cooper is in command of our army, whatever that army may be."

Solomon Barrow stepped forward again. "Hold on there, Margravine. Our Margrave is gone, and no one elected you to take his place, you... you..."

The Margravine crossed her arms. "Go on, man. Say what you feel."

"You *blasphemer*," Solomon said. "The Margrave warned us about you, about your people and your religion, and look what happened. You showed up, brought the evil with you, and now you think you can seize power here?"

Drasko took a step toward Solomon, but Solomon was not the type to back down—he raised his hammer, shook it.

"I killed a demon with this, Drasko—don't think I won't use it on you."

Councilman Poller stepped between the men, held up his hands.

"*Enough*," he said. "We are in a crisis. Someone has to make decisions, important decisions. Tinat and I are the remaining councilmen. We need to appoint two more, and someone has to replace the Margrave until we can hold proper elections."

Tinat puffed up his chest. "I am the most qualified to take over. I am not only a councilman, I'm also a warrior, and we are at war."

Several heads nodded.

Creen stepped forward. "Tinat, you've been on the council for, what... three months?"

Tinat's face flushed red. "Why is this *boy* speaking? Sit your ass down, Dinashin, or—"

"You'll do *nothing*," Ahiliyah said. She hadn't meant to shout the words, but she had. All eyes turned to her. No one spoke.

"You all think *I* saved you?" She shook her head. "Without Creen's discovery, *all* of you would be dead. Or worse. When he talks, you pay him the damned respect he deserves."

She waited for someone to argue with her. No one did.

Creen gave a theatrical bow. "Thank you, *General* Cooper. As I was saying, while Councilman Tinat's experience is vital to our survival, he's only been in governance for a short time. We need him in the fight to come, which he can't do if he's hiding away in the rear of the lines, being protected like a fragile imbid flower." Creen raised an eyebrow at Tinat. "Or am I wrong, Councilman? Do you need to be protected like an imbid flower?"

Everyone stared at Tinat. Tinat stared at Creen. The big man's fists shook.

"I do not need to be *protected*," he said through clenched teeth.

Creen raised his hands. "You see? We need Tinat as a councilman *and* the great fighter that he is. Which means someone else must lead the hold, and there is only one person here who has that experience." He pointed at the Margravine. "*Her*."

Preacher Ramirus stepped forward. "A *woman*? That's against the law. And she's not even one of us!"

Many heads nodded, Solomon Barrow's among them.

"Fuck that law," Councilman Poller said. "I suppose it's against the law for a humped gish to rule, but if a humped gish had the experience we need I would nominate it as our leader. Liyah is a woman, and without her we would be *gone*. I no longer give a damn what's between a person's legs, I want someone who will keep us alive. The Margravine was smart enough to put General Cooper in charge, and that's good enough for me."

That word, *General*, used twice in fast succession. Poller had used it, too. Ahiliyah could barely process that. It wasn't right—only Sinesh Bishor deserved to be called that name.

"Laws are *laws*," Preacher Ramirus said. "I won't stand for this."

Solomon stepped forward. "Nor will I!"

"Yes, you will," Poller said. "Because the two of you will fill the empty council seats. The very fact that you don't trust her will give us balance. What do you say? Will you both serve Lemeth Hold in the capacity until this crisis has passed, and we can hold elections?"

Ahiliyah knew little of statecraft, but Poller's move impressed her. Ramirus could say no, but would he pass up a chance to actually be *on* the council, instead of advising it?

Ramirus and Solomon exchanged a glance.

"I will shoulder this burden," Ramirus said. "As Poller says, for now, until we can have elections. Solomon, will you join me in this honor?"

Poller smiled a small smile—he'd known exactly what he was doing.

Solomon's face reddened, from embarrassment rather than rage. "Well, I mean, I'm just a foundryman. What do I know of running things?"

"You knew enough to question an outsider taking over," the Margravine said. "Or were you wrong about that?"

So subtle, so easy. If he argued with her, he would go back on his prior outrage. A sharper wit could have easily argued with her, but anyone talking to Solomon knew his strength—like his nephew Brandun—lay not with words.

"Solomon was right in that," Ramirus said. "However, Creen and Poller are also both right. Right now we need experience, *and* we need dedicated Lemethians to make sure the Margravine's rule lasts only as long as this crisis does."

It was amazing to see. In the midst of the corridors running red with blood, in the midst of a living nightmare, Ramirus let himself be manipulated by his naked ambition. But was Ahiliyah acting any different? She was willing to back anyone who would put her in command, because that was the only way she could make sure the demons paid for their evil. At that moment, her words had power, and she would use that power to do what needed to be done.

"Preacher Ramirus is right," Ahiliyah said. "Don't you agree, Solomon?"

Solomon looked like he wanted to be anywhere but there, but to his credit, he nodded.

"Yes, Liyah. He's right. I accept."

The Margravine bowed. "It is settled. Thank you for your trust in me. Now, let us prioritize our repairs, because the demons aren't finished. If they act like they did in Dakatera, in Keflan, there are more of them coming. We should first fix—"

"You made me the military commander," Ahiliyah said. "As such, I need to speak. Now."

The Margravine looked more surprised than upset at the interruption.

"Go ahead, General Cooper. Say your piece."

General. It didn't sound real. What would Sinesh have thought of this? It didn't matter what he would have thought—he was gone. Ahiliyah would fulfill his destiny.

"We should not waste time fixing *anything*," she said. "If we plug the holes, they will dig new ones. My strategy worked because of the corridors. The demons had to come right at our shields, they couldn't flank us." She gestured to the wide-open river cavern. "There are no corridors here. If they come here in numbers, we must go back to the corridors, where we can defend ourselves. But they'll be in there with us as well. Sooner or later, our torches will run out—we'll be trapped in the darkness with them. Sooner or later, they *will* get past our shields."

She took a breath, realized that everyone was looking at her. Not just the circle of important people, everyone along the river. Fifty years ago, Sinesh had shown the world what needed to be done. He had failed, but that didn't mean his idea was wrong.

He'd failed because he hadn't had the right weapon—a weapon Ahiliyah now possessed.

"If we wait here, we die," she said. "There is only *one way* for us to survive. We march to Black Smoke Mountain, and we kill the Demon Mother."

"They *slaughtered* us," Ramirus said. "You want *us* to go to *them*?"

Ahiliyah met his gaze, stared at him until he looked down. She'd saved the hold, not him, and everyone knew it.

"Tinat," she said, "you did a head count of our losses and how many can still fight?"

All eyes turned to the big councilman, his face still red from Creen's comments.

"The count is not yet finalized," Tinat said. "So far, we have five hundred and sixteen dead or missing. Not counting our old, our young, and those badly wounded, we have perhaps a thousand of us that can fight. That includes the Dakateran and Keflanian refugees."

Over five hundred people, dead or gone. From just a few dozen demons?

"The demons are coming back," Ahiliyah said. "Eventually, we won't have enough people to form an army. We must go to the surface and meet them on the ground of our choosing. We must fight *now*, before we don't have enough people to fight at all."

Up and down the plateau, all along the river, she saw heads nodding, saw faces harden. Many people were with her—they had tasted victory over their nightmares, and they wanted more.

"That goes against what you just told us, Liyah," Tinat said, "you—"

"It's *General Cooper*," Councilman Poller said.

Tinat looked annoyed, but he nodded. "Fine. *General*, you said we won because we had walls around us. There are no walls on the surface. They'll flank us and tear us to pieces."

The same problem Sinesh had faced, the same problem *she* had faced when she'd played Sinesh's wargames, but the battles in the corridors had given her the solution.

"They won't flank us," Ahiliyah said.

She picked up Sinesh's box, set it down in the center of the circle. Fighting back a sudden, crushing wave of grief for both Sinesh and Brandun's mother, Ahiliyah took out the game pieces and started setting them up.

"We need everything from the armory," she said. "All weapons, all armor… *everything*. We need to move fast, as we don't know when they will attack next. Gather around, I will show you how we will win. We'll make a phalanx that can't be flanked, because it *has* no flank."

Maybe God *did* give a shit—four hours later, the demons had not yet attacked.

Ahiliyah had given orders. Lemethians, Keflanians and Dakaterans had all rushed to do as she said. They believed in her, believed she was the one who could finally deliver them from the evil that plagued their world. Whether that was true or not, she didn't know, but she wasn't about to let this opportunity slip away. If they didn't fight now, it would be too late.

The Margravine and Tinat worked together to organize the wounded, the old, and the young, sent them—twelve hundred strong—marching north toward Biseth. If the demons attacked them on the way, there was nothing to be done for it, as Ahiliyah needed every fighter she could get.

The best way to protect the helpless was to make a stand on the plains near Lemeth Mountain and defeat the demons on open ground. Fighting on the mountainside wouldn't work—with the rocks and boulders and the slope, her phalanx would be jumbled and broken before the battle even began. The demons' delay had given her the opportunity to choose her terrain, and she was taking advantage of that.

Councilman Poller had overseen the emptying of the armory.

Craftsmyn were hard at work building flat-topped carts to carry the kettles, weapons, bolts, arrows and other supplies.

Creen and Tolio—with the help of many from the factory level—had prepared portable kettles in which they could make more poison. Both of Tolio's parents were missing, taken by the demons along with Chloe Jakobsen, Thomas Picayne, little Debbany, and so many more. Tolio poured his grief into his work. Ahiliyah would have liked to have comforted him, but there was simply too much to do to prepare for the demons.

Ahiliyah had led everyone who wasn't working on those projects down to the foothills. She'd picked her spot—a small hill with steep sides—and told everyone what she needed. They'd cleared trees and bushes, filled in divots to provide for more sure footing, and quickly built a ring of rocks near the hill's crest.

She'd sent runners to scout for the enemy. Jeanna Bouchard, Susannah Albrecht and Brenda Dafydd, all women—*girls*, really—because every man, even small men, were needed in the ranks. Ahiliyah hoped the scouts would all make it back, but doubted that would happen. The demons were fast, and coming in numbers—some of her fellow runners would die.

Atop the hill, in the early afternoon sun, Ahiliyah looked out over her forces. Everyone who hadn't fled, marched to Biseth, or gone out scouting stood in a thick circle around her. Her "army"—barely more than a thousand people.

Even Panda factored into her plan. She'd sent him back up to his observation deck, along with a shield team to protect him in case there were demons up there. Panda's job was to signal Biseth with a request for troops, and with the simple recipe for Creen's goop. Biseth would send that same request on to Takanta, and the Takantans would, hopefully, relay the message to Vinden. The Margravine had also given Panda a message to send, along with a code that proved the message came directly from her. Her message: *Send troops. This is our last chance, our only chance, to beat the demons. Act now, or face eternal night.*

Would any of those holds send troops? Ahiliyah had no idea. Biseth, Takanta and Vinden were about to learn that no hold was safe. Their only chance for survival was to join her in her quest. She had to pray all three holds would answer her call.

It was hard to think of anything they faced as "lucky," but she didn't have another word for the fact that the demons had stayed away long enough for her to choose her terrain and prepare for battle. If they'd attacked en masse while people were coming in and out of the hold, there would have been no chance.

Her people gathered on the hill. So many. And Dakaterans and Keflanians. In all her life, she'd seen *two* people on the surface at any given time. Now there were over a thousand.

If the Margravine was right, if the demons came in numbers, this was the place that the battle would happen. Not even ten warriors had survived—the fight would be won or lost by the citizens of Lemeth. Cooks, miners, metalsmiths, farmers, craftsmyn, the very people who had who had kept the hold alive for fifty years, would now be asked to give everything.

Tinat and Brandun came through the crowd, carrying something. A wooden stepladder?

They opened it, set it up at the very crest of the hill, next to the three barrels of caminus bush goop that would sit at the center of their position. It was more a portable platform than a ladder, with a square-yard top. The wood looked freshly sawn.

"Everyone is here," Tinat said. "Lemeth Hold is empty. All non-combat supplies are set up in a cache near here, as you requested. Hopefully you're right and they won't touch it."

She knew she was right. The demons didn't give a damn about carts, kettles and barrels of food and water. Everything the demons wanted was atop this hill.

Ahiliyah put a hand on the stepladder. "What is this for?"

"You're short," Tinat said. "This will let you see the battle, so you can make adjustments. I suggested Brandun here let you sit on his shoulders, but he insists on being in the front rank."

Ahiliyah didn't want him there—the people there were going to die.

"Brandun," she said, "I would like you to stay back with me. To protect me."

He wouldn't meet her eyes. "No. I need to fight."

He had already done so, and valiantly. Yet there was something off about him. She couldn't worry about that—after the battle in the hold, there was something *off* about everyone.

"As you wish," she said. "Go tell Creen to head up to the signaling station. I want him to help Panda, we have to get word to the other holds. Then come right back."

Brandun nodded, jogged toward the carts.

Tinat looked around at the mass of gathered people, then back to her.

"You need to talk to them, Liyah," he said, quietly. "They're terrified of what's to come."

And she wasn't? "You do it. I'm not much for words. You're a councilman and a warrior."

The way he smiled at her, so sweetly… it melted what was left of her heart.

"That's not how it works," Tinat said. "If you want these people to fight for you, *you* need to talk to them. Many of them won't see the sun set. And you are far better at words than you think. Talk to them." He glanced to the horizon. "And do it fast. I feel we don't have long."

Ahiliyah saw Creen jogging up the slope toward the hold. Panda didn't need help, but she had a bad feeling Creen wouldn't survive this battle—she needed his brain far more than she needed him to fight.

Brandun came running back. Would he be one of those who wouldn't see the sun set?

Ahiliyah climbed the ladder, stood atop it, pleased it felt so stable.

"Everyone, *listen up*," Tinat bellowed. "General Cooper speaks."

More than a thousand faces turned to look at her. They held shields, spears, crossbows, demon forks. Fear on those faces. Fighting in the corridors was one thing—a battle in the open was another. It had to be done. They wanted her to lead? Then lead she would.

"Demons are coming for us." Her words came out too quiet. She paused, louder. "The demons that ruined our world, that slaughtered our people, they are coming to slaughter us. But this time, we are not victims hiding in the dirt. When they come, we will kill them."

The words had sounded good in her head. She'd half expected a roar of agreement, like in the storybooks—she didn't get one.

"Look around you," she said. Everyone did. "The faces you see are the faces of the people who will fight by your side. They need you to be strong and steady, to keep them alive, just as you need them to be strong and steady, to keep *you* alive. Your place in the phalanx isn't about *you*, it is about them. We all fight as one. Listen to the commands of the warriors near you. As they stand firm, so will you."

They were hearing her. The fear on their faces didn't vanish— only an insane person would not be afraid—but it changed, became something she knew they would use.

"They can dig now. There is no longer any place for us to hide. If we run, they will come for us. If we stand firm, I promise you, this is only the beginning. When we win—and we *will* win—we march south, through Bigsby's Pass, across the Boiling Plains, straight to Black Smoke Mountain. We will kill them in their home just as they have killed us in ours. And we *will kill* the Demon Mother. We will end this threat, forever. Ataegina is *ours*, not theirs."

In the quiet, a distant voice echoed out. Ahiliyah looked up to Lemeth Mountain, saw a small, lone figure standing on a ridge. The figure waved a spear, pointed it south. Ahiliyah could just make out the words.

"They... are... coming!"

She recognized the voice... Jeanna Bouchard, one of the scouts.

"They... are... com—"

Her final word echoed across the mountain as a black shape pulled her back, out of sight.

"Phalanx, *form up*," Ahiliyah bellowed. "The time has come to fight!"

39

General Ahiliyah Cooper stood atop her stepladder, staring out over the curved wall of shields and spears. Five ranks deep, she had formed her force into a circle—a phalanx with no flank.

Inside those five ranks, a double circle of archers and crossbowmyn, two hundred strong. The hill's slope allowed them to shoot easily over the spearmen. The archers all had a half-spear at their feet. Once the demons reached the ring, the archers and crossbowmyn would be responsible for killing any demons that somehow made it through—or came over—the five ranks of spearmen.

Behind the archers and crossbowmyn, support personnel, those who would hand out replacement spears, arrows and crossbow bolts, who would pull the wounded out of the ranks, and who, if things went disastrously wrong, would step into the ranks themselves. The Margravine commanded the support personnel, freeing everyone who could hold a shield and spear to fight, freeing Ahiliyah to focus on the battle itself.

"Prepare yourselves," Ahiliyah said. "It won't be long now."

The demons came from the west. Perhaps fifty of them, spiny black shadows of death racing across the foothills, tearing past bushes, ripping through pokey plants, scrambling over rocks. Maybe they had gone up to the hold, found nothing there, and had come running.

Only fifty? Could she be so lucky?

"To the southeast!" The unmistakable, deep voice of Takwan Baines. "More of them!"

Ahiliyah turned, looked—another hundred, at least, ripping down the middle of Bigsby's Pass. Her circle would be tested early, and from two sides.

"Archers," Liyah yelled, "loose at will!"

Arrows and crossbow bolts flew. She realized, while the shafts were still airborne, that she hadn't assigned enough archers or crossbowmyn. The missiles rained down on the oncoming demons—most fell far short or went wide. A few landed amidst the streaking black, but only a few.

"There are too many," Takwan said. "This won't work. We have to run!"

He dropped his shield. He turned, tried to push through the ranks behind him. All around him, people shifted out of position, looked around as if searching for a place to run, to hide. Half of the archers stared at him, unsure if they should fight or flee.

Ahiliyah didn't know what to do. She'd named Takwan a section leader, counting on his experience gathered in commanding reserve troops. There were more sections than warriors, she'd had to assign the civilians she thought could do the job.

Takwan looked out, saw the demons closing in. He again tried to push through those behind him. His panic was infecting the others—the circle was going to break before the demons even arrived.

A fist the size of Ahiliyah's head slammed into Takwan's face. The man sagged, fell to one knee, his left hand flat on the ground.

Tinat stood over him. The councilman lowered his spear, held the blade inches from Takwan's throat.

"Get back to your position!" Tinat's voice was a roar, so loud it made Ahiliyah flinch. "Get to your position or *I'll kill you here and now!*" Tinat snapped out a foot, kicking Takwan in the ribs. Takwan whimpered and fell to his side. He covered up, hands in front of his face, knees to his chest, but Tinat wasn't done—the councilman kicked him again.

"Get up! Get back in line!"

Ahiliyah observed many things at once: the demons, now so close she saw their gleaming teeth; Takwan's face, smeared with blood; Tinat's wide back as he landed a second kick on the fat man; people looking at Tinat and not the oncoming enemy; Callow Winden, also panicking, trying to push his way back through the ranks, his sons Abrams and Duvall trying to stop him, to shove him back into place; the black streaks of intermittent arrows and bolts flying toward the oncoming enemy.

Everything was happening so fast, so much faster than it ever had in drill.

Tinat kicked Takwan again, in the head this time. The fat man fell limp—Tinat pushed through the ranks, picked up Takwan's dropped shield. The councilman knelt, held the shield in front of him atop the ring of stone, angled his spear over his shield.

"All right, you black bastards," he bellowed. "Come and get it! *Lock and raise shields*!"

Before the battle, it had been Ahiliyah's words that resonated. Now, with the demons seconds away, the people of Ataegina responded to Councilman Tinat, to demon-killer Tinat.

A fast cacophony of bronze on bronze sounded as the front rank's shields overlapped. Then the second rank clanked their shields down over the front. The third rank followed, their shields angled back. Finally, the fourth rank raised their shields high, almost parallel to the ground.

Through every tiny space in the shields, long spears jutted out—a ring of poison death waiting for its victims.

The first demon reached the circle, jaws open wide, black hands reaching out. It impaled itself on Tinat's spear, making the wood shaft vibrate. The beast let out an ear-splitting screech, tried to pull away, but the one trailing it slammed into its back, driving the first further onto the blade. The second one slid off, tried to come around fast.

Someone angled a demon fork, thrust the center tine into the beast's gut. The monster came on anyway, hands reaching out, but the shaft held—talons slashed at empty air.

The rest of the demons hit like a wave of midnight splashing against a shore of painted bronze. Black talons slashed at shields, tried to yank them away. Tailspikes slammed against metal. Spears thrust out, pulled back, thrust out again.

Spear shafts snapped. People screamed. Bodies tumbled backward.

The other demon wave crashed into the ring on the opposite side. Ahiliyah watched as the demons spread out, just as Sinesh had said they would. But there was no edge for them to find, no corner to turn.

A demon leapt through the air, trying to launch itself over the front ranks, only to impale itself on angled spears. The beast seemed to hover in midair, legs kicking, tail whipping, claws slashing at the wood, tearing free splinters until the shafts snapped. The beast fell. Wounded, spilling burning blood, it tried to rise, but met its end when the half-spears of a dozen archers sliced through it, pinning it to the ground.

All around her, over a thousand human beings fought for their lives.

"Hold strong," she called out. *"The poison will cut them down soon!"*

She turned in place, watching the battle, saw a spot where the circle had bent inward, demons clawing at metal and flesh alike. Abrams Winden fell back, his stomach torn apart, his hands clutching pinkish curls of intestine. A demon stood over him, two spear blades jammed into its side, some people trying to stab it, other flailing to get away from it. The rear ranks behind Abrams backed away instead of surging forward.

If the ring broke…

Ahiliyah drew her spearhead from its scabbard. She leapt off her stepladder.

"Fill the gaps!" She rushed the demon. It saw her coming, swung a claw at her. She stopped short, raised her blade—the demon's wrist hit the edge, and the black hand spun away. The severed stump gushed burning blood, on her, on Abrams, on the men around him.

Ahiliyah felt her skin burning even as the blood sizzled into ash.

The beast lashed out with its tailspike, plunging into the forehead of another man.

A spear jammed through the demon's neck. It stiffened, momentarily frozen. Ahiliyah lunged toward the nightmare, drove her spearhead straight into its open mouth, saw the blade-tip crack through the top of its black head. The demon sagged, fell on top of Abrams, whose face smoked with streaks of burning blood.

At a glance, Ahiliyah saw two more demons barreling toward the hole in the circle. The men on Abrams's left were pinned down by swinging, biting, whipping demons—they couldn't step sideways to fill the open space.

Ahiliyah dropped her spearhead, scrambled over the smoking Abrams and the twitching demon. A spear… she grabbed it, planted her foot behind the butt-spike, angled the point up.

For an instant, there was only her single spear, wooden shaft and sizzling metal point aimed out, aimed straight at the two demons already reaching for her, their jaws wide, so close that she could see their toothtongues in the back of their open mouths.

Then, like strands of rivergrass waving in the current, a half-dozen spears swung into place alongside hers as her people packed in around her—she was no longer one, single person. She was a single claw in a wall of longer-taloned fingers.

The first demon sprang high.

Ahiliyah saw it arc up, front and rear claws both extended—it landed on the spearpoints that angled up from behind her, three blades punching deep into the cracking black shell. The beast shuddered, making the wooden shafts wobble—a claw lashed out, snapping a shaft in half.

Burning blood spilled down on her, but shoulder to shoulder with her people she could not move. As the second demon rushed in, Ahiliyah squeezed tight the wooden shaft and roared, her lips curling back like those of the demons.

At the last instant, the demon tried to twist its way through, but there were too many spearpoints angled to meet it. One caught it in the shoulder, a glancing blow that tore through black shell and green flesh, then the full force of the beast drove home as Ahiliyah's spear point punched into its chest, so hard that she saw the spear shaft bend upward in the center, warping the coupling—wood shattered, leaving her with half a weapon.

The beast fell to the ground, jagged shaft sticking out of its chest, but still it tried to attack, trying to rip the spear out of its chest with one hand as it dug its toes into the soft earth and came toward her, sliding on its own blood across sizzling, smoking grass.

"*Shields*," a voice roared—Brandun's voice. "*Fill the gap!*"

Suddenly, he was there, stepping in front of her, kneeling, his shield filling the gap. Someone grabbed Ahiliyah, pushed her stumbling backward, away from the front rank, even as shields clanged home around Brandun's anchoring presence. Ahiliyah tripped, fell backward over the bodies of Abrams and the demon that had killed him. The leaves on her hands and knees sizzled against dirt soaked with burning blood.

A frozen moment—sitting on her butt, she saw the backs of her people, the ring of smoking bronze that back reflected back screams of pain, of rage, of hate, of death. The dull *gongs* of claws and tails and teeth slamming against bronze, the squeals and screeches of the demons trying to force their way in.

All through the ring, smoke rose up like a fog, carrying with it the stench of scorched dirt, burning flesh, and her own singed hair.

Ahiliyah scrambled to her feet. She rushed to the top of the hill, skirting the screaming wounded, moving around the dead demons that had gotten through only to be finished off by the archers, past the support personnel who slathered fresh goop on bleeding wounds, who handed forward fresh spears and shields.

Ahiliyah reached her stepladder—up she went, quickly turning to survey the battle.

All around the phalanx, the twitching bodies and still husks of demons, a black ring surrounding a jewel of battered bronze. She was shocked to see that most of the demons were dead or dying, their twitching convulsions ended by butt-spikes driven through their black skulls.

The ring had held.

A few demons fought on, their movements so slow that they quickly fell to the thrusts of multiple spears. Others staggered around, seeming almost drunk.

Ahiliyah looked down the hill, searched for bending grass, hoping there were no fresh demons rushing toward her and her people. She saw only one... and it was running away, a good fifty yards off, staggering through the tall grass.

"Brandun! Tinat! We have to catch that one!"

She again jumped off the stepladder. She grabbed the first weapon she saw—a halfspear, and sprinted toward the phalanx ring. Brandun was faster than she was, stepping in front of her with a hand up to slow her, stop her.

"You can't go out there, General," he said. "It's not safe. I'll catch it. It's got three bolts in it—why didn't it die as fast as the one I shot in the crevasse?"

Ahiliyah shook her head. "I don't know. We'll have to ask Creen about that."

The demon moved in a herky-jerky fashion, stumbling left, pausing, then moving forward and to the right. It paused again. The long black head angled up, as if it was looking to the sky for help.

"I've had my problems with Creen," Brandun said, "but right now, I want to kiss him."

"Go make sure it's dead first." Ahiliyah glanced around to see who was still standing. "Will Pankour, Ruslan Porter, go with Brandun, then all three of you get back here right away."

Brandun jogged out from the circle, waited for the two men to catch up with him, then closed in on the still-twitching beast.

Ahiliyah slowly turned in place, unable to believe that it was over. There had to be more demons. But if so, where were they? The sun shone overhead, leaving no deep shadows in which to hide. As far as she could see, from the mountains to the trees… no movement.

Tinat walked up to her, a bandage wet with gleaming caminus goop pressed to his left cheek. He held a similar bandage in his hand, pressed it to her head. She hadn't realized her skin was still burning there, not until she felt the instant cooling, until she heard the slight hiss of thinned acid turning to ash.

"You did it, General," Tinat said. "We beat the bastards! I have something for you." He reached into his webbing, pulled out a toothtongue. It was scored down the middle, a long, angled gash that had cracked the shell. "It's from the one you stabbed in the fucking face. Be careful with it, I don't think all the blood is out of it yet."

She took it from him, stared at it as if it wasn't real. Her *third* toothtongue.

Only a day ago, there had been but three toothtongue trophies in all of Lemeth Hold. Now there were well over a hundred. She and Tinat wouldn't be the only ones wearing the enemy around their necks.

"That was… horrible," she said. "Is it over?"

Tinat shook his head. "The fighting is, at least for the moment, but we have more to do."

He gestured to the people lying on the bloodstained ground—some moaning, some screaming. More than Ahiliyah could count. Had Creen survived? Had Tolio? She found she couldn't bear the thought of losing either of them. She focused, instead, on Tinat.

"We have wounded," he said. "And those who aren't dead yet, but will be before the sun sets. Gisilfred is getting me a tally of the demon dead." The big man put his left fist to his sternum. "By your leave, General, I'll see to preparing for a possible counter-attack."

He wasn't telling her what to do—he was asking for her permission.

"All right," she said.

Tinat strode away, barking orders to the others.

A hammer of fatigue slammed into her. She wobbled, had to adjust her feet to keep from falling. Her head throbbed, her skin felt hot. How close had she come to death? She'd been right on the front line, facing a wall of nightmares, yet she'd stood strong—she hadn't run.

Ahiliyah saw men and women staring at her. They'd seen Tinat's show of respect. The expressions on their faces—if any of them had doubted her leadership before the battle began, they doubted no more.

Her gaze fell upon the body of Abrams Winden. Duvall stood over him, spear in his hand, blade pointing straight up, butt-spike on the ground. And, kneeling over Abrams, shoulders shaking with sobs, his father, Callow Winden. Ahiliyah walked to them, knelt down on the other side of the body. Someone had dragged the dead demon away.

Abrams's face was a stinking mess of melted flesh. He'd been hit by far more burning blood than his thick coat of caminus leaves and smear of goop could stop. Parts of his guts clung to the frayed rope of his torn hidey suit.

"I'm sorry your son is gone," Ahiliyah said. "He died defending the hold."

Had those words sounded good in her head? Spoken out loud, they sounded idiotic.

Callow looked at her, his red eyes streaming tears. "It's my fault," he said. "He tried to stop me from running... because of that he wasn't ready, he..."

Deep, chest-wracking sobs cut off Callow's words. He fell atop his son, and wailed.

Ahiliyah felt herself crying. For Abrams? For Duvall and Callow? Maybe for all three. Callow had tried to run. Abrams had stopped him, yet Abrams was dead while Callow didn't have a scratch on him.

It wasn't fair. *None* of it was. And yet there was no time for forgiveness. She reached up, cupped the back of Callow's head.

"Next time, don't run," she said. "Or it will be Duvall crying over *your* death."

Her words brought fresh howls from the man. Ahiliyah hoped he'd learned his lesson, because the next time he broke ranks and tried to run, she would follow Tinat's example—she would kill Callow herself.

She would not let cowards stop her.

Nothing would stop her from getting to the Demon Mother.

40

"He'll survive," the Margravine said. "He is strong."

Ahiliyah watched her wipe a goop-covered cloth over Tolio's horrid wounds, neutralizing the last of the burning blood. He had served the hold and paid a powerful price. A tail or a claw had sliced through his right bicep. There was no way he could again hold a spear or draw a bowstring. As if that wasn't enough, a thick gout of burning blood had hit him in the face, enough of it splashing through caminus leaves and hidey-suit rope to overwhelm the goop smeared on his face. His eyeball had burst. The socket was a mess of burned, swollen flesh. Through the worst burns, she could see a spot of his skull, and another of his cheekbone.

"I'm sorry," Tolio said. "I fought as hard as I could."

Ahiliyah kissed his lips. "I know. Don't apologize. Margravine, give us a moment?"

The old woman looked as spent as Ahiliyah felt, but, like Ahiliyah, she would not stop. She stood, her knees cracking audibly as she did, and walked away without a word.

Ahiliyah stroked Tolio's hair, gently sweeping it from his sweat-soaked forehead.

She felt drained. Tinat, Brandun and the other warriors had given her this quiet moment, organizing the removal of the dead and forming the surviving forces into a tighter circle formation atop the hill. Shields and spears were close at hand. Some people lay on their backs, recovering. Others shook uncontrollably, some alone, some held by friends or family.

People with minor wounds were tended to where they were. For major wounds, though—both those who might survive, and those who clearly would not—Ahiliyah had ordered them carried on stretchers back to the Bitigan River inside the hold. Their constant screams had been demoralizing to the others—removing them was critical to keeping order, to stop people from running away.

A few *had* run, slipping off in the confusion that followed the battle, or carrying wounded into the hold only to run when they had a chance to flee. Those people were damned. Ahiliyah felt shame for wishing that demons found them. To run wasn't just individual cowardice, it cheated her out of another fighter. Every spear mattered.

"I can still fight," Tolio said, forcing his words through the pain. "I'll fight to avenge my parents. I will fight for *you*, my love. I will die for you."

Wounded, almost mortally so, and yet he refused to stop. While others ran and thought only of themselves, Tolio was willing to give everything for his hold. How had she ever doubted her feelings for this man? Seeing him hurt so badly, with injuries that he would carry for the rest of his life… something inside of her *changed*. In that instant, she knew what she wanted, and knew it wasn't some temporary thing.

"I'm afraid your fighting is done," she said. "You'll go to Biseth with the other wounded."

He started to protest, she put a finger to his lips.

"Tolio, my love, I need you to recover. Because when this is over, when we've won, I'm ready to have a family with you."

His one good eye stared up at her. His pain seemed to fade for a moment.

"If I'd known all it would take was an eye, I would have cut it out myself ages ago," he said. "I love you, Liyah."

This time, her response came instantly, effortlessly. "And I love you, Tolio."

He reached up, cupped her cheek. "Fight on. Kill the Demon Mother. Come home to me."

His pain returned all at once, scrunching his face into a mask of agony.

Ahiliyah kissed him again, quickly, once on the mouth, once on the forehead, then she left him there. Would he make it to Biseth? She didn't know. He might die on his own, or demons might get him on the way. She could not worry about him, not now.

She had a war to win.

Gisilfred and Tinat came jogging toward her. Ahiliyah tried to center herself. She had to appear strong, unbroken. People were looking at her differently now, like she was a hero. No one needed to explain it to her—she was the army, and the army was her. If she showed weakness, if she showed doubt, all could be lost before the next battle even began.

Tinat was no longer smiling. "Tell the General the count."

"General," Gisilfred said, "we killed one hundred and sixty-seven demons."

He opened his mouth to say something else, shut it. He didn't want to say what came next.

"Tell her all of it," Tinat said. "Liyah is no wilting flower. Tell her."

Gisilfred swallowed. "We have seventy-four dead. One hundred and eight injured to the point where they can no longer fight. And… twenty-seven missing in action."

Missing in action. A nice, polite phrase for those who had run away.

"We won, but at such a cost," Tinat said. "Do we still march on Black Smoke Mountain?"

Ahiliyah glanced around the hill. Most of those remaining were able and willing to fight, but she'd lost twenty percent of her forces. Only a handful of her remaining forces were trained warriors. The rest were smiths and farmers, cooks and craftsmyn—how long until they realized that anew?

"Maybe this was all the demons there were," Gisilfred said. "As far as we know, we just wiped them out."

Ahiliyah knew she had been lucky so far—or blessed—but there were limits to both things.

"Keflan, Jantal, Dakatera and Lemeth," Tinat said. "Many were carried off. If the Demon Mother magicked them all into black beasts, there could be *thousands* of them waiting for us just past the Boiling Plains."

If so, her people would die soon. If they waited, they would die later.

"We march," she said. "We won't stop until the Demon Mother is dead."

Tinat shook his head. "You can't make that decision alone. Not now, not with the losses we took. Gisilfred, gather the council, *now*."

Gisilfred ran off before Ahiliyah could say a word. Her anger flared.

"Tinat, don't be stupid. Ramirus and Solomon are on the council now. What if they sway the Margravine to say *no*?"

Tinat smiled. "You didn't mind when your little friend Creen started the power play that made you the commander. And I didn't hear you object when adding Ramirus and Solomon to the Council sealed the deal. I respect you, Liyah, but your ability to understand what's happening on a battlefield is far better than your ability to understand politics." He glanced to the afternoon sky. "So much has happened this day, and we still have hours before sunset. Come to the Council, General, and make your case. We will see what happens."

While Ahiliyah had played a part in it, she still wasn't sure how the Margravine had seized power. It seemed obvious that the woman intended to keep it. At the top of the hill, the Margravine was seated on a severed demon head, as if the hated enemy that had killed thousands was to her nothing more than a convenient stool. Those around her—Poller, Tinat, Preacher Ramirus and Solomon Barrow, still in their hidey suits with hoods down, sat on stones. Drasko stood behind the

Margravine, his arms crossed. One empty rock was obviously meant for Liyah.

Poller ran a whetstone over a spearhead; as Liyah sat, he didn't bother to look up from that work, continued on with the steady *snick, snick, snick* of stone on bronze

"Congratulations, General," the Margravine said. "Now we must decide what comes next."

Ahiliyah couldn't miss the irony—in a hold where women weren't allowed to hold power or serve as warriors, women had become the political and military leaders. How long would that last? She didn't know, and it didn't matter—she needed to lead only long enough to kill the Demon Mother and end her evil grip on Ataegina.

"We know what must come next," Ahiliyah said. "We march through Bigsby's Pass, to the Boiling Plains, and across them to Black Smoke Mountain. We will kill the Demon Mother."

Solomon Barrow fidgeted uncomfortably. "Liyah, we know we are alive because of you, but we have lost so many. Our people are hurt, they are tired, they are frightened. How much more can you ask of them?"

Ahiliyah glanced to the Margravine; she said nothing. No expression on her face. Would the woman back what needed to be done?

"We should march with our wounded back to Biseth," Preacher Ramirus said. "We could catch up to the young and old and those wounded in the initial attack, provide them protection. There could be more demons hunting them, we just don't know. Once we all reach Biseth, perhaps we can rally them to join our cause."

By *rally* what he meant was *find walls to hide behind*. The man was a disgrace to humanity. Ahiliyah never should have gone along with putting him on the Council.

"We march on Black Smoke Mountain," Ahiliyah said. "We kill the Demon Mother."

She would repeat it as many times as it took. The time for cowardice, for self-protection, had passed. People would die, of that there was no doubt. The question was, would anyone *survive*? With Ahiliyah's way, at least there was a chance.

"We need support from the other holds," Tinat said. "We can't do this alone. No word from our signalmyn yet."

Poller stopped sharpening. "Can we send runners? Most of our scouts made it back alive."

Did these people know nothing of the realities of running?

"We're looking at *five days*, minimum, to get word to and back from Takanta," Ahiliyah said. "Add another three or four days on top of that for word from Vinden. We can't wait here for days on end. If we are to win, we must move *now*."

Drasko stepped forward. "May I speak?"

The Margravine nodded.

"In my youth, I fought on the plains with the Bisethians and the Takantans against Northern raiders," he said. "The Bisethians are worthless, but Takantans are highly trained and well equipped. Better than us by far, I'll admit. Their archers and crossbowmyn are fast and accurate, the best in the world. If General Tasker is still there, they are well led. If we can wait for them, we should."

Ahiliyah felt embarrassed that she hadn't thought to ask about the *quality* of the troops from other holds. "And the Vindenians?"

"Their forces are comparable to ours," Tinat said. "If they send anyone at all."

"I believe they will, if we can reach them," the Margravine said. "Decades ago, they sent troops to join Sinesh. It's been many years since I visited either of those holds, but from what I know of them, once they learn of Creen's poison, they will realize this is their last opportunity to be rid of the demons."

Solomon tilted his head. "Margravine, *you* have been to those holds? Personally?"

"I have not always been in this wrinkled body." The Margravine reached her left hand inside her hidey suit. She grabbed the right shoulder of her dress, and with one yank, ripped the tattered fabric down, exposing her skin—and the sixteen faded slashes there. "In my youth, I was the best runner on the planet."

How different she was from the Margrave.

"If we wait, the demons can attack us again," Ahiliyah said. "If we lose another two hundred people, what we have left won't be worth marching at all. We must go *now*."

Ramirus shook his head. "Madness. If we wait, some of our

wounded will recover enough to fight. We can see if the other holds will join, *and* have more of our own."

The councilmen traded glances—they thought Ramirus made sense.

Ahiliyah tried to control her anger. "You must listen to me. The demons—"

A shout rose up from the base of the hill. There, she saw Panda and Creen, rushing up the slope toward her. When they reached her, they could barely breathe.

"*General* Cooper," Creen said, chest heaving, "we have good news! Panda, tell her."

Panda sucked in air. His face made him seem more pained than the people on the hill nursing actual wounds.

"We got word... from Biseth, they... they aren't sending troops, but they got word from Takanta. The Takantans are already on their way to help! Fifteen... fifteen hundred troops. And a thousand from Vinden as well!"

Hope surged through Ahiliyah, and vindication. "Where are they to meet us?"

"North of the Great Geyser," Panda said. "On the Boiling Plains."

She would march on Black Smoke Mountain with an army of *three thousand*.

"We will leave immediately," she said. "If we push hard, we can set up a defensive ring for the night, then march at first light and be at the Boiling Plains by mid-afternoon."

Ramirus held up his hands. "Hold on, we haven't decided anything yet, we—"

"Our *allies* are marching," Ahiliyah said. "Marching to join us, at our request. The decision is already made, Preacher. Run along to Biseth if you are afraid, but the rest of us are going to war. Councilman Tinat, gather the unit leaders. Creen, come with me."

She turned, walked down the hill. She didn't need to wait to hear the Council's decision. Now they had no choice—Ahiliyah was taking the battle to the demons.

Creen jogged to her side.

"Some of the demons lived a long time after getting cut," Ahiliyah said. "Why?"

He glanced around, took in the piles of dead—demon and human alike. "We're making the stuff as fast as we can. Out here I don't have the same level of control I did in my lab. Maybe the poison quality isn't as consistent. They'll all still die. It might take some longer than others."

"And while they live, they attack. We're marching immediately. Can you fix the problem?"

He rubbed his face. "We'll be brewing batches on the back of moving carts, Liyah. More variables. I don't know if I can fix it."

She stopped, grabbed his shoulder.

"*Figure it out*," she said. "Every minute a wounded demon keeps going is another minute where our people die. Our strategy depends on the poison working perfectly."

He stared at her, wide-eyed. "You won't get perfection out here. I'll do my best."

Frustration mounted, but she would not wait. She had to press her advantage.

"Don't let me down, Creen," she said. "You and Panda now make poison full-time."

She pushed him away, then stormed off to get her troops ready to march.

41

It had been fifty years since so many people had walked along the shores of Lake Mip. Fifty years since so many people had walked *anywhere* on the surface of Ataegina. For all that time humanity had been hiding away from a superior killer; from a stronger, faster, deadlier enemy.

Ahiliyah marched at the head of a column of crimson, a column eight hundred people strong. Mostly Lemethians, but Dakaterans and Keflanians as well. Every fighter wore a hidey suit thick with caminus leaves. Each spearman wore a bronze chestplate over a padded shirt. Along with bronze helmets and shields, the spearmen were as well-equipped as any army that had ever marched on Ataegina. They each carried a warrior spear and two spearheads, knowing the spearheads would sizzle away to nothing if there was more burning blood than a smear of Creen's goop could neutralize.

Plenty of weapons, plenty of armor. Ahiliyah wondered what kind of war King Paul had envisioned to store away so much.

She wore a chestplate as well, one that Crag Halden had modified for her, hammering it down to her smaller size. It was heavier than she liked, the leather shoulder straps that connected the front and back pieces digging into her shoulders, but considering what was to come, she would bear the weight and not complain. She hadn't decided about the helmet yet—after years of surviving because she could see everything around her, cutting off most of her vision seemed stupid, despite the protection she was giving up.

As for the shield… well, fuck the heavy thing. She would command the battle from her stepladder, not be in the ranks. The breastplate slowed her enough as it was.

There was a battle coming. Would it take place on the Boiling Plains? Closer to Black Smoke Mountain? Or in the tunnels below the mountain itself?

She would soon find out.

The column was ten people wide, eighty ranks deep. The first person in each rank acted as a unit leader. Most unit leaders were trained warriors but, as there weren't enough of them left alive, Ahiliyah had promoted those who had fought well in the hilltop battle, in the corridors of Lemeth Hold, or both—Councilman Poller, Councilman Barrow, and Nicole Mason among them.

People took turns pulling the three carts, one with the last of the replacement spears, shields and armor from the armory, one with barrels of food and water, and one topped with bronze shields turned into portable fire pits, boiling kettles above them in which Creen and Panda worked tirelessly to turn caminus leaves into demon poison.

As the column marched, they trained, constantly reviewing the signals that would be given, talking about the order of ranks, how to shrink the circle if too many people died, and who was responsible for what. There was no yelling, no screaming, no threats… there wasn't time for that. Nor was there a need. After Hilltop, no one had any illusions about what was to come. Everyone knew the stakes—victory or extinction.

The march along the shore of Lake Mip and into the pass that led to the Boiling Plains was so much easier than the hazardous mountain treks she'd become accustomed to as a runner. Every step fell on flat, solid ground… even at a steady march, it felt like she was sprinting.

Could this army of bakers, brewers, foundrymyn, cobblers, mushroom farmers, this army of young and old… could they win again? But they weren't civilians anymore, not really. Regardless of their past, they were *all* fighters now.

The strength of the phalanx is the spearman, the strength of the spearman is the phalanx.

She'd sent runners out ahead to scout. Just as with the Battle of Hilltop, she knew some of them would not make it back. She tried not to focus on that, instead centering her thoughts around the Margravine's words: *don't think of the ones you lost, think of the ones you saved.*

All the countless wargames with Sinesh. Training for the inevitable, perhaps. Anyone else could have led this war, a dozen leaders at a dozen times could have realized there was no hope in hiding away. But none did. Only Ahiliyah, backed by the Margravine.

And it had taken a slaughter to make this happen.

If only someone had realized this inevitability sooner, when thousands more people were alive, when hundreds of warriors hadn't already been killed.

None of that mattered now.

This was the army she had, and she was marching it to battle.

One way or another, everything would change.

42

Say one thing for her ancestors—when it came to naming things, they had been quite literal.

In the distance, Black Smoke Mountain belched a long, thin column of black smoke into the sky. All around Ahiliyah, the Boiling Plains bubbled with mud and intermittently spurted jets of steaming water. Some surged only to knee height before dying down, while others gushed up liquid pillars taller than three men standing on each other's shoulders.

The air had grown hot, and not just from the noonday sun—here, like in the depths of Lemeth Hold, the ground itself kicked out heat. While she had never seen the Great Geyser for herself—her one run to Takanta had followed the northern range above Lake Mip—others, including the Margravine, had, and assured her that when it let loose, there was no missing it.

Her column of eight hundred fighters marched across mostly dead ground, ground as black and rough as the demons themselves. Creen had taken a break from his cart, come to the head of the column and told her the cracked black surface was lava flows, which he described as *rivers of fire*. She asked if they would see any such rivers before reaching Black Smoke Mountain. Creen had said he hoped not, then returned to his poison-making duties.

The small geysers were a sight to behold. She was grateful for the chance to see such beauty before she died. Some geysers were nothing more than muddy holes in the ground that bubbled like soup. The larger ones spouted from ragged cones of various sizes—the bigger the geyser, the bigger the cone. All of them, cones and mud alike, *sparkled*, both from thick mineral deposits laid down over centuries, and from the water itself, which seemed to glow like the water of the Bitigan River. She found herself wishing she had arrived at night—in the darkness, what a sight these glowing plains would be.

The ground began to rumble.

Ahiliyah halted the column. She heard murmurs of fear from her fighters.

The Margravine—and her ever-present shadow, Drasko—came quickly to the front. She was smiling, her old face as cracked as the volcanic ground on which they stood.

"Don't be afraid," she said, waving her arms to the column to get everyone's attention. "Look south, toward Black Smoke Mountain, and you will see why it is called the *Great Geyser*."

Seconds later, Ahiliyah understood.

Perhaps half a mile away, the ground spit forth an impossibly tall jet of boiling water. Clouds of steam billowed from it, catching the afternoon sun. The water itself glowed with a bluish hue—a color that quickly faded. After only a minute, perhaps, the column of water died down. As the cloud it had birthed settled, Ahiliyah saw the gorgeous glow of a rainbow.

"I guess we're in the right place," she said.

The Margravine nodded. "Flat for miles. The Takantans will see us, to be sure."

If they came. Ahiliyah remained prepared to continue the fight without them. There was no going back, not now, not when she was this close.

She scanned the horizon, looking for any sign of forces from the other holds. Black Smoke Mountain was an hour's march away. Perhaps a little more, perhaps a little less.

Tinat and Brandun jogged up to meet her.

"The troops need rest and water," Tinat said. "If we're stopping, it's a good time for both."

Ahiliyah knew she should have thought of that. People were exhausted from the hot march.

"Get everyone into our circle formation," she said. "Spears and shields ready to be picked up at a moment's notice. One unit at a time can go to the water and food cart. We're close enough that demons could be on us fast."

Tinat nodded. "Each unit should post a lookout. Maybe fifteen yards out from the ring?"

"Do it," Ahiliyah said.

Brandun and Tinat jogged away, both like thick, moving caminus bushes, calling out orders that were quickly picked up and repeated by unit leaders. The ring formation formed, clumsily but quickly. Ahiliyah saw her people taking off helmets, resting shields on the cracked black ground, then sitting down. There were a few minor gaps—no one wanted to sit in mud.

Creen ran to her, a wooden mug of water in one hand, a hunk of bread in the other.

"A general has to eat," he said.

She took a big bite of bread, washed it down with water. She didn't know if Creen had any idea of what was coming next.

"There's nowhere to put you and Panda this time," she said. "You'll have to fight."

He glanced down. "I told you, I can't."

Sweat sheened his face. His hidey suit hung on him, caminus leaves limp and rope heavy from water absorbed from standing over the boiling pots. She loved him. She loved a lot of people who weren't around anymore.

"If you don't fight, you'll die," she said.

He shrugged. "We're all going to die anyway."

Ahiliyah cupped a hand under his chin, forced him to look at her.

"If I can do it, so can you," she said. "Don't disappoint me. And don't you *dare* run. You understand? I'll have to kill you myself if you do."

He forced a smile. "You can be one intense bitch. Anyone ever tell you that?"

"Only the people who won't stand and fight."

Creen huffed, shook his head.

Excited shouts rose up from behind them.

"*Ahiliyah*," Tinat called, "to the west!"

She looked west, and her heart surged. Across the shimmering heat of the black plain came a long column of people, spears raised high. Their polished, unpainted shields and helmets blazed in the afternoon sun. At the front, a man carrying a pole bearing the flapping standard of a green bow atop a field of caminus-leaf crimson.

The Takantans.

Cheers rose up from the circle formation.

Ahiliyah turned on them, furious. "Shut up! Be silent, you idiots!"

Unit leaders picked up her orders, understood her fear. They shushed their people. In an instant, the cheers died down, but the hopeful smiles did not. Ahiliyah couldn't blame them—*fifteen hundred* Takantans. And soon, another thousand Vindenians.

They were going to win. The Demon Mother would die. Humanity would be free.

Ahiliyah waved for Brandun and Tinat to join her. Both men came at a jog.

"Brandun, get some people and carry three barrels of poison to the Takantans, fast," she said. Brandun jogged back to the troops.

"That leaves us with only one barrel," Tinat said. "That's not much of a reserve."

Ahiliyah nodded. "Our troops have their personal ration. Creen is making more. We need the Takantans provisioned with poison in case the demons attack. Let's welcome our new ally."

They jogged toward the Takantans. Her chestplate felt heavier than ever. As they jogged, she glanced toward the smoking mountain. On the plain of black rock and steam, all seemed still.

"The Takantans are noisy bastards," Tinat said. "They sound like a thousand-legged beast."

Their in-step marching was loud, nerve-wrackingly so. It filled Ahiliyah with anxiety. This close to Black Smoke Mountain, if there were demons, they couldn't miss the sound.

The Takantans wore caminus-leaf-lined hidey suits, but as she approached, she saw the suits were of poor quality, cobbled together on short notice. Some weren't hidey suits at all, just normal clothes with bush branches jammed through cut holes. Ahiliyah's initial thrill at seeing so many warriors ebbed, slightly—those suits would provide little protection, and there were no caminus bushes on the Boiling Plains.

As a whole, though, the Takantans looked far more capable than her own force did. Almost all of the soldiers were good-sized men, armed with bronze shields, helmets and long pikes, even longer than the warrior's spears her people carried.

"Those have to be six meters long," she said. "Can they even use those effectively?"

"They can," Tinat said. "I've seen Takantans in action. They know what they're doing."

Ahiliyah and Tinat reached the column. A thickly built soldier stepped forward. Ahiliyah didn't realize the soldier was a woman until she bellowed out an order. The order echoed back through the ranks. Three unified steps later, fifteen hundred troops stopped as one.

In the wake of their footsteps, Ahiliyah heard a light wind whistle across the desolate Boiling Plains, heard the faint puff of a distant geyser.

"That's Tasker," Tinat said. "Older than I remember, but aren't we all?"

The woman strode forward, alone. She was thick with muscle beneath a coat of chain mail thickly threaded with crimson caminus leaves. She had a bow and a quiver slung across her back, a sword scabbard at her side. Her metal helmet had bush-leaf net pulled taut over the top and the sides—jutting from the helmet forehead, a bronzed toothtongue.

"I'm Anette Tasker, commander of the Takantan forces." She squinted her bright blue eyes, making the pronounced wrinkles at the corners furrow deeply. "I recognize you, from the campaign against the Northerners. Vinus Tinat, is it?"

Tinat smiled. "Good to see you again, General. And this—" Tinat gestured to Ahiliyah "—is General Ahiliyah Cooper, leader of the Lemethian garrison."

Tasker's gaze flicked from Ahiliyah's eyes to the three toothtongues resting on the netting over Ahiliyah's chestplate.

"So it's true," Tasker said. "A *girl* in command. No wonder your hold fell."

Why would Tasker, of all people, be so dismissive of another woman commander? Ahiliyah then understood—Tasker was judging on *age*, not gender.

"This *girl* drove the demons out of our hold," Ahiliyah said. "Then led the force that defeated over a *hundred and fifty* demons. How many have you defeated, General Tasker?"

Ahiliyah had faced down demons—she would not flinch at the bigger woman's glare.

"Hard to believe," Tasker said. She sighed. "But if Herriet validates it, I suppose it's true."

Ahiliyah glanced back to her people. The Margravine stood there, watching but not interfering, Drasko right behind her.

"The Margravine," Ahiliyah said. "You know her?"

Tasker nodded, her expression solemn. "Forty years ago, Takanta suffered a crippling outbreak of forgetter's syndrome. Hundreds died.

Thousands were sick. We didn't have enough labor to farm, to maintain the hold. My mother was ill, and pregnant with me."

The woman took off her helmet, revealing sweat-matted, gray-streaked black hair. She stared over Ahiliyah, stared at the Margravine.

"It was only a decade after the Rising—demons were everywhere, all around Lake Mip. Takanta was cut off from Keflan, which meant it was also cut off from Dakatera, from Dakatera's plinton fruit. Our runners tried to get there, to save our hold, but they all vanished. My father was one of them. He died trying to save my mother and me. When Herriet found out what was happening, she demanded her hold send runners. The Dakateran leaders refused, so she made the run herself—six times—carrying half her weight in plinton fruit each time. The best part is, Herriet had already completed her obligatory ten runs. She volunteered because she knew the route better than anyone else, because she knew she could save lives."

Running had once been mandatory in Dakatera, as it had been in Lemeth? When had that changed? Ahiliyah suspected it had ended when the Margravine came into power. Herriet Lumos had volunteered for extra runs, just as Ahiliyah had planned to do. Was it any wonder, then, that the Margravine had tried to lure Ahiliyah away from Lemeth?

"Takanta has not forgotten," Tasker said. "Our current Margrave, and our entire council, is alive because of her. As am I. Keflan, Jantal, Dakatera and Lemeth have fallen. The demons will come for us next. If Herriet Lumos says you have demon poison, that attacking now is the only way to save our hold, we believe her. We came because of her message."

Brandun and some of the other men walked past, set three barrels down before the Takantan column.

"That's the poison," Ahiliyah said. "Distribute it as quickly as you can. Make sure your people have enough to apply a thin coat to every blade, arrowheads included."

Tasker turned, pointed to the barrels. Takantan unit leaders barked orders. Soldiers quickly formed three fast-moving lines, one for each barrel. Each passing soldier dipped a small cup to scoop out a portion of goop. Fifteen hundred troops, and it would take only a few minutes for all of them to pass by the barrels. Ahiliyah couldn't help but be impressed by their organization.

Tasker stared at the barrels, doubt on her face. "I've seen a demon bristling with *twenty* arrows, and it kept coming. Is it true that, with the poison, a single arrow can kill one?"

Ahiliyah quickly told her of killing the demon in the crevasse, how Brandun's bolt had eventually killed it, of the Keflanian crossbowmen on Lemeth's deck, and how she'd learned from misusing her own archers and crossbowmen at the Battle of Hilltop.

"I hope your archers are more accurate," Ahiliyah said. "How many in your force?"

Tasker snorted out a laugh. "Takantans are born with a bow in their hands. Every warrior with me carries one, and every one of us can fire twelve shafts a minute."

"So *fast*," Tinat said. "Fifteen hundred of you, that's... that's..."

Tasker nodded. "Eighteen *thousand* shafts in a single minute."

Ahiliyah felt a surprising surge of hope that she might not only win, but also live to tell of it. As the Takantans passed by the barrels, armor and weapons creating a uniform, soft metallic rattle, their unit leaders spread them out in a long line six ranks deep.

"Form your phalanx into a circle," Ahiliyah said. "The poison doesn't work instantly, as I told you. If the demons come out to fight, some of them *will* reach us."

Tasker gave her a sidelong glance. "Girl, if my men are in a circle, then only *half* of them can see their targets. I don't think you understand what our concentrated fire can do. As we like to say, when the real fighting begins, why burden yourself with the weight of an unused arrow?"

Deep in her chest, Ahiliyah felt a sinking sensation. She glanced at Tinat, and it was clear he felt the same thing. He took a half-step closer to Tasker, drawing her attention.

"That works with people," Tinat said, "but the demons are far faster. You haven't seen demons attack in large numbers like we have. Ahiliyah's formation is proven, it will..."

His words trailed off as shouts of alarm rose from the Lemethian formation. People there were quickly getting to their feet, grabbing spears and shields—and pointing south.

Ahiliyah looked toward Black Smoke Mountain. For a moment, she couldn't process what she saw—the black plains, shimmering from the heat… were they… *moving*?

The image crystalized, and her belly turned to ice. In the distance, demons streaked across the plain. *Hundreds* of them, far more than she'd faced at Hilltop Battle, pouring forth toward her like a sheet of black water, sunlight gleaming off long heads and hard bodies.

Ahiliyah grabbed Tasker's arm. "Make a circle, or die," she said, then she sprinted for her troops, Tinat at her side.

Behind them, Tasker shouted commands.

Ahead, Brandun and the other warriors were screaming orders, calling the Lemethian archers and crossbowmyn into ranks in front of the quickly forming ring. Arrows nocked, crossbows cocked, sunlight reflected off scratches in bronze helmets and shields.

"Archers, coordinated fire," Ahiliyah called out. As she sprinted, she again looked south, saw that the demons had halved the distance, a moving puddle of black on black. Not hundreds of them, *thousands.*

She and Tinat reached the front circle as her archers let loose the first volley. A thin stream of arrows arced up into the air, flying toward the oncoming horde.

Ahiliyah heard Tasker's bellowing order, then her single-word command echoed by the deep voices of her unit leaders.

"Loose!"

A thousand Takantan bowstrings let go at once. A storm of arrows raced out from the long phalanx, like a hunting cloud that darkened the blue sky. The first volley hadn't even reached the demons before the Takantans sent a second volley arcing after it.

The crashing wave of missiles rained on the onrushing sea of gleaming black, a demon horde so thick that if any of them fell, Ahiliyah couldn't see them drop.

So *fast*—thirty seconds until they arrived, maybe less.

"Archers," Tinat called out, "loose, then to the center!"

The Lemethian bowstrings snapped, sending up another cluster of arrows that seemed pitiful compared to the continuing blizzard of Takantan shafts. The archers didn't wait to see the results—they turned and sprinted to the circle. Shields turned sideways as the ranks made space for the sprinting archers. Ahiliyah, Tinat and Brandun followed them in.

Brandun and Tinat banked away, ran to their units. Ahiliyah ran past an inner ring of spears that lay on the ground, spearheads pointed out, placed there in case she had to contract the circle during battle. The food cart, equipment cart and goop-making cart sat in the center of the formation, lined up side by side. Creen and Panda were atop the goop cart, positioning Ahiliyah's stepladder. Nowhere for the boys to hide away, this time—if the circle collapsed, they'd be in the same shit as everyone else.

Ahiliyah ran for the cart, saw Susannah Albrecht there, in her hidey suit like everyone else, nocking an arrow onto a bowstring.

"Susannah, to me," Ahiliyah said as she scrambled onto the cart and up the stepladder. She quickly turned in place, looking for problem areas, and realized how much smaller this circle looked compared to the last fight.

"Yes, General?" Susannah looked up, face blanched with fear.

Ahiliyah knelt on her small platform. "Run northwest, get clear of this battle, then track west. Find the Vindenians. Tell them to hurry."

Susannah glanced north. "Run… alone, General? With the demons coming?"

"You can do it," Ahiliyah said. "You're fast, aren't you?"

Susannah's expression hardened. "The fastest."

Ahiliyah slapped her shoulder. "Go, now!"

The girl dropped the bow and arrow, took off like an arrow herself. She wove through the ranks and headed northwest.

Ahiliyah stood, looked southeast, looked at the approaching horror.

"*They're coming to us,*" she shouted. "Shields, *up!*"

A deafening clang of bronze on bronze. Section commanders called for the ranks to lower. All around the circle, terrified but determined Lemethians, Dakaterans, and Keflanians readied their weapons. The spears of the first two ranks pointed straight out, horizontal to the broken black ground. The third rank's angled up at fifteen degrees, the fourth's at forty-five degrees. In an instant, her troops became an armored ring bristling with poisoned points.

The demon horde rushed closer.

Another dense volley of Takantan arrows landed. This time, Ahiliyah did see demons fall. Trailing behind the flowing black wave, she saw hundreds of stragglers limping or crawling along, hundreds more flat on the volcanic plain, thrashing in agony.

Ahiliyah realized she hadn't grabbed her helmet. Too late now. She looked east, to the horizon, hoping beyond hope that she might see a cloud of dust, the waving banners of a thousand Vindenians, arriving just in time.

Nothing—if they were coming, this fight would be over long before they got here.

The demon wave split, half flowing toward the circle, half flowing toward the long Takantan phalanx. They would reach the Takantans first. Ahiliyah could only watch.

"Liyah!" She looked down, saw Panda, eyes wide with fear, offering up an assembled spear. Creen was in front of him, cowering behind a shield that seemed bigger than he was. Instead of drawing her spearhead from her back scabbard, Liyah took the weapon Panda offered. Panda then ducked behind Creen's shield, his shaking hands starting to assemble another spear.

Ahiliyah rested the butt-spike on the stepladder's platform, then looked to the Takantans.

Like a single, living creature, fifteen hundred archers slung their bows. In a great, coordinated dance, they reached down, grabbed shields and spears. The spears pointed straight up as a wall of metal formed. Ahiliyah heard the distant shouts of orders—the *entire line* angled so that it would be perpendicular to the point of the demon wave.

Another muted command: spears lowered, first row, then second, pointing straight out, then the increasing angles of the third, fourth and fifth. Maybe Tasker knew what she was doing. Maybe it would work.

The black wave crashed against the Takantan phalanx, the first demons impaling themselves. Some wooden shafts snapped, but most held. The beasts behind the frontrunners crashed in as well, some trying to push through their brethren, some climbing up over them, most spreading out along the phalanx's length. Some leapt high, trying and failing to arc over the top. All along the line, claws, tails and teeth punished hard bronze, while spears in the second and third rows thrust forward and back through the wall of shields.

"*Here they come!*" Brandun, tearing Ahiliyah's attention away from the Takantans. The other half of the demons closed in on the Lemethian circle. She had a moment to see that many of the ebony monsters bristled with feathered arrow shafts, then the flood smashed against her ring, flowed *up* the angled shields, *around* the circumference.

So many... at least three times the number they had faced at the Battle of Hilltop.

At the initial point of impact, she saw the ring start to bend inward.

She pointed her spear to the spot. "Archer groups one through four, *reinforce!*"

Perhaps her people had become more seasoned by a pair of clashes, or knew the that smallest error could kill them all, but either way, eighty archers rushed toward the besieged spot, leaned against the backs of their comrades, legs pushing hard against the black surface. Their weight made an instant difference—the ring un-dented, moved back to its original range.

A single turn told her that the demons had completely encircled her circular phalanx. She shook a fist in morbid satisfaction. Instead of hammering on one spot, the demons had thinned their strength by surrounding the circle.

Spears thrust, talons clawed, spearheads stabbed, tailspikes slashed, shields slammed, teeth bit. All around the circumference, humans roared in rage or screamed in pain and panic, demons screeched and squealed, metal clanged. Blood—bright red and burning green—flew. The stench of scorched rope and flesh rose. People and demons died.

She saw her ring thinning in spots, and saw that the remaining reserve of archers were furiously trying to finish off wounded demons that had made it over the top. There was no one left to bolster the weak areas.

Ahiliyah drew in a deep breath, let it out with all that she had.

"*On my mark, push out, then backward to second position!*"

The warriors and unit leaders echoed the command even as they fought for their lives, for the lives of their family and friends, for the future of their hold.

"Three! Two! One! MARK!"

A combined human roar as hundreds of battered, smoking shields pushed out, knocking the demons back. As unit leaders screamed, the spearmen quickly shuffled backward, greatly contracting the circle. In an instant, hands dropped battered, broken and melted spears, picked up the fresh ones that had been laid down earlier. Ahiliyah had a moment to see dozens—possibly hundreds—of her people lying where they had fallen, some still twitching or crying out, then the demons closed the gap. Shields locked down and spears leveled a moment before the black wave again slammed into the ring of bronze.

Those that hadn't been able to step back were lost. Their screams didn't last long.

Movement on her right. She turned in time to see a demon launch itself high off the back of another with two spears driven through its chest. The beast arced toward her, clawed hands extended, silver teeth open wide. A spear thrust up into its chest as someone below caught it in mid-flight. The demon screeched. It shivered, stuck there for a moment, up in the air, then it lashed against the shaft, snapping the wood—the black body smashed onto the cart, rattling her stepladder.

The wounded demon scrambled to rise, but Panda was there, both hands on a short spear, driving the butt-spike into the long head. Bronze cracked through the black shell. The beast stiffened, and its tailspike flashed in, driving through Panda's throat.

Panda's hands spasmed. He let go of the spear, which tilted to the side. Blood sprayed from his wound. Ahiliyah heard Creen cry out. Panda fell—Ahiliyah forced herself back to the battle.

Death and chaos all around… but the circle was holding. The demons were thinning, their corpses stacking up before the wall of sizzling, melting shields. She blocked out all thoughts of friends and future, focused on what she saw—victory, or defeat, would be a close thing.

From her high position, she looked over the wall to the Takantan phalanx. It had thinned but still held strong, fighting up and down the length of a line of stacked, broken bodies, human and demon alike. The Takantans battled bravely, shield to shield, giving as good as they got, but the true threat wasn't the enemy bashing away at their shields.

Then, sickened, unable to do anything about it, she saw several dozen demons peel away from her circle. The group rushed toward the phalanx's right flank, barely twenty-five yards away. The Takantan commanders there saw the demons coming, screamed a command that made the end of the line pivot backward, making an "L" shape to try and fend off the onslaught. Against a human enemy, it would have worked, but while a dozen demons crashed headlong into that new front, the rest simply sprinted around it. Some curled inward, slashing at the back of the L, while others sprinted past and attacked the rear of the thinning main line.

The Takantan right collapsed almost instantly. What had been an orderly, disciplined wall of fighters disintegrated. Spears designed to hit the enemy from a long distance were hard to turn, and by the time they did demons were already well past the spearheads. Murderous beasts raged, claws and tails rending flesh down to the bone. The phalanx seemed to hold for one last, desperate moment, then it broke, and the rout was on. Takantans panicked—many dropped their spears and ran. Ahiliyah saw Tasker, standing there bravely, her face a warrior's mask of fury as she shouted at her men to fall in around her.

She went down under a leaping demon.

Some demons gave chase, slashing at backs and legs, cutting men down before pouncing on them to finish them off. Most of the demons, though, ignored the fleeing Takantans—instead, they merged into a tight pack and came straight back toward the Lemethian circle. A few of the beasts slowed, wobbled, Creen's poison finally catching up to them.

Some fell, but not enough.

Liyah looked around her circle, knowing all was lost, searching for a way to save her people. Her phalanx had thinned, almost broken in spots. Around the cart, broken spears, dead archers next to demons in spreading puddles of burning blood that sizzled when it expanded against puddles of red blood, the few remaining archers desperately fighting wounded, twitching beasts. So many *screams*, people crying out, gurgling, begging.

Maybe three hundred of her people were still fighting. She had to tighten the circle. If she did, she could make a dome of shields, try and hold on until the wounded demons died, then kill those that remained. It could work, it *had* to work.

"*On my mark!*" Her throat ached from screaming, from inhaling the fumes of burning blood. "*Push out, then backward five steps!*"

She waited for the warriors and unit leaders to echo the call—none did. She saw Tinat, using the edge of his shield to bash in a demon's head. Brandun, hole-ridden shield high on his shoulder, a screeching demon perched atop it. Will Pankour, on his back, dead eyes staring up.

Ahiliyah had to make her people listen, had to contract the circle. She started to scream the order again—then saw the demons that had slaughtered the Takantan line crash into her withering ranks. The few spears still angled up wavered this way and that. Ahiliyah watched, horrified and helpless, as demons leapt high, and there were no spears left to catch them. The beasts landed on their feet, instantly cut down screaming archers, turned and tore into the backs of the spearmen holding the line. Tumalo Ramirus went down.

Journay Barrow fell back, blood spraying from the cobbler's severed leg, and the first gap appeared. In the blink of an eye, a demon rushed through, brought down the tall warrior Galen Yates. The gap widened.

Spear in hand, Ahiliyah jumped from the stepladder to the cart bed, and saw Creen, tucked up under the stepladder, shaking madly. She leapt off the cart, rushed the gap, drove her spear into the back of a demon that was tearing Shalim Aniketos's blond-haired head from his body. The demon screeched, tried to turn toward her.

"*Close the line,*" she screamed. "*Close the—*"

A demon slammed into her, knocking her into the center of the collapsing circle. She landed on a body—human or demon, she didn't know—and rolled, tried to get to her feet. As she did, she saw the circle collapse. Andrey Baines fell, his legs slashed out from under him. Benji Johnson dropped his spear and ran, as did others.

Ahiliyah looked for a weapon. She saw a demon fork smeared with red blood, the shaft broken in the middle. She reached for it—something hit her from behind, driving her face-first onto the hard black ground. Dazed, blinking, she rolled to her back.

A demon landed on her chest. She knew she was dead.

A scream—more pure terror than battle cry—that Ahiliyah wasn't sure came from a man or a woman. The tines of the demon fork jammed into the demon's midsection, the blade penetrating, but not deep enough to do any real damage. Burning blood sputtered out, some sizzling on the bronze, some splashing against Ahiliyah. The demon's long head snapped up, looked away from Ahiliyah. A long arm lashed out. Ahiliyah glanced up and back just in time to see the black talons slash Creen's face.

The boy cried out—no question that this one was a scream, one of agony—and Creen dropped the demon fork, fell back, his hands at his face.

Ahiliyah had a selfish moment to think *go after him, take him not me* then the moment was gone. She tried to twist away. The demon reacted, long hands grabbing her shoulders, slamming her into the ground so forcefully her head smacked off the hard surface.

The beast's lips curled back, a gleeful smile of death. Jaws opened. The demon hissed, metal teeth glinting in the sun.

A shield flashed in the sun—the edge drove halfway through the side of the demon's head, knocking the beast to the side amidst a wild spray of yellow blood. A gout landed on Ahiliyah, some sizzling against her hidey suit, some against the goop still smeared on her face, some landing on spots of unprotected skin.

The shield yanked back, the leading edge already dripping, melting, smoking. Ahiliyah looked up to see Brandun, spots on his face sizzling, a snarl on his mouth just as primitive as those of the demons. Fifteen years old, and a boy no more—this day, he would die as a man.

Brandun kept the dripping shield, reached down with his right hand, grabbed the chest of Ahiliyah's still-burning hidey suit and hauled her to her feet. He turned, backed up against her, the shield protecting them both. Ahiliyah turned, back to back with him, saw Creen on the ground, rolling slightly, his face a sheet of blood. She grabbed his feet, dragged him closer. He scrambled to rise, managed to get to one knee.

Brandun pulled the demon fork from the still-twitching beast. He stood back to back with Ahiliyah and Creen. Smoke rose from them all, blood dripped from them all. The three of them had started this war. How fitting they would be together when it was lost.

The circle had shattered. She saw people dying, people running, demons dragging away the unconscious, the wounded. Every demon was wounded in one way or another, some with cuts from spears, most with arrows sticking out of them. Some tried to give chase to fleeing people, but the demons were slowed, seemed to understand their human prey was now too fast for them.

In the near distance, Ahiliyah saw the back of Drasko, the Margravine held in his arms. She hoped they would both get away.

An arrow-riddled demon crept closer. Brandun rotated to face it, but another rose up from the still-twitching body of Rinik Brennus, crouched low and crept closer.

Death all around. Piles of crumpled and twitching black mixed in among the ravaged, smoking human corpses. There were perhaps ten demons remaining—the heads of all of them turned toward Ahiliyah, Brandun and Creen.

"So close," Brandun said, grunting out the words. "We came so close."

Ahiliyah felt at her hip—inside her suit, her little friend remained in its sheath.

"They're all wounded, but there's too many of them," she said. "We need to kill ourselves before—"

Screeching, squealing and hissing, the demons flooded in. Ahiliyah reached into her suit to draw her knife. Creen's high-pitched scream. Brandun's growl of rage. Something slammed her backward. She landed hard, tried to scramble to her hands and knees only to be hit from the side so hard it knocked the breath out of her.

She had failed. Failed her friends, failed her people, failed Sinesh.

Ahiliyah opened her eyes to see the blur of a snapping toothtongue. She heard more than felt the impact.

Blackness swarmed—was *everything* black here?—then dragged her down into nothing.

43

Falling. Falling over rough ground. No... sliding across it.

Ahiliyah woke slowly. She woke to pain. Darkness. Something pulling on her left wrist. She wasn't sliding—she was being dragged.

Everything hurt. Her skin felt raw and ripped, hot in places as if someone held burning coals against it. Her muscles ached, every bit of her bruised and beaten. Rocks digging into her legs, her feet, her right shoulder. The hiss of dirt grinding against the bronze of her chestplate. So *weak*... she couldn't move, couldn't react.

Ahiliyah tried to opening her eyes. Her right eye refused. It throbbed, felt swollen shut. The left eye half opened, lids thick and dry and sticking to each other. Through the half-open slit, she saw heavy shadow dotted with strange bits of faintly glowing dark blue.

Night had fallen. The sound of her body being dragged reflected back to her, told her she was in a corridor. The blue light... glowjars? Broken glowpipes? Lemeth Hold didn't have blue light... which hold did? Humid here. And hot, as hot as Creen's lab.

The ground beneath her seemed to change, slightly. Parts of it seemed smoother, she slid faster. The sound of metal grinding lightly on metal.

Her shoulder screamed like her arm might rip out of the socket. Whoever held her wrist held it too tightly. Brandun? His grip felt hard, as if he was wearing an armored glove.

The stink hit her. Shit and piss. Wet rocks and moss. And something else, something thick—the stench of death, like she'd smelled in Keflan Hold.

Moaning sounds. Cries of pain. Coming closer. She was hurt, Brandun was dragging her to lie with the rest of the wounded. More of the blue haze. Not quite enough to see. The moans sounded closer, the smell of death grew worse, then both faded away, slightly, as if Brandun had dragged her past the wounded, leaving them behind.

The low groan of a man in pain, right next to her. Barely visible in the faint blue glow, she saw a man. Solomon Barrow? Limp, like her, his body sliding along.

Between Solomon and her, the feet of the person dragging them both. Not feet... not *human* feet... black, bony, claws for toenails...

Fractured pieces of the battle came back to her. The ring collapsing, demons swarming in.

Her body lurched to the left. That stench again, and the pained moans, lost groans of people battered just like her. More impressions of that faint blue glow, bits of it on the floor she was dragged across, soft hints of it in the air above her, in a mist that swirled with movement.

In a room of some kind. Black walls, gnarled and bumpy, some parts glowing that soft, deep blue. In the darkness, she saw the dim outlines of people leaning against the chamber wall. No, not *against* the walls—*in* them. Black growths across their arms, their legs, their chests, plastering them to the walls, holding them in place.

Her demon dragged her toward something sticking up from the floor, something... *egg-shaped* that lit the mist around it like a faded glowjar, a bit brighter blue than the wet walls or puddle-strewn floor. The glow came from *within* the egg-shape, showed the thinness of the opaque, leathery surface. As Ahiliyah slid past, she thought she saw a shadow inside it *move.*

Strong, hard hands lifted her like the limp ragdoll that she was. Ahiliyah pulled against the hands, found that some of her strength had returned. She tried to turn, to kick—her head smashed against the wall, making her already dark world spin with globs of fuzzy black and dark grey.

The demon roughly raised her right hand high, pressed her against the wall. The wall felt oddly lumpy, and the *stink*... even worse than her fractured memories of Keflan.

"The leaves." The voice, weak but familiar—*Creen*. "Liyah, Brandun ... eat the leaves."

She blinked, tried to get her wits. The voice had come from her right. Her head throbbing, she turned to look. Next to her, dead eyes staring out from an emaciated face. Faint blue light gleamed from droplets condensed on a white beard.

Margrave Aulus Darby.

His chest... ripped open, as if something inside of him had *popped.* Chunks of sagging, rotting flesh, stubs of hard, broken bone.

"The leaves." Creen, weakly calling through the dim light. "Eat... the leaves."

Something cold and wet on her right arm, the one held against the wall.

Ahiliyah fought against the thudding agony in her head, looked through the darkness, past the corpse of the Margrave—two demons there, tall and dangerous, both *part* of the shadows rather than in them. The demons held someone against the wall.

Creen. Dim blue light played off his pale, small face. He was... chewing?

One of the demons holding Creen bent down, started doing something to the boy's feet. Creen didn't struggle, didn't fight back... he turned his head, raised his shoulder, bit at the caminus bush branches woven into his hidey suit. He twisted his head, pulled leaves free, kept chewing as he bit down again to get more.

He'd gone mad. She wished she was mad, wished she was dead, that this wasn't happening to her. Where had Solomon gone? Was Brandun dead?

Ahiliyah felt her left arm yanked high. Through her hidey suit, she felt that same cold wetness there, like the demon was slathering it with clay or mud. The beast was right on top of her, so close to her face the scent of moss and stone almost overpowered the reek of decay. She couldn't look at it—she turned her head, looked left.

Someone there, encased in the wall. A Takantan. His chest armor lay in a battered pile on the chamber's wet, black floor. How strange. His undershirt remained, sweat-stained and dotted with blood. Something on his face, covering his eyes and mouth, something that reminded her of Sinesh's gnarled, withered body...

A spider. Eight long legs—four on each side—wrapped around the back of his head, a long tail coiled around his neck. The spider's sides swelled and receded.

Eat the leaves. The spiders. The Margrave's chest. Creen, the smartest person in the world. The caminus bush poison. *Eat the leaves*.

Ahiliyah craned her head, ignoring the pain in her neck and shoulder. Her face brushed against the leaves of her hidey suit. She opened her mouth, felt the leaves on her lips and tongue. She bit some off, chewed, tasted how bitter they were. The smell of them reminded her of home, of Lemeth, of steaming cups of tea, of Tolio.

Cold wetness on her thighs. Ahiliyah couldn't bring herself look at the nightmare in front of her. She did the only thing she could do: bite off leaves, chew, swallow.

Darkness, swarming over her, engulfing her, dragging her under. Ahiliyah fought against it, thought of how the Margrave must have felt when his chest exploded.

Hard hands cinched down on her ankles. Ahiliyah couldn't stop the moan of fear, couldn't stop her bladder from letting go. Tears came, unstoppable. Deep sobs shook her. She kept biting, kept chewing, kept swallowing.

She heard the ripping of twine, felt long fingers sliding between her chestplate and her body. Another hard tug, and another, the sound of leather straps breaking, then a rush of cool air against her sweat-soaked padding. A clang of metal. She waited for the talons to slice through her.

The cut never came.

Ahiliyah opened her eye. The demons were gone. If they were still in the chamber, she couldn't see them through the darkness and hanging mist. Her hands remained above her head. She tried to move them, found they barely moved at all. The clay or mud was like thick leather. She could feel it hardening. She redoubled her efforts. The material at her left wrist seemed to stretch, slightly, then her muscles gave out.

A man's voice, softly begging for God to save him—Preacher Ramirus, somewhere past the spider eggs on the far side of the chamber.

Ahiliyah felt a rumbling beneath her feet, in the walls around her. A tremor of some kind, perhaps. The tremor faded, then vanished, leaving her in blue-tinged darkness.

Fatigue hung on her, pulling her head down. She had nothing left with which to fight. She would die here, in the darkness and stink. The faint blue light dimmed, and all went dark.

She snapped awake, lost for an instant before pain pounded her from the inside out. She couldn't move. Hands and legs, bound. Panic clawed at her—she pulled hard, *harder*, felt the mud on her left wrist crack, giving ever so slightly. She tried to reposition herself, to shift her weight and pull harder still, when a strange sound froze her in place.

A brief, hollow, muffled rattling sound, like something moving inside a drum.

The sound came from a faintly luminous egg, only a yard away from her. Notches on top, two lines crossing, like four slices of pie meeting at the peak, crusts pursing like pouting lips. The egg's pale glow lit up the mist around it. Roots of some kind, stretching out from the bottom of the egg, stretching across the flat floor. Those roots crossed others, some leading to another egg, on her left, in front of the man who'd had the spider on his face. The four pie slices of that egg were peeled back—the egg was hollow inside. Water gathered in the bottom, glowing blue.

The spider had fallen off the man. It lay on the floor, near the man's mud-encased feet. The spider didn't move. It looked dead.

The hollow drum sound again. In front of her, in the glow of the egg, something quivered. Pie-flaps curled back, snot strings stretching from edge to edge. In the blue glow, the flaps' now-exposed undersides looked like raw vootervert steak, lined with white gristle.

A choking sound to her right. Creen, pinned to the wall, jerking and thrashing, a spider on his face, its legs wrapped around his head. Creen's fingers stretched out, closed. His left foot, the only part of him not bound, twisted left and right, toe pointed up, then kicked down.

In front of Creen, an open, hollow egg.

Ahiliyah shook in fear. She stared at the open egg in front of her, helpless, waiting.

From inside, a single, wet, bone-thin limb reached up. The trembling limb's tip tapped at the disgusting, meaty pie-flap, testing, exploring. It slid back, out of sight, then more delicate legs wiggled out, slick with blue wetness, a hand of evil pushing forth from a fleshy sleeve.

"God, *please*," someone whispered.

That someone was her.

Newborn legs twitching, the spider crawled out of the egg, pale skin glowing wet-blue.

The spider sprang. Ahiliyah saw thin skin stretched taut between reaching legs, then all went dark as cold flesh slapped against her face.

The legs stretched around her head, pulled the wet beast tight against her closed eyes, her cheeks, her forehead, her *mouth*.

The Margrave's chest… the spider wanted to put a demon *inside* her. Ahiliyah clamped her teeth tight. Something shoved her lips apart, until she felt that cold flesh against her gums. She thrashed, pulled at the bonds pinning her wrists, felt them cracking again, stretching…

The spider's cold tail wrapped around her neck.

Blind, bound, terrified beyond any sanity, Ahiliyah started to scream, stopped herself, kept her teeth clamped shut. The tail tightened. She thrashed harder, *pulled* harder, felt her own muscles tearing from the effort. No air. Her lungs began to burn. She saw black spots even though her eyes were covered, heard a roaring sound that came from inside her head.

She almost blacked out, fought her way back.

Ahiliyah fought against the urge to breathe, tried to yank feet and hands free. The cold noose cinched tighter. Her mouth betrayed her, opened to draw a breath—something hooked under her upper teeth, over her lower teeth, cranked her mouth open so wide she thought her jaw would snap. Something cold and firm pushed across her tongue to the back of her mouth. Ahiliyah gagged as it forced its way down her throat.

The noose constricted again.

As darkness finally took her, Ahiliyah Cooper thought she felt that cold something sliding all the way down into her chest…

44

Her chest burned.

Ahiliyah woke. Her eyes felt dry. Sticky. She lifted her head, blinked. Her right eye opened halfway, ached like she'd been punched. Exhaustion and sleep clung to her, clouded her, but she knew where she was—and she knew she was fucked.

Her throat, so sore she could barely swallow. A rancid taste in her mouth.

Across the dark room, someone cried out, a clipped, staccato scream of deep agony.

She looked toward the sound, was surprised she could see through the blue fog to the other side of the dark chamber. Her eyes had fully adjusted. Men and women were glued to the walls, encased in that semi-translucent demon mud. Just like she was.

A man lifted his head—Preacher Ramirus. He was crying, tears reflecting the faint blue light coming off the walls, ceiling and floor. His head was the only thing he *could* move. One hand glued by his hip, the other up above his head as if he were waving *hello*, dry mud holding him in place. Like her, his chestplate had been torn away, dropped in a useless pile on the chamber floor. Atop the chestplate, limp and flat against the bronze, an unmoving spider.

Ahiliyah looked down—at her feet, another spider, on its back, legs curled upward. It was dead. It had served its purpose.

A loud *cracking* sound drew her attention back to Ramirus. He shuddered, lurched against his unforgiving bonds. His head thrashed this way and that. He froze, stared out, wide-eyed, his body shivering. Another *crack*—his padded shirt tented out at the sternum, sank back, as if someone had rammed a spear through his spine then jerked it free.

In that spot, a black stain of blood began to spread.

Ahiliyah had an instant to tell herself this wasn't happening, that she was imagining this, that it was a bad dream and she was in her room in Lemeth Hold, that it wouldn't happen to her, *couldn't* happen to her.

The preacher's chest tented out again with a sound like breaking branches. The bloody padded shirt tore. Something *stuck out* of him, a pale worm streaked with dark wetness. Preacher Tumalo Ramirus made one final sound, a small cough with almost no air behind it.

The worm—abhorrent, repulsive, smooth head unmistakably like those of the demons—slid from the blood-soaked fabric. It fell to the ground, vanished among the faintly glowing eggs.

The preacher's left eye twitched. His head dropped. He did not move.

The sound of something small sliding through a thin puddle, then silence.

Ahiliyah trembled. Trapped, with a demon inside her. The spider, the worm... she was going to die, horribly, just like Ramirus had, like the Margrave had.

She would never see Tolio again.

Why had God allowed this to happen? Hundreds of thousands of deaths, each day a struggle against starvation, disease, her people hiding away in the dirt like insects, watching the last of civilization fade away... hadn't there been enough suffering?

Ahiliyah had done nothing but serve her hold, risk her life over and over again to make a difference. What had *she* done to deserve this? Nothing. She'd done nothing.

She could pray for salvation, for deliverance. Would her prayers be answered when even the preacher's were ignored? No, she would not beg to a deity that didn't give a damn.

Ahiliyah felt the flutter of an old friend—hatred blossomed, fought for space against the fear that consumed her. Hatred for the demons. Hatred for the god that had let this happen.

"God, if you're listening... go fuck yourself."

From her right, a weak but familiar voice.

"Not... helpful," Creen said.

Something about knowing he was there, knowing that a spider had violated him just as one had violated her, that he would soon die like Ramirus had, like *she* would... it broke the last splinters of Ahiliyah's will. Tears came, then sobs.

"Liyah, I'm so sorry." No snotty tone this time. None of the defiance that defined him. "I thought the leaves might... I don't know. I don't know.

"It's not your fault," she said, whispering even though there was no point in staying quiet. "It's not—"

She gagged, couldn't breathe. That burning in her chest... so *bad*. Not just in her chest, in her stomach as well, like a smoldering ember scorching her from the inside out.

"Liyah? *Liyah?*"

Bile in her abused throat, a throat locked as tight as if the spider's tail was still cinching tight around it. Her stomach clenched. Her mouth hung open, spit dangling.

Her belly convulsed—she was about to throw up. Her body lurched, hard, pulling her against the unforgiving mud. Something at her right wrist crackled, gave… she could move her arm a little more, but not enough to pull free.

Ahiliyah managed a fraction of a ragged breath, until a tickle at the base of her throat brought another constricting gag. That tickle rose, a fist pushing up, blocking any air.

Inside her neck, down her chest, something started to *wriggle*.

Tears in her scrunched eyes, she had to swallow but could not. She heard her heart in her ears, felt her pulse slamming through her neck and face and brain. Her stomach contracted again, driving the thing squirming inside her up through her throat to press down against her tongue, up against the roof of her mouth. It burned oh god it *burned* she couldn't breathe…

The fist pushed past her teeth, dangled there while still all the way down her throat. She gagged again, vomited, and felt the horrid thing slide up and out of her.

Ahiliyah sucked in a lungful of air. She coughed. The world spun. Another gasping breath, then another. Bile in her mouth. She blinked tears, tried to spit only to have strands of saliva and thick, burning fluid hang from her quivering lips.

Chest heaving, she looked down—there, by her trapped feet, a white worm, thinner than the one that had killed Preacher Ramirus. The worm looked misshapen… *melted*, like a candle burned from all sides at once. The creature twitched, quivered, then fell still.

This room of horrors… it was closing in on her. Maybe she was already dead. Maybe she'd died out on the battlefield, and this was hell. She was trapped here with the rotting dead, forever.

"Creen," she said, wincing at the pain in her throat. "What just happened to me?"

He didn't answer.

Ahiliyah leaned her head forward, looked past the Margrave's corpse. She saw Creen, lurching, his one free foot kicking. His jaw opened wide, *too* wide—a white thing slid forth…

…it stopped, filling his mouth. He was suffocating.

The hate and rage inside her rose up, possessed her—she would not let her friend die.

Ahiliyah pulled with her arms, her chest, her stomach, tried to bring her thighs up, anything to fight the mud pinning her wrists. She had to get to Creen. She yanked harder, relaxed, yanked again, over and over in a violent, stop-start motion that made muscle tear, that made bones feel like they were about to break.

The mud holding her right wrist crackled again… it started to give. She pulled, pushed, harder and harder, twisted and yanked, flexed and thrashed.

Creen made a choking sound; the motionless thing remained lodged in his open mouth.

Ahiliyah's muscles screamed at her to stop. She pulled harder and harder and harder, heard the mud crackle—her right hand ripped free.

Her little friend…

Ahiliyah reached to her hip, knowing it wouldn't be there, knowing she'd be too late to save Creen—her hand wrapped around the handle.

She drew the blade, jabbed the point at the black material holding her left wrist in place. She poked furiously, twisting the blade each time, breaking off thick bits of the mud, pulling hard with her wrist at the same time. She missed once, the point driving into the base of her thumb, but she did not slow.

Her left hand slid free.

Creen's choking sounds drove her. She jabbed at the mud covering her legs, kicked and pulled and thrashed. Left leg free, then the right. The last bits of mud mashed into her hidey suit twine snapped and split as she lurched away from the wall.

She rushed past the Margrave's encased corpse, saw the white thing crowning in Creen's strained mouth. Creen's face was a slashed, bloody ruin. Ahiliyah hooked a finger in the corner of Creen's mouth, pulled back to expose more of the white thing, then slid her blade in, turned it so the flat faced outward, and pulled. Enough of it came out for her to grab it with her left hand. Ahiliyah *squeezed*, leaned back— the nasty thing seemed to resist, then slid out of Creen's mouth all at once. It was as long as her forearm… and still moving.

Ahiliyah threw it to the floor. It landed across a black root. She stomped it, so hard her foot squashed the worm against the root—the white thing split, squirting out a long glob of thick fluid.

Creen heaved in a breath, let it out in a ragged whisper. "Brandun! Over there."

The boy tilted his head. Ahiliyah looked, and in the darkness, saw big Brandun, just as encased and helpless as Creen had been. Brandun's head hung down, but a convulsing gag brought him awake in an instant. He lurched, vomited, and chunks of quivering white fell from his mouth like half-chewed crelfish.

He blinked, drew in a breath as if to scream, and Ahiliyah was on him in an instant, covering his mouth with splayed fingers, her body pressed against his. Brandun did not scream. She felt his heart hammering against hers. He breathed deep, somehow controlling his fear.

Ahiliyah looked through the darkness, searching for a demon. Seeing none, she worked quickly to quietly cut Brandun and Creen loose. The three of them knelt at the wall, huddling together in a shivering, terrified trio.

Brandun saw Ahiliyah holding the knife. He seemed surprised, drew his own. He had a horrid gash across his right thigh, blood staining the pants beneath his hidey suit. And Creen's *face*—two parallel talon slashes ran from where his right ear had been down to just left of the point of his chin, slicing through cheek and lips, had torn away part of his nose. Blood, both dry and wet, caked his face.

"Creen," she said, "do you have your knife?"

He fumbled at his hip, shook his head. When he did, blood dripped down.

Ahiliyah glanced around the dark, misty chamber. Scattered bits of armor. Glowing eggs, some peeled back and hollow. Some still closed, and inside those she saw fluttering movement—spiders getting ready to leap out and find a victim.

"We have to get out of this room," she whispered.

Who knew what lay outside, but in here there was only death.

"Help me," Creen said. "Please."

Brandun reached for him; Ahiliyah pushed Brandun's hand away. With that leg wound, it would be all Brandun could do to walk on his own.

Ahiliyah slid under Creen's shoulder, helped him stand.

She looked around the dark chamber, repelled by seeing her people stuck to the strange, rippling walls, bloody holes in their chests. Steffan Andersson. Cruden Poller. Callow Winden. Theora Denisander. Solomon Barrow.

"All dead," Brandun said. "All except us. Creen, how did you know about the leaves?"

"They dragged us past other rooms," Creen said. He sounded as injured as he looked, and his lips didn't quite make the full *b* or *p* sounds. "People in them, just like here. I saw a spider jump on Leonitos. In here I saw the eggs, the Margrave's chest. It was obvious the spiders put something inside you, something that grew and ripped out of your chest. I thought if I had the leaves in my system, that might mess up whatever that something was."

And he'd been right. Creen's brilliance had kept them alive, at least a few minutes more.

The little friend in her hand. The demons hadn't taken it. Had they not known it was there, or just not cared? What else could they have missed?

She put her hand to her chest, felt what lay beneath her padded shirt. She lifted the toothtongue free. She sheathed her knife, pulled the cork—the goop inside reflected the chamber's faint blue light.

Brandun leaned in. "Is that what I think it is?"

Ahiliyah nodded.

"It's a small dose," Creen said. "It will kill one, two at the most."

Ahiliyah knew which one she wanted to use it on. "We have to search everyone, quickly see if anyone has weapons, or more goop."

Creen didn't argue, just shuffled to the first body. Ahiliyah did the same.

The walls... so strange. Furrowed black mud all over, making repetitive, curved patterns, but where the mud was not, the walls looked flat. She'd thought this a cave, but maybe not.

She focused on searching the bodies, her hands exploring around waists, feeling legs, sliding between corpses and walls to see if they had anything on their backs. The second time she reached behind a body and her hand hit something, cold, soft and putrid, she realized there was another corpse back there, one old and rotten—the demons had stacked the dead atop the dead.

Ahiliyah was oddly grateful there was nothing left in her stomach to vomit up.

She kept searching, tried to not look at the dead faces of her people, but she couldn't help it. Her friends. Her holdmates. She had failed them all.

Brandun limped to her, his face ashen. "Nothing. I found nothing."

Creen shuffled in, his wounds wet and horrid. He held up a spear case crusted with mud.

"Two halfstaffs and a coupler in here," he said. "No butt-spike."

Pain in his voice, pain he fought against. His face, a ruin… he had to hurt, *so* bad, yet he wouldn't give in to it. How long could he keep that up?

Creen pulled the halfstaff from the case. "Listen to this." He knelt, tapped the halfstaff against a flat spot on the floor—it made the unmistakable sound of wood clanking on metal.

"I don't understand," Brandun said. "They put metal floors in their burrow?"

Creen gestured to the walls, the ceiling. "I don't think this is a burrow. Or it didn't used to be. Either the demons are a lot smarter than we thought, or we're in an ancient lost hold. Maybe it was abandoned like the rest, or maybe the demons must have killed everyone, took it over."

King Paul's Ring of War holds had been abandoned for decades and had fallen into disrepair. The histories said Takanta Hold had been forgotten altogether, found only after the Rising, when people scattered into the mountains looking for shelter. Could this place be like that, only far older, from long before even King Paul's time?

"It doesn't matter," Ahiliyah said. "We need to get out of this room."

"Hold on." Brandun limped to where he'd been encased in the wall. He picked something up, came back holding his thick chestplate.

"They ripped the straps. Maybe I can tie it, though."

As if a chestplate would do any good at this point.

"It's bent." Ahiliyah tapped the right shoulder arch, which had been bent forward.

Brandun gripped it, tried to bend it. The metal wobbled, but didn't give. His chestplate was thicker than most—he had no problem with the heavier weight—but that made it far harder to fix without a forge or tools. He tried harder, snarling with the effort, yet still the metal resisted. Finally, he gave up.

"Leave it," Ahiliyah said. "Or get another."

"No. This one is mine. The others won't fit. I'll find a hammer or something."

"Please," Creen said. "Tell me you won't *hammer it*. Might as well ring a dinner bell."

"Shut up, both of you," Ahiliyah said. "Bring it if you want, but keep quiet. Let's go."

All that mattered was finding the Demon Mother and putting her down, once and for all.

Ahiliyah led her crew to the entryway.

45

In the chamber, dead people. In the passageway, dead demons.

The passageway was just wide enough for Ahiliyah and Brandun to walk side by side. Dozens of demons lay along its length, their black husks and metal teeth glinting slightly in the dim blue glow that came from wetness on the walls and puddles on the floor. Most of the monsters were dead, as rigid as the strange structure around them. Others weren't quite dead, but soon would be—limbs twitched, taloned hands clutched at nothing, jaws slowly opened and closed.

Some of the demons had visible wounds—spear punctures and scratches on their long heads, broken arrow shafts jutting from arms, chest, abdomen, or legs. More than a few showed gaping, raw holes, as if they had dug arrowheads out with their own talons. Others showed no overt damage, their wounds either hidden by their positions on the floor, or hard to see on black bodies bathed in low blue light.

"They lived long enough to drag us back here," Brandun whispered. "They were all dying. If we could have held on a little longer, we would have won."

Ahiliyah didn't want to think of the battle. She had failed. So much blood. Had Ramirus been right? Should she have taken everyone to Biseth?

No. Running would have only prolonged the inevitable. They had *fought*. They had killed hundreds of demons, maybe *thousands*, with more dying every minute. Maybe this was humanity's last gasp, but if so, she and her people had not gone quietly.

If only the Vindenians had arrived in time. With another thousand soldiers, could they have flanked the demons? Would the Vindenians have listened, formed a ring, drawn enough of the demons away that the Lemethian ring would have held? She would never know. Maybe the Vindenians were dead. Maybe Vinden had decided not to send anyone at all.

The ground vibrated under her feet. The vibration grew in intensity. She bent her knees to keep her balance, not wanting to touch the black walls. The shaking subsided, then faded away.

"The vibration is probably from a geyser," Creen said, his words a dry croak. "I felt roughly the same thing twice earlier, when I was... on the wall. The intervals are consistent."

Ahiliyah thought of the geysers up on the surface. "Is that what's making all this mist?"

"Most likely," Creen said. "I think we're under Black Smoke Mountain."

Under Black Smoke Mountain—the home of the Demon Mother. This was where she had wanted to come, with thousands of fighters at her back. Now it was just her, Brandun and Creen.

"If this was a hold," Brandun said, "they were really bad at carving tunnels."

The passage seemed relatively uniform—roughly the same space from floor to ceiling and from wall to wall—but it rose, fell and banked at odd angles, like an arrow shaft cracked and bent at several spots along its length.

"I don't remember which way they dragged me," Ahiliyah said. "Do you?"

Creen shook his head. Brandun pulled twine from his suit, tried to run it through the torn leather shoulder strap riveted to his chestplate.

"Fucking give that up," Creen said.

Brandun ignored him, glanced up. "It's a little brighter to the right. At the far end."

He was right. It was brighter, just a bit. Maybe it was an opening to the surface, or maybe a place where more water flowed, generating more light, like the Bitigan River back home. Whatever the reason, staying still did no good, so Ahiliyah led them down the passage toward it.

They moved carefully, cautious of their footing on the wet metal floor, along the passage's up-and-down angles, past dead and dying demons. Halfway down, the footing changed—it was the same black rock they'd seen on the Boiling Plains.

"Lava flow," Creen said. "No telling how old it is. Looks like it flowed through the wall."

If he hadn't pointed it out, she might have missed it. In the dim light, the fissure of rough black rock flowing down from the left-hand side didn't seem that different from the bizarre, curving, rippling patterns that the demons had made on the ancient hold's flat walls. Ahiliyah could imagine the *rivers of fire* from the legends pouring through a crack in the wall, dripping down, puddling on the floor, glowing orange until they cooled forever.

"Not much got in," Brandun said, pointing down the passage. "Flat floors up there."

They continued on, still moving toward the slightly brighter light. The dead demons were fewer and fewer, as if only a handful of them had made it this far after the battle.

The glow gradually changed, the faint blue on the walls and floor joined by irregular spots of pale yellow and faint green. Further on, those spots grew larger, overlapped each other, became brighter, merged with the blue until all surfaces glowed a pale, almost unified white—just like the Bitigan River. Still dark, darker than moonlight, by far, but brighter than the way they'd come. Even the mist seemed to glow.

"It's getting hotter," Creen whispered. "This environment is better suited to different kinds of bacteria, maybe."

Ahiliyah wiped sweat from her forehead. The humid air seemed to pull it from her.

Up ahead, a brighter patch of light, on the passage's right-hand side. It looked like an opening. Ahiliyah crept closer, her crewmates moving silently behind her. Yes, it was an opening, metal edges crusted with mud. She slowly leaned out, looked in—three yards past it, mud-encrusted handrails leading left and right. Beyond the handrails, what looked like a large, open, mist-filled space.

She dropped to a crouch. Brandun and Creen did the same. She gave them hand signals to remain silent, to follow her, to keep their eyes open.

Ahiliyah crawled through the opening. This floor was similar to the passageway in that it had odd angles yet seemed mostly flat, but the surface was different, almost... *woven*, like a metal net thickly crusted with mud and sparkling mineral deposits.

Up above, half hidden in the darkness, Ahiliyah had impressions of parallel beams, mineral-glimmering stalactites stretching down through them. One cluster of stalactites, off to her left, was much longer than the rest, a long, rough tooth biting into the mist.

She crawled to the rail, looked over. The deck was some fifteen feet or so above an uneven metal floor that swirled with mist, gleamed with pale white light anywhere water collected—wide puddles, small depressions, even trickling areas where condensed liquid flowed down from the wall. Large, strange shapes down there, boxy, like big carts encrusted with demon mud. Rust. Broken things. Jutting clumps of rock that had torn up through the floor.

Dotting the floor, sparse in some places, thickly clustered in others, Ahiliyah saw dozens of the horrifying spider eggs, glowing from within with the same pale light that luminesced off the standing water, that gleamed from the black walls. And among the eggs, demons. Most of the black beasts were dead or dying, victims of Creen's poison, but two of them—the biggest she'd ever seen—walked erect, seemingly uninjured in any way.

One spot on the floor glowed brighter than any other. A small pool, ringed with a thick crust of minerals, lying directly below the big stalactite. The gleaming water looked clear, enough for her to see a mineral-caked opening leading down like a narrowing funnel.

Creen nudged her, pointed to the walls, whispered: "This room is hex-shaped."

It took her a moment, but when she saw it she couldn't *un*-see it. The deck went all the way around the large chamber—the chamber had six tall walls, not four. The walls were bent and warped, but not so much she couldn't make out what Creen was saying. It was almost like the room, and the passageways they'd traversed to get here, had been... *smashed*, in some way. Like a shield dented by many, many blows.

Ahiliyah again looked down to the floor. To the right, near the ground, not quite under the curving deck, something moved. Something *big*. She fought an instant and powerful urge to run.

A demon. A *massive* one, so large it seemed beyond imagining. Backsticks as big and long as tree trunks. The body, heavy and *huge*, with a ridged, gnarled texture, like piles of blackened human bones laid out in a perfect pattern. And... was that its *head*? Flat and long, like a giant, heavy, decorative war shield, deeply notched on the sides, two curves on top that ended in points in the middle and at the corners. Long legs, bent at the knee, tucked up almost out of sight.

"It's *her*," Ahiliyah whispered.

The Demon Mother. Black, like the others, but she *shimmered* slightly, her hard surfaces gleaming with the faintest iridescence, as if her black contained all the colors that were. The iridescence reminded Ahiliyah of the rough rims around the larger geysers on the Boiling Plains.

"Those backsticks," Brandun said, his voice as thin as the mist, "there's some kind of... *rope* coming off them. They're... are they holding her up?"

With his words, Ahiliyah saw what the mist had partially obscured, what her own eyes didn't know how to process. Thick, yellowish bands—impossibly long animal skins, or tendons of some kind, perhaps—stretching down from the ceiling high above. The skins were wrapped around the backsticks, or maybe *part* of the backsticks: it was impossible to tell through the haze. And the backsticks weren't actually on her *back*, more near her narrow hips… and there was something leading away from her hips, something long, like an oversized grub or a fat snake, something that had to be full of water or fluid, because it glowed from within. Roundish things inside that snake, hard to make out through the mist, through the translucent surface…

Ahiliyah realized what it was. Icy disgust washed through her. "Eggs. She's full of eggs."

Creen squinted at the monstrosity. "Part of it is hanging under the deck. See?"

The same kind of yellowish skins that held the Demon Mother aloft ran beneath the egg sac as well. Some of the skins stretched to the ceiling beams. Other skins hung from the bottom of the deck, holding up a portion of the sac that was just below it.

Fear and frustration. Rage. *Hatred.* All the death, the loss, the pain, all her people had faced, it was all because of that thing down there.

Ahiliyah tugged on what was left of Creen and Brandun's hidey suits, guiding them back into the passageway. Brandun immediately started threading twine through his chestplate.

"We came here to kill the Demon Mother," she said. "We can still do that."

Creen started to talk, stopped, gently put his hand to the wounds on his face, perhaps to check if the damage was as bad as it felt. Ahiliyah could only imagine how much pain he was in.

"I want to go home," he said. "We lost. It's over."

There was no home left to go to.

Brandun tied a knot, started on another. "Liyah's right. We've lost everything. My mom is gone. We can kill the Demon Mother and free our people."

Creen sagged to his butt. He looked like he might not take another step.

"She's so big," he said. "I don't know if Ahiliyah's one dose will work."

Brandun slid on the chestplate. The bent shoulder arch made it hang at an odd angle.

"We can make more poison," he said. "There's still leaves on our suits, and leaves on the suits of all the others. Would it be enough?"

Creen shook his head. "I need a cauldron. And a fire. And *time*. We didn't kill all the demons—they're going to find us eventually."

Beneath them, the deck began to tremble. From the large room came a cacophony of demon screeches, including one louder and deeper than any she'd heard before—the voice of the Demon Mother.

As the ground shuddered, Ahiliyah crawled back onto the deck. Within seconds, the tremor seemed far worse than the one Ahiliyah had felt in the passage, which itself had been worse than the one she felt while encased against the wall. She had to grab the mud-encrusted rail to keep from being tossed about. Brandun grabbed the rail to her right, Creen to her left.

Down on the warped floor, the pool bubbled once, sloshing water across the crater-like ridge of minerals that surrounded it—a ridge just like the ones she'd seen on the Boiling Plains.

The pool… it was a geyser.

It erupted, water and steam roaring forth with the light of day. What had been a wonder to see out on the black plains was godlike in the chamber's closed confines. The column splashed against a cluster of stalactites, sprayed water all across the large room.

Glowing water rained down, searing Ahiliyah's head, her face, her hands, anywhere her skin was exposed. Creen whimpered. Ahiliyah ignored the pain. She wrapped an arm around the rail, put her hand above her eyes, and stared at her enemy.

Almost obscured by the swirling mist, she saw the giant beast waving four arms, saw the long head tilt back, and for the first time saw its mouth, easily large enough to bite a man in half. The Demon Mother let out a deafening screech—not of pain or fear, but of… *pleasure*.

The trembling slowed, ceased. The column of water died down, then stopped, as if some giant, hidden hand had turned a giant, hidden valve. Glowing water dripped from the ceiling, trickled down from stalactites. The rippling puddles on the ground were briefly brighter, making the eggs that rested in them look dark in comparison.

The ground's glow lit the Demon Mother from beneath, making her look even more ominous, even more unreal. Slowly, the light faded, returning the hexagonal room to an ethereal half-darkness. In the light that remained, Ahiliyah looked at her hand, at the red marks there growing to small welts.

"She liked it," Brandun whispered. Hate in his voice. And bloodlust. "That's why she's here. She likes the heat, the wet."

Ahiliyah let go of the rail, again crawled a few yards back into the passageway, well out of sight of the Demon Mother or the two large demons—her protectors?—down there with her.

"Creen, the geyser," Ahiliyah said, "was that water *boiling*?"

The boy sniffed, looked at the welts forming on the back of his hand. "It was damn near boiling when it hit us, after splashing off the ceiling. So even hotter than boiling when it came out of the ground. Had to be for that much water pressure."

She didn't ask him what he meant. After eating the leaves had saved her life, Ahiliyah was ready to take anything Creen said as gospel.

"We could lure her on top of the geyser," she said. "Would that cook her?"

Creen's one eye squinted. "Lure the Demon Mother. Over a geyser. *Cook* her."

Brandun nodded. "Boil her like a furgle."

Creen sagged. He shook from silent tears.

From the passage, past the entryway, a whisper in the dimness: "*Don't scream*."

Ahiliyah whirled, as did Brandun, who pointed the knife toward a man, a man on the floor, on his hands, legs behind him like he was just rising after a push-up. He wore strange clothes. No armor. No hidey suit.

"They are coming," he said. "Quickly, follow me."

Using only his hands, the man turned and crawled down the passage, his limp legs dragging behind him.

Brandun looked at Ahiliyah, confused, unsure what to do. She was confused, too, but in a hold full of murdering demons, she didn't have to ask who *they* were.

Ahiliyah hauled Creen to his feet. Pulling him along, she followed the crawling man. Brandun trailed behind, shield on his arm, casting fast glances over his shoulder.

From far back down the passageway came a low, long hiss.

The crawling man stopped, turned. Resting his weight on one arm, he reached up, slid his hand into an unseen hole in the demon mud. Ahiliyah heard a *click*, then a waist-high section of wall swung inward with a slight metallic screech, revealing a dark space beyond.

"In there," he said. "Quickly."

Ahiliyah hesitated. Who was this man? What waited in the darkness that lay through that space?

"Liyah," Brandun whispered, "I can see two demons, they're coming."

Creen pushed past Ahiliyah, vanished in the darkness. If something bad waited for them in there, it was too late to worry about it. She ducked down and followed him in. No light, not even the faint blue glow. She felt along the floor, moved toward open space. A bump from behind made her heart leap to her throat.

"Sorry," Brandun said. "But get out of the way!"

Ahiliyah crawled further forward, waiting for a bony demon hand to grab her, or metal teeth to bite off her searching fingers.

She heard the metallic screech again, then that metallic click.

The man's whisper in the darkness: "Be quiet."

Ahiliyah didn't move. No noise in here, so quiet she heard her own breathing, heard Brandun and Creen's as well. She turned, tried to look back the way she'd come.

The man had closed the weird wall-door. From beyond it, in the passageway, the sounds of clawed toes clicking against metal as a demon—or maybe two of them—scampered past.

She waited in silence, her hand on the handle of her little friend.

Then, a soft squeaking sound, a familiar sound—the sound of a spigot.

In the darkness, a soft white light. Water flowed into a clear glass jar held by the strange man, illuminating Brandun's wide eyes, Creen's awful wounds. The man turned off the spigot. He held up the jar.

"My name is Zachariah," he said. "Who are you?"

46

Ahiliyah's eyes quickly adjusted. The man was on his left hip, left hand flat on the ground, glowjar held in his right. The blue fabric of his shirt and pants, while threadbare in places, was a tighter weave than anything she'd ever seen. Clean-shaven. Red hair short, recently combed.

She quickly looked around the small room. Drawings all over the walls, pictures of demons, of people she didn't know, people also wearing strange clothes. Metal objects she didn't recognize. One small table, with a chair tucked under it, both made of a material she'd never seen before. Boxes all over, made of metal, perhaps. Some were open, most were closed. For some reason, the room reminded her of the factories in Lemeth's lower level.

"Don't be afraid of me," the man said. "I will not harm you. Did your ship land nearby?" The man waited. No one responded. He glanced at Brandun's chestplate, at Creen's face, then at Ahiliyah. "Do you understand English? Tu loquerisne Latine? Nǐ hui shuō?"

"I got the first part," Creen said. "The *do you understand*. Don't know the other words."

The man nodded. He set the glowjar on the floor, next to an empty one. He picked that up, held it under a tap sticking out of the metal wall, started filling it.

"I see that you are injured." He reached out, set the second glowjar on the floor in the middle of the room. "May I have permission to attend to your wounds?"

With the additional light, Ahiliyah saw that the right side of Zachariah's mouth didn't move when he spoke, yet his voice seemed unmuffled.

Brandun clutched at his thigh above his bloody cut. "Are you a doctor?"

"I have medical knowledge." Hand over hand, the man slid to a rectangular box. "It is one of the few areas of knowledge I still possess. It would be helpful if I knew your names."

"I'm Brandun Barrow," Brandun said. "He's Creen Dinashin, she's Ahiliyah Cooper."

"*Cooper*." Zachariah stared at Ahiliyah. "Are you a descendant of Samuel Cooper?"

Ahiliyah said nothing.

"Her father's first name was Vance," Brandun said. "We don't know a Samuel Cooper."

Zachariah looked at Creen, at Brandun. "Barrow. Cooper. Dinashin. Astonishing. To clarify, the three of you did *not* come here on a ship?"

Ahiliyah finally found her tongue. "The nearest shore is five miles away."

Zachariah sat silent for a moment. No expression. When he blinked, only his left eye closed. The whole right side of his face seemed oddly still, like it was… dead.

He dragged the box with him as he slid next to Brandun. Brandun's hand went to the handle of his little friend.

The man paused. "I can help you."

Brandun glanced at Ahiliyah. She didn't know what to tell him, this was all so strange.

"Let him," Creen said. "If he wanted to hurt us, he wouldn't have saved us."

Brandun considered this, looked warily at the man, then nodded.

"I will be as gentle as I can." Zachariah tore open packages, revealing thin white cloth inside. "You are in pain. On a scale of one to ten, how bad would you say it is?"

Brandun winced. "A… a five?"

Zachariah pulled something out of the box—a glass vial.

"These supplies are very old," he said. "I do not know how effective this will be. It will sting, but should help with the pain."

Zachariah pressed the vial to Brandun's leg. Ahiliyah heard a tiny clink of metal. Brandun hissed, snarled, swung a fist at Zachariah—the man caught Brandun's wrist.

"My apologies," Zachariah said. "It should only take a few seconds to work."

Brandun gawked at the man for a moment, then looked at his leg.

Brandun's fist opened.

"That… that feels better. Is it magic?"

Zachariah let Brandun go. "It's medicine. Let me bandage you up."

The man took another vial out of the box, held it near Brandun's leg. A bit of mist came out, coated the raw wound. Zachariah started wrapping the white cloth around it.

Brandun looked at his own wrist, where Zachariah had grabbed him, then at Ahiliyah.

"He's strong," Brandun said. "Stronger than… than anyone."

Zachariah finished wrapping the bandage around Brandun's leg, then slid to Creen, dragging his box with him.

"And you, Mister Dinashin. On a scale of—"

"A fucking *twelve*," Creen said. He was shaking. "Get to it."

Zachariah started pulling things out of the box. "I'm pleased to meet you all. Three hundred and nineteen years is a long time to wait, even for a synthetic."

He had saved them, but he was also clearly insane. Ahiliyah and her crew were trapped in this strange room with a crazy cripple.

"Three hundred and nineteen years," Creen said, speaking the words slowly. "You've been waiting that long. Are you saying you've been *alive* that long?"

Zachariah placed a glass vial against several spots of Creen's wounds. Each time he did, Ahiliyah heard that *clink*, and saw Creen wince.

"Technically, I'm not *alive*," Zachariah said as he worked. "I have very little memory of events prior to my being activated to land this ship, but I do know that my assembly date was three hundred and thirty-four years ago. I am the Zachariah synthetic companion, registration number WY2100023, manufactured by Weyland-Yutani in the Tokyo factory." He put the vial back in the box. "Does that feel better?"

Creen reached up, gently touched his wounds. "That's… *amazing*."

"I am glad," Zachariah said. "May I suture the lacerations? It will take a few minutes."

Creen's shaking stopped. He touched his face once more. He seemed awed.

"Sure," he said. "*Tokyo factory*. Where is Tokyo?"

Zachariah pulled more equipment out of the box. Ahiliyah watched him pinch Creen's sliced cheek together, hold a device against it. The device made a click sound—a tiny line of metal held that part of the cut together.

"I do not know where Tokyo is," Zachariah said. He slowly, methodically, stitched Creen's wound with the bits of metal. "*The Nan-Shan's* external cameras are long since lost, but three internals remain. I saw such a commotion among the Xenomorphs that I had to come out and see what all the fuss was about."

He spoke words that made no sense.

"Zee-no… what?" Ahiliyah's eyes narrowed. "Morph?"

"Xenomorph," Zachariah said. "I do not know why, but some limited information regarding the species remains in my memory. Scientific name, *Internecivus raptus,* although the term *Linguafoeda acheronsi* is also used. Are you familiar with either term?"

No one answered.

"Perhaps you've heard the term *plagiarus praepotens,*" he said. "Or, perhaps, *snatchers?*"

Ahiliyah stared, dumbfounded.

"I think he means the demons," Brandun said.

Zachariah paused in his clipping. "*Demons.* I will use that name."

He finished stitching the two long gashes on Creen's cheek, then examined Creen's ruined nose. No matter what this strange man did, Creen would have horrible scars—if Creen even lived out the day, which Ahiliyah doubted. She didn't think any of them would.

"You said *this ship,*" Creen said. "Do you think we are in a ship now?"

"We are. The *Nan-Shan.*"

"We're on solid ground," Creen said, wincing when Zachariah touched a spot on his nose. "Like Liyah told you, the nearest water is five miles south. We're nowhere near a coast."

"The *Nan-Shan* is an interstellar colony ship," Zachariah said.

Creen reached up, grabbed Zachariah's hand, looked into the strange man's eyes.

"*Interstellar,*" Creen said. "*Stellar,* as in, stars?"

Zachariah nodded. "I assume that is what a colony ship is designed to do."

Ahiliyah felt lost. Once glance at Brandun showed he felt the same.

"Other stars," Creen said, his pain seemingly forgotten for the moment. "Does that mean… other planets? There are worlds other than Ataegina?"

Zachariah gently turned Creen's head to face forward, went back to work on the nose.

"I assume so, but I cannot say for certain. Most of the ship's records were erased prior to my reactivation. When I was brought online, the *Nan-Shan* was in orbital decay. I was loaded with medical knowledge, the ability to pilot this ship, and little else."

The strange man pulled a small jar from the box. He opened it, started applying some kind of clay to Creen's nose, talked as he worked.

"I was reactivated by the captain and tasked with first landing this ship, then evacuating everyone I could. The *Nan-Shan* had suffered several acts of sabotage. All colonists aged eleven and up died while still in cryosleep. The crew was also dead, with the exception of the captain. There appears to have been in-fighting among the crew, resulting in casualties, and at least four crewmembers were killed by a demon."

Ahiliyah knew the Northerners' sailing ships had *crews*, but the word still had special meaning to her. To think that crewmates would fight among themselves, *kill* each other… in a way, that was even more hideous than what the demons did.

"Due to cascading system failures brought on by sabotage and internal use of firearms, I had very little flight control," Zachariah said. "The ship suffered extensive additional damage upon impact. I was able to awaken one hundred and nineteen children, all ten years old or younger. I got them off the ship immediately, as I knew that the demons on board might have survived the impact. The children left with nothing but the clothes on their backs and some seed kits I gave them. No tools, no weapons, no reference material, no computers. It was very rushed, very chaotic. I instructed them to get as far away from the ship as they could, as fast as they could, and to never return."

Zachariah closed the jar. He started wrapping white cloth around Creen's head.

"I have no personal memories from before my reactivation, but I retain all that happened since. Among the children who evacuated the ship were Kyle Barrow, Samuel Cooper, and Amy Dinashin. Those are, most likely, your ancestors."

"Told you that volcano story was bullshit," Creen said.

"Don't blaspheme," Brandun said, fumbling with his bent armor. "Not now."

Zachariah finished wrapping the bandage. He pulled another roll of white out of the box, started wrapping that around the bandage.

"The children had no idea what had transpired, nor did they have any knowledge of the demons or the dangers posed by the various phases of the demon life cycle," Zachariah said. "I wanted to protect them, so I had to paraphrase. The last things I told them—other than to never return, for any reason—was to hide if they saw a tall, skinny, black creature with no eyes and to stay away from large, egg-shaped objects. They had no idea what a face-hugger looked like, of course, so I told them that if they saw something that looked like a large spider with a tail, to run away as fast as possible until they could run no more."

He paused, glanced off. "I retain some information about other life-forms. Spiders. Elephants. Eels." He continued wrapping Creen's head.

Ahiliyah hadn't been sure what to believe, if she could believe *any* of what the crippled man said. Until he used the word *spider*. That resonated. She didn't know if what Zachariah said was real, but she knew that he believed it. All of it.

Zachariah tore the white wrap, pressed the end against Creen's head.

"That is the best I can do, Mister Dinashin."

Creen felt at the bandages around his head. His fingertips left spots of blood.

"You *seem* like a person," he said, "but you're not, are you?"

Zacharia nodded. "I am a synthetic companion. I was the property of the colonists. Considering that you are descendants of the colonists, I am now your property. I will assist you in any way I can."

Property? People weren't *property*.

"I don't know what that means," Ahiliyah said.

"It means I will do what you ask, as long as you do not order me to harm a human being."

Creen and Brandun both seemed much better. Whatever was in that vial had helped them. They needed a plan to kill the Demon Mother, but this man... so odd, so interesting.

"I have many questions," Creen said. "So many. If you've been here for over three centuries, what have you done with all that time?"

"Very little, I'm afraid. Ahiliyah? Are you injured?"

Her head throbbed. Her throat felt like she'd drunk boiling water. Muscles and bones ached. But she wasn't bleeding. At least, not anymore. She didn't want this man to touch her.

"I'm fine. Continue with your story."

"I spent the first few years trying to repair parts of the ship," Zachariah said. "Communications equipment, in particular, but what hadn't been destroyed before I was reactivated was damaged in the crash. I've spent most of my time since trying to keep myself functional. That, and studying this planet's native phosphorescent extremophile microbes—which are quite fascinating—and the demons. There really isn't anything else onboard."

Listening to him felt surreal. He spoke English, but some of his words made no sense.

Ahiliyah glanced at the drawings stuck to the walls. "You know a lot about the demons?"

"Honestly, I'm not sure," Zachariah said. "I have the ability to make detailed drawings, and to record data about their life cycle and habits, but I could not say if I know *a lot* about them. I have nothing against which to compare my knowledge base."

Brandun stood, tested his weight on his wounded leg. "If you've been in this hold with the demons all this time, how are you still alive?" He took another tentative step; his twine spun loose, he caught his falling chestplate before it hit the floor.

"I can fix that for you, if you like." Zachariah held out one hand toward him.

Cautiously, Brandun handed over the thick piece of metal. "And why are you still *here*?"

Zachariah took the chestplate, turned it in his hands, examining it. "When the captain reactivated me, he included in my programming that I am not allowed to leave this ship. I suspect the reason for that is I may have been involved in the sabotage."

Creen, his head and half his face covered by white bandages, looked around the small room. "That doesn't explain how you're still alive, or whatever the fuck you are. How have the demons not got you in over three centuries? You have to leave here to eat, shit and piss, right?"

"As a synthetic, I need to do none of those things." Zachariah said. He set the chestplate on the floor. "However, I frequently move about the *Nan-Shan*. Aside from a longer life span, I suppose, the one advantage to being a synthetic is that demons aren't that interested in me. As long as I don't present a threat to them, they don't attack. That has allowed me extensive access to study the hive's behavior. I have even been in the Queen's chamber, although I don't dare get close to her." He touched his legs. "I tried once. Her guards did not take kindly to the effort."

He put a knee on the chestplate, then gripped the bent tang and leaned on it. Ahiliyah, Brandun and Creen watched, stunned, as the bronze creaked and bent.

"He's strong, all right," Creen said.

Zachariah slid the chestplate across the floor to a stunned Brandun.

"It's somewhat better," Zachariah said. "May I ask a question?"

He wanted permission to speak? He was acting like they were in charge. If he was their *property*, maybe they were.

"Go ahead," Ahiliyah said.

"After the commotion began, I walked all through the ship. For the first time in fifty years, every single demon had left, except for the queen and her two guards. Even the demons that had been hibernating woke up. Well over a thousand demons marched out of the ship. Only an estimated twenty-four percent of those returned. Are the others dead?"

Ahiliyah nodded.

"Of the demons that returned, most were wounded," Zachariah said. "I saw arrow shafts and crossbow bolts in many. Others had deep lacerations. Am I correct in assuming those were caused by handheld weapons such as swords?"

"Spears," Brandun said. "We fought hard."

"Apparently," Zachariah said. "From what I have learned, it seems unlikely that you killed so many with basic weaponry. Did you also use firearms of some kind? Muskets, perhaps?"

Firearms. Muskets. More nonsense words.

"Our arms are not made of fire," Brandun said. "We used a phalanx, and Creen's poison."

Zachariah scooted to the wall, leaned against it. "Poison. May I ask how you made it?"

Creen glanced at Ahiliyah, waiting for her lead. This *man*, if that's what he was, lived down here with the beasts. She was hesitant to tell him anything. And yet, if he hadn't come up to the deck, she and Brandun and Creen would be dead, or again plastered to a wall in a room of rotting corpses, waiting for a spider.

She nodded at Creen.

"Caminus leaves," he said. "Something in them turns burning blood to harmless grey ash. I made an extract that protects our skin somewhat, but also coats our weapons. When a coated weapon penetrates the demon shell, I think the extract forms blood clots that kill the fuckers."

Zachariah considered this for a long moment.

"Native flora counteracts the acid," he said, finally. "Astonishing. The red leaves on your camouflage suits, are those caminus leaves?"

Creen nodded. "They are. When the demons took us, we ate the leaves and it fucked up the worms the spiders put in us. We puked them up. Everyone else died but us."

"I am sorry to hear that," Zachariah said. "But that reminds me that hatchlings—the *worms*, as you call them—will be fully grown demons in a few hours. Your evacuation will be easier if I get you off the ship before they begin hunting."

Ahiliyah's head hurt, and she'd never been so tired, so sore or so scared. Those things made it hard to focus.

"I must have heard you wrong," she said. "They'll be fully grown in a few *hours*?"

Zachariah nodded. "It's quite amazing. Their growth rate is exponentially higher than that of humans. Unfortunately, I don't know other species for a further comparative analysis, I—"

"*Shut up!*" Liyah felt the dread of both the battlefield and the fear of the egg room combine to clutch at her guts. "There were *twenty* people in that room with us, all with holes in their chests. That's seventeen worms—which means soon we'll have *seventeen more* demons to deal with if we're going to kill the Demon Mother."

"More than that," Zachariah said. "I have limited visual with the internal cameras, but I counted one hundred and thirty-seven human hosts brought back to the ship. The three of you apparently escaped, so I assume that at least one hundred and thirty-four hatchlings now roam the ship. I estimate the first of these will reach the predatory adult stage in the next two hours."

Ahiliyah's head swam. Just her, Brandun and Creen left, against over a hundred demons? Plus those two big ones in the Mother's chamber? Plus the Demon Mother herself?

"We need to kill her," Ahiliyah said. "Before it's too late."

Creen shook his head. "Fuck that. Let's *leave*. We get more people, we come back."

"No, we strike *now*," Brandun said. "She'll get more people, make more demons. We *saw* her. She's right here, we have to kill her."

Zachariah raised a finger. "Excuse me, but who is the *her* you're talking about?"

"The Demon Mother," Ahiliyah said.

His left eyebrow went up. "Ah. I see."

"Hold on," Brandun said. "You've been here all this time, watching them. Why haven't *you* tried to kill them?"

Zachariah blinked his one good eye. "Because no one has asked me to do that."

"I'm asking you now," Ahiliyah said. "Will you help us?"

"Of course, Ahiliyah. As I said, I am your property."

"We need to work fast," she said. "Do you have more paper? Can we sketch her chamber?"

"I can do better than that." Zachariah crawled to the wall, tugged off a piece of paper. He set the paper flat in the center of the small room, pinned it down with a glowjar. It was a top-down drawing of the Mother's chamber.

"It's to scale, of course," he said. "I had quite a lot of time on my hands." He pointed to a spot. "That's where the three of you were, on the catwalk overlooking her chamber."

Ahiliyah studied the drawing. "How can we get to her?"

Zachariah pointed to another spot. "That's the entrance at the lower level. It is hard to see from where you were. I'll tell you how to get there when we leave this container."

"We need weapons," Brandun said. "Do you have any?"

Zachariah shook his head. "There are no weapons. No guns, no knives, no explosives. Even fire axes were removed. I believe everything was confiscated during the crew's in-fighting. I assume all weapons were jettisoned. There is no fuel, nothing we can use to make incendiaries or explosives. I assure you, I have looked everywhere, and there is nothing you can use."

Zachariah took another piece of paper off the wall. It was a drawing of the demon queen, showing her in profile. He set it next to the room drawing. It reminded Ahiliyah of Creen's leaf drawings—exquisitely detailed, obviously the work of a genius. She might have liked more time to learn about Zachariah, but time was something she did not have.

"We've only got this much poison." She took off the toothtongue necklace, set it next to the drawing. "Creen, can we make more?"

He shook his head. "Not inside of two hours, we can't. And she's so *big*. I don't even know if the little bit we have will be enough."

It *had* to be enough. Ahiliyah refused to accept anything else.

"We need a spearhead," Brandun said.

Ahiliyah drew her little friend. "Can we use this as one?"

"Too small," Zachariah said. "A blade that size will not penetrate her armor."

Ahiliyah sheathed it, tapped the drawing. "Her egg sac, then. That's skin, not armor."

"Yes, but the skin there isn't thin," Zachariah said. "With all the fluid inside, it has to be thick to stand up to that pressure. I haven't been up close, but I would guess the egg sac skin is tough, like leather. You could stab through that, but with all that fluid your poison could become diluted. In addition, I don't know if her circulatory system will carry the poison to her."

Ahiliyah looked at Creen.

"He means the clots won't reach her heart," Creen said. "We got to stick her in the body to have a real chance."

Brandun glanced around. "There's metal all over, right? Can we make a spearhead?"

"I have no cutting tools," Zachariah said. "I am strong enough to tear off a piece of metal, but I have nothing that could grind a sufficient edge in the next hour."

He had bent Brandun's chestplate back into shape. Yes, Zachariah was strong, so strong, apparently, he could rip metal with his bare hands. There would be *some* edge to that piece of metal, but enough to break through the Mother's thick armor?

Creen adjusted the drawing. He traced his finger around the Demon Mother.

"Zachariah, do the demons ever fight each other?"

"Rarely," Zachariah said. "Ninety-two years ago there was another queen. I am not sure how that came to be. The hive split into warring factions. There were many deaths."

"They killed each other." Creen slid his finger along the Mother's tail. "When they fought, did they use their tails on each other?"

Zachariah nodded. "Yes, I see your point. It is possible a tail blade, with enough force behind it, could penetrate her armor."

"Then there are spearheads all over the place," Creen said. "If our knives are enough to cut those free. But we still have only enough poison for one shot. Someone has to get close."

"Me," Brandun said. "I'm the best fighter, I have the best chance."

"Against *three* of them?" Creen shook his head. "No chance."

"More than three if you don't move quickly," Zachariah said. "I now estimate you have less than sixty minutes before the first of the new generation reaches adulthood."

Ahiliyah had to make a decision. What gave them the best chance? Creen was right—Brandun wouldn't get close, not with the protectors there.

"Brandun," she said, "could you throw the spear from the catwalk?"

He scratched at the back of his head. "If the spearhead is a tailspike, it won't be balanced. We only get the one chance, so I wouldn't risk it. I need to go in there, Liyah."

"Fuck that," Creen said. "Let the synthetic do it! Why should *you* die, Dumbdun? He said he's been in the chamber. He can get closer than you can!"

Zachariah gestured to his legs. "I am strong, but not fast, I'm afraid. Yes, I can enter the chamber, or at least I could before you killed the entire population of demons. There's no telling how agitated the queen will be. And even if I can enter the chamber, as I've done before, I know from hard-earned experience that I can't get close to her. Not even close enough to try and throw a poorly balanced spear."

"We could distract the guards," Ahiliyah said. "They could chase Creen and me while Brandun slips in."

"*Double*-fuck that," Creen said. "I didn't live this long so I could get eaten."

Brandun turned on him. "We're out of time! We have to be heroes. We have to!"

"They can't be distracted," Zachariah said. "I've been watching them for centuries. The guards never leave the queen's chamber. If you want to get to her, you have to go through them."

Ahiliyah wished the pounding in her head would go away, just for a moment. Running out of time, no options but to go in on a suicide run, which she would do in an instant if it had any chance of working.

She had to think. Ahiliyah closed her eyes, and when she did, she heard Sinesh's voice.

When death comes, see the beauty in life.

She breathed in, slowly, fighting against the stress, the panic. Beauty. No mountains to look at here, she knew she would never see those again. Think. Every second mattered. Beauty. The Mother's chamber. The hanging mist, that was beautiful. She imagined the mist inside her, soothing her soul, calming her. The Demon Mother. Beautiful in her own way, when one thought about it. Far more beautiful if she was dead. The geyser, spectacular in its eruption…

"The geyser," she said. "Could we lure the Demon Mother over it? Would that kill her?"

Creen rolled his eyes. "Here we go with this again."

Unlike Creen, Zachariah didn't immediately dismiss her question. "I don't know if it would kill her. I've never boiled a demon before. But I would think so, yes. As for luring her over it, she's immobile. If she separates from the egg sac and can shed the secretions that keep her aloft, I think she can move, but why would she? Her guards will deal with any threat."

Ahiliyah stared at the drawings. Brandun and Creen stared at her. They were out of ideas.

But she had one more. "Immobile," she said. "Mother is stuck right where she is. Zachariah, you said you can enter the Mother's chamber."

"I can, but as I told you, I won't get near her. Her protectors will tear me apart."

Ahiliyah glanced at Brandun's chestplate. Zachariah had bent it. He could bend it again. He could probably bend it almost *flat*.

She pointed to a spot on the drawing. "Can you get *there*?"

Zachariah leaned closer. "Yes, I believe I can."

It could work. It could work, and Brandun didn't need to die for nothing. Neither did Creen. Neither did Ahiliyah.

"Creen, how long until the next geyser eruption?"

"Between seventeen and nineteen minutes," Zachariah said. "I've become rather familiar with the intervals over the years."

Zachariah's little room was so close to the Mother's chamber. There was enough time.

"Listen carefully," Ahiliyah said. "Here's what we're going to do."

47

Ahiliyah, Creen and Brandun hunched down at the edge of the deck. No, not a *deck*—Zachariah had called it a *catwalk*.

Slowly, carefully, Ahiliyah and her crewmates looked over the rail. She peered through the darkness and the mist, to the lower entrance

Zachariah had told her about. Just a patch of black in a dark, black room. No wonder she'd missed it. But in that spot of black, she saw him, saw Zachariah, slowly pulling himself along with his right arm. On his left arm and shoulder, he carried Brandun's chestplate.

A few agonizing inches at a time, Zachariah slid across the rough, wet floor, through puddles, past glowing eggs—toward the geyser pool.

One of the two big protector demons saw him, raced at him, going from a standstill to a sprint in a heartbeat. The speed stunned Ahiliyah—this one was faster than any demon she had seen as a runner, faster than any she'd fought against on the Boiling Plains.

"He's fucked," Creen whispered.

Ahiliyah thought Zachariah might panic, try to crawl away, but he simply stopped moving.

The demon reached him, slowed to a halt. The long head tilted, left, then right. Zachariah started crawling again, even slower than before. The demon walked beside him for a few steps, then it stalked back to the massive Demon Mother.

"Maybe he ain't got legs," Creen whispered, "but he's sure got balls."

Brandun turned to Creen. "He should be dead. What *is* he?"

"I don't know," Creen said. "But he's not like us."

Zachariah reached the geyser pool. Slowly, quietly, he set the flattened chestplate down edge-first into the glowing pool, just behind the spot where the water ran far deeper. He gripped the same piece he'd fixed, then bent it backward to make a handle. He adjusted himself, putting his weight behind the chestplate. With his free hand, he felt behind him, searching the lip of the steaming pool for a good handhold.

The deck began to vibrate.

"He made it," Creen said. "I hope he cooks that bitch to a crisp."

Ahiliyah looked to the Demon Queen. Her head angled to the side, tipped up… she seemed to be looking at Zachariah. No… she was looking at the chestplate.

"She just figured it out," Ahiliyah whispered.

The deck vibration increased. Ahiliyah held tight to the rails.

The geyser's surface stretched up in a swelling bubble.

"She can't know," Creen said. "It's impos—"

The Demon Mother screeched. The two protectors shot toward Zachariah.

The glowing bubble popped, splattering Zachariah with glimmering water.

The two protectors closed in—then the world erupted.

The geyser's column of brightly glowing water and steam hit the chestplate, slamming it against Zachariah. Scalding water spraying all over him, he leaned against the bronze, angling it over the erupting geyser—water sprayed wide at a sharp, shallow angle. Part of the jet caught one of the oncoming protectors, lifting it up off the ground, and throwing it backward to smash hard against a wall.

Steam billowed, and Zachariah vanished inside a cloud. Water sprayed madly in all directions, splashed against the other protector, seemed to confuse it, drive it off its direct line toward Zachariah.

Creen ducked his head, but Brandun and Ahiliyah squinted and held on tight. Brandun kept one arm on the rail—with the other, he reached across Ahiliyah's back, grabbed a handful of Creen's suit. Ahiliyah leaned into Brandun, desperately thankful for his weight, his solidity. She held tight to the rail with one hand, her other reaching out to Creen's hand, fumbling like a desperate fish until their fingers locked together.

Huddled as one, the three of them held on.

The cloud of steam thinned, the smallest bit, and in that fuzzy space Ahiliyah saw Zachariah squat down, lean the shield over the geyser like a lid touching one side of a pot and lowering over the opening. The jet of water angled down, down—the water and steam blasted into the Demon Mother's face and chest.

The great beast flailed as glowing water pounded against her arms, her chest, her giant head. Ahiliyah knew the bitch was screaming, but her death-cries couldn't be heard over the geyser's roar. The deck rattled Ahiliyah, threatened to throw her and Brandun and Creen all into the air, but she held on, and let out a scream of her own.

"*Die, you bitch—die!*"

Seven decades of hell, hundreds of thousands dead, civilization destroyed, and it was almost over. Even as the heat swirled around her, the steam soaking her, Ahiliyah embraced the hate in her soul, and embraced something else as well—victory. Sinesh had shown her the way, and now she had honored his memory, the memory of her mother, Brandun's mother… every person who had perished because of these foul vermin.

This monster had killed her people, had nearly wiped out humanity.

She would breed no more evil. First the Demon Mother, then the rest of the monsters, then the eggs—hard battles ahead, impossible odds, but Ahiliyah would win. *Humanity* would win.

The Demon Mother's screams faded. Moments later, so, too, did the vibration.

The plume of water died down to a burble, then cut off altogether.

Clouds of swirling steam hid the Demon Mother.

At the geyser's mouth, Zachariah crouched there, soaked from head to toe, steam rising up from him and the pool alike. He wasn't even breathing hard. He smiled his half-smile. He glanced at the chestplate, which gleamed like it had just been sand-polished at Solomon Barrow's factory.

All across the room, the water's glow began to die down.

Ahiliyah saw a protector demon slowly rise—rise, and move toward Zachariah.

She felt Creen draw a breath, knew he was going to scream a warning. She wrapped her arm around his head, covered his mouth with her hand. It was too late.

Zachariah saw the demon coming. He let go of the chestplate. It tipped over, fell into the pool, casting a shadow over the shaft's brighter light.

He didn't try to run. Maybe he knew it was too late. The protector's tail lashed out, the tailspike plunging through Zachariah's stomach. Ahiliyah expected red blood, but instead, white fluid sprayed. She didn't have time to think about it before the protector grabbed Zachariah's shoulders. The long head leaned in. The toothtongue shot out, crushing Zachariah's head. White fluid sprayed.

Zachariah's arms twitched, then hung limp. The protector released him. Zachariah's body splashed face-first into the steaming geyser pool.

"It doesn't matter," Creen whispered. "We got her."

Ahiliyah didn't know if she should feel bad for Zachariah. His bravery had delivered the final blow, and for that, she was grateful, but he'd also been a part of birthing this nightmare across Ataegina. And at any rate, he'd lived for at least three centuries—even trapped in this place for most of them, he'd enjoyed far more life than anyone on the planet he'd almost killed.

Ahiliyah squeezed Creen's hand. She leaned into Brandun, felt him lean back. They had done it. They still had to get out—and fast, if Zachariah had been right—but even if they died in the next few minutes, they all knew they would have given their lives for something far greater than themselves.

"Let's go," Creen whispered.

"Not yet," Brandun whispered back. "I want to *see* her dead. For my mom."

On the Demon Mother's side of the chamber, the steam finally thinned.

In the mist, Ahiliyah saw… movement?

"No," she said. "No, she's *dead*."

A waft of unseen wind carried away the steam, just for a moment, long enough for Ahiliyah to see, long enough for her heart to drop, for the taste of their hard-won victory to turn to bile in her mouth.

The Demon Mother wasn't dead. She gleamed under a coating of iridescent minerals, waves of color dancing across her shell. She was a living jewel—a massive, evil, living jewel.

"No," Creen said. "It's not possible."

The massive creature lifted one bent arm; chunks of drying mineral coating splintered, dropped away. She tried to extend that arm—it trembled, as if she was under great strain. Then, with a loud crack, the arm extended, more chunks spinning off to land on the glowing-wet floor among the eggs.

"All it did was slow her down," Creen said. "It's not possible. It's *not possible*."

Brandun reached behind him, grabbed his assembled spear shaft. He stood, stood tall, not even trying to hide. He turned the spear once—the severed, pointed, curved tailspikes lashed to each end glimmered in the pale light.

"Liyah," he said, "do it now."

Ahiliyah grabbed his wrist, tried to pull him back to kneeling. He was far too strong.

"*Now*, Liyah."

The deepness of his voice—the same tone he'd used on the battlefield while relaying her orders to his section. Before she could question herself, she pulled out the toothtongue.

He held one tailspike in front of her. "All of it."

She poured out the thick poison, smeared it across the black blade.

"We can run," Creen said. "All of us. If we get to the mountains, we can survive."

Brandun stared down. He seemed so tall. He smiled at her.

"Liyah, you showed me what it really means to be a warrior." Brandun turned his smile on Creen. "You're my hero, Creen. You always have been. I love you both."

With that, he turned and raced to the right along the warped catwalk as fast as his limping leg would allow. He raced toward the Demon Mother.

"Tell him to stop," Creen said. "Liyah, *order* him to stop!"

If she did, it would only slow him down. This was it—this was their final chance.

"Run if you want," she said, then she stood, cupped her hands to her mouth. "*Hey, you ugly motherfucker! Come and get me!*"

The protector's long head angled up toward her. Black lips curled back.

Creen stood next to her. "You can be one intense bitch, Liyah. Anyone ever tell you that?"

"Only my friends," she said.

Creen slapped his hands on the rail, screamed as loud as his ragged throat would let him. "Suck a sack of demon dicks!" He stomped his foot on the catwalk. "Oh, that's right, demons don't *have* dicks!"

The protector raced toward them, long legs pumping, tail swinging behind it, Zachariah's white blood still smeared on its black face.

"Oh, fuck," Creen said.

Liyah drew her little friend.

The protector leapt to the top of a rock outcropping and was about to leap when the Demon Mother let out an ear-piercing screech—the protector turned around in an instant.

Brandun banked around the catwalk. When he was above the Demon Mother's egg sac, he didn't even break stride—he held the spear with his right hand, used his left to vault over the rail. He dropped through the air, landed on the skin that glowed from within. The sac bent under his feet, the impact sending a glowing ripple through the thick fluid beneath, but it did not break.

The protector scrambled down the rock.

Brandun's foot slipped out from under him. He dropped to one knee. Ahiliyah's breath caught as he started to fall over the side, but he grabbed one of the hanging skins and yanked himself back to his feet.

"You gotta be shitting me," Creen said.

Ahiliyah watched, stunned, as Brandun Barrow—the boy she had trained as a runner, the man who had backed her up when she had given him no reason to, the friend she had fought shoulder to shoulder with, had bled with, had almost died with—walked along the top of the Demon Mother's egg sac, moving toward her glimmering body and head.

The Demon Mother screeched and squealed, tried to twist, her movements slowed by the hardened coating of iridescent minerals. Her two larger arms flailed slowly, awkwardly behind her—she couldn't turn to face her attacker.

The protector scrambled to the Demon Mother. She bent her long head—the protector grabbed the notches on her crest, scrambled onto the flat, hard surface as she tilted her head back, making a ramp for her progeny. The protector rushed off her crest, squirmed past the tree-trunk-like black growths on her hips, and—grabbing stretched skins as it went—raced across the egg sac to meet the oncoming Brandun.

Brandun held the spear with his right hand. With his left, he gripped a hanging skin. He crouched, waited.

"Come on, Dumbdun," Creen hissed, "*stick* him."

The protector closed the distance.

Brandun spun the spear, bringing the uncoated tailspike forward. As the protector reached for him, Brandun simultaneously backed up and rammed the black blade into the egg sac. A spurt of thick, glowing fluid burbled up and out.

The protector's foot landed near that slash, and tore through, black leg sinking in up to its bony hip. The beast lurched sideways, ripping more membrane—a great gout of gel splashed out, raining down on the eggs and floor below.

The protector started to roll off the side, but reached up taloned hands and grabbed a hanging skin. Black legs—one wet, one dry—swung free as it started to scramble back up.

Brandun leaned out over it, one hand holding tight to a hanging skin, the other hand holding the spear. With one perfect, downward overhand thrust, he drove the tailspike deep into the demon's upturned, eyeless face. Burning blood sprayed out, arced away, fell to the floor below. The beast shuddered, then dropped. It landed hard, crumpling, limbs twitching, smoke and steam rising up from the puddles around it.

Brandun pulled himself back atop the egg sac. He reached far forward, grabbed a hanging skin, tucked his knees to his chest and swung past the still dripping tear. He kicked out, came down just a few yards from the Demon Mother's tree-trunk hip growths. Brandun spun the spear so the poisoned tailspike faced forward, then continued forward, his feet pushing against the soft membrane. The sac had deflated some, slowing his progress.

Such balance, such *strength*.

The Demon Mother screeched and lurched, trying to twist around, her wild movements shaking the egg sac, making Brandun grab a hanging skin and hold on tight. Mother flung her long arms, only to have them bounce off the hanging skins that held her aloft, the impacts making the strands thrum like the strings of a deep-voiced musical instrument.

Then there was a new sound.

A sickening, *ripping* sound, like an animal being torn in two.

The Mother's body... pulling away from the egg sac, strands of membrane stretching, thinning, snapping.

Brandun rose up, taller, sprinted toward her before his footing could disappear entirely. The Demon Mother took a step forward, leaving the black tree trunks and her yet-to-be-laid eggs behind, glowing fluid spilling from her hips, chunks of mineral falling away from her joints in a shower of sparkling color.

The beast turned.

Brandun switched his spear grip to overhand, his right arm cocked and under the coupling, his left hand near the black tailspike tip. With the scream of a half-million hate-filled victims, he planted his right foot on a notch of the hanging black tree trunks, and leapt into the air.

The Demon Mother's huge arms reached up to meet him.

Brandun drove his spear forward. The beast's massive hands and splayed, glimmering fingers caught him in midair just as his tailspike blade crashed through her chest armor and plunged into the softer flesh beneath.

The Demon Mother let loose an ear-piercing squeal.

Her two huge, black hands held Brandun by his chest and waist, lifted him higher. He tried to grab the spear, but he could no longer reach it. He screamed, snarled, beat his hands against hers.

His head snapped backward—his legs kicked, his arms flew out, fingers splayed wide.

Blood sprayed from his mouth.

Her hands trembled for a moment, then Brandun's chest and hips caved in beneath her grip.

Ahiliyah shook her head; she couldn't believe what she had just seen. Brandun was dead. The Demon Mother had squeezed him to death, smashed him like a mushroom.

The beast tossed Brandun's corpse aside. The crushed body landed against a rock outcropping, a wet rag hitting solid stone, then sliding down to a pile that was only vaguely recognizable as human.

The Demon Mother's smaller arms reached up to her chest, gripped the spear shaft, and yanked. The shaft came free—but the tailspike was no longer on it.

The beast stiffened.

"It's in her," Creen said, sobs wetting his words. "The poison is in her."

The Mother's triangular head tilted back. Her huge mouth opened—it screamed, a piercing wail even louder than before, so loud Ahiliyah's hands went to her ears.

The monster's long legs extended. She stood, her head well over fifteen feet above the floor. Four arms flailed. Crusty minerals fell off her in a multicolored rain. Her gleaming head angled this way and that. Then the head turned toward Ahiliyah... and stopped.

Roaring in pain and anger, the Demon Mother lunged forward, huge legs covering five yards a step.

Ahiliyah and Creen turned and ran for the passage entrance. Footsteps thudding behind them, as loud as a geyser tremor. She shoved Creen through ahead of her, felt the catwalk shudder, heard the screech of metal bending and twisting. Ahiliyah leapt into the passageway, landed hard, felt the very floor vibrating beneath her; momentum rolled her, landed her on her butt facing back toward the chamber.

The Demon Mother's massive head filled the entrance, broken deck and twisted rails jutting out around her. Her mouth gaped open.

Ahiliyah scrambled backward. The toothtongue shot out, locked down on Ahiliyah's left foot, piercing flesh and breaking bone. Ahiliyah screamed, planted her right foot, tried to pull free—searing pain ripped through her foot, her leg.

Ahiliyah started to slide across the floor, toward the monstrous Mother.

Creen ran forward, leapt, landed on the Demon Mother's head, slammed his tiny fists against her crest. The toothtongue opened, freeing Ahiliyah's foot, and the beast's massive head twisted to the side, smashing Creen against the wall. Jaws snapped, trying to get him, but he grabbed the crest and held on. She angled her head, trying to shake Creen loose. The jaws snapped again, clacking on empty air.

The Demon Mother spasmed, her whole head shook. Her jaws clattered together as if she was freezing to death. She started to move back, taking Creen with her—his head lolled, he didn't know what was happening.

Ahiliyah lurched to one hip, then—like Zachariah—planted her left hand and lunged forward with her right. She reached... her fingers sank into the hidey-suit netting on Creen's leg.

The monstrous head slowly slid back out of the passage.

Tears in her eyes, searing agony coursing through her body, Ahiliyah heard the massive beast crash hard against the floor fifteen feet below.

Ahiliyah pulled her friend close.

"Creen? Are you all right?"

His eyes fluttered open. "Did we get the bitch?"

Ahiliyah listened, heard the faintest squeal of pain, and another chatter of teeth.

"I think so," she said. "Help me walk, let's go take a look."

48

If the baby demons weren't fully grown already, they would be soon, and there was nothing Ahiliyah could do about that. She could barely walk, and even then only with Creen's help. She realized, far too late, that she hadn't asked Zachariah how to get out of the hold, or ship, or whatever this place was. The new demons were coming. Before they came for her, she would see her hated enemy dead.

The Demon Mother lay on her side, her dying twitches sending ripples across the shallow water of the geyser pool. She'd fallen half across the pool, half on several eggs, smashing them flat. They lay broken, torn, the twisted legs of spiders sticking out in places.

The Demon Mother would lay no more of the eggs. A living god laid low.

Ahiliyah saw Brandun's crushed, bloody body, more bones broken than whole. His arms, shoulders and head remained mostly intact, the rest of him turned to pulp. His eyes were closed.

"He wanted poems written about him," Creen said. "Too bad we'll die here, or I'd write so many about him he'd never be forgotten."

What Brandun had done... could words even express it? The bravery, the skill, the strength—the *intelligence*. Never had there been a warrior like him. Never would there be one, either. He had wanted to be a hero. And so he was.

Ahiliyah leaned heavily on Creen. Her foot was a shattered, bloody mess. She needed to bandage it, and soon, but was there any point? Maybe it was better this way. She could bleed out, be dead before the new demons came for her.

As if she'd wished it into existence, a demon's distant squeal came from the dark opening.

"Well, fuck," Creen said.

Ahiliyah couldn't stop a dark, morbid laugh. "My sentiments exactly."

Creen had his right arm around her waist. He held out his left in front of her, palm up.

"We won't make it out of here," he said. "I know I told you I couldn't do it, Liyah, but that was before. I'm not going to let them take me. If you want, I'll end it for both of us."

She felt tears welling up, and not ones of pain.

"Yeah," she said. "I'm really tired. It would be better if it came at your hands, I guess."

She drew her little friend, placed the handle in Creen's palm. His fingers closed around it.

Another demon scream, from a different direction, this one louder than the first. There was no point in fighting. She had no strength left. She knew it, Creen knew it.

"Let me set you down," he said, his words cracking with sobs.

He lowered her, gently. She decided on her knees would give Creen the best access to her throat. At least Ahiliyah could go facing the enemy she'd helped to defeat.

"We did it," she said. "Brandun really killed her."

Creen's hand on her shoulder. "We all killed her. The three of us. Together."

The tears came now, and there was no stopping them. It would have been nice to see Tolio again, to have his baby, to live on the surface in a world free of demons. Yes, there were more, a few hundred, perhaps, but without the Mother… perhaps people could band together and kill those few hundred demons.

But that fight was not hers.

She, Brandun and Creen had done the impossible. What came next would be decided by others.

"I am your friend, Ahiliyah," Creen said. "Thank you for being mine. Are you ready?"

She reached a hand up to grasp his. His left hand. His right had a task ahead of it.

"Almost," she said.

Ahiliyah almost closed her eyes, but she kept them open, kept them fixed on the monstrous, dead body before her. She wanted the dead Mother to be the last thing she saw.

Somewhere inside, Ahiliyah felt her hatred finally let go.

"All right," she said. "I'm ready."

She felt Creen's hand squeeze down on her shoulder, knew it would be over in seconds.

Then, he let go. "Liyah… do you hear that?"

She listened, heard a demon screech… but also something else.

The yells of men?

"Maybe you should stand up," Creen said.

She reached up a hand. "Help me."

He did, putting an arm around her waist, grunting as she leaned on him.

The sounds—squeals and yells alike—were coming from the lower tunnel entrance.

Creen started laughing, a dark laugh full of pain, loss and bitterness, but also full of *life*.

"Amazing," he said. "I think the Vindenians finally made it."

A demon stumbled out of the tunnel, two thick gashes in its long head. It fell, started to twitch. Another demon rushed out of the tunnel, crouched to a stop, turned and sprinted back to the opening. Before it leapt, a wall of dented, smoking, heavily scored bronze shields came out of the tunnel, three across the bottom overlapped by three across the top. Jutting from between the small spaces, a hedgerow of warped blades, some still smoking. The men behind the shields were so thickly covered with crimson leaves they looked like walking bushes.

Ahiliyah recognized the symbol painted on the ravaged shields—the bright green V of Vinden Hold.

The demon leapt, squealing in rage as it flew, then in pain as three spear blades impaled it. It twitched and kicked, its tail lashed against the shields. Shields lowered, the spearmen put their weight on the spear shafts, pinning the beast down. One man stepped forward, a squat man nearly as wide as he was tall. Even covered head to toe in caminus leaves, Ahiliyah recognized his shape.

"Drasko Lemech," she said. "Who would have thought it?"

Drasko drove his butt-spike into the demon's head, once, twice. On the third blow, the beast fell limp.

"Wow," Creen said. "Good thing I didn't kill you."

Ahiliyah nodded. "Good thing."

More warriors came out of the tunnel, spread out with their shields in front of them. Wounded men limping in at the rear, helping each other along. Spearmen saw the Demon Mother. They re-formed their mini-phalanx and crept toward her.

Drasko pulled back his hidey-suit hood, revealing his helmet and sweat-covered face. Even from twenty away, Ahiliyah saw the burn marks on his skin.

He saw Ahiliyah and Creen. He looked from them to the dead Demon Mother, then back, his jaw hanging open.

Creen held up a hand. "Hey, Drasko. Yeah, we killed the bitch. Can you come help get Liyah out of here? I got to do something real quick."

Drasko ran over, big boots splashing through glowing puddles. Other Vindenians came running as well. Drasko scooped Liyah into his arms.

"I hope there are more of you," she said. "There's a bunch of demons yet to kill."

"Shield units are working through the tunnels now," Drasko said. "We have a thousand warriors. We'll kill every demon left in this place."

Ahiliyah nodded slowly. She felt so tired.

"That's good," she said. "I think I need a doctor."

Drasko laughed. "The Margravine assured me you were still alive! I thought she was mad, but here you are. You did it, General."

The Margravine had made it? That was nice.

"Smash all the eggs," Ahiliyah said. "Tell the men to be careful, there are spiders inside."

"I'll tell them, General, but I'm getting you out of here. The Margravine is out on the Boiling Plains. Vindenian doctors are with us, they'll see to your wounds."

She rested her head against his chest, closed her eyes. War made for interesting allies.

"Hey, Liyah!"

Her eyes fluttered open to see Creen, his head bandaged in blood-spotted white, the chest of his hidey suit torn open, standing atop the Demon Mother's head, his hands down at his crotch.

"Here's what we think of your kind," he said.

Creen Dinashin—the demon-killer—pissed on the Demon Mother's huge head.

EPILOGUE

"The strength of the phalanx is the spearman," Ahiliyah shouted across the plain.

"The strength of the spearman is the phalanx," her troops shouted back.

"Again," she said, "on my command."

In her right hand, General Ahiliyah Cooper held a spear, the heavy butt-spike on the ground, the business end pointed toward the blue sky above.

In her left arm, she held her baby.

She stared out at a scene she once could have only dreamt about. In the distance, men and women toiled away on large squares of farmland. Different colors for different crops—wheat, barley, and the glorious feathered tufts that were ears of corn, ready to harvest.

Closer in front of her, in the first group, stood men—and more than a few women—with shields and six-foot-long spears. Sixteen people across, three ranks deep. The warriors gleamed with sweat generated from the day's heat and from their constant drilling. Sunlight played off chestplates, mostly bronze, but a few new ones of the hard-iron variety as well.

The shields, however, were all new, all made from hard-iron, hammered out in the forges of Vinden, Jantal, Keflan, and Lemeth. Made in four different places, but they no longer bore the crests of individual holds—now each shield was painted with a sun rising above a stylized mountain range—the symbol for the unified nation of Ataegina.

Ahiliyah drew in a breath, barked out a command. "Front rank, *lower*!"

The front rank lowered their spears level with the ground.

"Second rank, *lower*!"

The second rank obeyed.

"Third rank, *angle*!"

The third rank lowered, their spears angling up at fifteen degrees.

Forty-eight people had just transformed into an armored wall of death. She had another three groups of forty-eight, and could have made her front line longer, but along with shortening the spears and utilizing the new hard-iron shields, she'd changed tactics. She gave orders to those groups, moving one to the left flank, one to the right, and keeping one in the center.

Some of these warriors had survived the battle against the demons. Some were Vindenians. Some were Takantans and Lemethians who had run—but no one cared about that. They were alive, and their experience was proving invaluable. For anyone who had survived that hellish day, their cowardice was understandable, and forgiven.

Most of the fighters, however, consisted of younger Bisethians, Takantans and Vindenians who were new to arms and combat. They all wanted to learn from the General, the one who had rid their world of the great evil.

"Slow *march*," Ahiliyah shouted.

The groups moved forward, counting off every second step, a marching hedge with two-hundred and fifty-six feet stepping in perfect unison. Were they ready? Ahiliyah hoped so. She would continue to drill them until they were.

She wondered if Sinesh would have been proud of what she was building. She felt that he would. She missed him, missed Panda, Brandun's mother… so many others.

Ahiliyah saw people approaching down the long trail that led up to Lemeth Hold—Susannah, running fast, her hidey-suit leaves rippling. Farther back, Tolio and two young baker's assistants, each laboring to carrying a large wooden crate.

"Formation, *halt*," Ahiliyah called out.

As one, the groups stopped.

"At *rest!*" Spears rose up. Shields lowered to the ground.

Despite nearly sprinting at least a mile, Susannah was barely breathing hard. Her face net was flipped back, exposing her blonde hair and deeply tanned skin.

"General Cooper," she said, "there's been a sighting of Northerner ships off the coast."

The words chilled Ahiliyah's blood. "How many ships?"

"Three," Susannah said, "but the scouts said they were a ways off. There could be more."

Susannah wore a hidey suit, but she wasn't a runner. Those positions had been done away with. She was a scout—one of the new warrior types Ahiliyah had implemented in her updated military structure. Susannah would never be big enough to fight in a phalanx, but she could run like the mountain wind, she never seemed to tire, and in her suit, she could hide so well you might miss her even if she were only a few yards away.

"Any sign of where the ships might land?"

"No, but Biseth garrison is alerted. Little Spider is on his way there now with a new device. He said he'll be able to see all the way to the coast and miles beyond."

Ahiliyah said nothing, let her glare communicate for her.

Susannah's smile vanished. "I'm sorry, General… I shouldn't have used that name."

"No, you shouldn't have," Ahiliyah said. "When you speak of the man who saved the world, you use his fucking *name*. Understand?"

Susannah nodded furiously.

"Good," Ahiliyah said. "What does he call this invention?"

"A *farglass*, General."

Yet another Creen invention. In the two years that had passed since the death of the Demon Queen, the boy—no, the *man*—had created a new kind of mortar that allowed for fast fixes to the ravaged mountain holds, had found a way to make iron harder and more durable than bronze, and able to hold a sharp edge for far longer, had designed the new city of Hellan with a grid structure of roads that made much more sense than the ancient city (which had gradually expanded with winding paths), had created a new style of plow that made farming far more efficient, and now, apparently, had a way to see enemies from far, far off.

Ahiliyah had led the army against the demons. Brandun had killed the Demon Mother. Together, they had given Ataegina a future, but Creen? Hideous scars and all, Creen Dinashin *was* the future. He continued to learn much from the wreck of the *Nan-Shan*, bringing that new knowledge to bear for all Ataeginians.

"Take word up to Keflan," Ahiliyah said. "Have them signal Dakatera, Jantal, Hibernia and Pendaran. I need the Dakateran regiment ready to march immediately."

"Yes, General," Susannah said. She tilted her head toward the baby. "May I?"

"Make it quick." Ahiliyah adjusted her position, careful not to put too much weight on her foot. It had healed, if one could call the twisted, scarred club of flesh *healed*, but these days her spear was more crutch than weapon.

Susannah took the baby boy. Her face lit up as she held him, making Ahiliyah realize anew how beautiful the girl had become. No, not a girl—a woman.

Soon, perhaps, Susannah would have a child of her own. Ahiliyah would lose a talented scout—for a few months, anyway—but Ataegina would have another citizen, and citizens were needed now more than anything else, even Creen's new iron.

Tolio arrived, flashing his twisted smile. He always seemed to smile. His light blue eyepatch was a perfect shade for the summer afternoon. Unlike Creen, Tolio didn't care about the scars he'd earned in battle. He held a food skin in his hand.

"Hello, Susannah," he said. "I'll take little Brandun."

Susannah handed the baby to Tolio.

"Go deliver my message, Susannah," Ahiliyah said. "You have done well."

The young woman put her left fist on her sternum. "Thank you, General," she said, and then she was gone, sprinting across the lowlands toward Mount Lemeth.

Tolio cradled the baby. "And good afternoon to you, General.

I brought your unit lunch. Your favorite—pumpkin fritters with vindeedee stuffing."

Ahiliyah kissed him, then opened the skin and inhaled the scent. She loved *anything* pumpkin, a flavor she'd never known until a few weeks ago, when the first harvest had come in.

She turned, called to her warriors. "Meal break. Approach in an orderly fashion, rear rank first, get your meal, return to your position, eat there. Spears and shields, *down*."

The warriors carefully lowered their equipment to the ground, then the rear rank quickly lined up to take food from Tolio's assistants.

"They look good," Tolio said. "Why aren't they all in a long line?"

"I've been working on new tactics," Ahiliyah said, talking through a mouthful of the delicious fritter. "The smaller groups let me react faster to changes, and when one has fought for too long, I can drop it back and move in another. I call the groups *modules*."

"Modules," Tolio said, trying out the word. "Are your people ready to fight?"

"I think they will be soon."

"Hopefully soon enough."

He was right about that. The Northerners. If peace could not be made, soon Ahiliyah's troops would live out the old ways—men fighting against men. She could say what she would about the demons, but at least they'd never slaughtered each other over a piece of land.

"I'm proud of you, General," Tolio said. "Will you be home tonight?"

Every single day, he told her he was proud of her, and when he did, he always used her title. She never grew tired of hearing those words from his mouth.

"No," she said. "Ships have been spotted off the shores of the Northern Plains."

Tolio's smile faded. "I wish we could send a demon or two to the North. Keep them busy."

"Even if I could, I would never use demons as a weapon," she said. "Only truly insane people could do such a thing."

Tolio leaned in, kissed her cheek. "If you come home tonight, I will be waiting. If not, I will come see you tomorrow. And I'll bring cupcakes."

He turned and walked away, jostling little Brandun in his arm.

Ahiliyah loved them both so much that it hurt. To keep them alive—to keep as many people as she could alive—she needed her troops to be ready. If the Northerners continued to focus on one long phalanx or shield wall, Ahiliyah was confident her modular system would defeat them. But only if her troops were drilled, disciplined, motivated and ready.

She waited a few minutes more, let her troops return to their positions, eat their meal, and have a moment to laugh with each other. Or to complain with each other—either way was a soldier's prerogative.

They had their prerogatives, and she had hers.

"Enough stuffing your mouths," she called out. "The enemy has been sighted near our shores, and we have much work yet to do. Shields, *up!*"

ACKNOWLEDGEMENTS

The author would like to thank the following Colonial Marines for their service in the creation of this novel.

Dr. Joseph Albietz

Clara Fei-Fei Čarija

Scott Middlebrook

Alex White

If the author has forgotten any brave soldiers who contributed to this book, the slight is not intentional. Stay frosty.

ABOUT THE AUTHOR

New York Times best-selling author Scott Sigler is the creator of seventeen novels, six novellas and dozens of short stories. He gives away his stories as weekly serialized audiobooks, with over 40 million episodes downloaded.

Scott launched his career by releasing his novels as author-read podcasts. His rabid fans were so hungry for each week's episode that they dubbed themselves the "Junkies." The first hit is always free...

He is also is a co-founder of Empty Set Entertainment, which publishes his Galactic Football League series. He lives in San Diego, CA, with his wee little dogs Reesie and Squeaky.

BOOK TWO

INFILTRATOR

*To the fourteen-year-old boy and his date who saw
the original movie in theaters and was
blown away by the experience*

1

He dreams of storms and flames, the heat of a thousand suns turning everything into molten nightmare. He screams, but the roar of the superheated beast drowns out his cries. His mother, his father, everything he ever knew consumed by something so hungry it cannot be stopped. Even as far away as he is, the heat blisters his face and burns away the hairs on his head. His tears prism his vision until his small universe is a kaleidoscope of fire.

The shuttle jolted him awake.

"Welcome to Pala Station," the pilot announced as the shuttle landed. The announcement could not have been delivered with less enthusiasm. Still, the welcome was a punctuation to a long journey for Dr. Timothy Hoenikker, who'd traveled too many light years, all at the chance of investigating a cache of newly discovered artifacts.

Alien artifacts.

For a theoretical archaeologist, who up until now had depended on modeling in order to advance his research, examining *actual* components of an alien race's past was beyond remarkable. This could be, he hoped fervently, the opportunity of a lifetime.

Wiping the dream from his eyes, he shoved the familiar fiend to the back of his mind.

His shuttle partner sighed heavily.

"Back to the shit," the man said. He'd introduced himself earlier as Logistics Specialist Steve Fairbanks. His eyes were haunted, his gaze far away, and he had the world worn look of someone who'd been in the thick of it, and still hadn't found a way out. Probably just short of thirty years old, he was average height and had black hair cut close to his bullet-shaped head. His nose was too thin for a flat face, but that wasn't his fault.

"Can't be as bad as all that," Hoenikker said hopefully, hiding his discomfort at being spoken to, and with the information.

"Just wait, sir," Fairbanks replied. "You'll see what Pala is about in no time."

The station was out on the edge of the known systems—but then, weren't all the places where new discoveries were possible? When Hoenikker had been recruited, he'd convinced himself that leaving the luxury of his cushy Weyland-Yutani corporate job was going to be worth the effort. Before leaving, he'd researched the jungle planet LV-895 and marveled at its exotic life. Sure, the living arrangements might not be what he'd been used to, and the day-to-day luxuries might not be there, but the payoff would be to lay hands on that which he'd only previously imagined.

This could be the opportunity, he knew, to become one of the foremost experts in alien anthropology. His pulse quickened as he imagined the data he could provide to those who would come after, his name synonymous with the greatest archaeologists of all time. Layard. Carter. Jones. Leakey. Evans. Schliemann. Navarro.

Hoenikker.

"Pala Station personnel should be waiting for your arrival," the pilot announced over the intercom. "One minute until doors open."

The thrill Hoenikker felt was tempered with a sick feeling that everything was going to go terribly wrong. He'd always been this way—feeling the desire to experience new things, yet dreading that reality wouldn't live up to his expectations. As had happened all too many times before, was he going to be disappointed, or would this be the greatest adventure of his life?

His friend Stokes, who he'd probably never see again, had argued long and hard for him to take this assignment.

"*You might never get this opportunity again,*" Stokes had said. "*Sure, you could stay here at your nine-to-five, going out for dinner on Fridays, seeing your therapist on Wednesdays. Or you could travel to the edge of the known universe, discover wonders no man has ever seen, and be better for it. Be boring and stay here. Or be dangerous and travel far.*"

Stokes always did the dangerous. He'd been a Colonial Marine, then a scientist traveling for the company. Always the center of any conversation. Even Hoenikker looked forward to listening to the outrageous stories the man continually shared—assuming they were all true. This was his chance, Hoenikker knew, to walk in the footsteps of his friend. But in reality, he could never be the person Stokes was capable of being.

The red flashing light switched to green. The rear door of the shuttle opened, revealing a single man waiting for them, holding a pad. He had dark skin, bald, about forty. Part of his right arm was a prosthesis.

Fairbanks was first off.

"Fairbanks. Steven," he said to the man. "Log. Back from emergency leave."

After making a few marks on the digital pad, the man nodded, but didn't say a word.

"Best of luck," Fairbanks said over his shoulder, then he hefted his duffel and disappeared around the corner.

"You must be Dr. Hoenikker," the man said. "I'm Reception Tech Rawlings, Victor, and I'll be inprocessing you. Is that all your luggage?" he asked, nodding to the single large bag on the deck.

Hoenikker nodded. Rawlings stepped over and grabbed the bag. "This way please."

Hoenikker followed, noting that the air in the hangar was humid. But that was soon replaced by the cool forced air of the interior, the buzz and hum of environmental equipment immediately making him at home. Facilities he knew. Jungles he did not.

"As you know, Doctor, Pala Station's existence is classified," Rawlings said. "I've been here a little over a year, and things don't hardly change. We prefer it that way. So, you're with the scientists?"

"Yes." Hoenikker didn't know how much he could reveal.

Rawlings laughed. "What you all do isn't a secret to those of us on the station. What with the black goo and all. We just don't like when your research subjects get loose. You understand."

"Does that happen often?"

"Once is too often," Rawlings said. He held up his prosthesis. "I've seen enough action. I'm just trying to get my retirement creds now."

There was the sound of rapid footsteps and three men rushed around a corner. As they did, the third knocked Hoenikker roughly into the wall. The man grunted, but kept going without saying a word. They all held long wooden rods.

"Sorry about that." Rawlings steadied Hoenikker. "We have a rat infestation. Station commander has us on a schedule for extermination duty, and no one is particularly happy about it." He nodded toward where the men had disappeared. "Their turn."

"Rats?"

Rawlings shrugged and gave a good-natured smile. "We're on the edge of nowhere, on a godforsaken jungle planet. Rats are the least of our worries."

They continued on their way, and Rawlings indicated several doors as they passed the various staff sections. Staff Section 1—or S1—was Manpower. S2, Security. S3, Engineering. S4, Logistics. S5, Med Lab. S6, Communications. And S7, Fabrications. He counted them off as they passed.

"Being as far out of system as we are, we can't just order a part. So S7 is in charge of producing everything we need to operate, from a knob, to a screw, to a laser-guided ass missile."

Hoenikker balked. "Laser-guided ass missile?"

"That was a joke. Sorry, military humor. Just know if you need something, they can make it. Anyway, you'll be dealing a lot with S7. Just don't get in the way of their feud with S3. It can get vicious."

They passed through a door and entered an office like many others he'd seen. The setup was familiar. A desk. Two chairs. A camera attached to a terminal.

"Sit there, please." Rawlings gestured. "We'll take your picture, retina display, biometrics, fingerprint, and DNA. Need to make sure you are who we think you are, and give you access to where you need to be later."

Hoenikker sat in the chair across from the camera, eyeing the cradle made for his hand. He could see several dozen minute needles, almost invisible to the eye, and didn't relish the idea of embracing it. Still, bureaucracy. He sighed.

"I think it started two years ago," Rawlings said, oblivious to his hesitation, "when Fabrications ran out of materials and there were no supply shuttles for six months. They were forced to take what they needed from everyone else. It wasn't that bad really, but Engineering—who feel self-important because they keep the lights and air running—began calling Fabrications by all sorts of names, to get under their skin. 'Acquisitions,' 'Infiltrations,' 'Reparations,' 'Thieverations,' and my favorite, 'Mastications.'"

Rawlings pointed. "Eye here, please. Thanks."

Hoenikker placed his right eye in front of the reader, and stared into the light.

"I know. I know," Rawlings continued. "It seems like a small thing, but all day every day for six months became too much. That's it. Thanks, Doctor."

Hoenikker leaned back.

"So, when Fabrications had the chance to turn the tables, turn them they did. Engineering needed Fabrications to create a water pump for the commander, which they did—but they put everything in backward so the pump exploded, and then they blamed it on Engineering. Even pulled out instructions they had clearly fabricated—pun intended—to imply a design flaw. Meanwhile, Engineering is completely overwhelmed, dealing with the effects the environment has on the station, not to mention the rats that are getting into the wiring.

"We're so far away from any supply depot, Fabrications is constantly fixing things that medlab needs, or producing the special glass used in the containment areas for your experiments." Rawlings rolled his eyes, and Hoenikker thought he detected a note of resentment in his voice. "I could tell you about the other staff sections, but we don't have that sort of time. Your fellow brainiacs will have to brief you up."

He gestured at the hand cradle. "Now for this. It won't hurt at all. I promise. Each needle is coated with a local anesthetic. You just have to press firmly."

Hoenikker held out his hand, but hesitated.

Rawlings reached out, gently but firmly grasped Hoenikker's hand, and placed it in the cradle. The reception tech's prosthesis was cold against his skin.

Hoenikker sucked in air, ready to shout out.

The tech was right. No pain.

Rawlings maintained his grip as he made a few selections on the display with his left hand.

"And don't get me started on the commander," the reception tech said, and this time his ire was obvious. "He's completely useless, spending more time trying to get the hell out of here than trying to do his job." He glanced over, and nodded as if Hoenikker had said something. "I know. I know. The deputy should step up, but he's oblivious—too in love with the flora and fauna outside to pay attention to what's going on." He sighed. "It's our own fault, really. We're all professionals—if we weren't, the place would *really* fall apart. The fact is, each section operates on its own, without supervision. It's not like this is brain science, you know? But no one's paying attention to the big picture."

He released the hand, and Hoenikker hoped it meant he could go. So much gossip...

"Alright. You checked out, and you're checked in." He handed Hoenikker an ID badge on a fob. "Wear this at all times, and Security will leave you alone. Same goes for the synths, but I doubt you'll even see them."

"Synths?" Hoenikker asked, realizing upon hearing his voice that he hadn't spoken in a long while.

"Sure. You know, 'state-of-the-art,'" Rawlings said, delivering air quotes. "Special Security Chief Wincotts maintains them, but we've never seen them in use. No need, I guess. Probably stacked in a closet somewhere, covered in glass with a big sign that says, *Break In Case of Emergency*." He laughed.

"It all sounds a bit intense," Hoenikker said.

"Oh, no—not really," Rawlings said, standing and urging

Hoenikker to do so as well. "I've been in units where the tension is so thick you're worried someone's going to pop off a pulse rifle. Or we could be crawling in mud, on patrol on a new LV. Hell, I could be on sentry duty! No thank you, sir. I'll take the politics of Pala Station anytime." He looked Hoenikker square in the eye. "Just know where you are and who you're talking to before you say something you can't take back." He patted Hoenikker on the shoulder. "But hell, that's the same everywhere, no?"

Hoenikker nodded as he felt himself being guided gently out of the room.

"Now, let's get you situated."

They passed several more doors and went down enough corridors that Hoenikker lost track. Then they came to a door with his name on it.

"Only you and Security will have access. Just place your palm on the access panel." Hoenikker did so and realized the numbness had already passed. The door slid open, revealing a room that was large enough for a desk and chair, a bureau, and a narrow bed.

He turned to Rawlings. "Bathroom?"

The tech pointed across the corridor. "Communal. For brainiacs only. Sorry, Doc. If you wanted a private bathroom, you should have applied to be the commander."

Hoenikker sighed.

"Listen," Rawlings said. "Unpack. Get situated. I'll be back to get you in an hour."

Then he was gone, leaving Hoenikker alone. All he could hear was the pumping and hissing of forced air.

The silence was blissful.

2

When Rawlings returned, Hoenikker was sitting on his bed, hands in his lap. He had folded and refolded his sparse collection of same-color shirts, pants, and lab coats and placed them in their appointed places in the bureau. Pulling out his personal display he had placed it in the middle of the desk, hooking up to the station's comms so he could have access to news, vids, and mail. He'd stripped the bed to check the state of cleanliness, then had remade it.

Now he was ready to get to work.

During the short walk from his quarters to the area that housed the labs, he heard three arguments, saw four rats, and witnessed a man yelling something that sounded like, "I've had it up to here with this shit!" So, when he arrived in the quiet contemplative reception room that led to the labs, detecting the familiar antiseptic smell, he grinned inside. It felt more like he'd escaped from the streets into a house of worship.

For Hoenikker, a lab *was* a house of worship—a place to worship facts, critical hypotheses, and discovery.

A narrow man approached, wearing all black with a severe Mandarin collar. Somewhere between sixty and seventy, he had a white goatee and white hair that ran into a ponytail. He held both hands behind his back, and his chin was slightly raised.

"Dr. Timothy Hoenikker, I presume."

Hoenikker stood straight and nodded. He didn't like shaking hands, and assumed by the man's posture that the sentiment was mutual. The man in black nodded to Rawlings, who returned the nod and walked away, leaving the two men staring at each other. Despite the awkwardness, however, if anywhere was home, this was it. Whether it was in the center of a city or on the edge of the known universe, all labs were alike.

"I am Mansfield," the newcomer said. "We expected you a week ago."

"B-but…" Flustered, Hoenikker couldn't help but stutter. "But I, I have no control over transportation. Weyland—"

A hand suddenly appeared and cut him off by chopping the air. "You will find, Doctor, that we don't care for excuses around here. We care about results. Now," he said pausing for dramatic effect, "are you checked in and ready to assume your duties?"

Hoenikker gritted his teeth and nodded. Then he softened. Perhaps the man had trouble dealing with new people. Hoenikker could easily understand this. He had the same problem. So instead of responding with anger, he tried another tactic.

"Thank you, Dr. Mansfield," he replied. "When you recruited me, offering an opportunity to work with verified alien artifacts, I dropped everything and came as fast as I could. I'm eager to begin…" He cleared his throat. "…and I apologize for being a week late."

There. That should ameliorate his new boss.

"You are incorrect, and on two accounts, Doctor Hoenikker. To begin, I am not a doctor, although I am the person to whom you will report. And you will not be working on alien artifacts. We have other tasks in mind for you."

Hoenikker tensed, but tried not to show it. He didn't want to argue with his boss on the first day, but working with alien artifacts was the primary—the *only*—reason he had taken the job.

"There must be a mistake," he replied. "The reason I left my previous position was the promise of working on genuine alien artifacts, to compare them with my archaeological modeling." Despite the attempt to maintain his composure, his words became louder. "If you knew that I wasn't—"

Another hand chop.

"Lower your voice, Dr. Hoenikker," Mansfield said. "I am well aware of the promises that were made. They will be kept. Alien artifacts are closer than you think. However, our mandate is threefold." He began ticking them off on his fingers. "One, create technology with which to defend against the Xenomorphs. Two, to create related tech which the military can use to actively combat any opponents, including the Xenos. And three, discover the nature of the pathogen to determine if it can be used in a positive manner—for example, to cure disease in humans. As it now stands, we've scored some notable successes creating acid-resistant armor. We're also optimistic about the prospects of Leon-895."

Hoenikker had heard rumors about strange things happening at LV-895, but no hint of a biological substance that was the focus of their efforts. Before Mansfield could elaborate, however, a thirty-something woman approached. She had brown hair tied into a bun, and a pleasant face. Mansfield gestured in her direction, but she didn't say a word.

"This is Dr. Erin Kash. She will be your team lead, and will bring you up to speed." Mansfield stepped back. "Is this all clear, Dr. Hoenikker?" He spoke in a way that didn't invite an answer.

Hoenikker understood indeed. Bait and switch. He should have known. And this Mansfield was a real piece of work. He pictured Stokes in his mind, and asked himself what his friend would do.

"Move on," Stokes would say. *"Do your best. Be famous."*

Hoenikker nodded once.

Mansfield turned and walked away. When he was out of earshot, Dr. Kash finally spoke.

"Did he ask you why you were late?"

Hoenikker nodded.

She grinned and glanced behind her. "He does that to everyone. It's his way of establishing the upper hand. Ignore it. He's simply a bureaucrat Weyland-Yutani put in place to ensure that we create something they can sell. In this case, armor to protect Colonial Marines against the exigent threat of the new Xenomorphs."

"Xenomorphs?" he said. "Are those the creatures the rumors speak of?"

"You've never seen one?" She clapped her hands. "Doctor, you're in for something special. We don't have any at the moment, but are due for a new shipment. That said, we *do* have some interesting experiments currently under way. Come. Allow me to introduce you to the rest of the team." She led him through a door.

The lab was larger than Hoenikker had anticipated, given what he'd seen of the tight confines of Pala Station. After the reception room came a central area boasting distinctly top-of-the-line lab equipment—though none that he hadn't seen before. Besides digital testing devices, there were the usual old-school beakers, flasks, and test tubes. Old friends.

Two men worked at the central station, injecting something into a tabletop containment device. One had to be pushing three hundred pounds, while the other couldn't be half as much.

"We call this central area Grand Central," Kash explained. "Étienne, Mel, allow me to introduce my new lab partner."

The pair turned and regarded Hoenikker with good-natured

expressions. Reaching out with his hand, Hoenikker introduced himself, as did they.

Biologist Étienne Lacroix was the thinner of the two, and spoke with a French accent. About fifty, his skin was olive and he exuded the confidence of three men.

Chemical engineer Melbourne Matthews was the larger man. Even when Étienne was speaking, Hoenikker noted that Mel muttered to himself and had trouble making eye contact. He was younger than his associate, balding, and white.

"What we're doing here, Dr. Hoenikker," Étienne said, "is trying to determine the nature of the pathogen—that's what we call the black goo—and its effects on various Old Earth diseases. Fun stuff like Ebola and smallpox and shingles."

"Please, call me Tim," Hoenikker said. "Or if you must, just Hoenikker."

"I do like Hoenikker," Étienne said, making a fist. "It's quite a robust name. You must be quite proud of it."

Mel muttered something that sounded agreement.

"Aren't you afraid you might create a super bug?" Having spent his entire career doing computer modeling, Hoenikker thought it was an obvious question to be asked. To his astonishment, Étienne clapped.

"We can only hope, *mon ami*."

Hoenikker pointed to the box. "But I mean, what if—"

Étienne shook his head quickly. "That would never happen. One press of this button—" he gestured, "—and the experiment goes *poof*."

There was a cough, and all three men turned.

"Thank you, Étienne," Kash said. "Thanks, Mel."

"*Mon plaisir*, Erin." He turned back. "Welcome to the team, Hoenikker." Then he clapped Matthews on the back, and they returned to their experiment, Étienne peering through a lens while Mel input notes on a display.

Beyond Grand Central, through an open doorway, there was a single corridor with what appeared to be two containment areas on each side. Each was roughly ten-by-ten-by-ten and had a floor-to-ceiling glass front. A portion of each front could be opened, to allow personnel to enter and leave, and some of the rooms had doors between them. A workstation stood at each containment area, with a keyboard and various knobs and buttons.

"We call this Broadway," she said. Then, seeing the look in his eyes, added, "We had a scientist working here early on, a guy named Deneen who had minored in Old Earth History. New York City was a favorite of his. As far as I could tell, these are the names of landmarks there." Continuing on, she gestured. To the left, nearest them, stood a tall, muscular dark-skinned man who wore his hair in an Afro.

"Here we have Dr. Mark Cruz, testing environmental effects on a pathogen-infected rat." Inside what was labeled as Containment Room One was a creature that Hoenikker guessed had once been a rat, probably from the station itself. While he had always found rats to be arguably cute, the goo's effects on this one were unmistakably arachnid, creating a furry beast with gnashing teeth and six two-foot-long spidery legs.

"Dr. Cruz, allow me to introduce Dr. Timothy Hoenikker. Cruz is one of our xenobiologists, and the staffer who's been here the longest." Cruz didn't turn. He seemed to be focused on making entries into the workstation.

"I heard what Étienne said. 'Robust.' Gotta love the French." He shook his head, then his voice went serious. "If you're going to get along around here, Hoenikker, you need to find something you enjoy doing. I'm not talking about playing cards or whacking off, but something that contributes—that's beneficial to society."

Hoenikker didn't know how to reply. Before he could, Cruz continued.

"Fire and ice. Watch this," he said, in a way that Hoenikker could tell the man was grinning. He tapped a couple of the controls, and water cascaded onto the creature, causing it to twitch. Then he turned a knob, and the water quickly iced over. The gnashing teeth slowed until they didn't gnash at all. Frozen.

"Cruz—" Kash said.

"Easy, Kash," he replied, cutting her off. "It's still alive. This is the sixth time I've done it. The pathogen allows the creature to survive temperatures ninety below zero, maybe more, without cellular deterioration. I'll warm it up in a few moments, and we'll re-examine." With that, he focused on his notes again. Kash guided Hoenikker further along, to a man standing in front of Containment Room Four.

"You might have noticed that Cruz enjoys his work a little too much," she whispered, her mouth conspiratorially close to his ear.

"I heard that," Cruz shouted.

"I figured you would," she shouted back. "Still, it's true."

"Remember, Hoenikker," Cruz said. "Get your pleasure where you can."

The new man was the youngest one yet, probably early thirties. He was bald and fit like an athlete, with high cheekbones and bright blue eyes. He turned and grinned when they approached.

"I see you've met the welcome wagon," he said.

"Mansfield?" Hoenikker said. He thought *a real piece of work*, but bit it back because he didn't yet know the politics. The man laughed.

"I meant our resident psychopath, Cruz."

"I'm actually more of a sociopath," Cruz shouted, still without looking up. "It's not psychopathic if the creatures you enjoy torturing want to kill you."

"There's got to be a better word for it," the young man replied loudly. Then he shoved out a hand. "Mark Prior. I'm the other xenobiologist."

Hoenikker stared, and almost didn't respond, but at the last moment shoved his own hand out. He was immediately disappointed in himself when he wet-fished it, rather than returning the strong, confident grip that Prior had presented. When they released, he glanced into the containment room and saw that it was empty.

Prior pointed. "Do you see it? Can you find it?"

"What? Where?" Hoenikker asked.

"Leon-895. It's in there, I promise. See if you can find it."

Hoenikker had been curious since Mansfield's previous cursory mention. Squinting as he examined the ten-by-ten-by-ten-foot room, he saw nothing but the gray interior. Then something shifted, almost imperceptibly. A slightly lighter shade of gray. He blinked and adjusted his position, but in doing so he lost it. Shaking his head, he grinned self-depreciatingly.

"You saw it," Prior said.

"Only for a moment, and I didn't really see it. I saw the outline of something."

"Here. Let me see if this helps. The one problem with Leon-895 is the inability to change color at low temperatures."

He turned the same knob on his workstation as Cruz had used when lowering the temperature in his containment room. The creature's outline began to form, then the rest of it as it returned to its natural color. It was hairless, and the size of a housecat, but that's where all resemblance stopped. It also had six legs and a mouthful of razor-sharp teeth.

"Hoenikker, meet Leon-895. It has the same ability to change color as many of its Earth-origin cousins. This xeno-chameleon has a superficial layer of skin which contains pigments, and under that layer are cells containing guanine crystals. Color change is achieved by altering the space between the guanine crystals, which changes the wavelength of light reflected off the crystals, thus affecting the color of the skin."

"So, this is one of the Xenos," Hoenikker said.

"Yes and no." Prior turned to him. "There's Xenomorph with a capital X, and xeno with a lowercase x. Big-X Xenos are the gnarly beasts that bleed acid. We don't have any of them right now, but we expect a delivery soon. Small-x xenos are any creature not of Earth origin. Leon-895 is a small-x xeno." Recognizing the questions on Hoenikker's face, he added, "You'll see the difference when we get our first face-huggers down here."

"Prior is doing important work," Kash said. "He wants to see whether the ability to change color increases or decreases with the application of the pathogen. If we could harness the color-changing effect and marry it with the acid resistant armor we've already produced, we might have soldiers who are invisible to the human eyes."

"Where did you get the pathogen?" Hoenikker asked.

"No one knows for sure." Prior grinned tightly. "It came down from corporate."

"Rumor has it that it came from a ghost ship," Cruz shouted. "Found floating in space and of unknown origin."

"Or it could have come down from corporate," Prior said, rolling his eyes.

"Or both," Cruz persisted.

Placing a hand on Hoenikker's arm, Kash showed him down a side corridor, then another bordered with multiple containment rooms. Other creatures of unknown origin resided in different rooms, scratching at the impenetrable glass, trying to get out. Seeing the monstrosities, he began to realize that he was as trapped as the creatures. He was in a closed environment where there were a lot of things that could kill them. Things that came from outside Pala Station.

He wondered how far he'd have to go in order to finally get hold of the alien artifacts he had been promised.

He wondered if he'd live to see them.

3

Night. Everyone who should have been was in bed, except Cruz. He couldn't sleep. He'd been having more and more flashbacks recently, and rather than lie there staring at the ceiling, he decided to work a little.

No one could ever accuse him of not working. He'd grown up in a ghetto of storage containers on a Weyland-Yutani distribution planet that doubled as an intergalactic trash dump. Most of the residents of LV-223 were destined to search the dump for rare metals or, if they were lucky enough, get a job hauling product into awaiting containers bound for out-system LVs.

Cruz wanted none of that. At the time he'd been proud. Too proud. He'd laughed at his father and mother as they struggled to feed him. He'd told them they were lazy and should have found a way to get off planet, so he'd have a better future. When he became old enough, he managed to stow away, only to be discovered and jailed at his destination. He'd been given a choice then to either remain in prison or join the Colonial Marines.

Not really a choice.

At marine training he'd discovered what it was like to finally work hard, sweating and bleeding in equal amounts. He'd relished turning his body into a killing machine and learning how to use a weapon—a pulse rifle. He'd enjoyed his first and second deployments, each one bringing down an insurrection from a planet just like his own, and people just like his own. He'd seen from the other side the squalor in which they were forced to live, realizing for the first time that they *couldn't* leave. They had no means of changing their destinies.

They'd been given their lot and had to make the best they could.

He tried to reach out and speak with his family, to apologize to his father and mother, but all efforts at contact failed.

Then, on his third deployment, he encountered xenos.

He shook the memory away and donned his lab coat. As he entered the lab, the lights came on automatically, attuned to movement. He went immediately to Containment Room One. Cruz wanted to increase the amount of black goo he'd been injecting into his current specimen—what he'd come to call Rat-X. It scowled at him, the front two of its six legs held in the air. He needed to immobilize it, so he turned the temp all the way down.

The others thought he was crazy. Probably even the new guy, Hoenikker. Perhaps Cruz *was* a little crazy. Anyone who'd seen combat was changed by it, something his fellow doctors had no way of understanding. They'd grown up entitled.

Through a hardscrabble life and being the agent of his own actions, Cruz managed to parlay military service into a collegiate opportunity and finished with a graduate degree in xenobiology.

Crazy? No, what he was doing with Rat-X was as important as anyone else's experimentation, including Prior's specimen-of-the-moment Leon-895. Pala team still had a lot of questions, including how to freeze Xenos so their blood was no longer acidic. Would the nature of the acid change with thawing? Could they create a freeze weapon that would make Xenos easier to kill with conventional weapons, while preventing the blood from dripping through a ship's hull? They were fresh out of big-X Xenos, but they had the rats and they had the goo and they had the time.

Once Rat-X was frozen, he turned off the temperature controls.

Before it thawed and awoke, he'd have more than enough time to do what he had planned. Grabbing a biopsy needle from a nearby drawer, and a clamp, he toggled open the containment room door. There was a click, then he stepped inside. A residue of cold made him shiver for a moment. He attached the clamp to a spot along the back wall, then lifted the frozen creature and put it into the clamp, which actuated. Four padded arms enveloped the creature, holding it fast.

Cruz held onto one of the long chitinous legs and shoved the biopsy needle into the abdomen. What he sought was more of a core sample than a blood sample. If he'd wanted the latter, he would have put the Rat-X to sleep using gas. But this was easier and, frankly, made him feel better.

Suddenly, he's back in the wretched darkness—a darkness to which he's returned, over and over. A darkness that won't leave him. One that lives inside of him and somehow forever avoids the light.

Pulse rifles light up the night, turning the events into an old-time movie. Reality flickering from light to dark to light again over and over as the pulses from the rifles strive to save them. They'd been assigned settlement protection on LV-832. Carnivorous moose-sized creatures with tentacles charge their position. Their hooves the sound of thunder. Their howls like musical horns. Pulses from the rifles illuminate the creatures in nightmarish flashes. The forward observer dies first.

Back in the lab, he snaps off a chitinous leg.

The lieutenant tries to be a hero. No one wants a fucking hero. They fire and fire until their rifles choke. Still the creatures come. Trampling.

Snap!

Snyder hurls into the air, propelled by the tentacles wrapped around his torso.

Snap!

Schnexnader screams as his right arm is bitten off. Blood spurts on all of them as he spins madly.

Snap!

Correia is grabbed and slammed repeatedly against a tree until blood and organs explode from his body.
Cruz screams, then cries.

Back in the lab, he realized he was holding a leg in each hand, ripped from the creature's body. He was making a low sound like a continuous groan, felt incredibly drowsy, and wanted to lie down.

The rat began to move, then cried out in pain, the sound of a cat caught in a vice. Rat-X writhed and squirmed. Twisting, it freed itself from the clamp and, with its remaining three legs, latched itself onto the front of Cruz's lab coat.

Cruz madly knocked it off.

It careened to the floor, righted itself, then scrabbled toward him.

Cruz backed away, but the Rat-X grabbed his pants leg. In a spastic one-legged dance as he tried to shake the creature free, Crux made it back toward the containment room door. Rat-X lost its grip and flew against a wall. Then Cruz spied the biopsy needle. He'd dropped it during his blackout. Realizing he still held two of the creature's legs in each hand, he threw first one, then the other at the creature, which backed away.

Diving for the needle, Cruz managed to grab it, but Rat-X surged between his legs toward the open door. From his knees Cruz reached out and grabbed the monstrosity from behind. The creature gnashed its teeth at him, but Cruz managed to narrowly avoid being bitten. He jerked the creature over his head, slamming it into the back wall. The motions threw Cruz to his knees, and he crawled frantically through the door. Twisting onto his back, he kicked the door closed just as Rat-X faceplanted on the glass.

The creature stared daggers at him as it slid to the floor.

Cruz climbed wearily to his feet, and placed the biopsy needle in a drawer. He'd take care of it later. Pulling aside a button cover, he revealed a big red ABORT button. He pressed it, and the containment room filled with flames from top to bottom. Rat-X squealed for a second, then folded in on itself as it first turned to cinders, then ash. When the flames died, Cruz searched the room for any other debris that might represent the legs.

He thought he'd got them all.

Wearily, he headed back toward his sleeping quarters. The night had almost been a disaster.

4

An hour before first shift, everyone else was asleep—but not Logistics Specialist Fairbanks.

Ever since he'd returned to Pala he'd been a nervous wreck. His blood pressure had to have been through the roof. His head ached from the constant pounding, and he couldn't get his hands to stop shaking. He'd thought that maybe he would have been searched when he returned from emergency leave, but Security hadn't so much as glanced at him. That had been an immense relief, but still he couldn't help but wonder if he wasn't being watched.

Although he knew from his work as a logistics tech that there were only a few instances of internal surveillance, his paranoia made him wonder if perhaps Security had planted some devices without him knowing. Just the thought of it made him want to hyperventilate, so before he was able to do what he'd planned on doing, he had to sit and try to control his breathing.

Finally, he was able to stand, his legs still a little shaky. He believed he'd feel better once the deed was done, yet couldn't help but feel as if he was doing something terribly wrong. Just the thought of it made him sit again. He wasn't really an infiltrator, was he? He wasn't a bad guy. He was a victim—a victim of corporate greed. He was a bullet fired from one corporation to the other.

In this case, Hyperdyne firing at Weyland-Yutani.

What they wanted him to do wasn't so bad, he supposed. After all, it wasn't like he was going to hurt anyone. It wasn't as if someone might die because of what he was being made to do.

Yes. He was the victim. He'd been given a part to play in the Corporate Wars and he'd play it then move on with his life. It wasn't as if he had a choice, either. He'd threatened to go to Security, to tell them what had happened while he was away. His blackmailer's response was to remind him how long an arm Hyperdyne had, and how they knew where his family resided—especially his mother. Had it been a threat? Most definitely. So, they had him. There was nothing he was capable of doing except follow through.

Fairbanks stood, reassured about what he was going to do. He nodded to himself, straightened his spine, and strode toward his dresser. Opening the top drawer, he reached toward the back. Beneath his underwear and socks was a thick package. He pulled it free, peeked inside, then closed it.

Still alive.

Good.

Grabbing a pack off the side of his desk, he shoved the thing inside. He slung it over his shoulder, opened his door, and glanced up and down the corridor. Clear. Stepping outside, he closed his door and headed quickly to his left. Three turns later he was in the right corridor. He hurried to the end and stopped alongside an access panel about three feet tall. Checking left, then right, he pulled out a tool and opened the panel, letting it come to rest on its lower hinges.

Inside were several wires and an opening in the ductwork. He slouched out of the pack and rested it on the open panel, pulling free the package and opening it. Inside were three dozen specially designed baby rats provided courtesy of Hyperdyne Corp. He shepherded them into the ductwork, watching as they scampered madly away, probably elated to be free of the dark confines of the package.

Once the last had gone, he put the empty package back in his pack and pulled out a vid display unit. He attached it to some wires, then hammered out a message—code he'd memorized that Hyperdyne would pick up. They'd ensured him that they'd already hacked station comms.

His task complete, he wedged the vid display behind a cluster of wires, used the tool to close the access panel, and placed the tool back in his pack. He was about to leave when a security specialist turned the corner. She stopped and stared in his direction.

"Identify yourself." She had a hard face and short-cropped blonde hair. Her muscles were twice the size of his. Even if he thought he might try and escape, there was no way he'd be able to get away from her. "I asked your name."

He stood at attention, his back against the wall.

"Logistics Specialist Fairbanks."

"What are you doing here?" she asked, eyeing the access panel, then his pack.

Enabling Hyperdyne Corporation to spy on you. He blinked. His mouth was a desert. His head pounded and he wanted to pee. "I thought I heard something in there." He glanced toward the access panel. "Maybe rats?"

She shook her head. "We have rats everywhere. I mean, what are you doing in this corridor? You have no reason to be here. This leads to the underground."

"I—I was trying to get some exercise, prior to shift. I wasn't paying attention to where I was."

"And the pack?" she asked, pointing to it.

"Uh, have some trash in there. Going to dispose of it after exercise."

She held out a hand. "Let me see."

Just his luck to get the most thorough damned security specialist in all of Pala Station. He shrugged out of the pack. She opened it and pulled out the package, checked inside and saw it was empty. Shoving it back in the pack, she pulled out the tool.

"And this?"

"I'm a log specialist." He shrugged and tried to laugh, but it came out as more of a bark. "I use it every day."

She tapped it against her hand a few times then, frowning, placed it back in the bag. She handed it back to him. He accepted it with two hands and held it.

"You were the one went on emergency leave, right?"

"Uh, yeah." He felt his eyebrows raise. "I had to get to a place with better comms."

"So you could call home?"

He nodded.

Her face softened. "That's the main problem with being out so far. That, and the knowing that you'll probably never see your family again." She stared down the corridor and millions of miles farther. Then she turned back to him. "How was it you were allowed to go? What was it, seven weeks' travel?"

He thought of Rawlings, and how the reception tech had hooked him up. Just a few fake signatures and a compelling narrative.

"Lucky, I guess."

She frowned, "I don't believe in luck." She stepped close and poked him in the chest. "Now, get out of my section and go exercise somewhere else."

Just then the sound of something rustling came from inside the access panel.

She shook her head. "Fucking rats everywhere."

He nodded, then backed down the corridor. When he reached the intersection, he hurried down the new direction, eventually finding his way back to his room. Stepping inside, he closed the door and fell against it, breathing heavily. He hurled his bag onto his bed, then bent over double. He'd never make a good criminal.

Hell, he barely made a decent infiltrator.

5

Reception Tech Rawlings entered his office, sporting a grin and a cup of coffee. He took a sip as he sat behind his monitor.

Any day at the ass end of the universe is better than being in the suck.

That was his motto for pretty much every occasion. Glancing at his prosthesis, he chuckled. Some do it for the medals. Some do it for the money. "*Come. Join the Colonial Marines. See the universe.*" Shoot things and break things and we'll pay you for it. While his left hand ached with arthritis, his prosthetic right one felt nothing at all. The bright side of a dark day.

He took another sip, then dialed up the dailies.

Staff sections had reported a hundred percent. As it should be. If someone went missing, it meant something bad had happened. Pala Station was a closed station. No one was allowed to go anywhere without the station commander's approval—except of course the deputy commander, who seemed to spend more time off station, hunting and exploring, than he did on duty. Even built a lodge out there. Not many people knew about it.

Nicoli was already at her desk. She was in charge of personnel management and would soon be forwarding the daily accountability to the commander. She also had some disciplinary notes to attach to several personnel folders. It seemed as if the good folks over in Engineering had made their own hooch. Such a thing normally wouldn't have been a problem, but when one of them coded the station lights to flash on and off to the beat of an old rock song, they went a bit too far.

Brown was also at her desk. Her function was readiness management. It was getting to the end of a cycle, and she had to ensure that team leads entered their employee progress reports into the Weyland-Yutani database. Corporate was always about the lure of promotion. Do well, rat on your peers, use their backs for your own stepping-stone, and we will promote you.

Rawlings, meanwhile, had to prepare for the incoming specimens about to be delivered to the scientists and their personnel. The *San Lorenzo* had towed *Katanga* refinery into orbit, and soon they'd have some visitors. It was Rawlings' job to ensure that all inbound had the correct security clearances and personnel files. This caused him to have interaction with Security, which he didn't mind at all. Several of them were former Colonial Marines, trading in their knowledge of infantry operations for security operations.

Rawlings spent an hour at the terminal preparing digital paperwork, then once he was finished, he stood.

"You leaving us again?" Brown asked.

"Going to Security, and then to Fabrications."

"You do know you can just call them, right?" Nicoli asked.

Rawlings grinned merrily. "I prefer the personal touch. No offense to you two ladies, but I do like to see other faces in the flesh, now and again."

Brown shook her head, returning to her screen.

Nicoli shook hers as well. "I just don't understand you, Rawlings."

He smiled wider. "Nothing to understand. What you see is what you get." He saluted her with his empty coffee cup and exited the office.

Cynthia Rodriguez was security chief, and a Wey-Yu corporate troubleshooter. Her deputy for internal security was Randy Flowers, a relatively new addition to the station, still finding his footing. Rawlings had known Randy in the service. Captain Flowers had been a solid no-nonsense marine. They'd deployed together on the mission where he'd lost his hand.

It was less than a five-minute walk to the Security offices. When Rawlings arrived, he found Flowers and coordinated the transfer of personnel, ensuring that there would be follow-on files for him to peruse and store. He grabbed some of their coffee and headed out the door. Right before he left, Sec Specialist Reyes approached him.

"What does a girl gotta do to get off station?" she asked.

He'd always liked her. Although never a Colonial Marine, she had the square jaw of a tough person. He could imagine her in uniform, firing a pulse rifle at some incoming enemy.

"Only the station commander can authorize off-station travel," he said.

"Word has it he'll sign whatever you give him."

"Is that so?" He sipped at his coffee, wondering where she was going with this.

"I bumped into Fairbanks this morning," she said cryptically.

Rawlings nodded slowly. "He had a family emergency."

"Is that so?" She grinned.

He grinned back and sipped his coffee. "Company policy is that if you have a compelling need, you can have up to ten weeks LWOP—leave without pay. It's just finding the compelling need."

She stared at him thoughtfully.

"Is that all, Security Specialist Reyes," he said, "or are you going to frisk me."

"Yes. I mean no. I mean, yes, that is all."

Rawlings saluted her with his coffee. "Compelling need."

"Compelling need," she repeated, gaze turned inward as if she was trying to figure out exactly what need was compelling.

Next stop was Fabrications. When he entered, they were playing a board game. Something having to do with logistical supply lines to spaceships. Fabrications was the smallest staff section. Tom Ching and Brian Mantle were the specialists, while Robb King was in charge. When he entered, all of them groaned.

"You do know that you eventually have to work, right?" he said.

"We've spent three days on rat duty," King said. "That's work enough."

"How would you like to do *real* work, like actually fabricating something?"

"Don't tell me," Ching said. "The brainiacs need more glass for their containment rooms."

Rawlings saluted the smaller of the three. "Got it in one try."

"How come they need so much of the special glass?" Mantle asked. "It's not easy to blend it with tungsten, and still make it transparent. Why not just use tungsten walls and have a video camera on the inside?"

"Ever seen those things they work on—the ones sent ahead from *Katanga*?"

All three of them shook their heads.

Rawlings offered them a grim smile. "It would rip that camera down in a second. Plus, I'm told it bleeds acid."

All three of the men mouthed the words, *it bleeds acid*.

"Knowing the why is nice, but you fabricate because it's your job." Rawlings nodded. "If I were you, I'd get ahead of the game and see if you can prepare some glass. Plus, if you have work orders, you can't really be rat hunting, now, can you?"

All three of their faces lit up.

"That's true," King said. "That's very true."

Rawlings saluted them with his coffee cup, then went in search of Comms. Three minutes later he was saying hello to Comms Chief Vivian Oshita. Inside the section HQ were three workstations, each occupied by a comms tech. Buggy, Brennan, and Davis. It was Buggy he was there to see.

"Bugs. Share a cup of coffee with me?" Rawlings asked.

"What is it you want?" the tech asked suspiciously. He was about fifty, bald, with pockmarks on his cheeks. Rawlings knew he had a prosthetic right leg, lost during his tour in the marines.

"I'm trying to get a bunch of us together to form a group of... common concern," he said.

"A group of common what?"

"A group of common concern," he repeated. "A club, sort of. One that's filled with former Colonial Marines."

Bugs shook his head. "I don't want to be in any club. I've put the marines behind me."

Rawlings laughed and nodded as he poured Bugs a cup of coffee. He passed it to him. "It's not that kind of club. We don't have parties or dues or wear funny uniforms. We did all that before in the marines, right? No, this is just about us getting together to... to be there for each other." He glanced at Bugs, who was taking a sip of his coffee. "I don't know about you, but sometimes I need to talk about shit, but none of these civilians would understand." He waited for that to sink in. "Plus, in the event that things go bad, we need to stick together."

"What do you mean, *in the event things go bad*?"

"You're in Comms. You know what kind of fucked-up creatures they have on *Katanga*. They're bringing more of them down soon. Have you ever thought what would happen if they got out?"

Bugs gave him a swift glance.

"Wouldn't be something I'd care to happen," Rawlings said without waiting for an answer. "Want your life to depend on station security? Or do you want to depend on guys who went through the same things you did?"

Bugs eyed him as he sipped coffee. "You're making more sense than I thought you would. How many of us are there here?"

"Less than ten. Not a lot of us, but I've managed to get with Logistics and stash away an emergency supply of weapons, just in case."

"Aren't those tracked?"

"Sure they are," Rawlings said, grinning.

"Oh, I see."

"You know that any Colonial Marine worth his or her salt would have a Plan B."

"And *we're* the Plan B," Bugs said. He stared into his coffee for a long minute. "You know, I really thought I wanted to put all my military time behind me. I lost more than people know. But can we really do that? Isn't it who we are?"

Rawlings held up his prosthesis. "I know what you're saying. Every time I do anything with my hands, I'm reminded of what I lost—but then I remember what I've gained. I remember the comradery we had. I remember the highs I had while serving and fighting with my mates."

Bugs absently rubbed his prosthetic leg. "Yeah. It's easy to forget the good times. Sometimes the bad times just outweigh everything. So, what is it you propose? Do we have meetings? Do we have a secret sign?"

Rawlings laughed. "Maybe get together every now and again. We'll play it by ear. I just wanted to see if you were up for it." A moment later he added, "My gut tells me we need to stick together."

"Well, if I can't trust the gut of a Colonial Marine, I don't know what I can trust."

"That's what I was hoping you'd say." Rawlings nodded. He began to back away, saluting Bugs with his coffee cup. "Until next time." Then he turned and was out the door.

6

Hoenikker spent the morning helping the other scientists clean the lab and check the integrity of the containment rooms. Several of them needed replacement windows. Fabrications said it would be a day or so before they could make them. Mansfield, to his credit, ordered enough to replace all of the glass, based on the upcoming delivery of capital-X Xenos.

After a thirty-minute lunch of questionable substances in the mess hall, Hoenikker returned to the laboratory and began to shadow Kash. He'd found her a dedicated professional. One who should be emulated. He'd enjoyed his association so far, and looked forward to more interaction.

As a primer for what they'd be doing later on, she'd arranged the lab table so she could show him firsthand how the pathogen interacted with living matter. While they worked, he eyed Cruz down the corridor, sitting in front of Containment Room Two.

"What's his story?" he asked in a low voice.

"Cruz?" she said. "He's efficient." She withdrew a sample of black goo from a secure container. "A little sadistic, but then, he was a Colonial Marine."

"How did he go from being a Colonial Marine to being a scientist?"

"Education. Not everyone wants to spend their life in the military."

"I know, I was just…" He glanced at her. "I don't know what I wanted to know. He just seems like a different sort of person to be in a laboratory."

"He's definitely not what you'd expect, but he has an amazing mind. He was the one who made the breakthrough that enabled us to develop the acid-resistant armor. That alone would enable him to run any Weyland-Yutani lab in the known systems."

"Yet he stays here."

"You know how it is. In the central systems, everything is safe. It's all modeling and algorithms—but out here you get to work on live specimens, in an environment that pushes the boundaries. Rules aren't necessarily rules. They're more guidelines, which promotes more out-of-the-box spectacular thinking."

"Hence the breakthrough."

"Hence the breakthrough. Even Mansfield leaves him alone."

"Mansfield," Hoenikker said, the word more of a sigh.

"Typical Weyland-Yutani bureaucrat. He's a constant reminder that we work for a corporation, and not for ourselves."

"How bothersome is he?"

"Not as much as you'd think. As long as we're producing and following security protocols, he leaves us alone." She glanced at him, smiling. "After all, he really has no idea what we're doing."

"Seems like an interesting mix of scientists," he said.

"All are at the top of their game. Étienne is more than what he seems. He's all suave, but he's extremely serious. As is Muttering Mel."

"There's one of him in every lab," Hoenikker said.

"Yes, but what he lacks in social ability, he more than makes up for in concentration. He's best doing repetitive experiments, or creating algorithms to prove or disprove a supposition. He can do those on the fly. Eerie the way he's able to just lean in and do the math."

"Prior seems to be a good guy."

She glanced down the corridor to where Prior was working.

"He is, but he has a back story no one really knows. All I could gather is that when I came on board, Mansfield felt he had to inform me that Prior had once been in prison, and asked if I'd be comfortable working with him."

"Prison?" Hoenikker stared at the man, who seemed to be so nice and polite. "What was he in for?"

"Murder, if you'll believe it."

"Murder?" Hoenikker whispered. "Who did he murder?"

"His wife, but there were extenuating circumstances, I'm told. He was released after an appeal."

"Extenuating circumstances?" he whispered. "If he murdered her, then what could those have been?"

"Your guess is as good as mine," she said. "I'm curious as well, but it's not something that comes up in casual conversation."

Hoenikker couldn't help but stare at the man. Prior looked up. He grinned and waved, then went back to what he was doing.

As quickly as he could, Hoenikker looked away. The man knew they were talking about him. Hoenikker felt like an idiot. Still, a murderer? If anyone had asked him who was the murderer in the lab team, he'd first deny that any of them were capable of it. Then, if pressed, he'd have nominated Cruz. That seemed so obvious, but it was clear that what seemed obvious was anything but.

"They lured you here for alien artifacts."

Hoenikker snapped out of his internal dialogue and nodded vigorously. "They promised me I'd be able to investigate them firsthand. Indicated that they had an extensive collection." He looked around. "But I don't see anything like that, unless it's covered by the jungle canopy."

"I wouldn't be surprised," she replied. "There's definitely more going on here than I know. Did they tell you about the synths?"

"I heard mention."

"Let me just say that they're spooky. When you see them you'll know what I mean."

"Where are they?"

"That's the thing. I don't know where they keep them. It's as if they have another wing that we don't know about."

"I haven't walked the whole station, but it doesn't seem to be that big."

"It isn't. Which begs the question, where are the synths?" she asked, her blue eyes wide. He considered that, and vowed to himself to walk the corridors and get a better lay of the land. After all, he might need it some day.

"How long have you been at Pala Station?" he asked.

"Six months. Previously I worked at a hospital. I also have a medical degree."

"Medical? As in eye, ear, nose, and throat?"

"More trauma surgeon. We were near a mining rig, and there were a lot of crushing injuries." She sighed and looked away. "You couldn't imagine the number of amputations I've had to make. I needed a break—needed some pure science. Weyland-Yutani was looking for an epidemiologist, and I was looking for a change of scenery." She spread her arms. "So here I am.

"What's your story?" she continued.

He sighed. "I'm probably one of the most boring people you'll ever meet. Never been married, no brothers and sisters. I was an orphan who had good enough marks to get a full ride at university."

"You were really an orphan?"

"Yes." An image of fire tried to roar to life, but he stomped it down. "Which is why I suck at relationships." He glanced at her. She raised an eyebrow.

"I didn't mean it that way," he said quickly. "What I meant was that I never really had someone to love, and I was never really loved, so I don't think I understand the concept." He blushed, feeling his face turn hot and red.

"Timothy Hoenikker, are you blushing?" she asked, a smile forming on her face.

He was furious at his traitorous body. Why was he even talking about love? He was worse than "Muttering Mel."

"I don't know what's going on," he replied. "I don't know why I told you that. It's not as if you asked."

"I did ask," she said. "I asked what your story was, and you told me part of it. We all have these things that make us who we are. I was married once. My husband found that he had a better time with nurses than he did with a fellow doctor, so I let him have it his way."

"You were married to a doctor?"

"I thought we'd have something in common. As it turned out, we had too much in common."

A cry went up to their right, and he peered down the corridor. Cruz was backing hurriedly away from the containment room window.

"Protect yourselves," he shouted. "It's going to go!"

7

Rather than running away from the problem, Hoenikker ran toward it, and he didn't know why. He found himself beside Cruz, both of them breathing heavily.

He was just in time to see the glass melt as the Rat-X inside continuously pelted it with acidic spittle. A hole formed. Hoenikker backed away as the creature's chitinous forelegs grasped the opening and it pulled itself through.

The creature landed on the floor. About two feet tall and three feet wide because of the legs, it was a formidable little beast. Not big enough to intimidate, but not small enough to ignore. If one didn't know it could spit acid, they might take it for granted and approach it.

Kash went to hit the alarm button.

"Don't do that," Cruz shouted. "We can take care of it here."

She paused.

The creature saw her, and began to scuttle toward her, propelling itself with its chitinous rear legs while holding up its forelegs in a menacing fashion.

"We combined DNA from a local spider to see what the interaction would be," Cruz said. "Hence the legs, but the acid was an unpredicted result brought on by the pathogen."

Kash circled around the other side of the central table, putting it between her and the creature.

"Are you going to do anything, Cruz?" she asked, eyes wide, looking ready to bolt.

"Just don't let it get near you," he responded. "I have an idea." He dove for a closet and began to pull something out.

Rather than follow her around the table, the creature jumped onto it. It spit a wad of acid at her, but she was able to dodge. The wall behind where she had been standing began to melt in the spot where it hit.

"Cruz! You need to do something now!" she said, edging her way toward where they were standing. Cruz exited the closet wearing something with a tank, a hose, and a long metal nozzle.

"Flamethrower," he said. "I put it here in the event a xeno escaped." He passed Kash. "Get behind me," he said, ushering her back with his arm. He held out the nozzle and was about to fire when the door to the lab opened.

Mansfield stood in the doorway staring at the Rat-X.

"What the hell is going on?"

Before he was able to move, the creature leaped off the table, spit acid at his leg, and scurried out the door. Mansfield screamed as the acid ate away at his clothes and skin. Kash ran toward him, grabbing a med kit from the wall as she did.

Cruz ran out the door and disappeared to the right.

Against his better judgment, Hoenikker followed him. Out in the corridor, he was ten feet behind Cruz as they chased the creature. It hissed and raised its front legs whenever it saw a threat, but seemed more intent on fleeing than harming. His eyes went wide as it jumped onto the wall, and then onto the ceiling, running with as much an ease as it had on the floor.

They began to encounter other people in the corridor. Each time Cruz seemed about to fire, Rat-X would jump down or around something or someone.

They approached a corner, and a clique of people appeared, chatting together. The creature seemed to have decided it had done enough running, and leaped onto the face of a young man in the middle of the group.

The rest screamed and fled, leaving their comrade on the ground, kicking with his legs, trying to pull the thing from his face. It punctured the man's face and neck with the spikey ends of its legs, over and over.

He tried to scream, but the creature spit acid into his mouth.

His legs and arms danced along the ground.

Cruz fired the flamethrower and a jet of fire encompassed both the man and his assailant. The burning creature tried to flee, scrambling up the side of a wall, but Cruz was on it. He fired again, this time hitting it squarely.

It fell to the ground, its legs curling on themselves.

Hoenikker looked on in appalling fascination as the man still rattled the floor with his arms and legs, even as he was on fire, his face melting onto the hard-composite surface beneath him. The image fanned the flames of his own memories, and he found himself backing away.

Cruz turned and opened a gout of flame onto the man's face, and kept firing until his legs and arms stilled.

Hoenikker fell to the ground. He pushed himself back until he was against the wall. Then he turned, hiding his face, but feeling the heat of the burning figure. When it was all over, Cruz slumped against the opposite wall.

"Jesus H. Christ," was all he said.

Security ran up, shadowed by a med tech. One look at the man, however, and they knew there was nothing that could be done. Someone doused him with flame retardant until the fire was out.

The stench of burning hair and human flesh was one of the most horrible scents Hoenikker had ever encountered.

"Is that the only one?" a security officer asked.

Cruz nodded. "Just this one."

Hoenikker shook, peeking through his hands as if he were five, and barely alive. Cruz reached down and grasped him gently by the elbow.

"You okay, Hoenikker?" he asked. "Did you get hurt?"

Hoenikker realized he'd been crying, and wiped his face with his free hand. He allowed the bigger man to pull him to his feet and gently guide him back to the lab. The taller man was shaking, almost imperceptibly—he could feel it through the grip.

When they got back into the lab, Cruz shrugged out of the flamethrower and set it heavily on the chair. He held out his hands and saw they were shaking. He crossed his arms and put his hands under his armpits, and rocked back and forth.

Prior came up and put a hand on his back.

"Wasn't your fault, brother. Was the glass. It's just not made for what we have in there."

Cruz nodded. "I know. It's just—it's just it took me back to where I didn't want to be." Hoenikker looked on but didn't know what to say. It had taken him to such a place as well.

Kash brought Cruz a glass of water, which he drank in one long shaking gulp.

"The PTSD has been bad lately," Cruz began. "I know I can be rough around the edges." He stared solidly at the middle of the table. "But until you've lost all your friends in a battle, you'll never know what it's like." With still-shaking hands, he pulled up the sleeve on his right arm, revealing names tattooed there. "Snyder, Bedejo, Schnexnader, Correia, Cartwright. They all died. We were trying to protect a settlement, and these giant four-legged xenos with tentacles and way too many teeth attacked. We fired and fired until our pulse rifles locked up from the heat. They killed all my friends."

"How did you survive?" Hoenikker found himself asking. Cruz jerked his attention toward him. He stared hard at Hoenikker. When he spoke, each word dripped with disgust.

"I fucking ran. I saw that all my friends were dying, and I fucking ran. I've always been the fastest, and I used that to save myself."

"Your rifle wasn't working anymore," Kash said. "What could you do?"

"I could have *not* run," he said, staring off into the distance. "I could have stayed with my friends."

"You would have stayed and died," Prior said.

"So what? At least I could live with myself."

"Uh, you mean you'd be dead," Hoenikker said.

Cruz stared at him again. "You say that as if it's a bad thing."

Étienne and Mel rushed in.

"Is everything okay?" Étienne asked. "We heard one got away."

"As good as it could be," Kash responded. "One of the glass fronts failed."

"Damned Fabricators," Étienne said, punching his hand.

Mel went over to examine the hole. As he did, Mansfield returned, fuming. His leg had been wrapped in a bandage.

"What the *hell* did you do?" he roared. "You almost had me killed!"

Cruz took one look at the man, and lunged. Prior and Étienne grabbed him to keep him from pounding Mansfield.

"He saved lives," Kash said. "Without his quick thinking, the creature would have killed more."

"He let the thing escape!" Mansfield said, still red in the face.

"He did no such thing," Prior said. "It's the glass. It's worn out. The Rat-X burned a hole in it, and escaped on its own."

"As if it knew how," Mansfield spat.

Cruz shrugged out of the grip that held him.

"I'm fine. I'm fine." He brushed at where they'd held him. To Mansfield he said, "Make sure that before you accuse someone of something, you know what the hell you're talking about." Then he turned and left.

8

Two hours later, everyone was commanded to be present in the lab.

Security Chief Flowers and Deputy Station Commander Thompson called them to attention. To Hoenikker, Flowers was the image of an old-school retired Colonial Marine general with a face as lined as a topographical map. He wore his hair in a high and tight, and stood ramrod-straight. Although he'd never heard him speak before, he could imagine it as the sound of gravel being chewed in an echo chamber.

Thompson, on the other hand, was the direct opposite. As Hoenikker had heard it, the man had never served in the military. He slouched as he stood, staring at his manicured nails. All of his clothes were tailored and had an expensive sheen to them. He seemed bored, as if he wanted to be somewhere else.

"I understand that yours is the core mission for Pala Station," Flowers said to the group in a voice like Hoenikker had imagined, "but you've put everyone at risk, and the very idea is unacceptable. As it stands, Weyland-Yutani now has to explain to a family why their loved one was bitten by a creature, and then set on fire. You have security protocols in place. You knew you were to sound the alarm. You've practiced regularly, for just these circumstances. So why didn't you follow the protocols?" When there was no answer, he continued, "Clearly there has been a breakdown at all levels."

"If I may interject—" Mansfield started.

"You may not. I place the blame at your feet, Mr. Mansfield. That death is on you. Had you practiced shutting down the lab and locking it down enough times so that it was muscle memory for your scientists, this never would have happened. Did you expect your team to get it right the first time?"

Mansfield shook his head and stared at the floor.

"I'd fire you on the spot, but there's no one to replace you." Flowers turned to Thompson. "Sir, is there anything you want to add."

Thompson nodded. When he spoke, his voice was rich and polished and bored.

"If you're seeing me, then something terrible happened. You should *never* see me. You shouldn't even know what I look like. I certainly don't want to know what you look like. Frankly, I'm too busy to deal with your messes. There are larger problems that demand my attention. We need food for the infes— the creatures on *Katanga*." He paused. "Someone has to lead the hunt for local fauna. Incidents like this take away from the time I need to accomplish what needs to be done." He gave them a disgusted look, then started to leave.

"So inspiring," Cruz said under his breath.

"Wait a moment, Deputy Commander."

Kash stepped forward.

The man stopped and turned, glaring.

"We need better support from the station," she said. "This isn't a fault of the lab. If we had better containment room maintenance, this never would have happened."

Thompson stared. "You're saying it's the station's fault?"

"We sure as hell didn't build these." She pointed at the containment rooms. "They are the tools we use. We take as good care of them as we can, but it's up to Engineering and Fabrications to make sure they're new and functioning."

"So it was a failure of equipment, rather than the personnel." He looked dubious. "Is that what you're saying?"

"That's *exactly* what I'm saying," Kash said.

Thompson flicked his gaze over to Mansfield. "Get a status report on my desk ASAP." Then he left.

Kash breathed a deep sigh.

Hoenikker hadn't been on the station long, but he could tell she'd broken protocol. Yet of all the scientists, she probably had the best chance of not getting her head ripped off, perhaps because of her gender. It seemed like a patriarchal system, as backward as that was.

"She's right, of course," Mansfield said to Flowers. "We could have a hundred protocols in place, but if the equipment fails, then there's nothing we can do about it."

"If you had followed your protocols," Flowers growled, "the creature never would have escaped into the corridors."

"And we would have died," Cruz insisted. "I feel for the family of the deceased, but would you rather lose one or two station personnel, or all of your scientific staff?"

Hoenikker held his breath.

Flowers gave Cruz a hard stare. "That's a pretty cocky statement, Dr. Cruz."

"Remember, we are the reason you are here," Étienne said. "You are here to support us. If we are dead, you have no mission."

"You say that as if it's a bad thing," Flowers snapped, echoing Cruz's earlier comment. To Mansfield he said, "Your team is quite talkative."

"When you have the smartest people in the station, and they have something to say, you tend to let them say it," Mansfield replied. "It's also best to listen."

The bureaucrat's stock rose in Hoenikker's mind.

Flowers nodded. "Get that status report ASAP, Mansfield." Then he was out, the door sliding closed behind him. Everyone let out a sigh of relief.

"Why is it they have to be such assholes?" Cruz asked.

"Not so fast," Mansfield said. "Flowers was right about one thing. What about the security protocols? Why weren't they followed?"

"I wasn't able to press the abort button," Cruz began. "It just happened so fast."

"I was trying to get to the lockdown button by the door," Kash added, "but between Rat-X chasing me around the table, and you entering the lab, I just wasn't able."

"I can vouch for that," Hoenikker said. "It was a perfect storm of unlikely events."

Mansfield listened, then pointed his finger at each of them in turn.

"Remember your security protocols. I don't want you to have to practice them over and over, treating you like a bunch of bad kids. You're adults. You're scientists, for God's sake. But you should know them and be able to apply them." He looked up, as if past the ceiling. "We have new Xenos coming from the *San*

Lorenzo and *Katanga*.

"I'm going to get Engineering and Fabrications in here to fix the problems. Kash, Étienne, I want both of you to inspect everything, and make a list of anything we need repaired or replaced. I need it in two hours. I'm going to attach a service request to the status report, to put Deputy Station Commander Thompson on the hook for everything we need."

Kash and Étienne nodded.

"On more thing," Mansfield said. "No new experiments without proper approval."

"Wait. What?" Prior asked.

"Yeah," Cruz said. "*Now* you're treating us like children? No offense, boss, but there's not a scientific bone in your body. You don't know what we're doing here."

"Then school me," Mansfield replied. "Tell me your plans, and explain the benefits."

"So you can decide if the experiment is necessary or not," Kash countered.

"That's my job. You are the brains. I'm in charge. Had Weyland-Yutani felt that a scientist would be a better chief, they would have assigned one. Instead, you have me." Seeing the looks on the scientists' faces, he added, "You could do worse."

"I don't know how," Cruz murmured.

Mansfield stared at him a moment, then turned to leave.

"Two hours," he said over his shoulder. "I need that service request."

As soon as he was gone, Kash and Étienne partnered up and began to check the serviceability of everything in the lab. Cruz left, saying something about he'd be in his room. Prior and Mel began to clean up.

Hoenikker decided it was time to figure out the security protocols. He didn't know what they were, so he moved to his desk, spooled them up on the display, and began to read.

9

Three hours later, with the service request turned in, they were once again hard at work in the lab.

Étienne, Prior, and Mel stood at a table screening a new collection of station rats that had been captured. They needed to confirm that each had a clean bill of health before it was injected with goo. Any infection present in a rat could affect the interaction with the pathogen, and skew the results of an experiment.

Hoenikker and Kash stood behind Cruz, who'd signed out a rifle from Security. Since Containment Room Four was no longer functional for its stated purpose, they used it as a rifle range. As it turned out, the hole created by the xeno's acid was large enough to aim through. They'd affixed the new acid-resistant armor to the back wall, and were currently exposing it to various temperatures for testing.

Cruz fired again, while Hoenikker and Kash recorded the results.

"Looks like you're enjoying that," Hoenikker said.

"Never underestimate the medicinal value of the simple act of firing a weapon."

"I've never fired one," Hoenikker said. "Is it difficult?"

"You've never... get over here," Cruz said.

"I wasn't asking to, I was just—"

"No excuses. The last thing we need is for you to need to use a rifle, having never even fired one."

Hoenikker wished he hadn't said anything, but there it was—he had. Against his better judgment, he handed his tablet to Kash, who gave him a conspiratorial grin.

"Go ahead. It's fun," she said.

Hoenikker stepped next to Cruz, who held up the rifle. The weapon seemed twice the size it had just a few moments ago.

"Now, you don't need to know every detail about the M41 Pulse Rifle, just know this. It fires ten times 24mm caseless ammunition. The stock is the big end and it goes in the pocket of your shoulder. You hold it like this." He demonstrated. "Note my finger. This is called trigger discipline. I never put it in the trigger well unless I'm going to shoot. Do you know why?"

Hoenikker thought for a moment. "So I don't accidently shoot someone in the back?"

"So you don't accidentally shoot someone in the back. Yes. You got it on the first try. Well done. Now, look at the carry handle. You'll never need to touch it. The battery that operates the electronic firing system resides there. Now, look at the barrel. Note that underneath is a grenade launcher. We're not going to use any grenades, or even load it. We're inside a station. Grenades should *never* be used inside. On the right side of the barrel you'll note there's a charging handle. You pull it back to either clear a breach, eject and empty a shell, or to load ammo. Watch me."

Cruz placed the stock snugly into his shoulder, then moved his right hand to the trigger housing. His left hand gripped the rifle underneath the mounted grenade launcher. He aimed through the hole, slowly moved his finger into the trigger well, then slowly depressed the trigger. His shoulder flexed as the rifle fired with a loud report.

"Easy as pie." Cruz held out the weapon. "Now it's your turn."

Hoenikker took a step back.

"Don't be afraid of it. It's nothing more than a tool. Are you afraid of a scalpel?"

Hoenikker shrugged, then shook his head.

"Sure, you're worried about the blade. You don't want to get cut, right? So, do you hold it by the blade?"

Hoenikker shook his head again, beginning to feel foolish.

"Here." Cruz held out the rifle. He grinned. "Just don't hold it by the blade."

Hoenikker grasped the rifle as if it was made of something breakable. It was both heavier and lighter than he'd thought it would be. He turned to grin at Kash, but Cruz stopped him. Hoenikker noted that the barrel was now pointing directly at Cruz.

"Oh. Sorry." He turned back.

"Always take care where the working end of the rifle is pointing. Here, it should always be pointing into the containment room, or what we call 'down range.' Now, sink the stock into the pocket of your shoulder."

Hoenikker did, and Cruz helped him adjust. Then he moved his right hand to the trigger housing and grasped the barrel with his left. Cruz adjusted his grip on the barrel. As it turned out, Hoenikker had grabbed it on the top but Cruz wanted him to hold it from the bottom. It certainly felt better. Probably offered superior stabilization, as well.

"Aim down the barrel and line up the groove in the carrying handle, pointing it toward the target."

Hoenikker noted the groove and lined it up so it was piercing the air between the center of the armor and the barrel. He moved his finger into the trigger well, blindly found the trigger, and pulled it back. When it fired, Hoenikker was surprised at the noise and at the recoil into his shoulder. All that said, he also realized he was grinning. Releasing the trigger, he pulled it again. This time he was ready for it and he was able to tense his shoulder to take more of the recoil. He grinned wider and fired again. He was about to fire a fourth time when Cruz tapped him on the back.

"Okay, killer. That's enough for now."

Cruz reached out and grabbed the rifle gently by the barrel. For a second, Hoenikker didn't want to give it back. He now understood what it was like to fire a weapon. It was actually fun. Reluctantly, he relinquished it.

"Thank you," he said. "I never knew."

"Most folks don't. Less than one percent of people ever serve in the Colonial Marines, and with gun restrictions—unless you are a marine or know one—there's no way you're ever going to be able to fire an M41."

Hoenikker nodded. "I hope I never *need* to fire one, but I'd like do so again someday."

Cruz held the rifle with his left hand and clapped Hoenikker on the shoulder. "After this next round of Xenos, we'll all get together and I'll see if we can't try out a real rifle range. I know Security has one. We'll see if we can borrow it for a day."

"Hey, guys," Prior said. "Get over here. We've made an... interesting discovery."

Cruz leaned the rifle against the workstation at the front of the containment room. They all gathered around the table, where the rats were segregated into six small glass boxes with holes for them to breathe.

"What have you got?" Kash asked.

"MPDTs. In the rats. All of them." Hoenikker didn't know what MPDTs were, but he hoped they weren't contagious—at least not transferable to humans.

"All of them?" Kash asked.

"Who would put them in rats?" Cruz asked.

"Are they signed?" Kash pressed. "Were you able to find a copyright on them?"

Prior shook his head. As did Étienne.

"What is an MPDT?" Hoenikker asked, more uncertain than ever.

"Micro-personal data tracker," Kash said. "We all have them in our badges, and in our shoulders."

Hoenikker remembered when he'd first been assigned to Weyland-Yutani and he'd had to have a tracker surgically implanted. They hadn't called it an MPDT—just a "chip"—and it was so long ago he'd forgotten all about it.

"Every weapon has one," Cruz added. "It's to track them and make certain we know their location at any given time."

"And the rats have them?" Hoenikker asked.

"Yes, miniaturized versions of them, and we don't know why."

Mel muttered something. No one else picked it up.

"He's right," Hoenikker said. "They must be for mapping. The rats are being used to map the station."

"Why would anyone need to do that?" Étienne asked no one in particular.

"I think we need to get the security chief down here, now," Cruz said.

Five minutes later, an impatient Security Chief Flowers, accompanied by Security Specialist Wincotts, stood peering at the rats. Mansfield stood off to the side, looking none too happy.

"These are state-of-the-art trackers?" Wincotts asked. Short and dark-skinned, he was in charge of "special security," which according to Kash meant the synths.

"Yes, sir." Prior said.

"How long has this been going on?" Flowers asked.

"Has to have been recent," Prior said. "We didn't pick this up before."

"Have you found the locus of access for the rats?" Hoenikker asked. Both security chiefs looked his way, and shook their heads.

"There's no way to determine how they're getting in," Flowers replied.

"Maybe if you hack the signal of the trackers," Hoenikker suggested. "I assume they are transmitting data. The trick would be to get your own data, and see if perhaps the trackers have memory storage, then see where they all started."

Everyone was looking at him now and he didn't like the feeling.

"Of course, you could also try and determine where the data is being received." He felt his face turning red because of the attention. "That wouldn't be too hard, I'd imagine, if you have some comms personnel with up-to-date training."

"That makes perfect sense," Wincotts said. He turned to Flowers. "Let me handle this, Randy."

Flowers nodded. "Have at it."

Wincotts rubbed his hands together. "Our rat infestation just became an infiltration. Can't have that," he said, leaving the lab. "Can't have that at all."

10

Communication Specialist Brennan was bored out of his mind. He'd been tasked with deciphering the model and type of MPDTs they'd found on the rats. It was a job anyone could do. Buggy and Davis got the cream job.

They were assigned to hack the devices so that they could get the log history of the data contained in the memory. Brennan would have loved to do that, but he'd been on Oshita's shit list for a long time. So, out of spite, Brennan ignored his assignment and returned to playing his Colonial Marine first-person shooter. He'd played this before. Hell, he played it every day—it was the only thing keeping him sane in a station at the ass end of the universe.

Brennan was on level forty-three of a fifty-level game when his screen blinked red. He had no choice but to pause his game in progress.

Checking the warning, he noted that there was an unauthorized signal going out. He'd seen it before, but had been unable to pin it down. Now that it was live, he would be able to trace it. He actually grinned as he realized the envy Buggy and Davis would have when he solved this one himself. It didn't take five seconds to see that the signal was coming from a comms closet at the end of a dead-end corridor.

Brennan saved his game, grabbed his portable display, and headed out. He passed Rawlings, who saluted him with his coffee cup. That guy was never in his office. Plus, he was far too nice. There had to be something the man was hiding—but then, Brennan thought that of pretty much everyone.

Four corridors later and he was at the access panel. Pulling a tool from his belt, he removed the top two screws and let the panel fold open on its lower hinges. Rats immediately poured out of the wiring and onto the floor, causing Brennan to back away, almost tripping, wondering where the hell the rats were coming from. He began shooing them away with his feet, landing a couple of solid kicks. When the way was clear, he approached the access panel and quickly noted a vid display unit secreted behind the wires. Pulling it out, he tried to access it, but it required either a code or a fingerprint to enable. Common security practice.

Whoever had been sending out the signal had definitely used this terminal. Which meant that this vid display was probably used to send either a burst or an encrypted transmission. If he could determine whose device it was, then he'd know the perpetrator. He grinned as he came up with the word *perpetrator*.

Buggy and Davis were going to be *so* envious.

He hurried back down the twists and turns of the corridors.

Five minutes later Brennan was in the entryway for Logistics, standing at the counter that separated him from the staff. Fields, Fairbanks, and Chase each sat at a terminal.

"Still playing the game, Brennan?" Fields asked. He'd been an actual Colonial Marine, and liked to make fun of Brennan's pretending.

"That old thing?" Brennan said. "Quit that a long time ago."

"It's not too late to join the real corps, you know," Fields persisted. "You're still young enough."

"What, and give up all of this?" Brennan widened his arms to take in the room.

Fields laughed and shook his head.

Fairbanks eyed Brennan and came over to the counter.

"What can I do for you?"

Brennan held out the vid display. "I need to figure out who this belongs to."

Fairbanks stared at it. "Where did you find that?"

Brennan's eyes narrowed. "Doesn't matter. I need to know who it belongs to. It's locked so I can't log in."

"Then I don't know if we can help you," Fairbanks said, still not touching the device.

"What do you mean? Don't you have inventory control numbers?" Brennan asked.

"Maybe whoever owns it is looking for it. Have you considered putting it back?" Fairbanks asked.

"Putting it back? What?"

"Wish I could help you," Fairbanks said.

Chase came over. "What's going on?"

"Guy took a vid display from where someone left it, and doesn't want to put it back," Fairbanks said.

"Guy? Who are you calling 'guy'? It's Brennan, Fairbanks. We've known each other five years. What the fuck's going on?"

"Why don't you put it back?" Chase asked.

Brennan had thought this was going to be easy. It was anything but. If he had to guess, he'd think they were trying to make it harder.

"Listen," he said slowly, trying to calm himself down. "I can't get into the security details, but this vid unit was used to contact someone outside the station. I need to know who it belongs to."

"Why didn't you say so in the first place?" Chase nodded.

Brennan wanted to choke someone.

"Hand it over," Chase said. "I'll check the inventory control number."

That's what I said in the first place, Brennan thought, but he handed it over without saying so.

Chase took it to his workstation, sat down, and pulled out a micro reader. He focused it on a rear corner of the device. After a moment it beeped and a number appeared on the micro reader screen. Chase pulled up a document and compared the numbers.

"Found it, but you won't like this."

"What do you mean I won't like this?" Brennan asked.

"This unit isn't assigned to anyone. It's extra, and should have been in storage."

Brennan thought about that for a moment, noting that Fairbanks was still standing behind the counter, staring at the device.

"Who was the last one to inventory it?" Brennan asked.

Chase punched at his own screen. "That'd be you, Fairbanks." He turned to look at his fellow log specialist. "That would be you."

"I just listed it in the inventory," Fairbanks said. "Anyone could have taken it."

Chase glanced again at his screen. "It was supposed to be in Supply Room Six. That's dedicated to high-value long-term supplies. We keep it locked."

Brennan couldn't help but feel that Fairbanks looked as if he was going to jump out of his skin.

"Someone must have broken in," Fairbanks said.

"I don't think so." Fields swiveled his chair around. "I was just in there yesterday, and there was nothing wrong with the lock. What's the access log say?"

Chase tapped the screen a few more times. "It says that you accessed the room, and before you it was Fairbanks, the day he came back from leave. Why'd you go into the supply room, just when you returned, Fairbanks."

"I... I..."

Brennan's eyes narrowed. Could it be that simple?

"Fairbanks?" Fields stood, holding out the unit. "What did you do?"

"I... I..." Fairbanks gulped. "I swear to you, I didn't do anything. I took a display with me when I went on leave. I know I wasn't supposed to, but I needed something to do on the shuttles. I was just putting it back."

"You know you can't use station equipment for personal use," Fields said. "What if we had a surprise inspection?" He stood and approached his coworker. "Next thing you know, you'll be playing first-person shooters and pretending to be a Colonial Marine." He laughed and patted Fairbanks on the back.

Chase rolled his eyes.

Fields went back to his workstation and sat.

Fairbanks made eye contact with Brennan, but quickly looked away. Brennan stood in his spot for a moment, then shook his head and turned to go.

"What are you going to do now?" Fairbanks asked in a hushed voice.

What *was* Brennan going to do? What was there to do? He guessed he'd report it. Maybe go back and track down the signal again, and see if he couldn't decipher it. Brennan shrugged.

"I don't know," he said without turning. "Maybe nothing."

Then he walked out the door.

11

Shit. Shit. Shit.

It was all Fairbanks could think.

All the effort. All the worry.

And it was Brennan. Fucking gamer Brennan, who never did any work, who'd found him out. How could that even have happened? What had he done to the universe to deserve such a thing? And now Brennan was probably going to make a beeline to Security, and turn him in.

"Fairbanks, what's wrong?" Chase asked.

"If you're worried about us turning you in to Section Chief Jamison, forget about it," Fields said. "We got your back. Just don't do something that stupid again."

Just don't do something that stupid again. Famous last words.

"I got to go," he mumbled, and headed to the door.

"You got cleanup tonight," Fields said loudly. "Don't forget. Come back from wherever you're going, so you can clean up."

Fairbanks waved his hand to acknowledge and almost ran out of the office. He went down one corridor, then another, searching for Brennan. He didn't know what he'd say when he found him, but Fairbanks needed to stop him, or things would get out of hand.

"Looking for me?" Brennan asked. He was leaning against a wall when Fairbanks turned the corner. Fairbanks halted, eyes wide, breathing heavy. What was he going to say? What *could* he say? That he was committing industrial espionage? That everything would be fine? *"There's nothing going on here. Please run along."*

"It was you, wasn't it?" Brennan looked him up and down.

Fairbanks didn't know what to say, so he merely nodded, blinking rapidly.

"What is it?" Brennan's eyes narrowed. "Who are you communicating with?"

"I can't say," Fairbanks said.

Two security guards turned the corner. A man and a woman. They were chatting, but stopped when they saw the two men. All four eyed one another as the guards passed. Brennan waited several seconds, long enough for them to get out of earshot.

"You have to say something," Brennan whispered. "What happened, Fairbanks? I thought you were a standup guy?"

"I am a standup guy. I just… I just—"

"You just what?"

"I just got in the wrong place at the wrong time." He felt a sob pushing free and he swallowed it. No way was he going to cry about this. "What are you going to do?"

"By all rights, I should go to Security." Brennan shook his head.

Fairbanks felt his stomach sink. He didn't want to go to prison.

"In fact, that's what I'm going to do." Brennan turned and left.

Fairbanks tried to speak, but nothing would come out. So instead, he returned blindly to his quarters. He was almost to his door when he felt the bile rise in his stomach. He ran to the bathroom across from his room, hurled the door open, and spewed into the toilet. The door shut behind him, leaving him on his knees as yellow bile swirled against the metal. The smell of it made him retch again, his back arching with every heave until nothing came out.

After a few moments, he reached out and used the toilet to help him get to his feet. He washed his face and hands, but didn't have the courage to look at himself in the mirror. After wiping his hands and face, he exited the bathroom, used his handprint to enter his own room, and slouched onto the bed.

He wasn't sure how long it would be before they came for him. Five. Ten. Fifteen minutes.

Three knocks.

He glanced up and stared at the door.

Hyperdyne Corporation had given him a vial. They said to take it if he was caught. It was a way out. He stood and shakily pawed through the clothes in the top of his dresser.

Three more knocks.

Just as he was about to give up, his hands curled around the small glass vial. He removed it and placed it in the palm of his hand. It wasn't any longer than a section of his middle finger, and held an amber liquid.

Three more knocks. Insistent.

Try as he might, he couldn't bring himself to take it. He shoved it into his pocket, then went and opened the door, ready to accept his fate.

To his surprise, it wasn't Security.

Brennan stood in the doorway. He pushed his way past Fairbanks and into the room.

"I thought you went to turn me in," Fairbanks said, closing the door.

Brennan walked to the back of the room and turned. The foot of the bed was to his left. The small desk and chair were to his right. He grabbed the chair, spun it around, and sat on it cowboy style.

"Sit down," he said, gesturing to the bed.

Fairbanks glanced at the door. "Are they coming here?"

"I said sit down." Brennan rolled his eyes. "I didn't go to Security, okay? Jeez, relax why don't you?"

"Then what…" Fairbanks sat down slowly, never taking his eyes off the other man. "I don't understand."

"It's simple, really." Brennan spread his hands. "We're going to make a… a transaction. I don't make an issue about this with Security, and you'll be around to provide me with whatever I want. I'm tired of living like a prisoner. I know you have backups for all the swag the section chiefs and the station commander have. I want some."

"You want some—wait. You're blackmailing me?" Fairbanks asked. His fear evaporated as if it had never been there. It was replaced by an equal amount of anger.

"Call it what you want." He shrugged. "Just so long as we come to an agreement."

Fairbanks stood. "What if I went to Security and gave myself up, and told them about the blackmail?"

Brennan grinned. "That's easy. I'd tell them that you tried to offer me a bribe, and I refused. But you could wait until you give me stuff, and then I *couldn't* go to Security. I'd be culpable."

"Or by the time I give you stuff it's too late," Fairbanks said, "because you can say it's a bribe that you didn't want to take, but were forced to." His mind was racing.

Brennan's grin grew wider.

Fairbanks wanted to slap it away.

"That's pretty smart of you, Fairbanks," Brennan said. "You'd make a good criminal. Correction, you *are* a good criminal. That's probably why they picked you."

"I am *not* a criminal." Fairbanks took two steps forward.

Brennan stood. "Sure you are… or do you prefer the word 'spy,'" he said with air quotes.

"I'm neither." Fairbanks balled his fists.

"Then what are you?"

Fairbanks thought of the way Hyperdyne was blackmailing him. He thought of what Brennan was trying to do to him. He knew what he was, and he said it out loud.

"I'm a victim."

"Oh, please." Brennan snorted. "Save it."

That was it.

Fairbanks brought his right fist around and slammed it into the side of Brennan's face. The man stumbled with the blow.

Fairbanks hit him again.

Brennan fell to his knees beside the desk.

Fairbanks grabbed his head and began to slam it, over and over, against the side of the desk. Blood splattered the wall. A moment later pieces of gore began to litter the desktop. At first Brennan tried to speak, but all he could do was grunt each time his head slammed against the hard surface.

Five more times until the grunting stopped, then Fairbanks let go of the man's hair. Brennan slumped to the floor like a bag of meat. Fairbanks stared at his hand, then at the body.

What had he done?

He'd killed the man.

But his anger still fueled him. He'd do it again if he had to. He was tired of being a pushover. He was tired of being forced to do things that he didn't want to do.

He heard a groan.

Was he still alive?

Brennan's hand twitched. His fingers moved like the legs of a dying spider. He tried to roll himself over, and just managed to do it. His eyes were crossed. Teeth had broken through his cheek.

Fairbanks shuddered. Had he done that? The enormity of it hit him like a brick. He stumbled back. He should get help. Maybe they could still save him.

Brennan spit out several teeth along with a bubble of blood.

Fairbanks shoved his hand into his pocket and felt the poison vial. He pulled it out and stared at it. A small glass filled with amber liquid. Really just the size of a tooth. Without thinking it through, he opened the stopper, knelt, and poured the syrupy fluid into Brennan's open mouth.

The dying man choked once, then swallowed to clear it. An eye found Fairbanks and seemed about to cry.

Then everything went still.

Fairbanks hurriedly pushed himself back so he was sitting with his back against his bed, and buried his face in his hands. He sat there for a long moment, then he began to chuckle. Just a titter at first. Then actual laughter. Soon he was giddy with the moment, as full-blown guffaws rocked the inside of the room. He realized two things.

One, Security wouldn't be looking for him anytime soon.

Two, he needed to find a place to hide the body. When he thought about it, he laughed harder. *Hide a body.* He'd never once thought he'd have to think those three words, much less carry through with them.

Hide.

A.

Body.

Life was so hilarious.

12

Cruz shuddered beneath the sheets.

The tentacles are wrapped around Snyder's torso. Surprise and terror battle on his face. The tentacles squeeze, and the sound of ribs snapping is like gunshots. Blood shoots from Snyder's mouth in a waterfall of red that only a dream could create. Blood and more blood and more blood until it covers everything, the world a red-dripped Rorschach.

Cruz begins to gasp, then choke.

He's drowning. Can't breathe. The blood covers all but his reaching hand. Then he breathes it in, becoming Snyder, enwrapped by the tentacles, feeling the impossible strength of the monster as it squeezes out everything it means to be alive.

Cruz shot up to a sitting position. Consciousness returned, and he slid his legs off the bed. He dropped his head between them as he began to hyperventilate. Sweat dripped from his face, falling to the floor. His heart was galloping as if he'd just completed a run. What the hell had just happened?

Damn dreams. Damn Snyder.

It was the marine's own damn fault for not following orders. Cruz realized that it was more than sweat dripping to the floor. He wiped his eyes, then furiously shook his head. Standing, he opened his door and strode across the corridor into the common bathroom. Found a sink and dashed water on his face.

Behind him came the sound of someone flushing. The door to a stall opened and a bleary-eyed man staggered out. When he saw Cruz, he stopped cold.

Cruz turned around. The man wasn't saying anything, just standing there.

"What the fuck do you want?" Cruz said.

The man blinked.

That was when Cruz realized he'd forgotten to put clothes on, and was completely naked. He shook his head.

"Never seen a naked man before? Get back to bed, you." Then he turned back to the sink and stared at himself in the mirror.

His almost-black skin hid many of his wounds, but he knew every scar and pock. He could trace the lineage of the wounds as if he'd inflicted them himself. To a point he had, by joining the Colonial Marines. Back then, when the drill sergeants saw him, they knew he'd be an effective killing machine.

He picked at his Afro. He really needed to get it cut, but there wasn't anyone qualified on the station. Soon he'd have to settle, and probably shave it. The hair was getting knappy.

Throwing water on his face, he headed back to his room, where he pulled on clothes, used a pick to fix his hair as best he could, then donned his white lab jacket. He was on his way to the lab before he knew what he was going to do. He passed two security specialists making the rounds, nodded to them, and they nodded back. When he entered the lab, the motion sensor turned the lights on.

Cruz immediately went to work. The effort of combining the radioactive plutonium with the pathogen wasn't difficult, but because of safety protocols it was time consuming. Not only did he have to make sure that he reduced his exposure to the radiation, but also to the lab itself. So, it was all black box work, the radiation kept inside a lead-lined box with video sensors that allowed him to manipulate arms that were doing the work for him.

Mansfield's voice rang through his mind, reminding him that there were to be no experiments without his permission.

Fuck Mansfield.

The man wasn't even a scientist. All he wanted was for them to toe the line. Didn't he know that it was the mavericks that made the best scientists—that it was the mad geniuses who effected the greatest advancements? The Mansfields of the world would have stopped the discoveries of penicillin, and nuclear fusion, and antimatter, and faster-than-light travel. The Mansfields of the world would have humanity still landlocked to a single planet, instead of out in space going cutting edge.

Yeah. Fuck Mansfield.

Cruz pressed a button, and a syringe with the irradiated pathogen ejected from a side drawer on the black box. Donning lead-lined gloves, he took it and moved to the containment room where Leon-895 was kept. So far, the effects of the goo had been impressive. The size of the creature had increased fivefold, as had the appearance. A new set of legs had appeared, giving it a new and strange presence.

At the containment area, Cruz didn't even try to locate it. Instead, he immediately lowered the temperature. The creature appeared in the top left corner, and he watched as the image of it solidified. Once a coat of frost covered it, he entered the containment room, injected the creature with the irradiated pathogen, then exited again. He wasn't about to have the same problem he'd had last time, when he'd allowed his PTSD to get the better of him.

Once back outside the room, he removed the gloves and returned them to where they belonged. He placed the syringe back in the black box, to dispose of it later. Irradiated as it was, he couldn't just throw it away. There was a process. There were the sacred protocols. Then he returned to the containment room, raised the temperature to normal again, and sat back.

They'd installed a prismatic light system to measure the speed of Leon-895's ability to change color. So far that ability, while impressive, had been slow. Cruz hoped that the irradiated pathogen might cause it to autocorrect sooner. Now, all he had to do was wait.

An image of Snyder returned to him. Not dying, but living. They'd been preparing to go to a cold-as-hell planet for guard duty. The day before, they'd let loose. Snyder had brought his girlfriend and they'd all begun drinking yards of beer—an old German tradition to which his family still adhered. Snyder had always fancied himself a drinker, but he was really just a lightweight.

They'd all been at Sgt. Bone's quarters. Cruz, Snyder, Erica— Snyder's girlfriend—and Foxie, an old buddy of Bone's. It was the usual bout of drinking games and blowing off steam prior to setting off for a nearby LV. Everyone was having a good time until Erica challenged Snyder to a drink-off.

Cruz had come to believe that it was premeditated.

Snyder wasn't about to let his girlfriend get the better of him. So he matched her yard for yard, drinking down an impressive—by anyone's standards—amount of beer. Cruz didn't know from what alcoholic DNA Erica had been spliced, but she seemed impervious to the alcohol. She drank and drank and the only way to know she'd drunk so much was her need to pee. It was on the eighth yard that Snyder spewed the contents of his stomach all over Sgt. Bone's kitchen, then proceeded to pass out on the bathroom floor. Cruz had taken care of his friend as best he could, then cleaned up the mess.

Meanwhile, Erica, none the worse for wear, started cuddling up to both Sgt. Bone and Foxie, laughing and acting as if she wasn't anyone's girlfriend. Once the mess had been cleaned up, Cruz grabbed Snyder and carried him back to the barracks.

They'd left the next morning without ever seeing Erica again. The cherry on top of the memory was that Snyder hadn't packed before he'd gone out drinking, so he only had one extra sock in his 'go bag.' He'd ended up getting trench foot during the mission, and almost had to have his feet amputated.

All because of a girl.

Once Cruz had left the Colonial Marines and taken up his education, he'd learned that there were substances that could render the alcohol of a liquid into pure sugar. Upon discovering that, he'd become certain that was how Erica had beaten Snyder. Cruz wondered if it was just to make her safe from an alcohol overdose, or if it had been a ploy to get next to Sgt. Bone. He'd never know, because Erica had never been seen again and Sgt. Bone had died in a shuttle explosion reportedly caused by a faulty fuel wire.

Cruz sighed. Such were the symptoms of living two lives. The other scientists didn't have his problem. They'd grown up, gone to college, and become scientists of their own accord. They didn't have a life before this one. But Cruz did. In spades.

He checked the temperature of the room and the temperature of Leon-895. Both had achieved stasis. He toggled a switch on the control station, and watched as a light in the containment room slowly began to cycle through three primary colors.

Leon-895 remained visible without any change.

Damn. Had he used too much radiation? Please say that he hadn't used too much. Please show that the creature wasn't dead. Mansfield would have his ass.

Checking the creature's vitals, he noted that they were slightly lower than usual, but not drastically so. It should be attenuating. He waited a few tense minutes, then Leon-895 began to cycle slowly through the three colors—red, green, blue... red, green, blue... red, green, blue.

There.

At least he hadn't killed the damned thing.

He began to cycle slightly faster, and was joyed to see Leon-895 skip a beat, then match the speed of the color change. Then he added three more colors—yellow, brown, and black. A beat skipped again, then Leon-895 began to adapt. Cruz watched for several minutes as the creature changed color with the change of light, pleased at its progress.

Finally, he dialed up a dozen variations, then a hundred, then a thousand. Hell, *two* thousand. Each flash of light, Leon-895 changed, conforming to its new colored reality as easy as if it was breathing.

Cruz turned up the speed so Leon-895 was changing in three-second intervals. He pulled a chair over from the central table and placed it in front of the containment area. For the next two hours he sat and watched his own personal disco as the creature flashed color after color after color, while images of Snyder being squeezed to death *rat-a-tat-tatted* through his mind.

13

Security Specialist Wincotts convinced Mansfield that their experiments should be put on hold, so they could focus on the MPDTs. The scientists were far from thrilled with the turn of events. They each had their own projects, and were loath to stop.

Hoenikker hadn't yet been assigned an individual project, and was seconding several of his peers. Although he didn't have as much emotional or intellectual investment as his fellow scientists, he still felt the frustration and the pull of real science.

Cruz had been the most vocal.

"We've developed a brand-new species here in Leon-895—one that could change the nature of how a Colonial Marine goes to war. And what do they have us doing? Dissecting rats."

"There's nothing to do about it," Mansfield responded. "We rely on the goodwill of the station so that we can operate freely—*especially* after one of your experiments got loose and killed station personnel."

"That's likely to happen again," Cruz countered. "Where's Fabrications? Why haven't they replaced the windows?"

Mansfield nodded. "They claim that they're short on tungsten, and don't have enough to replace all of the glass."

"Then at least replace the worst ones." Cruz stood from the chair he'd been sitting in, and pointed toward the containment rooms. "Jesus, there's so much infighting on this station it reminds me of primary school. Everyone taking sides. Engineering won't talk to Fabrications. Fabrications won't talk to Logistics. Can they just fucking do their jobs, so we can get back to business?" No one responded, and he lowered his voice.

"Sorry for yelling," he said. "I'm… passionate."

Mansfield just nodded, folded his hands behind his back, and left the lab.

"Don't you get tired of all that yelling?" Étienne asked.

"It's part of his personality," Prior said, flashing a smile toward Cruz. "It takes all sorts of us to effectively science. Take Matthews here," he said, putting his arm around the bigger man's shoulders. "He doesn't say much, but he sciences hard."

Mel muttered something that sounded like a thank you, then went back to his microscope.

"Why isn't Comms working on this?" Étienne asked.

"Oh, they are," Mansfield said. "We're working in tandem. So far, they haven't found anything."

Kash clapped her hands together loudly, and Hoenikker jumped. She moved to where everyone could easily see her.

"Let's get to this, so we can return to our experiments," she said. "What's the one thing every piece of tech has?"

Prior and Cruz glanced at each other. Both shook their heads.

Mel didn't look up.

Étienne chewed a fingernail.

Hoenikker had no idea where she was going with this.

"Okay, let me make it easier. What does every piece of art have on it?" she asked.

Étienne was the first to answer. "A signature."

"Right." Kash nodded. "A signature. Tech doesn't have signatures—"

"—but it does have inventory control numbers," Hoenikker said, finishing her words. She snapped her fingers.

"Yes. Or something similar. Weyland-Yutani doesn't make anything without slapping its name on it. They want the world to know that the products they're using were made by their favorite corporation."

"Wouldn't the size of the trackers make that hard to do?" Cruz asked.

"If they can make a device that size, then they have the technology to sign it." She pointed to Hoenikker. "You will run Team B. This is where your theoretical modeling comes in handy. Prior and Cruz will work with you. You're going to find out *why* they are being used." She pointed to Étienne. "You are in charge of Team A. Myself and Mel will be part of your team. We're charged with determining where the MPDTs came from."

"Why aren't *you* in charge of Team A?" Étienne asked. "Don't get me wrong, I love being in charge. I do bossy well."

"Let's try and minimize the bossiness," she said. "I chose you because of the way your mind works. I think you're the right solution for this problem." She turned to everyone and said, "Right. So, let's get to work."

Hoenikker turned to Cruz and Prior. "We don't need to be here to discuss this. Let's carve ourselves a corner in the mess hall and discuss it over coffee."

Cruz nodded. "Finally, a good idea."

Ten minutes later they were ensconced in the mess hall. Cruz and Hoenikker blew on hot black coffee. Prior drank soda through a straw. Because it was midmorning, the place was almost empty. Only one other was working there. Hoenikker recognized him as Reception Tech Rawlings. He was on the other side of the room, drinking coffee from a portable mug and going over something on his vid display. When they'd entered, he'd saluted them with his coffee, but hadn't tried to get into their space.

The mess hall was pretty rudimentary. On one side of the room was the drinks table that offered everything from tea to coffee, soda, soymilk, and water. The other side of the room held the buffet, currently empty, and the entrance to the kitchen. There were a dozen tables. The gray walls were adorned with posters from Weyland-Yutani regarding security warnings, the need to respect your fellow workers, and the infamous, "SEE A PROBLEM, FIX A PROBLEM."

"So, what are we doing?" Cruz asked.

Hoenikker had become more and more impressed with the man. Where at first he'd felt that Cruz had been someone who gleefully heaped abuse on his specimens, it was clear now that he had multiple layers.

"We have the simplest job, frankly," Hoenikker said. "That's why I wanted us out of there."

"You've solved the problem?" Prior asked.

"I believe I have—and if you think about it, you could solve it as well."

Prior sipped loudly through his straw and gave him a dubious look. Hoenikker took a sip of his coffee.

It was hot and terrible.

"Let's pare it down to the basics," he said. "Each of us has a PDT implanted in our shoulder. What are they used for?"

"To keep track of us good little Weyland-Yutani employees," Cruz said.

"And how do they keep track of us?" Hoenikker asked, raising an eyebrow.

"Reception nodes placed around the facility. We walk by them, it logs who we are, along with a time-and-date stamp," Prior said. "Everyone knows that. And like Cruz said, it's how they keep track of all their good little employees, while making sure we don't go to places we shouldn't go."

"Then what good would the PDTs be on the rats if they were from another company? If this is some sort of industrial espionage, then how could they log the rats as they passed a reception node?"

Cruz sat up. "Unless they hacked the system."

"They'd have to have a man on the inside," Prior said.

"I'll bet if we went to Comms, they could find the signal," Hoenikker said.

"They might have already found it and ruled it out as a glitch," Cruz offered.

"Interesting hypothesis, but it doesn't have any legs," Hoenikker said. "Come on now. Let's keep with the scientific method."

"Why is it you went straight to industrial espionage?" Prior asked.

"What else would the rats with MPDTs be good for? If I'm right, they're being used to map the station, and the results are being broadcast to someone on the outside."

"Might be a hostile takeover," Cruz said.

"You do realize that you were the most recent person to come on station," Prior said to him. "Which makes you suspect *numero uno*." He grinned and sipped at his soda.

"While that may be," Hoenikker said, "why don't we run on over to Comms, and ask them about outgoing signals?" His associates nodded, and all three stood. They exited the mess hall, leaving Rawlings behind.

Five minutes later they were chatting with Buggy and Davis. The third comms workstation was empty.

They'd been able to hack the MPDTs and found the information logs. The rats had been everywhere, strengthening Hoenikker's supposition. He told them what he believed was going on, and they agreed that it made the most sense. When asked if they'd discovered any outgoing signals, they both shook their heads.

Hoenikker asked them to check.

Davis went to his workstation, and after a few minutes came back. As it turned out, Brennan had flagged two occasions. Both had been burst transmissions, the last one taking place only a few hours earlier. Only Comms and Security had access to the employee PDT log system. Hoenikker asked where Brennan was, so they could question him about it.

When they queried Brennan's location, it showed him in his room. Buggy commented that he was usually playing first-person shooters, even at work, which had earned him a spot on Oshita's shit list.

Together with Buggy, Hoenikker, Cruz, and Prior, they went to Brennan's room. They knocked, but there was no answer. After repeated attempts, Buggy used his override code to enter the room.

It was empty.

"But the signal said he was in here," Cruz said.

Prior glanced under the bunk.

Buggy checked in the closet.

Hoenikker stared at the pillow. It had been fluffed, but was off center. Why would someone take the time to fluff it and not make sure it was straight? He went to straighten it and noted a spot of red on the white sheet. He lifted the pillow, then dropped it and backed away. His heart rate immediately went through the roof as the blood left his face.

"What is it?" Cruz asked. "Looks like you've seen a dead man."

"The pillow," Hoenikker managed. "Look under it."

Cruz grabbed the pillow and lifted it. Beneath it lay an identification fob and a section of skin with a small rice-sized piece of metal embedded in it.

A personal data tracker.

Brennan's personal data tracker.

Which meant that more than likely, Brennan was dead.

Either that, or he's *the infiltrator*, Hoenikker thought, *and removed his own PDT so he couldn't be tracked.*

He voiced the possibility, and they called Security. Each of them was interviewed in turn, to give a thorough account of how they had arrived at their macabre discovery. Once they were allowed to go, Buggy returned to Comms to brief Section Chief Oshita, and the others returned to the lab.

Mansfield was already there. He'd heard through the command channel what had happened. Hoenikker briefed him on their discovery and suppositions.

Étienne's team had continued their work, to a degree of success. They'd discovered where the MPDTs originated. Each MPDT, Étienne explained, had its own inventory control number. Without any information regarding the origin of the device, however, the number was useless.

Under normal circumstances.

Matthews observed a pattern in the placement of hyphens on the MPDT IDs, distinctly different from the inventory control numbers used by Weyland-Yutani. A quick search of the lab yielded equipment produced by other manufacturers, and Kash noted that one of the microscopes was a Hyperdyne product. Its numbering convention matched those of the MPDTs.

Even with this epiphany, they didn't know who had brought the rats into the station, used them to map it, then sent communication bursts to a nearby receiver. Nor were they any closer to finding Brennan... or his body.

There was one thing they did know.

Only two people had come to the station recently, and Hoenikker had the feeling he knew what was certain to happen.

They sent Security the results of their investigation, and not fifteen minutes later a pair of officers entered the lab. With hardly a word they cuffed his hands behind his back without trying to be gentle about it, while the rest of the scientists looked on.

Cruz began to protest, and moved toward the officers and their prisoner, but Kash stopped him with a hand on his shoulder. She didn't look any happier about it than he did, though.

14

To say that he was pissed-off was an understatement. Hoenikker knew he was innocent, and expected everyone else to see it as well. It was *obvious*. He'd always followed the rules—well, *almost* always—and what rules he'd failed to follow had been inconsequential.

The very thought that he was being accused of espionage turned his face red, and caused his skin to prickle. As he was marched down the corridor, however, he wondered what would happen if he wasn't able to *prove* his innocence? He'd heard of innocent men and women who had been incarcerated, their fates based on their abilities to convince someone—the *right* someone—of their innocence. People who'd probably already made up their minds.

The thought was chilling.

"Faster," the officer said, pushing him hard in the center of his back. They propelled him down a hallway he'd never seen, and through a door marked SECURITY. The long room had office cubicles along the sides, and a large conference table in the middle. Guards and other staff members occupied the cubicles, and some sat at the conference table. They did more than glance up when he entered.

They stared, each gaze an indictment—a judgment.

Hoenikker was marched through the office and down an interior corridor, passing several doors with heavy locks and no windows. At the end of the corridor stood an open door, and he was pushed inside. The room held a table and four chairs. One chair was already occupied. It was the other guy who had been on the shuttle.

What was his name? Fairbanks?

The door slammed behind him.

A large glass mirror faced him from one wall. He'd seen enough vids to know it was a one-way glass window. Security personnel were probably on the other side taking notes and recording his activities. Judging him.

"They grabbed you, too," Fairbanks said. "Remember when you said Pala Station couldn't be as bad as all that?" He spread his hands. "What do you think now?"

"I think once I explain myself, they'll let me get back to work," Hoenikker said, almost believing his own words. He began to pace.

"You might as well sit down. They're going to let you steam and cool for at least thirty minutes." When Hoenikker shot him a quizzical look, he added, "I used to date a security guard. He ran me through the steps. Said it makes us more malleable, because we spend all of the time running back and forth in our own minds, either trying to find out what we did to get caught, or trying to figure out a way to talk our way out of the room—or both."

Seeing the logic in his advice, Hoenikker took the seat next to Fairbanks. He assumed that the two empty chairs on the other side of the table were reserved for his interrogators.

He remembered what Stokes had said.

"Be boring and stay here. Or be dangerous and travel far."

If there was a moment he wanted to be boring, this was it. He didn't want to be dangerous. Not to *anyone*. He just wanted out of this room. And out from under any judgmental observation so he could go back to his modeling. He wondered, if he hadn't solved the MPDT problem, would he still be free? Then another part realized that one of the other scientists could just as easily have worked it out, so the result had been inevitable.

He could almost hear Stokes in his ear.

Just relax, everything will work out. You're a good guy, Hoenikker. Nothing bad is going to happen to you.

Nothing indeed.

Like being detained for espionage.

The door snapped open and he jumped. Two security personnel entered. One man. One woman. The square-jawed woman wore her hair short, and looked as if she could gut punch a landing shuttle. The man was lanky, and wore a smirk as if he knew the universe's private punchline.

Rather than taking a seat, the woman leaned against the wall in the corner, crossed her arms, and gave him a death stare. The man sat across from them and introduced himself as Mr. Tacker. His voice was pitched lower than Hoenikker would have expected from someone so thin.

He asked for Hoenikker's full name and employee ID.

Hoenikker gave it.

Tacker did the same for Fairbanks.

He gave it.

Then the man did nothing. He merely sat and smirked at the two of them until what must have been ten minutes had passed. All the while, Hoenikker felt his nervousness increasing, which in turn made him angry. The effect they desired, sitting silence, and he hated himself for falling for it.

"You're angry," the man said finally. "Angry at being caught?"

Hoenikker shook his head. "Angry at being a part of this. You know very well that I had nothing to do with it. In fact, I was the one who figured it out."

"The easiest way to influence the information is to be close to the investigation."

"Influence the information?" Hoenikker snorted. "I *broke* the case." At least he thought that was the terminology. "You wouldn't even know about the espionage if it wasn't for me."

"Broke the case," Tacker said. "Interesting choice of words. Do you like detective fiction, Mr. Hoenikker?"

"*Doctor* Hoenikker."

The smirk widened. "Do you watch the criminal vids, *Mister* Hoenikker? Are you a fan of docudramas? Have you invented your own, so you can have a starring role?"

Hoenikker had never wanted to punch a man in the face more than he did at that moment, and Hoenikker had never punched anyone in the face. He probably couldn't even make a proper fist. Still, he wanted to punch this man in the face.

"Listen," Hoenikker began, "I don't know what you're trying to accomplish here. We both know you have access to station logs, and you can track my movements anywhere. You've probably already been over them. If you want to question me about that, feel free. Better yet, why haven't you tracked Brennan's PDT? After all, we know someone cut it out of him. Where did that occur?"

Ha! He thought. *Answer me that!*

Tacker listened patiently the entire time, giving Hoenikker a heavy-lidded stare. Still, his smirk never wavered. Without answering, he turned his attention to the logistics specialist.

"And you, Fairbanks," he said. "You had a convenient trip off planet."

"Nothing convenient about it," Fairbanks said. "Unless you like shuttling back and forth, and experiencing short-term cryosleep. I don't."

"Was it you who brought back the rats? Was it you who started the infestation? Sec Specialist Howard here said she saw you near the comms access panel—the one that was used to send a signal outside. You were wearing a backpack. What was in the backpack, Fairbanks?"

Suddenly, Hoenikker wanted to know what was in the backpack as well. Was Fairbanks the spy? Was he the infiltrator? He hadn't seemed like one, during their shared trip. But then, how could anyone tell?

Fairbanks glanced at Howard, then back at Mr. Tacker.

"Nothing. Just bullshit."

"Sec Specialist Howard, what was it Fairbanks told you?"

"He said he was out for some exercise, and that the pack was full of trash."

"Was there trash in the pack?"

"Just an empty package, and a tool."

"Could that package have contained the rats?" Tacker asked.

"It could have," she said.

Even to Hoenikker it sounded fishy. Tacker pulled a vid display unit out of his pocket and dialed something up.

"Know what I'm looking at, Fairbanks? I'm looking at your PDT tracking logs since you returned to the station. There's only one time you were up before everyone to *exercise*. Once."

"I pulled a muscle," Fairbanks said. "Should have stretched more."

"'Should have stretched more,'" Tacker repeated. He stared at his vid for some time. "I have you in your room yesterday afternoon, when you were supposed to have been on shift."

"I had some personal issues to take care of."

"Were they personal issues with Brennan?" Tacker asked. "We tracked him into your room at the same time."

Fairbanks glanced at Hoenikker, and then Howard, before staring at his steepled hands balanced between his knees.

"That's personal."

"Personal? You gave up having a personal life when you signed your company contract. I'll ask you again, Logistic Specialist Fairbanks. What were you and Brennan doing alone in your room?"

Hoenikker realized he'd been leaning forward, and sat back in his chair. He understood. He could see it in Fairbanks' eyes. He was sure that Tacker understood as well, but clearly the man wanted Fairbanks to admit it. Hoenikker felt embarrassed for the young man, and looked away. His gaze met Howard's.

She looked as if she was ready to pounce.

"Fairbanks, I'm talking to you," Tacker pressed.

"Listen," Fairbanks began, his voice hoarse and low. "Brennan wanted to be together with me. He wanted to have a relationship. I—I didn't want it." He licked his lips and closed his eyes. "He got mad and stormed out. Maybe he took off? I don't know."

Tacker sat silently for a moment. "You're saying that he left your room of his own accord?" he said. "More likely he spurned you, and you got angry."

Fairbanks shook his head. "It was nothing like that. As I said, he left. He called me terrible names. He was angry. I stayed in my room."

"We have a record of you following him," Tacker said.

Fairbanks stared with tears rimming his wide eyes. "Fine. I followed him to his room. We talked some more. I tried to make him feel better, but… but he wouldn't listen. So I left."

"You left." Tacker's smirk grew again.

Fairbanks nodded, unwilling or unable to meet the interrogator's gaze.

Hoenikker wondered if they'd forgotten he was there.

Fairbanks cleared his throat. "Come on, Tacker. My personal life has nothing to do with this. Plus, if you had anything on us, we'd be in a cell by now. Can we just get back to work?"

Hoenikker nodded. That added up. Tacker was fishing. He must not have any evidence against them. He just figured because they were the last two persons brought to the station that it had to be them.

"How do you know it's not station security personnel who did this?" Hoenikker asked, breaking the silence. He regretted it immediately, but there it was.

"Why would security personnel do this?" Tacker sat back in his chair. "For that matter, what *is* 'this'?"

"I don't know," Hoenikker answered. "You tell me. Why would a scientist who begged for an assignment here, *begged* to study alien artifacts, come here and put everything he had in jeopardy?"

"Maybe you work for someone else," Tacker said. "Maybe you were blackmailed, or *very* well paid. Do you have any evidence that station security was involved?" The smirk was still there, yet Hoenikker knew he had to choose his words carefully.

"As much evidence as you have against me," he said. "Maybe more. After all, there must have been security personnel who were away from the station repeatedly in the last few weeks, with the *San Lorenzo* on the way. They could have met up with another corporation, and been given a bag of rats with MPDTs to bring back into the station."

"What do you mean 'away from the station'?" Tacker asked.

Hoenikker leaned forward. "When Deputy Station Chief Thompson goes on his hunting trips, does he go alone?"

Tacker's smirk died a thousand deaths.

As childish as it seemed, Hoenikker wanted to jump up and point, saying, *I got you!* Instead, he fought to control his facial features and just stared. He wondered how proud Stokes would have been for this moment.

Tacker slid his vid display back into his pocket and stood.

"We're done for now," he said. "Be prepared to make yourselves available."

"It's not like we have anywhere to go," Fairbanks said.

Then Tacker and Security Specialist Howard left the room.

They left the door open.

15

The next day Hoenikker was relieved to get back to the lab. Being in custody had soured him enough that he'd considered putting in his transfer packet. What with the absence of the alien artifacts he'd been promised, and the sheer state of paranoia on Pala Station, he'd feel much more comfortable back in a corporate cubicle, working nine-to-five, creating models based on his own theses.

The argument convincing him to stay had an unlikely source.

Cruz. The man was operating on a combination of caffeine and excitement. He hadn't slept much and had come to the lab for some distraction. And he got it.

As Hoenikker stood before Leon-895, he was sure the creature had grown to at least five times its size since he'd last seen it—what he *could* see of it. Cruz had the lights flashing through a prismatic color sequencing and the creature matched it with barely a pause. It was in that pause that Hoenikker noted spikes jutting from its top and sides, like an old-world porcupine.

"I haven't yet tested the effects of temperature fluctuation on color attenuation, but the fact that it can change so fast is absolutely incredible," Cruz said, more than a little giddy. "Imagine if we had armor that could allow our Colonial Marines to blend into any surface. They'd be virtually invisible. Combat efficiency would skyrocket, as would the survival rate. This is groundbreaking."

"It's a great first step, Cruz." Hoenikker could appreciate the man's excitement—but they were scientists, and far from any viable conclusions. "Next we need to replicate your findings with other Leon-895s, to identify the new standard. Then devise a method of copying the creature's modified guanine crystal cell structure, and apply it to armor."

"Of course. Of course." Cruz nodded. "But isn't this fantastic?"

"It is," Hoenikker admitted.

Off to the side the lab door opened, and Fairbanks stepped in, followed by two log specialists Hoenikker didn't know. Kash stepped away from her station, approached one of the specialists, and began to speak. Hoenikker moved closer to hear what was being said.

"—from *San Lorenzo* soon. I'd like Engineering to inspect the integrity of each of the glass fronts, to determine which ones need replaced, then get Fabrications working on them ASAP."

"I've checked the inventory, ma'am," Fairbanks began, glancing at Hoenikker, then quickly away. "I'm not sure we have enough tungsten to replace all the glass fronts. We may have to triage."

"Why on earth wouldn't you have enough tungsten?" Kash asked. "Who else uses tungsten in any quantity?"

"Well, Deputy Station Chief Thompson has been creating his own ammunition for his hunting rifle. He uses nothing but station tungsten."

"My God," she said. "How many bullets does the man need?"

Fairbanks stared at the ground. "I'm not sure, ma'am."

Kash placed a hand on his shoulder. "Of course you aren't. We'll just do the best we can. Please, take the team to the back of the lab and work your way forward. Don't interfere with any of our experiments, though, and do not—I mean do *not*—touch any controls on the workstations."

"Yes, ma'am," he said. He and the other two slid past Hoenikker and headed toward the back.

"What's that all about?" Hoenikker asked, sidling next to her.

"We're retrofitting as best we can before more Xenomorph samples arrive. They should be here within forty-eight hours, and I'm not convinced the glass fronts can contain them."

"I've never seen the Xenomorphs—not firsthand," he said. "Are they that bad?"

"Take every nightmare you've ever had, mold it into a ball, and sculpt the worst thing you can imagine. The Xeno won't be it, but it will eat what you imagined. That's how bad they are."

Hoenikker gulped.

Mansfield entered, his hands folded behind him.

"I heard you were questioned."

Hoenikker frowned. "The entire experience was ridiculous."

Mansfield nodded. "That's the thing about knowing there's an infiltrator on station. It could be anyone. Leads to paranoia."

"I didn't see them questioning *you*?" Kash said, coming to Hoenikker's defense.

"Mark my word," Mansfield began, "if they don't identify the guilty party soon, all of us will have a turn. It's not something I relish, and I didn't relish it for you, Dr. Hoenikker. I would have stopped them if I could."

Hoenikker stared at the bureaucrat.

Was that empathy?

"Now for what I came here to do," Mansfield said, his voice suddenly hard. He marched past Kash and Hoenikker until he was standing behind Cruz. "Dr. Cruz, may I please have a moment?"

Hoenikker and Kash eased forward a little.

"I've made a breakthrough, Mansfield." Cruz turned, his smile still firm. "You see, I couldn't sleep last night, so I—"

Mansfield held up a hand. "Dr. Cruz, did I or did I not place a moratorium on any new experiments? Did I or did I not indicate that *any* new experiments had to be cleared through me?"

"But you've got to see what I've done. You need to—"

"I don't need to see anything, Dr. Cruz. *Did you not understand me?*"

Cruz straightened. His smile fell. His eyes went dead, like those of a Colonial Marine who knew how to play the game.

"I understood you," he replied, all excitement gone from his voice. "Did you understand me when I indicated that I may have had a breakthrough that could substantially increase the survivability of Colonial Marines in combat?"

"Dr. Cruz, you cannot be trusted," Mansfield replied. "You are relieved. Return to your quarters and stay there."

The bigger man blinked as if he'd been slapped. "What did you say to me?" Cruz growled, stepping toward Mansfield.

"I told you to return to you—"

Hoenikker surprised himself, and leaped to grab Cruz, as did Kash—who put herself between the scientist and Mansfield.

"What did you say to me?" Cruz shouted, muscles jumping in his arms and shoulders. Hoenikker wanted to be anywhere but where he was. Still, he held the bigger man as best he could.

All eyes were on Cruz.

Prior's.

Matthews'.

Fairbanks'.

The two specialists stared, as well.

Mansfield didn't move. He stared into the face of a man who could beat him to a pulp. Hoenikker admired his bravery, though he questioned his good sense. Cruz looked dangerous when he was mad. Hell, Cruz looked dangerous when he was happy.

"I believe I gave you an order, Dr. Cruz," Mansfield said evenly.

Cruz stopped, tensed, and tossed off Hoenikker's hands as if they were nothing. He backed away, chewing the inside of his cheek. Then he turned and marched out of the lab. Mansfield eyed both Hoenikker and Kash. After a moment he spoke.

"Isn't there something you should be doing?"

"Come on." Kash grabbed Hoenikker. "Let's go help Prior and Matthews with the inventory." Hoenikker allowed himself to be pulled away, as long as it was away from Mansfield.

So much for empathy.

16

They found the body the next morning.

All of a sudden the medical lab became the popular place to be. In addition to Dr. Erikson and the body, it hosted Security Specialists Howard and Tacker, Reception Tech Rawlings, and Casualty Operations Specialist Edmonds. Slight and introverted, Edmonds wasn't at all suited to looking at a dead body. Rawlings, on the other hand, had seen plenty of dead bodies from his time in the Colonial Marines.

Brennan lay naked on the table. From the neck down, the only damage was the ragged hole in his shoulder from where the PDT had been removed. The body bore the same white flaccid complexion to be expected from a lifetime of working inside various stations.

His head and face were another thing altogether. It looked as if someone had beaten him to death. Pieces of his skull were missing. Teeth poked through ruined cheeks. An eye had hemorrhaged. His nose was a twisted mess.

Rawlings drew an imaginary line down the center of Brennan's face and noted that one side hadn't been hurt at all. Rawlings had been in enough fights to know that Brennan's head had been immobilized, probably by someone grabbing his hair in a tight-fisted grip.

"The damage is extensive," Dr. Erikson said, even though it was obvious to everyone in the room. "I removed metal shavings from inside of his mouth and skull. My techs reviewed them, but they're from the common composite used in the fabrication of the station, and much of the furniture."

"Was there anything on his clothes that might have indicated where he was?" Howard asked.

"He was found naked, his clothes already removed," Rawlings said, having seen Brennan *in situ* where he'd been stashed. The body had been found in a rarely used supply room.

"We'll need to do a search for the clothes," Tacker said, "but they've probably already been put in the incinerator. We'll do a tracker pull to see everyone who had access to it in the last six hours or so."

Howard nodded. "Then we can determine if Hoenikker or Fairbanks was anywhere near where the body was found," he said. "It seems convenient, finding the body right after we released them from custody." She pulled out her vid display unit and began to punch up information.

Rawlings considered her logic. Not finding the body might have been better. Whoever had killed Brennan, if they could have made it to Fabrications, they could have used the section's industrial-sized incinerator. That would have predicated them carrying a body through corridors teeming with people—much easier to spot in the video record. No, if Rawlings had to guess, Brennan hadn't moved far. His body had been stuffed in that room for convenience. Most likely the killer waited for a time during the night when the corridors were emptier, to move the body as quickly as possible.

"Hoenikker was in his lab the entire time," Howard said. "But Fairbanks fell off the grid again." She eyed Tacker, who nodded.

"I think we have a suspect," he said. "Do you think it was a lovers' quarrel?"

"If what Fairbanks said was true," she began, "then yes, it could have been a crime of passion."

"Wait a moment," Rawlings said. "Are you saying that Brennan and Fairbanks…" He laughed. "Can't possibly be."

"Fairbanks told us that Brennan came to his room so they could hook up," Howard said.

"I don't know why Brennan went to his room, but I can tell you that Brennan wasn't inclined that way. In fact, Brennan is—was—pretty much asexual. He spent every waking hour playing first-person shooters, video games. His file is full of reprimands from Comms Chief Oshita."

"How do you know about his sexual orientation?" Tacker asked. "It's not something we keep in personnel files."

"I just know," Rawlings said. "Small things. Phrases used. Words used. We're close units in the Colonial Marines. We know each other's inclinations. Not that it matters, but we know it. It's the same here." He stared straight at Howard. "I know everyone's inclinations. I pay attention."

She broke his gaze to stare at the body.

"Let's pretend you're right," Tacker said. "Then why? Why is this body so battered?"

Rawlings shrugged. "I'm not Security. I just know the people in my station."

"Where's Fairbanks now?" Tacker asked. "Or is he off the grid again?"

Howard attended her vid display. "No. He's on the grid. We have him currently in the laboratory, providing support to a Fabrications team." She paused again. "Looks like they're replacing some of the glass fronts on the containment rooms."

"Put security outside the lab. No reason to go in there if we don't have to. The last thing I need is Mansfield complaining to Flowers," Tacker said. "Let's go take a look at Fairbanks' quarters. And get someone from Logistics to join us."

"One more thing," Dr. Erikson said, holding up a hand.

Tacker stepped from foot to foot. "What is it?"

"Comms Specialist Brennan was poisoned."

"Poisoned?" Tacker stopped moving. His eyes narrowed. "How?"

The doctor turned Brennan's head. "Note the blackening of the tongue and the petechia of the eye. Nothing else could cause this. What type of poison it is? We're not sure at this point, but it's not anything we have on the station."

"Why would someone poison a guy they just beat to a bloody pulp?" Howard asked.

Rawlings wanted to know the same thing. It made no sense.

Tacker chewed on his cheek for a moment, then nodded slightly. "Perhaps the beating was out of rage, but then when the killer realized he hadn't completed the job, he used poison." He leaned over to stare into Brennan's mouth. "That's the only explanation I can come up with. But where did the poison come from?"

"Why not just choke him, or beat him some more?" Howard asked.

"Maybe the killer didn't want to be a killer. Poison is a lot less hands-on," Tacker said. Then he turned toward the door. "Come on. Let's go to Fairbanks' quarters."

Once outside the medlab, Rawlings realized how tense he'd been. Dealing with bodies always took him back to his days in the Colonial Marines. He held out his hands. The one on the right, metal, emblazoned with a Weyland-Yutani stamp. The one on the left, flesh and blood, trembling slightly as his nerves flared, memories of the bodies, his friends, dead and in ditches on a far-away LV.

Looking up, he noted that the others had already reached the end of the corridor and turned the corner. He wanted to be with them and see this through. So, he hurried after them, arriving at Brennan's room just as Tacker and Howard did. They were joined by Buggy from Logistics.

Tacker entered the room first. He went to the middle of the room and stood. Not touching anything. His gaze raking over everything.

From the doorway, Rawlings could see a perfectly made bed on the right. On the left were a metal bureau and a small desk and chair. A room like any other. A room like his own. So mundane. It would have been difficult to believe a murder had taken place here, had he not seen similar scenes before. Like the church they'd found sitting serene in a forest glen. A place of worship, a center for gathering, the church had been a locus for community and religion for three decades. Then they'd opened the door and found the missing villagers inside, bloody, draped across the pews, dead where they had been shot, bodies ravaged by the M41 Pulse Rifle used by an AWOL Colonial Marine.

He shook his head to chase away the memory.

Tacker sniffed the air. "Smell that? Disinfectant."

Howard stepped into the room. She sniffed as well. "Heavy duty cleaner." Stepping over to the desk, she pulled on plastic gloves, bent down, and touched the edge. She straightened. "This desk is new."

Buggy bent down, and ran a scanner over the inventory control sticker underneath the desktop. He read the results.

"Nope. This is the one assigned to the room."

"Can't be." Howard shook her head. "Know what I think? I think Fairbanks put his old inventory control tag on a new table, and put the new one on his old table. It's probably been put back into storage. Maybe even cleaned up. He'd have wanted to make sure there wasn't any evidence left on it."

Tacker knelt down, peering at the wall beside the table.

"Is it me, or are those spots?" he said, pointing.

Howard joined him. "We can have those tested."

"Let's do it," Tacker said. "Meanwhile, let's go have a chat with Fairbanks. I think we have a better understanding of what went on here." Both he and Howard strode out of the room, leaving Buggy and Rawlings alone.

"Did you see the body?" Buggy asked.

Rawlings nodded. "It was pretty bad. Face bashed in and all that."

"How you holding up?" Buggy asked.

"A little anxious. Brought back memories." He grinned as the interior of the church was superimposed on the room, the body of an elderly woman twisted and staring at him, the unasked question, *why did you let him do this to us*, hanging in the air. "To be expected, I suppose." He turned toward the door. "What I need is some coffee. Want to join me?"

Buggy hesitated, then grinned as well. "Sure. I'll join."

They left the murder scene behind and headed to a better place.

17

Fairbanks was in a personal hell.

He never should have let Hyperdyne Corporation blackmail him. He should have informed Security the moment he returned to the station. That would have been the proper thing to do, but his cowardice hadn't let him. Instead, he hid and did their bidding and installed software into the system until even the most inadequate and incompetent comms specialist had tracked him down.

And then instead of turning him in like he should have, the guy had the temerity to try and blackmail him again. How could Fairbanks have allowed that to happen? Once was bad enough, but to let himself be blackmailed two times…

How could he look himself in the mirror?

Yelling began at the front of the lab.

Fairbanks spun to the sound, but it was only the large black-skinned scientist, screaming at his boss. Fairbanks watched in fascination as the smaller man just stared into the face of the violent man, until, with barely a few words, the larger of the two was storming out of the lab.

That was the kind of strength Fairbanks appreciated. Strength from silence. Strength from a perceived position of weakness. Fairbanks had never been a big man, nor would he ever be, but to be in a position to know people and have people do your bidding—that was an envious position. Like Rawlings. Sure, the man had been a Colonial Marine; and sure, he'd lost a hand. But he knew everyone and everyone knew him. If he were to ask around, he doubted there was a single person who had a problem with him.

Fairbanks wanted to be someone like that. He didn't want to be a traitor. He didn't want to be an infiltrator. He just wanted to be someone good, whom others respected.

"Get your head out of the clouds, Fairbanks," Glover said. "Are you taking notes or what?"

Fairbanks jumped, and attended his vid display.

"This is another one that needs to be replaced. We have pitting and scoring in three of the four quadrants."

Fairbanks looked nervously inside the containment room, at the rat with large spider legs. He shuddered as he imagined the creature crawling over him.

"Fairbanks?" Glover said. "Are you with me?"

"Uh, yes. That, uh, makes seven out of the nine we've checked, and we still have six to go."

The third specialist spoke up. "No way are we going to be able to provide that many fronts. Do you realize the process?" His name was Ching, and he worked in Fabrications.

"Don't you recycle any of the tungsten from these fronts?" Fairbanks asked. "Can't they be recovered?"

Ching sighed and looked as if his lunch wasn't sitting well. "Recovery is a long procedure. Even if we did recover the tungsten, the degradation would be too much."

"But added to what I can supply now," Fairbanks pressed, "if you recovered what's in these, would it be better than what we have?"

"Yes." Ching nodded grudgingly. "Marginally."

"If 'marginally' is the best we can do, then I say we do it," Fairbanks said.

They moved to the next containment area, where lights were strobing in different colors, for no apparent reason. This unit appeared to be empty, but just as Fairbanks was going to dismiss it, he spied the spiky shape of a large creature that was blending into the background.

The door to the lab opened and Security Specialists Tacker and Howard entered. Fairbanks caught them in his peripheral vision, and turned away. The last thing he wanted was for them to notice he was there. So far he'd been able to steer clear of them. If he could just keep it up—

"Fairbanks," Tacker said. "Can we have a word?"

He looked into the eyes of Ching and Glover. Both of the men had the odd combination of curiosity and accusation. Was it that easy to accuse a fellow worker? They didn't know what he'd done. He shouldn't be thought of as being guilty, just because of an accusation. Where was the brotherhood?

"Fairbanks. I'm talking to you," Tacker said, closer.

Ching backed away.

As did Glover.

Without turning, Fairbanks said, "I'm in the middle of an inventory. If we can do this when I'm finished—"

"You are finished," Tacker said.

Howard appeared next to him and gently but firmly removed the vid display from his hands.

Fairbanks turned.

Everyone was staring at him.

His face burned red.

"What is it you want?"

"You're accused of the murder of Comms Specialist Brennan. You will come with us."

"Come with you?" he asked, his voice rising several octaves. "I don't know what you're talking about."

"Fairbanks, we've been to your room. We found the table you replaced. We've scanned the blood you failed to clean up. You killed Brennan, and now you need to be held accountable."

In that moment, everything he'd ever dreamed of accomplishing died, and he let out an awful groan.

Tacker sighed. "Howard. If you will?"

Howard reached for his elbow.

Fairbanks panicked. He punched her in the face—to no effect except to hurt his hand. He backed into the workstation in front of the containment area. He looked down and saw several buttons.

"Don't touch anything," one of the scientists warned.

One button said ABORT.

The other said RELEASE.

He glanced up, and everyone seemed to be moving in slow motion. "Don't do it," Hoenikker cried.

Fairbanks punched the RELEASE button and dove.

The door sprung open but nothing seemed to happen.

No one moved for a good ten seconds.

Then Ching went to close it, and as he reached for it, his arm disappeared.

A creature came into existence—large, four legs, the front two as striking claws. Tentacle-like protrusions from its mouth chewed at Ching's arm, then spit it to the side. It blinked at everyone as if seeing them for the first time, then leaned back and let out an awful roar.

Then it disappeared.

"It's Leon-895," someone shouted. "The idiot let it out."

Mansfield backed toward the door. "I'll seal the room," he shouted.

Howard tried to pull her weapon, but was decapitated before she could complete the move. Her head rolled to Fairbanks' feet and he screamed like a child, even as the woman's blood fountained into the air.

Two of the scientists were hurled to the floor.

The "Leon" materialized above one of them, the fat one, ripping at the scientist's chest with its claws. He fell to his knees, grabbing his chest.

Another of the scientists, Hoenikker, ran toward the exit. The creature could barely be discerned chasing after him, knocking things and people down as it loped.

Mansfield tried to escape through the door. He hit the button and the creature was on him, ripping great gouts of meat and muscle from his small boney frame. Blood flew and covered part of the beast, and even as it chameleoned to the colors of the laboratory behind it, the red swath marked it as a killer.

The door opened and Hoenikker ran through it.

The creature followed.

Fairbanks saw his opportunity. He bolted from the room and took off the other way.

18

Hoenikker paused to catch his breath. Had that really happened? Had that dumb shit really opened one of the containment rooms? The one that contained Leon-895?

A scream sounded from behind him.

Hoenikker spun and watched in terrible fascination as a specialist had his throat ripped out by the Leon. The only parts of the creature he could discern were those covered in blood.

For one brief dreadful instant, the creature materialized. No longer did it blend into the background. Now it was merely the horrific creature Cruz had helped create. Almost the size of a human, with four legs, the center one propelling it forward while the outside legs helped it to maintain balance. It began to move toward Hoenikker with a slow, steady gate.

"Shoo," he said. "Shoo!" He batted the air with his hands as he backed away. Why was it following him? What had he done to deserve its attention?

"Out of the way!" A security guard ran up and pushed him aside.

The woman held up a pistol.

She fired but missed.

The Leon winked out of sight.

Hoenikker could track it because of the blood, but the security guard didn't know what had happened. She straightened and looked around.

"Where did it go?"

She flew against one wall.

Then the other.

Then the ceiling.

Then the floor.

Her face condensed upon itself as a great muscular weight was applied and the head was crushed into a parody of itself.

The smell of her death hit Hoenikker in the face, the distilled essence of blood and offal and brains. His back arched as he retched. Just the sight of her face being crushed was enough to change him. But he had to get away. Hoenikker turned to run, and crashed into a group of people.

"Hey, now."

"Watch where you're going."

He picked himself up off the floor and tried to push past, but they held him firm.

"Looks like he's running from the devil," one said, laughing.

"Let me go," Hoenikker begged. "It's coming."

All eyes turned to stare down the corridor.

"There's nothing th—" The speaker was snatched forward, then slammed into the wall.

Suddenly the alarm sounded.

"I don't see it," someone said. Then he too was thrown back.

Hoenikker managed to push past, then was knocked into the side of the corridor as the others turned and fled, jostling him with their urgent need to survive. He fell to one knee, but hurriedly struggled to his feet. He had his own urgent need to survive.

Another security specialist appeared. This one was a man carrying a pulse rifle. As deadly as the weapon seemed, Hoenikker knew it wouldn't be enough.

"Run," he said, voice cracking.

"I got this," the man said, suicidally obtuse.

But there was nothing to get.

No target.

Only a corridor with dead people.

Still, Hoenikker backed away.

The Leon materialized above the security specialist.

Hoenikker was about to shout for the man to look up, but it was too late. The Leon grabbed the man by the neck, lifted him up, and snapped a bite out of the top of his skull, the brain bleeding like it was the top of a man-size ice cream cone.

The smell hit Hoenikker again. He was so used to the disinfectant aroma of a lab. Even outside of the work area, the station had a clean metallic smell, despite the rats and the close proximity of humans. It was the air scrubbers and the filters that did the job. But here, next to a hunter, the smell of the dying combined with the new scents of internal organs and sweetbreads made him want to vent everything that was inside of him.

Another alarm sounded, this one higher pitched. This one was matched by the sound of running feet.

Five guards turned the corner, only they looked different. Their faces, all identical, were devoid of emotion. Their bodies were the color of the walls and floor—their own form of chameleonism, he supposed. Each held a pistol in his right hand. Their movements were too fluid. Too neat.

Synths.

One grabbed him and put its arms around him. Like a hug, but one he couldn't escape. Hoenikker wasn't sure if the gesture was meant to protect him or detain him. He struggled briefly, but found it almost impossible to even move. The synth spun and pinned him against the wall, shielding him with its back. Hoenikker craned his head to watch.

The remaining four synths fanned out in the corridor, looking back and forth, trying to find a target.

"Switch to infrared," he shouted. "It's invisible to the naked eye."

All heads swiveled to him, then each other, then to a spot near the corner of wall and the ceiling. Hoenikker saw the swatch of red just as the synths opened fire.

The Leon materialized like static, as each round found a home. It backed away and they chased after it, around a corner in the corridor.

Now was the time Hoenikker should have been trying to run, but he wanted to know what was happening. The science part of his brain fought with his need to survive.

Two synths crashed back into sight, against the wall, as if thrown. The synth that was holding him let go and rushed around the corner, immediately opening fire with its pistol.

Hoenikker heard a dozen shots as he crept forward.

He was about ready to turn the corner when a great invisible beast rushed past him, knocking him to the ground. It held him there, its terrible maw and gnashing teeth mere feet from his face. All the creature had to do was lean down and take a bite, and Hoenikker's life would be ended.

Three synths turned the corner, raised their pistols, and fired.

Leon-895 took off.

They ran after it, chasing it down the corridor and around the corner.

Hoenikker lay on his back, trying to gather enough sense to stand. He'd been inches from death. He didn't know *why* he'd survived. Was the creature interested in him? Was there a sentience inside Leon-895 of which they'd never become aware?

Kash appeared above him.

"Hoenikker? Tim?" she said breathlessly. "Are you alright?"

He felt himself. Somehow, he'd gone unscathed. The creature had seemed to fixate on him. Why was that? Why had it followed him, or had Hoenikker just been unlucky enough to have been in the way of its retreat? Had it been pure coincidence? Would it have followed him had he turned left instead of right?

"Tim," she said, kneeling and gently shaking him by the shoulders. "Are you alright?"

"Yeah," he said, softly. Then with a little more strength he repeated, "Yeah. I think I am."

He sat up.

"What about the others?" he asked.

She shook her head. "Dead. So many. Dead."

19

The number of dead was unimaginable. All from a single Leon-895, something no one on the station knew existed until now. To think that a simple creature captured from the jungles of LV-895 could have wrought so much havoc.

Rawlings made his usual rounds, exchanging coffee for gossip, and could detect fear circling the edges of every conversation.

It was only going to get worse.

He also had it on good authority that the next day would bring not only wholesale changes to the way Pala Station was being run, but more of the Xenomorphs on which the scientists had experimented before. He'd only ever seen one of the adults, but that had sent chills through him as he watched it chase down a sample of local fauna, its jaws extending from its body to rip the creature in half.

Which was why he'd called the meeting. He hadn't anticipated needing one so soon. When he'd first divined the idea of creating a group of common concern among the station's veterans, he'd thought they might benefit from a group of close comrades, to vent about various issues that only they could understand. As a group they were all older than their peers, and age brought with it a certain worldliness and weariness.

Now it was more than that. His gut told him that they might need the group to survive.

They met in the mess hall, gathering between breakfast and lunch. A few workers were refilling some of the drinking containers, but other than that, they were alone. Buggy from Comms sat across the table from him, sipping soda loudly through a straw. Flores and Dudt sat beside Buggy, both from Security, and both new to Weyland-Yutani corporate, so basically fresh off the boat.

McGann from Engineering sat beside Rawlings, with Chase from Logistics. They were only waiting on Dr. Cruz to arrive to establish their quorum.

"Any news on Fairbanks?" Chase asked the two security specialists. Flores shook her head and glanced first at Dudt before answering.

"It's like he disappeared. There's no pings from his PDT. Nothing."

"I bet he ripped it out," Dudt said. He had red hair and skin so white you imagined he'd never been in the sun. "That's what he did to Brennan."

"There are ways to hide the signal," Buggy said. "In special services, we had devices that adhered to the outside of the skin where the implant was. That blocked the signal, and it scrambled it so even if something leaked, nothing could read it."

"What are they saying in Log about Fairbanks?" Rawlings asked Chase.

"We're all pretty stunned," he replied. "Fairbanks was a standup guy. We never knew he was into espionage. I mean, why would you even do something like that—and then to kill Brennan? I heard Fairbanks did a number on his face."

"It wasn't pretty," Rawlings said.

Chase's eyes brightened. "You were there?" Then he nodded to himself. "Of course you were. You go everywhere."

"I just try to pay attention." Rawlings sipped from his cup of coffee. "What about you, McGann? Heard anything?"

A thirty-something, acne-faced woman with a dark ponytail, she shrugged. "We're always hearing things. Seems the rat problem is finally under control. We haven't had to pull any extra duty." She knocked on the table for luck. "But there's some talk about the incoming Xeno specimens. Between us and Fabrications, we're concerned about containment."

"Yeah," Chase said. "Don't those scientists have any security protocols? I mean, that Leon should have never gotten out. The lab should have been locked down immediately."

"Security has an answer for that," Flores said. "They're putting two synths in the lab, so if there's another problem, they can take care of it before it gets out of hand. Word has it that there will be no more breaches. Before that happens, the station commander will order all the specimens killed."

"Not that we've heard from the station commander at all," Chase said.

Rawlings took a sip of his coffee. "He's on the outs. It's the incoming commander who said that. We get to meet him tomorrow. Get ready for an ass reaming."

"We've already been warned down in Security," Dudt said. "The ass reaming has begun by remote control."

"Do you think that's going to be enough?" McGann asked, her eyes as hard as flint. They were surrounded by laugh lines that seemed seldom used.

"It's going to have to be," Cruz said, entering the room. He grabbed some iced tea and a straw and pulled up a chair to sit at the head of the table. Rawlings nodded to him.

Rawlings had been the highest ranking when they were in the Colonial Marines, rising to the rank of warrant officer. But here on Pala Station, the scientists were the big men on campus. The station staff were all about supporting them. So, Cruz was *de facto* in charge of their little group, even though it was Rawlings who'd created it.

"How are you guys recovering?" Rawlings asked. He'd helped process the bodies, so he knew of the decimation the scientific staff had experienced.

"Not good," Cruz said. "I feel like shit that I wasn't there to help."

"I heard Mansfield relieved you," Rawlings said carefully. Cruz glanced at him for a sharp-eyed second, then shrugged.

"Difference of opinion. You know the deal. Fucking civilians."

The others all nodded. Each had experienced their own run-ins. Each one knew what it was like to be in the shit. They might all be fucking civilians now, but their muscle memory was still as marines. For a moment everyone had a faraway look, as if remembering another time and another place, when things were different.

"Mansfield isn't going to be relieving anyone soon," Rawlings said.

"We also lost Prior and Matthews. Matthews was a thumb-sucker," Cruz said. "Don't know how he got the job, but Prior was a solid scientist. He knew his shit."

"I heard Matthews wasn't touched," Chase said.

"He wasn't. Heart attack. Mind you, I might have had one too, had I seen Leon in action," Cruz admitted.

"And they still haven't found it," Dudt said. "It's still somewhere on the station."

"What about the synths?" Rawlings asked. "I heard they were doing patrols."

"Even with their advancements, they can't seem to find it," Flores said.

"I fucking hate that it killed people," Cruz said. "I know there are those who blame me, because I was the one who experimented on it. But can you imagine if we can harvest the chameleon ability of the beast onto power armor?" He smiled and leaned forward. "Imagine going into combat being invisible."

"All in the name of science," Chase said, rolling his eyes.

Cruz gave him a hard look. "Yes. In the name of science. Listen, people die. Shit happens. We're not here at the edge of the known universe to fuck around. We're here to develop technology that will save marines."

Rawlings held up a finger. "That, and something else, my friend. We're here to develop technology sold by the Weyland-Yutani Corporation, for a handsome profit."

"The man's got to get paid," Cruz said. "That's for sure." He leaned back. "Enough of the small talk. Why did you bring us together? I mean, I'm all up for a group of 'common concern,' but I wasn't planning on having weekly meetings. I have a laundry list of things to do, not to mention seeing if we can fix the damage done by Leon-895."

Rawlings looked around the table. Everyone was staring at him, waiting for a response.

"Here's the deal," he began. "We all know there's been two containment problems with the lab. We also know that the containment fronts aren't what they should be. Log, and Fab, and Engineering are working on it, but there's only so much they can do—and now we're about to bring down the second round of specimens from the orbital mining facility *Katanga*. It's been in space for more than twenty years, and has been the station's source of Xenomorph specimens. These are the real deal. As bad as Leon-895 was, these are far worse. Do you remember that feeling you got in your guts before a mission, when you knew for certain you were going to be shot?"

Everyone nodded their head.

"I have that feeling now," Rawlings said. "I can't quantify it, I can't science it, I can't prove it, but I know some serious shit is about to go down, and I want to make sure we at least have a chance at surviving it."

"What do you think is going to happen?" McGann asked.

"Murphy," Rawlings said flatly. "Murphy's Law is going to happen. We're going to have all the protocols in place, we're going to have plans for how to mitigate problems, and still bad shit will ensue, and we won't have any control over it whatsoever."

"Murphy," mumbled Cruz.

The rest did the same.

"So, what is it we can do?" Flores asked.

"Be aware of what's going on. Constantly check your six," Cruz said. He glanced at Rawlings, then at the others. "I've had the same flutters in my stomach, as well. We need to be careful. Who here has personal weapons?"

No one raised their hands.

"Come on. No bullshit," Cruz said. "I have body armor, a pulse rifle, and a flamethrower—don't ask. What about the rest of you? No Colonial Marine, current or former, would let themselves be caught dead without a weapon. So, give."

"Dudt and I each have a full complement of weapons we were issued, that we store in our hooches," Flores said.

"Can you get more if necessary?" Rawlings asked.

She glanced at Dudt, who nodded, then nodded to the group.

"I have two pistols," McGann said.

"I have a pulse rifle, but hardly any ammo," Chase said.

"What about you, Rawlings?" Cruz asked.

Rawlings sipped from his cup of coffee.

"I have three pulse rifles and five thousand rounds of ammo."

"HFS," Chase said.

"How'd you get so much?" Flores asked, suspiciously.

Rawlings grinned and shrugged. "I just asked for things. People gave them, and sometimes when people leave, they leave stuff that hasn't been inventoried. No big deal. I'm not looking to overthrow anything.

"I'm just looking to survive."

20

All the essential staff were packed into the mess hall. The tables and chairs had been removed so everyone was standing shoulder-to-shoulder, butt-to-butt, uncomfortable in the indescribable way that can only be understood by being in that situation.

Security personnel lined the walls. Although they didn't carry weapons, their demeanor was deadly serious. The scientists—or what was left of them, at least—had been placed in the front row. Étienne, Kash, Hoenikker, and Cruz, whose suspension had been negated by the death of Mansfield. Ironically, because of his seniority, he'd been put in charge.

Hoenikker didn't care who was in charge, but it seemed to him a little like the fox guarding the henhouse.

The section chiefs were lined up at the head of the room, silently facing out over the crowd, and they didn't look happy. Several heads were down. Conspicuous by their absences were Station Chief Crowther and Deputy Station Chief Thompson.

Finally, a newcomer—a man—entered wearing a white uniform. He stopped in front of each chief, shook hands, and said a few words the rest couldn't hear.

"Let the ass reaming begin," Cruz said under his breath.

"Anyone know about this guy?" Étienne asked.

"Not a word." Kash shook her head.

The man turned and centered himself in front of the section chiefs. He had piercing blue eyes and the chiseled face of someone who spent a lot of time at the gym. His figure beneath the uniform seemed to tell the same story.

"Men and women of Pala Station, I am your new station commander," he said so all could hear. "My name is Vincent Bellows. Station Chief Crowther has been relieved for cause, and will be taking a long voyage back to headquarters." His words were neither angry nor endearing. They were delivered in a flat, businesslike manner to be expected of a senior Weyland-Yutani executive.

"Deputy Station Chief Thompson has also been relieved," he continued. "He will be joining Crowther on his journey. But that's irrelevant, as far as you're concerned. I'm here to point out to all of you that the mission of Pala Station is research. Everything we do here, everything *you* do here, is to advance Weyland-Yutani capabilities, and to increase corporate profits.

"Every time someone dies, we have to pay out death benefits. Every time something breaks, it needs to be replaced. Our job is not one of dying and breaking, it is one of discovery.

"To date, we have managed to develop acid-resistant armor technology which we can sell the Colonial Marines," Bellows said. "As briefed by Dr. Cruz, we also have another opportunity to improve armor through the creation of biological stealth technology, although that specimen seems to have disappeared. I have been informed by Security Chief Rodriguez that motion sensors are being positioned in order to try and track the creature. If you see it, do *not* engage. Note the location, get to safety, and inform Security."

He paused, likely for effect, Hoenikker guessed.

"Up to now, it seems as if your greatest single shared asset has been incompetence. Let me assure you that this will cease. If I relieve you from duty, I will ensure that you are on the slowest ship back to corporate, and that any bonuses you've earned during your time here will not be paid. Pala Station needs to produce. To do that, I need everyone's very best. From Logistics to Personnel. From Fabrications to Engineering. From Security to Medical. I need everyone to know their job, and perform it perfectly.

"As for the scientists, I need you to follow scientific safety protocols. If any more specimens escape, I will hold you personally responsible. I will shut down research until I can get more qualified scientists. Certainly, corporate will be mad at me, but I'm used to people being mad at me. If there's one thing I know it's Weyland-Yutani policies, and trust me when I say that I have enough policies in my back pocket to ensure my own continued survival. So, do not—I repeat, do *not*—tempt me to shut something down, or kick someone off the station.

"I'll do it in a corporate minute.

"Finally, there will be no more hunting trips outside of the station, and no need to maintain an external facility. We have enough work to do without leaving to find something else." He placed his hands behind his back as he leaned forward. "Now, are there any questions?"

Silence.

"Any questions? Come on. Now is your chance."

No one responded.

"Alright, I can see that the lot of you are nervous," he said. "So, I will answer the most obvious concern. What is happening next. The *San Lorenzo* arrived in orbit two days ago. That's how I got here. Right now, synths are acquiring specimens from *Katanga*. They'll be shuttling them down later this afternoon.

"As you know, these specimens are some of the most dangerous creatures we've ever encountered, which is why Pala Station is in the middle of nowhere. We don't want any of the specimens getting into population centers. What does that mean? It means they are dangerous. They are *beyond* dangerous. To that end, I will be posting extra security in the lab, in order to protect station personnel."

He stared at the assembled mass, nodded once, then turned on his heel and left. The moment he was out the door, the room let out a collective sigh. Everyone began to move toward the exit.

The section chiefs left first, single file out the door, heads still down. Hoenikker wondered if they didn't have another, more private meeting where they would each be told in explicit terms what was expected of them.

Cruz and Kash headed out the door, and Hoenikker would have followed, but Rawlings stopped him.

"A moment," Rawlings said.

Hoenikker stared into the scarred black face of the reception tech. The man's smile always seemed to be in place. Perhaps the way he went through life. Certainly better than frowning, he supposed.

"Sure," Hoenikker said. "How can I help you?"

"I just wanted to let you know that things are going to get a little bit jumpier around here."

"Jumpier?" Hoenikker said. "Than what?"

The smile faded a bit. "Folks are going to be quicker to get angry, and quicker to react. What with our new station chief and a new group of specimens, the staff are going to be worried. They know what these things can do if they get out, and what they don't know, they make up."

"I'm not sure why you're talking to me about this," Hoenikker said, glancing back to the doorway and freedom.

"It's just that you will be closest to the action. Closer to the danger. You're going to be one of the first ones to know if something isn't right."

Hoenikker nodded.

"So, if you find yourself needing a place to run, or needing to tell others it's *time* to run, I'm that person. I can keep you safe in the event…" He didn't finish.

Hoenikker frowned. "In the event of what, exactly?"

Rawlings' smiled widened again. "I don't rightly know, but my guess is that when it happens, you'll know."

Then he left, leaving Hoenikker standing in a room that had quickly emptied.

Two times specimens had gotten free, just since he had arrived. Would the same happen with the Xenomorphs? *Could* the same happen with Xenomorphs? He was so lost in the possibilities of it, he didn't notice the mess hall staff trying to put the room back together and prepare for dinner, until one of them came up to him and politely asked him to leave.

21

Cruz was in charge, and he wanted everyone to know it, making Hoenikker feel vaguely like a Colonial Marine instead of a scientist. They'd been waiting for him, and he felt this heat from Cruz's gaze as he entered the lab, the last scientist to do so.

While Hoenikker hadn't exactly liked Mansfield, at least the Weyland-Yutani bureaucrat knew how to keep things organized. Now Cruz was the boss. Cruz—the same person who enjoyed frosting and roasting specimens. Hoenikker glanced at the others as he took his seat.

No one was looking at Cruz. They'd all found their own horizons at which to stare.

"Now that we're all present," Cruz began, clearing his voice, "here's how things are going to be. Prior and Matthews are gone. It sucks, but that's the way it is. Their… departure makes it harder on us."

Hoenikker watched Étienne mouth the word *departure*.

"Now we have to perform the functions of six scientists with only four. While it's easier to replace Prior, because I'm a xenobiologist, replacing Matthews—no matter his individual eccentricities—will be much more difficult. His chemical engineering skills will be missed. So, we're all going to have to buck up and take on more responsibility. Frankly, if the rest of the station was run the way we're going to be running the lab, starting immediately, we'd all be in much better shape."

Étienne formed the words *better shape*. This time, Cruz saw him.

"Is there something you want to share with the group, Étienne?"

"No." Étienne shook his head, and stared at the floor. "I'm fine."

Cruz sneered. "You don't look fine. It looks like you have something you want to say."

Étienne sighed, then glanced up. "Don't you think you're taking this 'being in charge' bit a little too seriously?"

Cruz's face hardened. "Too seriously? People have died, Étienne. This is *very* serious."

"You might have died, had you not been sent to your room for malfeasance," Étienne replied. "You were just lucky enough to have been kicked out of the lab."

"Malfeasance?" Cruz quickly rose to his feet. "Who the hell do you think you are, you little French cocksucker?" He moved toward where Étienne sat, but Kash stood and placed a palm on his chest.

"Dr. Cruz? Is this really the way you wanted the meeting to go?" she asked, her voice low and level. He tried to push past her, but she kept in his way, gently but firmly pressing her hand into his chest, trying to lock eyes with him. Finally, he looked at her. "Let's all sit down and apologize, okay? After all, we're scientists, not brawlers."

Cruz glanced from her to Étienne, then seemed to sag.

"You're right of course." He returned to his seat, smoothed down the front of his lab coat, and smiled the sort of smile someone might wear if he or she were disemboweling a cat and enjoying it immensely. "I'm sorry that I called you a French cocksucker."

Étienne smiled as well, his the sort Hoenikker would expect an enemy to provide at the funeral of their rival.

"I accept your apology." He paused a moment, then said, "And I'm sorry I've been thinking you're an overbearing psychotic windbag who shouldn't be in charge of yourself, much less a team of scientists. I'm sorry that I know we're pretty much all going to die because of your need to self-medicate your PTSD by killing specimens. And finally, I'm sorry you weren't in here when Leon-895 escaped, because I'm sure either Matthews or Prior would still be alive."

His eyes going wide, Hoenikker turned to watch Cruz as Étienne spoke, waiting for the bigger man to launch himself across the table. But the reaction was anything but what he expected. Instead of getting angry, Cruz began to laugh. Full-out guffaws that made Kash look at Hoenikker with eyes that asked, *Is he crazy?*

"That's good, Étienne," Cruz said. "That's rich. You reminded me what it was like back in the barracks when we used to exchange *your* mama jokes. You've got to learn to get as good as you give." Cruz glanced around the table. "And you're right about Leon-895. It probably would have come for me, so in a strange way, I owe Mansfield my life. That said, I'm still in charge, and we need to pull together.

"Speaking of Leon-895," he added, "has there been any news?"

"Security is doing a search, and placing the motion sensors," Kash said, "but their number one priority is to make certain the specimens from *Katanga* arrive safely." She glanced at Hoenikker. "Wait until you see them. Going to make you wished you'd stayed in your office."

Hoenikker swallowed hard. He really just wanted his alien artifacts. After all, they couldn't bite back.

"I'm putting Kash in charge of the Xenomorph experimentation," Cruz said. "We're already aware of their morphology, so we need to make certain we experiment during all phases. Hoenikker, this is all new to you, so keep your eyes open and your hands in your pockets. Don't do anything unless Kash gives you the go-ahead."

Hoenikker nodded, feeling a bit like he'd shown up three weeks late for kindergarten.

Cruz had a few more words, then directed Étienne to supervise the insertion of the new glass fronts for the specimen containment areas. As it turned out, Engineering and Fabrications had put their heads together and determined that they did, indeed, have enough tungsten, as long as they spread the mixture more thinly than before. They assured Cruz, however, that the barriers would still be within safety protocols.

Cruz left to meet with Security about the specimen transfer.

Which left Hoenikker and Kash alone.

Then the engineering staff arrived, accompanied by a pair of synths. The two scientists watched as the fronts to the empty containment rooms were removed, one by one, and replaced with new ones. The process was laborious, made even more so by Étienne's insistence that everything be just right. Hoenikker didn't mind it at all, though. The safer they were, the better he felt. After they'd watched the removal and installation of two fronts, Hoenikker turned to Kash.

"What's the story about *Katanga*, anyway?" Hoenikker asked.

"It's been hanging over our heads like the Sword of Damocles for more than twenty years," Kash said. "It was originally created as a facility for a terraforming planet. The problem was that the colonists encountered Xenomorphs on the planet, and were forced to flee to the mine. Then, of course, the mine became infested, and all was lost."

"By the same creatures that were on the planet?" he asked.

She nodded. "Appears so. These particular Xenomorphs like to use human bodies to gestate. When it's time to give birth, they just about ruin everything on their way out."

Hoenikker shuddered, trying not to picture what he'd just been told.

"So, then they built Pala Station."

"No. Evidently," Kash said, "Pala Station was already here. They transported the mine from another solar system to this one."

"I thought it was purpose built for the Xenomorphs?"

"Nope," she said.

"Then why put Pala Station here? What makes this planet so important? I thought Pala was built to support research into the Xenomorphs on *Katanga*? But if Pala was already here, then it had to have been built for a different reason."

Kash shook her head. "I can't tell you for sure. But every now and then Mansfield would bring in an artifact covered in strange glyphs." His pulse quickened at her words. "There are also areas of the station that are off limits to everyone but Security. I mean, if the station was built for a purely scientific reason, then why wouldn't they allow us full access? Cruz believes there's an entire other crew doing side-by-side experimentation in the part of the station we aren't allowed to enter."

"That seems a little far-fetched," he said. "But he seems the sort who would buy into conspiracy theories."

"I agree, on both counts, but there's something they aren't telling us," Kash said.

Hoenikker scratched his head. "So, for the past twenty-plus years the *San Lorenzo* or some other ship supplies us with specimens?"

She nodded. "I heard that they originally sent scientific teams to try and collect specimens, but that didn't end well. Since then, they've had military research teams that collect Xeno specimens in their egg form, and cryochamber them to us at regular intervals. My predecessor said that they only had one delivery during his tenure at Pala Station. So far, this would be my third."

"I thought there had been only one other," he said.

She made a sour face. "Security protocols forced us to kill them all before we could really begin testing."

He eyed the two synths standing against a wall, almost blending into the machinery. Having seen them in action, he knew how fast they could move. Yet as fast as they were, they'd been unable to capture the Leon. He hoped they'd fare better with the Xenomorphs.

The scientific part of him was interested in their morphology.

The human part of him was scared shitless.

22

The next morning the scientists were in the lab before sunrise. They checked the integrity of all the glass fronts, as well as the workstations at each containment room. Rawlings brought them all coffees, with the exception of Kash, whom he brought tea. He hung around, watching and nodding occasionally as one of the scientists passed. The arrival of the Xenomorph specimens was like Christmas, and he wanted to be in the center of it all.

Security was abuzz. Word had spread that Bellows had lit into them, promising each and every one that if there was a security incident during the transfer, they'd be on that long journey back to Weyland-Yutani, *without* cryosleep. Rawlings wasn't sure the commander had the authority to do such a thing. Anyone traveling without cryosleep would age accordingly. But the threat of it seemed to put a spring in Security's steps. The ones he could usually chat up were close-mouthed and all business.

So, he posted himself in the lab, hoping no one would notice him and kick him out. He wasn't let down.

They came two-by-two from the loading docks. Each pair of security personnel carrying a cryosealed container about three feet by three feet by three feet. Hypercold air leaked from the seams of the containers in a dull hiss, creating a ground fog that swirled and danced as they moved through it. The personnel wore special gloves that insulated them from the cold. Each team placed a specimen inside a containment area.

Étienne Lacroix made certain the doors were sealed and security locks were set. Once all twelve containment rooms had been filled, the security persons went away.

With the exception of the two security synths. Although they seemed to blend into the background, Rawlings knew they could activate in a split second.

He took a sip of coffee.

This was getting good.

Cruz and Étienne went to separate workstations and, using articulated arms, began to open the cryosealed containers. As the tops came loose and were placed to the side, an egg-like shape could be seen in each container.

"They're called Ovomorphs," Kash said. "This is the first stage of a Xenomorph's existence—essentially an egg laid by the queen. They're still cryo'd until we remove the lower case. After that, they'll 'wake up,' so to speak.

"They're kept in stasis during transit," she continued, "because studies have determined that the eggs have the ability to detect biological organisms around them. Inside each Ovomorph is a stage one Xenomorph."

"Go ahead and call them by their real names," Étienne called over his shoulder as he removed yet another container lid. "Stage one Xenomorph sounds so boring by comparison."

"They call them face-huggers," she said, nose scrunched at the word. "Imagine two giant skeletal hands," she said, putting her wrists together, locking her thumbs, and waggling her fingers. "And a spine-like tail. The tail wraps around the victim's throat and the stage one Xenomorph essentially hugs the face until it can implant the highly mutagenic substance known as *plagiarus praepotens*. We're going to work with this substance and try and determine the effects of the pathogen on it. Mutagenic substance vs. mutagenic substance."

"It's going to be lovely," Étienne called.

"How does the er… face-bugger stay in place?" Hoenikker asked.

"Once over the mouth of its target, the *face-hugger* controls the host by rendering it unconscious using a cyanose-based paralytic chemical similar to dimethyl sulfoxide, administered simply through skin contact."

"It's also been able to suppress the host's immune system," Étienne added, "so that the body can't fight against the invasion. Once the mutagen is set, the 'face-bugger' releases, having done its job of delivery. Then comes the fun part," he said. "Stage two." He made a fist near his chest then opened it dramatically while simultaneously making the sound of an explosion. "Chestbursters."

Hoenikker shook his head.

Rawlings took a sip of his coffee to hide his expression.

"But we're not going to have to worry about that," Kash said. "We're going to focus on the Ovomorphs and try and entice mutagens from them without face-huggers."

"About that," Cruz said. "There's been a change of plan."

"What do you mean?" Kash asked. She turned, hands on her hips. "The plan has been in place for months."

Cruz finished removing his last container lid and stood, straightening his lab coat, then wiping his brow with a sleeve.

"Bellows has other ideas. He wants Xenomorphs. The acid-resistant armor is a game-changer. We need more tech like that, and he thinks that testing the mutagenic effects of the pathogen on the various stages of a juvenile and adult will give us the best results."

"But he isn't a scientist," she said. "What did you tell him?"

"I told him I'd do what he said."

"You what?" Étienne cried out. "You didn't even stand up for our agenda?"

"What was I supposed to do—on my first day? Disobey a direct order? We'll have other chances to do things the way we want. For now, we need Xenos."

"But that requires…" Kash looked around. "Oh, no, we are *not*."

"We are not what?" Hoenikker asked.

Rawlings knew exactly what her concerns were, and he had the same problem with the sudden change of plan.

"Bellows has a cache of criminals," Cruz said. "Don't worry, they've all signed waivers, and it's perfectly legal. He assured me of it."

"Do you hear yourself speaking?" Étienne said. "A cache of *people*? People can't be cached."

"Don't get all high-and-mighty, Dr. Lacroix," Cruz said. "Weren't you the one just now dramatizing the chest bursting to Hoenikker here?"

"That was before I thought—" He glanced at Hoenikker. "He's right. I shouldn't have been joking. It's a terrible thing to watch."

"Have you seen it?" Hoenikker asked.

"Only in videos," Étienne said. "Say, can we send these back, and get fully formed Xenos?"

"Do you want to lead the team to try and capture them?" Cruz asked.

"What happened last time?" Hoenikker asked.

"We received several infected humans who were pur-portedly 'explorers.' Our containment areas weren't as secure then, so we never saw the actual chest bursting," Kash said.

"Another time, we received several adults in cryogenic stasis," Étienne said.

"And now we have twelve Ovomorphs," Hoenikker said. "Which means we'll need—"

"Stand aside," Bellows commanded as he entered the room. Behind him came a flow of civilians dressed in dirty gray jumpsuits, accompanied by security personnel.

"You going to do this now?" Cruz asked.

"We don't have the capacity to keep them anywhere else." Bellows glanced at the other scientists, then planted himself in front of a containment room so he could admire the Ovomorph. "Might as well begin testing, or whatever it is you do here. I count twelve eggs, and we have twelve volunteers."

"Wait a minute," Étienne said, his voice rising. "Just wait a minute. I didn't sign up for this."

"Nor did I," Kash said.

"Nor did I," Hoenikker echoed, looking like he might be sick.

The twelve humans stood with their heads down. Three were women—two in their mid-thirties and one near sixty. The rest were men of various ages and ethnicities. All of them shared the same look of world-weary rejection, as if they just wanted to be done with it all.

"Oh, look, the new scientist has an opinion," Bellows said without turning around. "Listen and listen good, people. You will all perform your functions as per your contract with Weyland-Yutani. Any ideas you might have not to work will be met with the severity only a corporate giant can impose.

"Dr. Hoenikker," he continued, "we are aware of your sister and her troubles. These can either be exacerbated or corrected. Likewise, Dr. Kash. You were unhirable when you came to us. Do your partners in science know that you were once called the Angel of Death? And Dr. Lacroix. You are a very happy scientist to not be in prison. Prison isn't a luxury for anyone. Just look at the twelve volunteers we have here.

"I do not threaten anyone. I merely provide realities. Right now, your realities are as scientists aboard Pala Station. Those realities can change if you feel they must, but for the moment, you have jobs to do and I expect them to be performed to perfection."

He turned, hands folded behind his back, and regarded the three scientists. Then he turned to Cruz.

"Doctor? I expect a report first thing."

Cruz nodded. "Yessir."

Bellows left the room, walking stiffly past the doomed. Cruz nodded to the security personnel, who walked each one of the humans into a chamber that contained an Ovomorph. One man and one woman had to be physically restrained as they began to shriek, and begged not to be put in the room. But to no avail. Ultimately, Security managed to get them where they were supposed to go, closing the doors.

The shrieks became muffled.

When the security personnel left, Cruz turned to his team.

"To your stations," he said, his jaw tight.

Hoenikker had a look of horror on his face.

Kash held a fist to her mouth.

Étienne's focus was more precise, anger curling his lip.

"I said *stations*," Cruz said.

Étienne whirled on him. "How can we just do this?"

"What do you want me to do?" Cruz asked. "You heard the man. You heard what he said. He talked about realities." Cruz pointed at one of the containment rooms where an older man sat in a corner, hugging his knees, staring at the egg in the middle of the room. "They volunteered. They want to change their realities—the realities of their families. Don't ruin it with sentimentality."

"Sentimentality?" Étienne asked. "It's not sentimental, not wanting someone to die."

"They're going to die so that others may live," Cruz said. "The Colonial Marines who benefit from this might never know, but each of you will know what they've given—what they've sacrificed."

"I think I'm going to be sick," Hoenikker said.

Kash put her hand on his back.

Cruz continued his monologue. "As a former marine, I can tell you that the sacrifice will not go unappreciated."

"That's not something we can grasp," Kash said. "It's hard for us to get past the idea that these people are going to die, and we can't stop it." She paused. "It—it just feels wrong."

"You're going to have to get past it, Kash." Cruz nodded in turn at each of the scientists. "All of you are going to have to find a way to get past it. Now, get to your stations. We need to inject the pathogen while we're still able."

The scientists remained in place for a moment. Then one by one, each of them moved to their station.

Cruz noticed Rawlings.

"You? Do you have a place to be?"

Rawlings nodded.

"Then get there."

Rawlings was glad to leave. Part of him wanted to watch the process, intrigued by what that was about to happen. But another part knew there were some sights that couldn't be unseen. An alien bursting out of the chest of a young woman was one of them.

He hoped he'd never see such a thing again.

The coffee tasted weak in his mouth right now.

He needed something stronger.

23

The last time Rawlings had been this drunk before noon, he'd just been fitted with his second prosthesis. The reason he'd needed a second prosthesis was because in a drunken fit, he'd thrown his first mechanical arm into traffic, and it had been run over.

He'd forgotten the reason he'd hurled it into traffic, but thought it might have had to do with his girlfriend of three years taking off with all his stuff and leaving him with a dead plant, a fishbowl with dead fish, and the trash strewn all over the room.

He'd forgotten why she'd taken off as well, because he'd been on a four-day bender.

They'd forced him into detox after he received his second prosthesis, and he hadn't really drunk much since then. He'd been happy to partake of coffee and contemplate the good qualities of a life outside of the Colonial Marines—even with a corporation such as Weyland-Yutani.

But that was before he'd watched a group of human beings trade their lives for what was the most gruesome experience possible. Rawlings had seen it happen.

Hell, he'd almost fallen victim to it himself.

Pouring the rest of the bottle of whiskey into his coffee cup, he screwed the top in place, took a sip, stumbled, then straightened. Wouldn't be right if anyone saw him stumbling around the station. Wouldn't be right at all. He managed to hug the walls all the way to the Comms section before stumbling a little as he entered the office.

Brennan's desk was still empty, as was Davis's, but Buggy was still there, which was good because that was why Rawlings came.

One look at Rawlings and Buggy was out of his chair and helping the reception tech back the way he'd come. When he got Rawlings to his room, he eased him onto the bed and closed the door.

"What the hell, Vic?" Buggy asked, taking away the cup, smelling it, then wincing at the smell. "Anyone see you drunk on duty, and Bellows is going to have your ass."

"Do you know what they're doing here?" Rawlings asked.

"Everyone knows. It's not our business."

"Why not? Isn't it our job to protect those who can't protect themselves?"

"Easy there, Vic. You're not a Colonial Marine anymore."

"Who says?" Rawlings shouted. "Once a marine, always a marine!"

"Easy, now. Keep it down. Listen, I'm going to get the others."

Rawlings began to hum cadence he hadn't marched to in a dozen years. Buggy made a few calls on the wall communications panel. Within minutes, McGann and Chase had joined them.

Rawlings watched it all through amused eyes. He wasn't as drunk as he could be, but he was definitely impaired. He'd wanted them together anyway, so this was as good a way to accomplish that as not.

"What is it—a flashback?" McGann asked, checking the bottle.

"How'd he get the booze?" Chase asked.

"You'd be surprised at the sorts of things I have," Rawlings said. "When people leave here they don't always take everything." He clapped his hands together and pounded the bed beside him. "Have a seat. We need to make plans."

"Plans?" Chase asked. "What plans?"

"He thinks he's still a Colonial Marine," Buggy said.

"Once a marine, always a marine!" Rawlings shouted.

"What the hell, Rawlings?" McGann said.

Chase went to the desk and picked up the cup. He smelled it first, then took a tentative sip. Once he was sure what it was, he took a deep draw.

"Easy there, Chase," Buggy said. "You don't want to end up like Rawlings."

"Not enough in here to end up like him. Just enough for a stiff drink." He took another, then held it out. "This is some good shit."

McGann took it and slugged back a mouthful. She sighed after she swallowed, then held out the cup to Buggy.

Buggy stared at it for a moment, then grinned. "What the hell. You only live once." He held up the cup and said, "Semper fi," before kicking back the last of the whiskey.

The others repeated it back to him.

"*Semper fi!*"

After a few moments of silence, Rawlings spoke. "You know what that means, right? 'Semper fi.' *Semper fidelis.* It means, 'always loyal.' Like us. Always loyal to the corps. But it's more than that. It's also always loyal to your friends. Your fellow humans, even."

"Fellow humans?" Chase glanced at McGann. "What's he getting at?"

"The alien eggs and the twelve people who are going to get infected," Buggy explained. "It's messing with his head."

"Wait. What?" McGann asked. "No one said anything about infecting humans. Who could force someone to do that?"

"They've volunteered," Buggy said. "Some had life sentences commuted, so they could die early."

"I heard one of the women is doing it to get her husband out of prison," Chase said. "She has some disease, and doesn't have long to live, or something like that."

"It's still fucked up," McGann said.

Chase nodded hurriedly. "Definitely fucked up."

"So, what are we going to do?" McGann asked.

"What is there to do?" Buggy said. "Just do your jobs."

"We need to be ready," Rawlings said. "Bad shit's coming, and we need to be ready."

"You can't know that," Chase said.

Rawlings stared at him. "Know that feeling in the pit of your stomach before a battle? Know that itch on the back of your neck when you're on patrol? What about that catch at the back of your throat, or the snap of your teeth together, unable to release them because they're more ready for an impact than you are?"

The others nodded, looking to their own memory horizons.

"I ever tell you how I lost my hand?" Rawlings asked.

They shook their heads.

"Just another LV. Just another patrol. You know how it goes. They send you into space and you're sent to keep someone or something from killing settlers, or miners, or agro-farmers. In this case it was a mining colony. People were dying mysteriously, so they sent for the marines. Same-o, same-o."

"If I had a hundred credits for each colony I'd gone to, I could vacation for a year," McGann said.

"Exactly," Rawlings said. He nodded toward the cup. "Any left?"

Buggy shook his head.

Rawlings sighed, and lowered his head to his chest, puffing out his neck. White scars could be seen on his dark skin. "Probably just as well. Where was I? Yeah. We were on this LV, I forget which one. Mining colony was losing miners and support staff. Turns out some of those eggs were found deep in the mine. Same eggs we have in the lab right now. We never did get the chance to see what the eggs looked like, just heard about them. Instead, we had full-on adult Xenomorphs. I'll never forget them. I watched them plow through six marines like the creatures were hot knives and the marines were butter."

Everyone's eyes were on him. Leaning forward.

Part of this story, and part of theirs.

"We didn't come down without firepower, though. We had a pair of M577 armored personnel carriers."

Buggy gave a low whistle.

Rawlings looked at him and nodded. "Yep. A pair of synchronized RE700 20mm Gatling cannons. We were able to back the Xenos into a corner of the mine and opened fire with all four cannons. We didn't care for shit about the flechettes. We gave them all we had in HE rounds. Imagine six thousand eight hundred high-explosive armor-piercing rounds slamming into the dozen Xenos that were preparing to charge. Brothers, we turned them into mush. They covered the walls, the floor, the ceiling. We fucking obliterated them."

"I don't get it," Chase said. "I thought you were going to tell us how you lost your hand."

"But wait… there's more," Rawlings said. "We waited, and once the thermal imagers and ultrasonic motion trackers gave us a consistent negative reading, we prepared to open the hatch and exit. I was the first out, opened the hatch, and as I did, some of their fucking Xeno blood fell onto my hand. Must have been dripping from the ceiling.

"The pain was immense. I watched as my hand just turned to liquid and fell away. I remember screaming and falling back inside the carrier. I ordered the driver to put it in reverse and get us the hell out of there. Once we were back in daylight, we got the medics to take a look. The wound had cauterized itself, which was good, but I had no hand. Gone. Just like that. From a few drips of blood. Now imagine what a whole pool of that blood will do to something—do to someone?"

All eyes were wide.

The smile on McGann's wide face was anything but friendly—more a grimace than anything.

Chase looked ready to bolt.

Buggy's jaw was set into a firm frown.

"And the M577s," Rawlings continued. "In the light of day, the armor had been pocked by the Xeno blood. It hadn't made it all the way through, but it might have, had we let the ceiling continue to drip on it. As it was, there were holes you could put a fist through."

Rawlings pulled himself up from the bed and went over to his dresser. He opened the second drawer and pulled out a bottle that was only a third full. He took a deep draught and passed it around. Each of the others took a deep draw, as well. When they passed it back to him there was enough for one more, and he took it. He held the empty bottle in his artificial hand.

"And that, gentlemen, is what we have in the laboratory. If any of those get out, not only do we need to kill it, but we need to watch after, because their blood is as deadly to us as they are alive."

24

Fairbanks hadn't eaten in three days. He hadn't drunk anything either. A container of his own urine stared back at him, begging him to take a sip. He'd read and seen planetary survival vids where people had been forced to drink their own urine in order to live, but he'd never thought he'd be one of them.

An hour or so ago—he'd lost the ability to keep track of time—he'd gone to it and lifted it to his face, but the smell had overpowered him and made him gag. With nothing in his stomach, it was little more than dry heaves, but the attempt had left him exhausted.

When he'd fled, he hadn't been sure where he was going to go. All he knew was he needed to get away. He needed to be able to think— to come up with a plan. After all, he wasn't a bad guy. He'd just been caught up in the middle of bad things. He'd been blackmailed, pure and simple. Was it his fault? No. He was a victim.

He'd go to the grave believing as much.

But he'd needed a place to plan. Because of his work in Logistics, he knew where things were kept. He knew the layout of the storerooms, and knew which ones were never inventoried. Which ones were so inconsequential that they didn't have sensors. He'd chosen one of those, certain that he couldn't be found. He'd made himself a hiding spot behind some old bedframes and boxes of paint.

What it lacked in the comforts of home, it more than made up for in its spartan qualities.

After he'd overcome his initial fear at being caught, he'd fallen into a deep pit of boredom. No vids. No games. No books. Nothing. Just him and his mind, replaying the events of what turned out to be a pretty pathetic life. Somewhere during the second or third replaying of his school years he'd decided that if he ever got out of this situation, he'd make a wholesale change. He'd find a way to leave Weyland-Yutani, maybe buy out his contract, then sign on to a terraforming mission or a pilgrimage. Life wasn't meant to be lived inside the cold steel walls of an outpost like Pala Station. Life was meant to be lived outdoors, under wide open skies. Life was to be lived with people.

He knew this last part was because of his loneliness. Ever since he'd come aboard the station, he'd found it hard to make friends. The idea of having a boyfriend or a girlfriend was even more ludicrous. The funny thing was, the one he was most drawn to was the blonde security guard. She could probably break him over her knee, but he'd enjoy her doing it. He'd once had a boyfriend in college who was twice his size. He'd thought he'd loved him, but it turned out that he'd become codependent. The guy was addicted to stims, and could be quite the bully. Eventually, Fairbanks realized that he'd spent more time trying to placate his partner than being with him on his own terms. Or were those his own terms?

His head jerked.

Was that a sound?

He stopped breathing and listened for the door to open.

Nothing came.

Maybe he hadn't heard anything.

Maybe it was all in his mind.

But there it was again. Not the sound of the door, but something smaller. Something like a scratching noise. What could it be?

He scooted so his back was in the corner where the urine container was. He glanced around for a weapon, scrambled toward one of the bedframes and grabbed a piece of metal that had been dangling. He gripped it and began to wrench it back and forth, making more noise than he believed possible.

The scrabbling came again, this time nearer to him.

He wrenched faster and managed to come away with the twelve-inch piece of metal just as a creature leaped onto the bedframe in front of him. He fell back, colliding with the urine container, the putrid liquid sloshing up, wetting the back of his shirt. He gaped at the creature.

It had been a rat once, for sure. But instead of small rat legs, it now had long segmented chitinous legs that held up an enlarged torso. And its face. Its face held a maw with serrated teeth that looked capable of shredding his arm. The entire creature was the size of a station cat, which meant it had to have increased in size no less than ten times. But how could that be?

A high-pitched laugh escaped him.

Was this something Hyperdyne created? Or was it something they wanted?

No. He couldn't believe it. More likely it was something that escaped from the lab. Hadn't there been a breach before the Leon-895? Either that or… or what if the regular rats had come into contact with the blood of one of the escaped specimens? Could that have done this?

The creature leaped to the ground, landing five feet in front of him.

Fairbanks let out an, "*Eep!*" and kicked out with a shoe.

The creature easily avoided the move and leaped atop the leg. Fairbanks bit back a scream as he began to shake his leg furiously, trying to remove the thing, but as hard as he shook, the creature wouldn't let go.

He managed to climb to his feet while still shaking his leg. The creature had its long legs wrapped around it and was trying to chew through the fabric of his pants. Shoving the length of metal against the creature's torso, he tried to dislodge it, but it wouldn't move. He tried again, this time poking harder. The creature looked up and snarled at him, then went back to trying to… bite him? Eat him?

Stepping forward he kicked his leg against the metal bedframe. It made a calamitous noise, but the creature still held fast.

"Fucking hell!"

Fairbanks kicked five, six, then seven times, pummeling the creature against the metal until it finally released. He fell back against the wall. His leg ached with the kicks. He held out the metal, this time prepared to defend himself.

The creature had landed on its back and it took a moment for it to right itself. When it did, it glared at him and bared its serrated teeth.

"Fucking hell," he repeated, this time his voice low and filled with dread. "Stay back you little fucker," he said, punctuating his words with the metal.

It took a step toward him, then another, then before Fairbanks could do anything, it leaped. He swung with the length of metal and missed. Instead, the creature landed on his arm. He was surprised by the weight, and even more surprised by the pain as it bit down on his hand, separating tendons and breaking bones.

He couldn't help himself as he screamed and dropped his makeshift weapon. He spun to the wall and began to smack his hand against it over and over. The creature seemed to become weaker and weaker with each battering, until finally it fell to the floor, knocking over the urine container.

Fairbanks didn't hesitate. He stomped the damn thing until he saw its guts come out of its mouth. Once he was sure it was dead, he backed away from it, chest heaving, out of breath from both exertion and fear. After a few moments, he looked at his savaged hand, and almost retched.

It looked as if a wild beast had just taken bites from it—which was true. He straightened and removed his shirt, but couldn't rip a bandage from it with one hand, so he used the entire thing to wrap his wound. When he felt the wetness, he remembered the shirt back had been soaked with his own urine. He could only hope it held some sort of antiseptic property.

With the creature dead, he sat and stared at it, resting in a pool of urine. Was that it? Had he become infected with the same thing that mutated the rat? Was he going to grow long legs and rollick about the station, trying to eat people? The idea made him giggle. The impossibility of it made him laugh—but what if it was true? He didn't know anything about science or biology, but wasn't that how it worked?

He sat thinking like this, losing track of time, when an idea came to him.

The longer he'd sat staring at the creature, the more he'd been reminded of his own hunger. And as far as he looked at the situation, it was a win-win. If the creature was infected, it had already infected him, so eating it wouldn't do any more damage. If he *wasn't* infected, then the creature couldn't infect him, which meant he could eat it and nothing would happen. Except he'd finally have something in his gullet.

But he'd have to get the guts out. He couldn't eat guts.

And he couldn't eat the skin, so he'd have to gnaw the meat.

He wished he had some way to cook it, but that would be impossible. The smoke alone would set off alarms. No, he'd have to eat it raw. Thinking about it, he realized he'd already made up his mind.

Using the ragged piece of metal, he crawled over and hacked at one of the spider legs. Once it came off, he sat back and began to gnaw on it. It tasted bitter and vile, but that was probably the urine. If he could get past that, the creature might actually taste good.

One thing was for sure. He wasn't going to starve.

Like he'd thought, this was a win-win.

25

Hoenikker hadn't said a word for the last four hours. Neither had Étienne, his efficient movements accentuated by the death stares he gave Cruz when the "chief" of the lab wasn't looking.

No one was happy to be there, but after all, they were scientists and needed to concentrate on the task at hand. At least, that's what Hoenikker said to himself, to make everything they were doing seem reasonable... ethical... moral. Because it sure hadn't felt that way.

Even as Kash quietly directed him to take samples from the exterior of the eggs and store them for further examination, he couldn't help but glance at the human test subjects who would soon be used as incubators to propel the alien's morphology along.

Hoenikker had tried to send a message back to Weyland-Yutani corporate, begging for a transfer, but Bellows had put a block on all outgoing comms while the Xenomorphs were on station. According to Buggy, the very existence of the Xenomorphs was supposed to be classified. That they'd only been rumored to exist demonstrated that there were active controls on the information.

Kash handed him another sample.

He took the metal tube, tagged it, logged it, then put it into cryogenic storage.

To keep sane, he'd have to concentrate on the scientific method. Used by scientists across the known systems, the method hadn't changed since the 1700s—conduct background research, construct a hypothesis, test the hypothesis through experimentation, analyze the data, draw conclusions, then communicate the results.

They had little knowledge regarding the pathogen and its interaction with organic beings. What they did know was that the goo tended to exacerbate naturally occurring characteristics of the test subject, and weaponize them. He'd read the data from when they'd created the acid-resistant armor. The goo was definitely the catalyst, but how it had been used was genius. Now they were going to try different levels of irradiation, as well as a serum developed from Leon-895. If they could give the armor a cloaking or chameleon quality it would make the wearer near invincible.

One of the questions they needed to address was, how did the Xenomorphs see? Was it through thermal imaging? Did they have some sort of motion detection? So many questions, with elusive answers on the horizon.

Truth be told, the scientific method excited him.

What didn't excite him were the prisoners.

Especially Test Subject #3.

Cruz had insisted that each of the human test subjects remain anonymous, so that the scientists could retain some semblance of objectivity. The problem was that some of the test subjects looked like people they knew from the past, which erased some of the subjectivity. Like Test Subject #3. She looked like an older version of Hoenikker's steady girlfriend during the first two years of university.

Her name had been Monica Enright. She was blond, introspective, but eager to please as if it had been drilled into her by her parents and she couldn't turn it off. In the end, that had been the problem. No matter how Hoenikker messed up his life or his grades or his relationship, she forgave him and wanted nothing more than to make him happy—in order to *be* happy.

It had been toxic for him, and just as toxic for her, he'd convinced himself. In the end, he'd walked out.

He'd always wondered if he'd done the right thing. Was it her fault that she'd loved so unconditionally? Was that something he deserved? It certainly didn't make her a bad person. The opposite had been true—she was a great person. He could still see her face as he left, not understanding, unable to fathom why he was leaving when she would do anything for him.

Perhaps that was the problem. A relationship couldn't exist without some degree of conflict. He'd *needed* her to be angry. He needed balance. Still, he wondered what his life would have been like had he stayed with her, married her.

Shaking his head to clear it, he glanced up at Test Subject #3. She was looking at him.

No, staring.

Could it be her?

He had to know.

He went to Cruz. "Can I have a moment with you, Doctor?"

Cruz paused at his workstation. "I'm a little busy now, Hoenikker. Can it wait?"

Hoenikker nodded and began to back away.

Cruz returned to his work.

Hoenikker stared at him for a moment. "You know what? No, it won't. I need that moment now."

"Fine then." Cruz sat back from his pad, eyebrow up at Hoenikker's intrusion. "What it is?"

"I need to know who the test subjects are."

Cruz gave him an impatient look, and prepared to get back to work. "I already explained. We're not doing that."

"Wait." Hoenikker surprised himself by putting his hand on Cruz's shoulder. "Wait. I—I think I know one of them."

Cruz stared at him, then the offending hand.

Hoenikker removed it and took a step back.

Cruz appraised him. "You've been nothing but trouble since you got here."

Hoenikker shook his head, thinking of all the specimen therapy Cruz had been doing off the clock. But he let that go.

"That's not true at all. I was promised alien artifacts. I'm not used to live specimens. It's not my specialty."

"Take that up with Mansfield," Cruz said. Then he added, "Oh, wait. He's dead."

Hoenikker felt himself becoming exasperated. "What are you talking about? All I want to know are the names of the test subjects."

"Because you think you know one of them."

Hoenikker nodded. "I'm almost sure of it."

"Do you know what the odds are for that? Come on, Doctor. Do the math."

"Math be damned. I think I know Test Subject #3. I think she was my… was my girlfriend in college." Cruz glanced at the test subject in question for a long moment, then shook his head.

"She's no one to you, Hoenikker. I'm not going to release the names."

Hoenikker opened his mouth to argue, but Cruz beat him to the punch.

"Enough of this. Get back to work. She's not who you think she is."

"But you don't understand—"

"I understand everything." Cruz stood, towering a full head above Hoenikker. "You want to save the test subjects. Everyone does—but the universe doesn't work like that. Those people signed a contract, much like *you* signed a contract. Weyland-Yutani owns your ass. Weyland-Yutani owns them. It's a contract. They get to be part of a complex experiment to try and help save the lives of Colonial Marines, and in turn Weyland-Yutani does something for them." He poked Hoenikker in the chest as he said the next words. "Just. Leave. It. Be."

Cruz sat, returning to his work.

Hoenikker stood for a moment, his hand rubbing where he'd been poked, then he turned and walked back to where Kash was working.

"What was that all about?" she asked.

Hoenikker stared at Test Subject #3 and she stared back at him. She cocked her head, shook it as if to say no, then looked away.

He gasped.

"Tim. What is it?" Kash asked, her eyes round with concern. "What's wrong?"

He opened his mouth to speak, but nothing would come out. He couldn't even breathe. The cocking and shaking of the head was pure Monica. She was the only person he'd ever seen shake her head that way. Twenty years had passed, and now they were back together, only to have her die in front of him.

For the sake of a Weyland-Yutani experiment.

When he could finally breathe again, he gasped. The room swayed around him. He put his hand out to grab the table to keep him from falling. He had to free her. He needed to get her out of there and to a place of safety. But how? How could he save her? Where could he take her?

The room snapped straight and he could suddenly breathe.

And think.

He knew exactly who to talk to.

Without comment, he hurried out.

26

It took him three tries to find Reception Tech Rawlings' room. If there was anyone who would know what to do, it would be the guy who knew everything.

The first time the door opened it was a female security guard who'd been sleeping in the nude. He'd barely processed her nakedness, apologized, then hurried away.

The second room turned out to be a storeroom and was devoid of human occupancy. The problem was the corridors. He still didn't know the layout of the station. His paths went from his room to the bathroom, the mess hall, and the lab. He really hadn't paid attention to what was in between.

As he approached his third try, two men and a woman came through the door. He recognized Buggy from Comms, but the others he didn't know. They nodded at him and he nodded back. Once at the door, he knocked and waited for it to open.

After a moment, Rawlings opened it wearing nothing but underwear.

"If you're looking for more hooch—" he began, then stopped talking when he saw it was Hoenikker. Rawlings glanced down at his naked black torso and Weyland-Yutani underwear. "You. What do you want?"

"I need your help." Hoenikker pushed past him into the room. He paced to the end of the room, then turned. Rawlings closed the door and scratched near his crotch.

"Can't you see I'm under the weather?"

Hoenikker spied the empty bottle on the desk. "Looks more like you've been drinking."

"Lots of things can make you under the weather," Rawlings replied. "Drinking is one of them." He went to the edge of his bed and sat on it. "I'd offer you something, but as you can see, we're fresh out."

"I'm not here to drink."

"Then what can I do for you, Doctor?"

"It's her. I know it's her." Hoenikker paced back and forth from the door to the wall and back again. His normally ordered thoughts were a jumble. "How do I make them understand? They can't kill her. They just can't. Maybe I still have a chance to make it all up. Maybe I can be there for her now."

"Whoa now, killer. I thought I was the one who'd been drinking. What's got you all juiced?"

Hoenikker stopped pacing. "Her. I told you. It's her."

Rawlings shook his head. "You haven't even introduced her."

"Monica. My girlfriend. She's here!"

"Well, that's great, my friend. You and her can get some nookie, and have a great old time."

"No." Hoenikker shook his head furiously. "You don't get it. She's in the lab."

"She's in the lab? But only scientists are in… the…" Rawlings blinked quickly. "She's one of them?"

Hoenikker threw up his hands. "That's what I've been *telling* you. She's there in the lab. Test Subject #3. Containment Room Three."

Rawlings rubbed his face, continuing over the top of his skull. "Oh, Doctor." He shook his head. "You've got to be mistaken. It can't really be her."

"Oh, it is. At first, I was like you. 'It couldn't be.' But then when I saw her do some of Monica's mannerisms—mannerisms I haven't seen replicated in twenty years—"

"Okay." Rawlings patted the air. "Let's say that what you're claiming is accurate. Let's say that an ex-girlfriend of yours from twenty years ago somehow got crossways with Weyland-Yutani, and became a test subject at a science station at the ass-crack end of the universe. What do you intend to do?"

Hoenikker straightened. "Rescue her."

"Rescue her?" Rawlings stood.

"Yes." Hoenikker nodded. "Rescue her. With your help."

"My help?" Rawlings sat back down. "I picked a doozie of a day to start drinking again." He smacked his face several times, then closed his eyes and opened them. "Damn. You're still here." He paused a moment as if in thought. "So, what do you propose?"

Hoenikker shrugged. "I don't know. Hide her in a room? Steal a shuttle? Something. *Anything.* I mean, we have to do something, right?"

"We don't have to do *anything.* I know you want to do something, but look… We don't even know if it's her."

Hoenikker leaned in. "Can you check?"

"Can I check? Shoot. I have access to everything. I can even tell you what Bellows is reading right now." Rawlings got to his feet, went over to his desk, and sat down. He began to fiddle with his vid screen. Punching numbers and swiping until he got to what he wanted. "What did you say her name is?"

"It was Monica Enright," Hoenikker said breathlessly.

"So, here's what I have. I have no first names, just initials. Then I have last names. I have two Ms. One M. Russel and M. Trakes. Sorry, Doctor. It's just too vague."

Not to be defeated, Hoenikker asked, "What's the background on M. Russel?"

A swipe and a few moments later, "Okay. Gender is female. Forty-three years old. From Earth. One son. Not married. She was arrested for murder aboard a Weyland-Yutani space station six years ago."

Could that be her? "You say she has a son. How old is he?"

"Thirteen. Sorry, Doc. Can't see that it could be yours."

"Of course not." Hoenikker felt dizzy with the information. "What about the other one?"

"M. Trakes. Also female gender, but thirty-four years old."

Hoenikker nodded. "With cryosleep, she could be any age between thirty and forty-three." He nodded. "Go on."

"M. Trakes has two daughters." Rawlings punched a few digital keys on the screen. "Aw. I see it now. One of her daughters has a rare disease. Costs a fortune to get it taken care of. The company has offered to take care of it. They chose this one specifically because she's AB negative."

"That's the rarest blood type."

"Wait a minute." Rawlings punched a few more keys. "All of them are AB negative. Must have been difficult to track down that many volunteers with the world's rarest blood type."

"Any more information about M. Trakes?" Hoenikker asked.

"She's from Earth as well. Her daughters are with her husband." Rawlings shook his head. "I'm afraid this wasn't much help."

"I don't know," Hoenikker said. "She could be either of the two. The only way I'm going to find out is by asking her, it seems."

"And you think Cruz is going to go for that?"

"He won't have to. He won't be there." Hoenikker began to pace again. "We're going to need a distraction."

"And then what? What is it you're going to do? Steal a shuttle, you said? Hide her?" Rawlings picked up the empty bottle, tipped it upside down over his mouth, then grimaced and put it back on the table. "This is the Weyland-Yutani machine you're up against."

"I understand that, but I—"

"Do you really understand? We're talking *Weyland-Yutani*. They could disappear this whole station, and no one would even blink. They're probably the most powerful corporation in the known sectors, and you want to go against them. Even if I were to help you—and I'm not saying I will—how many others on the station would help? Because we're going to need a goddamn lot of them."

"Maybe when they hear my story—"

"They'll what? Be willing to lose their jobs? Be prepared to go to prison? All because Doctor Timmy Hoenikker found out that one of the *voluntary* test subjects used to be his girlfriend?"

Hoenikker stopped pacing and stared at the floor.

"Then what is it I'm supposed to do?"

Rawlings stood and placed his hands on Hoenikker's shoulders as he faced him, naked down to his underwear.

"What do you do? Nothing, Doctor. There's nothing to be done. This is merely the irony of the universe, that you two might have met near the end."

"I can't—" Hoenikker gulped. "I can't accept that."

Rawlings gave him a look a mother might give a child who'd just discovered he wasn't the center of the universe.

"You're going to have to. This is out of your hands."

27

The next morning was set for the experiments to begin. According to the plan, they'd remove the lower half of the cryogenic travel cases so the Ovomorphs would awaken. Then, sometime between ten and thirty minutes later, each Ovomorph would detect the presence of another biological organism, and would deliver the face-hugger, who would then find the organism.

Pitting human against face-hugger, there would be no winning for the human. It wasn't even a challenge, especially since there was nowhere for the humans to run.

Cruz insisted that all doctors be present to acknowledge the sacrifices the test subjects were making, but Hoenikker believed that was all a ruse. Cruz wanted them all there for cover, so he wouldn't be the only one gleefully observing the destruction. Still, Hoenikker couldn't deny that the lab was finally functioning like an actual lab, as if Cruz had been able to spin it into his own, as easy as running a Colonial Marine platoon.

Hoenikker would be there, but first he had something he had to do. At four in the morning, after a sleepless night, he entered the lab. The lights were in maintenance mode and cast the room in a barely lit gloom. He noted the two synths watching him, but ignored them. He wasn't going to do anything that would cause them to come alive.

He approached the workstation in front of Containment Room Three and sat before it. The chamber was dark, except for the blinking lights on the cryogenic travel cases. He dialed up the vid display and toggled infrared, noticing immediately that Test Subject #3 was sitting up on the rear ledge and facing in his direction. So, he wouldn't have to wake her up after all. He toggled the lights up to fifty percent to reveal that she was staring back at him.

He turned on the intercom. His mouth felt dry. He'd planned a speech. He'd practiced in the mirror.

All that came out was, "It's you, isn't it?"

She wore her blond hair short. The wide space between her eyes accentuated her features. High cheekbones made it seem as if she was always on the verge of a smile. Her green eyes mesmerized as they caught the light and changed.

She nodded.

He bit his lip.

"I knew it from the moment I saw you."

She cocked her head and shrugged.

"Will you talk to me?"

She stared at him for what seemed like forever, but was only thirty seconds.

"What is it you want me to say?" she replied, her voice as soft as he remembered. "That you broke my heart? That you walked out on me—on us?"

Twenty years and a hundred parsecs flashed through him. He remembered them holding hands in college, going to class, concerts, even the library terminals. Her kiss tasted sweet because she was always sucking on one candy or another. Even the smell of her clothes burst through him in a timeless hurricane of scent memory.

She'd make him dinner most nights. Nothing special. They were students. But just the effort of someone making him instant noodles or instant rice was a convenience he'd taken for granted. And her smile. She always smiled at him as if not to smile would drive him away.

Now, looking at her, he could see her without a smile, yet she was still beautiful—and he'd left it all behind. Had he thought that it would be too much? That he'd end up behind a desk doing something corporate and meaningless? Had he been afraid that his dream of becoming a scientist would be lost, because he'd have to settle with her as soon as she became pregnant or decided she was done with school?

Or was it just that he'd been a selfish prick who didn't understand that he'd had it good.

"That was twenty years ago," he said.

She regarded him with side eyes. Then she stared at the egg resting in the cradle of the cryo travel case. She didn't seem to be afraid of it.

"Ever wonder if your life would be different if it wasn't for a single decision?" she asked.

Had his leaving started her on a path from which she couldn't return?

"Me leaving?" he asked.

She sneered. Then she stood and walked to the glass, putting her hands on it.

"I'm over that. I mean the decision I made when I decided to kill the man I was with, for his money."

Hoenikker, who'd been leaning forward, sat back hard. He'd hoped she'd been the one with the terminal illness, but she was the murderer.

"What? You didn't know?" she asked, adding a little vinegar to her sugar. "I've killed many a man. Turns out I like it."

All he could do was shake his head.

"Turns out I've always been this way. My desire to please was nothing more than an emotional placeholder. When I pleased people, they would return the gesture, and it would fulfill something in me. But what I found is that a man begging for his life is even more of an emotional rush—the idea of pleasing them because I might allow them to live filled me with a certain ecstasy."

He couldn't parse her words with the memory of her. They didn't match. It was as if his old girlfriend had had her mind wiped clean and replaced. She couldn't have been like this when they were together.

"What are you saying?" he asked.

"I can see you there, feeling sorry for me, and wondering what would have happened had you not walked out. I'm not exactly sure. You might have become my first victim or you might have kept me from killing—although, I have to tell you, Timothy, murdering is *such* a fucking rush."

Hoenikker flicked off the intercom. This wasn't his memory. This was someone else entirely. Sure, it was Monica, but it was as if something had invaded her body, changed her.

He sat and stared for several moments as her lips continued to move, not even wanting to know what she said.

"Not exactly what you expected is it?"

The voice came from behind him.

Hoenikker spun.

Cruz sat back in an alcove, where Hoenikker had missed seeing him, his attention so focused on Test Subject #3. Cruz held a glass in one hand and an unlit cigar in another.

"I knew you'd come around," Cruz said. "I just wanted to see what you would do."

"I thought about trying to free her."

"Anyone with a scintilla of decency would do the same, if they were in your shoes." Cruz took a sip of amber liquid. "I'd expect nothing less."

"But what you said before—"

"Was absolutely right. We need to approach this as scientists. Not as regular people. We can't afford to be regular people. We have a responsibility to try and make the Colonial Marines safer. *Everyone* safer, and if it takes twelve people sacrificing themselves, then so be it." He held out the glass. "Have a sip of this. You need it."

Hoenikker stood and went over, accepted the glass and took an angry sip. He felt so manipulated. How was it other people had such a better handle on their emotions? He knew the answer, of course. Other people used their emotions more often. They practiced at it. Hoenikker had spent most of his life trying to avoid emotion. As the liquid burned through him, so did his anger.

"She's not the same person," he said, turning to regard her.

"Does that make any difference? Would you save her for the person she was?"

Hoenikker shook his head. "She just made me remember things. Regrets."

"Oh, Doctor Hoenikker, we all have regrets. We can look back and hear them following us like footsteps if we listen close enough."

"What's she getting out of being a test subject?" Hoenikker asked, passing back the glass. Cruz accepted it, made a motion for cheers, then took a sip.

"She was facing a life sentence, and bound for a terraforming prison work detail. Dangerous work. Nothing I'd wish on my worst enemy. This is her way out. This is how she is escaping her fate."

"Escaping her fate," Hoenikker repeated. "Just like I did when I walked out, all those years ago."

She knocked on the glass.

He thought about turning the intercom back on, but what was there to say? She was a different person. He stared at her for a long moment, trying to revitalize his feelings for her, trying to return to his need to save her, but that emotion was irrevocably lost. So, instead, he shook his head, turned, and left the lab.

Hoenikker needed to get some sleep. The testing began in the morning, and he needed to be there to record the data.

Once again, he retreated to the scientific method.

It was easy.

It was safe.

He couldn't get his feelings hurt.

28

Hypothesis #1: The pathogen, when irradiated and injected into the Ovomorph, will positively affect the Xenomorph morphology.

Hypothesis #2: The pathogen, when irradiated and injected into the human host, will adversely affect the Xenomorph morphology.

With the hypotheses in place, the scientists began their experimentation.

Hoenikker was asked to stand back and record data for this first group of tests. Étienne and Kash would be the primary researchers while Cruz supervised the process. Kash would be taking readings, as well.

Hypotheses one and two were tested on the subjects and eggs in Containment Rooms One and Two. Containment Room One saw the injection of the irradiated pathogen into the Ovomorph. There the test subject was an elderly female of African lineage.

Containment Room Two saw the injection of the irradiated pathogen into the test subject—a morose looking man in his forties or fifties who was severely overweight. The injection must have made the process seem more real, and he became agitated almost immediately.

After fifteen minutes, the remainder of the travel cases were removed, and the Ovomorphs began to approach room temperature. Hoenikker could tell immediately when they had recovered from the effects of the cold. The top of the egg structure began to twitch and quiver, as if it could smell the presence of the human test subjects.

The test subject in Containment Room One didn't run or act agitated. She merely sat with her back facing the egg, perhaps unwilling to face it. She appeared to have made peace with her situation, and was just waiting to play her part. Hoenikker considered her smart. If it had been him, he wouldn't have wanted to face what was coming next, either.

He stole a glance to Containment Room Three where Monica sat, watching them like a cat might, sitting in the window of a home. She wore a disinterested look, almost laconic, as she observed everything around her. Hoenikker wondered if, when the time came, she would be like the woman in Containment Room One, or like the man in Containment Room Two, who, even now, scrabbled at the glass, begging to be let free, his stomach bobbing as if it had been filled with too much jelly.

The intercom was turned off, but there was no mistaking what he was screaming. Hoenikker prayed that if he was ever in that position, he wouldn't behave the same way. But then, he couldn't be sure how he'd behave when faced with the inevitable prospect of being face-hugged by a Xenomorph. Although he'd rather be like the elderly woman, he feared he might end up like the fat man.

Each of the test subjects had been fitted with transmitters that provided live health data. Hoenikker made sure these were streaming as his vid display recorded the results.

Then, as inexorably as he'd been told, the top of each Ovomorph began to peel back, and a creature began to appear. At first it was the tail, whipping about, snapping, the end cracking the air. This he knew would eventually wrap around the test subject's neck to hold the face-hugger in place. He'd read the literature and watched the vid, but seeing it in person held him fast. Not only was he observing the morphology of an alien entity, he was also witnessing the impending death of a human being.

The face-hugger in Containment Room Two was faster—perhaps because of the behavior of the test subject. Although he had nowhere to run, the face-hugger didn't yet understand the parameters of its captivity. Not only did it whip itself free of the egg, moving in a blur, but it attacked the man's back, scraping him, forcing him to spin, thus making the job of the face-hugger that much easier.

The creature attached itself to the man's face, so Hoenikker couldn't see his expression, but he could imagine the wide eyes and the strangled scream, quickly silenced by the pressure of something entering the throat. The tail came around and wrapped itself once, then twice around the man's enormous neck. He clawed at the Xenomorph, but it was of no use.

Staggering to the center of the room, he spun one hundred and eighty degrees until he was facing toward them. His face was completely covered by what looked like the carapace of a large crab. He staggered again, fell to his knees, then onto his side.

Hoenikker checked to make sure the health data was still streaming, and shuddered.

The man was still alive.

Over in Containment Room One, things were moving a bit slower. The woman still sat with her back to the Ovomorph. The face-hugger had already crawled out of the egg and seemed to be regarding its imminent host. In no hurry, it moved to her. When it touched her back, she tensed, but otherwise made no move. She knew there was nowhere to go. Knew it was her end. She just didn't want to have to see it happen.

When it did, it happened fast. The face-hugger's tail latched around her neck and it propelled itself around in an arc, like a rock climber with a rope, landing on her face as if it were the face of a mountain it wanted to conquer.

She fell backward.

Her body twitched several times.

Then the tail tightened.

All the while, Hoenikker ensured that the data was recording. After a few moments, Kash approached.

"It's different seeing it in person," she said, wiping sweat from her upper lip. Hoenikker realized his mouth was dry. He swallowed and licked his lips.

"Sure is."

"Some believe they were made to do this," she said. "Others believe that it was evolution."

"That evolution could create something that needs another creature to survive makes the universe seem cruel," he said.

"Tapeworms, roundworms, and flukes have been invasive to humans since the dawn of time," she said.

"I don't see them busting out of their hosts' chests."

"They don't, you're right. But give it a million years. Who knows?"

"How long does it take?" he asked, then followed up by being more specific. "I mean, to go from face-hugger to chestburster."

"Not as long as you'd think. The gestation period is brisk. Far faster than one would believe. But then, the host doesn't need to survive the transition."

"I'm sure it wreaks havoc," he said. "Crash and burn the system."

"That's all we really are, just a bag of DNA," she replied. "The process doesn't care what's left."

He stared at the woman lying on her back, the face-hugger doing what it did, the tail wrapped around her neck.

"But for the moment it knows to keep the host alive. The evolution seems too impressive to be natural. It seems engineered. I couldn't imagine a better way to create an army. Gestate in the bodies of your enemies, then be reborn with acid for blood."

"Maybe that's why they're here."

"If they're part of an army, then who is the general?"

She didn't answer, nor did he expect her to. She moved on, recording data as it came.

"How are you holding up?" Cruz asked, stepping up beside Hoenikker. He glanced at the taller man, surprised at the attention.

"Better than I expected." He hesitated as he watched the body in Containment Room Two twitch and shudder. "I thought it would bother me more, but knowing they're doing this with intention helps mollify my apprehension."

Cruz nodded, observing both test subjects and their face-huggers. Then he turned to Containment Room Three.

"Will you still feel the same when we get to her?"

Hoenikker glanced over, then looked down. How could he know until they did it? He wasn't sure how he'd react. His feelings had changed since they'd spoken. He realized that so much of what he'd felt was like an echo of how he'd felt so long ago. He wasn't even sure if he still felt the same way—was the idea of loving her, or being in love, a force of habit he'd failed to break even after all these years? It was as if when he'd stopped seeing her, he'd just shelved his feelings, and never dealt with them.

"What is it we're going to do with her?" he asked.

"Irradiated pathogen for both her and the Ovomorph," Cruz said. "We're still in the data accumulation phase. We got lucky with the acid-resistant armor. We're hoping that after we accumulate enough data, we'll be sufficiently informed to use Leon-895 DNA to try and create some sort of biological cloaking mechanism to add to the acid resistance."

"That would be beneficial for sure," Hoenikker said, realizing how hollow the words sounded. "Have they found the missing Leon?"

"Not yet," Cruz said, frowning as he answered. "We never attached a transponder or a PDT to the creature. Had we done something as fucking simple as that, we would have been able to track it. We're not going to have that problem anymore. All of the test subjects have been tagged with PDTs, as will the chestbursters."

"With all the tech we have, I'm surprised it hasn't been found."

"You'd be surprised how big this place really is," Cruz said absently. Then he turned to Hoenikker. "Keep plugging in the data. Our algorithms will make sense of it, and we can move to the next step." Then he walked out of the lab, the door closing behind him.

Hoenikker stared after him, thinking of what the man had shared. Was the place bigger than it seemed to be? Kash had mentioned on several occasions that it was, but he'd never followed up. Why was that? Even as he asked himself, he knew the answer. He was Timothy Hoenikker. He toed the line, didn't ask questions, didn't buck the system. He did as he was told.

Well, maybe that all should change.

Maybe he should be a little more discerning.

Maybe he should ask a few more questions before he blindly followed directions.

Kash called for him, and he turned to assist.

In Containment Room Two, the woman's body lay still. At less than six beats a minute, her heart was barely functioning. The face-hugger itself had crawled away and lay dead in a corner. That meant the embryo was in place.

"Any time now," she said.

Hoenikker stared at the woman, and then the data, trying to see patterns in the numbers. Not knowing what to look for didn't stop him from his attempt to understand. He was a scientist through and through, and trusted in the process. He knew that eventually the pattern would reveal itself, but until then he'd record and push the data.

"On Earth, there is a wasp that lays its eggs in a live tarantula," Étienne said as he approached. "Most call it a tarantula hawk because of its size, but *pomplidae* is definitely a wasp. It first paralyzes the spider, then drags it to a hidden site for brooding. Once there, it lays a single egg on the underside of the tarantula—which isn't dead, mind you. It remains alive as the larva grows and then hatches. Once hatched, it burrows a hole into the tarantula's body and begins to eat its way through, avoiding the large organs until the very last. The idea is to keep the spider alive as long as possible, because it's the larva's only food source."

Hoenikker shuddered at the idea of being eaten alive from the inside.

"I often wonder which is worse," Étienne said. "Being eaten from the inside, or dying a quick death as an alien bursts from your chest." He gestured to the containment room with the man. He was sitting up and scratching the side of his head as if nothing was wrong. There, again, the face-hugger had crawled away to die. "Do you think he's being eaten from the inside, like he's a tarantula?"

"I think being eaten from the inside out has to be the worst," Hoenikker said. "Knowing that something is inside you has to be terrifying."

"But look at him." Étienne pointed at the man, who was now standing and peering into the empty egg. "Does he look scared?"

Hoenikker checked the data. "I show a doubling in serotonin production."

"Maybe that's the solution. Like a frog in a pot of water that slowly comes to a boil. Make someone happy that they have a parasite in their body, and they won't mind as much."

"Is that what the Xenomorphs are? Parasites?"

"What else would you call them?"

Monsters was what Hoenikker wanted to say.

The waiting seemed worse than the implantation had been. They remained at their stations for what felt like an eternity, but was in reality a little more than eight hours—tense the entire time with anticipation. Cruz didn't return, but Hoenikker, Kash, and Étienne didn't dare leave.

Then it happened.

More suddenly than he'd expected.

One moment, she was still; then she arched her back and her chest erupted as two sets of telegraphing jaws pierced free to the air. Claws gripped the pieces of ripped chest and the chestburster pulled itself free. The woman's blood pooled as the creature moved off and onto the floor, more tail and teeth than anything else.

Her vitals hit bottom as death overtook her.

Meanwhile, the creature moved to the back corner of the containment room and huddled there, a hatchling programmed to protect itself until it grew larger.

The man in his containment room remained unaware of what had happened to the woman. He'd finished idly inspecting the egg and had moved to the glass. He was in the process of testing it with his fingers when he suddenly got a look like he was about to vomit. He doubled over, then straightened.

Then his chest exploded.

Blood spattered the glass as the chestburster shot free. One moment the man was staring in surprise down at the hole in his chest, the next he was sagging to his knees, falling on his side as gravity stole his mobility, forever and a day.

29

The next day found them doing the same thing.

As well as the next.

And the next.

The scientific method and data modeling.

Hoenikker spent the nights watching one video in particular. The taking of Test Subject #3.

He'd been through the data dozens of times, but never tired in disassembling her destruction. Which was strange, considering what they'd once shared. At first, he'd felt concerned about his lack of emotional response. But then, after watching it, he'd felt as if she'd gotten what she wanted—some semblance of finality to her place in the universe.

Monica had never really been happy. She'd always needed someone else to make her complete. That she'd once chosen him to complete her showed her own inability to make the correct decisions. A broken bolt twisted by a broken tool into a broken system—doomed to failure.

In the end, her death had been more similar to the woman's than the man's, in that she never saw it coming. Sure, when the egg had released the face-hugger, she'd stood her ground. Balled fists down at her sides, straight backed, she'd only flinched a little as the thing attached itself to her, wrapping its tail three times around her slender neck. Instead of falling, she'd backed toward the ledge near the back of the containment room and sat, resting her fists in her lap as she leaned on it for balance.

Her stoicism was what kept him coming back to the video. That she seemed so accepting of her situation demonstrated how much she'd changed in the intervening years. He'd rewatched the first half of the video no less than twenty times, trying to see if there had been any other reaction he could discern, but as often as he'd watched, he couldn't see any.

The second half of the video was hardest to watch.

She hadn't fared as well in the last three minutes and forty-seven seconds.

The face-hugger had been long gone and her serotonin levels were maxed when the thing inside of her began to move. She felt it, and tore her shirt away. Her breasts hung heavy, nipples pointed down and no longer in the bloom of youth. He'd known and mapped them when they were younger, but they weren't the focus of his attention. Instead, he stared at the lump that continually pressed against the inside of her chest and abdomen. Tentative at first, the chestburster wasn't ready for the full Monty. Instead, it pressed its face and jaws against the inside of her skin, revealing itself even before it broke free.

Each time it moved within her she'd shriek, then force herself to stand still. It was as if her single *fuck you* to the universe was to try not to panic, instead provide as much of herself to the witnesses as possible. For the sake of science? It had to be for the sake of science, because no one could possibly get off on the destruction of a human being in such a way. No one he'd ever want to know, anyway.

After three minutes and forty-seven seconds of it acting as if it wanted to be free, it burst out of her chest, falling to the ground where it lay stunned for long enough that they might have thought it was dead.

The first several times his eyes were on the chestburster, wondering if it was going to live, then somehow insanely pleased that it had. Later he'd watched her, and noted that she hadn't died immediately. She'd managed to live for almost thirty seconds longer, her hand coming up and feeling the gaping hole in her chest, her fingers feeling around inside. Then falling to her knees. Staring out the containment room window, her face pinched with pain but also angry, as if asking if this was what they wanted her to do—be a tool for someone's experiment, allowing an alien to gestate inside her all so a mega-corp could create something from which it could profit.

He told himself this and then he argued with himself, even knowing it was specious.

She died for a reason.

Monica died because she *wanted* to.

She died because she'd murdered someone, and had to pay the price.

It was almost as if she'd had the last laugh. He might have been projecting, but even if he hadn't known her, he would have understood her stance and wondered at his own morality—of allowing a thinking and breathing human being to be used in such a manner.

The corporation be damned.

The Xenomorphs grew amazingly fast. The first three had already reached full adulthood and stalked back and forth inside their containment rooms. The bodies and the vestiges of the previous morphology had been removed via mechanical means.

Cruz kept the temperature near freezing in those containment rooms. Although the Xenomorphs were seemingly impervious to extremes, he was hoping that if needed, they could reverse the temperature with superheated fire to shock their systems. Sustained fire would kill them, and repeated shocks to their exoskeletons might make them more docile.

At least, that was Cruz's hypothesis.

The creatures salivated profusely, ribbons and rivulets dripping from their mouths. Cruz mentioned that he'd seen some with the ability to spit acid, but as yet this hadn't been an issue.

The two Xenomorphs in Containment Rooms One and Two appeared normal, their torpedo-shaped heads immense on a frame that even at two meters tall seemed too small to support them. Likewise, the tails and extended vertebrae nodes seemed normal, based on the records from previous encounters.

Things began to change with Test Subject #3. Although she'd become a drone like the previous two, her skin was dark and leathery with an odd striping, the texture evident from many meters away. The overall effect was different, this Xenomorph seeming more malevolent.

Test Subject #5 grew an extra set of arms. These mostly hung down at its sides, but the hands seemed to face behind it, so when it raised them, it was capable of holding items in either direction. Étienne was especially excited about this, wondering if the duopolistic condition also carried forward to its senses.

Test Subject #7 was perhaps the strangest augmentation. Although the head was the usual smooth torpedo shape of the drone Xenomorph with nary a mouth or any other visible sense organs, the body was translucent. Almost white. What one might call an albino.

The body was more human-shaped as well, the knees and torso larger than a human's but functioning just the same.

Étienne wanted to introduce this test subject to the others, to see how they'd react. His hypothesis was that this could be a super-drone, capable of leading the others. But Cruz was adamant that security protocols should be observed, so no comingling of test subjects was possible. Still, Étienne worked on several ideas to accomplish his goals, and determine if his hypotheses were correct.

Four test subjects had been reserved for Leon-895 experimentation. Security had managed to procure one of the creatures on an approved hunt, and Cruz was determined to inject its blood, combined with the pathogen, into the four subjects, while incrementally increasing irradiation. His hope was that they could create a Xenomorph with chameleon-like properties, and then transition the science to armor, much as they'd previously done with the acid-resistance experimentation.

That breakthrough had been based on the Xenomorphs' resistance to their own acidic qualities. One of the strongest corrosives in the known universe, the creatures had it inside their bodies both as a defense mechanism and to carry nutrients. How something could eat through metal, and not eat through skin and organs, had flummoxed the scientists until the late Matthews had analyzed the Xenomorph DNA. He had been able to pinpoint the gene that made it possible.

Thus gene-splicing armor was made from the lab-grown skin of a Xenomorph.

If they could do that, Cruz proposed, why couldn't they then identify the genes that enabled chameleon abilities, and use them in the creation of a new and improved Xenomorph? Hoenikker, while appreciating the idea, thought that having a nearly invisible, utterly impervious killing machine was a perilous idea, and was reluctant to have anything to do with it.

Which was why he was happy to play transcriber, while his associates manipulated the most dangerous genes in the galaxy.

30

Cruz didn't like where the experiments were taking them. Sure, they were seeing results that they could manipulate, but not the results they *needed*. They needed something they could monetize.

Bellows had already called him into the office. The station commander stressed the success of the acid-resistant armor, and demanded that they continue in that direction. The problem was, that last breakthrough had been the proverbial lightning in a bottle, and trying to replicate it might prove to be impossible.

Still, they'd been working on gene mapping, and had ideas where to go.

Then everything was put on hold.

The missing Leon-895 had gotten hungry.

Folks had mostly forgotten about it, many hoping it had found a way outside, where it wouldn't be a problem. Ironically, Edmonds of Casualty Operations had gone mostly missing. His ID and a magnificent amount of his blood had been found on one of the corridor floors. Bellows had insisted that every operation come to a full stop, until they were able to find and sequester the predator.

Cruz strode down a corridor, flanked by a synth and two male security guards with pulse rifles. One of the guards had a motion detector that was pointed toward the ceiling. The other had an IR viewer pointed in the same direction.

The synth faced backward, protecting their rear.

"I'm still not sure why I need to be part of the team," Cruz said, not liking at all that he wasn't allowed a weapon. He also knew that they'd never have been in this position had he been in charge from the beginning. It was the ineptitude of the bureaucrat Mansfield that had allowed the creature to escape. Not that he'd paid with his life, but still. Cruz should have been in charge from the very first moment he'd appeared on station.

"Not my business," security guard number one said. "Bellows is the one who put the teams together."

"I get that," Cruz said, trying hard not to roll his eyes at the commands of yet another bureaucrat. "But what is it you expect me to do?"

"Whatever you think will help," security guard number two answered. Which left Cruz scratching his now bearded chin.

He'd created Leon-895, but wasn't keen on its hunting techniques. He'd never seen it in the wild, had never interacted with it outside of a containment room. His intent had been to enhance the creature's innate ability to blend into the background. Just a little black goo behind the ears and *poof*—invisible.

They moved a few feet and stopped. The idea wasn't to search, but to hold an area. Other teams like theirs were in other corridors, waiting for evidence of the creature. If this didn't work, they'd have the synths go from room to room while they held their positions. One way or another, they were going to find the Leon.

The radio chattered.

One of the security guards responded.

Nothing more than boredom.

Cruz had seen it enough during his time in the marines. Standing around and holding a rifle wasn't anyone's dream job. Guard duty sucked, pure and simple, no matter where you were, but it was something that had to be done. He'd just figured, with his improvement in paygrade, that it would no longer be him.

Fifteen minutes later the radio chattered again. This time the words were punctuated by the sound of pulse rifles.

"What's going on?" Cruz asked, again wishing they'd given him a weapon. After all, he was probably more familiar with one than they were.

"Sighting," security guard number two said. "Corridor. Over by Comms section."

More chatter.

More pulse fire.

"Is it headed this way?" Cruz asked.

As if in response, the security guards spun and aimed their detectors at the ceiling. Both devices went off, and began to wail. Cruz watched as the Leon appeared, rushed by overhead, using the metal beams of the ceiling to propel itself forward. As it passed, it reached down with one appendage and tore free the head of the synth, the body falling to the floor, nothing more than a pile of useless invention.

Then Leon was gone again. The security guards fired blindly, defeating the purpose of the detectors. If they hit anything, there was no indication.

Cruz shook his head.

Why couldn't they just have a platoon of Colonial Marines, instead of private security? Reaching down, he snagged the pistol the synth had been holding. At least now he was armed. He felt better.

"Did you hit it?" Number One asked.

"I think so," Number Two said. "What about you?"

"Definitely."

Cruz pushed them both aside, grabbed the motion indicator, and headed after the Leon.

"You boys didn't hit shit."

"Wait? Where are you going?" Number One asked. "We're supposed to stay here, in the event—"

"You mean if it comes this way? It did. It came, and it went." Cruz continued walking. "And I'm going after it."

"But we're supp—"

He turned the corner before he could hear any more of their bullshit. He'd never been good at guard duty because he could never follow directions. The idea of staying in one place and staring into a pre-described space seemed as interesting as sticking a pen in his ear.

Cruz bumped into another security team that seemed as clueless the last one. Hoenikker stood with them, looking as out of place as an ice cream cone in a gun factory.

"Did it pass?" Cruz asked.

Hoenikker nodded. "Didn't see it. Just heard it." His wide eyes betrayed his attempt at courage.

"Give me a pistol," Cruz said to the synth on the team.

The synth handed it over.

"Hey, wait a minute," one of the security guards said.

"Enough. Give me your radio," Cruz said. He didn't wait. He snatched it from the guard, who looked as if he wanted to fight for it, but Cruz was the larger of the two and a station scientist. He handed the extra pistol to Hoenikker, who stared at it like it was about to go off.

"Safety is off. Jut aim and pull the trigger."

"What am I aiming at?" Hoenikker asked.

"Oh, you'll know." Then Cruz spoke into the radio. "All stations this net. Listen, find something liquid. Paint. Blood. Whatever. When the Leon passes, cover it so we can spot it easier. Right now it's doing laps around us. Paint it with something that sticks, and we can take it down."

"What are we doing?" Hoenikker asked.

"We're going to stand by and listen. Stand back to back and aim at the ceiling. I'll tell you when," Cruz said.

Hoenikker did as he was told, and pressed himself against Cruz until their backs were touching. They stood there for a few moments, listening to the crackle of the radio.

"Sorry about the way I've treated you in the lab," Cruz said.

"What? Oh. It's okay," Hoenikker said. "Things have been… well… a little frightful."

Cruz listened to the chatter, tracking the action. "None of this is what you expected, is it, Tim?"

"I can't say I planned on this. Mansfield promised me alien artifacts."

"How about actual aliens?" Cruz asked.

"Not so fond of living creatures, no offense to them," Hoenikker said. "I was just hoping to apply my specialty."

"You do see the importance of our mission, don't you?"

"Of course." Hoenikker shifted his pistol to his other hand. "I mean, protecting people is important, but… well… never mind."

"No, what is it?"

"It's just that, knowing the history behind many of the civilizations that preceded us could better inform our way forward on both a macro and micro level. Imagine the advancements we could make, researching the successes and failures of those who've come before."

Hoenikker had made a valid point, but Cruz knew research of that sort wasn't what made Weyland-Yutani the corporation that it was. Discovery of the Xenomorphs, and their attempts to own the morphology, spoke volumes about the company. They'd monetize breathing the air if they could validate it in court.

Hell, given the filtration systems, they already had, he supposed.

"Hold on," Cruz said, hearing harried curses on the radio. "It's coming around again."

"Which way?"

Cruz listened, then spun so that he and Hoenikker were facing the same direction.

"This way."

"Is it coming?"

"Yes—and some brainiac actually listened to me."

Pulse rifle shots from around the corner.

Cruz held his pistol and began to fire even before he saw anything. Aiming for the ceiling rail because that was what the Leon would be using to propel itself.

Reports were that it had been shot. When it appeared, it almost shocked him. Someone had managed to cover it in pink paint, defeating its camouflage ability in a mockery of science. His rounds snapped into the Leon as it hurtled around the corner, blood mixing with the paint, splattering against the wall.

Beside him, Hoenikker turtled, hunching protectively inward, the pistol clutched in two shaking hands.

The Leon fell to the ground and began to crawl toward them. Slowly, on its last breaths. But Cruz was out of ammo. He dropped the hand holding the pistol and backed up a step.

"Shoot it," he shouted to Hoenikker. "Kill it."

The terrified archaeologist held out his pistol with shaking hands, and just as the creature reached him, pressed it to its head and pulled the trigger. Brains went everywhere.

Then Hoenikker threw up.

31

It wasn't all a loss. At least they were able to harvest mature stem cells from the dead Leon-895, which Cruz felt could better manipulate the Xenomorph morphology.

Hoenikker played along. He was so out of his element, he just wanted everything to be done so he could get back to his *real* research. Dealing with aliens hands-on wasn't what he'd signed up for. He wanted artifacts. He wanted models. He wanted constructs.

He wanted stone and metal and composite, and not the biological messiness that came with living beings.

Instead of losing a full day, they'd only lost a few hours. Bellows was beyond pleased. With one synth and two guards lost, he called it an unmitigated success. He'd lauded the effort over the intercom, boasting his idea for so long that people started to ignore it and went back to work.

Back in the lab, they finalized several variations of the stem cells to inject into the last three Ovomorphs. The other containment rooms all boasted grown Xenomorphs. Their menacing pacing and scratching against the glass served as reminders that only slim engineering protected the scientists from certain death.

The Xenomorph in Containment Room Five had already shown overt aggression. Cruz was having none of it. He spent an hour burning it with flame and freezing it with ice, until finally the hideous beast retreated to a corner and cowered beneath its four clawed hands. One set was pointed weirdly outward. Hoenikker had been afraid that Cruz might be borrowing trouble, but the results were undeniable.

Étienne and Kash asked him to join them at the examination table near the front of the lab. They had their vid screens laid out, displaying some data they'd been debating. They needed an impartial assessor, and he'd been their first, last, and only choice since asking Cruz was out of the question.

They all perched on stools. Étienne had his hands placed on top of each other, his eyes entreating. Kash sat sideways, as if she'd been forced into the conversation but felt she had to be part of it.

"We need interaction," Étienne said firmly. "We need to put two of them together." Hoenikker glanced at Kash, who rolled her eyes. He looked back at Étienne.

"What does interaction provide that you can't have now?"

"I want to test how their pheromones change when they are in proximity to one another."

"I still don't understand," Hoenikker said. He looked at Kash again, but she just shook her head.

"They were either developed or evolved to become prime hunters. Definitely the alphas at the top of the food chain," Étienne said, his French accent a little stronger when he became more assertive. "Yet they have no discernable eyes. There have to be additional ways they can identify friend and foe. Some have hypothesized that echolocation is one means to identify prey, as it is with bats. Others believe they can see through the carapaces, and have a much wider view than we suspect."

"It's too dangerous," Kash said, interrupting. "What you plan is too dangerous."

"No. No. *Mademoiselle*, what I plan can surely be done. We need to shock their systems, then they will be—"

"We don't even have a handle on human pheromones," Kash said. "We've been studying those for centuries, and it's still pseudoscience."

"Then how do you explain some of the perfumes used to draw men or women? It's no longer just pleasant smells. I had a friend from medical school who was working on the idea of capturing sweat and recreating it in labs." Étienne rubbed his armpit, smelled his hand, then held it out for the others. "To someone, this is as sweet as the most expensive perfume. In it, there is a science of behavior we can finally understand."

Both Kash and Hoenikker leaned away from his offer.

"This is more than just the smell of sweat," Étienne continued. "It will tell you if I am afraid. It will tell you if I am in love. It will tell you many things—our problem is that we have an imperfect method of evaluating and translating the information."

Kash put her hand on his arm. "I get that, Étienne. I really do. Please, put your sweat away, and hear me out. Trying to evaluate the chemical properties of the perspiration on an alien is about as esoteric a concept as one can imagine." She glanced back to where Cruz sat at a workstation, and jerked her chin in his direction.

"Plus, he will never go for it."

Étienne grinned and smoothed his mustache. "*Ma cherie*, I have always been one to ask forgiveness first, and ask permission later."

Kash gave a sigh of frustration and almost turned away.

"What's the primary benefit that can be derived from this experiment?" Hoenikker asked.

"Primary benefit?" Étienne replied, his eyes off and into the distance.

"*Oui. Quel est le principal avantage?*" Hoenikker asked.

Étienne's eyes lit up. "*Oui. Oui.* I see what you have done here. Who knew you spoke French?" He waggled a finger. "You have been keeping this from me. *Le principal avantage*, hmm. If we are able to capture the scent of a Xenomorph in close proximity to another Xenomorph, perhaps we can create a chemical compound that is a deterrent? It could be replicated, and used as a protective spray."

"They can still tell that we are human, or at least not of their species," Kash said.

"If we look human but smell Xeno, wouldn't that give them pause?" Étienne asked. "Come on, Erin. This is all scientific method. This is a hypothesis. At least give me a chance to prove it before you dash it on the rocks of common sense."

"Do you really think you have the ability to break down the scent of a Xenomorph?" Hoenikker asked. Étienne stared at him for a long moment, then placed his hand on Hoenikker's shoulder.

"Yes. Yes, I do."

"Then let's do it," Hoenikker said. "But first, we have to clear it through Cruz."

Étienne's face fell. He threw up his hands.

"Then this will never happen."

He got up and walked away.

But Hoenikker had another idea. He felt that Cruz would go for it. It was all in how he sold it. Even the worst pill could be swallowed if given with something sweet.

An hour later, they were preparing Containment Rooms One and Two. Like the other rooms, these had accesses in the rear and were joined by a common door. No Xenomorph would need to be removed. Instead, they would just open the door between them.

"How'd you get Cruz to go for it?" Kash asked as they prepared for the experiment.

"I made him think it was his idea. I also pointed out that if it worked—and if Weyland-Yutani could monetize it—every Colonial Marine, and miner, and settler in the known systems would want a spray bottle of Xenomorph Defender."

"Did you come up with the name?" Kash asked, her smile wide and appreciating.

"I did," Hoenikker said. "Think it's too much?"

She laughed. "No. I think it's perfect."

None of them were sure what was going to happen when they raised the door between the containment rooms. Would the Xenos attack each other? Would they see each other as allies? Given their source, the scientists believed that the Ovomorphs came from the same queen, so the adult Xenomorphs were essentially siblings. They *should* be able to interact without killing each other.

In fact, Étienne was sure of it, but the moment the door slid open and the two creatures turned to face each other, the lab was filled with tension. No one said a word. It wasn't until they rushed at each other, then circled like dogs might have, sniffing each other, that Étienne pounded a victorious fist into his palm.

"Yes!" he said.

The creatures moved together for a moment, then switched rooms, each Xenomorph investigating the newly opened space. Their movements were sudden, much like a display on a vid that jerked due to an irregular signal—stuck one moment, and then having already moved the next.

Having inspected their new surroundings they met again, touching each other, tails whipping, jaws drooling. The scientists watched while they continued in this way for an hour, then when each Xenomorph found itself in its original containment room, they shut the door between them.

What came next was unexpected. Each containment room boasted a suite of utility arms that could detach from the walls, floor, and ceiling. Whenever they tried to release one, the Xenomorph would attack it. The hypothesis was that once they became aggressive, the pheromones would change.

So it was with a deft hand that Cruz operated the workstation. He pumped in music that might be present in the mess hall or waiting in a med suite. Whether it was to calm the creatures or himself, he never said. Then he fired an arm from the ceiling of the room that wiped the torpedo skull of the Xenomorph with a length of cotton. The creature whipped around, some of its drool striking the wall, ceiling, and cloth. Then Cruz snapped the utility arm back into the ceiling.

He sat back and grinned.

"Okay, Étienne. It's time to get your science on."

Étienne looked surprised.

"Don't pretend this wasn't you," Cruz said. "I know Hoenikker, and he'd never think of pheromone sprays. Trust in a Frenchman to want to make a cologne."

"*Oui.*" Étienne grinned. "*Oui.* Time for science."

32

Things were humming.

Kash was continuing her painstaking observations.

Étienne was working on his pet project that might actually *be* something.

And Cruz was doing what he wanted—supervising the team, and he had his own project with the Leon. All the Xeno eggs had hatched, including the last three they'd saved for the Leon-895 stem cells. Mixed with varying amounts of pathogen, each egg was injected with a serum in an attempt to see if they could replicate the chameleonic abilities in a Xenomorph.

The most difficult gestation to watch had been Test Subject #11. For a few days he had begun to exhibit a hope that had never been there. He'd been fed and kept comfortable for so long that he came to believe they might actually have commuted his sentence. But when they'd finally removed the bottom of the cryo case, he'd run to the glass and banged against it until his fists left streaks of blood.

When the face-hugger finally did emerge, he ran, then fought the creature, actually managing to grab the tail as it whipped around his arm. He began to beat the arm against the wall, hard enough to break it. Bone could be seen protruding from the injury. He tried to pry free the face-hugger, but the creature was having none of it.

Then the Test Subject did something completely unexpected. He placed the tip of the bone against the side of his neck and rammed himself into the wall. Once. Twice. Three times. Then on the fourth he managed to puncture his jugular. He went down, blood pumping furiously.

Cruz could have sworn that the man smiled, dying as he did, having outfoxed the face-hugger, who wouldn't be able to implant a chestburster inside a dead man. The face-hugger tried to attach itself to the dead man's face, but its own biological imperative wouldn't allow it. It needed something living, and there was nothing in the room to which it could attach itself.

It scrambled around, seemingly frantic, bouncing against one wall then another, plastering itself onto the glass that fronted the enclosure, until it slid miserably to the floor.

Cruz turned away. Unless they had a spare prisoner, Containment Room Eleven was a wasted opportunity. While part of him had rooted for the man to survive, and part of him had saluted the man for giving the big middle finger to Weyland-Yutani, the waste of an Ovomorph wasn't going to play well with the boss.

Bellows had handed him his ass, or at least tried to. Drill sergeants and commanders had handed Cruz his ass on various platters, so he took what Bellows gave and pretended he had enough hurt feelings to mollify the station commander.

Shit way to run an operation, he thought angrily. *Someone should show them how it ought to be done.*

Someone like him.

Hoenikker, meanwhile, was busy helping where he could. While Cruz hadn't really liked the man—probably because he was so entirely different from a Colonial Marine—he'd come to appreciate his work ethic. Even Étienne had backbone. Kash had backbone. Hoenikker... Cruz just wasn't sure.

Even now, the archaeologist carried samples back and forth for Kash, acting more like a third-year lab assistant than a fully credentialed scientist. What was a theoretical archeologist, anyway? Didn't really sound very scientific.

Étienne approached. "Remarkable. Do you know how complex these beings are?"

Cruz nodded. "However they came to be, they have some remarkable tendencies. What have you learned?"

"I examined not only the sweat you gathered from the carapace, but also the salivation we managed to capture. I think there's a sympathetic symbiosis between the two, as many of the cells I found were exactly the same."

Cruz grinned. "Can they be replicated?"

"I think so."

"Then what's the next step? Are you going to lather up and walk into one of the containment areas?" Cruz asked.

Étienne gave him a look. "That isn't funny," he replied. "We'll figure it out once we are able to replicate. Until then, I'm not even going to worry about it."

Cruz shook his head. "You can't go through your life being an inflight spaceship repairman."

Now it was Étienne's turn to grin. "Of course I can. It's worked for me so far." And then he was off, back to his microscopes. Cruz enjoyed the man's energy and his confidence. If only every scientist had the same.

He approached the Xenomorph in Containment Room Seven, observing the smooth, elongated head and reticulated jaws that continually snapped at the air. The human-shaped body was also intriguing. They'd been able to conduct scans and noted a biology that seemed to share components of both humans and Xenomorphs. With no eyes and no nose, it had to somehow detect the presence of others and note its surroundings through its mouth, using echolocation, or perhaps tasting the air.

Maybe Étienne was onto something. Perhaps pheromones were the missing link to understanding these complex aliens.

The longer Cruz stared at the creature, the more he wondered at its genetic origins. A static at the back of his brain started to rise, as if he'd tuned in to some new broadcast. The adult Xenomorph drones on either side of Seven began to spit acid at the glass. Their jaws launching forward, their tongues following like alien stilettos. Cruz felt a need to *do* something. He *wanted* to do something, but he didn't know what it was.

Cruz blinked and shook his head. The feeling remained, but it lessened a bit. Was he feeling contact from Seven? Had it told Six and Eight to attack the glass, and was he able to listen in to part of it? Or was he imagining it?

Hoenikker paused to stare at the glass of Containment Room Six.

"Should they be doing that?" Captain Obvious asked.

Cruz heard but didn't say anything. Instead, he listened and attended to the feeling. Was Seven communicating somehow with the others? Was the feeling inside his own head a broadcast of some sort, or was it literally inside his head?

Hoenikker approached him.

"Dr. Cruz, I don't think that—"

"Shut up and listen. Do you feel it? Do you *sense* it? Use your brain and embrace the science instead of the fear, Dr. Hoenikker. Seven is trying to communicate." Cruz looked past Hoenikker's hurt feelings and saw Kash working diligently in the front of the lab. "Erin. Do we have anything to measure frequencies?"

She paused and stared thoughtfully at one of the supply closets. "We don't, but I bet Comms does."

"Can you get us something, please?" he asked. She stared for a moment, then nodded.

Kash understood the need.

She wasn't scared like Hoenikker.

Then she left the lab.

Cruz's head buzzed with some sort of purpose he couldn't quite work out. He felt the energy. He felt a directive, but he lacked the translation to understand what it meant. He turned to Six and watched it spit acid repeatedly at the same spot. Over and over. Acid. On the glass. Then he turned to Eight and watched it doing the same thing. Directed. Focused.

Then Cruz understood.

Seven was smart.

Seven was the brain.

Seven wanted to escape.

It didn't have the capacity itself, but it did have a way to influence.

Cruz stepped over to Containment Room Seven's workstation. He sat and stared for a moment at the gray-skinned Xenomorph, so different to the others. Was it really a byproduct of irradiated pathogen—an accident of nature? Or was it designed to be this way? Had they unlocked something?

Kash had wanted to introduce this drone to the others, to see how they'd react. Her hypothesis was that this could be a super-drone, capable of leading the others. Cruz believed she might be right.

He watched as the other Xenomorphs attacked the glass for a few more moments, then he pressed a button. Fire rained down on Seven, causing it to flinch and fall back. And the other two Xenomorphs?

They stopped their attacks on the glass, instead investigating their demesne as they had been—in menacing whirls and jerks, tails whipping, no longer concerned at what they'd just been poised to do.

Cruz nodded.

Kash had *definitely* been right. Whether by design or accident, Seven was a creature to be watched.

33

Life in the lab continued anxiously, four scientists doing what eight should do.

Hoenikker was beginning to like this life a lot more since the chestbursters had turned into adult Xenomorphs. Even as he thought it, he felt bad for the thinking of it. For the adults to be present meant that humans had to have died, but he'd been working on coming to terms with it. He'd forced himself to accept it. He hadn't been in charge, and had no control over the process. Because of this, he'd been able to detach himself from the morphological step that required the incubation of humans.

Even the idea that Monica had now become an inglorious Xenomorph was an acceptable fact in the face of the idea that he finally had a race of alien entities for which he could create an archaeological model.

He pored over the data they had about the lifecycle of the Xenomorphs, curious about the relationship between the drones and the warriors and the queen. It was too easy for him to make comparisons to a beehive or an anthill because of the use of the term "queen." He needed to realize that the imperfect word was meant as a description for an unknown to adhere to a known, and wasn't truly identifiable. "Queen" was nothing more than a placeholder until a better scientific term could be found.

By using the term, he locked himself into a certain train of thought. The use of "queen" meant there was a sort of worship and respect. That all other beings of the same genetic model would intervene on her behalf, and do her bidding. But the term "mother" could also be used for that.

Or another term, not yet determined.

One of the issues with archaeological modeling was that unless he used the exact terms in the target species' language, he was doomed to be wrong. Bringing human terms to a model of Xenomorph anthropology was akin to bringing a knife to a gunfight. Sure, he might succeed, but there was so much he had to overcome to do so.

Not that they had a queen to study, which Hoenikker found himself wishing they had. He'd love to study the female Xenomorph, and its ability to control the males of the species. In that, the Xenomorphs were interesting because they didn't parallel carbon-based mammals as much as they mirrored an insectile sociological structure. Which brought him back to the bees.

With a female being at the center of all activities, and perhaps even directing them, how would the eleven Xenomorphs they held in their containment areas create their own sociological interactions, unless there was some sort of genetic marker that identified one as being superior to the other?

While examining Seven, Hoenikker couldn't help wondering if the Xenomorph might not have been genetically triggered *because* of the absence of a queen. Could nature be predisposed to fill a vacuum? He had been fascinated by Seven's apparent ability to silently manipulate or direct the other Xenomorphs. But now, after three more days of having to flame Seven because the others were spitting acid on their glass containment fronts, the humanlike Xeno was becoming a pain in the ass.

Cruz wanted to get rid of it, but Bellows wouldn't allow it. They'd already lost Eleven, and Bellows didn't want to have to explain to Weyland-Yutani why they kept losing hyper-expensive corporate resources. So, Cruz was left with continually trying to stop Seven from influencing the others.

Meanwhile, the creature's reach had grown, and it became able to influence Four, Five, Six, Nine, and Ten, all of which would randomly begin attacking their glass barriers. Every time they started, one of the scientists would have to move to Seven's workstation and actuate the flame system.

Worse, there was no way to measure damage to the glass. Fabrications came to take a look, and their idea of help was to stand around with blank looks in their eyes, gaping at the Xenos, scratching their heads and saying, "*I don't know.*"

When faced with this new problem, Bellows' solution was to have the two synths already assigned to the lab flame each of the Xenos whenever they started spitting acid at the glass. As logical as it sounded, the synths were suddenly in everyone's way, racing from one workstation to another as they tried to stop all the creatures.

What upset Cruz the most was that Seven seemed to be influencing the new Leon-895 he'd been able to create using the stem cells he'd mined from the original creature. At the same time as the Xenomorphs began to spit acid, the Leon would begin cycling through the colors of the spectrum in a dizzying display of camouflage. This ate into Cruz's experimentation time. His frustration was evident in the way he would take it out on the others. He'd begun to talk to Hoenikker as if he were a lab assistant.

"Give me a hand, will you?" Étienne said, jolting Hoenikker out of his reverie.

"What do you need?" Hoenikker asked, eager to do something. Étienne held up a beaker that had several ounces of clear liquid.

"Smell this."

Hoenikker hesitated, then leaned forward.

"There isn't any scent."

"No. Nothing that we can smell. However, watch this."

With an eyedropper, Étienne took a sample. Two cages rested on the table, a rat in each cage. He pulled the rat on the left free of its cage and placed two drops on its back. The rat squirmed for thirty seconds and almost got free, but went still. Étienne put it back into its cage. The rat circled a few times, then stopped.

"What am I supposed to see?" Hoenikker asked.

"Nothing yet. Wait for it."

Étienne then pushed both cages together. The other rat immediately ran to the side of the cage farthest from the first rat, and began to tremble visibly.

"We can't smell the liquid, but these rats can."

"Why didn't the first rat react?"

"Oh, it did. You saw it trying to get away. It wasn't trying to get away from me. It was trying to get away from itself. Somehow the pheromone merged with that of the rat, and it calmed. That's not unlike what happens when a face-hugger calms its victim. Or else the rat's brain sensed that there was no obvious threat. I'll need to experiment further to figure this out."

Étienne took the cage with the unchanged rat over to the workstation in front of Containment Room One. He glanced at the Xenomorph, who was prowling the other end of the chamber. Removing the rat, he opened a small hatch to the bottom right of the glass, placed the rat inside, and closed the door. Then he depressed a button on the workstation, an access panel slid to the side, and the rat fell into the room. It immediately found the nearest corner and started scratching where the glass met the wall.

The Xenomorph's torpedo-shaped head whipped around. It spun, impossibly fast, tail ripping through the air. In three steps it was upon the rodent, jaw opening, then telescoping out to snap the mammal in half. The alien rose to its full height and stared at Étienne, red and silver saliva dripping to the floor. It snapped its jaw out one more time, this time catching the glass, the teeth scraping it as a lance-like tongue tapped against the barrier.

Étienne grinned, got up, and returned the cage to the table.

"That was fun," he said.

Then he grabbed the other cage, containing the rat that had been subjected to the pheromone. He took this to the workstation and repeated the process. In a moment, the rat was in the cage, just as frantic as the other, scrambling over the remains of the first as it tried to claw through the window.

Xeno One watched the whole thing, and in a single bound hovered over the rat, saliva dripping onto it, making it frantic with terror. Curiously, though, the predator didn't attack the tiny creature. Instead it crouched, reached down, and grabbed it in a clawed hand. It held it there as if examining it. Then it stood took two steps back and hurled the creature as hard as it could into the glass.

The rat exploded as its skin parted with the force of the contact and its organs burst forth. Hoenikker, who'd come forward to observe, backed away in horror. Meanwhile, Étienne clapped his hands and laughed.

"Isn't it wonderful?"

"What do you mean? The Xenomorph still killed the rat."

"Yes, but not for the reason it killed the first one."

"But they're both still *dead*."

"The second one lived longer than the first. Why is that, Timothy? Why would the creature let it live, even go so far as picking it up and examining it?"

Hoenikker shook his head with disgust. "And then throwing it against the glass."

Étienne turned. "You're letting your emotions get in the way, and missing it. The pheromone I reproduced had a definite effect. We've achieved something measurable." He hurried back to the workstation. "Now to record the data and see if I need to manipulate the strain."

Hoenikker remained in place, his gaze on the streaks of blood and guts that were slowly sliding down the vertical surface of the glass.

Archaeological modeling.

No blood in that science.

Just clean facts and clear suppositions.

He shook his head and turned away, wishing he'd never taken this job.

34

Rawlings would rather have been sitting behind his desk, drinking his third cup of coffee of the day. He'd already had two, one before breakfast and one after.

Or better yet, in the mess hall. Today was Salisbury steak day, one of his favorites, but he'd be lucky if he even got leftovers. Both he and Webb from Engineering had been assigned to find a missing box of data chips that were required to fix the air conditioning in the commander's quarters. Engineering swore they knew where they were, but as it turned out—not so much.

And Rawlings. Hell, he wasn't doing anything. Might as well get him to do something that's not his job because someone else lost a box of data chips. Sure. *"Get Rawlings. He's just here to take care of pretty much everything."*

They'd gone through two rooms thus far, and had twelve more to go. He sighed.

"And you should'a seen the walls of the old deputy's quarters," Webb continued. "He has heads of creatures I didn't even know had heads. So much outside'a Pala Station. I understand people hate it inside, but the outside is hella more dangerous."

Webb was a little over five feet tall, with an immense chest and arms. Fabrications had to make special tops for his uniform so they would fit. He was a gym rat and was always asking Rawlings if he couldn't get them to requisition more exercise equipment. But as big as he was, he had a higher pitched voice than was normal, and was the station's center of gossip.

Rawlings nodded as he used his security card to open a third room. Webb hadn't shut up the entire time they'd been searching. This room had belonged to Comms Specialist Brennan, and had been filled with boxes of supplies brought down from the *San Lorenzo*. Each box bore the name of the ship from which it had come, along with a barcode. Made of composite metal-plastics, they were both heavier and lighter than seemed appropriate.

They had to move them aside as Webb used his scanner to find the box they were looking for. He'd scan, the device would beep, he'd look at the readout, and shake his head. All through it, he never stopped talking.

"This was Brennan's room, wasn't it? I heard he died. Some say he was murdered." He glanced at Rawlings, dimples on his face as he grinned. "What do you know about that?"

"Really not supposed to talk about it."

"Aww, come on. We're just passing time. You know you can trust me to keep a secret."

Now it was Rawlings' turn to grin.

Webb saw it and added, "When have you ever known me to share a *real* secret." *Beep.* "Sure, I might pass some info around about this or that." *Beep.* "What about that time there were bugs in the food? I was the one who broke the news and saved the station." *Beep.* "You act as if I'm never helpful." *Beep.*

"You're helpful," Rawlings said. Half the Salisbury steak was already gone. He was sure of it. "I just can't talk about it."

"Well, it's not as if Brennan wasn't going to get in trouble anyway." *Beep.* "Everyone knew he spent most of his work time playing a video game." *Beep.* "What was it called? Damn if I remember." He stood up straight. "Whelp, it looks as if this room is clear. Let's go."

They moved to the next room that was being used to store supplies. This one was farther away from the active corridors, and near the blockaded area where station personnel—other than security services—were unable to pass. Rawlings spied a rat scurrying down the edge of the corridor, but ignored it. He'd tired of the constant presence of the creatures, and was loath to report it. After all, he might be the one chosen to be on extermination duty. Searching for a missing box was bad enough, but that would be even worse.

He slid the security card over the door and it opened, sending a rush of putrid air that quickly surrounded them and threatened to make the coffee return for a second showing. Webb turned his head.

"Something die in here? Jesus." He pulled his collar over his mouth and nose.

Rawlings covered his face with his left hand. Surely they hadn't stumbled on something dead? He recollected that there was a thing called a King Rat, where rats in a nest got their tails so intertwined that they couldn't move, and ended up dying of starvation. Was that what this was? Had they stumbled upon the mother of all King Rats?

"You first," Rawlings said nasally, trying not to breathe.

"Hells no." Webb shook his head and backed up a step. "You want to go in there, then you go."

Rawlings felt a flare of anger. He was missing breakfast because the engineers lost a box, and now their chosen representative didn't want to go into a room because it stank. What the fucking hell?

Webb must have seen his face because he patted the air, palms out.

"Okay. Fine. Be that way. I'll go in first."

"You did lose the box," Rawlings pointed out, not willing to let it go. "I'm just along for the ride."

Webb gave him a sour look, but said nothing more. With a ham-fisted hand he pushed open the door. The room was like the others, filled with boxes nearly to the ceiling, except this one felt as if it was an animal's burrow.

"Jesus. What lives in here?" Webb asked.

Rawlings had no idea and didn't care. He expected there had been a carton or two of food that had been meant for the mess hall, but had either been mislabeled or mis-stored or both. Just thinking about it, he was reminded of the meal he was missing. Any goodwill he might have felt toward the pit bull of a man in front of him went away.

"What are you waiting for?" Rawlings asked. "Let's get this done."

Webb began scanning the inventory tags. He'd kept his T-shirt over his mouth and was breathing through the cloth, so he wasn't talking. Rawlings was thankful for the silence, but not thankful for the stench.

Webb hurried through the first two rows of boxes, then he and Rawlings had to move several aside to create a lane toward the back of the room. It was then that they noticed there was a large open space in the far-left corner. When they stepped through to continue scanning, they saw what appeared to be a dead thing lying in a large clump upon the ground.

Rawlings tried to make sense of it. What looked like giant segmented legs were folded in on it. Beneath them was a body, possibly human. He stepped closer and leaned in. There were arms, too, folded in on themselves. He didn't see any hands. Nor did he see a head.

"What the fuck is that?" Webb asked, stepping beside Rawlings.

"I have no idea. Looks like something with legs. Think it could be something from outside the station?"

"It sure could be," Webb said. "But the question is, how did it get in here?"

Rawlings examined the ceiling and upper corners of the room. He didn't find any openings or broken ceiling panels. Nothing to explain the presence of the dead creature in front of them.

"We should call this in to Security."

"What are they going to do?" Webb scoffed. "Need to get a maintenance crew to take out the trash."

Then the thing moved.

Both Rawlings and Webb jumped back a step.

They looked at each other and, after a moment, Webb laughed nervously.

"What do you think?" he asked.

Rawlings examined the ground around the thing. A pile of filthy blankets. Small bones scattered on the floor. A container stained yellow. Possibly from urine. Whatever the thing was, it had been here for some time. He surmised from the bones that it had either starved to death or died from dehydration. There were no water sources, so the latter was certainly possible. Then again, it could be both.

Then he stopped.

He backed away slowly.

A single eye stared up at him through the mass of legs.

"Webb," he whispered.

"You know, it looks like a giant spider of some kind," Webb said. He held his scanner out as if to prod it.

"Webb," Rawlings whispered a little louder.

The pit bull straightened and turned toward him.

"What? Why are you whispering?"

With a rustle like wads of paper being stuffed into a box, the thing rose on its feet to its full height. It wasn't dead. It wasn't even wounded. It was completely alive and terrible to behold. It was as if a human had sprung long chitinous legs from the hips. Its human legs had withered and were a third the size they should have been. They swayed as the thing moved.

From the waist up, the creature looked almost human, but the nose had disappeared because of the enlarged mouth that took up nearly half the face. Twin rows of jagged teeth rimmed the inside of the jaw. Oddly, the eyes remained human enough for Rawlings to identify the man.

Fairbanks. Or what was left of Fairbanks.

Whatever had happened to him, he'd become a monster.

Webb must have seen Rawlings' eyes widen, because he began to turn around—but he never made it. Before he could move more than a few inches, the Fairbanks monster grabbed him by the head and bit down on it, coming away with a round bit of skull and brain matter. The creature chewed quickly as the legs adjusted themselves to stay balanced. Standing on those new legs, the creature's head nearly brushed the ceiling.

Rawlings couldn't take his eyes off Webb's face. The eyes were wide and the mouth was open as if he were about to scream. Then the eyes narrowed and his lips curled down as if he were confused and about to cry. All the while the creature chewed mechanically.

Feeling his way backward, Rawlings used the boxes to help him navigate. Oh, how he wished he had a pistol at his hip, or a pulse rifle slung across his back. The monster watched him as he began his retreat, its hands still on the side of Webb's head.

Just as Rawlings reached the door, the Fairbanks monster tossed Webb aside and rushed, the four chitinous legs propelling it incredibly fast. Rawlings spun, keyed the door open, and sprinted left down the corridor, more afraid for his life than he ever had been as a Colonial Marine.

35

Too late, he realized he should have shouted a warning. He plowed into two maintenance workers, knocking them both to the ground. Instead of helping them to their feet, he spared a quick glance behind him and saw the monster closing fast. He turned and ran, leaving the two workers to the creature, hoping they would slow it down and condemning himself for feeling that way.

"Shit. Shit. Shit," he said under his breath, his cursing keeping time with his pounding feet. He came to an intersection. He hadn't been in this part of the station in a long while. He chose left, immediately saw a blank wall blocking his way, and knew he should have turned right. He backpedaled and peered down the corridor.

The Fairbanks monster was dragging one of the maintenance workers by her long black hair. Her arms hung limp. The creature eyed him and let out a scream that was eerily human.

Rawlings shot down the right corridor, feeling all forty-two years of his slightly overweight Colonial Marine veteran body. He saw a fire alarm and pulled it. The alarm immediately began to ring from every speaker in every corridor, hammering at all thought.

It was the least he could do.

He had to warn people.

But it backfired.

Instead of being fearful, the alarm made everyone open their doors and step out into the corridor. They looked around, concerned as Rawlings ran past.

"Where's the fire?" one asked.

"Monster," he yelled, out of breath. "Run."

"What about the fire?" someone else asked.

Then the creature turned the corner, moving rapidly and still dragging the woman by her hair. It screamed once, then lifted a leg and brought it down on the chest of a man, pinning him to the ground.

Rawlings had to stop. He stood with hands on hips, trying to get his wind as he watched the monster reach down, pull the man up, and bite his face off.

That was all it took.

Everyone in the corridor screamed as they turned and ran.

He started running again as well, allowing the wave to carry him along as they all funneled through the corridors. It was pure panic. Others joined them, not knowing what they were running from, but understanding the need. Those with more sense opened their doors, saw the stampede, and closed them again. A man tripped, sending those behind ass-over-elbows. Rawlings had to step on one to keep his balance, almost going down himself. He knew that if he had, he'd never be able to get up again. No. He needed his balance, so he took short running steps, his hand close to the man's belt in front of him.

A security guard appeared with a pistol drawn, but she was flattened by the mob before she could even open her mouth.

Someone, somewhere, turned the alarm off.

As they came to various corridors, the mob began to dissipate, some taking the corridors, some continuing forward, some finding unlocked rooms. The problem with the station was that it was essentially a closed loop. A giant set of rectangles that had you turning and turning until you were back to the place you began. If the monster had only realized this, it wouldn't have tried to chase after its prey. It could just stand still and let them race toward it.

A stitch hit Rawlings' side like a stiletto driving into his lung. He lurched to a stop, his hand held to the place of greatest pain. He leaned against the wall as those few who remained behind him flowed past like water might go around a rock. He was done running.

Staggering back, he saw that the Fairbanks monster was about forty feet down the corridor. It had stopped. It had finally let go of the maintenance worker's hair and was busy eating the face of the downed security guard.

Rawlings gasped for air as silently as he could. It couldn't come fast enough. His lungs burned. He remembered when he could run five, even ten kilometers in full battle rattle. Now he couldn't run ten meters without the threat of passing out.

He spied the pistol on the ground about midway between him and the monster. He staggered toward it and managed to grab it before the monster registered his presence. The safety was off. Raising the pistol, he sighted down the length, aiming for center mass. Then, noting the legs of the security guard fighting for traction, he adjusted his aim, and pulled the trigger.

Blam!

Blam!

Blam!

He fired until she stilled.

Nothing worse than being eaten alive.

Probably.

The Fairbanks monster dropped its meal and glared at him.

Rawlings raised his pistol and aimed, but his hand was shaking from the adrenaline bleed. He brought his left hand up and steadied his aim, then pulled the trigger three times in succession. Two rounds hit, knocking the creature back several steps. The legs threatened to fold in upon themselves for a moment, then they righted, and the creature skittered backward and out of sight.

The sound of boots running toward him filled the silence.

"Put it down," someone commanded from behind. "Put the gun down now."

He relaxed his two-handed stance and let his gun hand fall to his side, but he didn't let go. He turned. Two security guards faced him. One with a pistol drawn and aiming at his face. The other rushed past to the downed security guard he'd just put out of her misery.

"I said put the gun down," the guard with the gun said. The name tag on his shirt read MAHMOOD. He had dark skin and even darker close-cropped hair. A scar tore through the skin under his left eye.

"She's been shot," the other security guard cried. "He shot Fredericks in the back."

Mahmood stepped forward and pressed the barrel of his pistol into Rawlings' cheek hard enough to click the teeth through the skin.

"Why the fuck you shoot Fredericks?"

"Tell the other asshole to look at her face," Rawlings said. Seeing the look of doubt in Mahmood's eyes, he said, "Ask him. Come on. *Ask him*."

Mahmood shouted over Rawlings' shoulder. "This one says to look at her face."

After a few seconds, "Oh shit. Something's been eating it." The universal sound of retching came next. Mahmood's eyes went from what was happening behind Rawlings to his face.

"A fucking monster is loose and it was eating her face when she was still alive." Rawlings pushed the pistol away. "So yeah. I shot her. Wouldn't you have?"

Mahmood walked over and stared down at Fredericks. Rawlings joined him. Whatever her appearance had been, there was no trace of it anymore. One eye dangled free. The other was missing, along with the nose, lips, and cheeks, revealing open jaw, gums, and teeth as if someone had tried and failed to stuff a human skull into a flap of skin.

"What kind of monster did this?" Mahmood asked.

"I don't have a nomenclature for it. I've been calling it the Fairbanks monster because whatever it is now, it used to be Fairbanks."

"Fairbanks as in the missing comms specialist?"

Rawlings nodded. His legs felt like lead. "The same, except this one has giant fucking spider legs and a mouth with enough teeth to eat a cow."

"And it's loose in the station?" Mahmood asked.

Rawlings nodded and kept his snark in check.

Mahmood grabbed the radio from his belt and called to put the station on alert. Rawlings straightened and headed off in the direction the monster had gone.

"Where are you going?" Mahmood asked.

"There's a monster on the loose," Rawlings said without turning. "Don't you think we oughta be trying to kill it before it kills someone else?"

"Uh, yeah," Mahmood said, running up beside him. "Let's go get the damned thing."

Shoulder to shoulder they moved down the corridor. Finding the creature didn't prove as hard as it could have been. Rawlings had hit it squarely, and it had left a trail of blood. They found it two corridors to the left, munching on a fabrications tech. It must have preferred the soft skin of the face, or maybe brains, because once again the creature was concentrating on the head.

Mahmood called it in on his radio.

Rawlings leveled his pistol and began to pull the trigger, but he only fired two rounds before he heard an unsatisfying click.

The monster spun and ran.

Rawlings still felt the stitch in his side.

He wasn't going anywhere.

36

The ruckus was intense. The noise mind-blowing. Every single Xenomorph in every single containment area had begun attacking its glass with fervor. Acid spitting, hand clawing, tail banging, anything they could do to attack the glass.

The only containment rooms that were silent were the one with Seven and the one with Leon-895-B. Seven stood implacable, staring blindly outward. Étienne, Kash, Hoenikker, Cruz, and the synths were busy trying to stop the creatures from attacking the glass. Cruz privately feared they'd break containment at any moment, and was considerably worried that all of his security plans wouldn't be enough to stop whatever had gotten into Seven.

They'd heard a fire alarm, but then it had gone off.

Cruz got word through the command channel that some creature was loose in the corridors, and people were dying. In the meantime, they were on lockdown and had their own problems.

"When are they going to stop?" Étienne asked, shouting over the din.

"I don't think they're going to," Kash hollered back.

"But that means…" Étienne didn't have to finish the sentence. Everyone knew what that meant. Cruz cursed. He went over to Seven and stared at the damn thing a moment.

"You want to be the first one to die, you bastard?"

He opened the cover on the abort switch. The difference between the flames they'd been using and the flames from the abort was astronomical. Nothing could survive it, jets of fire firing from all angles, microwave beams designed to cook something from the inside out.

His hand hovered over the switch.

The Xenomorphs suddenly stopped.

The only movement was the constant drip of saliva from their mouths and the swaying twitches of their tails. Hoenikker leaned back in his workstation, out of breath. Kash stared wide-eyed at Cruz. Étienne leaned forward, draping his arms over his panel.

Just as he thought.

Cruz nodded at Seven.

"The next time you do that, I will begin with you, and work my way up." He replaced the cover on the abort button. "Heed my words." He had no idea if the Xeno could hear him, or understand.

The command channel on his vid beeped, indicating an incoming call. Cruz answered it. Bellows was on the other end. The station commander's face was beet red, his eyes wide and veined.

"What the hell have you done to my station, Cruz?"

"What are you talking about?"

"Your damn specimens. They're in my corridors." He looked away from the screen for a moment, then back. "Reports are that the dead and dying are everywhere."

Cruz put a hand up to the side of his head. What was the man thinking? "I'm telling you, sir, that all of my specimens are present and accounted for."

"That can't be. You should see my station."

"There may be something out there, but it's not from the lab. I can show you if you—"

"You can stop right there." Bellows held up a hand, and looked at Cruz sadly, like a father might to a lying child who was caught in his falsehood. His chin lowered, and he stared down the length of his nose. "My synths have already reported that one of the containment rooms is empty. Number twelve."

"An empty..." he said. "There's no empty containment room. That's where Leon-895 is. He's not visible!"

Bellows shook his head. "You're not the right one to lead this, Dr. Cruz. Not only are you not to be believed, but you failed to warn us that a specimen escaped."

"Bellows. Seriously. Listen to me," Cruz said. He couldn't fucking believe he was having this conversation. "For the love of Christ, there is no escaped specimen. All my containment rooms are occupied."

"That will be all, Dr. Cruz." The station commander stared at him for a long moment, then shook his head. He moved to turn the vid off and paused. "Oh, and Dr. Cruz?"

"Yes, sir?"

"Don't take the Lord's name in vain, to try and explain away your incompetence."

Cruz blinked several times. "What? What do you mean?"

But the screen was blank.

Cruz looked up and noted that everyone was staring at him.

"What was that all about?" Kash asked.

"I think I've been fired," Cruz said.

"But why?" Hoenikker asked.

"Why would he fire you?" Étienne asked.

"That's just it." Cruz tossed the vid display onto the table. "I don't really know." He turned to stare at Seven, who stood silently in the middle of its containment room, arms hanging at its sides. The creature was as still as a statue. Was it looking at him? Was it *laughing* at him? Did it even understand what was going on?

Suddenly the two synths came to life. They'd retreated to the wall when the Xenomorphs had stopped harassing the glass, but now they moved to the workstations for Containment Rooms One and Two. Each of them opened the cover for the abort button.

"Whoa. Wait!" Étienne cried. Closest to them, he reached out for the synth at the workstation for Containment Room Two, and was thrown back as the automaton backhanded him. Étienne fell hard to his back, face bloody.

"Stop," Cruz yelled. "Don't!"

The synths ignored him.

Each of them depressed an abort button.

Flames from all angles poured over the Xenomorphs. They began to scream and flop, their arms and legs rattling on the ground as they were consumed. Invisible microwave radiation baked them from the inside. Their animal cries were almost human in their terror, the heat they were experiencing unimaginable. Their skin was on fire, causing the fluids in their bodies to boil, acid dripping into the flames.

The synths remained in place, their hands over the buttons, protecting them, finishing the job, not moving until the creatures had been aborted.

Cruz realized what was happening. Bellows wasn't taking any chances. Whether or not the creature loose in the station had originated from the lab, none would escape now. The station commander had ordered the synths to destroy them, knowing that the scientists would balk. What a fucking idiot. On one hand, he refused to let Cruz abort Seven because of its value to the company; and on the other, he decided to abort *all* the Xenomorphs out of fear.

The synth who was sitting at the Containment Room One workstation stood and moved to the workstation for Containment Room Three.

Hoenikker was already there with a fire extinguisher.

"No!" he cried, and he brought the extinguisher around.

The synth deflected it, then pushed Hoenikker to the ground.

But Hoenikker wasn't done. As the synth gathered itself into the seat, Hoenikker climbed to his feet and brought the fire extinguisher down on the synth's head. The synth fell forward onto the workstation control panel. Hoenikker brought the fire extinguisher up again, but felt it ripped from his hands.

The other synth was up and protecting the first. Hoenikker spun and found himself being thrown into the air and onto the worktable in the center of the lab, scattering vid displays, beakers, and various scientific equipment.

Then all hell broke loose.

All the Xenomorphs resumed their attacks on the glass. If anything, their frenzy was multiplied. The glass fronts smoked with acid as each of the creatures spit and slammed their teeth over and over, each into a single space. They raked the glass with their claws so quickly that had they been attacking a human, the skin would have been flayed down to tendon and bone in a matter of seconds.

A crack appeared in the glass of Room Four.

The Xenomorph redoubled its efforts.

Étienne took up the fire extinguisher and began to hammer at the synth Hoenikker had hit before. Its head was canted as if it had lost the ability to straighten.

Kash helped Hoenikker to his feet.

Cruz stood in the middle of it all, watching as crack after crack appeared in the glass fronts, spidering, growing and running to the ceilings and walls and floors. A feeling began to grow in his stomach. A feeling he'd last felt when his squad had been overrun and torn apart.

The Xenomorph in Containment Room Four died at the hands of a synth; at the same time, the glass from Containment Room Five shattered. Cruz backed away and grabbed Étienne by the shoulder as he did. The Frenchman stopped hammering, noticed the broken glass, and let himself be dragged away.

Out stepped the Xenomorph known simply as Five.

But it ignored the scientists. Instead, it stepped tentatively toward the containment room holding Seven. It stood there, saliva falling from its jaw and the occasional twitch of its tail showing that it wasn't some hellish statue that suddenly appeared in the midst of the laboratory.

They watched as Seven and Five seemed to have some silent exchange. With the glass between them, it couldn't be Étienne's pheromone that allowed them to communicate. It had to be something else, and the only thing he could think of was some form of telepathy. He remembered the buzz in the back of his head. If his brain had been wired in the same fashion as the Xenomorphs', he'd have known what it had been trying to say.

Five moved to the workstation and depressed a series of buttons.

He's been watching, Cruz thought. Then another thought struck him.

Seven might be better at management and org-anization than all the bureaucrats on Pala Station combined.

The surviving synth pulled its pistol and fired several rounds into Five. The creature turned, pushed one more button, and the glass front slid aside.

Damn. How had Seven known the complex combination of buttons needed to do that?

The synth fired again, approaching the Xenomorph. Its implacable expression didn't reveal anything. If it had been Cruz or any human approaching such a monster, fear—and perhaps determination—would have been plastered over his face. But the synth was eerily passive.

Five whirled and grabbed the synth by the side of its head, bringing it in close. Its jaw telescoped and scored the synth's metal head. The synth punched the body of its attacker, then brought a palm up, slamming it into the underside of the Xenomorph's jaw.

"Cruz!" Kash whispered urgently.

The Xenomorph threw the synth across the room, bending one of the wall lockers into Rorschach origami.

"*Cruz!*" she whispered again.

He snapped out of it. "What?" He glanced at the other scientists. All scared. All desperate to leave. Étienne was grabbing a container of some sort. Hoenikker looked like he wanted to cry.

"We can't leave."

More crashing from behind.

"They put us on lockdown," Étienne said.

Cruz glanced behind him.

Another Xenomorph had freed itself.

They were all going to die.

Still, they had to try. "There's an override," he said. "Try 198473 in the access panel. *Hurry.*" He turned back just in time to see Seven step from its containment room. It turned to face him, standing in the middle of the lab as chaos raged around it.

The synth had managed to kill the Xenomorph from Five, but it was surrounded by three more. Leon-895 flashed in the background. That meant all the containment rooms had been breached. Cruz laughed. Bellows would really be pissed now.

Fire roared from Containment Room Eight. The glass had already broken and even this far away Cruz could feel the heat.

Then the door to the lab *sssked* open.

Seven stood there. It didn't say a word, nor did he expect it to, but by the buzzing in the back of Cruz's head, he would swear it was smiling.

He turned and ran.

37

Hoenikker flinched as Étienne poured liquid from the beaker over his head, all the while giggling like a child. If the pheromone was going to work, it was do or die.

Kash pulled at Hoenikker's elbow.

"Come on," she said. "We need to leave, now!"

Now out in the corridor, Hoenikker stared into the lab. He had lost count of the Xenomorphs, but they all seemed to be swarming around the strange white-colored one known as Seven. Hoenikker found himself looking for Three—what had formerly been Monica. For a moment he thought she might have already died, but then he saw her, the light striping on her arms and torso so different than the others. She held the head of the last synth in her hand, before turning and hurling it toward him.

Both he and Kash dodged the missile.

Kash grabbed him one last time.

This time he followed her lead.

They ran into a pair of security guards, who grabbed Kash's free arm to stop her. They ended up swinging around so their backs were to the door of the lab.

"What happened?" one asked.

"The Xenomorphs," Hoenikker said. "They're all free."

"The fuck you say?" the other replied.

"Go see for yourself," Kash said. They turned to leave, and the first security guard stopped them.

"I wouldn't go that way."

"Why not?" Hoenikker asked.

"Another fucking monster is why," the second guard said. Hoenikker stared at him. How many monsters were out there? What had happened to the nice peaceful station they'd had?

Who was he kidding? The station had been infested since the moment he'd set foot on it. Once again, he wondered why the hell he'd left his cushy corporate job to come to this godforsaken place.

Just then a Xenomorph shot into the corridor, grabbed the first security guard, and jerked him back into the room. It all happened in the blink of an eye, and the man didn't have a chance to make a sound. The other guard turned and looked from side to side.

"Barron? Where the fuck are you?" He turned back around. "Where did he go?"

It had happened so fast that both Kash and Hoenikker stood like idiots with their mouths open. Then another Xenomorph grabbed the second security guard and jerked him inside the lab before he could even reach for his gun.

Kash and Hoenikker glanced at each other. They prepared to run…

"*Frère Jacques, Frère Jacques. Dormez vous? Dormez vous? Sonnez les matines. Sonnez les matines. Din din don. Din din don.*"

Étienne came walking out of the lab. Somehow, some way, the Xenomorphs hadn't taken him, or even noticed him. The pheromones had *worked*.

A Xenomorph popped into the corridor in front of Étienne, who stood swaying gently from side to side as if he were on a ship.

"I once saw a man in India reach out and pet a King Cobra," Étienne said without a trace of fear. Hoenikker wondered if he'd gone insane. "The idea was to lull the snake into a false sense of security. He would sway from side to side and the snake would mimic him."

Hoenikker watched in horror as Étienne reached out with his hand. The Xenomorph wasn't swaying from side to side. It was leaning forward, saliva dripping, tail snapping the air, claws opening and closing. But Étienne wouldn't stop. He reached out and ran a hand down the side of the torpedo-shaped head.

"There now, *mon frère*." He waved jovially at Kash and Hoenikker, then turned and walked the opposite way, soon lost in the curve of the corridors. The ghost of the song leaving a trail of musical breadcrumbs behind him. "*Sonnez les matines. Din din don. Din din don.*"

"God loves drunkards and fools," Kash said.

"And evidently Frenchmen," Hoenikker added.

Then they did run, but they didn't get very far.

They almost tripped over the first body they came across. Blood smeared the walls. The head was missing. One leg bent at an unnatural angle—but it couldn't be from the Xenomorphs. Those were behind them, or at least Hoenikker thought they were. Then he remembered the harried video call from Bellows, believing that it was one of their Xenos who had escaped. That was what had started it all. So then, what kind of creature were they going to encounter?

Screams came from behind them.

They both turned toward the sound.

Then came a roar from the way they'd been heading.

Hoenikker knew he was close to his room. He grabbed Kash's wrist and tore off down the corridor toward the roar, praying. When he approached the intersection, he saw coming the other way the creature that must have wreaked havoc in the corridors. With the face of Fairbanks and the legs of a giant spider, it came for them, nine feet tall and impossible fast.

Kash screamed.

Hoenikker jerked her hand as he pulled her the other way. When they reached his door, he palmed in, pulled her after him, and closed it behind them. Instantly Kash ran to the end of the room, fell to the ground, and pulled her knees to her chin. He joined her, and they sat staring at the door as scream after scream came and went, individual Doppler effects of terror.

Another alarm sounded, drowning out most of the screams.

They sat that way for several hours, anticipating that the door would burst open, one of the monsters from the lab coming to get them. Or worse yet, Three coming to give him a warm hug.

When the alarm finally silenced, so did the sound of screams.

"No one is ever going to know," Kash whispered.

"Know what?" Hoenikker asked.

"Everything. Nothing. What we've done here." She waved her hand around. "It's all going to be forgotten."

"Not if we survive," he said, not really feeling the hope he was trying to project.

"Survive?" She snorted. "We're not going to survive this. Even if we do, we can't be sure they got them all. Besides, this whole event will be a wart on Weyland-Yutani's success. They'd rather nuke us from orbit than expend the moral credits needed to save us, and explain how they failed."

"You're painting a bleak picture."

"It's a watercolor made of blood depicting the end of all things." She shook her head. "The first group of specimens we had were different. They hadn't been subjected to the pathogen. The black goo did something to Seven. Made it smarter. Made it more in control."

"I was thinking about that. Perhaps because there isn't a mother, some DNA we thought was junk turned on instead, to create a leader."

She nodded. "It was made to help them survive."

"I've been modeling what we know of their society. They need a mother. A leader. They *want* a leader. Without one they're nothing more than a wolf pack without an alpha. Renegades." He chuckled. "Ronin. Like the masterless samurai who used to roam feudal Japan."

"The Xenomorphs have a lot more weapons than a samurai."

"Don't be so sure." Hoenikker stood, cranking his neck until it popped. "Weapons weren't allowed in feudal Japan. The samurai were like modern tanks. To the common man, they were weapons of mass destruction. Which makes me believe more and more that these alien Xenomorphs were purpose-made. They're too perfect. A bipedal version of ancient samurai who spit acid."

Kash stood as well, putting two fists in the small of her back as she bent backward.

"I hate to break it to you, Tim. These aren't samurai. We *wished* we had samurai." She pulled her hair out of the bob and shook her head. She went over to his bed and lay down on it. "I'm just so tired."

He grinned. "Me too." He laughed.

"What's so funny?" she asked.

"I was thinking about that hard-ass, Cruz. Know what he'd say?" he asked. "Probably something like, 'No napping during Armageddon, Hoenikker.'" He bellowed, trying his best to imitate the man's voice.

Now it was her turn to laugh. "Do that again."

"There ain't no napping during Armageddon, Hoenikker," he said again, his voice a full-on parody of a military bellow.

Suddenly, there came a banging on the door.

Kash shot out of bed and stood near Hoenikker.

He stood still, staring at the door. He felt like a kid who'd just gotten caught making fun of their parents.

The banging came again.

38

A maintenance closet was the last place Cruz imagined himself. Wedged between cleaning supplies and a floor scrubber while others fought and died. It was as ignoble a position as he'd ever experienced. He'd never been one to turn tail and run, he'd always been ready to fight.

Or at least, he wished he'd been that person. He deserved to be that person, with all the hard work and dedication he'd put into being a Colonial Marine. But then LV-832 happened. Moose-sized xenomorphic quadrupeds with tentacles happened. Snyder, Bedejo, Schnexnader, Correia, and Cartwright happened.

He closed his eyes to calm himself, smelling the sharp tang of cleaning solution.

That was then. This was now. He could make up for it. He could save his crew. He'd run away leaving his previous crew to die, but now he had a chance to redeem himself. He had Kash and Étienne. He even had Hoenikker. Although he didn't like the man, this was war, this was survival. He was human and the damned Xenomorphs were not.

Plus, he had to get all of their research out, or it would be irrevocably lost.

Bellows and Security probably thought they could retake the station, but Cruz had heard and seen enough that he felt it was a fool's bet. The Xenomorphs were the universe's chosen killing machine. It was nature's way of ridding space of humanity. How dare humans assume that, just because they possessed something like an LV, it was theirs? Bellows would learn. His security guards would learn, and in the meantime, Cruz would help his team escape. There were a shuttle and the *San Lorenzo* orbiting above. They still had hope.

First, Cruz needed to find a way to get back into the lab. So, he waited, and began to prepare himself. He spent ten precious minutes hacking his vid display into station security using one of his command controls. He needed to know what was going on.

At first the screams came fast and furious, matched by the sounds of running feet and what could only be humans being ripped apart. A pool of blood seeped beneath the door. He moved back as far as he could, but the puddle reached and surrounded his feet.

He searched through the station vids until he found one near his door, where he saw several station personnel running, while being chased by a juvenile.

Eventually the sounds became fewer and fewer, long stretches of silence punctuated by occasional screams of the dying. After hour three had passed he put his ear to the door and, upon hearing nothing, palmed it open, hoping that the vid display showed him the door to the maintenance room he was in. The sound of it opening seemed impossibly loud in the silent corridor.

He looked down and saw Comms Chief Oshita lying in a pool of her own blood. Or what was left of her. Her hair had singed away, leaving her scalp raw and ugly. Her face was locked in a grimace, probably from the intense pain from exposure to Xenomorph acid. Her chest cavity was empty, and her body still smoldered, thin curls of smoke wafting upward. The Xenomorph saliva that had dripped on her gave her an unholy sheen.

He glanced at the vid display and saw an image of himself. He looked up, then down, then nodded. This would come in handy.

Stepping over her, he frowned as his feet squelched in her blood. Looking left, then right, he gripped the steel handle of a floor mop, the only weapon he could readily find, and took three steps down the corridor, squelching less and less with each step. He had about thirty meters to go to get back to the lab. The mop would do little as an offensive weapon, but it might just give him a chance to flee. He was hoping to find a dropped security weapon along the way.

Cruz kept his back to the wall as he slid sideways down the corridor, clocking each door in case he had to find a place to hole up.

The dead were plentiful.

A maintenance worker, gutted from stem to stern.

A fabrications tech, chest hoved in, neck sliced, lying in a lake of blood.

He recognized former Colonial Marine Fields from Logistics, his head crushed and separated from a body that looked as if the Xenomorphs had had an end-of-the-world rave on top of it. Then, finally, a literal pile of security guards, each owning their own version of death by alien monster.

He set aside the mop, overjoyed he hadn't had to use it, and gathered three pistols and a pulse rifle. The pistols he shoved into his belt and pockets. The rifle he shouldered after checking to see if it was loaded and had power. The ammo counter read 99, which meant the poor schmuck hadn't even had a chance to fire. Must have been surprised either rounding the corner or coming from behind.

Yeah, Bellows was full of shit if he thought that he could retake the station.

Then a thought hit him that made him worry. What if Bellows already knew that and had decided to leave? What if the shuttle was already gone? He glanced back the way he'd come. The shuttle bay was at the far end of the station. He should check first, but the lab was closer, as were his team. He shook his head. He'd have to chance that the shuttle would still be there.

Sliding sideways several more meters, he came to an intersection. He searched left, then right, then jerked his head back. A Xenomorph stood down the corridor, munching on something that looked remarkably like a human heart. The problem was that he had to go that way to get to the lab.

He checked the rifle again, set it to four-round bursts, then eased the barrel around the corner and sighted over the top of the carry handle.

The Xenomorph was no longer there.

Which meant it either went in the other direction, or was…

He pushed the barrel all the way around and saw the Xenomorph coming toward him along the wall. Blood dripped from its left hand where it had gripped the organ. Pink-colored saliva bubbling from its maw.

He aimed and fired at the side of the carapace and grinned as the bullets punched through. But the creature kept coming. He fired twice more, eight explosive-tipped rounds finding their mark in the side of the Xenomorph's head.

It fell to the floor, propped on a knee, but continued toward him, making a hollow sucking sound as it came. He aimed again and it leaped at him.

Cruz was barely able to get back around the corner.

The monster sailed past, hitting the ground and rolling to its feet, already facing him. He put a four-round burst into its chest, creating four neat little acid-dripping holes. The alien went down with a single loud squeal.

He turned and ran. No telling whether or not the sound of the pulse rifle would draw any others. He made it to the door of the lab, which was held open and continually trying to close on the body of a synth whose head was missing. He pushed the synth out of the way with a boot, then slid inside as the door closed. He breathed a little easier, but only a little. He still didn't know if there were any creatures left in the lab.

Which was trashed.

He went to the mainframe, grabbed the backup drive, and slid it into his pocket. Then he switched the rifle to full auto. If he encountered something in the lab, he wouldn't have the luxury of picking it off from a distance. It would be full-on close quarters combat, and he'd need to overwhelm a Xenomorph with the sound and fury of an M41A pulse rifle on full automatic.

Lucky for him, there was no need. The lab was clear. Even Leon-895 was gone. Or at least, he thought it was.

Setting aside the rifle, he grabbed two things. The first was the prototype acid-resistant body armor, which he put on. The helmet was a little tight around his large hair, but with a little shoving he got it to fit. Based on an M4X body armor frame, the acid-resistant polymer coating was an upgrade to the limited acid-resistance of the old M3 vest. The armor provided full body protection with sleeves, gloves, and a full-face helmet capable of withstanding light velocity rounds. The armor was augmented with a complete body frame to help with balance when the wearer was struck by tremendous force.

The second thing he grabbed was the flamethrower, or M-240 Incinerator Unit, comprised of a large capacity napthal backpack tank and attached firing nozzle. It felt heavy, and he had to adjust the shoulder webbing to allow the tank to sit higher on his shoulders.

Now he felt better prepared.

Grabbing the pulse rifle from where he'd left it, he slung it over his shoulder. He'd use the Bake-A-Flake for now, trying for wet shots at first for distance, and flamers for anything close in. He exited the lab, taking one last look at the place he'd called home for three years, a place he'd been put in charge of, now destroyed because of events that were beyond his control.

There was a noise from the way he'd just come. He couldn't place it for a moment, but then it all came together. Singing.

Someone was singing.

He strode down the center of the corridor, stepping over and around the occasional body or piece of one until he saw the Xenomorph he'd shot. Inexplicably, Étienne was rubbing himself against the ruined torpedo-shaped carapace.

"*Frère Jacques, Frère Jacques. Dormez vous? Dormez vous? Sonnez les matines. Sonnez les matines. Din din don. Din din don.*"

Cruz approached. "Étienne? What are you doing?" The man kept singing and rubbing himself against the alien skin. Cruz couldn't fathom what the man was doing, unless...

Pheromones.

"Étienne? *Ça va?*" Cruz asked. "What's going on?"

"*Mon ami*, isn't this wonderful?" *Étienne* grinned from ear to ear as he climbed to his feet. "I am invisible to them. I can walk through them. I can move past them. They do not see me."

Had it really worked? He'd have to see it to believe it. To all appearances, it looked as if the Frenchman had experienced a break with reality.

"Étienne, come with me. I'm going to get everyone out."

The scientist shook his head. "I am not done yet with my field study. I need more data."

"You have enough data," Cruz said. "This is too dangerous."

Étienne grinned again. "Not for me." He made a shooing motion with his hands. "Now, you go. I am busy. I will catch up to you." Then he turned and walked down the corridor, singing the old children's song about Brother Jack. Over and over. Crazy like a scientist holding a hypothesis in a death grip...

Cruz stared for a long moment, then turned and headed back, past the lab and toward their rooms. Twice he spied a Xenomorph, but they were all moving the other way. Once he saw something totally unexpected that looked for all the world like a person with giant spider legs, but by the time he'd shaken his head and closed and opened his eyes, it was gone.

Reaching the corridor with all the scientists' rooms, he went to Kash's door first, but then moved on when he heard a loud voice coming from Hoenikker's room.

That's not smart.

"There ain't no napping during Armageddon," the voice said, somehow sounding similar to Cruz's. Smiling, he banged on the door.

He could only imagine what they were wondering inside.

When they didn't answer, he banged again.

"Who—who is it?" Hoenikker said.

"It's Cruz. Open up."

The door opened and Cruz pushed his way inside. When the door closed behind him, he turned to stare at Hoenikker, well aware of what he looked like in the power armor and with the flamethrower.

"Now, what's this about Armageddon and napping?"

39

Hoenikker about peed his pants. Cruz looked more like a battle robot than a scientist.

"How'd you get through?"

Cruz began removing his gear and putting it on the desk. "The corridors are mostly clear. I don't know where the Xenomorphs have gotten off to, but I did see a few. I also saw something else."

"That would be Fairbanks," Kash said. "I posit he was somehow exposed to the pathogen."

Cruz frowned. "That's not advised."

"No." She shook her head. "Not at all. What are you doing here?" she asked, then added hurriedly, "Not that I'm complaining."

"I came to save you."

"Me?" Hoenikker asked. "Us?"

Cruz placed his large hands on Hoenikker's shoulders. "I might not like you at times, Timmy, but you're one of us. You're on my team, and I need to take care of you."

The gesture incited the warmth of belonging combined with the smarting of not being liked. But then, Hoenikker never really cared about being liked anyway. Science wasn't about liking things. Liking things was about emotion. Still, he'd prefer to be liked than not, at least by his coworkers.

"Thank you?" he said, the words sounding more like a question.

"What's the plan?" Kash asked.

"We'll need to make a beeline to the shuttle bay." Cruz pulled out three pistols and laid them on the table, then sat in the chair. "Assuming it's still there. But Étienne is a problem."

"Last time we saw him, he was singing French and heading down the corridor in the opposite direction," Hoenikker said. He eyed the chair Cruz had taken and sat on the edge of the bed instead.

Cruz nodded. "He's still doing that. He was also rubbing himself against a dead Xenomorph. Know anything about that?"

"During the chaos, he poured a beaker of pheromone over his head and lathered himself up," Hoenikker said.

"And did it work?"

"Yes," Kash said. "We watched as a Xenomorph approached him, and then moved on."

"Fascinating." Cruz scratched the side of his head. "If only we'd had more time to study."

"The containment rooms weren't solid enough to hold them—" Hoenikker began, but a sharp shake of Cruz's head stopped him from continuing.

"There's never going to be a containment room that will keep them, as long as there's something like Seven. Each of the Xenomorphs is its own boss, determining how or when to fight. They don't coordinate with each other. They don't plan. There's no strategy. Unless they have someone to lead them. In the absence of a queen, it has to be a mutation."

"Do you think that's what they're doing now?" Kash asked. "Organizing?"

Cruz looked critically at both Kash and Hoenikker. "There are things you aren't aware of. For instance, there are a lot more eggs that we have in cryo travel cases."

"More eggs?" Hoenikker asked, eyes widening. "How many?"

"Dozens. Maybe as many as a hundred," Cruz said. "And each egg begets a face-hugger, which begets a chestburster, which begets a full-blown adult Xenomorph killing machine."

"We haven't heard any screams in a while," Hoenikker said. "Do you think..." His eyes widened.

"Go ahead and finish the sentence," Cruz said.

"I was going to say, do you think that they might be collecting people to create Xenomorphs? Do you think Seven is that smart?"

Cruz stared at the floor as he smiled grimly. "Either that, or all the Xenomorphs are dead, and I just can't believe that."

"We have to do something." Kash looked at Cruz in horror. "We can't just let them all—"

"What is it you would have us do?" He grabbed a pistol and tried to shove it into her hand. She wouldn't grab it at first, so he closed her hand around it and let go. "Do you want to go face down a Xenomorph, or a dozen or two dozen, to save the lives of the few remaining humans on the station? Then go ahead. Be my guest." He leaned back in the chair and stared at her down his nose. "But I'll tell you this. You'll die. You'll die horribly, or you'll be an incubator for a Xenomorph."

She stared at him for long grim moment, then carefully laid the pistol on top of the bureau.

"So, your plan is to run? To get to the shuttle then call for help from space?"

"Damn skippy," he said.

"I remember you telling me about the last time you ran. You have the names of your team members tattooed on you, is that right?"

"Careful where you are going."

"Let me just say this," she said. "I don't have enough skin on my body to tattoo the names of everyone we're going to leave behind. So, when we do, can I borrow some of yours?"

Hoenikker stared at Kash, and Cruz for the longest. He didn't know what Kash was talking about, but it hit home. Cruz had gone from red to pale, his frown deepening. For a second he thought the man might strike her.

"What you're saying," Cruz began slowly, "is that our team is bigger than us four. You're saying that all the humans on Pala Station form a team. Is that what you're saying?"

She nodded slowly.

"You're right," he said. "I can't run again. My conscience couldn't survive that. We'll see if we can save them first. We'll do what we can. But if we find out there's nothing we can do—that we'd die trying—then we go back to the original plan. Is that good for you?"

"Damn skippy," she said, reaching for the gun.

Hoenikker wasn't sure what just happened, but it felt like things just went from bad to worse.

"First, we need to go back to the lab, to get our work," she said.

Cruz grinned slightly. "Got it right here," he said, patting his side pocket.

"Then all we need to do is grab a gun and head out. We're certainly not going to save anyone dicking around here," she said. "Hand me that pulse rifle." When he just looked at her, she added, "What? You get the flamethrower *and* the rifle? I don't think so."

"Can you handle one of these?"

"I dated a Colonial Marine once. His idea for a first date was to go out shooting."

"Sounds like a Colonial Marine." He handed it to her.

"What about me? Hoenikker asked.

Cruz raised an eyebrow. "You date a Colonial Marine, too?"

Hoenikker snarfed. "No. I mean, what does that have to do with anything?"

Cruz handed him a pistol. "Point and shoot. Just keep your finger off the trigger until you're ready to fire. Understand?"

Hoenikker accepted the pistol, and the first thing he did was examine it by looking down the barrel.

"Tim. Stop," Kash said. "That's where the bullet comes from."

He looked at her and cocked his head. "Oh. Of course." Then he looked back at the gun and hurriedly turned it away. He should have known better.

Before this week, Hoenikker had never fired a gun. He'd never even held a gun, but he'd seen the popular movies and knew the basics. Hold, aim, point, shoot. It couldn't be brain science. After all, if Colonial Marines could do it, so could he. He practiced aiming down the barrel at his bureau, which he figured was about as wide as a Xenomorph.

"You don't need to squint," Cruz said, standing. He took two quick steps and took the gun away from Hoenikker. "Try it this way." He held the gun with two hands, chest high, arms thrust out in front of him. "If you hold it like this, you will shoot whatever you're facing."

Hoenikker studied the man's grip, then nodded.

Cruz gave him back the pistol.

As best he could, Hoenikker imitated the way Cruz had held the gun. His fingers fought to find a place to rest, but eventually he realized that one hand's fingers fit neatly into the spaces between the other hand's fingers. Yet as he imagined actually using it, butterflies began to crash into the sides of his stomach, bouncing to and fro. He felt sick and light at the same time. He was going to have to shoot something.

Shoot or be dead.

Even if he did manage to shoot a Xenomorph or, God forbid, that monster Fairbanks had become, he might still be killed. After all, his handgun couldn't possibly have the stopping capacity of a rifle or that flamethrower.

"Is everybody ready?" Cruz asked as he began putting his armor back on.

"Does Weyland-Yutani fuck people over?"

Cruz gave Kash a raised eyebrow.

"I used to date a VP at Weyland-Yutani," she muttered. Then looking up, she said, "What? You never dated anyone?"

"Whoa there." He held up his hand. "Not judging." He finished putting on the armor, including the gloves, then used the table to support the backpack tank and bent down and slid into the straps. When he stood, he let out an *oof* before adjusting the straps and the placement of the tank on his back.

He noticed Hoenikker staring at him.

"What? Never seen a man in combat armor before?"

"No. It's just that I feel so underdressed." Hoenikker grinned.

Cruz laughed and patted him on the back. "Funny, Timmy. Very funny."

40

Rawlings wanted nothing more than to drink himself into oblivion. Some nice whiskey to soothe his shattered soul. Maybe just a little bit of go juice to make his jitters dance away. Perhaps a few shots to soothe the savage beast inside of him, screaming to come out.

The bottle on the table in front of him had a devil doing a jig on its artsy label, the artwork reminiscent of a French advertisement. The more he stared at it, the more he could have sworn the devil was staring back at him.

The memory of his right hand being burned away by acid thrashed once again through his head. The pain had been so intense he'd fallen to the ground and rolled to try and get away from it. Then it was gone as the acid seared the nerve endings, the absence of pain a black hole to his soul in the shape of a hand that had loved and hated and created. A bright image of the hand cradling his mother's cheek right before she died.

He reached for the bottle.

The door opened. McGann and Buggy slid inside.

McGann's black hair was tousled like she'd just gotten out of bed. She held a pulse rifle in one hand and a pistol in the other.

Buggy's bald pate was slick with sweat. He had a pistol jammed into a holster, one he'd clearly stolen from the Colonial Marines when he'd been in the service. But then, hadn't they all. Rawlings had weapons he'd made sure to procure before he left the service. He was about to say something to Buggy, but the guy went straight to Rawlings' bottle and grabbed it by the neck.

"Got no time for this shit," he said, shoving it into the trash compacter and pressing the button.

Rawlings' eyes went wide. The finality of the trash mechanism struck him in the gut, and he sat back in his chair. He wanted to bitch. He wanted to complain. But he knew Buggy had done the right thing.

Damn him.

"Come on," Buggy said. "Get your ass up. We need to plan."

"There's too fucking many," Rawlings said. "Did you see what they did to the mess hall?"

"They're organized as fuck," McGann said, pacing back and forth in the small space of the room, talking mostly to herself. "I thought these were like drones. The way they lined up those men and women, and fed them one by one to the face-huggers, it was too much." She stopped and stared. "Who knew they could do that?"

Rawlings had found a place to hide and watch as it happened. The scientists had called the Xenomorph leader Seven. Standing in the middle of the mess hall, Seven had commanded the others to do things he was pretty sure they shouldn't have been able to do. Rawlings had watched at first in fascination and later in terror as the other Xenomorphs first moved the tables and chairs against the wall, then brought out egg after egg. All the while a gaggle of humans was herded into a far corner and guarded. Then, after a time, a Xenomorph would grab a human one by one and force its head to face into the egg until a face-hugger wrapped its tail around the neck and found a home.

The victims were then stacked like cordwood on the other side of the mess hall, which was what eventually sent him to his room for a last and final date with his bottle of Scotch.

"I don't think this is normal," Buggy said.

"We need to get out of here before the juveniles hatch," McGann said, pacing.

"They're already hatching," Rawlings said. "Not in the mess hall, but from somewhere else. I saw them."

"We need to do something," Buggy said.

"What?" Rawlings asked. "What is there to do?"

Buggy smacked Rawlings across the face. "Get the fuck up. You were the one who brought us all together. You were the one who warned us bad shit was coming. Well, bad shit paid us a visit, and it isn't leaving anytime soon. You need to decide whether you want to sit here and feel sorry for yourself, or join us and see if we can't ride this out."

Rawlings snapped his head around and stared at Buggy, then at McGann. The comms tech was right. He needed to get up. He needed to do something. He got to his feet.

"What's the plan?"

"Right now, Security is spread thin," Buggy said. "They have a cluster of security techs around Bellows, and another group of external security techs in the landing bay, pretty much keeping everyone from taking the shuttle and getting the hell off the rock."

"So, we can't escape even if we wanted to," McGann said.

"I have to admit, the shuttle looked like the best choice," Rawlings said. "Without it we really don't have much choice… unless…"

McGann stopped pacing. "Unless what?"

Rawlings wiped the side of his face where he'd been smacked. If Buggy was going to say he was sorry, the moment had passed. Anyway, they were marines. It didn't matter.

"Well, there's one possibility, and for the life of me, I don't know why Bellows didn't take it."

"If you have an idea, then share," Buggy said.

"What about Thompson's hunting lodge?" Rawlings asked.

"Hunting lodge?" Buggy asked.

McGann wrinkled her eyebrows. "Yeah, what lodge?"

Rawlings nodded. "I thought you'd know, Buggy. After all, they had major comms set up in there—or at least, that's what I read on the installment order."

"I have no idea what you're talking about."

"Well, unless it's a lie—I've never actually seen the place— Thompson wanted a place to stay outside of station so he could spend more time hunting. He had a lodge built. One of the reasons we were so short on tungsten. I'm not sure where, but in addition to the communications array, I'd imagine it has everything we'd need to survive. So all we'd have to do is find it, get there, and lock the fucking door until help comes."

Buggy shrugged. "Sounds like a plan to me."

McGann nodded. "Who do we ask where it's at?"

Rawlings shook his head. "We *don't* ask. If we start spreading the word that there might be a safe place outside of the station, we'll be lucky if there isn't a riot. We don't know about the food and water stores in the lodge. I'm assuming it'll have enough for the three of us. Four, if we can find Cruz, but that's it. No more."

"Then how do we find out where it is?" Buggy asked.

"That's a good question," Rawlings said.

McGann scratched her head. "If it's getting power, then Engineering would have electrical schematics, showing where it attaches to the main power grid."

Rawlings nodded. "That's a great start." He grabbed his own pulse rifle from where it leaned against the wall. "Then all we have to do is make our hundred-meter dash to freedom." He held his rifle at the ready. "Who's first?"

"It was my idea." McGann headed toward the door. "I'll go first."

"Then lead the way," Rawlings said, almost happy he hadn't drunk his courage, like he'd planned.

He, McGann, and Buggy posted at the door in that order. They'd done this a thousand times, although never with each other, but that didn't matter. Every Colonial Marine did it the same way. There was only one technique to conduct CQB, and they'd all learned it in the same bloody crucible.

Each of them held a pulse rifle at the ready, trigger fingers disciplined to stay off the trigger until needed, lest they shoot each other in the back. McGann palmed the door open and they moved like a three-coiled snake through the corridor, hugging the right side. Dead body to the left. Pieces of a dead body to the right. Rawlings' universe was sixty degrees of nothing.

Until there was something.

The Xenomorph couldn't have been five feet tall—a juvenile by all accounts. It snapped at him and twitched its tail as it exited a room, almost oblivious to their presence. Rawlings opened fire, giving it seventeen free automatic bullets, more than half of them finding a home in its chest, a spray of blood and acid in their wake.

It died and they continued to move, three becoming one, muscle memory taking them over. Rawlings felt the fear of the unknown, the fear that they might all die, but he also felt the comfort he'd known only as a Colonial Marine. They'd had the same training, the same experiences, the same shit-cloaking tear-shedding training, each of them emerging better than when they'd begun. Their civilian skins forever shed, to be replaced by the pride and capacity of a Colonial Marine.

McGann cornered into a corridor and opened fire.

Buggy fired from behind.

For now, Rawlings didn't need to fire. He had no targets. His sector was clear.

41

Cruz liked the hug of the armor against his skin. It made him feel invincible, even though he knew he wasn't. He held the pulse rifle ready. Hoenikker and Kash huddled behind him, hiding behind his size.

They'd come to a place in the corridor where they couldn't go any farther. Furniture had been piled in the middle from floor to ceiling to block all traffic, whether alien or human. A few rifle barrels sprouted out of the available openings, hints of movements behind them.

"Let us pass," he said to no one in particular.

"Where'd you get the armor?" a voice responded.

"Stay where you are," another voice said.

"The armor is mine," Cruz said. "What the hell is going on here? We need to talk to Station Commander Bellows."

"He's not talking," the second voice said.

"Who am I talking to?" Cruz asked, deepening his voice like a Colonial Marine non-commissioned officer would to a misbehaving private.

A pause. "Security Tech Francis. Security Tech Hardon is with me."

"Francis. What's the deal with the station commander? Why won't he speak with us?"

There was another pause, the sound of whispering.

"He's locked up in his suite with most of the external security personnel."

"Jesus. What's he doing there? Hiding beneath his bed? I have information I need to give him."

"He won't listen," Francis said. "He's not listening to anyone."

"How much you take for your armor?" Hardon asked.

"Not for sale," Cruz said flatly. Then he added, "Try and take it, and I'll make you wish you were facing a roomful of bugs."

"Easy, big fella," Francis said. "It was just a simple question."

"Where's the rest of Security?" Cruz asked. "Why aren't they clearing the corridors?"

"That's beyond my paygrade," Francis said. "I was just told to guard this point."

Fucking paygrades. Being an enlisted soldier, or a security technician, was just like being a mushroom. You were kept in the dark and fed shit. Cruz didn't respond to Mr. Paygrade. Instead, he backed away and around the corner, keeping Hoenikker and Kash protected. When they were safe, he found a supply room and ushered them inside. Once the door was closed, he removed his helmet and placed it on a shelf near some floor cleaner.

Kash lowered her pistol.

Hoenikker did the same with his, holding it uneasily in two hands.

"Things are worse than I expected," Cruz said. "We might have had a chance if it wasn't for the commander."

"What do you mean?" Hoenikker asked.

"If we could do a sweep of the corridors, we could create safe zones. The problem, though, is that we have islands of efficiency. The commander has turtled up in his suite and decided to wait out the infiltration. Same thing happening in the shuttle bay. Security locked it down and are keeping us away from the one way off the rock." Seeing the look of surprise in their eyes, he said, "There are things you don't know—things I was briefed about after Mansfield became fertilizer, and I was promoted. We're worse off than you think we are, especially now that the security staff have been OPCON'd directly to the commander."

"OPCON'd?" Kash asked.

"Sorry," Cruz said. "Operational controlled. Yeah. This means he's either taken over the role of security chief, or the security chief is dead. The commander could do his job and we could rid ourselves of the Xenomorphs, or at least keep them locked in the mess hall."

"Wait?" Hoenikker asked. "What's going on in the mess hall?"

"Seven is what's going on." Cruz shook his head. "They've turned the mess hall into a Xenomorph factory."

"What?" Kash's mouth dropped open. She glanced warily at Hoenikker.

"Here," he pulled out his personal vid display from where he had it secured under his armor. "I patched it into the security cams. Just take a look how organized the Xenomorphs are. It's going to blow your fucking mind." He handed it to Hoenikker.

The screen clicked on. The Xenos were still at it. Only a few humans remained in one corner of the mess hall, kept there by a twitchy adult alien that snapped and drooled at them every few seconds. They cowered, hugging each other, and even though the display had no sound, it was obvious they were crying and begging the universe to save them.

Even as they watched, a Xenomorph held a red-haired young man over an Ovomorph, its wide-clawed hand on the back of his head, locking it in place. They watched in horror as the Ovomorph opened like the petals of a terrible flower, then the snap and twist as a face-hugger launched out of it, wrapping its tail around the man's neck, its claws grasping the man's head for purchase.

"Jesus," Hoenikker said, jerking back. "This is terrible." Then he leaned back in. "How do you think it's communicating?" he asked, turning to Kash.

"I don't even care," Kash said. "We have to stop it." She turned to Cruz, her eyes pleading. "We have to stop it. Can we go stop it, now?" Her lips tightened and trembled as she spoke.

"What's to stop? Look at the others, stacked over there like logs. They've been at this for hours. It's as if Seven and the other Xenomorphs knew where the other eggs were—but that was a well-kept secret." Cruz shook his head. "Best we can do is lock the doors to the mess hall, and keep them trapped inside."

"And then what?" Hoenikker asked. "Then what do we do?"

"We need to hook up with Rawlings and the others. There's several of us Colonial Marines who planned for something like this. I have an algorithm running that will let me know when they show up on one of the security cameras."

A subdued *ding* came from his vid screen. He grabbed it from Hoenikker, punched up a different view.

"Just as I said." He saw two men and a woman moving down the corridor, then into Engineering. The last one in line turned to check the team's six, revealing the face of Buggy. Cruz turned to the others and grinned. "We're heading to Engineering."

Pulling up a schematic of the station, he found that there were two routes they could follow. One would take them near the mess hall, though, and he wasn't sure he wanted to get that close to the breeding ground. He glanced at Hoenikker and Kash. No, not with two civilians.

"Alright, you two. Stay on my six. We're going to join the others, and we're going to be moving fast, so keep up." Cruz slid the vid display back under his armor.

The other two scientists stared at him, terrified.

"Nod if you understand," he said.

They both nodded.

Hoenikker licked his lips.

Cruz put his helmet back on and checked the ammo counter on his rifle. All was good. He palmed the door open, looked left, then right, then left again. After a moment, he turned right and took off at a small jog. The body armor was heavy, but he'd run in much worse conditions. He could be running outside. At night. In the mud and rain. Enemies firing at him. This was nothing more than a jog down the—

He ran full tilt into an adult Xenomorph.

Before he could bring up his rifle, the beast turned to him and shot forth its multiple jaws, spraying him with acid and knocking him to the ground. The armor bore the brunt of the acid. He tried to scramble to his feet but the Xenomorph whipped around, the barb on its tail catching him in the side and throwing him into the wall. He lost his grip on the rifle, which twisted out of his hand.

The Xeno turned to face the scientists.

Both backed away, pistols aiming at the floor.

"Shoot the damn thing!" Cruz bellowed.

The Xenomorph took three quick steps toward them and began to open its mouth.

"*I said shoot!*"

They raised their pistols so slowly it was like they were moving through water. Cruz knew right then they were going to die. First the other scientists and then him, because like a raw recruit he'd lost control of his rifle. *Fucking damn it all to hell.* He twisted into a sitting position and reached for his rifle. It was his only chance.

Someone screamed.

Then the sound of two pistols opening fire.

He spun to the sound. The scientists had finally done it, sending dozens of rounds into the face and chest of the Xenomorph. Its body jerked and twisted with the impacts. Acid and spittle flew from its face, landing on the walls and ceiling. Where it hit, the surfaces sizzled. Finally, it fell backward, its blood blistering the ground beneath it. Had the floor been made of metal or something less solid than concrete, he was sure it would have melted through. Even so, pockmarks appeared.

Cruz kicked out to get away from the spreading pool of acid, then managed to get to his feet. He checked the armor, which didn't seem worse for wear, snatched his rifle off the floor, and nodded at the pair.

They both stood wide-eyed and open-mouthed, staring at the dead Xenomorph. Cruz approved. They might be good for something after all. Chances were they were going to get killed pretty quickly if the shit hit the fan, but at least they'd been blooded, and knew the working end of a pistol.

"Good job." He turned and stepped around the dead predator. "Okay. Let's go." He started his jog again, this time slowing down a little at blind corners. About a minute and a half later they were at the door to Engineering.

He palmed open the door.

Three hard-looking persons turned to greet him with their pulse rifles.

Then they all grinned.

"Howdy, Marine," Buggy said.

Cruz mock saluted, made sure the two scientists were in the room, then palmed the door shut.

Rawlings pointed to the scorch mark on the chest plate of the body armor.

"Ran into a little trouble, did you?"

"Score one for the scientists. Thing took me by surprise." He cranked his neck. "Damn those things are strong." He noticed that McGann was studying a particularly confusing schematic. "What is it you all are doing?"

"We need some place to turtle," Rawlings said. "Shit's going to get a lot worse before it gets better. Not to mention we can't even get to the food storage now."

"Wait until those assholes in the commander's suite run out of food. They'll start eating themselves, sooner or later." When Rawlings shot him a questioning look, Cruz related what he knew, and the conversation he'd had with Security Tech Francis.

"So where's the place you think is such a good candidate to hide?" Cruz asked.

"Thompson's hunting lodge. I heard there was one off station," Rawlings said. "And 'off station' means we get away from the Xenomorphs. Even better"—his face brightened—"it's supposed to be fully stocked."

"If I remember right, there were enough dangerous things outside of the station to keep us on lockdown," Kash said, joining in.

"That was before the Xenomorphs," Cruz said. "Plus, if it belonged to Thompson, then it probably has a lot of firearms. Something tells me we don't have enough."

Rawlings nodded, pointing at his scorched armor.

"Something tells me you're right."

42

Hoenikker felt the shaky aftereffects of the adrenaline rush. He'd never fired a pistol point blank into an alien that could kill him in the blink of an eye. At first, he'd frozen and couldn't move. A voice screamed from the inside, telling him to lift the pistol, but the only muscles working had been his leg muscles, propelling him backward.

Then his scream became real and his arms unlocked. He could still hear the sounds of gunfire and see the rounds impacting the Xenomorph's head and chest. The way it stiffened and fell back with each impact.

Realizing he was still holding the pistol in a shaky hand, he set it down on one of the desks. He wiped sweat from his forehead, bewildered that a body could produce so much, and glanced over at Kash. She seemed to be processing the same emotions, but was taking it better. Still, he could tell by the slight tremble in her shoulders that her adrenaline was bleeding away as well.

And Cruz? He seemed to be impervious. Daunting in his power armor, his dark skin, sharp features, cutting the perfect image of a Colonial Marine. He stood with one leg jutting out, one hand on his hip as he spoke confidently with the others. Moving from the maintenance closet to Engineering had been a walk in the park for him.

Hoenikker straightened his spine. If he was going to survive this, he needed to emulate the man as much as possible. Cruz noticed his movement, glanced at him, nodded, then returned to his conversation.

Evidently former Deputy Station Chief Thompson, prior to being unceremoniously removed from his position by Bellows, had used station assets to build his own hunting lodge about two kilometers from the station. His own outpost where he could play safari. If what the others said was right, they'd have enough food and weapons to last until a company of active Colonial Marines could come.

"Does anyone know if there's been an SOS?" McGann asked.

Buggy, who was a comms tech, responded, "Here at Pala, we don't have the capability for deep space transmissions. We sent SOSs to the *San Lorenzo*, but we have no idea if their radio systems are set to auto-forward, or if there's a comms tech doing the work. We can't raise anyone, and have no way to go find out unless we take the shuttle up."

"The shuttle is out of the question," Cruz said, "for now."

"That means no one knows what's happening here," Hoenikker said.

Buggy nodded. "That's exactly what it means."

"All the more reason to get out of here," Cruz said. "Let Security fight the Xenomorphs until either one side or both are dead." He pulled out his personal vid and groaned. The screen had cracked in two places. He tossed it onto a desk. "It's all about water and food now. Napoleon knew that an army traveled on its stomach. It's why he almost conquered all of Europe. He didn't have to master warfare— he only had to master logistics. The two groups that are holed up are probably experiencing hunger pains. Infighting is going to follow."

Kash began to rummage through the desks and the lockers.

"What are you doing, ma'am?" McGann asked.

"I don't know of a single office that doesn't have munchies. Snacks. We should gather up what we can, when we can—don't you think?"

Hoenikker agreed. He began on the other side of the room. Let the marines make their plan. At least he could be of use.

Before long they had several bags of chips, some crackers made from some sort of seaweed, and nuts. Then Hoenikker hit the motherlode in Engineering Chief Dudman's office. Dudman had a minifridge that contained a bunch of food ranging from fruit to some sort of mystery meat in gravy. Hoenikker left it in the fridge, but grabbed a pad and a pen and made a note of what was there. Then he returned to Kash.

"Looks like with the six of us, we have about two days of food," she said. "Three if we ration even more."

"That gives us enough time to get to the lodge," Hoenikker said.

"About that..." McGann began.

Hoenikker recognized the tone, and worry immediately set in. Everyone turned toward the engineering tech.

"Might as well tell us," Cruz said, a frown already deepening in his face. "News is like a dead body. It don't smell better with age."

"As it turns out, there's... one of three ways to leave the station," McGann began slowly. "The first is the shuttle bay. There's an exit by the venting system."

"That's out," Cruz said. "Unless we can talk our way in."

"Then there's the mess hall. Backside of the kitchen is an exit door."

Hoenikker shuddered. That was the last place he wanted to go, no matter how intriguing their interaction was from a scientific point of view.

"Might as well lay down and get face-hugged," Cruz said.

Everyone nodded.

Buggy shuddered.

"Then there's the command suites. They have an emergency hatch that allows for them to escape." She pointed at the screen of the desktop vid. "Good news is that it hasn't been activated, and it does have power."

"So you think the commander doesn't know about the lodge?" Hoenikker asked.

"When he kicked the commander and deputy commander off station," Buggy said, "I doubt there was an exit interview. External security would know about it, because they were the ones who guarded

Thompson while he was outside. They must not have told Bellows, for some reason known only to them."

Everyone stared. The best guess Hoenikker could make was that the security personnel wanted the lodge for themselves.

"So no matter which way we go, we have to fight," he said, putting words to what they all must be thinking. "Either the security forces or the Xenomorphs. Am I getting this right?"

"Afraid so." McGann nodded.

Cruz leaned over and stared at the screen. He tapped it thoughtfully. Hoenikker wondered what was going through the man's mind. His critical thinking skills might be sharper even than his sadistic tendencies.

Cruz pointed. "Can we shut down power to various doors from here?"

"Sure," McGann said. "But what good will that do?"

"Well, first thing we can do is secure the doors to the mess hall. That will keep Seven and his merry band of killers in there for as long as it takes him to figure a way out. Hopefully, that will be long enough for us to blow this popsicle stand."

"And second?" Buggy asked. "You said first, so I figure there must be a second."

"Second, we lock down *all* the doors. We're in Engineering. We have special access. Perhaps we'll get to the point where we have something we can trade for safe passage out of here." He turned to Kash. "How much food did you say we had?"

"Two days. Three days max."

"So, we have seventy-two hours to figure this out. They should be good and hungry by then." He tapped the screen. "My guess is that the guards in the shuttle bay will blink first. The command suites probably have decent food storage. But the shuttle bay and loading docks? Naw. They're going to get hungry."

Hoenikker looked askance at the food on the table, and thought about the stuff in the fridge. He'd never had to ration before—never been told there wasn't enough food to eat. He glanced at the other men, all bigger than him. Surely they'd need more calories than he would to survive. They'd have to eat more food.

What would happen in three days if they couldn't negotiate their way out? Things were going to get worse. Would they actually draw straws, like he'd read about in old books, or would they just kick him out the door? Certainly, he'd be first. After all, what good was he in a firefight, compared to them?

Times like these, one's ability to survive trumped any other academic or God-given skill.

Cruz noticed him looking at the door.

"I know what you're thinking," he said. "It's not going to come to that."

Hoenikker stared at him, blinked several times, and wondered how the man could possibly know what he was thinking, unless he was thinking the same thing—only from his own point of view.

That wasn't reassuring.

"We're going to get this handled," Cruz said. "First step is to remove power from every door. That'll keep them from being able to rewire. Then we sit back for a day and let them freak out. At the end of that day, we get on comms and let them know what their choices are."

Kash shook her head. "The longer we wait, the more time the Xenomorphs have to breed. Right now we're facing seven or eight. Soon there will be several dozen."

"Well, let's hope that's the station's problem. We'll let the security forces sort it out if and when the Xenomorphs are able to leave the mess hall," Cruz said.

"I'd say *when*, not *if*," Kash replied.

"I'm afraid that you're right."

"Say? Anyone seen Étienne lately?" Hoenikker asked.

Everyone looked at him.

"I can't see how he survived," Cruz said. "I guess he went out like he wanted to."

Hoenikker thought of the man singing, walking down the hall past the Xenomorphs. He couldn't help but smile at the sheer lunacy of it, and hoped Étienne *had* found a way to survive.

43

The first day seemed longer than normal.

It was nothing to remove power from all the doors. Rawlings imagined that for the first few hours, people were trying to figure out why the lights and the air systems were still running, yet the doors wouldn't open.

By midday, someone tried to hack into the engineering systems. Buggy stopped them in their tracks and sent several Trojans into the computers, shutting them down. He was gleeful in his ability to outthink and outmaneuver them.

Rawlings was happy for him.

Hell, he was happy for all his new best friends. Cruz had become a scientist. McGann had become an engineer. Buggy had become a communications specialist. A lot of people never found a life after the marines. Far too many couldn't take civilian life, ending up on a penal planet or eating the barrel of their own gun. To see some vets achieve success was a testament to their drive and desire.

Which also made him sad. All their efforts, all their training, would be ruined because some of them weren't going to survive. It was the law of combat. You go in thinking you'll probably die, and come back happy to be alive. Those who go in not wanting to die made mistakes or were too slow to react.

His eyes went to the two scientists—Hoenikker and Kash. *They'd* hesitate. They'd go in wanting to live, and die for it. But him and the others... sure, they might die, but they had a better chance of living because they accepted the possibility of death. They were ready for it. Hell, they'd gladly do it, if it meant they could save their fellow marines.

By that afternoon, Rawlings was bored to tears. More importantly, he wanted a drink. He began pacing around, eyeing the desks and the layout, wondering where the best place would be to hide a bottle. Kash had been right that every office had snacks hidden in desks— and every office had liquor hidden somewhere.

The office was divided into four rooms: the bullpen, the project room, the water closet, and a private office. All three desks used by the engineering techs were in the bullpen, which was the large space next to the exit. The desks faced each other, so if anyone was to drink, the others would see him. So then where?

McGann lounged at her desk, looking like she was about to fall asleep, head back, eyes almost closed. Behind her was a storage area with shelves and cabinets. Rawlings went through each one of these, careful not to make much noise. He searched the best he could, but didn't find what he was looking for—just cables and couplers and everything in between. He even checked behind each one for spaces in the wall.

Nothing.

How could an office not have any booze?

He turned around, frowning and a little bewildered. McGann was awake and staring at him.

"How long?" Rawlings asked.

"Long enough," she said. "Do you really think this is a good time?"

So, she knew.

"Is there ever a bad time?" Rawlings countered.

"When we're about to go into battle," McGann replied. "I'd call that a bad time."

"But we're not." Rawlings grinned. "We have more than two whole days. A few nips now, and by the time we need to be sober, we will be."

McGann gave him a long look, then shrugged.

"Fuck it. You're your own man. You want to get shit-faced, then get shit-faced. Bottle's in the chief's office, bottom right drawer of his desk."

Rawlings winked. "Thanks, pal."

He passed by the project room. Cruz had laid his armor, weapons, and flamethrower on the table and was asleep beneath it. Kash had pulled two chairs together and was curled up on them, her elfin arms and legs drawn into themselves. He walked softly past them and into the office.

Hoenikker was fast asleep on the couch that sat in front of the desk, his body turned facing the cushions. He'd taken off his shoes and placed them in front of the couch. His knees were drawn up and his right hand rested on the side of his face.

The office was spartan. A map of the facility was hung on the wall behind the couch. Open shelving housed several dozen actual books, each of them antiques. Their topics ranged from astrophysics to non-Euclidian topology. Wedged within them was a book of poetry. Leaning in to get a closer look at the name, Rawlings noted that it was by Walt Whitman.

That name was familiar, though all he knew of the man was that he lived in the 1800s back on Earth, and wrote the poem 'Oh Captain, My Captain', which he'd heard spoken at too many Colonial Marine funerals. How did the end go?

> *My Captain does not answer, his lips are pale and still,*
> *My father does not feel my arm, he has no pulse nor will,*
> *The ship is anchor'd safe and sound, its voyage closed and done,*
> *From fearful trip the victor ship comes in with object won;*
> *Exult O shores, and ring O bells!*
> *But I with mournful tread,*
> *Walk the deck my Captain lies,*
> *Fallen cold and dead.*

It always had been a miserable damned poem.

He turned, gingerly pulled out the chair, and sat in it, noting the softness. *Must be good to be a section chief.* Then he reached down and pulled open the bottom right drawer. Sure enough, a liter flask lay there. He plucked it from the drawer, opened the lid, and sniffed. His head jerked back. It might as well have been paint thinner. Jesus, but it smelled strong.

Taking a tentative sip, he sat back as a nuclear holocaust occurred in his mouth before searing his throat and then slamming into his stomach.

McGann stood at the door, grinning.

"What the hell is this stuff?" he asked, whispering.

"Shine," McGann whispered back. "Dudman bought it from a guy in Fabrications."

"What percentage alcohol is this?"

"All of it," McGann said. She strode over and took the flask. She took a swig and her face turned instantly red. "Jesus. How can anyone drink this?"

"Practice," Rawlings said, accepting it back. He took a sip and then set the flask on the desk. "Something tells me this is our last hoorah." He touched his mechanical hand and flashed back to when he'd lost it.

"Probably." McGann nodded. "But then I've had a good run. I've had my share of women. I've been places I'd never dreamed of—done things I'd never thought possible."

"I've had my share of women, too," Rawlings said, eyeing the one in front of him.

McGann sneered. "I bet I've had more than you."

Rawlings shook his head. "I won't even touch that bet." He paused a moment, then asked, "Don't you want to do just one more thing?"

"Like what? I mean, sure, it's nice to be alive, to taste something wonderful, watch a vid that stimulates. But haven't we really done everything?"

Rawlings considered. He had done more than he'd ever thought. He'd shot, fucked, and fought across a galaxy that seemed to be getting larger by the day. Maybe he should treat this as sport. Maybe killing the Xenomorphs should be a final game, one in which the loser *really* loses.

At least that way he'd be motivated.

McGann was turning away and about to leave when Rawlings spoke. "I bet I nail three of them before I bite it."

McGann turned, grinning like a fool. "Three, you say? Then I'll bag four."

"Adolescents count as much as an adult," Rawlings added, swigging.

"Adolescents count as much as adults." McGann nodded. "Sure."

"We get to call our shots, too," Rawlings said.

"Well, if one of the creatures is a danger to all of us, then we're all opening fire." McGann nodded again. "But I get your point. If we see one at distance and you want to call it, you just have to say it ahead of me."

"What about Buggy? Think we should get him involved?"

McGann shook her head. "He's way too serious for all of this. We'll just make sure he has our sixes."

Rawlings took one last drag, noting there was still plenty more for later, and leaned back. Yeah. Shooting Xenomorphs at the end of the world. This was going to be hella fun. He imagined killing Xenomorphs until the flask was empty. Then he turned around and puked in a waste basket. He wasn't feeling very well.

Hoenikker was sitting up when he turned around.

"Was that you?" the scientist asked.

"Whuth? You nether saw pipple puthing?" Rawlings vaguely realized that he couldn't move his tongue.

Hoenikker stood suddenly, covering his nose and mouth with a forearm.

"Oh. The smell." He hurried out the door.

"Gud riddith," Rawlings said, then he staggered toward the couch. He had passed out before he even hit it.

44

Cruz keyed the audio. Thirty-six hours had passed since he'd put everyone on lockdown, so he imagined they were eager to get out. He glanced at those around him, then began.

"People of Pala Station," he said. "By now you've figured out that you can't move from where you are. All doors have been locked. There are no drop ceilings. There are no secret passageways. What you see is what you get. Many of you might be hungry and or thirsty, as well.

"The problem is that Security have hunkered down, and aren't doing what Security are supposed to do," he continued, "which is clear the station. I will open the doors for the next hour, and observe through the security cameras, to see if Security are doing their job. If not, then I will close the doors again."

He glanced at McGann. She keyed in a command.

"The doors are open."

He sat back. "Now let's see the chaos."

They had five vids running—outside the command suites, outside the shuttle bay, outside the mess hall, outside Engineering, and inside the mess hall. They counted three distinct Xenomorphs roaming the corridors. The rest were in the mess hall pretending to be wet nurses for the humans who had woken after being face-hugged.

Security techs with pulse rifles poured out of the shuttle bay, searching this way and that for targets. They looked scared and confused. Their hair and uniforms were in disarray. Much different to the security techs coming out of the command suite, who looked professional and military. They moved with purpose and allowed Cruz and his companions to view them for exactly five seconds before someone shot out the camera.

Cruz hadn't unlocked the mess hall doors. He wasn't *that* crazy. But he wanted to see what the security forces would do. Word would spread, and shortly everyone would know about the activities in the mess hall. So, it was either turtle up in each end of the station, or become proactive and kill the monsters in the corridors. In addition to the three Xenomorphs outside of the mess hall, there was the missing Leon-895, as well as the Fairbanks monster. Neither of them had been seen or heard from.

"Someone's trying to access the escape hatch in the command suite," McGann said.

Cruz nodded. As he'd suspected. He'd turned on power, but had locked the door. He just wanted to see what they had planned.

"Remove power," he said.

McGann did as she was told.

Hoenikker and Kash hovered over the vid display showing the inside of the mess hall, murmuring to each other. It was all they could really do. Cruz might have liked to have joined them, but he'd partitioned that part of his brain and was now firmly once again a Colonial Marine. He had to be, or else they would all die.

Buggy was furiously warding off attacks on the comms servers. They were becoming more and more sophisticated, but he seemed to be up to the task.

And Rawlings?

He was passed out on the couch in the chief's office. The old warrant officer had needed to blow off steam. Two good things came from his bender. The man had been able to voice his issues so he could get right in the head, and they were now officially out of alcohol.

The others had argued with him about whether or not he should have let them out. They were afraid everyone would make a beeline for Engineering and try to take them out. But Cruz needed Security to patrol the corridors and remove the threats. He also knew it was a matter of time before Seven would figure a way out of the mess hall. That Xeno had an agenda, and Cruz hoped he wasn't playing checkers while Seven played three-dimensional chess.

If that was the case, then they were all doomed.

Several security guards from the shuttle bay reached the mess hall. They tried to palm open the doors, but found themselves locked out. Cruz watched as they argued amongst themselves. Then he leaned forward. Either it was a trick of the light, or the wall had moved.

Then the wall moved again.

Or something the same color as the wall. Just as he was about to form the words "Leon-895," it partially materialized and grabbed one of the security guards. The creature took a huge bite from the top of the man's head, and then dropped the body.

One of the remaining security guards turned and fled.

The other fired blindly—once, twice, then turned to run.

He didn't get but ten feet before he was jerked off his feet. The top of his head disappeared, as did his brain, in a shower of blood, bone, and gore. A fleck of gray matter landed on the security camera bubble, creating a blind spot until it dripped off, leaving a wash of red film to see through. Clearly the Leon preferred brain matter over any other body parts.

A security force appeared outside the Engineering section door. He'd anticipated that. Curiously, they didn't shoot out the camera that covered the entryway.

"McGann, want to get suited up?" Cruz suggested. She nodded, ran to the project room, and shrugged on the power armor and the flamethrower.

Several security techs from the command suites were trying to palm the door open. One pried open the control panel and began to work on it. He jerked backward onto the floor as if pulled by a rope, a line of electricity following him from the box. McGann had made it so that the only thing hooked to the panel was the main power line. Although it was genius, it could only work once. The circuitry inside the access box was completely fried, but it would deter others from trying.

Cruz grinned and keyed the microphone. "You're going to have to do better than that," he said, his voice booming throughout the station.

The comms console buzzed.

It was an incoming call, and the ID flashed **COMMAND**. He guessed Bellows was ready for a parlay, and opened the line of communication.

"What the hell are you doing, Dr. Cruz?" Bellows demanded.

"What needs to be done," Cruz responded calmly. "Are you finished hiding in the corner, or are you ready to get Security out so they can do their job?"

"Hiding in a corner?" Bellows blustered. "I'm doing nothing of the sort. I'm conferring with the head of Security to identify the best way to deal with the problem, while you're playing evil overlord and locking down all the doors so we can't get anything done."

"So, you hatched a plan?"

"Of course we hatched a plan. That's our job. To protect the station."

"I noticed the Weyland-Yutani company personnel inside the mess hall weren't part of your plan," Cruz said, a grim note entering his voice. "Had you done something sooner, they might be alive."

Bellows paused. "We took that under consideration. Security felt the situation was untenable."

"You mean you couldn't convince them to put their asses on the line," Cruz said. "Or didn't try." Another pause. This one longer. Cruz wondered if perhaps Security Chief Rodriguez wasn't beside him, listening in.

He decided to press it.

"Are you safe, Station Commander Bellows?" Cruz asked. "Are they holding a gun to your head?"

"No one is holding a gun to anyone's head, Dr. Cruz," Cynthia Rodriguez said, each word tightly enunciated.

"That's good to know," he replied. "Because when help eventually arrives—and it will—you need to make sure you've been acting aboveboard and for the benefit of the station, and not for yourself and your security technicians."

"They'll understand why I did what I did."

"History judges decisions in a far harsher light than the present. You'd better hope so." Then he said, "Commander Bellows?"

"Yes."

"If the Xenomorphs manage to get outside the mess hall, without Security having a plan to keep them in or kill them, all that's going to be left of the rest of us is piles of smoking acid. They're breeding, and soon there will be a lot more of them. Do you really have a plan?'

Silence.

"Bellows?"

Silence.

"Bellows?"

"I think he disconnected," Buggy said.

"Just as I figured." Cruz turned. "Okay, it's time for round two."

"What's that?" Hoenikker asked.

"We turn off the lights."

"How does that help us?" Kash asked.

A few seconds later, the security techs in front of Engineering found themselves in the dark. None of them had thought to bring night-vision devices like the one on the camera in the corridor.

Cruz pointed at the three milling bodies outside their door, now illuminated in green night vision by the cameras. "They've made their points clear. They want what we have. The only way to get that is to kill us."

"But won't they die?" Kash asked. "What about the Xenomorphs?"

The security techs fumbled around for several minutes, then panicked and began to open fire. The terror in their faces was lit by the strobes from their pulse rifles.

Then there were two.

The flash of a whipping tail and fangs.

Then there was one.

Then silence.

As the Xenomorph marched on.

It was truly every man and woman for themselves.

45

Six hours later, Cruz turned the lights back on.

His chin rested on his fist as he stared at the screen. There had to be a reason they hadn't shot out the camera in front of Engineering. If it had been his plan, Cruz would have shot out *every* camera, blinding those who had control over power and the doors. So, what was the reason? What were they planning where they needed to be seen? What subterfuge was in play that he couldn't recognize?

If he didn't figure it out, he might fall victim to it.

Then it happened.

A woman.

She arrived breathlessly at the door, glancing back fearfully, banging on the composite metal as if her life depended on it.

Cruz knew immediately what it was, and was disappointed. It was as if they thought he was stupid. She had to be a Trojan horse. They should have known that he'd know, too. Was that it? Were they counting on him to double-think?

He leaned forward, intrigued.

Twisting the camera around, he checked to see if there was anyone else down the hall. It was empty. Then he hit the control and let her in, the door *snicking* open fast enough that she fell forward.

Three security techs rushed into sight.

He closed the door. They weren't fast enough.

McGann grabbed the newcomer by the back of her neck and pressed a pistol to her head.

"What's your name?"

"Susan," she said breathlessly. Medium build. Mousy brown hair. Brown eyes. A face that had probably been pretty when she was younger, but had fallen victim to middle age. She wore a blue jumpsuit. Interesting. No one on the station wore blue jumpsuits.

She glanced feverishly around the room—or was she taking inventory? Making a map of everything, so she could go back and inform Bellows or Rodriguez or whoever was in charge.

"Last name," McGann asked.

"McCune. Susan McCune. What the hell's going on with the station?"

Cruz raised an eyebrow. "What do you mean?"

"We just arrived on Pala Station. The security techs in the shuttle bay said you have control of the whole facility. They refused to escort us, and something took down my copilot. I never saw it. One moment he was here. The next... nothing."

So, that was their ruse. An unplanned shuttle.

Interesting.

"Buggy, get Rawlings up," Cruz said. "I need him. Meanwhile, McCune, you just sit there."

"No can do," Buggy said. "I need to monitor comms. There are incoming like you wouldn't believe."

Cruz growled. "Will someone wake Rawlings the fuck up?" Kash nodded and stood, then went into the office.

"What's your copilot's name?" Cruz asked.

"Ernest Withers."

"What type of vessel do you hail from?"

"Merchant ship. We received an emergency hail from the *San Lorenzo*."

"We did get the word out!" Hoenikker's normally dour face lit with excitement. Cruz shot him a look.

"Are you Weyland-Yutani?" he asked McCune.

"Private contractor. We've worked with Weyland-Yutani before, but not currently."

"What's your cargo?"

"Ore. Primarily magnesium and cesium."

"What's your compliment?"

"Sixteen. The others are in cryosleep. Withers and I were awakened when the emergency beacon contacted our ship. Listen, what exactly is going on here? Why the interrogation? I'm just following the rules of open space. If we hear an emergency beacon, it's our duty to investigate."

Rawlings staggered into the bullpen. "My mouth feels like a family of rats took a shit inside, and then smeared it everywhere." He looked like hell. Bloodshot eyes brimmed with liquid atop a bulbous, red-veined nose. His dark skin was the color of old clay.

"Rawlings, I need your full attention," Cruz said.

"Yeah?" He blinked several times and rubbed his hand on the back of his neck. "What is it?"

"Do you recognize this woman?"

Rawlings peered at her through bleary eyes, then shook his head. "Never seen her before."

"So, she's not from the station?"

"Nope. I know everyone. It's my job. She's not from here."

"Can you please explain to me what's going on?" McCune asked.

Cruz held up a hand. "Run her face through biometrics," he said, handing Rawlings a personal vid unit. The reception tech fumbled with it for a moment, then keyed in instructions. He held it up to her and took her picture, then ran it through biometrics.

Everyone looked at one another in the silence, no one really wanting to be the one to break it. The only sound other than breathing was Buggy punching his monitor, his hands moving fast enough that he could have been playing a piano.

Finally, Rawlings shook his head. "No record of her being on the station. No record of her being in Weyland-Yutani. Looks like we have a certified stranger."

"What about her PDT?" McGann asked.

Rawlings shook his head again. "I remotely scanned everyone's in this room. We all have one. She doesn't."

"Does that mean she's really here to help us?" Hoenikker asked.

Now Cruz *really* was intrigued.

"Who were the security techs outside?" he asked, meaning the three who had rushed the door. "Did they bring you here?"

She shook her head. "I don't know what you're talking about."

Either salvation had just appeared at their doorstep, or she was a great actress and somehow had been working on the station like a ghost. Still, it didn't entirely make sense. If there had been a shuttle landing in the bay, then command would have wanted access to both the pilot and the shuttle.

And there wasn't any way to check out her story. He was blind in the bay and in front of the command suites. Then again, he *wasn't* blind, was he? Every door and access point on the station could read a personal data tracker, and everyone on the station had PTDs implanted in their bodies.

"McGann, I think it's okay to lower your pistol," Cruz said, then he turned to the engineer. "Follow me." He and McGann walked into the office, and outlined his idea. McGann nodded, grinned, and confirmed that it was definitely possible. Then she sat down behind the desk.

Cruz called in Buggy, who joined them. They chatted for a moment, and Buggy disappeared into another room. Cruz returned to his seat in the bullpen.

"What do you know about Xenomorphs?" he asked McCune.

Her eyebrows twisted. "Xenowhats?"

"Xenomorphs. Brought to us care of the *San Lorenzo*, which towed a facility that was infested with them. Creatures capable of using a human as a gestational host from which to transition and grow. They enter the human host through the mouth, then burst from the chest, then grow at an alarming rate until they become full-size killing machines." He grinned flatly. "What do you know about them?"

She shook her head, but displayed no emotion. "This is the first I've heard of them," she said evenly.

"The security techs in the shuttle bay didn't warn you about them when they let you into the station?"

"All they said was that there were monsters," she replied. "I thought they were nuts."

"So you and your copilot—"

"Withers."

"Yes, you and your copilot Withers just entered the station, and made a beeline to Engineering rather than the command suites."

"The shuttle bay techs said that the people in charge were in Engineering," she replied. "They gave us directions."

"You came unarmed."

"We're a private ore hauler. We don't have weapons."

"And you've never heard of Xenomorphs."

"That's what I said."

Cruz stood and went over, gesturing to shake her hand. She held hers out automatically as she stood.

"Excellent," Cruz said. "I'm going to let you be on your way, then—I'll provide you with directions to the command suite, and you can talk with them regarding assistance."

"I don't understand," she said. "I was told you are in charge."

"Only the lights and power," Cruz said. "McGann? Are we ready?"

"We're on it."

"Let's hit the lights before she leaves."

"Lights off," McGann said.

"Excellent." He turned to their visitor. "Well, are you ready?"

"It's too dangerous," she murmured.

"I have good news," he lied. "Xenomorphs need light to survive. They hibernate in the dark. Just don't bump into one, and you'll be perfectly fine." Hoenikker stood and was about to say something, but Cruz snapped his fingers to shut him up. Buggy came over with a flashlight. He snapped it on and off in his face.

"This should get you there." He handed it to her. "And hey, thanks for saving our asses. We really appreciate it." Wearing a confused expression, she looked from one to the other, her hand on the flashlight, her thumb turning it on and off absently.

"Will one of you come with me?" she asked, her voice small and breathless.

"Sorry," Cruz said, returning to his seat. "We've got too much work to do. But like I said, you'll be okay. The Xenomorphs hibernate. They're usually against the walls—they do that to keep from falling down. So walk down the middle of the corridors, and you'll be alright."

"I heard there might be other monsters."

"That's not what you said," Cruz replied, adding a curious note to his voice. "You said, 'all they said was that there were monsters.' You never said anything about there being more than one type."

She glanced from one to the other including Hoenikker and Kash, then she frowned, her face going ugly.

"You fucking sonuvabitch."

"Just as I thought." Cruz nodded. "McGann, what do you have?"

"Four of them around the corner."

Cruz got up and went into the project room. He returned thirty seconds later wearing the flamethrower.

"You can't possibly," McCune said, staring wide-eyed at the lick of flame dancing at the end of the barrel.

"Oh, I absolutely can," he replied. "What did you think you would do to us? Have one of us follow you, or find a way to open the door? I knew you were a Trojan the minute I saw you. How you're on the station without us knowing about it is another thing entirely. For now, though, we'll let the station understand we mean business." He adjusted his shoulders and spoke to Hoenikker and Kash. "You two might want to get over there," he said, nodding to where the storage was to the right of the door. "McGann, when you're ready."

The door *snicked* open.

"Here they come," McGann called.

Cruz depressed the actuator just as they came into view. Instantly the four men were consumed at the entrance to Engineering. One managed to get a shot off into the ceiling, but the others became flaming imitations of men, their arms waving, legs dancing, then crumbling as each one of them tried to scream, sucking flame and superheated air into lungs that burned from within.

They never made it inside.

McGann closed the door, leaving only the smoke and the smell of human flesh to remind them of what had occurred. They were still visible on the vid, which showed a smoldering pile of would-be attackers.

"I can't believe you did that," McCune said breathlessly. Cruz turned toward her.

"Don't go getting sanctimonious on me," he snarled. "You would have done the same to us, given the chance." She seemed unable to stop staring at the display.

Cruz left her there, took his flamethrower back to the project room, and set it on the table.

46

"Who *are* you?" Cruz demanded, his face stone cold with purpose.

Hoenikker felt as if he was an outsider looking in. He'd thought they were fighting against the monsters, but as it turned out, they were *all* monsters. The Xenomorphs, the Leons, and the humans. Their capacity for killing could not be underestimated, nor could it be ignored. There was no safe haven here. There was no place to hide. Enemies were all around, some of them fleshed in the bodies of "friends."

"I gave you my name," she said, tight lipped, sweat beading on her brow. She sat in a chair, her hands bound behind her with cable straps.

"Susan McCune, why aren't you on the station rolls?" Rawlings asked.

She turned to him and frowned. "That's above your paygrade, Warrant."

Rawlings grinned at that. "So, you know I was a Colonial Marine, and you know my rank. Good for you."

"Nothing is above *my* paygrade," Cruz said. "Answer the man."

She seemed to consider the question. "Let's just say there are doors you can open, and doors you can't." She paused. "And there are doors you don't even know exist."

"Does that even make sense?" Buggy asked.

She just sneered.

"You know you're going to prison, right?" she said to Cruz. "You killed them in cold blood. I'll be a witness at your trial."

Cruz laughed hollowly. "There's never going to be a trial. You're not going to survive what's coming. Fuck. *None* of us might survive what's coming, except Rawlings and Hoenikker here. After all, God favors drunks and fools, and those who don't understand what's going on."

"Hey," Hoenikker said. He certainly didn't feel like a fool. For the most part.

"No offense, Doctor," Cruz said, nodding in his direction, then he addressed McCune again. "My point is that if the two groups of security techs don't get together, to plan a way to defeat Seven and his Xenos, then we're all screwed. You'd be lucky to make it ten feet by yourself, much less all the way to a corporate court."

"Chief Rodriguez assured me we have this handled," she replied. "She has a plan. We just need access to Engineering."

"And how much experience does Cynthia have with Xenos?"

"She's dealt with them before. She knows their weakness."

"Their weakness? Susan, you're talking to a group of scientists who have been studying them for weeks, trying to find their weaknesses." He pointed at the door. "Those things have no weaknesses. They have no natural enemies. They were created to attack a host, gestate, explode from a chest, and become a battle-raging acid-spitting machine." He laughed. "You and yours. You think you know more about these creatures than the scientists—and I get it.

"I was a Colonial Marine," he continued. "I felt like there wasn't anything I couldn't fight, fuck, or kill. Then I ran into something none of those verbs worked against. Yes, there's shit out there in the universe that we don't ken, and we should run from it as fast as we can. Xenomorphs are at the top of the list, only Weyland-Yutani wants to 'monetize' the impossible."

No one spoke for a moment.

Finally, Kash broke the silence.

"Susan, what's the plan?" she asked.

"I'm the one talking to the prisoner," Cruz said.

"The hell you are. I've sat back and tried to convince myself that you all are doing this the Colonial Marine's way." Kash said the last like it left a horrid taste in her mouth. "But I doubt their way is to kill four Weyland-Yutani security techs in cold blood."

Cruz began. "But you don't underst—"

She whirled on him. "Listen to me, Buster. No more killing station personnel. Not unless they try and kill us first."

"You might not get that chance," Cruz said, his voice low and carefully controlled.

"I—*we'll* take that chance." She pointed at the vid screen. "Better to die a human than a monster."

Cruz was about to say something, when Kash turned back to Susan. "Again, I'm asking. What's the plan? Right now, ninety percent of the threat is in the mess hall. Have they considered setting up units at the doors?"

McCune stared, then seemed to come to a decision.

"Rodriguez believes that we can induce stasis in the creatures by alternating the frequencies of light," she said. "According to her, it worked before."

"Disco lights?" McGann said. "She wants to use *disco lights* to defeat the monsters?"

Hoenikker considered. It might actually work, but they hadn't tested it. What Rodriguez had seen in the wild—outside of a controlled experimental space—might have been the result of anything. Not being a scientist, she could have applied the vector inaccurately. It didn't pass his logic test, but that didn't mean it wasn't possible.

"Hoenikker, you might be the smartest of us," Cruz began, avoiding eye contact with Kash. "You look like you're working this out in your head. What do you say? Is it possible?"

He stared at Cruz, and couldn't shake the image of him setting afire the four living human beings who had tried to burst in.

"We don't have enough data, but we could always conduct a controlled test," he suggested. "After all, the Xenomorphs are in a single space. We could create an algorithm to adjust the light variance, and record what effects they might have on the ability of the Xenomorphs to conduct regular activities."

"What did he just say?" Buggy asked.

"He said we can test it out," Cruz said.

"Then why didn't he just say that?"

"He did, doofus." Rawlings took a swig of water from a jug.

"Easy on that," McGann said. "We don't have much left."

"Cottonmouth. I can't help it."

"Last cottonmouth you're ever going to have," Buggy said.

"Fuck, I hope not."

Cruz leaned forward to talk to the prisoner, but looked to Kash first, who gave him a hard nod. "McCune, did they even consider attacking the mess hall?" Cruz asked.

"Not once," she said. "They don't want to be directly involved with the creatures. As Weyland-Yutani employees, they—we—don't feel like it's our responsibility. After all, that's what Colonial Marines are for."

"I'm not sure if you've noticed," Rawlings said, "but there's a current shortage of Colonial Marines."

"They'll come eventually," McCune said.

"Oh, really—and how will they come?" Cruz asked. "Has anyone called them?"

"That's above my paygrade."

"You and your fucking paygrades," Rawlings said.

"Easy, Warrant. You'll blow a gasket," she said.

Just then the power snapped off. A couple of them shouted their surprise, and a couple more swore. Darkness surrounded them all, and Hoenikker was afraid to even move. Finally, it was Cruz's voice that rose above the rest.

"Everyone fucking shut up." Once the chaos ebbed, he added, "Rawlings and Buggy, grab rifles and attend the door."

A light blinked from a desk.

"McGann, what's that light?"

"Master control. We have a direct line to a single power cell, in the event of an EMP or anything that disrupts the main power feed. It's shielded."

"Can you get on there, and figure out what happened?"

"I think so." A dim figure in the near-absolute blackness, she hurried to the blinking light. There was the sound of a chair being moved, followed by a halo of light shining on her face as a screen lit.

"Hoenikker, Kash, find flashlights. Check the shelves."

Hoenikker could barely see, but he knew where the shelves were, so he zombie-walked in that direction, hands out to be his eyes as he used his fingertips to sort through the detritus of the Engineering department.

Kash was the first to find one. She snapped it on and handed it to Hoenikker, then she grabbed three more. She passed one to Buggy and the other to Cruz, and held onto the third, snapping it on and flashing the beam over everything, including their prisoner, who was still in place but struggling to free herself.

"I don't think that's a great idea," Kash said to her.

"Make sure her bonds are secure, please," Cruz said.

Hoenikker walked over to the screen where Cruz stood with McGann.

"Looks like a power node was disrupted here," McGann said, pointing at the screen.

"Disrupted how?" Cruz frowned.

"With the exception of the master, all of our power comes from solar cells on the roof and a massive solar array we have on the south side of the station."

"So, the node is an intersection?"

"Yes. I can reroute the power, but it will take a bit of programming."

"What could have caused the outage?" Hoenikker asked.

"Yeah, what he said," Cruz added.

McGann furiously punched in commands. "I can't be sure." She shook her head. "It could be anything."

"Where's the node located?" Hoenikker asked.

"Near the south side of the station."

In his mind, Hoenikker mapped what he knew of the station. When he thought he had it figured out he turned sharply to Cruz.

"It's the mess hall. That's on the south side."

Cruz's eyes narrowed in the glow of vid light. "Where are the nodes located?"

"On the roof," McGann said. "Only way to access them is from outside."

"Can you go through the roof to access them?" Hoenikker asked.

McGann answered. "Sure, but you'd have to—fuck." She glanced at Cruz, then Hoenikker. "Do you think that's what happened?"

"What else could it be?" Cruz asked.

"I suppose, depending on their ability to detect ion energy, they might have been able to detect directional energy." Hoenikker looked up as he continued talking. "I mean, being close to a power conduit might be the same as being next to something that's magnetized. If they have, or have developed, the ability to detect power, and understand what it is, then perhaps they could track and destroy it."

Perhaps this is one of the mutations Seven has acquired, he thought. *Given his heightened sensory capabilities, like telepathic communication.*

Even if the rest aren't so advanced, he could direct them. The thought made him shudder.

"Ever wonder if what we've done here might be the doom of the entire universe?" Kash asked, joining them. "The experimentation with the pathogen, combined with the irradiation, might have helped create even better killing machines."

"My thoughts exactly," Hoenikker said.

"Enough of what we shouldn't have done," Cruz growled. "We did it. We were paid for it. We wanted scientific advancement at any cost." He shook his head. "Just look at what we did to our fellow humans. We allowed them to become victims of the creatures. Despite what I said, I was as disgusted as the rest of you. But Bellows had put me in charge. If I didn't follow his instructions, it might have been one of you, or some front-office flunky."

The lights suddenly came on again, dimmer than before.

"Okay," McGann said. "We have power, but it's not full. Something's siphoning what power I have, and I don't know the reason why."

"Hurry. Check the mess hall," Cruz ordered.

McGann dialed up the cameras on her vid display. She gasped and showed it to the rest in the room. They gasped.

"What's wrong?" Rawlings asked from the door. "What do you see?"

"They're gone." Cruz ran a hand over his face. "Every last Xenomorph is gone. All that's left are the bodies, and the husks from the face-huggers. I don't know how they did it, but they found a way out."

"What about the other cameras?" Buggy asked. "Like the one in front of our door?"

McGann punched the screen a few times.

"There are no other cameras," she said. "We're blind."

"That devious bastard," Cruz said.

"What's devious? Who bastard?" Kash asked, her face still red from their previous interaction.

"Seven. He killed the screens. He's mocking us. He's warning us, because he doesn't think there's anything we can do. He's saying, *ready or not here I come.*" He shook his head. "We had him trapped in a cage, and now he's returning the favor."

Hoenikker stared at him, knowing that what he said was true and wishing that it wasn't. He glanced around, and found where he'd laid his pistol. It seemed so small and pathetic. Was it going to be enough? Would it keep him from being killed? Dear God, why had he ever come here? He backed away from the desk on two stiff legs.

"And now we are the hunted."

The sound of claws scraping against metal came from the door. Hoenikker spun and stared, just like the rest.

He had an overwhelming sense of having to pee.

47

"Alright. Everyone get geared up," Cruz said. "This is the end game—both humans and monsters are going to be coming at us. I don't know which is worse, so we have to be ready."

Kash handed Cruz his helmet. "Sometimes humans *are* the monsters. This is your chance not to be one."

"Humans are always the monsters," Cruz said, not meeting her gaze, "but there can be monsters more dangerous than us, and we've just spent weeks making them better." He fit into his gear and then turned to the others. He knew how he looked. A Colonial Marine in full battle rattle was a bad enough sight to behold, but one carrying a flamethrower was enough to send them running.

Rawlings, Buggy, and McGann all had pulse rifles, with pistol backups. Hoenikker and Kash had pistols, which was about as much as they could handle. Then there was McCune, the invisible resident of Pala Station.

"What's it going to be?" he asked.

She crossed her arms and tried to look brave, but he could see the nervousness in her eyes and the way she tapped the toe of one foot. Probably meant it to show her impatience, but he'd seen enough people about to go to battle that he knew what it really indicated.

"What do you mean?" she said.

"Well, you came all up in here with a handful of lies that fizzled when the Xenomorphs took your queen."

"You're mixing your metaphors like a drunken AI that's been head-smashed at a Humans First rally," she said.

"Maybe I feel like mixing them, especially since I need to decide whether to tie you up and leave you here as alien food, give you a pistol and ask you to join us, or send you packing to find your own fate."

"Will you give me a gun if I want to go back?" she asked, foot tapping double-time.

"You can pull one off a dead body on the way," he said. "Besides, we need all our guns and ammo. Not sure what's going to happen, and we need to have our contingency plans at the ready."

She stared at him, the corners of her mouth curling. She was close to tears, but she controlled it. Held it back and swallowed hard.

"Would you trust me with a gun if I joined you?"

"Would you really choose to shoot us over the Xeno-morphs?" he countered. "Your safety rests in our numbers. The fewer of us there are, the greater chance you'll die."

"You didn't answer my question."

He knew the answer. He just didn't want to have to voice it.

"Probably not."

She raised an eyebrow. "Probably?"

"Okay." He grinned tightly. "No. I wouldn't."

"Then I know what I have to do," she said.

He nodded. "I suppose you do." He turned to the others, wiping her from his concern. "Order of march is me up front with Buggy alongside. Behind us will be Hoenikker and Kash. Rear guard will be McGann and Rawlings. Watch your rate of fire. Count your ammo. Don't shoot anyone in the back." He stared pointedly at the two doctors. "And for God's sake, watch out for their blood. Even a little will burn through you until it finds daylight."

Everyone adjusted themselves. Hoenikker and Kash nodded to each other, as if sharing courage.

Another scratch came from the other side of the door.

"This is it," Cruz said.

He nodded to Buggy, who palmed the door open, revealing an adult Xenomorph. Its head in profile, saliva dripping onto the floor, sizzling where it landed. It made a sound of heavy breathing as the head began to turn toward them. Cruz lit it up with a gout of flame and Buggy opened fire, putting ten rounds into its chest and torso. Then he palmed the door closed.

Cruz turned and grinned at Buggy.

Two former Colonial Marines working as a team, wordlessly understanding what was needed to complete the mission. This was the way it should be.

After a thirty count, Buggy palmed the door open again. They were greeted with the stench of burning carapace.

The alien lay off to the side, curled in on itself, half burned, blood eating at the floor beneath. More importantly, it wasn't moving.

"With me," Cruz said. He stepped into the hallway, turned right and moved out. Buggy strode a little behind him, not wanting to be in the range of the flame, but ready to use his pulse rifle at anything within a 120-degree forward arc.

They didn't get ten meters before a juvenile Xenomorph popped out of an open door. Compared to the adult, this one could have been a toy at an amusement park. Something a kid could ride. Tempting to think it wasn't as deadly as the full-sized version. Then it leaped toward them, arcing through the air.

Cruz caught it in a plume of fire, then backed up to give the cute little monster space to land. But he didn't have much room to do so. Fire from two pulse rifles sounded from behind him. Rawlings yelled for them to move. Cruz kicked the smaller Xenomorph against the wall, regretting it immediately. Acid poured onto his foot. He tried to shake it off, but the pain was so intense he couldn't help but cry out. He didn't dare look, though, to see how much damage he'd done to himself.

He needed to move forward.

Two more juveniles appeared up ahead, probably drawn by the sound of gunfire and his scream. Buggy opened fire, rounds ripping into both of the Xenos. Blood and body parts sprayed the corridor until pieces of the nasty little monsters clung to every inch of the walls, floor, and ceiling.

"This isn't so hard," Buggy said, turning to Cruz and grinning.

Then the comms tech was jerked into the air and began flying down the corridor. He screamed, trying to shoot his invisible attacker.

"Let me go. Let me go, you fucker!"

They couldn't see how he was being held, but it had to be the escaped Leon. Cruz raised his nozzle to fire, but then lowered it. He couldn't do it without frying Buggy. As best he could, he began to run after them, pulling his pistol from its holster.

Buggy managed to get his rifle around and pulled the trigger. The Leon let go and he fell to the ground, landing with a loud grunt. The rifle skittered away.

Cruz saw blood on an otherwise blank surface, raised his pistol, and fired seven times. The Leon screamed, and disappeared around the corner.

Hoenikker ran up to Buggy. "Are you okay?"

Buggy had claw marks on his back and shoulder, but otherwise he seemed fine. Hoenikker helped him to his feet.

"Son of a bitch," Buggy said.

From behind them came a scream.

Punctuated by another.

And another.

They were the screams of a woman.

No one needed to ask whose they were.

McCune, the mysterious woman who shouldn't have been on the station, was no longer on the station. Cruz wondered where she'd come from. Surely there were places here they knew nothing about?

How many more of her type were there?

48

Rawlings didn't like pulling rear guard. Facing that direction, it meant he was backing into unknown danger. He had to trust in those behind him, but it had been a few days since he'd been a

Colonial Marine. He was no longer used to having his life depend on someone else.

Back in the marines, the idea of partnership had been ingrained through exercise after exercise, until it was muscle memory. On Tuesdays during one training phase, instead of doing the morning runs like normal people, they ran backward. The first time they'd tried it, it was a clusterfuck extraordinaire.

They couldn't keep their spacing, tripping and falling blindly over one another, each unable to see the rest—and it was because they didn't trust their fellow recruits. The space was constantly changing, and they were constantly looking over their shoulders.

Until they accepted that nothing bad was going to happen. Then it started to work. Still running backward, each stared at the next person, who stared at the next, peripheral vision keeping track of the person to the left and right, maintaining the spacing.

Trust was what would keep them alive.

But could Rawlings trust the scientists? They'd never been through training. They were civilians through and through, and didn't know how to operate in sync.

Sync.

Synth.

What about the synths? Where were they, and why weren't they clearing the station so that the humans didn't have to. They were probably guarding the command suites, which made Rawlings wish he was there. Not only would he be safe and sound, he'd probably have access to top shelf liquor.

Abruptly they came to a halt. Buggy had been skied by a Leon, which seemed to want to take him to its nest, wherever that was.

Rawlings didn't like being at a halt.

He wanted to move.

"I don't know what's taking them so long," McGann said beside him.

"Picking their nose or something," he called back over his shoulder. "Hey up there. We moving, or what?"

"Easy back there," Cruz called. "We're moving in one mike."

McGann cursed.

As did Rawlings.

A lot of shit could happen in a minute.

A juvenile appeared, this one grabbing ceiling pipes and pulling itself above them.

"Like fucking cockroaches," McGann said. They both opened fire, each plugging it with a handful of pulse rounds. The creature hung on for a moment, then fell to the ground.

Rawlings stepped forward and put two more rounds into its brain pan, careful to avoid the spray and glad he did as it sizzled and popped the paint on the walls. This was actually easier than he'd thought it would be. He was afraid it was going to be wall-to-wall Xenomorphs, but as long as they came at them one after the other, it was a shooting gallery.

What was the old term?

Easy peasy—

"Oh, shit," McGann said, grabbing Rawlings' collar and pulling him back.

An immense creature came skidding around the corner, slamming into the wall. Huge chitinous legs supported it so the head almost touched the ceiling. One of its four legs looked broken, and it walked with a limp. The central figure was human, with withered human legs dangling uselessly beneath it. Twin rows of jagged teeth took up most of the face—except for the eyes, which remained disconcertingly human.

Rawlings' eyes widened.

Fairbanks.

Or rather, the Fairbanks monster. He'd forgotten completely about it.

The creature roared. Reaching out with its claw-tipped human arms and hands, it rushed them.

Rawlings and McGann opened fire, but it was as if the creature was fast enough to dodge the pulse rifle rounds. Its legs propelled it along the walls and across the ceiling in the blink of an eye. Wherever they fired, the monster wasn't.

There wasn't enough time to call for help before the monster grabbed McGann by the head, slamming her into the wall and dislodging the pulse rifle. She managed to hold onto it with one hand, but the left hand released. Then the creature backed away and folded in on itself, using McGann as a shield.

"Shoot it," Buggy cried.

But he couldn't. Like one of those long-legged house spiders that looks impossibly large, it was able to fold itself into a smaller size, virtually hidden behind McGann. The battering had all but rendered her unconscious. She held onto the grip of the pulse rifle, probably automatically. Not knowing what it was. It might as well have been a stick.

"What do we do?" Hoenikker shrilled.

Rawlings tried to find the right angle, but it was as if the creature knew and adjusted each time, spoiling the shot.

"Shoot!" Buggy called again.

"Just watch our six!" Rawlings shouted back. "I got this."

McGann woke screaming.

"*Ohmygod*. OHMYGOD."

Then the scream of someone being eaten alive. Her eyes were all whites and her mouth was all red. Her neck strained as she screamed, over and over.

"It's *eating* her," Kash cried.

By God if it wasn't, while still using the body as a shield. Rawlings fought the urge to shoot, just to put her out of her misery, but he wasn't sure if it was too late to save her.

Fuck it.

He ran forward, zigzagging as he tried to get an angle.

One of the monster's legs wasn't all the way hidden—the broken one. He fired and scored a hit. The monster brought its leg in, and as it did, its left shoulder hove into view. Rawlings shot two rounds into it, the impact sending the monster back. He moved in for the kill, but the monster righted itself impossibly fast, and continued eating.

McGann was screamed out, glass-eyed and staring, but still alive.

Rawlings felt a presence next to him.

Cruz.

He had a pistol in his hand, and fired into McGann's head until the glass eyes turned dead.

Rawlings jumped with each impact. When he realized that his friend and comrade was dead, he raised his pulse rifle and put twenty rounds through her. The first five ripped a hole through her chest. The second five found the monster behind it. The final ten created a flesh-and-bone free-for-all as pieces of McGann and Fairbanks exploded outward in all directions.

What was left of McGann sagged to the right, revealing the monster. It was gasping through its twin rows of sharp teeth.

Buggy raised his rifle again, but Cruz put his hand on the carrying handle and gently pushed it down. Instead, he holstered his pistol and raised the tip of the nozzle. First he gassed the flamethrower, letting out a stream of wetshot, thickened fuel misting both McGann and the struggling creature. After a few seconds of that, he clicked on the burner in the nozzle and the stream became a gout of flame.

When the flame touched the targets, they erupted in a *whoosh* of fire, reaching all the way to the ceiling and walls.

Then Cruz turned and glanced once at Rawlings.

"You need to do a better job at watching our six."

He pushed through Kash and Hoenikker, both of whom were ogling the sight of the burning beings, and resumed his place at the head of the squad.

"If y'all are ready, we still might make it out alive."

49

Cruz was trying not to limp. He sure didn't want to see what the acid had done to his foot. Even if he looked, it wasn't as if he could do anything about it. They still needed to get to the lodge or—if they could—the shuttle. By now, he didn't know which one was safer. What was it called when the shit hit the fan after the shit had already hit the fan?

Whatever it was, this was it.

They'd lost McGann. They'd probably lose more before it was over. As it was, they'd been lucky. The flamethrower was like a weapon of mass destruction against pretty much everything biological. As soon as he'd learned that the deputy commander was going out hunting, he'd arranged through an associate in Security to, at a steep price, slip this last-generation M240A1 flamethrower into a requisition.

Problem was, he was down to a third of the requisite napthal fuel. He shouldn't have flamed McGann and the monster, but he'd been so frustrated by the loss that he couldn't help but wetshot the whole clusterfuck.

Moving through the corridor was easy for the moment. Soon they'd be in a much more vulnerable position. By his estimation, they were less than a hundred meters from the shuttle bay. There was a junction of corridors ahead that he'd expect to be occupied by at least one Xenomorph. So, he'd held the squad back, waiting to hear sounds of movement.

It wasn't long before they heard screams and the sound of pulse rifles. He couldn't tell if it was human on human, human on alien, or a combination thereof. Whatever the case, something was going on. There was dying, and that was going to help them get past, so it was to their benefit to wait.

The firefight was long by marine standards. A few stray rounds scored the corridor walls in front of them, but they were in no danger. A piece of Xenomorph and a human arm skidded to a stop in front of them, swirls of smoke coming from the arm, acid-splashed and skin melting.

Human on alien, then.

Kash and Hoenikker whispered behind him.

Then Rawlings opened fire.

Cruz glanced back. A juvenile had skidded around the corner and slammed against the wall, scrambling on the slick floor to get back to his feet. Rawlings evidently wasn't taking any chances. He opened fire and laced the beast, so that when the next one slammed into it, its skin and carapace were splashed with acid. But then it stood, unfazed.

It regarded them, torpedo-shaped head pointed their way. Its tail whipped absently behind it as it took a few tentative steps toward them. Rawlings fired.

Nothing happened.

"Oh, fuck me," he said. "Jammed."

It was as if the Xenomorph understood English. The words were like a switch and it went from zero to homicidal in 2.2 seconds.

Kash and Hoenikker both began to fire. Hoenikker's trigger discipline made his barrel jerk all over the place. If the ceiling had been the enemy, it would have been dead. But Kash stood with a two-handed grip and fired round after round, catching the Xenomorph in the chest with each round.

At the last moment, before it plowed into them, Rawlings cleared his jam and opened fire, catching the juvenile in the side, throwing it into the wall.

Acid rained down and caught Kash on her wrist and Rawlings in the face. Both of them gave sharp intakes of breath, but refused to scream. Kash vigorously wiped her hand on the wall next to her.

Rawlings pulled out a water bottle and leaned forward, dousing the area to clean out the acid. Then he checked his pulse rifle. Cruz approved. It would do no good if it jammed again. Regrettably, when Cruz had flamed McGann, he'd also ruined the dead woman's pulse rifle. Melting it was a rookie move.

The firing in the junction had stopped, but the screeching sounds of the Xenos continued. Cruz tapped Buggy on the shoulder, then made the sign instructing him to move ahead and recon. Buggy nodded, lowered himself into a tactical stance with the barrel of the pulse rifle pointed to the floor. He would be able to raise it quickly in a time of need. The butt of the rifle was deep in his shoulder. His trigger finger lay across the trigger well, not in it.

He inched forward until he reached the corner. Once there, he glanced back, then did a quick snoop around the corner before he jerked his head back. He turned to the group and made a fist, palm forward. Then he held up three fingers and shook his head.

Three.

They could take three.

The idea was to get past them and hit the lab, where they should be safe for a time. Cruz could have kept the group where they were in Engineering, but he was afraid that they'd be OBE. Overcome by events. He also didn't want anyone to take the shuttle or the lodge before they could, so he had to gauge where and when the pleasant folks from the command suites would make a break for it. His hope was that they'd make a run for it and get cut down by the Xenomorphs commanded by Seven. Some were bound to get through, but it was relatively unlikely that those would have the shuttle code.

It was a wild guess, but one based on hundreds of military operations, wargame scenarios, and an understanding that humans wouldn't allow themselves just to stay in one place. The oft-asked question was, "Why did they do it?" It's because they had to. Their DNA forced them to.

Only Colonial Marines were capable of resisting their genetic urges, because it was trained out of them. Where others would run away from danger, marines would run toward it, because they knew they had to eliminate the danger on their own terms, before it came at them on *its* terms.

"Okay," he said softly. "Buggy and Rawlings. Lay down fire into the intersection. Controlled bursts. Five seconds total, then back away and get behind me. We'll see what happens with whatever you don't take down."

Rawlings made his way forward and exchanged hand signals with Buggy. Buggy took high, and Rawlings took low. On their silent count, they cornered with their barrels, then fired into the intersection, controlled bursts of four rounds each. After a five count, they stopped firing and backed away until they were behind Cruz. Rawlings faced the rear. Buggy continued facing forward.

"I think we got two," Buggy said.

Cruz waited for the third.

And he waited.

And waited.

A minute went by.

Fuck it. He edged forward and peered around the corner.

And was attacked for his efforts.

A full-sized adult Xenomorph had been waiting for him. It lashed out with its tail, catching him in the legs. Cruz went down hard on his back, the naptham reservoir making him cant to the left. The creature mounted him, acid and saliva dripping onto the armor. Cruz couldn't help but feel the terror trying to creep its way from where he'd hid it. That the armor worked was a testament to their science. The appreciation aside, he was in grave danger.

The Xenomorph's mouth telescoped once, then twice, trying to get through the acid-resistant prototype helmet to the soft spot of Cruz's face. Still, Cruz twisted and jerked at each attack, unwilling to trust a recent development against a creature that had been made eons ago to destroy the universe.

Suddenly the sound of pulse rifles and the impacts of the rounds sent the Xenomorph thudding off him. Cruz rolled to his left, and was able to get up on one knee before he was slammed face first into the floor.

The sound of pulse rifles continued. Still two, then only one.

The Xenomorph continued its attack.

What *was* this thing?

Then it stopped.

Cruz glanced up just in time to see the alien grabbing Buggy's arm and ripping it free. The sloppy wet sound was compounded by a short, slushy *crack* as the bones snapped. Tendons and sinews trailed from the top part of the arm, and ribbons of red blood gouted thickly from the hole in his shoulder. The arm still gripped the pulse rifle, and the alien threw it aside.

Hoenikker and Kash rushed forward and fired point blank into the Xenomorph's mouth. The alien shrieked and fell back, its tail lashing, knocking both of them down. Its movements were frantic, as if it knew it was going to die.

Then it was still, and the only sounds were Buggy's screams.

As Cruz scrambled awkwardly to his feet, his chest dripping acid onto the floor, Rawlings grabbed Buggy and tackled him. The alcoholic comms tech forced the blood-pulsing stump into a pool of acid. Buggy's scream rose so high it couldn't be heard. The blood burned away in a singe of disgusting redolence that made everyone want to gag.

Hoenikker did, turning as he hurled. Still, Rawlings held the stump in the acid until finally Buggy was able to kick free. But the acid had done its job. The wound had been cauterized. The communications tech slumped to the wall as the adrenaline bled off, communing with a pain he'd never imagined.

Cruz clambered to his feet and checked the dead alien to make sure it was indeed dead, then glanced over at the intersection. For now, it was empty. He'd have loved to stay where he was and lick his wounds, but they needed to move. They needed to get to the lab, so they could reassess and plan for their next phase.

"We're going to move, and move quick," he said. "Everyone stick behind me. We're going to the lab. Pick up any ammo or weapons you find along the way. We can make it in thirty seconds if we move out. On my command. Are there any questions?"

Hoenikker wiped spittle from the side of his face, and shook his head. Kash's eyes were wide with the rush of her adrenal glands. She shook her head, as well.

Rawlings slung both his and Buggy's rifles on his back. He helped Buggy to his feet. The wounded man moved sluggishly, but moved nonetheless. For one traitorous moment Cruz considered leaving him, but knew he couldn't. The mantra of *don't leave anyone behind* was too ingrained in his martial DNA.

"Okay. Then follow me."

And he was off, his nozzle ready to spray hot wet death at whatever got in his way.

50

As they tumbled into the lab, Cruz and Kash immediately cleared the central table so they could lay Buggy on it. Hoenikker ran to the first aid station and pulled out bandages and searched for morphine, but couldn't find any. Then he remembered that there was little or no difference in the analgesic response and safety of intravenous morphine versus fentanyl for adult trauma patients. So he snatched up some fentanyl lollipops.

At first the injured man resisted the medication, but the outside of the lolly became slick with the man's saliva, and became easier to administer. After a few moments of the analgesic taking hold, Buggy allowed it to stay.

Meanwhile, Kash addressed the cauterized wound that still smoked from the acid.

Rawlings and Cruz grabbed several carts and stacked them at the entrance. It wouldn't stop any intruder, but it would slow them down long enough that they could grab their pulse rifles and deter them with rounds.

Hoenikker stood back and surveyed the scene. He was beyond wishing he'd never come here. He'd shot and killed things he never knew existed. He'd run and fought like some hero from a docudrama. All he cared about now was the next few minutes. To care any farther into the future was a luxury he couldn't afford.

In their thirty-second rush to freedom they'd passed piles of dead station personnel and Xenomorphs, and a few ripped-apart synths. They hadn't seen anyone living, so Cruz's strategy seemed to be working. Everyone else was doing the fighting.

They'd managed to pick up several pulse rifles and bandoleers of ammunition, so they might be able to make it to the shuttle bay after all.

He turned to survey the lab. He'd spent so much time here—more than a place of work, it had become a place of inspiration. A place of *perspiration*. He'd loved and hated coming to work here. Sure, he wished he could have stayed with computer modeling, but by being forced to live outside of his comfortable box, he'd learned so much more about the scientific method, and about himself. He'd actually *miss* the place. Coming to work to find out what craziness Cruz had done during the night, or the constant wonder that Étienne tried to project, or the confidence that Kash owned in everything she did.

Buggy moaned from the table.

Kash made soothing sounds.

And then a sound came so unexpectedly, his eyes went wide. He spun, and waited to see where it was coming from.

"*Ami Mark, lève ton verre. Et surtout, ne le renverse pas!*"

Friend Mark, raise your glass, but definitely don't spill it.

"*Ami Timothy, lève ton verre. Et surtout, ne le renverse pas!*

"Amie Erin, lève ton verre. Et surtout, ne le renverse pas!"

Étienne was there, just out of sight behind some equipment. In the rush to address the wounded, they'd missed him altogether. Kash rushed over to him.

"Mon ami. You're alive."

Étienne laughed. "Yes. It is me. Alive like a walking ghost."

The Frenchman looked worse for wear, however. The hair on one side of his head had burned away. The face beneath it was pocked and scarred from contact with acid. His clothes were covered in someone else's blood. Still, his eyes were bright, and he held a beaker of something liquid in his right hand.

"The pheromone worked?" Hoenikker couldn't help grinning from ear to ear.

"Eh, my friend." Étienne put an arm around him. "It worked until it didn't. Looks like it had a time limit before it wore off. My estimate is that it was about two hours. Still, what a discovery, no?" He took a sip, and offered it to Hoenikker.

Hoenikker accepted, and almost fell down with the strength of the liquor.

"Ack. What is this? Embalming fluid?"

"Just some hooch I found in Fabrications when I was hiding there."

Hoenikker held him at arm's length. "What's all the blood from?"

"Alors, once the pheromones wore off, I was forced to hide underneath some bodies. There was one hell of a firefight. Acid flew everywhere, which accounts for my new look." He turned to show his mangled face. "You like, yes? I look, how you say, rakish?"

Hoenikker frowned. "I'm sure it's lovely."

"Enough of the hugging and kissing," Cruz said, stepping over. He'd removed his armor and flamethrower. The clothes beneath were sodden with sweat and stank of battle. "You still crazy, Étienne? What was all that *frère Jacques* nonsense?"

Once again, the Frenchman grinned. "It was, how you say, ballsy, yes? I wanted to see if they detect each other through sound, or if the sound might counteract the pheromone. As it turns out, it didn't matter what I said. They left me alone until the pheromone wore off."

Then his face turned serious. "We need to get this out. We need to make sure that Weyland-Yutani can replicate it in their labs. Just think how we can better protect the Colonial Marines."

"I'm picking up what you're laying down, Étienne, but we need to survive the infiltration first," Cruz said. "We're a three-minute sprint to the shuttle bay from here. We need to find a way to ascertain where everyone is, and what they're doing."

"Would a radio help?" Étienne asked, his face as innocent as a babe's.

"All the comms are down," Rawlings said, joining them, his eyes immediately going to the beaker.

"Then why are they still talking?" Étienne asked, pointing behind him.

Rawlings glanced at Cruz, then hurried to one of the empty containment rooms. He returned with a portable comms unit that was abuzz with conversation.

Cruz frowned, and pointed at Rawlings. "Monitor what they're saying. We need to know where everything stands." To Étienne, he said, "Where'd you get that?"

"There was a battle. Security from the other end of the station tried to get to the shuttle bay, and didn't make it. One of the dead security guards had this, so I took it. I thought it might come in handy, *ça va*?"

"Drunks and fools," Cruz said, shaking his head, the shadow of a grin appearing beneath his mustache. "Drunks and fools and Frenchmen."

Étienne saluted him with the beaker, and took a sip.

Cruz took it from him, took a sip, then shook his head and made a sound somewhere between satisfaction and dying. He handed it back. "Definitely embalming fluid." Then he turned. "Come with me, Hoenikker."

Hoenikker followed, as did Étienne.

Buggy looked no worse on the table. His eyes were glazed from the fentanyl, but it was helping him with the pain. The stump of his right arm no longer smoked. Kash had wrapped it in a gauze bandage.

Cruz looked at her and said, "I need you to look at my foot."

She paused for a moment, then motioned him to one of the workstation chairs, which had a back. A stool would have been too difficult for balance. Cruz sat in the workstation for Containment Room One and spun it so that she could have access to his foot. He tried to remove the boot, but it had melted to his skin. He tried to peel it away, but it was as if the rubber and the skin had molded into a new element. He glanced to where his toes should have been and didn't see any.

Leaning back, he groaned.

"Tell me what you see," he said.

Kash leaned in. Hoenikker stood over them and stared at the vile mess of the man's foot.

"I don't know how you've been walking," Kash said after a few moments. "You've lost all of your toes and the front third of your foot."

"What you're saying is I now have a pod," he said humorlessly.

"Does it hurt?" she asked.

"Now that the adrenaline has worn off, fuck yes."

"We're not going to be able to do anything about it here. We need a proper medical suite. I'm sure there's one on the *San Lorenzo*, but for now, all we can do is treat the pain."

Hoenikker was already on it, and handed him a fentanyl lollipop.

Cruz pushed it back. "I don't want to—"

Kash pushed it toward him. "You asked for my help, and this is it. We need you to get us out of here. None of us are equipped. Sure, we'll point and shoot at whatever you tell us to, but without you, we don't know what to do. We have no strategy. We have no tactics. Our way of surviving is to follow the Great Cruz. So, you *will* take this this fentanyl and you *will* suck on it! It'll make you a bit high, but it will also allow you to function."

Cruz stared at her for a moment, then took the fentanyl in his mouth. "You had me at 'the Great Cruz.'" Then softly, "I'm sorry for the way I acted before."

She shook her head. "You'll have to answer for it if we survive. I won't forget."

He stared at her for a long time and then just nodded, looking away.

"There's something going down." Rawlings ran up, excited. "What's left of the command suite security forces are making a final push to the shuttle bay. The synths seem to have abandoned them. They don't know or they won't say why. So, there's only nine security techs left, and Bellows.

"Here's the thing," he continued. "They're going to have to pass by the lab to get to the shuttle bay. We can invite them inside, and then go as a larger force, or we can just stand by and see what happens."

Even though he wasn't a tactician, Hoenikker understood the pluses and minuses. Having more targets for the enemy would increase their chances of survival; but then again, if they got themselves killed, and took out more Xenomorphs in the process, then it would be better for Cruz and his crew.

It was both a win-win, and a lose-lose.

"What'll it be?" Rawlings took a swig of the beaker, which he had commandeered. It was half empty.

Cruz sucked on the lolly for a moment. "If they're all moving forward, who are they speaking to?"

"Seems as if there's a contingent of security forces forward of the command group, trying to clear the way. Bellows is there and he may have some security with him, I just can't be sure."

Cruz nodded. "Let's listen in, and see what happens."

As if on cue, the sound of gunfire came out of the tinny little speaker, accompanied by screams.

51

Cruz asked for the radio. He depressed the call button.

"Break. Break. This is Cruz. We have safe harbor in the laboratory. Repeat, we have safe harbor in the lab." Then he handed the radio back to Rawlings, stood a bit unsteadily, and asked for help clearing the door.

They moved the blockage, and then Cruz drug-fumbled his way into his body armor. He left the flamethrower sitting on a side table, but checked the ammo in the pistol at his waist.

The sounds of screams and pulse rifle fire began to diminish until it was only a single scream and a single rifle firing. Then there was silence. Pure and utter silence.

"What do you think happened?" Hoenikker asked.

Cruz knew exactly what happened.

"Let the cowboys and Indians fight amongst themselves," he said. "There's less we have to deal with between here and our objective. As for the station commander, he had a choice he decided to ignore. Now, he's run out of resources—and guess where he's going to be coming."

There was a banging at the door.

"This is Station Chief Bellows." The voice came through the radio, as well as through the door. "I demand that you open this door."

Rawlings looked at Cruz. "Doesn't he know it's unlocked?"

Cruz grinned around his lollipop and spoke into the radio. "We don't accept any demands. If you want a rescue, we might be able to accommodate."

Buggy moaned and tried to sit up. Kash asked Hoenikker to help her, and they held him down.

The banging came again. "*Let me in.*"

Étienne laughed. "Not by *zee* hair of my chinny chin chin." Cruz couldn't help but smile. Goddamn but he loved the Frenchman.

He paused.

Where did *that* come from?

He pulled the fentanyl candy out of his mouth. Yeah. That was it. He popped it back in and sucked on it. He couldn't feel his foot, which was all he cared about at the moment.

"Fucking hell." Rawlings took a swig, handed the beaker to Étienne, then strode to the door. Just as the commander began to pound again, he opened it, jerked the commander in, and closed the door behind him. Bellows fell to the ground, his jacket still smoking from an acid burst. He scrambled to get up, but Rawlings put his foot in the middle of the man's chest and drew his pistol.

"Now, tell me what the fuck you think about us now?"

Before the half-drunk warrant officer could shoot the station commander, Cruz stood. He figured the only reason the security techs hadn't taken the shuttle was because they didn't have the access code. Now that he had the commander, they could get the code and get the fuck off this rock.

"Ease off, Rawlings," Cruz said. "Let Bellows get to his feet. After all, his men are all dead or dying, so all he has is us." Rawlings glared at him, then sighed and backed away. He holstered his pistol and walked around the table next to Étienne.

Bellows huffed as he got to his feet, opened his mouth, and seemed about to launch into a diatribe. Then he saw the looks on the faces that surrounded him. He closed his mouth, his confidence fled. He looked like a deflated old man, his once bright, confident eyes engulfed in fear and self-doubt.

"How'd you survive?" he asked.

"Skill, planning, and luck," Cruz said. "What about you?"

Bellows shifted his feet and put a hand on his lower back.

"We didn't fare as well."

"It's because you had a larger force," Cruz said, and the commander shot him a confused look. "You didn't consider conservation of resources. You chose to try and bludgeon your way through, rather than strike at sensitive areas of the enemy until it could no longer fight."

"How do you…" Bellows laughed hollowly. "That's right. You're one of the Colonial Marines." He looked at Rawlings and Buggy. "They were, too. Smart. You got together."

"It was Rawlings who got us together. At first, I thought it was going to be nothing more than a club where we reminisced about old times. Rawlings had a gut feeling, though."

"A gut feeling?" Bellows asked, staring at the reception tech as if for the first time.

"Yes," Rawlings said. "A gut feeling that the station was so poorly run that it was only a matter of time before everything went to shit, and it was every man for himself."

Bellows jerked back as if slapped. "Well now. Don't hold back."

Enough of the small talk, Cruz thought. "What's the disposition of your forces?"

"What forces? Everyone's gone. Or if not gone, in hiding."

"What about the group at the shuttle bay?"

"They might be there, or not. We lost contact with them an hour ago." Bellows' eyebrows creased as his eyes narrowed. "What *is* that thing you created? How did it know what do to? Did you see the mess hall? Did you see the death factory it created?"

"We saw. We don't understand it, but we saw."

"If it wasn't for that piranha-headed Xenomorph, we might have been able to retake this station," Bellows said. "It has more than animal instinct. It has intellect."

Cruz liked the piranha-headed comparison. It fit.

"How many Xenomorphs did you see?" Hoenikker asked.

"At the end, none. I was too far back. But your head alien is holding the area in front of the shuttle bay." He glanced at the vial, and licked his lips. Étienne passed it to him and was thanked with a nod. "Honestly? There can't be that many left. Four. Five. Seven tops."

"Is that thesis supported by evidence?" Kash said.

Bellows pointed at the door. "Well, missy, the evidence is out there. You want to find it, I assure you, I won't stop you."

Hoenikker stepped forward, grabbed the commander by his lapel, and pushed him up against the wall. Cruz didn't know who was more surprised at the move, Hoenikker or Bellows. He was about to jump in, but wanted to see it play out.

"What? No threats?" Hoenikker asked. Bellows tried to disengage, and he pushed him against the wall again. "You think it's as easy as all that? You think it's our fault?" He leaned in. "Who's the asshole who brought in human beings to be experimented on?"

Bellows glanced toward Cruz, who just shrugged.

"I was just doing what corporate told me to do," Bellows mumbled.

"Just doing what you were told to do?" Hoenikker's voice rose a pitch. "You think that's a fair excuse to kill people? And what about the threats you made—to *all* of us?"

"Threats?" Bellows asked, his voice small.

"You were going to tell everyone about my sister. Do you want me to tell them now? My sister is a drug addict. We've been trying to cure her, but she steals to get money for drugs, and is on a prison planet." Hoenikker waved his fingers in front of Bellows' face. "Oooooh, that's so *awful*."

Cruz had to laugh.

"Hell, she might have been one of the people you made us kill," he continued. "And then you called Dr. Kash—one of the finest humans and scientists I have ever worked with—the Angel of Death. What the fuck was that about? And our friend Étienne? You said he should be in prison?"

Hoenikker pushed Bellows hard into the wall, released him, then backed away.

"And now you want our help. You want us to forget all the terrible things you've said and done, because your guards are all dead and you're *scared*. You are pathetic. No, you're *worse* than pathetic. You're what looks up to pathetic, and wants to be pathetic."

The station commander didn't reply. No one spoke.

"Enough," Cruz said, finally. To Hoenikker he said, "You're what looks up to pathetic?"

Hoenikker's gaze went to the ground.

"It was all I could think of."

"No, no." Cruz put a hand on the archaeologist's shoulder. He liked it when members of his team stood up for the others. Hoenikker had come a long way. "What you said was good, and it was needed." He pinned Bellows with a look. "But now, it's time to leave. Everyone gun up and be ready."

"Am I coming with you?" Bellows asked, glancing at Hoenikker.

"Only if you don't want to stay here," Cruz said. "But before you go, what's the command code to release the shuttle."

The room went as silent as a tomb.

"If I tell you, you'll leave me behind," Bellows said evenly.

Cruz shook his head slowly. "I'm a Colonial Marine. We never leave anyone behind."

Bellows seemed to consider. "But you're a *former* Colonial Marine."

Rawlings stepped forward. He wobbled a little, but Cruz didn't think Bellows noticed.

"Once a marine, always a marine," Rawlings said.

Bellows frowned. "Is this the condition for me coming with you?"

"It is," Cruz said.

"Fine." Bellows sighed. "Fuck it. One-nine-seven-five-three."

"Alrighty then," Cruz said. "Let's go."

52

As they prepared to leave the lab, Cruz moved to the back. He insisted it was because he was concerned about the amount of fuel he had left for his flamethrower. Hoenikker studied him with a frown. The man's foot was basically gone, though if they survived this, he could probably obtain a prosthesis much like Rawlings had for his hand.

They put Bellows next, giving him a pistol. Hoenikker wasn't sure of the logic—they hadn't trusted McCune, after all—but by the way he held it, it seemed as if he knew how to use it. That might prove to their advantage. Étienne stood next to him, a pistol in his hand, an expression of joy on his face.

Then it was Hoenikker and Kash, next in line. They were given the choice to carry rifles or pistols. Kash chose to take the rifle. Hoenikker thought about it. He'd fired one before, thanks to Cruz, but ultimately decided that he'd be better off carrying a pistol. He was more familiar with it, and felt that changing weapons might be to his detriment.

Buggy and Rawlings were in the front. Hoenikker didn't know why either of them should be there, but they'd insisted on it. Rawlings was eight-ways-to-Sunday drunk and could barely speak. Buggy was as high as he could be after two fentanyl lollipops, and only had one arm—his firing arm.

Even so, they'd argued and Cruz had decided that if they wanted to go first, then they could go. Buggy held a pistol in his good hand. Hoenikker realized that it meant he and Kash were the *de facto* front line, but they were almost to the shuttle, and they had the command code. All they had to do was make it there, lock themselves in the craft, and they'd be home free.

In the instant before going out the door, Hoenikker remembered Stokes' comment when Hoenikker had asked whether he should take the job.

"You might never get this opportunity again. Sure, you could stay here at your nine-to-five, going out for dinner on Fridays, seeing your therapist on Wednesdays. Or you could travel to the edge of the known universe, discover wonders no man has ever seen, and be better for it. Be boring and stay here. Or be dangerous and travel far."

Once again, he wished he could opt for "boring." If he ever got out of this, he was going to go back to his friend Stokes and punch him in the gut. The image of it made Hoenikker smile. Yeah, he was ready.

Let's get this show on the road.

Rawlings reached for the door, and they all tensed, ready for an attack.

Nothing was there.

Turning left, they kept a tight formation. They couldn't go a foot without stepping over the corpse of a human, or that of a Xenomorph. It was as if the floor was carpeted with the dead. Had it been his first week on station, Hoenikker would have found himself on his hands and knees, vomiting at the sight and stench of it. But the weeks he'd been here had made him into sterner stuff.

They didn't have far to go before they saw the enemy.

Seven stood in the middle of the corridor. It was as if he was staring into the distance. His jaws worked furiously, dripping saliva and acid. Around him crouched eleven juvenile Xenomorphs. Seven didn't seem to be looking at them, but finally it turned to them, and as it did, so did the eleven monsters. Their tails twitched and their jaws worked. Saliva dripped like waterfalls of death and sizzled onto the floor.

Beyond them lay the shuttle bay doors, and freedom.

Hoenikker could taste it. He could almost imagine lying down in a cryo-sleep cradle and drifting off, only to wake up to a place that had a paucity of Xenomorphs and an abundance of great wine. His own personal heaven.

"Hoenikker," Étienne said from behind.

"Yes?"

"It was nice knowing you, *mon ami*."

Hoenikker gulped.

Then the juveniles attacked.

Buggy began firing with his left hand, one round after the other. Rawlings, who had a hundred rounds and another hundred to load, began firing full-automatic in what Cruz had referred to as the "spray and pray" method. Rounds flew by the dozens, catching Xenos in midair and on the ground.

Only there were too many of them. Hoenikker tracked a juvenile who walked the walls and then the ceiling as it raced toward them. He fired, and Kash did as well. She caught it in the head, but as it died it rained blood.

Buggy and Rawlings both screamed as the acid fell on them. Buggy went down hard, his skull melting as the majority of it landed on him. Rawlings reeled into the wall, still pulling the trigger, but went down on one knee.

Kash and Hoenikker kept firing until the juvenile fell to the ground in front of them.

It twitched once.

Then twice.

Then stilled.

Rawlings glanced back, his face running as the skin sloughed off. He tried to speak, but his lips burned away before he could. He fell face first into the dead Xenomorph and continued melting into it.

Hoenikker looked away, and was stunned to see that the other Xenomorphs had stopped attacking. In fact, they'd moved back to protect Seven, squatting next to him like children would their parent. He counted four more dead or dying juveniles on the ground. Which mean it was now seven against five. But half of their firepower was now gone, with Rawlings and his ruined pulse rifle down for good.

Staring at Seven, Hoenikker began to feel the familiar buzz. The Xenomorph was broadcasting something. What it was, he didn't want to know. He just wanted to see it dead.

Then he became aware of a new sound.

Crying.

It was Bellows behind him, blubbering. He was like a child, all tears and snot and not wanting to be here. Hoenikker glanced at Étienne, who was all business. The look on his face was one that Charlemagne probably wore when he faced the Byzantine Empire.

"Fuck me to tears," Cruz said from behind.

"What?" Kash asked. "What's going on?"

"I'm going to have to charge," Cruz said. "You all stay where you are."

"What exactly do you mean 'charge,' *mon frere*?"

"Exactly what I said. Listen, when I get close, fire at the reservoir on my back. Trust me. It's our only hope. I can take them all out without issue."

"But that's suicide," Hoenikker said. He didn't like this at all. He'd rather continue the firefight, and let the chips fall where they may.

"I was never meant to make it off this rock. My entire job was to lead you scientists. I know, I know, I'm a scientist too—but at heart, I am a Colonial Marine. I want to go down fighting. Sometimes to survive isn't enough. If you're the sole survivor, it means that everyone you've loved has died. They're in a place together, and you're alone. Every day I wish I'd died with my friends. Every day I hate myself for surviving. Every—single—day. I don't want to outlive you all.

"In fact, I refuse. So, this is my choice."

"But you can't," Kash said.

"You can't stop me."

Kash growled. "I wouldn't even try."

"Thank you, Erin."

Cruz pushed Bellows aside and edged between Kash and Hoenikker. He glanced down at Rawlings and Buggy, and shook his head. Then he toggled off the igniter and prepared to run.

"Ready or not, here I come," he said, just loud enough for them to hear. Then he sprinted, spraying wet napthal out the end of his hose, shouting, "This is for you, Snyder, Bedejo, and Schnexnader. This is for you, Correia and Cartwright. I'm coming home.

"Flame on!" At the last, he flicked the ignitor and all the fuel he'd been spraying suddenly exploded into flame. He stood in the middle of it, in front of Seven and his *children*, who were burning. They screeched, but could do nothing.

"Shoot now," Cruz cried.

Seven reached out for him, grabbed him, and pulled him in.

Cruz let go of the nozzle and fought the creature, but even from where he stood, Hoenikker could see that the big man was overmatched. He glanced at Kash, who was locked in a trance, and grabbed the pulse rifle from her. She let it go without a struggle. Hoenikker planted the butt in his shoulder and stared down the sights, just as Cruz had shown him. Then he took a breath.

Cruz began to scream.

Hoenikker fired at the reservoir of fuel. When it exploded, they were knocked off their feet.

53

He climbed to his feet, using the rifle as a crutch. The explosion had left him fuzzy. Hoenikker flashed back to his arrival at the station, then to the Rat-X going free, then to the Leon-895 chasing him, then to the memory of the girlfriend he'd once had.

To Cruz sacrificing himself. It was funny how the man he'd once thought of as a sadist had shown the most humanity of them all.

He coughed, the air thick with smoke.

The corridor ahead of them was completely in flames. There was no evidence of Cruz, or Seven, or the juveniles. Just a flaming pyre of death that the air scrubbers couldn't diminish. He was forced to kneel and get down low so he could breathe.

Hoenikker glanced around.

Étienne and Kash were rising slowly, rubbing their heads where they'd hit the ground. He helped them and pointed to the dark haze of smoke near the ceiling. They nodded, understanding that they shouldn't stand.

Bellows was already up. He gave Hoenikker a hate-filled grin, then pushed him aside as he raced toward the blaze. To the left side there was a section free of fire, and this was what he was aiming for.

"Stop him," Hoenikker cried.

Kash unholstered a pistol and aimed at the fleeing man.

But she didn't have to.

A burning arm came out of the fire—a Xenomorph arm—and it pulled him in. His screams came fast and repetitive, until they stopped completely.

No one would mourn the man.

"What now?" Étienne asked.

"We escape to the *San Lorenzo*," Hoenikker said.

He felt weird. He felt like the *de facto* leader. Up until now, he'd looked to others to make decisions, but now—now he couldn't help but notice the way that Kash and Étienne looked at him. They wanted his guidance. They wanted his approval. How the hell did he earn such a position? Was it merely survival?

"Follow me." He crouched and held the pulse rifle like he'd seen Rawlings do it.

Moving quickly but carefully, he went toward the left side of the blaze. When he was near enough, he opened fire and sprayed the flames with twenty rounds, just in case another hand was waiting to grab them. When he made it around the pyre, he waited for Kash and Étienne, who followed without a problem. Then the three of them approached the shuttle bay.

On the other side of the door was an abattoir. Blood and acid mingled in smoking pools. The bay floor was carpeted in bodies. Hoenikker could almost relive the battle by the size of the clumps of humans and Xenos.

"Be careful. Be ready," he said. There could be survivors.

They turned a corner, and there, like a religious icon, sat the stubby frame of the shuttle. All their hopes and dreams had rested on it, and now they were here.

Hoenikker turned to Kash.

"What about the lodge?" he asked.

"We don't even know if it really exists," she said. "We have this in front of us. I say the shuttle."

"*Oui. Oui,*" Étienne said.

Then it was settled.

Hoenikker checked the outside of the craft, underneath it as well as on top. All seemed clear. He entered and found it empty, except for the single dead body of a woman in the hold. They pulled her free and left her on the bay floor. Once the three of them were inside, he figured out the toggles and closed the door.

He asked Kash to punch in the command code.

One-nine-seven-five-three.

She did and the engines responded. Before long they were ascending. He felt like cheering, his grin from ear to ear. They'd made it. Thrilled to be alive, they held hands.

"I can't believe I made it," Étienne said.

"Drunks and fools and Frenchmen," Hoenikker said, mimicking what Cruz had said earlier.

"Thank you," Kash said.

Hoenikker shook his head. "I didn't do anything but what I was told."

"I thought about running so many times," Kash said.

"I did as well," Hoenikker admitted.

"If it wasn't for Cruz, we'd all be dead," she said.

"I will buy everyone a drink, once we return to civilized space," Étienne said. "We will raise a glass to him." Abruptly the shuttle lurched, and they all froze for a moment, then broke into laughter.

"Probably leaving the ionosphere," Kash said.

Hoenikker was laughing when he saw death appear. More precisely, he saw the Leon-895 change its camouflage appearance so it could be seen. He was about to cry out when it snatched Étienne and hauled him backward. Before Hoenikker could even scream, the creature bit down upon the Frenchman's head, ripping free the skull plate with a sickening crunch. Then it dipped its face into the skull and began to chew.

"No!" Hoenikker screamed, finally able to move. He raised his rifle and fired until there was nothing left to fire, the pulse rifle clicking over and over and over as the battery tried to find a round to fire.

Both the Leon and Étienne were riddled with bullet holes. Neither had a chance at living.

"What have I done?" Hoenikker asked, falling to a knee. "I killed him."

"No, you saved him," Kash said.

Hoenikker folded in upon himself until he was sitting on the deck, the empty rifle beside him. Étienne had come so close to freedom. It wasn't fair. It could *never* be fair. He sat that way for a long time, staring at his friend, the look of utter surprise on the Frenchman's face that had appeared as his brain was being eaten by a creature they'd created from the fauna on the planet's surface.

"Why did you say what you said?" Kash asked eventually.

Hoenikker looked at her, feeling drained.

"That I was the best person and scientist you've ever known," she added.

He shrugged. "I don't know. The words rang true."

"But you don't even really know me."

"I know you well enough."

"You never asked why I was called the Angel of Death."

"I figured if you wanted to tell me, you would have."

"This wasn't the first time I was involved in human experimentation," she said, looking away.

He shrugged. "We all have things in our past."

"Oh, yeah? What was yours?" she asked. "You're about as clean and pure as the best of us. Hell, you might *be* the best of us."

"Don't count on it," he said.

"*Prepare to dock with the* San Lorenzo." They jumped at the computerized voice, then both took their seats. Just as the docking sequence commenced, the shuttle rocked as if with a blow.

Hoenikker looked toward the place where they'd been hit and saw that it was the broad front window. Instead of space—which is what he expected to see—he saw a fully adult Xenomorph with light stripes along its arms and torso.

Monica. How had she—

Even as he watched, she brought her clawed hands up and pounded a windshield already weakened by her acid. She chewed at the glass, and drooled on even more of it as she pounded.

"Will it never end!" Kash screamed.

Hoenikker glanced behind him at the body of the Frenchman and noted that it was completely alone. The Leon was nowhere to be seen.

Either it had camouflaged itself in death, or it wasn't as dead as he'd thought it was.

There was a *thump* as the docking sequence concluded, and the rear door opened. They raced inside. Hoenikker headed left and Kash followed. He bypassed several doors and found the bridge. There the door responded to his palm, so the place wasn't on lockdown.

Still, it was deserted.

"Watch my back," he said. "I'm going to send a distress signal." He found the communications array and looked for a way to send a signal. It took a few moments, then he found it. A switch underneath a red protective cover that said **EMERGENCY**. He lifted the cover and pressed the switch. The screen in front of him came to life with several choices.

```
1 - Evacuate Ship
2 - Vacuum Ship
3 - Send Emergency Message
4 - Destruction Sequence
```

He selected number three. Waited. When he saw what looked like a microphone flashing green, he spoke.

"Anybody out there. Anybody. This is Dr. Timothy Hoenikker from Pala Station. Everyone is dead. Please come. I am on *San Lorenzo*. We have an infiltration of—" He noted that the microphone was no longer flashing, and had switched to red. The message would have to be enough.

He turned and said, "Okay, let's find us a place to—"

Monica had Kash, a claw over her mouth.

The Xenomorph had made it on board.

He reached down and discovered that he was weaponless. He'd left the pulse rifle in the shuttle—but that had been emptied.

Kash squirmed free, fired several times at her captor, then screamed as the acid washed against her, cascading her chest.

"Run, Tim!" she gurgle-screamed. "Save yourself."

The Monica Xeno hissed as it twitched toward him. Acid-laced saliva slapped Kash's face, and she screamed. Then it cocked its head, just as Monica had done what seemed like eons ago.

Hoenikker didn't know what to do.

Kash managed to fire again, and the shot was a wake-up call.

Hoenikker stepped backward, then found a way around the struggling pair, and bolted through the hatchway. He watched the walls for guidance and was soon aft. His only hope was to find a place to hole up until help arrived. He noted a pedestrian tunnel that said **TO KATANGA**. The place where they harvested the Xenomorphs. *Oh, hell.* He hesitated, but then heard another of Kash's screams.

Katanga might be dangerous, but the thing that had been Monica was right behind him.

Racing down the tunnel, he reached the door and palmed it open. Behind him there were more shots, and more screams. He considered going back, but what if Monica was still alive? He gave an insane little laugh at the idea that an old girlfriend had turned murder machine, and wanted to kill him.

He ran down one corridor, and then another, not paying attention to where he went. Eventually he was out of breath and the screams came closer. They clearly weren't human. He stopped at a random door, palmed it open, then closed it and threw himself into a corner. He was almost to the point of hyperventilating, and forced himself to slow his breathing. Concentrated on the act until it was back to normal, his mind still racing at how he was going to survive.

He thought of Kash, and wondered if she'd been killed. But then, when he remembered the acid that had bathed her bosom, he knew better.

A claw scraped the outside of his door.

Was it Monica?

Was it something else?

He waited for it to repeat, but it didn't.

As quiet panic set in, he reminded himself that he'd made it. He'd survived. Against all odds, he'd somehow been the one to live at the end. But that thought was squashed by Cruz's words right before he'd made his mad dash to suicide to save them.

"If you're the sole survivor, it means that everyone you've loved has died. They are in a place together, and you're alone. Every day I wish I'd died with my friends. Every day I hate myself for surviving. Every single day."

And then he'd called out the names of his comrades.

Was that what Hoenikker was destined to do? Was he going to go out like Cruz, calling the names of his own dead?

Prior.

Matthews.

Lacroix.

Cruz.

Kash.

Monica.

A claw scraped across the door again, making him jump.

Sometimes to survive wasn't enough.

He'd never wanted to die more than the moment he thought he was going to live.

ACKNOWLEDGEMENTS

Being part of the *Aliens* universe had always been a dream of mine. My dream was first realized when I was invited by Jonathan Maberry to write a story in *Aliens: Bug Hunt*, an anthology of Colonial Marine stories. The dream was fully realized when Titan editor Steve Saffel contacted my agent, Cherry Weiner, and asked if I had time in my schedule to write an original *Aliens* novel that was not only to be canon in the universe, but also to be a prequel to a new video game. What a dream. What an honor.

As most of you know, I am best known as a horror author. Even when I write science fiction, it's dark-as-hell science fiction. But that's okay, because *Aliens* has never really been science fiction. It's always been horror. The terror of losing control of one's own body. The fear of becoming something impossible. Ridley Scott said it best in the tagline of his 1979 groundbreaking movie, *Alien*. "*In space, no one can hear you scream.*" So, thank you to Jon, Cherry, and Steve.

Thanks also to the Titan crew, Nick Landau, Vivian Cheung, George Sandison, Davi Lancett, and Dan Coxon. I'd also like to give a shout out to Carol Roeder and Nicole Spiegel at Fox, and the hardworking gamers over at Cold Iron Studios, including Craig Zinkievich, Jared Yeager, Chris L'Etoile, and Sylvia Son. Finally, I'd like to thank the fourteen-year-old version of myself, my date, and her brother, for braving possibly the scariest movie of the 1970s and creating the embryo of a young man who would later xenomorph into a horror author.

ABOUT THE AUTHOR

The American Library Association called Weston Ochse, "one of the major horror authors of the 21st Century." His work has won the Bram Stoker Award®, been nominated for the Pushcart Prize, and won four New Mexico-Arizona Book Awards. A writer of more than thirty books in multiple genres, his Burning Sky duology has been hailed as the best military horror of the generation.

His military supernatural series SEAL Team 666 was once optioned to be a movie starring Dwayne Johnson, and his military sci-fi trilogy which starts with *Grunt Life* has been praised for its PTSD-positive depiction of soldiers at peace and at war.

Weston also published literary fiction, poetry, comics, and non-fiction articles. His shorter work appeared in DC Comics, IDW Comics, *Soldier of Fortune* magazine, *Weird Tales*, *Cemetery Dance*, and peered literary journals. His franchise work included the X-Files, Predator, Aliens, Hellboy, Clive Barker's Midian, Joe Ledger, and V-Wars.

Weston held a Master of Fine Arts in Creative Writing and was a professor at Southern New Hampshire University. He lived in Arizona with his wife and fellow author, Yvonne Navarro. A 37-year United States veteran, he passed away in November 2023, and was laid to rest with military honors in Arlington National Cemetery in Virginia.

BOOK THREE

VASQUEZ

Dedicated to all the Castro women in my family
and my beloved daughter

El riesgo siempre vive. The guts to take a risk is the dream, even if your corazon must become as combustible as a grenade

PART I

JENETTE

1

"VAS-KEZ, you dumb fuck!"

Jenette didn't respond.

"Whatever," he continued. "Here, your name is Recruit. If you're *good enough*, that is. Now move!"

The man who assumed he was Jenette's superior flicked his eyes from her breasts to her sculpted arms, then to her face, giving her the type of look she'd received all her life.

"You won't make it."

"Who do you think you are?"

The patronizing glare rolled across her with the pressure of a two-ton space rover, bone crushing. She stepped into the elevator that would take her to the training pit. The metal doors closed, leaving her in a vacuum of silence with only her reflection staring back. Her brown skin shimmered from the sweat that managed to escape the red bandana across her forehead.

Before this moment she'd been on the scantest of MRE rations, had hiked every day for five hours, and stayed up writing a paper to the court arguing why she deserved a chance in space.

Take all those self-destructive tendencies and take aim, mujer, she told herself. The tattooed teardrop next to her eye appeared to slide in the dim light. All she had in this life was the woman staring back at her. Neto's words echoed in her mind.

"Us against the ugliness in the world. You think they want any of us to make it? If they did, we would see it. Nah, we fucking take it any way we can," he'd said. *"They protect their territory like they the*

gangbangers. Believe that. Put it on your waist and in your piggy bank."

Then she thought of Leticia and Ramón.

It was as much for them as it was for her, even if she'd only held them long enough to give them names. That had been the most difficult battle she imagined she would ever face. Her Mesoamerican ancestors believed that if you died in childbirth, you would be given a warrior's welcome in the afterlife. She hadn't died, despite the agony she endured alone, bearing down with her heels in stirrups and hands tearing at the hospital bed sheets. The two babies ripped her flesh as they crowned. So many battles she'd already fought sola. The journey to that test had been worthy of the fabled underworld Mictlan.

Jenette wondered what gods or demons were left to be met in her life. She'd believed she would die in prison, but was released into service to the USCM—the Colonial Marines. In just her first trimester, it had been a machete through her guts when she signed away all rights to her unborn children. There had only been time for one final kiss and glance before they were whisked away. Then came the enforced sterilization process.

Jenette was a warrior, had walked the warrior's path, even if it was wayward at times where she stumbled with bad judgment. Now in this final test for the Marine Corps, she had to muster all the ganas of every soldier in her family who served before her. In this moment her bones weren't made of calcium and marrow, but of steel. They would be steel for as long as she needed to get what she wanted.

A second chance.

No fucking way would she die behind bars. Too many like her had lived and died there, in a fungal cocoon of hopelessness for petty shit or things they didn't do. You want to kill a soul, cage it. Want to show people their place in the world? Four bare walls without real care or rehabilitation can be as cruel as it is a statement. Monsters are created.

Don't be surprised when jaws snap your neck.

She didn't like bullfights or rodeos, but she'd studied old video recordings of both, preparing for this battle that would determine whether or not she would make it into the Marines. With matador concentration she held her pulse rifle, and cocked it.

Alright, papi, swing those balls my way.

Like any recruit, she'd had to run a gauntlet of weapon prep, marksmanship, survival skills, physical fitness, and hand-to-hand combat. Every challenge she accepted with her bandana worn low and gold cross shining. Without failing a single one, she'd moved forward in the Marines with the stealth of a dark horse—even when she received recognition in two different rifle competitions.

This challenge wouldn't be an exception. Jenette crossed her body in the shape of the crucifix and braced for the attack from an android opponent who would be twice her size and programmed to make this anything but easy. The mistake she saw time and time again in this cumbia of "win or lose" was arrogance, the lack of respect for the opponent.

No one was going to make it easy for her. No one would give her *anything* in this life.

Don't underestimate the instinct *that is survival.*

Respect was everything—getting it and keeping it. Now was her time to burst through every barrier and run hard.

The metal door opened. The training pit was dark. The silence was what she imagined space might sound like. Lights began to appear dimly overhead, and the temperature of the room increased to that of a desert at the hottest point in the day. She flicked her eyes to the top of the pit at the one-way glass in the walls, knowing every movement would be watched and judged. The scrutiny on her performance would outweigh the others. This controlled evaluation was meant to test strength, senses, and ability to think on your feet—all in the space of ten minutes.

Doors opened on the opposite side of the room. There he stood. The android was six feet one inch of pure synthetic muscle, holding the same weapon as she. His eyes remained blank, without a flicker of life or sympathy. He only knew the instinct of his programming. A timer on the wall above his head flashed a countdown in red blinking lights. As it hit zero, he would come alive with one intention, to make her fail or give up. But these assholes had forgotten that when you grow up in a system rigged for your failure or to devalue you, you replace skin with an exoskeleton of having nothing to lose.

In her mind's eye she saw the faces of those who had locked her up, of dead family members languishing in ill-equipped and overrun hospitals, the babies she would never know, the guards who had wanted to rough her up. All of it was butane for her fire-breathing nostrils.

Bulldoze him like a tank. Smoke him. Be *the goddamn tank.*

Don't forget you come from soldaderas.

Zero.

Jenette aimed her gun with ease—as if it were an extension of her arm—and fired. The android mirrored her actions, forcing her to tumble to the side to avoid getting hit. Those suckers hurt. Many times, in afterhours training, she'd been walloped courtesy of Drake.

She kept moving and continued to fire as she ran around the circular perimeter, but *goddamn* he was fast for his size, with speed more minotaur than man. Then again, he wasn't human. There was no emotion on his face, no tell she could pick up on.

All she needed was one clean shot in the sandstorm of rubber bullets. The two of them couldn't keep running with the dizzying motion of a carousel. *They* would make sure of it, because combat wasn't no game of ring around the roses. In real combat, someone always died.

She stopped abruptly and darted toward the android while taking aim. Her shot hit his left shoulder. The blow slowed him down, with his body jerking backward, but it wasn't enough to offset his shot to her pulse rifle, which flew from her hands upon impact. It clattered to the ground. Without missing a beat, she grabbed a smaller gun attached to her waist. This time her shot hit the android in the center of his right hand. The malfunctioning digits seized, giving her enough time to take another shot.

He dropped the pulse rifle.

Jenette kneeled for the kill, aiming for the head. One huge stride toward her, coupled with a roundhouse kick, knocked the pistol out of her grip. The bones cracked and her flesh stung with the feeling of a hot iron, but she held her scream between gritted teeth.

It ain't over till it's over, motherfucker.

Without hesitation Jenette propelled herself straight into his body. The sudden impact made him stumble back. On her right ankle she had stashed a switchblade, the kind she carried as a kid and the one grandfather Seraphin told her was the weapon of choice for the pachucos of old. Jenette flipped it open then plunged it as deep as she could in the part of his lower belly not covered by the protective vest, then swept it across. He shoved her to the ground while pressing a hand to his body where it was leaking white liquid.

Booming broke out above her head.

Then simulated gunfire.

The temperature decreased rapidly, accompanied by a simulated rainstorm. The lights strobed across the pit. This was *their* way of saying *"Are you going to win or lose? You decide… now."*

The android took the opportunity to strike again, but this time she was ready to end it. When he lunged for her, Jenette drove her boot straight into the hole in his belly. He pushed closer, ignoring the boot in the cavity of his midsection as he grabbed her by the neck. With her opposite leg she attempted to kick him as hard as she could anywhere her foot would land, trying to rupture his wiring or something. The water made her boot slip.

Thanks to the bandana her vision hadn't blurred. Her wounded hand was all but useless, however, and already beginning to swell. Jenette could feel her windpipe closing as his fingers constricted around her neck. It was now or never. No way would it end like this—nothing and *no one* could grab her by the neck. She squeezed her abdominals hard to lift her closer to the android. She still had the switchblade in her good hand, and with one hate-fueled swipe she caught him across the throat.

White paste flooded from the gash. His face contorted from the damage. His grip softened. Jenette took that moment to grab his wrist and pull him to the ground, securing his torso with one knee as he convulsed from his two wounds.

"Adios," she said as she dropped the knife and yanked out the cables inside his neck. White liquid flew into the air and splashed across her face and chest as sharp electric shocks ran through her fingertips.

The lights went up and the shower ceased. A robotic voice spoke.

"Congratulations. J. Vasquez. You are the victor and have successfully passed your final evaluation. Please make your way through the open doors."

She lifted her gaze to the tinted rectangular window at the top of the training pit and nodded. With her good hand she stowed her switchblade in the left thigh pocket of her fatigues. You couldn't go wrong going back to basics, your roots.

Every muscle ached as she lifted herself from the ground. Her mouth was a cottonfield beneath the blazing sun.

Drake greeted her when she stepped out of the elevator, standing with the rest of the recruits waiting for their evaluation. A large screen in the holding area showed each showdown. He gave her a large grin as she walked out. It was nice to have a friendly face after staring down an emotionless android.

"I knew you had it in you," he said. "You made that shit look easy… I can't wait to get a crack at that dildo. He won't know what the hell hit him."

"What choice do we have but to make it?" she said. "This is it for me. No plan B and no trust fund—and careful with that 'dildo.' He has some moves. You might get fucked if you don't stay on your game." Jenette rubbed her neck, hearing her voice strained from the android's grip.

"Don't I know it, sister. You ready to celebrate tonight?"

"Hell, yes," she said. "Let me shower first and get this hand wrapped. Tell me when and where?"

"Will do. I'll send you a message later. We're gonna get lit tonight, like the good ole days."

She gave him a confident smirk. "Good luck, man." Then she slapped his hand, even if the reverberation made her want to wince. *Don't let nobody see your pain.. Don't let your own sweat sting your eyes, otherwise you won't be able to see, and that's what your enemy wants. They want you to be blind. ¡El riesgo siempre vive!*

Abuelo Seraphin always had the good advice.

A commanding officer stopped her before she could make it out of the waiting area. If she hadn't known better, he could have been the brother of the android she just destroyed. "Vasquez, you did major damage to the android with that switchblade. No one knew you had it on you. It's not USCM issued."

"No one said I couldn't improvise," she replied. "Send me the bill." He stared at her without expression.

Then he reached into his pocket. "You showed creativity, tenacity, and that you're a hell of a fighter. Remarkable strength. Here." He handed her a square patch with "USCM" embroidered on it. "Welcome, Vasquez. You're going to the stars."

"Thank you, sir!"

"We are your family now." He turned on his heels to return to the observation chamber, where he would watch the rest of the evaluations.

Jenette's heart galloped. It was just a patch made from cloth and thread, yet the weight of it could carry her places she never imagined.

She walked back to her training quarters with head held high, feeling like a Roman gladiator. In the bigger scheme of things, they were all pawns to benefit the higher-ups orchestrating wars, politics, and "building better worlds," as they put it. Pure entertainment for the new gods, puppet masters stitched from the flesh of dead soldiers and colonists, the strings forged with gold coins and credits.

Gangbanger, she had been called. The whole system was rigged by a gang of suits. Everyone belonged to a gang in this world, wanting only to protect their barrio.

Jenette pressed the button to close the door to her tiny efficiency quarters. Her wobbly legs managed to make it to her single bed before giving way for her body to crumple, now that the adrenaline had faded. Her boots had to come off, but suddenly she lost all energy to move or control the sobs escaping from her chest without warning.

Eyelids fluttered, hoping they would set free the overwhelming emotions in that moment. She removed the sodden red bandana from her head, Abuelo Seraphin's bandana. She brought it to her eyes and squeezed them shut. Her hands clutched it until her knuckles went white. She had to keep her palms to her face to prevent the brown mask of bravado from slipping off with her sweat and tears. Tears and sympathy were a luxury not reserved for her type. Her injured hand didn't register the pain with the explosive fission escaping from her heart. She needed something to remind her this moment was real.

There would be nothing more to prove.

One door of destiny shut as another opened.

She had done it. No one believed she could or would—just another Brown number in a white jumpsuit when she signed on the dotted line to be released early for a murder she hadn't committed. She'd sacrificed it all and only had herself now.

Wiping her tears, Jenette exhaled. With the overwhelming emotions purged as much as she would allow, she pulled off her combat boots. There were no more tears from her eyes except the one permanently marked on her face.

Jenette removed the switchblade from her pocket. It was still wet with the white mucus from the android. Back in wartime 1940s Los Angeles during the Zoot Suit riots, you were either a zoot suit-wearing pachuco called a gangster with a switchblade, or a military man fighting the good fight. Blood from both spilled during those riots. Jenette—where she came from and who she was—possessed the spirit of both now. She was a Marine, but she also remembered that street life.

Placing the switchblade on the bed, she messaged Roseanna the good news. A photo flashed on the screen, of two small children covered in mud, playing with a litter of baby pigs.

Roseanna responded immediately.

As if there was any doubt!

Can't take it away if it wasn't yours to begin with, Jenette thought.

She belonged to the Marines now, likely the only family she would see in the flesh until the day she died. At least she had her homie Drake with her. Small blessings and shit. She stood up and ran her fingers through her short hair until they touched the nape of her neck.

Damn it felt good.

Time to shower, get her hand seen to, then raise hell—or maybe just the roof that night.

2

2166

As far back as Jenette could remember, she had always wanted to be a soldier. Her father, her great-great-uncle Roland who was buried with a Purple Heart for his service in Vietnam, her grandfather, and great-grandparents, all with roots that began as farmworkers on Earth, moving farm to farm like many Mexicans emigrating to the US hundreds of years ago.

"*¡El riesgo siempre vive!* That is what my grandmother would say to me," Seraphin told her, "and what she heard from the women before her. Did you know the military could be for you, too? You have a distant relative who was a soldadera and fought in the Mexican Revolution. Those soldaderas were a bad group with their rifles and bandoliers. Chihuahua, watch out!"

Abuelo Seraphin liked to repeat this story time and time again. "People risk their lives and the lives of their children for a chance at something more. It's a story told across Earth for centuries, and it carried people into space. There has been much tragedy, so many lost in the oceans, rivers, and deserts, but also there is hope. Never lose your hope even if you lose your way."

Her grandfather said this while polishing his old combat boots with a round black-and-gold tin of black polish and an old T-shirt made into a rag. His memories and nuggets of wisdom also were shared while he tended his garden of chilis and squash, a red bandana across his brown forehead. His pride had continued long after he retired, and he was buried with all his military gear.

Most of the men in the family joined the military to be educated through the GI Bill. The cost of everything on Earth was sky-high, even back then. Someone had to carry on their military tradition, the slow bachata toward upward mobility wherever it could be found.

Growing up in Los Angeles, Jenette had liked making forts, playing guns, watching ancient reruns of *G.I. Joe* or *She-Ra*. She'd tease her sisters, brother, and cousins with insects and small animals while the children did their homework in a silent circle at the kitchen table. She captured centipedes, and crickets squirmed in a jar as she crept up to unleash them on the table. They all roared in fright, and she with laughter.

"Jenette, I'm *telling*! You're so necia all the time!" they would whine. Her mother, Francisca, stood by, giving her a look of disapproval.

"Why can't you be like other girls?" Mother said. "Look at Roseanna and Carmen. Come with me. If you can't behave, I'll keep you busy with the housework."

Despite her mother's protests, Jenette would run around the house, imagining new worlds with monsters to kill. This earned her the title of Disaster Master. She would walk into the kitchen to see a broken toy in her mother's hands.

"Did you do this? You want your father to work himself to death trying to provide, when all you do is cause trouble by breaking things. You will clean all the bathrooms for a month."

The only time she wanted to sit still was at Easter.

Cascarone time.

For months Francisca would gingerly break the eggs at the top end, creating a small opening to allow the slimy contents to slip out before jumping from the heat of a pan sizzling with red chorizo fat. The shells would be rinsed then placed upright in an empty egg carton. The eggs with jagged mouths lined up on the counter until there were rows and rows of them. Sometimes spiders or flies would find their way inside and crawl in and out. The sight made Jenette shiver.

A few days before Easter it would be time to dye them different colors, fill each one with confetti, and cut squares of tissue paper to be glued at the top.

The great annual Easter cascarone fight would ensue. Jenette stalked the house with a carton tucked beneath one arm looking for unsuspecting victims. The element of surprise was essential. No one was safe from having a cascarone smashed hard on the top of their head. Her victims expected to be picking confetti and eggshells out of their hair for days.

Nothing was ever safe in her wake.

Abuelo Seraphin's favorite granddaughter was shaping up to be a big bad Marine.

A quinceañera, a tradition for hundreds of years, was the last thing Jenette wanted when her mother Francisca brought it up on her thirteenth birthday.

"You are now a teen, and in two years we will have the most amazing party for you!"

"I'd rather die than have one of those," Jenette responded, "like a doll or a little pet you dress up for your friends." Her mother didn't speak to her for days after that.

To add insult to injury Jenette took her defiance a step further. All her life she had kept hair that fell to her waist. The traditional dolls she received from Mexico had two braids with ribbons interwoven with the hair, long black yarn tied neatly to the sides and wearing a traditional dress to the ankles. Her mother and grandmother loved the thick tendrils that had been a family trait for generations.

This beautiful hair was cumbersome, so she cut it all off.

Jenette did not want to be one of those Barbie dolls presented at girl parties—the ones suspended in the middle of a pan with the dress made from cake and topped with piped pastel icing in the shape of flowers. Barbie was only released when every morsel was eaten, and only crumbs remained on her bare body.

"Jenette, por favor! Why did you do this?" The gasp from her mother's mouth, followed by a shake of her head and the pious crossing of her chest, told Jenette she would never hear the end of it. "I should have stopped Seraphin putting all those ideas in your mind." How would she ever find a husband now, her mother seemed to cry.

She didn't give a shit. She loved the feel, the same freedom as the guys.

Jenette was already at a disadvantage, being a Brown female with no family name or fortune, so why not make her life easier? Jenette wanted to be accepted as the best of the best, with the ability to smoke an enemy as fast as any of the men. And despite what her mother might have thought, the short hair looked good.

* * *

Jenette would have given anything for those harsh words from her mother's lips, because at least there would be a hug again when her mother's frustration subsided. It was better than a bunk bed in a stranger's house.

Without any regard for the small dramas in the lives of everyday people, the world came to a halt for millions.

A gruesome, highly contagious sickness raged through the population before anyone knew what was happening, and before it could be brought under control. The "flesh-eating bacteria," they called it, and the description fit. The vaccine supplied by Weyland-Yutani came too little too late for many, the priority given to anyone leaving for the most valuable colonies in space, and supplies sent to keep the colonies free from infection. She saw her father Pablo and Seraphin for the last time as they were wheeled into an ambulance, writhing in agony, knowing it would be the only goodbye they would get. No one—barely any of the doctors or nurses, even—came out of it alive or without permanent damage.

Her sister Roseanna was on the front lines of death, and when not in the hospitals she was in a bottle of booze or pills to cope with the stress and to stay awake. One evening in their mother's home she was slumped on the couch with a beer in her hand.

"Mama, it's hell out there," Roseanna said. "I feel like an undertaker and not a nurse. I need Santa Muerte's spirit to take over me. Otherwise, something else is driving me too fast somewhere I don't want to go. I can feel it."

"Don't be silly, Roseanna. It will pass, and you're an angel. No more bad talk and no more cerveza. You're saving lives. After all this you'll get into that program to be a doctor—I just know it—and then we will have a big party… since this one didn't want a quinceañera." She nodded toward Jenette. "It's what your father would want, too. He worked long hours, but it was to provide. He was so proud of you, even if he didn't say it enough."

"Maybe I'm meant for something else." Roseanna stared at the wall. There was a vacant shadow in her eye as she took long gulps from her beer. Her skin was red raw from the hot showers and antiseptic soap she had to use after a shift at the hospital. "What if I don't want to be a doctor anymore? They're just as fed up and overworked…" Her voice trailed off.

Some of the hospitals offered bonuses for taking on extra hours. Two days later Roseanna crashed her vehicle on a run to an emergency call. She was alive when paramedics arrived but placed into a coma for her recovery. No one knew if she would make it.

Jenette wondered what being heroes did for any of her family.

Before her accident, Roseanna stole a spare dose of vaccine, only managing to do so because she was a health worker. Francisca kept it safe in her bra and underwear drawer for weeks while she monitored the news of her daughter. One evening she slid the green inhaler across the dinner table, her fingers trembling, toward Jenette.

"Take it," she said with sweat rolling down both temples, her skin a plastic sheen of smaller beads of sweat.

Jenette put down her fork of twirled chicken ramen noodles.

"No. It's for you."

"Stop being so defiant and take the damn thing!" Francisca raised both balled fists to her chest and took a deep breath. "For once do as you are told. Everything I have done has been for you… *all* of you. I've tried my best to keep you, Carmen, Sandro, and Roseanna out of trouble. One day you will understand how hard it is to stay true to your roots, while trying to reach for the stars, whatever those stars look like.

"We are the people from the soil, it is true," she said, "but we don't have to stay seedlings. I just wanted you to be seen as a good girl because we are seen as so many other things. I should know. Maybe trying to keep the old traditions was wrong. I'm sorry. El riesgo siempre vive. I am risking my own life now to spare yours. You have a purpose. Live to see it through."

The flesh hanging from her cheeks and desperation in her eyes scared Jenette. Her mother had never spoken to her with such fervor—

or honesty. Jenette complied, sticking the inhaler all the way up one nostril and inhaling the vaccine in an explosion of burning magma. A single tear rolled down her mother's face.

"Thank you." She clutched the hem of her blue T-shirt before running to the toilet. Jenette heard her vomiting in the bathroom, then shuffling back to her bed and the warm comforter that awaited her there.

Two days later Jenette found her under the comforter, no longer retching… or breathing. She held on to the pillow on which her husband had slept, and clutched a family photo album and rosary. Jenette turned away, left the room, and closed the door.

How was this reality?

She couldn't be left alone in this world.

When her father died, she had cried for her mother's sake. He had worked more than he spent time with her or her siblings, and always felt like a stranger because of the odd hours he kept as a foreman and lead tech liaison for the android factory. They came from generations of thinking that when times are good, then you have to take advantage of it. Surf that wave because you never knew when you might get knocked on your ass, or the work would dry up. The need for androids never relented, new models were created all the time, yet the fear of *"what if"* burrowed with the hunger of a parasite.

If Father wasn't dealing with labor disputes, then it was the day-to-day with the factory.

Now she looked around the house. Everything remained the same, but suddenly it seemed hollow, without any soul. Something had fled from this space she no longer recognized.

Her shock turned to a typhoon of rage for not having any control over any tiny crumb of what her life could or should be. Through hysterical sobs she grabbed up all the plates and glasses on the drying rack next to the sink and threw them to the floor until the shards resembled Easter confetti. Then she turned over anything that wasn't secured to the tiles in the house—which was everything. Jenette screamed and shrieked with not a soul in range to stop her. Carmen and Sandro were floating in space for the Early Learners Terraforming Program offered by their school, and Roseanna lay in a coma. All others in her family had been claimed by the spinning wheel of fate called death.

When there was nothing left for her to destroy or any voice to scream, she walked into the bedroom to remove the gold cross from her mother's neck and placed it on her own. She couldn't have the paramedics stealing it. Before calling an ambulance, she gave her mother's cold temple one kiss.

"I love you, mama. Thank you. I'm sorry if I didn't tell you enough."

What would she have left to cling to?

Nobody wanted to feed and look after a teenager. Jenette was sent to live in a foster home.

Roseanna survived the accident, but her blood work indicated a cocktail of alcohol and medication. Instead of facing any time, she chose to be transferred to Texas for rehab and a contract to work in a rehabilitation facility. Even though all the remaining family assets were transferred to Roseanna, taking care of Jenette was out of the question. She could never handle medication, would never be a nurse, but she would be trained as a counselor.

For Roseanna and Jenette, the familiar life they knew was gone in the time it took to sneeze.

If this was it then, Jenette figured, what was the point of anything? If she mattered so little in this world, what did it matter what she did?

Taking risks took on a new meaning.

She was settled in a modest home with nice enough but neglectful guardians, Timothy and Hazel Hall, who fostered a bunch of kids. There she met another teen named Liberty Love, a beautiful girl of sixteen wanting the glamour of gang life, a real buchona with impeccable makeup, thick fake eyelashes, and curves on show. When Jenette asked her where her family was, she shrugged while filling in her plucked eyebrows with dark brown pencil.

"Fuck if I know. My mom died and my dad couldn't get work after losing his business," she said. "We used to live large, amiga. He sent me to live with my cousin until he could find his feet again, but all of it fucked with his mind after a while. My cousin gave me to the state when I refused to get a job, so I could give her the entire check. If I'm going to wear some ugly ass uniform with married pervy dudes trying to pick me, then at least I get to keep my dinero. That outbreak, it hit a lot of us hard, fucked us all up gacho. People getting sick without enough healthcare."

Jenette felt like she had found a kindred soul in grief and heartache, yet they couldn't be more different. Jenette was more of a tomboy, always causing trouble, running the streets in Dickies and sometimes a slick red lipstick, if the mood struck.

A week later another kid, P-Wee, came to stay. He was a skinny half gringo and half Mexican, too shy to be tough, yet winning everyone with his sense of humor. The three musketeers went to local parties and started mixing cheap vodka with 7UP. Jenette was the homegirl with an attitude, someone the girls wanted to smoke with, and the boys wanted to fool around with because they could tell she was a "wild one."

"Hey, I want you to meet some friends," Liberty said. When Jenette looked doubtful, she added, "Don't we all just want real family again?"

"You don't want to stay a neutron." P-Wee pursed his lips and shot Jenette a confused look.

"What does that mean?" Jenette asked.

"It means you don't belong to any gang. We'll see what the Inca has to say."

"That's a great idea, P." Liberty leaned over and kissed him hard on the lips. "You know I love how you think."

"Yeah, you love my weed…"

"That, too."

Jenette looked on as Liberty kissed him. She wanted something, too.

"Who are these friends?"

"I know I said friends, but I mean *familia*. They helped me get through the worst of times. I'm in with Las Calaveras. I want to introduce you to them."

* * *

"This is for you," P-Wee said from the driver's seat. The music played loudly. "Damn It Feels Good to be a Gangster" by the Geto Boys, the pioneers of horror core rap in the twenty-first century. Liberty Love sat next to him in the passenger seat. Neto was in the back with Jenette.

She leaned toward Liberty's ear.

"Why do they call him P-Wee?"

"Because when he used to get high, he was obsessed with the old Pee-Wee Herman show. He's clean now, building his business, and never watches them, but the nickname stayed."

Liberty wore her tightest jeans and low-cut ribbed bodysuit with a sweetheart neckline. In the sepia of the streetlights and whirlpools of smoke, she could have been a caterpillar sitting on top of a mushroom. No worries and no rushing. Jenette couldn't help her eyes straying across the beautiful body, the sumptuousness of it.

Jenette had made out with boys before, and liked it fine, but the curiosity to explore a body like her own grew stronger the older she became. Desiring *both* felt normal. Lust was as amorphous and complicated as an uncharted galaxy, and depending what direction you find yourself floating, it was different for everyone.

P-Wee pulled up to the house on a residential street of large homes that bordered the blocks of Los Angeles projects in a neighborhood that once was called Downey—high-rise buildings with murals meant to inspire, but which had eroded over time. On the opposite side of the street were the blocks of tents where the homeless set up their own hood with whatever materials they could salvage. By day, do-gooders roamed the area, talking about Jesus and the perils of space while handing out clean water and energy bars.

Jenette waved off the residual smoke wafting from the blunt Liberty smoked in the front seat. The grassy scented eddies made her feel lightheaded. Ever since what happened to Roseanna, she hadn't been one for drugs.

"Hold this." Neto reached back and placed a small pistol on Jenette's lap. Her heartbeat ricocheted in her chest with an alien sensation, and she ran her fingertips across the cold metal, an instrument of life and death. There was a vibration of power, even if it was the type that stole innocence. Being in the car with the people she was supposed to consider family made her feel physically less alone, but in that instant the only thing that felt real, or had any weight, was the gun resting on her thighs.

When she was growing up, guns had been banned in their home because her mother always feared they would be stolen or used against them. Even Seraphin had complied.

Finishing whatever he was doing, Neto reached down and took it from her, then aimed it out the open window. P-Wee slowed the car down.

"This is just a warning shot," he said. "Those cabrons better stop straying into our damn neighborhood. ¡Las Calaveras, pendejos!" he shouted out the window.

"Las Calaveras!" Liberty Love echoed loudly while throwing up a crown with her right hand.

The succession of pops made Jenette jump, then Liberty chuckled at the screeching wheels as they picked up their speed. It was an old car, so the engine roared. She extended the blunt to Jenette, who shook her head, so she pulled it back and took a deep hit. With heavy lids topped with thick black eyeliner and wispy fake eyelashes, she fixed her gaze on her friend.

"You know you're still a future," she said. "You won't be with us until you go on a mission of your own. It could be anything. Then you can shake up with me. Live and die for each other, familia. We can even go to the juntas together. It's mostly boring stuff, like what's happening in the neighborhood, dues, who wants to move up the ranks."

Neto placed the gun on Jenette's lap again. Poles of light and shadow crossed his face as they sped through residential streets then onto the freeway, where there was little traffic.

"Every gang requires some sort of sacrifice, a test," he said. "I remember you telling me you come from military. You think those boys don't do the same here or up there? A uniform or suit, fucking Dickies and tube top like Liberty over here wears, it don't matter. Dinero, territory, space, food, fucking medicine. Shit's only legitimate because someone with authority says so—and most of the time that authority is a weapon, or money."

"Then what makes Las Calaveras different?"

"Because we wear a crown with five points. Love, sacrifice, honor, obedience, righteousness. And every motherfucker will want to tear it off your head. Don't slip up. Respect your brothers and sisters. Respect your hood. Respect yourself. No cocaine, no heroin, no crack. P-Wee had to learn the hard way."

"Yeah, I had to take a neck down for five minutes from the meanest on the block," P-Wee said from the driver's seat. "Those bruises did not go away quick, but it sobered me the hell up. Can't make the hood look weak for nothing or nobody."

Jenette didn't say anything, rolled down her window to get fresh air in her hair, the beat of the music filling her head like the weed. She wondered where this life would lead.

"How much did you smoke, Neto?" Liberty Love joked.

Jenette turned to Neto. "You going to show me how to use this gun?"

He leaned back and kissed her on the cheek. His lips were slightly dry, but the softness on her skin made her neck go warm. Was it so bad to like both Liberty Love and Neto? The feelings were the same, because in her eyes both were equally attractive, just in different ways. Their bodies capable of different types of pleasure. They didn't cover those emotions in health class, or the few times she went to Sunday school.

He pulled closer and placed his arm around her shoulders.

"Of course," he said. "We're familia, and you need to know how to use a hood gun at some point. Us against the ugliness in the world. You think they want any of us to make it? If they did, we would see it. Nah, we fucking take it any way we can. They protect their territory like they the gangbangers. Believe that. Put that on your waist and in your piggy bank."

Jenette relaxed her body into the crook of Neto's arm. There was the faint scent of body odor and knock-off cologne clinging to his Dodgers jersey, but having the warmth of someone else was comforting. There was a sense of safety.

"I feel you. I believe that."

Jenette celebrated her sixteenth birthday by drinking at a house party while listening to twenty-first century hip-hop in the backyard. It was Neto's place, and a spread of vodka, Modelo, Coors, and tequila covered a card table along with cartons of fruit juice mixers. The music moved from old school rap to norteño. It wouldn't be a party without Los Dos Carnales belting out corridos. The stars were out, and they were all feeling good—either high or drunk or both.

Life was beginning to appear normal again for most folks.

Liberty Love and Jenette lay on a blanket in the bed of a rusted Toyota pickup truck without any tires. Whenever Jenette looked up at the stars, she thought of the last real conversation she'd had with her mother. She wondered what Carmen and Sandro were doing?

"I hope we don't get the cops called on us. It's getting a little loud."

"No shit," Liberty said. "Sounds like people moving into the streets, too. I think the end of summer has everyone going a little crazy, and after a year of bad news and dead bodies."

Liberty Love rolled toward Jenette and kissed her lips, the heaviness of her breasts pressing against Jenette's chest.

"I know you look at me," she said. "I like it. Figure this would be a good birthday surprise."

"You just doing me a favor then?" Jenette gazed into her eyes, then pulled away. "No thanks. Plus, don't Las Calaveras have some whack rule about this?"

"Maybe we can change that rule. Also, it's not like that. It's a present for me, too."

Liberty's tongue was soft. Her mouth slightly sweet and bitter from the alcohol and weed. Her body as supple as Jenette had imagined as she touched it with care.

Sirens wailed, along with the sound of screeching wheels.

"Fuck, I *knew* it!" Liberty put out the blunt hanging between two fingers she held at their side. "Let's go." They jumped from the back of the truck and ran through an alley to reach the street parallel to the one in front of the house. Others had the same idea, and there were other partygoers running down the street, hopping over fences, or jumping into cars parked curbside. Engines customized for noise roared to life.

Liberty hurled forward, face-first to the ground, when someone they didn't know crashed into her, running away from the police. Blood streamed from her nose and cut bottom lip as she lifted herself from the asphalt. She sat upright and began to cry as she looked down at her blood-soaked tank top.

"Damn it! My clothes, my lip feels busted." Jenette kneeled next to her and grabbed her upper arm.

"C'mon we got to go."

A police vehicle silently pulled up and blocked off one side of the street. They had to move fast between houses, or hide. To their right an officer came bolting through the alley, before they had a chance to run.

He pointed his gun at them.

"Don't you move."

Jenette put both her hands up. The last thing she wanted was trouble, even though she figured she already looked like trouble to him. All that mattered was getting out of here, and getting Liberty Love to a doctor.

"She's hurt. We didn't do anything! Help us."

"You shouldn't be here then."

Jenette looked up and down the street, then to the houses to her immediate right and left. People ran past, caring only about their own skins, desperate to not get trapped in the teeth of the law. Cars roared and shouts rang out around them. She hoped someone was watching between the blinds and recording it all.

Fear made her realize that, despite the people she ran with, she was still just a skinny kid no one wanted—except a sister who couldn't have her. She became conscious of her own body and Liberty Love's curves that might be too noticeable to this man who stood before them with a gun, taser, and badge. As a female in fight-or-flight, she realized her anatomy became acutely important.

True fear.

It was why her mother never wanted any of them to walk alone. Now she understood. She didn't know what to do.

From the house next to Neto's the screen door slammed open. A group of Las Calaveras charged in their direction with an officer chasing behind, shouting at them to stop. Two shots exploded between the shouting and sirens. So close, Jenette and Liberty Love ducked from the gunshots. Jenette glanced up at the cop who'd had his weapon pointed at them, pulling the trigger.

The body of the pursuing officer and a kid she had seen in the neighborhood thumped to the ground. Both were bleeding from the wounds to their torsos. Muffled moans faded with the flow of blood. Their eyes lost all life, until they stared back at her with the coldness of the merciless elements of space.

The cop looked at Jenette, then to the fallen officer.

His gun was pointing at her.

"You!"

"Fuck you, man. I saw what you did."

"Shh, don't say anything, Jenette," Liberty Love pleaded in a whisper through lopsided lips. "You'll make it worse for us."

The cop dashed toward Jenette, knocking her to the ground.

"Stop it!" she shouted. "Don't touch me!" She tried to push him off with her arms and legs. His bulk overwhelmed her and his limbs were those of a spider trying to wrap her into a web for later consumption.

"Help!" Liberty Love screamed, still bleeding from the mouth and nose. "Someone help us!" The houses were dark, with people minding their own, not wanting to incur the wrath of the law.

The officer pushed his weapon into Jenette's hands. She grabbed her switchblade from her back pocket and pressed the button hard to open it. Without thought of where it would land, she tried to slice him just enough to get him to move away. It only served to stoke his conviction.

"Now you'll really rot in prison," he growled.

He overpowered her by placing a knee between her legs and his forearm across her chest. The pressure made her breasts feel as if they might burst. His body weight made it difficult for her to move. Between sobs, Liberty was still screaming down the empty street. He grabbed the switchblade, tossing it away.

Liberty snatched it from the ground, closing it, then put it in her bra before grabbing the officer's neck to pull him off Jenette. Sirens made them all pause for a beat, then the officer started to hit Jenette in the face. A police vehicle and ambulance came to a screeching stop in front of them. Two more cops jumped out, and one pulled Liberty Love away.

The cop kept punching Jenette in the face, spittle spewing from his mouth.

"¡Mira! Stop him! It's not right!" Liberty shouted. "Why is it always us on our asses, having to fight up? *Why us?* Fucking do something!"

All Jenette could do was attempt to grasp his forearms as her head slammed right to left. She could see her own blood flying into the air, then felt it land back on her face. A paunchy officer with a thick straw-colored mustache stood next to her.

"What the hell is going on, Jason? Get up now."

The cop stopped his assault to look up. "This punk skank took my gun and shot those two."

"No she didn't!" Liberty roared. "He's lying!" She lunged from the officer holding her back. Her tank top was a mural of mascara black and blood red. "Look what he did to her!"

Paramedics from the ambulance rushed to the officer and young man lying dead in their comingling blood. They didn't look twice at Jenette with a swelling eye, or Liberty's broken nose and sliced lip. The mustached officer shook his head.

"You didn't have to take it this far. Go on. We'll take it from here."

The cop, Jason, rose from the ground, releasing Jenette. With one eye swollen shut she took a good look at him. He had a few pockmarks around a forehead topped with light brown hair that receded slightly. Only a few telltale wrinkles around the eyes and mouth to give away that he was an hombre who had worked too long in a job he probably hated, but couldn't give up. The only power he had—that gave his existence any weight—was this.

Did mutual hate cancel each other out, or did it just accumulate to create something more vicious they couldn't see? He looked down on her without any remorse.

"Take them both in, and check that one for a knife. She tried to stab me after shooting them."

Jenette remained silent, having no fight left in her as she stared devoid of emotion at the night sky. Not a scrap of fucking will left. Blood from her mouth dribbled down her chin and rested in the fold of her neck, staining the gold cross she wore. Each blow had done more than inflict pain—there was the fear that this is how she would spend the rest of her life.

How many blows are we supposed to take in one lifetime? she thought. If there was a God, why did it seem like the world she lived in was one big beating into submission. She sat there powerless, the one without a badge, a cock, a gun, money, family, hope. *Where is my hope, Seraphin? Where are the spirits of the soldaderas?*

I need them. I need you.

Before Liberty was taken away she screamed once more, but this time directly at Jenette.

"Whatever happens, homegirl, keep your head down and take whatever they give you. Don't make it worse. Just get out. Some of us have to make it. Swear to me!"

Jenette could barely open her lips to whisper.

"I swear it on the Vasquez name."

The judge had too much foundation and plastic surgery. Jenette could only see her through one purple-and-yellow-ringed eye. The other was swollen shut. Her bones ached even though nothing was broken but her heart.

"You were found with a weapon. A switchblade you gave your friend to hide after threatening the life of an officer."

"No, I did not give it to her," Jenette answered. "But yes, it was a switchblade, and the dead officer was shot. I told you it was another officer who did it, his name was Jason. Let me show you who it was. Please believe me. Doesn't he have a camera on him?"

"The officer in question stated that it was switched off because it had been quiet all evening. His shift was nearly over. There is no proof of what you have told me. It's your word against his."

Jenette's body tensed.

"My word isn't worth anything?"

The judge stared at her with little concern bordering on boredom. "It's very clear that you have no direction, so we are going to course-correct for you. You will remain incarcerated. You don't want to tell us details about the Calaveras? No problem, but this is the consequence for that decision."

"I told you I don't know details," she said. "I wasn't a full member. And if I was, I wouldn't snitch."

The judge didn't blink. "This matter is closed."

"Closed? That's it? How can you sleep, lady?"

The judge didn't give her a second glance before closing the case file and gliding out of the courtroom in her black robe.

Even at that age Jenette knew the world was divided between the people who carried the consequences of their actions and the ones who didn't. The hearing had been held behind closed doors, with her court-appointed lawyer making the decisions for her. There she was, stuck and totally fucked like one of those sad worms at the bottom of shitty tequila bottles the gringos like to take photos with in border towns, or corny fake Cinco de Mayo celebrations used as an excuse to get drunk.

Her lawyer turned to her.

"I did the best I could," he said. Then he added, "There's a program, but you're too young right now. You just might get out in a few years. Until then, do what you've got to do to survive. Your kind always do…

"I'd suggest doing research on the Marines."

With that the lawyer walked away. He wore scuffed shoes and a suit jacket that made his shoulders look like they were sliding off his body. The poor shit probably got paid peanuts for being a public defender, or he had done something wrong and this was *his* punishment.

The Marines.

Among the grief, partying, wanting to disappear, chaos, she'd almost forgotten about that small dream. Now she would have nothing but solitude to focus on it. Maybe it was a false promise he'd made to soften the blow. If there was any chance at a life outside of here, she would take it.

"You ready?" A guard with the most sympathetic look she had received since the incident tapped on the table to get her attention. "I don't think you'll give me any trouble."

Jenette nodded in numb shock. He guided her away without cuffs or excessive pressure on her body when she had to be guided from the courtroom to the van that was waiting to take her away. After he helped her into the vehicle, with his hand still on the sliding door, he looked at her straight in the eye.

"It doesn't have to be the end. Don't go in there thinking it is. Whole planets have been formed with nothing but patience. You feel me?"

"Thank you."

"De nada, sister."

The door slammed shut, and she was off.

3

Jenette lay on her single bottom bunk with her back against the concrete wall and her legs pulled close to her chest. She had tossed and turned most of the night. Her body felt so small, as if she took up no space in this world, and the cell amplified that feeling. Her right cheekbone still ached from the punches.

No wonder a gun had felt so good.

A voice came from above her. "You kept me awake down there," it said. "I know it's hard to sleep when you're new, but all you need to know is they're trying to maintain their image. We're as disposable as sanitary products. Too many people with not enough choices—no way will they admit it was friendly fire."

Jenette had been so locked in her own thoughts she forgot someone else shared her space.

"How do you know about me?"

"Gotta fill the time with something. Gossip is one of the ways." A pause, then she added, "My name is Daisy Paxton."

"Jenette."

Daisy climbed down from the top bunk. "It helps to have a clique in here. You ran with Las Calaveras, so you should be alright."

"And you?" Jenette wasn't expecting a pretty white girl with freckles and brown eyes. "What are you in for?"

Daisy sat on the edge of Jenette's bed. "I caught my cousin stealing my dad's diabetes and pain medication. He was also taking my underwear. So I hacked his car. He got into a bad accident and almost died. I'm shitty at being a criminal, and didn't bother trying to cover my tracks."

"Shit, my sister was in a bad accident," Jenette said, "but she was trying to save the world, while doing everything she could to shut it out." She thought about it. "Damn. Small world."

"Yeah, too small. That's why there is a place up there called space. So many worlds to escape to, if you get the chance."

The metal door to their cell opened for her first breakfast in prison. The only daylight came from the small window that overlooked the staff parking lot, and farther off a sallow field. Knowing the sun and moon existed was a small comfort—otherwise it could be anywhere at any time of the day.

"With nothing else to do, you'd think they would at least let us sleep until a decent hour." Jenette rolled out of the uncomfortable bed, moving sluggishly. A shadow eclipsed the light coming from the corridor.

"Hurry up! Fucking cockroaches move faster than this. You're new and need to know the way of things in here. We run a tight schedule. You can't be lazy anymore."

The uniformed guard wasn't much taller than five feet nine, with black eyes and a puff of hair spilling from the neck of his uniform. He barged into their cell, stashing the personal device he'd used to open the door, and grabbed Jenette by the scruff of her blue sweatshirt so that her forehead bashed against the railing of the top bunk. Remembering what the cop had done to her, she fought the urge to kick and scream.

Who knew what would happen behind bars.

"I heard you're a cop killer," the man said. "A tough, gangbanging, murdering cunt. Well, you're nothing in here. Don't try anything on my watch."

"Leave her alone, Hanson!" Daisy shouted.

"Shut up, hoe. You can't protect your new girlfriend." He continued to drag Jenette to the door of her cell, controlling her movements with one hand on the collar of her sweatshirt and the other hand digging his thumb and forefinger deep into her neck. "When lights are up it *means* lights up. You hear me, girl? Don't even look like a girl."

He shoved her one more time toward the entrance. "Now stay, bitch." He sniggered before swaggering into the corridor to shout insulting profanity inside other cells. Jenette shot a glance in Daisy's direction.

"Can he do that? Treat us that way?"

The light in her cellmate's eyes dimmed as she looked off to the corner of the room.

"No one stops him."

"Damn. I feel smaller than before, weak." Jenette peered out through the bars. "Like a dead leaf being blown away, no way to tell where I'm going to land."

"Then don't be." Daisy took a step toward Jenette and gently rested both hands on her shoulders. "Fuck being small. Be the tree that don't move, with deep roots, and if you do get blown away, make sure you make some noise when you're falling, or take something down with you."

Jenette held back the tears mounting in her eyes and looked at her feet to hide her emotions.

"*Please make an orderly line outside,*" the intercom blared in a calm, inauthentic voice from the corridor.

"I guess we need to go. Thanks for the pep talk, roomie."

"I got you," Daisy said.

There was more than enough time to think about their crimes, but Daisy and Jenette lived out their desires in secret, finding solace at night in each other's arms. Daisy was real, solid, but Jenette still tried to hold on to her dream.

The Marines.

She wouldn't get lost again.

When she closed her eyes, she revived her memories of the soldiers in her family. As painful as it was to remember, she saw old Seraphin in his baggy jeans held up with a leather belt and large silver belt buckle in the center with an intricate design of a buck. He punched the air with his fist whenever Bruce Springsteen's "Dancing in the Dark" began to play, like it was his working man's anthem to a better existence, knowing it was there but just out of reach.

For a little dramatic effect, he added cumbia steps to the song and a twirl like he was spinning a beautiful woman in a dancehall. In her visions he always wore his red bandana and black ribbed tank top.

She imagined the soldaderas with their long braids, practicing their aim for their country, wearing big skirts and fighting to be a voice in a society whose fate was just as much theirs as anyone else's. She wanted to know *more*.

Nothing but time on her hands so why not learn something new, she decided. The meager prison library, smelling like moldy paper, was like a jumble sale with odds and ends of donations. The books she sought out explained survival techniques, military history, any type of fighting or combat. There were videos of rodeos and bullfights that kept her transfixed with the concentration the people had to maintain in the ring.

Then there were the books on physical training and anatomy. She touched the still-tender bone beneath her left eye as she watched. Who would look after her if she couldn't do it for herself?

When made to feel small, pliable, meek, muscle became a form of power, just like knowledge. Taking up physical space made Jenette feel as if her presence would be known. Lockup was a battle against a beast with no heart or eyes, only teeth. Not a goddamn thing was going to push her around or grab her by the neck.

Daisy taught art every Monday to a small group of interested prisoners. She was a tattoo artist, as well, and Jenette asked her to tattoo a single teardrop on the corner of her eye. Not for a murder, but if they wanted to think that, then let them. If the Marines panned out, she would become a cold-blooded machine with a weapon always hot in the most dangerous position.

She decided this would be the last tear she would show for her past, or for herself out of pity.

The gym was the perfect outlet to satisfy her need to take control of something in her life *and* fill the hours. Jenette wanted weight in this world that didn't come from her hips, tits, and ass. And if everyone thought she was a murderer, then she might as well play that part. The prison facility was mixed to accommodate everyone's gender—it was one of the few places all genders mixed.

The walls were lined with mirrors behind plexiglass that couldn't be broken, even from a weight hurled across the room. Cameras monitored from the four corners and there were two guards on watch at all times. It wasn't anything fancy, with only the basic equipment you would find in any budget gym.

A young gringo with dirty blond hair and skinny arms sat at the edge of a weight bench. There was a nasty scar extending from the corner of his left eye. He looked as lost as she felt as he scratched at the small pimples on his neck and next to his ears. His gaze passed her before doubling back.

"Want this bench? You need someone to spot you?"

Jenette looked around and realized he was talking to her. "I can't front," she said. "I have no idea where to begin. Mostly read a bunch of books."

"Yeah, this room is a little overwhelming, considering the terrible accommodations in the rest of this place." He gave her a crooked grin. "You ready to go hard? I'll spot you. Put that stuff in your cabeza to good use."

Jenette raised an eyebrow and crossed her arms. "What do you know about going hard?"

He shrugged. "I don't fucking know. Trying to figure it out myself. Look, if I'm not gonna spot you, do you mind spotting me?"

Jenette glanced around the room again. The other inmates either talked among themselves or seemed happy to be solo knowing what they were doing. Then she looked back at the gringo. He seemed decent enough.

"Sure, what do you want me to do."

"Cool," he said. "Put on another fifteen pounds." As she moved to do so, he added, "What's your name by the way? I should know before you have the power to crush me under a barbell."

"Jenette Vasquez. You?"

"Mark Drake. Thanks for partnering up. It's tough not knowing anyone, and not knowing who to trust."

"No shit," she said. "If this works out, maybe we can do it on the regular."

"Cool," he said again. The scar at the corner of his eye puckered when he smiled. Jenette wondered what kind of fight had made that. Didn't matter. The past had to be the past, otherwise she would remain in a mental prison. This one was bad enough.

If Drake showed her respect, she would return it in kind. And lifting heavier weights would require a partner at some point, anyway. No one would lay hands on her, ever again. Resilience in body, spirit, and mind—even if no one could see or feel it but her.

It worked out, so Drake and Jenette developed a routine. They met every day during recreation time. There was something she loved about the concept of tearing her body down to the smallest fibers, for the promise of building it up bigger and better.

Stagnation was a cell within the mind, she knew. Stay too long, and it was hard to leave. No, she had to keep up her regimen with Drake, especially on the days when the monotony of lockup hatched hundreds of monstrous larvae to tear apart her sanity.

One bash against the cell wall and it could be over.

Then she remembered the officer Jason, the judge, and in here, Hanson. No way would she give these motherfuckers the satisfaction. Sometimes one stand was all it took.

They alternated upper and lower body exercises day to day, with fasted cardio twice a week. After heavy lifting, the burn for one or two days gave her some sign there was change, movement toward a goal.

"Come on, dude." Drake lay on the bench press with his arms wobbling as he reached for the bar again. Jenette stood behind with her bandana around her forehead. "You got this."

"Well, technically, you do if I don't."

He was halfway through his reps when a familiar voice shouted toward them.

"The two pussies of the joint found each other."

"What do you want, Hanson?" Jenette didn't bother looking up. "This is our time. And your breath smells like salami. Back off."

"It's whatever I say it is, and you're whatever I say you are." Hanson walked over to the bar and placed an extra ten pounds on each side. The entire room slowed their workouts to watch. Some stopped altogether.

"Show us what you got." Hanson hovered over Drake with a malicious sneer. "Or are you only hanging with Vasquez cuz you're a little bitch, too?"

Drake leered back at him then gripped the bar. His arms quaked under the strain as he took the bar overhead and lowered it toward his chest. His face changed from light pink on only his cheeks to bright red from the neck up as he began to lift it again. The veins in his lean forearms and biceps bulged as thick as his triceps. He gritted his teeth with sweat rolling onto the bench.

"C'mon, man," Jenette whispered. "You can make it. Fuck this prick."

"Who you calling a prick?" Hanson spat. "You're next."

Drake managed to just place the bar back on the rack. He exhaled loudly as he lifted himself from the bench. Those in the room clapped, with some whistling.

"Get on there." Hanson attempted to shove Jenette into the bar, but her frame didn't budge as she tensed. Hanson's narrowed eyes ran the length of her body when he couldn't push her forward.

"She's never lifted that high, man," Drake said. "Let me spot her." But Jenette slapped his midsection with the back of her hand.

"You want to be a bad man, Hanson? Just watch."

"You sure are cocky without a cock," he replied. "But with that hair and body…"

Jenette spat on the floor at his feet, just missing his shoe. She made her way to the bench then lay in the puddle of sweat left behind from Drake. One big breath, followed by adjusting her white bandana. It had to be white to avoid gang colors. She could hear the crowd murmuring, some placing bets of commissary and cigarettes.

Fuck you all, she thought to herself.

She wrapped her fingers around the bar, then wiped her hands on her sweatpants before taking hold of it again. She lifted it slowly until the weight of it was directly over her head. One second of wavering and it would give new definition to the exercise they call a skull crusher.

Stored in that bar, this was the culmination of the weight of the last few years, and the beginning of the years she still faced in lockup. If the weight fell, no one would be left hurting but her. Or she could try as hard as possible to make that one rep. Rise above the sorrow and disappointments. Slowly she lowered it toward her chest. God her arms wanted to give way, give up.

"Go on, Vasquez. Let everyone who didn't bet on you lose," Drake whispered. The bar reached just above her breasts.

Now was the real test, lifting it up again.

With every ounce of muscle, energy, and determination, she tightened her abdominals. There was a sudden awareness of the soft cotton of her bandana, absorbing her sweat. Then she pushed. Even if the metal melted from the heat in the palm of her hand, she would accomplish this—not for the crowd or Hanson, but for herself. She could do it. She continued to drive it upward, allowing one groan escape before placing it back on the rack. As metal hit metal, a cheer louder than Drake's filled the gym. Bets were won and lost.

Hanson stood over her.

"You still ain't shit," he growled. "It's just one rep. Don't mean a damn thing in the real world."

Jenette sat up, feeling every muscle in her body sigh in relief. As much as part of her wanted to break into tears from the exertion and humiliation, she knew this was the point of no return with Hanson. No more tears. She stood to meet his gaze.

"Let's see what you got, pendejo," she said. "You wanna play big dog, ese, then show us those big balls. This *pussy* has no respect or time for shrimp dicks, dickhead."

The room erupted into hoots and howls. He sucked his teeth.

"On duty. No can do."

There was sniggering from those still watching the standoff. More bets being placed if there would be a fight between the two. Hanson looked around, and found all eyes on them.

"Everyone get back to your own fucking business. Time's almost up." He turned his attention back to Jenette and Drake. "That goes for you, too."

When his back was turned to walk away, Drake held his palm up to Jenette.

"Hey, I didn't mean to doubt you. Just tryin' to look out. And damn, chica... mad respect."

She gave his palm a friendly slap. "I understand. No harm. I would have done the same."

"Think I'm done with lifting for the day," Drake said, trying to make it sound like a joke.

"Same. Let's just get on the bikes like we're somewhere cruising—but tomorrow back at it."

"You got it, sister. You want to stick with the bench press?"

She shook her head. "Nope, I want to do that." She pointed. "If I can lift my own body weight, I can carry anything."

Drake followed her pointed finger to the pull-up bar.

"Hell, yes," he said. "Mañana."

The next time she saw Hanson he hassled her less, opting for the hard stare when she passed. She could live with that and matched his glare. There was no harm or foul with exchanging a "fuck you."

Roseanna regularly sent her messages and money for her commissary. The notes always ending with her apologizing profusely. Jenette had no beef with her, or anger. How could she, when they were all they had left in this world, sharing blood yet destined to be worlds apart.

The world wasn't done with the Vasquez name. Jenette knew that for certain, but goddamn she needed a win. She had respect, puppy love, the body of Adonis with tits, read nearly all the books in their sorry excuse for a library that only existed as a charity. Prison libraries were never fully funded—it was so much bullshit.

With Daisy lying in her arms, she would stare at the metal lattice of the bed frame or window, hoping for a way to slip through.

Rumors ran like wildfire through the cellblocks, and she ignored most of them for the bullshit they were. One piqued her interest, though—the Marines were recruiting. Something was going on out there, where new colonies were cropping up. Some said it was the different countries, each trying to snap up new territory before the others could get there. Others claimed it was the companies, always looking for new ways to take your money.

It didn't matter who it was. Not to Jenette.

Please let this be the day something comes through, she would pray, whenever the moon could be seen outside her small window. She wondered what had become of Neto, and Liberty Love. That lawyer had left her with hope, and she held on for dear life to it. *When life gives you limes, make a damn margarita and dance in the dark until it's dawn again.*

4

When the day arrived, it fell on a Monday—not that the days of the week held meaning, since each one was exactly the same as the previous. Only holidays stood out, and those only because of the dessert served at dinner.

Jenette stood in the middle of her cell tossing a hacky sack around with her foot. After that, she would use the hand grip to build up her strength further. A female guard opened the door.

"Vasquez," she said. "You got a visitor. Looks like the law."

A part of her panicked, wondered if it was bad news, because what else was there? *Please don't let it be Roseanna. Please, God. I'm asking for a blessing or a miracle.* She walked the corridor that seemed to be buzzing with a hushed excitement. There was extra movement and chatter. This gave her a glimmer of hope that it might be something besides another slap in the face from life.

"Hello, Ms. Vasquez." Behind the glass of the visitation unit sat the disheveled lawyer from her trial. She vaguely remembered him as Tom or Tim. He still wore a terrible suit, and had bags under his eyes. "Wow, you've changed. Do you remember me? Today is your lucky day. I have an offer for you."

"I'll take it." Jenette didn't bother to smile or offer any pleasantries. "I just want the fuck out."

He shook his head. "You don't even know what it is."

"I remember you, and I remember what you said about the military. I've been reading about it, in here. Working out. Keeping my head down. I'm no dummy."

He raised both eyebrows in surprise, then reached into the metal briefcase on his lap.

"That's perfect—I'm glad you remembered." He pulled out some papers, stapled together. "Here is everything you need to know about becoming a Marine. Just read through it, and if you agree, place your hand on the glass and I'll scan it."

He slid a contract through the small opening beneath the partition. He remained silent while Jenette read the letter, and the more she read, the more she wanted to cry—for once, tears of relief and joy.

This was her shot.

She was going to take it.

Jenette couldn't wait to share the news with Roseanna, Drake, and Daisy. She'd see Daisy when she got back to their cell, but wouldn't see Drake until just before dinner.

Through blurred eyes she scanned the small print. She could do all of this. Without looking up, she placed her hand on the glass. He took out a small device and used it to scan her palm print—just as the cops had done when she was arrested. This time, however...

"Alright," he said. "Looks like you're all signed up. You turn eighteen in a few months, and as soon as you do you will be a free woman—at least somewhat. Between now and then they'll perform a basic physical on you. Good luck." He looked as if a weight had been removed from his shoulders.

"Wait. Why did you come back to me? There are thousands of us."

He took a deep breath and exhaled. "You believe in luck or destiny? The number assigned to you in here was picked at random. I was given a stack of people to approach, and here you were. Get paid by each completed contract. So, thank you."

Jenette watched him leave, not caring about destiny.

She was getting the fuck out. Freedom.

Grinning at everyone she passed as she swaggered back to her cell, Jenette was dancing inside to the mental beat of any Cypress Hill tune. Even Hanson got a wink and a smile, out of pure spite, as she passed him in the corridor.

"Adios," she said loudly as she flipped him the middle finger. She hoped he already knew. She was scanned as she approached the cell, the door opened, and she bolted inside.

"I have some good news!" she said, bursting with excitement. "I'm going to be a Marine. Once I'm eighteen, it's fucking *adios* to this place."

Daisy sat with her legs dangling from the top bunk. To Jenette's surprise, she stared out the window without a smile or hint of joy.

"Shit, they must need more bodies," she said. "After you left, I could hear a few guards talking about a big recruitment push. A bunch of you, it sounded like. I figured that was the news you were getting." She fell silent, then added, "A second chance."

"Be happy for me," Jenette insisted. "I'm not wasting any more time in this hole, all for something I didn't do. I'm not stupid, though I wonder whose hands are getting greased for recruiting people in lockup. What a racket it has to be—these places are a business like your local bodega." Then she shook her head. "Don't matter. I'm gonna do this. I *want* to do this. It's part of my family history. This isn't just a second chance, it's my chance to be a real soldadera."

Daisy looked at her with tears in her eyes. "You do what you have to do."

Jenette dialed it down, and stroked Daisy's leg. "You can't be happy for me? What about you?"

"I've got multiple sclerosis in my genetics. Chances are I'll get it at some point. They have all of our information, from when we were arrested. They only choose the ones that can make it—at least make it long enough for whatever war is going on." She looked out through the window again. "I guess I'll have a new roommate."

"What did you expect, Daisy? El riesgo siempre vive."

Daisy climbed up onto her bed and rolled onto her side, facing away. "Go hang out with Drake. He'll give you the high five you want."

Jenette didn't know how to react. This offer was the hope she had been waiting for ever since the seed was planted in her head. It had grown at the same rate as the strength in her body, the confidence she could still be who she wanted to be, or at least figure out who she was. Freedom.

Recreation time arrived, and it was a relief to get out of the cell. Jenette spotted Drake on the pull-up bar. He'd come a long way in their regular training. She jumped on the spot next to him. Without any words they synchronized their movements.

"Yo, I have some news."

"Me, too. I'll be damned if it's the same news." Through the exertion, he flashed her a mischievous smile.

"Marines?" She groaned as she matched his large grin.

Drake nodded, then jumped to the ground. Jenette did the same. He extended his open palm, and she slapped it harder than usual.

"¡Órale!" she said. "Good thing we already have the bodies for it."

He lifted both biceps and flexed. "We're gonna run that gun show, baby!" Drake's excitement got her pumped up again. This felt right.

"Maybe we can go in together," she said. "Fuck this place. I can't wait to see Hanson's face when we walk out that door. I swear if I ever see him on the streets…"

"Save it for training!" he joked.

Jenette felt free for the first time in a long time. She left lockup with the small bag of belongings she'd had when she went in—including the switchblade. It felt good in her hands and reminded her of her real family.

They had a week before the training began. Unfortunately, Roseanna couldn't leave her job to fly out to visit before Jenette had to report. All they could do was exchange smiles and tears of joy over a video call.

"Have fun," Roseanna said as her parting words. "Live your life. Sometimes taking a risk is the dream. Your dream as a kid was to be a soldier, and here it is. Things that are meant to be always come around."

Nothing would be off limits. The last few years had been pure discipline and teetering on the tightrope of hope, trying to not fall in the chomping maw of despair, its hot breath always licking her heels. Tonight, the new crew of Marine recruits was heading to The Rooster, a known watering hole for the Corps.

Everyone knew the drill, the uncertainty in wartime, which meant this was a guaranteed good time. There was no one to tell her to not drink until she blacked out, or smoke cigarettes until her lungs burned, or fall into bed with a stranger or three. There was nothing like a tight ass in fitted jeans.

The price she'd paid for this freedom was to sign the rest of her life away to the Marine Corps. She'd gone into juvie just a kid, and was leaving as a young woman. She wanted to pick up where she left off, but this time instead of throwing up a crown with her right hand to honor her gang, she would be wearing the USCM insignia.

Drake was already at the bar and two drinks in, messaging her to hurry the hell up, he needed his wing man. The place heaved with hot bodies ready for one last lay before heading to wherever they would be sent with the possibility of never coming back.

Bruce Springsteen's "Dancing in the Dark" played over the din of the crowd. It reminded her of Seraphin and when she was younger. Old Seraphin in his bandana tinkering with blades or reading one of numerous newspapers on his tablet. The nostalgia made her feel alive again. As she passed the bar and the long mirror behind it, she ran her fingers through her thick pompadour. Fitted Levis, Timberland boots, and a cropped black halter with thin straps tied behind her neck. The only jewelry she wore was the gold cross around her neck.

Damn, she looked caliente, if she could say so herself. Jenette wanted to listen to hours of oldies, and get drunk.

Drake stood at the end of the bar talking to two very attractive women. Jenette had to smile. He knew her type. Drake looked up, caught her eye, and waved her over.

Then *a stranger* moved next to Drake.

She caught his eye immediately—it was obvious. She'd worked hard for the muscle, and she liked to show off the chiseled lines of her traps, shoulders, and biceps. No more baggy, used jumpsuit. Jenette knew exactly the power that was the curve of the female silhouette. One advantage of having nothing but a jumpsuit for a Friday night was growing to love your skin for what it really is.

Jenette loved her body, what it was capable of. Her muscles may have been hard, but the soft folds of womanhood still as delicate as a newly sprouted petal. She looked him up and down to let him know she might be interested. Just depended on what came out of his mouth.

The two women were obviously into Drake.

"Vasquez, you finally made it," he said. "Meet Tawney and Pam."

Jenette gave the two women a short nod. They smiled with eyelids heavy from day drinking. The one named Pam ran glitter pink nails down Drake's chest like a territorial beast. Jenette wouldn't be a cock block.

"You three have fun," she said. "We can catch up later, Drake."

As Jenette turned to walk to the bar, the good-looking stranger was right in front of her.

"You look a little young to be hanging out here," he said.

Jenette smirked. "If I'm old enough to be sent somewhere to fight and die, then I'm old enough to have a drink." She let that sink in, then added, "I'm Jenette."

He raised one eyebrow and wrapped his thick lips around a bottle of Coors. "Lorenzo Sanchez. I'm a new recruit, finishing up courses at community college so I can jump to a higher position once my training is done. Only way to climb that rope is through a degree, or who you know—but let's be real, it's mostly who you know."

Jenette could feel herself become flush. The scent of his sweet aftershave when he moved closer to hear her better. The shape of his pecs and arms visible through his tight T-shirt. She wanted to reach out and touch his chest, then trail her hand lower. Before lockup she had only fooled around with Neto, who was two years older and gave her an informal education in weapons. Over beers counting ammunition he'd asked her to be his girlfriend.

Other than Neto, and making out with Liberty Love, it wasn't until juvie she met Daisy. They'd had a physical relationship and experienced young love together, until she broke the news she was leaving.

"Well, Jenette," Lorenzo said. "Can I buy you a drink while you tell me all your dreams?"

"Yes, you can buy me a drink. Make it a shot, because I'm celebrating."

"Really? I'm intrigued."

He finished the last of his beer and stared into her eyes. Jenette knew where she would lay her head that night.

By midnight the crowd had thinned. Drake was long gone with both women. She had given him the condoms she brought, because Drake always seemed short on cash.

She found herself slow dancing to Guns N' Roses "Knockin' On Heaven's Door." They were both drunk, already floating in the oblivion of space. Why put limitation on life, she thought, when the only outcome is death. She wanted Lorenzo, and wouldn't take no for an answer. Her mind needed a release…

He tilted her chin toward his mouth and kissed her. His tongue pulled more sexual greed from her longing body. One hand squeezed her hip.

"My place?" he said, then he pulled back a little. "But I am being deployed soon. Cryo for two years. This will be whatever it will be."

"Any place, as long as we have nothing on." Her hand crawled to his ass. "El riesgo siempre vive."

She all but moved in with Lorenzo until it was time for him to leave.

The days were spent running the perimeter of the base and challenging each other on the obstacle course. At night her body cracked in the darkness like the striking of a whip as she surrendered herself to freedom. Lorenzo handled her in the ways she and Daisy couldn't allow for themselves, what with the guards and cameras. In lockup, it all had to be under the sheets and hushed in the dark.

Jenette wanted to make up for time lost.

The present was all that mattered until his deployment to one of the brewing conflicts out in space. They both knew departure day would arrive, but the time passed too soon, and it came with both of them still wanting more.

They stood at the curb outside his place.

"I guess this is it?" he said, trying to keep his voice light. "Maybe we will meet up there, in the stars." Then he looked her straight in the eyes, and turned serious. "Thank you for making the last few weeks magic. *You're* magic. A real bruja. Don't ever forget that, and kick anyone's ass that tells you otherwise."

Jenette held back her emotions. Daisy had refused to say goodbye on that final day. That lack of closure still hurt, as if what they shared meant nothing. At least she could close this chapter with Lorenzo.

"Thank you," she said finally. "You will always be part of me. I'm sure of it."

He kissed her one last time before getting into the automated taxi that would take him to the base. Part of her soul was pinched with grief of what could have been. Then she reminded herself that people crossed paths again all the time. Grabbing her own duffel, she headed back to the base. Drake had been lonely and slightly jealous without his best friend for training.

"Wait, do it again."

Eight weeks later she found out she was pregnant during a routine drug test. In shock, Jenette sat in front of the nurse.

The nurse stared back at her.

"I did... three times. I'll have to report this," he said, almost apologetically. "In the meantime, you need to go for a scan. Now." He wrote down on a notepad what they needed to do at the base clinic. Jenette's mind was beyond that already.

How would she get in contact with Lorenzo, already frozen and floating toward a who-knew-what? She didn't want to tell Drake or anyone, not just yet. Her main worry was fucking up her one shot—and for what?

On the bus to the clinic, anger burned her to the marrow as she chewed on the skin around her nails. No way would she go back, serve the full term of her sentence. They *had* to allow her to terminate. It was still her body and her choice.

Sinking in her thoughts, she nearly missed her stop.

Whatever happened next was in the hands of fate.

She lay on the table with the red rectangular light moving across her body. The projection against the wall revealed two sacs. Twins. Her heart thumped harder than in any training session. She didn't know if she wanted to scream or cry, so she lay there while the tech made a call to someone. When finished he turned to Jenette.

"You can pull down your T-shirt and pull up your jeans. I was informed that you need to return to the barracks until an emergency hearing on your status is scheduled. You can expect it within a day or two."

Jenette just nodded—she had no questions or anything to say, given the severity of the situation. As she walked out, she messaged Drake and Roseanna. Whatever the outcome, she would need someone to lean on.

Drake messaged back.

Damn. Lorenzo?

I've got your back, whatever you decide.

See you at the barracks.

Twenty-four hours later Jenette stood in front of the judge, not wanting to look her in the eye. It's not like she hurt anyone or went back to running with the old crowd in the streets. Never touched drugs in her life. Yet the grief wouldn't stop.

"You just can't stay out of trouble," she said, her voice full of condescension. "All of you are products of arrested development."

Jenette's cheeks felt hot.

"Yeah, well maybe stop arresting and start developing." Her temper was a cluster of Roman candles set alight while still in her hand. God help anyone if she pointed it in their direction.

She wanted to explode.

The judge flipped through a file. "Now, do you understand what this means? This is a violation of your terms of service. We can't force a decision on you, but either way, once you reach the outcome you will be sterilized. History can't be allowed to repeat itself." While Jenette tried to understand what was being said, she continued. "If you choose to remain pregnant, then upon the birth your placenta will be claimed, along with your womb and eggs, for use by the government as they see fit. This will help to compensate for the cost of the procedure."

"What?" she said. "Sterilized? Taking my organs? For what purpose? So, I don't even get a choice later on? You want to take that away from me, too?"

"Given your position, you ask a lot of questions," the judge replied. "As I stated before, everything that's recovered will be put to use as the government sees fit. In terms of your military service," she continued, "by behaving as you have, you're taking away from someone who would be more appreciative of the opportunities."

"Have you ever been locked up, your honor?" Jenette asked. "And not just locked up—for something you didn't do? You got any clue what it's like in there?"

"I'm not going to dignify your first question with a response," the judge responded flatly. "As for your innocence... that is not for you to decide. If we took the word of every convicted felon, then *everyone* would be 'innocent.' So I suggest you be quiet, and take the offer that's on the table.

"You will find I am very generous," she added. "I have a soft spot for your kind."

Jenette took her advice, and remained silent.

If there hadn't been so much hanging in the balance—returning to jail, kicked out of the Marines—she might have spat in the judge's face and told her to fuck herself because she obviously needed it.

Sometimes power didn't require any physical force at all. Rendering your opponent silent is enough.

"I want to think about it."

The judge gave her a fake smile. "Sure," she said. "You have twenty-four hours. If you are not back here by then, we will come and find you, to take you back to prison to serve the full term. You are in control of your future, Ms. Vasquez. I will place in the record my recommendations, should you decide to not terminate." The judge waved the bailiff over to hand Jenette a document. "These are the terms for keeping a pregnancy during training."

Then she gestured for Jenette to approach, and handed her a note. It was folded, indicating that it should be read in private.

Twenty-four hours to make this life-altering decision. Jenette needed to talk to Roseanna. Her sister had hit rock bottom before, had been forced to brave her storms, day in and day out. She also counseled people for a living. If anyone could provide some clarity, it would be her.

She went immediately to the barracks to make the call.

"That isn't much of a choice," Roseanna said bleakly. "Either way they will enforce their so-called 'right' to alter your body, just to suit them. Sterilized? Fuck them."

"I never thought much about kids," Jenette admitted, "but tell me I can't have them… Maybe I don't deserve them…"

Roseanna couldn't come on such short notice, so she had to remain an image on a screen. In front of the camera, she lit a white seven-day candle and placed it on her altar next to the photos of their relatives.

"I'm sorry, Jenette," she said, then took a moment to compose herself. "I know I have apologized to you more times than I can count, but I will never stop. And believe me when I say that I have had my own one-night stands and brief affairs. Don't you dare apologize for it."

"Fuck those clowns." Jenette ran her fingers through her hair. "I would terminate, if I knew I could choose later—but there won't be any later."

The candle on the altar crackled. Roseanna turned to look at it, then back to a fidgeting Jenette.

"I'll take them," she said. "I *want* them. If that is what you choose. I will also accept your decision, if you choose terminating. You…"

"What?" Jenette looked straight into the camera.

"*I want your babies*," Roseanna repeated. "To keep them in the family. Should you ever want to see them… You can trust me. We all deserve options, the right to make choices. We aren't just our pasts. We learn and move forward, wiser… sometimes it's just with another scar or tattoo."

Jenette thought about what her hermana had said. Let it sink in.

"I know I can trust you." Then she added, "Are you sure?"

"You know me better than that," Roseanna responded. "I wouldn't say it if I didn't mean it. This is unfinished business for me, because I couldn't be there for you. But what will you do, when you can't train like the rest? What did they say?"

"The first trimester, I can train like everyone else," Jenette explained. "I'll be spending the second half of my pregnancy in the armory. I will be living and breathing big guns. Not a bad gig. Then after they are born, I get a few weeks to catch up on what I missed with the rest of the training." She paused, then said, "If I terminate, then it's business as usual, but I will never have a chance to have my own, if I want that later."

Roseanna shook her head. "I'm fucking sick of all these tests."

"Tests and timing, sister. These are the pieces we are given for the board."

The candle continued to crackle and burn bright. Jenette hung her head and clasped her hands. Teardrops fell one by one with the slowness of blood drawn from a pin prick.

"I want to go through with it, Roseanna. I'll tell the judge you have all the rights. But as far as seeing them… I have to make this sacrifice count. I have to make myself and the family proud. Make *them* proud."

"You will, Jenette. Keep that soldadera spirit alive."

Jenette raised her head. "After they are born, I'm going to the top, the stars. Nobody is going to stop me. They can take my children, and organs, they can't have my soul. I'll make it to the stars, you wait and see."

Roseanna nodded and brought her hands to a prayer position. "Rewriting our history in our own blood, by changing the future."

5

2179

It was now or never if they wanted to escape this hell of a planet and the demons who seemed determined to claim their souls.

Jenette reacted instinctively, pulling the trigger on her pulse rifle, filling the tunnel with gunfire as she moved backward, trying to follow Ripley and Newt. She fired until the pulse rifle was dead. Dropping to the ground she went for her pistol.

The Xenomorph continued its pursuit. Then from an open tunnel above, one of them lunged downward. She gritted her teeth and pulled the trigger. As it fell, she pinned it to the wall with her boot. Without hesitation she unleashed a spray of bullets until bursts of the Xenomorph's acidic blood burned through her ankle.

Jenette screamed out in pain. She had to make it out. With both arms she pulled herself through the tunnel, while releasing the clip in her gun.

"No, no, *no*," she cried out.

The pain shot through her legs, making it difficult to move faster than a crawl. She heard Gorman call her name, then he was behind her and grabbing her beneath both arms. From a distance they could see a Xenomorph trying to burst through a metal wall. Gorman shot in its direction until he ran out of rounds.

The sound of skittering on metal revealed Xenomorphs coming from all sides.

Fuck, she thought. *This is it. I wish I had more time.* For a fleeting instant, she thought of Roseanna.

Ramón.

Leticia.

Reaching behind, he pulled out a grenade.

"You always were an asshole, Gorman."

He held the grenade in front of them and flicked off the safety. As he hit the button, she clamped her hand over his. Despite what was coming, neither of them closed their eyes. They would both die with honor. Jenette would earn her place with the soldaderas who came before her.

PART 2

FAMILIA

6

The true cost of energy and habitable land could only be counted in blood, the cries of those left behind, and decayed flesh left to fertilize the hardened ground.

Dr. Brenda Moon never expected to accept a position in weapons, but it was one of those offers she could not refuse, that would create generational wealth in her family. Wealth, what everyone vied for on an Earth spiraling into decay, with people struggling to cover even the basic necessities of living.

Generational wealth equated to the wealth of opportunity.

That was why she sacrificed herself to this new Weyland-Yutani planet that had been in the making for years, with intensive terraforming and the harnessing of its immense geothermal energy, similar to Iceland on Earth.

The planet was so secret it hadn't even been given an LV designation, a pet project launched by Meredith Vickers, who had died before she could create her own kingdom here. She had a great-grandson named Jacob who was only tangentially involved with the company. From what she knew, he lived in England. Brenda didn't know what Vickers' plan had been for the planet—no one did. She'd had a good eye for potential, though, because once the terraforming was complete, it became the perfect location for a scientific outpost.

The terrain was rough with sharp mountain ranges, plentiful water, and geysers to naturally surround the location of the facility. The landing station had been deliberately placed in front of a large swatch of brown and yellow sulfur fields filled with potholes of bubbling mud and burping water spurting plumes of sulfur into the air for hundreds of feet. It burned with the intensity of acid as it fell.

Large mud vents, some the size of a man, expelled smoke. Nothing grew there. Passing this section of the planet made her gag from the stench, even as her mind filled with possibilities for research. Only someone intent on reaching the facility would dare cross this unpredictable and treacherous road without special equipment, making it the perfect place to dispose of dangerous biological materials. The heat was enough to destroy anything.

Even the oceans on the planet were death traps with skyscraper-height waves and undertows powerful enough to drown a whale. Thus, the main facility was situated between the coastline and the sulfur fields. Perfect. Their research could be conducted far from the eyes of the competition, independent watchdogs, or government regulation.

The small group of scientists working here were a dedicated team who fully understood that they most likely would never leave the facility—nor would they want to. They would be tagged as the ones who had written a new chapter in humanity. Not everyone would understand.

They say the only constant in life is change, Brenda mused.

War should be added to that list.

Brenda stood in front of the glass, half staring at her own reflection as it merged with the grotesque sight of a body that resembled a blackened charred log, despite the fact that it hadn't been exposed to a matchstick. Their synthesized bacteria was a different type of fire. Nearby lay a nameless human guinea pig whose chest had become a wide chasm of liquified organs and congealing blood.

Given what she had just witnessed, Brenda felt just as grotesque inside. The human hadn't felt a thing, with a powerful sedative cutting off their pain, but they did witness with their own eyes the creature that had emerged from their chest, tearing through organs and past shattered bones. A creature that had become the object of the weapons development efforts, and had died a painful death, never knowing what had killed it.

Her colleague, Dr. Gilda Patel, joined her as a team behind the glass removed every speck of blood spatter, vomit, and fecal matter from the walls and floor. No trace of the bacteria could remain, even if its origins were in part native to Earth—a variation on the once-rare "flesh-eating bacterium" known as necrotizing fasciitis. The original had been recorded as far back as the eighteenth century.

The other component was a black mold, the origin of which remained unknown to her team. She knew better than to ask.

Xenomorphs had a sophisticated immune system unlike anything she had ever witnessed. Nature was the mother of the cruelest creations, she supposed, depending on where one stood in the hierarchy of things. Creating the right combination of elements, getting past that amazing immune system, had been the greatest challenge of her career. They were still a long way off pinning their hopes on every experiment. Sometimes the experiments worked, and other times they did not.

"I hope this time it pans out," Gilda said. Then she enthused, "You're going to be rich—I can't wait to get my bonus! Our shares will be worth a fortune. I wonder where I'll buy my first property. And all it took was a deal with a living, breathing devil.

"What will you do with your share?" she added.

Brenda had to hold back the urge to vomit. Her stomach cramped as it pushed lunch up her gastrointestinal tract.

"I'll tell you when I'm paying the price in hell—but let's not get ahead of ourselves. We have to be careful. There can be no accidents, no data leaks. We're not there yet. We know the bacteria works on the creature while it's still in the host, but there's still a long way to go before we can collect that check."

Like I'll ever get to spend it, she added silently.

As she moved toward the area where they would conduct phase two, Brenda could feel the world contracting tightly around her neck, laying its evil eggs of self-doubt.

When she declared she was going into space, accepting a major promotion with a biological research team, her family in Guyana wanted to know where she was going. She'd had no answers, not because she wouldn't tell them, but because she *couldn't*. She'd had no idea where she was being taken.

Despite its lethal history, Brenda didn't fear the bacteria. During her time teaching at the London School of Hygiene and Tropical

Diseases after leaving her home in Guyana, the CDC, and UNICEF, she had encountered all the worst bugs known to humans. She had seen firsthand what they were capable of doing. She was happy to flee Earth, to work in isolation from the chaos, and she didn't need to be there to make certain her family was still looked after financially.

The bacterium was only one of the projects they were developing. In this very facility they had created a newly engineered parasite based on the humble pork tapeworm. They gave it real teeth. She would rather contract Ebola than have it inside of her. But her mother hadn't raised her to be a fool. Every product could be neutralized.

Except these other creatures. The Xenomorphs, as they were called, were unnatural things they had no business trying to harness—not in their natural form. The longer she studied them, the less she slept. She kept her doors to her office and apartment double bolted. She checked all safety protocols twice after each experiment and when leaving the research wing for the night. No one she hadn't personally vetted was allowed near the creatures, even the small ones, chestbursters. Pale phalluses with jaws, yet the damage they caused to their hosts was something she hadn't been prepared for when she first witnessed the viciousness of it.

There was no recovering from that.

Unlike humans, these things could not be manipulated with money, power, sex, drugs, contracts. Humans had nothing to offer these things within the concept of our world or existence. The exact opposite. All they saw was carnage and survival. Their life cycle was an act of destruction and death.

They could not travel on their own—their expansion depended on others passing them around with the same ignorance of a host coughing out a pathogen on a crowded train. These things had no inkling of time. They only existed for the sake of it. They seemed immune to everything.

Until now.

Brenda paced her steps as she made her way to phase two. Each research lab was separated from the next by walls that could not be destroyed by anything short of a tank or blast from artillery. She stood beneath the globe scanner until the door opened. Inside, Gilda stood by the glass waiting for her. Brenda checked a tablet that registered the growth of the Xenomorph. The dosage had to be precise.

"All checks complete?"

"Twice. Just as you like it."

Brenda removed a small fob from the pocket of her lab coat.

"Good. Do it."

Gilda swiped on the console inlaid in the glass. A light came on behind the clear partition, illuminating what lay beyond. A young Xenomorph thrashed around the polytetrafluoroethylene-insulated chamber designed to withstand their acidic blood.

Brenda knew that at some point she would have to allow a test subject to get bigger, but she would avoid it as long as possible. If she had called the shots and held the purse strings, they would not grow beyond this point. But she didn't. Before long she would be forced to allow them to grow.

If all went according to plan, this next five minutes would tell the tale. From the back wall, a small ball the size of an orange rolled from an opening just large enough to accommodate it. They didn't dare anything larger. As soon as the ball entered the room the Xenomorph screeched and backed away. Its head lolled in confusion, with strings of viscous saliva pouring from snapping jaws filled with teeth.

The remotely controlled metal sphere continued to roll closer until the Xenomorph could no longer maneuver past it in the small barren room. Brenda pressed the fob in her hand.

The sphere exploded.

Projectiles sprayed from the orb to pierce the Xenomorph's armored exterior. The monster convulsed, waving its small arms as the bacteria invaded its body. The large mouth snapped at the air as if it was choking, until its body fell to the ground like the husk of a cicada from a tree. The bacteria caused toxic shock in the Xenomorph faster than in humans. It could lie there for hours in a delirium as the microscopic invader took over its system.

Today, however, they needed live samples.

She peered at the creature that could have been made of glass, a horrid Lladró from the depths of space. Brenda pressed another button on the fob. A man in full hazmat walked through a side door into the chamber, carrying a small rubber mallet in one hand. At the front of his waist were three small cylinders. Hoisted to his hip was a pulse gun, there in the event the test subject attempted to move.

Kneeling in front of the incapacitated Xenomorph, he extended a single finger to graze the limp inner mandible hanging out of its main jaws. The Xenomorph's teeth snapped, but not fast enough to catch the man's flesh. He stumbled backward onto his ass. That last movement by the Xenomorph caused another violent seizure before it slumped to the ground. Ashy blots bloomed on its exterior.

Brenda swiped her tablet to activate the intercom.

"What are you waiting for?"

The man remained sitting at a distance. *"Did you see what it just did?"*

She rolled her eyes, even though he could not see her. "It was an automatic response. The color exhibited on the skull tells me it's fine to proceed. We need the sample while it's still alive. Hurry. Unless you want to do this again."

Lurching back to his feet, he kneeled next to the Xenomorph and delivered a soft whack to the skull. Instantly the body cracked and crumbled. The inner tissue was deteriorating rapidly and that made it easy to destroy. He picked up the smaller pieces and placed them in the three cylinders on his waist. The last shard he brought close to the clear square visor on the helmet, giving it a few twists and turns before looking at the window, giving a thumbs-up.

Brenda smiled. The bacteria had neutralized the acidic blood of the Xenomorph, which led to its death. But so far it had only been tested on the young, the small ones. She didn't want to think about trying it on a full-grown Xenomorph... or a queen. One of the young queens they possessed she had named La Reina.

When fully activated, this bacterium could also be sequenced for use on humans. It would be lethal to everyone at any age. Yet even if the bacteria were sequenced to attack human DNA, they could be rendered harmless with the right antidote—currently under development.

For that matter, the bacterium might also be placed in a human without it being fully activated, and thus remain dormant. Humans could be the engineers of anything they wanted. Developing weapons like this could help mankind avoid long, protracted wars of tit for tat. One show of this weapon, and no one could stop you.

But Brenda hadn't been born yesterday, nor did she labor under idealistic delusions. She stayed as much for the money as she did to try to keep the Xenomorphs under control. The bacterium would offer some semblance of protection, even if it meant playing a shitty game to get ahead in the universe.

What was the old saying?

"Hate the game, not the player."

The humans they used in their research had "volunteered" to be a part of their program, and once they reached their inevitable end, they were dumped in the sulfur fields. No trace remained on the premises, and no one would go fishing in the fumaroles that were more than a hundred degrees Celsius. One of the scientists had suggested they toss the expired Xenomorphs into the treacherous oceans that were unsafe for anything or anyone.

"Absolutely not, not under any circumstances," she replied. "The only good Xenomorph is a pile of ash without anything recoverable from it." Even dead, the creatures came from unknown origins. She wouldn't run the risk that the remains might interact with any indigenous species.

Brenda prided herself on a degree of level-headed thinking, but where the creatures were involved, her imagination tended to run wild. Nature and science had taught her humility, but the world of men taught her how bad things could get when it was least expected.

"Dr. Moon, we're ready for you. *She* is ready."

Brenda didn't like this at all, but it was now or never.

"Take me to her majesty."

She walked along the narrow corridor and stopped to face a blank section of wall. A camera dome hidden in the ceiling scanned her, and a section of the wall opened into a windowless room known to a very select few. There was nothing inside except a single pane of reinforced plexiglass, filling the far wall.

"La Reina," Brenda whispered.

Her entrance alerted the team on the other side. In the middle of the sterile room lay an infant queen Xenomorph. She was one of three. Her hood was only starting to develop and wing back. She writhed with her arms, legs, and tail bolted to a PTFE gurney. Because of her blood, everything in the chamber was made from polytetrafluoroethylene. Above her head, a large heated glass sphere of black-and-blue bacteria particles floated in plasma.

As if sensing the threat, the queen paused in her struggles.

"Time to give La Reina her crown."

A scientist walked behind the Xenomorph, pushing a trolly that held five white bullet-shaped PTFE cylinders, each the size of a shotgun shell. He attached one to the top of a handheld drill, then placed it against the skull of the Xenomorph. With a hard jolt the first cylinder broke through the young creature's relatively soft cranium, leaving part of the cylinder protruding. The PTFE could avoid being absorbed deeper in the softer tissue.

La Reina shrieked loudly, thrashing and attempting to free herself. The scientist continued this process until each bullet was embedded, creating a circular crown. The Xenomorph increased her protestations with each insertion. Each bullet contained a chip that could be activated to release the bacteria.

Yet that wasn't the intent.

Time for the next phase.

A scientist to the right switched on a laser scalpel. The red tip burned through the bottom half of the creature's jaw, leaving the long inner mandible swinging side to side. The scientist then removed half her tail with a clean swipe, followed by both hands. The bottom half of each leg was removed at the knee joint. This left her utterly incapacitated.

The only thing they required of La Reina was for her to reproduce. Brenda took a deep breath. Their queen would now be placed deep within the facility, in a new throne that would eventually be her tomb.

"How do we know this will accomplish anything in the long term?" Gilda said.

Brenda took another deep breath as she continued to look at the small queen. "We don't." Seeing Dr. Patel's expression, she continued. "Look how many versions of androids there have been. *Nothing* is perfect—including science. But science is what we have, and we couldn't have survived this long as a species without it. Hell, we wouldn't be up here in space without pushing the limitations."

"So you're betting on that she—I mean all the queens—will just grow to accept their chopped-off pieces? Giving up and giving us their limbs, their eggs, and their DNA until we kill them off?"

"I don't know," Brenda admitted, "but there's one thing I *do* know. If the slightest hint of a threat appears, before La Reina has a chance to do anything she will be executed, hence the crown. One press of a button and *poof*."

"What comes next?"

"We wait, and we see if she begins to produce eggs." Brenda and Gilda stood there in silence, watching as La Reina was wheeled out and a scientist removed the globe of bacteria. Its purpose had been served.

Gilda turned to Brenda. "Coffee?"

Brenda chortled. "Make it an Irish coffee, and you're on."

7

Roseanna Vasquez's small ranch in Texas, a few hours north of the restored Gulf of Mexico, had a pale blue, two-bedroom, one-story house on three acres of land dotted with pecan, oak, and mesquite trees, with its own small pond. The beautiful foliage and wide-open space from which she could watch the sunrise and sunset encouraged calm and gratitude when memory eclipsed her mind, sending her into dark corners of not wanting to live.

She had purchased it from a man named Robert Boone, a tall Black vaquero who had two children close in age. It had been instant chemistry when he opened the door, and even more when he showed her the property. This patch of paradise enabled her to stay sober and find a sense of purpose. A collection of wind chimes hung from the beams in the front and back of the house.

The wild spirit of nature was all she needed to put her back into alignment so she could help others in their daily struggles.

* * *

In the final fight to live, as she lay on the operating table, she had wondered if she should just let go and let herself die. The world would continue to turn without her in it. Floundering in life wasn't enough. It had to have meaning, or she just wanted to go quietly into the night like everyone else in her life.

The din of the medical equipment, surgeons, nurses sent her to sleep as they fought to save her. She felt herself drifting off with one final thought.

Fuck you, God. You want me alive then make your move.

This is my white flag.

I'm exhausted.

To her surprise, she woke up wrestling between gratitude and anger. Perhaps being awake was a sign itself.

At that moment all she could remember were nightmares about the androids she had encountered during a visit to the factory with her father at about ten years old. Their life-like appearance frightened her, considering they were devoid of life. The coldness in their stare as she passed bordered on wicked curiosity.

In her nightmare, one chased her between rows and rows of their nude bodies hanging on what looked like meat hooks. It always ended with her seeing a group of them slicing open a screaming human with a shriek of something not of this world. But that was just a nightmare.

Roseanna's injuries seemed to have healed more than she would have expected. She asked a nurse how that could be.

"You've been in a medically induced coma for almost two months. The nightmares were a side-effect." The nurse's eyes shifted to her right and looked away—she wouldn't meet Roseanna's gaze.

"What is it?" Roseanna asked.

"I'm not authorized to tell you," the nurse replied. "When you're up for it, I suggest you read that." She gestured, then quickly left the room.

On the small table next to her bed lay a thick stack of paperwork with the city emblem on the top. After a time, she took it in her hands, not knowing what to expect. It was from the courts and the hospital giving her the options she had to choose from as a consequence for the accident.

Her mother was dead.

Jenette had been put into foster care.

As understanding sank in, Roseanna clutched her chest and heaved with hysterical mourning. Tears poured from her eyes. The pain in her body was nothing compared to the shredding of her soul.

Finally the grief passed, and exhaustion caused her to sleep again. When she woke, she mulled over her options, and realized she had none. She would have to relocate to Texas for rehabilitation and, hopefully, employment. Once there she would find a way to do right by Jenette.

That her sister was still alive told Roseanna something that buoyed her spirits—the one dose of vaccine she had stolen must have saved Jenette's life. She should have known Mama would refuse to take it herself. Every day humans made billions of choices—as vast as the canopy of stars—and each decision was connected to another. Francisca Vasquez had chosen her path, and now Roseanna had to choose, as well.

She had to stay alive.

Counseling proved to be as natural and fulfilling to her as walking around the pond on her property. She would tell the new members of the rehab program, "The accident took away my nursing career and the possibility of becoming a doctor—something I thought I would do until the day I died—but it led me to my true calling and to you beautiful people today."

Roseanna embraced the eccentric, getting into crystals and meditation. Buddha and Ganesh hung out side by side with La Virgen and Jesus on her windowsill in the kitchen. A gold cross always hung around her neck on a gold-linked chain. Unlike her sister Jenette, she practiced curanderismo, traditional healing and spiritual beliefs. They helped get through the bad days, to work through the remaining echoes of trauma.

Thanks to the car accident her right leg was held together with a metal rod, and she had a scar from her hip to the ankle. Like her favorite artist, Frida Kahlo, the accident left her physically unable to carry children, not that she had ever harbored an overwhelming need to have them. Now that the choice had been taken away, however, it hurt somewhere deep.

Then she received the most unexpected news of all.

She was going to be an aunt!

"That isn't much of a choice," Roseanna said, nevertheless trying to stay as positive as she could. "Either way they will enforce their so-called 'right' to alter your body, just to suit them. Sterilized? Fuck them."

"I never thought much about kids," Jenette said over the video connection, "but tell me I can't have them… Maybe I don't deserve them…"

As her sister spoke, Roseanna lit a white seven-day candle and placed it on her altar next to the photos of their relatives. This gave her time to think, as well. Then she turned back to the screen.

"I'm sorry, Jenette," she said. "I know I have apologized to you more times than I can count, but I will never stop. And believe me when I say that I have had my own one-night stands and brief affairs. Don't you dare apologize for it."

"Fuck those clowns," Jenette said angrily, running her fingers through her hair. "I would terminate, if I knew I could choose later—but there won't be any later."

The candle behind her crackled, and Roseanna turned to look at it. She made yet another decision—one which would change her life forever—and her voice was firm when she spoke.

"I'll take them," she said. Jenette looked surprised, but before she could say anything, Roseanna added, "I *want* them. If that is what you choose. I will also accept your decision, if you choose terminating. You…"

"What?" Jenette's eyes were wide.

"*I want your babies,*" Roseanna repeated, trying not to roll her eyes. "To keep them in the family. Should you ever want to see them… You can trust me. We all deserve options, the right to make choices. We aren't just our pasts. We learn and move forward, wiser… sometimes it's just with another scar or tattoo."

There was a long silence, and Roseanna worried what might come next.

"I know I can trust you," Jenette said, adding, "are you sure?"

"You know me better than that," Roseanna responded. "I wouldn't say it if I didn't mean it."

As she prepared for the journey to California, to collect Leticia and Ramón, Roseanna understood that she would have to love herself enough to love them. Only then would she be able to do what was going to be needed.

When she finally got to see them, they were cradled in small carriers. Fast asleep, both dressed in all white and looking nearly identical. Two little doves. Jenette was already back in the barracks, and any contact was strictly prohibited. It seemed unreasonably harsh, and Roseanna wondered if anyone else would have been treated that way.

They hardly made a sound the entire time, and once she was back in Texas, she dropped to her knees on her front porch, and looked to the sun.

"Please don't let me fuck this up," she said. "Of all the trials. Of all the tests. Guide me, ancestors and spirits. Guide them. Stay close to Jenette, as well, because where she is going, none of us can follow."

The wind chimes adorned with conch, oyster, and other seashells blew in the wind. The noise momentarily roused the babies, but they settled again.

Roseanna closed her eyes.

Thank you.

She would raise them the best she could. Most of their family was dead—as far as she knew, these were the last of the Vasquez seeds. Their little mouths, puckered in the shape of small butterfly wings, sucked instinctively. Roseanna didn't know how this would work, but she felt called to do it.

The Vasquez name had to be carried on.

Roseanna would tell them about Jenette, and do the best she could, one day at a time.

8

Leticia grew to inherit her mother's adventurous spirit, including an insatiable curiosity about space and mankind's push to colonize distant worlds. But before they were even ten years old, word came that Jenette had died on a distant world. All the children would have of their mother was a faded photo.

Roseanna wanted them to have as normal a childhood as possible. The money sent to her after Jenette's death was meant for them alone, and she would do everything she could to make sure it lasted. Each week, with pocket money in hand, Ramón and Leticia waited for the van that sold pickles, salt limon, and always saladitos—shriveled salted plums so sour it puckered their lips until they burst into laughter at the faces they made.

There were the usual birthday parties with a piñata and playdough. Summers meant raspa and colorful tongues. They ate them fast before the ice could soften the white paper cone to mush. Roseanna taught them both to cook, preparing them to take care of themselves when they were older, but without any expectation that either of them would like it. Determined to raise them equally, she refused to treat Leticia like a doll, remembering the pressure that had been placed on Jenette.

Leticia adored the open space with chickens, a small pond, and more than enough trees to climb. Ramón, on the other hand, hogged all the Lego to create detailed, extravagant buildings and worlds where his mother and father had trained to go. La Llorona herself would have been scared at the screams that came from his little body if anyone dared destroy something that took him weeks to create.

There were the unsuccessful attempts to get them to play together, which would have made her life easier, but Ramón wanted Leticia to play *his* way. Frustrated, Leticia stomped on his creations with one foot while tossing other parts across the room. Fights would ensue, then they both would run to Roseanna for her attention and affection, demanding that she declare one of them right. The only fair solution was to send them both to their bunk beds until they could get along.

After the appropriate amount of time Roseanna would peek in.

"Look, we are all we have," she would say. "This is our little gang, and no one can break it up. If you give each other a hug, I'll make popcorn and we will watch a movie together."

Begrudgingly, they would agree. Leticia and Ramón hated sharing a room even when they were in a period of truce. Ramón claimed the space for his own by cluttering it with his things. There were his science experiments, posters, stacks and stacks of books on every subject. He knew how to manipulate and did his best to get what he wanted, especially from his sister.

Leticia retreated to the small bunk with her own belongings. Sometimes in the middle of the night she would climb into Roseanna's bed.

Finally one morning, Roseanna took Leticia aside.

"Stand up to him. Say no. What is yours is *yours*. Don't let him talk you into giving him the remote for the TV, or your pocket money, or the last bite of dessert. You deserve as much as him. Do you understand?"

Leticia nodded in understanding, and to Roseanna's delight she did as had been suggested. It didn't take long for Ramón to get the message, and before long a status quo was reached.

The same couldn't be said for Ramón's relationships at school. The students there didn't appreciate Roseanna's nephew for the brilliant child he was, and he was treated as an outcast of sorts. He announced at a young age that to have what he wanted, he would need to build his own worlds.

And be rich.

When the twins were twelve years old Roseanna built another bedroom and small bathroom with a shower for Leticia. She would need her privacy soon to have the freedom to blossom into the young woman she was born to be.

It was autumn again, and just before their seventeenth birthdays. The leaves on the property created a carpet of fire that offered a deconstructed reflection of the trees.

As above, so below.

Roseanna always kept an altar in the house to represent their deceased family members, including Jenette. There was a photo of their brother Sandro and his wife Blanca. They were gone, having died closer to God in space, but their eight-year-old son Cutter survived and was still up there somewhere.

From the beginning Roseanna made it a point to bring Leticia and Ramón into her Dia de Los Muertos ritual to honor the family, especially their mother. She taught them that physical death didn't have to be the end, unless it was what they wanted it to be. Through cloning, science had imposed itself upon the spiritual interpretations.

During the ritual there were white pillar candles and tea lights, fresh marigolds, roses, and a small red-robed figurine of Santa Muerte holding a cornucopia of gold coins. A small skull of obsidian rested next to a photo of Jenette alongside decorated sugar skulls. And finally a bowl of fresh strawberries because Jenette joked she was afraid she would forget what they would taste like traveling in space. Leticia, Ramón, and Roseanna stood before the altar, and Leticia's tears were hot as candle wax as she quivered inside like the crackling flames of the tea lights.

Dark shadows danced across the photos of her mother with the viciousness of dark beasts, she thought. The beasts invaded Leticia's mind, stripping her of everything but sorrow. Every year since she was fifteen years old, she had promised herself she wouldn't cry, and every year she couldn't help it. Ever since Roseanna had told her the whole truth about her parents, Leticia's birthday and Dia de Los Muertos had left her emotionally drained.

Roseanna had been honest, telling Leticia and her brother that lying wasn't the solution to easing the pain that came from loss. She didn't want any secrets between them, since they were all they had.

"It's okay to cry, mija," Roseanna said quietly. "The veil is thin. We feel everything, and we should. Let it pass through you and teach you something about yourself—it's the best thing we can do. I get the chills all day every year on this day," she continued. "They are close, I promise. When I first got the news about your mother, the two of you were the saving grace in my sobriety. She lived on with you."

Roseanna placed her arms around Leticia and Ramón.

"I appreciate your kind words of wisdom, tía, but there is nothing out there," Ramón said, ever stoic.

"Callete, Ramón!" Leticia barked, her eyes puffy. "You're so cold."

"No, it's okay." Roseanna patted her shoulder. "You're entitled to your beliefs, Ramón. All I can tell you is when I was battling alcohol, I was barely alive. It took dying to my old life and self for me to live again. Your mother wasn't perfect, but she lived without fear. She cut off all her hair to become the person she wanted to be, and not what she was told was right or acceptable. You both may feel you are dying inside sometimes, and that is okay. You need to grieve, and will go through personal struggles, but know that you have your lives to be lived."

Ramón broke away. "Whatever. She lived a textbook, stereotypical life that got her killed. A gang member? Prison? That is not for me. I have work to do." He moved toward the door. Leticia opened her mouth and moved to stop him. Roseanna gently squeezed her arm.

"Mija, let him go," she said. "We all have to work through things in our own way."

"He puts so much pressure on himself to succeed," Leticia protested, "like some sort of Atlas."

"That's because we are judged by the stories that came before us. He doesn't just carry his own desire for success, he also doesn't want to be written off before he has accomplished anything. Those are the limitations that are set for us, before we are even born. When that happens, we grow with them, believing them."

"Fuck that."

"That is exactly what he is trying to do," Roseanna said, "but it's eating him at the same time. Ouroboros, eating his own tail." She ran a hand through her hair. "Anyway, it's almost your birthday. What do you want to do?"

"I don't know." Leticia wiped her eyes. The longing faded, as it always did. "Just hang out with my friends. I'm getting old for a party."

"I guess no tres leches cake, either?" Roseanna quipped.

"No!" Leticia cried. "I didn't say that. Maybe we do cake, and a movie in the evening?"

Roseanna kissed her on the forehead. "You got it. Now go do your homework, too."

The Pleasanton Mall was quiet, with half the shops shut down. Most things were in short supply depending on which countries were fighting with each other, disrupting the supply chain. This made it difficult to keep stores filled with stock.

Leticia roamed aimlessly with Erika, Joslene, and Nadia. They were their own little clique, sharing secrets over sodas in the quad at lunch and sending text messages to each other in class without getting caught. Here they were dressed casually, in jeans and T-shirts, though Leticia wore some charcoal mascara.

"What are we doing, birthday girl?" Nadia asked as she took a short video clip of Leticia on her phone.

"Nothing crazy," Leticia responded, trying not to look into the camera. "Let's just get food and check out the sales. I could slaughter some sticky chili tofu and noodles. And put that away! My birthday isn't a big deal."

Nadia put the phone away. "It's a shame that hot brother of yours won't be joining us."

"Eww!" Leticia scrunched her nose. "I do *not* want to hear that. He's my brother, and I have to smell his farts and burps."

Nadia laughed with Joslene. "¡Cochina! So many girls like him, but he really doesn't care. Does he have a boyfriend?"

"To be honest, I don't know or care. He can be with whomever he wants—it's his business. The only female he hangs out with regularly is the mom of a kid he tutors. He never talks about boys or girls."

"Well give him my number!" Nadia said, and she giggled.

Leticia rolled her eyes, then stopped in front of a small boutique called Magnolia. In the window were second-hand and new designer clothes, cosmetics, and accessories.

"Damn, that's cute." She spotted a brown suede leather jacket with tassels hanging from the chest and extending to the back. *That would look good with the turquoise and silver teardrop earrings Roseanna gave me this morning*. The card with her gift also said from Ramón, too, but she knew better.

"C'mon, it's your birthday." Joslene tugged on her hand to drag her into the shop. The others were behind, so there was no use resisting. "We're all pitching in to get you a gift." Leticia gave in without any real protest.

The shop floor was half full, but the girls still browsed as if they had free run of the place, bantering without the care of disturbing anyone. It was a birthday after all. The only shop assistant, a girl in a straight bob and dyed cherry red hair, not much older than Leticia, gave them a long stare as they entered. Her sour face made Leticia feel uneasy, and spoiled some of the fun.

Trying to ignore her, they moved on, but she followed them. Leticia had grown used to Ramón and his hovering, with endless questions about her progress in school. It felt like that as they opened and closed different samples of lip gloss and pulled out the price tags of various items of clothing before tucking them back. In the back of her mind, anger began to burn.

With another slit-eyed glare, the shop assistant let Leticia know she didn't like them, and wanted them out.

An ember became a flame.

"You can't just try every lipstick," she said in a snarky tone.

This moment had been stalking Leticia in the shadows of her mind. It was a bubble of teen angst, sorrow, and resentment that would burst and scald whatever was closest. There was still a rawness from Dia de Los Muertos.

"We can do whatever we want." She stepped closer to the girl. "It's a free country. At least that's what I'm learning in school."

The shop assistant gave her a sarcastic smile and squinted. "Fucking we—" she began under her breath.

"Don't you dare say it, pendeja." Leticia reared her head and narrowed her black-lined eyes. "The Rio fucking Grande dried up to a trickle. It doesn't exist anymore. Watch the news, or read a book."

"Whatever," the girl responded, refusing to meet her eyes now. "I saw you put something in your pocket. I'm going to call security."

Leticia squared up with her.

"I didn't take anything."

The pain of the moment reached deeper than the words. Flashes of memory blinded her. Images of her mother burst in her mind with the explosiveness of a grenade. Leticia lunged and grabbed a handful of the girl's hair, giving it a hard yank. Her ears were plugged with vitriol that made her oblivious to her friends shouting at her to stop.

She would be the one in trouble.

Another hard pull and a large clump of hair was left balled inside her palm. The assistant screeched in pain and fear, ran to the counter, and slapped a button next to the till.

Leticia's fist held her rage and sadness in a tight orb of cold space where her parents' souls now resided. She ran for the assistant again, and her friends attempted to pull her off, but she continued to pummel the girl's face that bled from the nose. Leticia screamed obscenities as tears left charcoal mascara streaks down her cheeks.

Two security guards rushed in, each grabbing an arm and pulling her back.

"Don't tell me who I am, bitch," Leticia shouted, sobbing. "Don't you fucking *dare*. All of you. Fuck you all!"

One of the guards pulled her to the side.

"Show us your pockets, miss."

Leticia didn't move, and looked at her friends who all wore fear on their faces. That brought her back to the moment, and she did it for them. They shouldn't get into trouble because of her. She complied and turned up her pockets, with nothing to be found. The other guard opened her small handbag, proving that there were no stolen goods.

"She still assaulted me," the assistant said, holding the crown of her head. "I want to press charges." Nodding, the security guard grabbed Leticia's upper arm again.

"Let's go," he said. "You can call your parents after the police arrive."

"I'm going." She snatched her arm away. "Don't touch me."

Joslene ran behind her. "We saw it all. We heard what she said. I'll stick up for you. Just tell us what to do."

The guard turned to Joslene, causing her to stop.

"Step away, unless you want us to take you, too."

"Go, Joslene. I'll be alright."

Behind her, Leticia heard Nadia knock over a stand with a box of bras. She glanced over her shoulder as her friend flipped the assistant the middle finger.

"I'll be talking to the manager about this, bitch. You just wait."

Walking through the mall with guards on either side of her, Leticia felt ashamed—not for sticking up for herself, but for what Roseanna would think. Her tía did her best for them, and now this. Roseanna didn't deserve the heartbreak or worry.

By the time they reached the mall entrance a police officer was waiting. Her pulse quickened. She didn't want to get in the police car, but what choice did she have.

9

Roseanna stood in the station entrance when they brought Leticia out from a three-hour wait in a holding cell. They made eye contact, but she remained silent while they walked out the front door into the night. The radio was on in the car, and Roseanna turned it off, then turned to her niece.

"I spoke to your friends," she said calmly. "They told me what happened, and I believe them. I also believe you wouldn't lash out unless you were feeling something... big. You want to tell me what's going on?"

Tears streamed from Leticia's eyes.

"I don't think I know myself," she said. "Just feel lost. Ramón has it all figured out. Most of my friends have some idea. I know there's something for me, but what? Where?" She paused to wipe her eyes. "I get good grades. Never had any trouble with the teachers—but for what? Where does it lead? Dorothy at least had a yellow brick road. Alice had a bunch of animals to guide her."

The tears came again, and she composed herself.

"Does Ramón know? It's just going to make him act like even more of a jerk."

"He doesn't know," Roseanna said. "Your friends agreed to not speak about it at school, either. If you don't want me to tell him, I won't. To be honest it's none of his business. How you were treated was unacceptable, but so was the extent of your reaction. But I know, you swallow that bullshit long enough, and all you want to do is *La Exorcist* that pea green shit back into their faces. I understand. When I was in nursing school and applying for jobs, I got it all."

Leticia stared down, feeling undeserving of Roseanna's understanding. Even that made her fall deeper into a chasm of grief. Roseanna placed a hand on her knee.

"We're going home, and I suggest you take some time alone to think about it. I'm not grounding you or punishing you. I think how you feel is enough. You know this behavior is unacceptable."

They spent the rest of the journey in silence. Leticia's mind and body were numb. She leaned against the headrest, watched the world pass by, and had an overwhelming desire to sleep. Where the hell in this world did she belong?

When the car came to a stop, Leticia threw open the door and rushed to her room to avoid making any contact with her brother. She flopped face-first onto her bed.

Two hours later a knock on the door roused Leticia from her self-pity and tears. To her relief, Roseanna was on the other side.

"You okay?"

She couldn't avoid her forever, and to tell the truth she wanted a little comforting. She knew it had been wrong to lash out violently, but something inside of her was begging to be expressed. She opened the door. Roseanna had two mugs of steaming manzanilla tea in her hands.

"Not really," she said. "I'm sorry and embarrassed. I don't want to be a burden. It just made me so *angry*, the way that girl treated me." The sweet aroma of the tea mixed with a little honey made Leticia feel slightly better.

"Thank you for the apology," Roseanna said, "but never say that you're a burden." She sat on the edge of the bed and handed a mug to Leticia before pulling a folded piece of paper from the front pocket of her brown flannel shirt. "I was supposed to give this to you when you were eighteen, but I think the time is now. You said in the car that Dorothy and Alice had guidance to find their way. So do you. It's already there… inside.

"You don't need to look outside of yourself," she continued. "Listen to it like a wind chime. Your mother was always going to be a soldier. Didn't happen the way any of us thought, but destiny had to be fulfilled. When the right words, or song, story, or bumper sticker speaks to you, it sets a little flame off in your soul. Then you will know. Don't let self-doubt stop you. El riesgo siempre vive. The guts to take a risk is the dream, even if your corazon must become as combustible as a grenade."

Leticia placed her mug on the nightstand to take the letter into her hands.

"It's from your mother. She was always a chingona, and in her defiance she wrote a letter for you and Ramón. She bribed a nurse to stick them in your baby carriers when you left the hospital."

Leticia began to open it, but Roseanna stopped her.

"This is for you alone to take in and to work through. If you need me after, then I'll be here. There is a box with items from your mother that goes with it, but I'll give that to you later. I'll leave you now."

Roseanna closed the door, and Leticia opened the letter. The fear of what it might say was greater than seeing the police officer. This was someone who had been a dream, a phantom all her life. Now Leticia had in her possession the words her mother had written with her in mind. She took a deep breath before beginning to read.

My dearest Leticia,

To you I am stranger, or some type of ghost if you share Roseanna's beliefs. You've probably heard things about me that aren't so great. Like everyone, I'm not perfect. Never been a saint, but I always tried to be real.

When you read this, you will be on your own journey. Our family so many years ago traveled farm to farm, and my greatest hope was to travel planet to planet. I have always wanted to be the highest-ranking Marine in the Vasquez family. When you both kicked in my belly while I worked in the armory, I knew you both were fighters, even if you didn't choose the military. I hope the power in your choices will carry you through life and to your dreams, your destiny.

Even things we see as failures can be delayed blessings. Maybe you can be the first to do what has not been done. Life brought me you and your brother, and my plans took a little detour. I always felt insignificant to the point that I knew if anything should happen to me, that the world would keep spinning. Not many people would care or cry, and those who did would get over it quick enough and keep spinning in their own little worlds.

Know you are worth making an impact. Believe it more than I believed in myself. Don't forget, like I did for a little time, that we Vasquez women are daughters of soldaderas, Mexican fighters. You are the next generation of soldadera.

With this letter you will also receive a switchblade. It has seen me through the good and bad times. I'm leaving it here because I don't think there is anything I can do with this little thing in space. So I leave it for you.

Never think I didn't love you with all my soul, just because I didn't know you. Whatever anger you have, put it in your work. Do that with everything you feel. Create something spectacular with your life. I wanted it all because I believed normal people like us deserve to have it all. Be the best of the best.

Look out for your brother. I have written a letter to him and told him to do the same. Be there for each other even when you don't like each other.

And remember, real freedom starts with you. It doesn't matter what they call you, where they try to tuck you away, whatever barriers are in your way. See the light at the end of the tunnel and there will be light.

We are familia. Siempre.

Love,

Jenette Vasquez

Descendant of Soldaderas, Marine, Mama

Leticia pulled the letter to her chest. It answered questions and teased apart complicated emotions that hardened like smoky quartz when she focused on of them. This went beyond thought. It was a feeling.

Her mother didn't want her to settle for less than accomplishing her goals. This she knew and felt. It was the boost she needed, from beyond the veil. It came at just the right time, like Roseanna said. Despite the challenges, the barriers the world put in her way, trying to steal away every opportunity and make her buoyancy the weight of lead, Jenette Vasquez had followed her path.

Quietly Leticia left her room and went to sit in front of the altar with the letter in her hand. There was a patch there with the Marine Corps insignia, and she picked it up. Her fingers rubbed against the stitching, and she had the feeling of having tea with a ghost. Years ago, Roseanna had told them their mother's entire story.

Not much could be found on her father—who had died in one of the wars—or any information concerning his family. Maybe it would happen in time.

Leticia had researched the Marines, but casually, still with a hesitation. There were no guarantees in such a profession, not in the world on which they lived, and certainly not once you ventured past the stars. She had so many questions, coupled with not knowing the direction her young life might go. It had become like the fabled La Lechuza, an ugly creature with the face of a haggard witch and the body of an owl. It perched outside her room in the darkness waiting to pounce with spears for claws. Higher and higher it took her into the night before letting go as she tumbled to death.

That was what the uncertainty felt like.

The words *unfinished business* popped into her mind as she stared at the patch. Reading a letter written in her mother's own words had unlocked her fear of taking a risk. There was no reason, with all her advantages, that she couldn't succeed and go beyond what her mother achieved in her short life. Leticia knew then, the average challenge would not do.

She wanted to be admitted to the Raider Regiment, which specialized in special operations. Not an easy place for good girls to survive, or thrive. Their patch was a skull, like Santa Muerte, and no wonder.

It would be another year before she could enlist.

This was it, the flame, the heat that would melt the wax of doubt. She tucked the letter and the patch beneath the lace cloth on the altar and picked up a photo of her mother. One year. A sense of urgent purpose gripped her as she sat there with the ancestors, looked at the photographs of their Brown faces in uniforms.

There was one more thing—it had been on her mind since she was fifteen. Leticia wandered the rooms of the house to find Roseanna. Ramón had his door shut, but she could hear him practicing his Spanish. He was also becoming fluent in Chinese and wanted to conquer Japanese and Russian. Him and his "arsenal of languages," he called it.

Other times he played Pink Floyd. "Money" and "Wish You Were Here" were his favorites that played on a loop.

Leticia stepped out onto the enclosed back porch and found Roseanna in her armchair, reading on a tablet. The air smelled of the citronella candles lit to fight off the mosquitos at that time in the evening. Wind chimes sang their song along with the chirping cicadas and crickets in the long grass.

"Tía, can we talk?"

She raised her head, wearing the usual calm smile on her face.

"Of course."

Leticia took a deep breath and sat on the ottoman next to her.

"I read the letter."

"And? How do you feel?"

Leticia nodded. "I want to have her close to me, a reminder. I was thinking of getting ink." She held her breath expecting a no, or some sort of chastisement.

Roseanna's face didn't change. "Of what?"

Leticia raised the photo of her mother. "Her," she said, "on my left arm, and what is written on the back of this. What you said. El riesgo siempre vive."

Roseanna's eyes softened seeing the photo. She took it into her hand. "You will probably do it eventually, so why not now?"

Leticia jumped from the ottoman. "Really!"

"Yes, really. You want it done by hand or automated? I know someone I trust. When do you want to do this?"

"I prefer a human touch, the artistry of it. When can you make the appointment?" Leticia gave Roseanna a wide grin, knowing she might be pushing her luck again.

"I'll do it now."

Leticia's smile faded. "Why are you being like this? So cool about everything?"

"Don't think what you did was cool. You know how wrong it was. I know you. But instilling more shame in you than the world will try to do will only mix you up inside. Jenette told me about lockup. It does the exact opposite of what humans need. You need to learn how to manage yourself. People need tools and compassion."

"Thank you." Leticia wrapped her arms around Roseanna. "It won't happen again. I promise." She ran back to her room to get to the homework waiting to be completed. The Marines weren't just about physical strength. She needed to flex the biggest muscle of all to make it to the top.

Three days later Leticia walked into the tattoo parlor expecting pain. There was a heady smell of incense, and a woman wearing rubber gloves greeted her.

"Leticia? You ready? I received the scanned photo, and we are ready to start now."

She looked back at Roseanna, who had accompanied her.

"Thank you."

Roseanna chuckled. "I would say have fun and enjoy, but it hurts. You might regret asking for it."

Leticia sat down, feeling her heart begin to pound when the needle switched on. She braced as she stared straight ahead. Sure, machines could create a tattoo in half the time, but then it didn't feel like art to her. Her mother had her tattoos done in lockup, and it was a guarantee there was no machine service in there.

Roseanna sat next to her, holding the hand of the opposite arm. Leticia squeezed shut her eyes when the stinging hit her skin. Every line etched would be a tribute to the name Vasquez, all the women going back to the beginning of their bloodline.

When it was complete, she lifted her head to the side to look at it in the mirror. Mother and daughter, one face above and the other below. They shared the same high cheekbones and full lips. Roseanna kissed her on the top of her head.

"Wow. It's beautiful. You look very similar."

"I love it. Thank you both!"

When they returned home Ramón stood in the kitchen with a glass of orange juice in his hand and stared with a sneer at her glistening raw skin.

"You've got to be kidding me. This is how you remember her? By getting a tattoo? What will people think when they look at you?" He paused, and she hoped he was finished. No such luck. "It's unprofessional and doesn't do her any justice. She would be disappointed. It's a little desperate and pathetic."

Leticia could feel the same anger she had experienced at the shop. The spirit of La Lechuza inside of her, wanting to scratch him deep to match the way his words hurt her. Without thinking she slapped Ramón hard, leaving the imprint of a red handprint across his cheek.

"You aren't my father, it's not your body, and she wouldn't approve of your arrogance," she replied. "It will be your downfall one day, and maybe even your death. And don't get it twisted, I get grades just as high as yours. You can't call me pathetic!"

"Are you really that stupid?" His body twitched as he fought the urge to slap her back. "First a tattoo, and now you want to do the very thing that killed both our parents." Her eyes went wide. "I saw the Marine Corps letter printed in the kitchen. *Why?* Why would you do that? That's not making the most of your life, Leticia. It's called repeating the same mistakes. You'll die a broke soldier—you know how many vets are on the streets and never taken care of?"

"No, Ramón," she said. "I'm going to get it right. I'm going for special ops. I have the grades and the strength for it. Marine Raiders all the way."

Ramón's face changed after she said this. A small shock, and perhaps even respect, she thought.

Roseanna rushed in from the other room. "Stop it! Both of you. You aren't children anymore." They looked at her but didn't say anything. "Something has to change. Maybe you both need jobs to help you mature a bit." Before they could object, she continued. "Robert has space on his ranch—we were talking about it over dinner the other night. There are horses, and if you are serious about enlisting, Leticia, you can learn to shoot."

Ramón threw his hand into the air above his head. "I can't afford the time for a job right now, tía. Please. I'm on track to be Valedictorian, and the school counselor just gave me a list of scholarships. It could save you so much money, plus I could earn more with the tutoring on the side. I kind of already have a job." Roseanna placed her hands on her hips. "You know I don't like farms," he added.

"That boy's mother does spend a small fortune on his education," she admitted. "You're always helping out over there."

"She's doing it all alone." Ramón looked into his glass to avoid eye contact. "Sometimes she needs a second pair of hands to do stuff. If I'm already there, then why not? You're always telling us to help others."

For once Leticia could hear real pleading in his voice, and fear. It was so thick she thought he might choke on it. Sometimes she hated his guts, but at the end of the day they only had each other.

"He's right, Roseanna," she said. "And he always seems to have money—but I *do* want a job, and shooting sounds hella fun. Any extra experience might go a long way when I enlist."

"Thank you, Leticia." Ramón looked sheepish, that his sister had taken his side. "I'm sorry for being rude. It's just that these exams... I'm stressed." He started toward the door. "Anyway, I have homework."

"Wait," she said. "I'm sorry I slapped you. It was wrong."

He shook his head. "Nah, I deserved it. I was mean. Sometimes even I need sense knocked into me. You do whatever you want to do." When Ramón left the room Roseanna turned to Leticia.

"You slapped your brother? Leticia, you're on thin ice. If you continue that behavior..."

"He was being nasty about my tattoo," she said. Then, "I apologized!" Roseanna's gaze didn't leave Leticia's face.

"Leticia, you *both* need to channel your anger."

"I know and the farm sounds great. Thank you."

Roseanna was about to leave when Leticia stopped her.

"When are you and Mr. Boone just going to get engaged and move in together? You only have the hots for each other, and it's been years."

Roseanna raised an eyebrow. "This doesn't detract from your outburst, and I'm *not* talking to you about my private time. You're lucky I let you get that ink. But yes, Robert and I have been discussing our future together."

10

Lucinda and Avery Boone waited on the front porch of their home, standing with their father Robert Boone. Leticia had to admit that he was exceptionally handsome with dark skin and a square jaw covered with salt and pepper stubble, all beneath a tan Stetson that matched dusty boots. Straight Wrangler jeans accentuated his long frame.

He towered over Leticia and she could see why Roseanna was so hot for him. A millionaire rancher with one of the last horse farms in the country, apparently he was one of the best Tejano dance partners she'd ever had, too. He kept it quiet, though, and lived a low-key life.

The main house was a simple four-bedroom, single floor made from red brick, without flashy cars in the driveway or much to draw attention to it. There were a lot of desperate people on Earth, and there were also those choosing to live life without the technology that drove others to space. As people died or became severely ill, entire cities came to a complete standstill. Goods were no longer delivered at regular intervals, the demand for androids skyrocketed over the years, but with only skeleton crews to create more goods, prices increased.

The Boone family had always been farmers, and continued to live that way. There had never been a time when more people wanted to learn horse-riding, or purchase their own. He was also increasing his herds of goats and sheep.

Living the simple life was paying off.

"Welcome, Leticia," he said. "It's been a long time since you were here, and we're glad to have you back. Make yourself at home. Your aunt and I have a horse show later today, so Avery and Lucinda will show you the ropes. Help yourself to lunch with these two."

"Thank you, sir."

"No need for 'sir' just because you're at my house. You know this."

Leticia nodded. Usually when he came over, both she and Ramón made themselves scarce, feeling awkward exchanging small talk. Sometimes when they awoke in the morning, he was leaving out donuts and squeezing a fresh mix of grapefruit and orange juice. That, too, was weird, but strangely comforting.

Lucinda gave her a warm and welcoming grin. "How old were we when we last played together?" she said. "Why so long? It will be good to have another girl around. Between my dad and Avery, it gets to be pretty boring."

Leticia gave them a shy smile, especially when her eyes shifted toward Avery, who wouldn't stop staring at her face. He was just as good-looking as his father, and wore the same jeans and boots. Leticia and Ramón had spent time playing with Lucinda and Avery when they were younger, even staying over at the farm when Roseanna and Robert spent time together.

Once they hit middle school, however, they had to go to different schools and were no longer interested in "playing." They met new friends and drifted apart. Leticia was happy to meet up with them again.

"Thanks for having me," she said. "It feels like years since we caught frogs in the pond." She looked around. "Where do we start?"

"Wow. I almost forgot about that," Lucinda said. "Now it's swatting off frogs trying to kiss me. Roseanna said you have military in your blood, and plans to enlist—how exciting! You want to learn to shoot? We can do that after lunch, and start the chores tomorrow." She raised both eyebrows and grinned even wider while nodding.

Leticia had to chuckle. "I guess. Show me the way."

The memories Leticia had of the ranch were those of a child. Everything had seemed huge, an endless field of exploration from one of the older barns close to the main house to the creek at the edge of the property. She still had a scar extending from her left ankle to the knee from bouncing on two wires suspended between trees over a creek.

Lucinda had claimed they had always been there, probably some sort of property marker. They were rusted old things, completely unsafe but irresistible to a curious Leticia when she gave both a hard tug. A light rain was falling, but they seemed safe enough to cross. As she shuffled sideways, her foot slipped and metal cords ripped through denim and skin.

It felt worth the pain once they made it to the other side. She hobbled back to the main house, wincing yet feeling like a victor of sorts. Ramón had stayed in the barn that day reading a book and playing *Ages of Conquest* and *War Vol. II* on his hand-held game device.

One of her fondest memories was of Robert and Roseanna creating a large fire pit to roast marshmallows for Halloween. The scent of smoking meat from a grill had filled the air.

Today it was a normal farm, where play would be replaced with manual labor beginning at dawn on the weekends and once a week after school. She didn't mind. Only one more year before leaving Texas for what could be a very long time, especially if she traveled into space.

In the barn where they had played hide and seek among the hay bales, now there was a wall of reinforced locked metal cabinets roughly five feet high. Lucinda's eyes glittered as the doors opened to her handprint. The locker was filled with hunting knives, a crossbow, and several .22 rifles, 20-gauge shotguns, and a pair of pistols.

"It's nothing like the fancy stuff you'll get in the Marines," Lucinda said, sounding slightly envious. "We only keep what's needed to run the ranch. It's still good practice, though. Why don't I add you to the users? Put your hand here." Lucinda typed on the screen inside the cabinet then stepped aside for Leticia to scan her handprint. Once it had been recognized, she reached out to touch these weapons she had only seen, yet never held.

This was where her mother found her soul, Leticia mused, a sense of power and deep interest. These were also her companions in the final months of pregnancy, when she couldn't do rigorous training. Her expertise had blossomed, despite being shut away.

"Next weekend we should go camping," Lucinda suggested. "If you can survive with nothing but a knife and your wits."

Leticia shook off thoughts of her mother.

"Camping sounds fun," she said. "We've never done that. Ramón always had some bum excuse about needing to study or do this or that project, and Roseanna had to ferry him here and there to his different activities and study groups. But I thought this was a job," she added. "You're making it sound more like summer camp!"

"Damn, girl, we have a lot of catching up to do. There's something really empowering about going back to basics—and don't you worry about work. There's a lot to do all day."

There was a sound behind them, and Leticia looked to the open barn door. Avery stood there with a tray of coffees.

"Since it's the first day, let's take extra coffee breaks to get reacquainted," he said.

"Sounds good, as long as we can get to work tomorrow."

"Be careful what you ask for. We have to reinforce a temporary fence to keep the coyotes away, clear a patch of land for a new septic tank out by the horses, and paint the outside of an old barn at the far end of the main property. The horses have fancy new digs, and the smaller one will be converted to a type of studio. Pop is looking to hire someone to stay watch full time, to avoid thieves now that we're expecting foals and a few other new additions. He's finally broken down to put in a proper security system throughout the outer perimeter property. Those horses are as much his babies as we are. The coyotes are always trying their luck around the chickens, so the farthest ends of the fencing will be all electric. Will be good before lambing season, too."

"Let me guess," Leticia said, "he wants you guys to pitch in, just to teach you a little something he learned growing up."

"You got it." Lucinda rolled her eyes. "He says we won't appreciate what we don't work for. This is the 'legacy' he wants to leave to us. He can afford to hire a team to do everything, but he wants us to be 'involved.'"

Leticia nudged Lucinda's arm. "Well I'm not complaining, especially about getting paid."

"I'm glad someone is!" Avery chimed in. Standing there with coffee in hand, the three had a good giggle. Then Leticia took a sip, deep in thought.

"You mentioned coyotes. Do I need to worry about them? Will they attack?"

"No." Lucinda shook her head. "They're the least of our worries— but if you run across one, or a few, you have to give that animal respect. Same goes for wolves. It doesn't understand anything but territory, hunger, and survival. You make yourself as big as possible and maintain eye contact. No sudden moves as *you* get out of their way, very slowly."

"Good to know. If only people were that easy to understand."

Childhood memories of play fast forwarded to hard work. Each morning Leticia woke up to her phone alarm, and Roseanna drove her to the farm just as daylight was breaking. By the end of the day, she smelled of sweat, hay, splattered white paint, and horse feed.

At home the trees left blankets of leaves she had to blow into piles with the leaf blower strapped across her chest. This was something she also did on the Boone property. It made her feel like she carried a flamethrower as the burnt orange and brown leaves flew into the air. Avery and Lucinda bagged them afterward.

It was peaceful on the farm. There was hardly any traffic on the road that ran along the perimeter. Occasionally she saw a truck go past, but it moved too slowly to be of any concern.

She loved visiting the horses, stroking their brown coats with taut muscles flexing and relaxing to her touch. When hauling and painting, her anxiety subsided and the future held less weight. Her mind gave way to the moment without worrying about what Ramón or other people in school were doing.

When they practiced shooting, Avery stood behind her and guided her aim at pumpkins, soda cans, and—even scarier—scarecrows. In the back of her mind, she knew that one day it might not be old clothing stuffed with hay standing before her. It might be a moving target of flesh-and-blood, intent on killing her.

At the same time, his breath on her ear and hands teaching her how to hit a bullseye affected her in ways she'd never experienced before. It caused inner confusion, because she couldn't tell if it was from the explosion caused by pulling a trigger, or the young man showing his affection for her day after day.

Good morning and *Good night* messages from Avery filled her phone. He gave her books on horses and shooting.

Leticia read at home, and practiced shooting at the Boone farm, even when she wasn't scheduled for any work. Robert and Roseanna didn't mind. Ramón scarcely noticed, doing his own thing and making his money with his side hustle. He kept his bedroom door closed and a small whiteboard tucked away in his closet.

The small barn the farthest from the main house was looking good, given that neither Lucinda nor Leticia was a professional painter. Robert didn't want his place to be ostentatious, since so many had lost so much over the years. Keeping the farm simple was part of that plan.

Lucinda stepped out of the barn while Leticia rolled the last of the paint in her tray. Her body was tired from the work, satisfying as it was.

"I don't know about you, but I'm starving. Dad said Thai was fine, so I just put the order in."

Leticia stopped her rolling. "Will he be joining us?"

"Not sure. He said he was on his way home with Roseanna. I know it's early but damn it's getting dark fast." Leticia looked to the indigo sky deepening in hue by the minute, with a breeze kicking up without the sunshine.

"I know," she said. "It'll be the holidays before we know it."

Lucinda kneeled to replace the tops of the paint cans. "Let's get these inside. I'll soak the sponge brushes. Don't want to be out here when it's too dark, with the critters running around."

A single light in the barn provided illumination as they rushed through cleaning up.

"Right, looks like we're ready," Lucinda said. "Time for Thai and to see what's streaming on TV tonight." Leticia loved spending time with Lucinda. There was less pressure than with Avery, who made it no secret how he felt about her. She'd probably made a mistake by making out with him when no one was watching, but what could the harm be in a little fun?

"I'm not going to bother locking it," Lucinda said as she closed the barn door behind her. "Nothing in there anyone wants." They walked briskly with the half-moon overhead and stars coming in and out of view with the gathering clouds. "Hear that?"

Leticia didn't want to stop for the sounds of the nocturnal animals that lurked in the trees nearby.

"Foxes mating. There might be a few coyotes on the prowl, too."

Leticia shivered, only partly because she was wearing a thin long-sleeve T-shirt. The fall leading into winter in Texas was pleasant during the day, sometimes hot. The night brought cooler temperatures.

"I'm too chilly to stop and listen."

Lucinda was no longer by her side. She stood in the muddy road, patting her body.

"Shit. I forgot my phone. I need to run back. You go on ahead. The food will be here soon, and I'm hungry."

"You sure?"

Lucinda was already skipping backward. "I've never been attacked by a coyote! Not once."

Leticia shook her head and continued to walk. The sounds of the night were natural, had been there long before any of them. Still the unknown of the darkness, like deep space triggered fear. She looked back again, expecting to see Lucinda running toward her. Nothing. The light in the barn was still on. The longer she walked in the dark the more nervous she felt.

A coyote howled in the distance. Her mind began to wander. She glanced back again. The larger barn near the house was just a few feet ahead. She took out her phone and dialed Lucinda's number. After two rings it shut off. She stopped in her tracks to think about what that meant, and what to do. Then she broke out into a jog before sliding open the door and running straight for the gun cabinet.

A small pistol. Surely nothing more would be needed to calm her nerves or shoo away an animal, but that didn't make sense with the phone. She locked the cabinet and jogged back to the small nearly white barn. No Lucinda in sight, and her friend wasn't the pranking type.

Her heart began to beat faster than her feet. As she approached, the light from the barn showed dried tire tracks in the mud. She had noticed them the previous day.

Her head jerked to the side as she heard a crash from inside, and she knew something was wrong. She had to be smart about this, and approached the door with caution. There was a muffled voice that was not Lucinda. With a heaving chest she threw the door open with one hand, then rushed inside with both hands back on her pistol.

A skinny guy with dirty jeans and boots was fastening tape around Lucinda's mouth. Her feet and hands were bound. Two paint cans were tipped over and oozing white paint across the floor.

Leticia swallowed hard. She had never been in a situation like this, real fear standing in front of her, shaking her to her soul. But to show that fear would only be used against her.

"Take your fucking hands off her."

The guy stepped away from Lucinda. His hands were dusty, with nails caked with dirt. He smelled of hay and manure… and horse feed.

"What are you going to do, little girl? Maybe I need to show you what you need, to be a woman. An extra lesson… for both of you."

Leticia's arms began to tremble. Part of her wished Avery was here, but at the same time, just because a man was by your side didn't promise safety. She had figured the intruder would back off, with a gun pointed at his face. Instead, he took a step forward with his left hand on his belt buckle. His greasy hair was tied into a short ponytail. His smile looked like he chewed tobacco.

What would Jenette do?

You're a Vasquez woman.

A soldadera.

"You want to try me, motherfucker?" Leticia cocked the pistol. "I said step away from her, and take your hands off your buckle. Nobody wants to see your pinkie finger. Not that there's anything to see."

"That's a dirty mouth, little girl. I'm gonna wash it out with my—" As he reached to the back of his jeans, Leticia fired three shots toward the ground. Two bullets hit his left foot and the other the floor. He cried out and collapsed into the paint, dropping the Bowie knife he'd pulled from his waist.

Her breathing and heart seemed to be in sync with the gunfire. The fear evaporated with the lightness of gun smoke. It felt like the most natural thing in the world to pull the trigger.

"Next time I'll aim higher."

He lifted his face, half covered in dripping paint, toward her as he groaned in pain. Both his hands clutched his bleeding foot. Half of the spilled white paint was now tinted to pink. Leticia kept her gun aimed at him while slowly making her way to the knife. With one foot she slid it closer to her and picked it up.

She kept her aim to his face.

"I'm bleeding bad," he said. "You have to help me. You'll go to prison for this. Who do you think they'll believe?"

"You'll survive, you piece of shit," she said. "I promise you that. You *will* pay for this."

He looked at her with a fury that filled her with fear and a matching animosity. Is this what the world would look like? Combat? Until now her world had been sheltered. It made her think of what her mother might have experienced.

Lucinda already had her hands lifted for Leticia to slice through the tape. The knife was sharp enough to cut through with ease. Once free Lucinda removed the tape to her mouth and cut her legs free. She reached for her phone. As they waited for emergency services to answer, Robert and Roseanna came running through the barn. Robert held a shotgun. His eyes went wide as he pointed his weapon at the bleeding intruder, still holding his foot.

Roseanna ran to Leticia's side. She still aimed the pistol. A single tear rolled down her face.

"Leticia, are you okay?"

"I'm fine, but it's a good thing you showed up, because he might not be."

Roseanna lowered Leticia's quivering arm. "You got him, mija. There are four of us and one of him."

Sirens wailed in the distance. Lucinda moved to Leticia's side.

"Thank you," she said. "You're going to be the best of the best."

Leticia turned to Lucinda and gave her a tight hug. "I'm glad you're alright."

"How did you know to come back?"

"I saw a truck passing by the farm for the past few days, but it's been going slow. Too slow. It held us up the other day on our way here. I thought I'd sound silly if I mentioned it. Then earlier in the day I noticed tracks outside the fencing. None of us have been driving around here. Something felt off when you didn't come running out. I called your phone. I don't know... I ran as fast as I could to the barn and back."

"Watch out, Marines, there is a new colonel in town," Lucinda said as she slapped Leticia gently on the back.

Leticia had to crack a smile. "We will see. I feel like I'm ready for anything, because I really don't know anything. There is a whole other world—and worlds—out there."

An officer entered the barn with his gun out. Something about him was strange. He looked at Robert, who wore a tracksuit and sneakers, then the intruder who lay on the floor bleeding. The guy shrieked with a cracked voice.

"That little whore shot me, and this big asshole would've done worse."

"Whore?" Leticia lunged toward the man "Who's lying on their back? Not me, cabron."

Robert lowered the shotgun to his side. "There was some sort of incident, officer," he said. "I'm just protecting my own. This is my farm, and I have no idea who this man is with my underage daughter and her friend. We arrived home when I heard shouting, then the gunshots."

The officer, who had no name tag, kneeled next to the intruder, removed a handheld device from his front pocket, and scanned the man's face.

"Sir, do not try to persuade me with any bias you may have," he said. "I am an android programmed to uphold the law. According to this, you are a known criminal and match the description of someone sought in other robberies in the county. I will get you the medical assistance you need. However, I will not tolerate any more obscenities from you. You are under arrest, and I will now read you your Miranda Rights."

"The fuck?" The intruder moved his head from Leticia to Robert. "What is this country coming to?"

More sirens wailed in the distance. Another officer and a paramedic arrived.

"You may all go into your residence," the first officer said. "Once the criminal is secure, I will take a statement. Thank you."

Roseanna nodded and placed her arm around Leticia.

"Robert, girls. Let's go. I'll put on some tea and hot chocolate."

Two days later Leticia and Avery sat on the top of a round hay bale, watching the sun set. In the clear sky of lavender and pink the moon was a glowing crescent. The tree line of barren branches stretched toward the sky like claws attempting to choke the heavens.

Whenever Leticia looked to the sky, she thought of her family. It was a nice distraction from the realization that she had been prepared to take the life of another human, without a second thought. She still saw his paint-covered face and the fury in his eyes. That moment haunted her—the lack of remorse for injuring him after he threatened her. Then the sense of power welling inside, knowing she could. The deep sense of satisfaction knowing she could do whatever it took to survive. It scared her.

"So you are really set on going up there?"

"After I smash all my goals here, yeah. I'd like to go out there."

"I have to admit, going up there doesn't appeal to me at all. I don't want this place to fall into the wrong hands when my dad is older. He and Roseanna won't be young, or here forever."

Leticia knew this. It weighed on her, but she couldn't ignore the wind chime that blew her passion farther afield. Roseanna would never dream of holding her back, either. Still, part of her wanted to give back to Roseanna what she had given to her and Ramón.

When Leticia didn't respond, Avery spoke again. "No way I could convince you to stay in Texas? I mean why would anyone want to leave?" He chuckled and playfully pressed his arm into hers. "There are androids and machinery for everything now. I guess my dad wanted to teach us how to get on without any of that—you never know when the lights might go out." She still didn't answer, so he continued. "I like the idea of having my feet firmly planted on land I own. Hopefully grow the farm, then maybe grow some babies."

Leticia turned to him with a quizzical look.

"Not now!" he protested. "Later for sure… with the right woman. We'll work as a team in business and in life."

"I'm all about the team, Avery, but I want to play up there." Leticia shivered, now that the sun was nearly past the horizon.

"Why don't we go in, and I'll make you dinner."

"Avery…"

"No, I insist."

Leticia leaned toward Avery and kissed him on the cheek. His eagerness and attention were flattering, almost intoxicating. This sensation of young love was as soft as lamb's wool with the awkwardness of a foal's first steps. He was strong, yet tender with good looks and a good soul. She knew she had to tread carefully, to not break his heart.

"Hey, I just want to thank you for showing me the ropes with shooting," she said. "It felt good to have control over a situation that could have been very, very bad."

"No problem. It's all you—you're a natural. Guess that's why you might make a good Marine one day. It's in your blood."

11

2190

An entire year passed with the slowness of a pregnancy. Her time helping out at the farm was done soon after the incident. Roseanna only worked mornings so she could be there in the afternoons for her and Ramón. Once a week she led an AA meeting. Robert paid for an android to stand watch and a security system throughout the entire farm, to be installed without delay.

Leticia was still welcome to shoot side by side with Lucinda, and they took camping trips out to Big Bend for hiking. When not at the farm she pored over the Marine Corps and Raiders training videos.

Her high school friends busied themselves with studying for exams and applying to college. They still took the time to gossip in class or wander the halls, but there was a sense of needing to have a plan in place well before graduation. Leticia took up any opportunity to push herself physically on Roseanna's three acres or on the Boone farm. She felt awful about turning down Avery's advances, but she didn't love him. Sure, he looked impossibly cute feeding baby goats with a bottle, and attended to all her needs. He was one sexy vaquero. However, it was telling that in their many conversations he often led with, "Things don't always go to plan… but life with me on the ranch is a sure thing. You'll be safe."

He didn't mean it maliciously and maybe he was right, but safe wasn't what she wanted. She owed it to herself to find out in her own time and way what was truly meant for her.

The niggle to get more ink cropped up with every time she passed the altar, the statue of Santa Muerte catching her eye in the glow of the candle flames. Roseanna's response when she asked her was simply to put her hands up.

"It's your body, and you are nearly eighteen. You need to know how to listen to your inner voice and do what is right and good for you. Your choices are your own."

Wearing a black bandana like a head band, Leticia went to the same tattoo parlor that smelled of incense. It reminded her of the woody and fragrant palo santo Roseanna burned every full and new moon when she did her limpias. Lucinda followed her in.

The tattoo artist Brandy greeted her with gloved hands. "Good to see you again," she said with a wide smile. "I appreciate you going for the hand of an artist, instead of a machine. You ready?"

"If it's done by a machine," Leticia replied, "can it be considered art?"

Brandy threw up one hand. "Never was one for philosophy. I'm just doing what I love. Glad there's still enough work for me to keep going."

"And that's why I am here." Leticia removed her shirt, then leaned into a chair face forward. She pulled the bandana tight around her shoulder-length brown hair to create a ponytail, then used bobby pins to secure the rest in a bun. Settling in place, she put in her ear buds. Metallica would have to get her through the next few hours of patience and excruciating pain.

Lucinda found a seat along the wall, and did the same.

Brandy laid an imprint of Santa Muerte that covered most of her back. It was what Leticia wanted before joining the Marines. This tattoo was an act of faith, seeing and believing it would happen. Santa Muerte was the saint of death, depicted as a skeleton in long luxurious robes, associated with the afterlife and protection. The needle glided across her back with little pain to start, until Brandy had to double back and fill in the image. Then Leticia maintained her breathing, and the music helped her focus on thoughts of getting through bootcamp, the elation of reaching the goal.

It would happen. It *had* to happen.

Santa Muerte had her back, after all.

Leticia returned home with most of the tattoo complete. All that remained were the red roses at the feet of Santa Muerte, and they would be done another time. The Eagles played in the background and Roseanna took pizzas out of the oven.

"Hey, great timing," she said. "I have a few things for you. Have a look on the table, then show me the ink."

On the kitchen table sat a cowboy boot shoe box, with a rattlesnake on the front beneath a leather boot. Its fangs dripped with venom. The picture gave her the chills. She quickly removed the top and began to pull out each item with care, one by one. A collection of different colored bandanas, photographs, an old Bruce Springsteen *Born in the USA* T-shirt. "Dancing in the Dark" had been Jenette's favorite song, she knew. Leticia brought the T-shirt to her nose to detect any memory of scent. Nothing but fabric softener.

She still held it close to her chest.

"This means so much to me. Thank you."

"She would be proud of you. Your grades, your hard work on the ranch and dedication to getting into the Marines."

Leticia turned around. "Here. Careful when you lift the T-shirt. Lucinda laughed at me the entire way because I sat hunched over, not wanting to rub off the covering."

Gingerly Roseanna lifted the shirt, and gasped.

"Mija, it's beautiful. I can't wait until you get the roses done. Nobody better fuck with you. They would have to answer to a Vasquez woman with Santa Muerte on her back."

The doorbell rang. "Already? I thought we could shove a few slices down first."

Leticia walked toward the door. "I don't think this will take long."

A tall man stood in the doorway, carrying a large bag. "I take it you are my victim tonight."

Leticia couldn't hold back her laughter as she pulled out the pins and hair tie that secured her long brown locks.

"I am. We have hot pizza first."

"I love pizza."

After dinner Roseanna stood next to Leticia while she sat in their living room with Bernard, a friend of Roseanna's from the rehab center. Leticia held up a photo of her mother, from when she ran with the Las Calaveras. Bernard looked at the photo, then Leticia.

"That's pretty short, but you have your mother's bone structure," he said. "She's beautiful. You can pull it off. I get a lot of people chopping off their hair and regretting it. Takes time to grow back. Are you sure about this?"

"How else are people going to see all this beautiful art on my body?" Leticia replied. "And I don't want to mess with it during basic training. Do it. *El riesgo siempre vive*."

The long strands fell to her lap with the ease of a snake shedding skin. Leticia felt lighter, a little closer to her destination, even if it was still uncertain. She had to do something to keep the faith in what she wanted more than anything. When the floor was covered with silky brown threads, he brought a mirror to her face.

"You're ready for what comes next," he said. "No hair to keep you weighed down or get tangled in some helmet."

Leticia ran her left hand across her head to the nape of her neck.

"Ready to settle unfinished business."

She showered to catch the rest of the remnants of fallen hair, then sat at the white desk she and Roseanna had found at Bussey's Flea Market one Saturday morning. Together they had sanded it down and painted it. That was a project she loved doing.

The application for the Colonial Marine Corps was open on her tablet, and nearly complete. This was it. She hoped it would be enough to get past the first hurdle—to not just be a grunt, but part of the elite. The Raiders. Leticia brushed her fingertips across the switchblade that had belonged to her mother. Perhaps the sharp end would point her in the direction of her destiny.

The front door slammed.

Leticia looked at the time. Roseanna was already in bed reading. She walked out to find Ramón appearing disheveled. He stopped as he inspected her new look. There was a startled sadness in his eye.

"Now they *have* to let you into the Marines. You look just like her."

Leticia could see something peeking from his T-shirt collar. She walked closer to him and pulled it down slightly, but he jerked away.

"You and that boy's mother?"

He continued to stare at her haircut and face.

"What I do is none of your business."

"Ramón, we are the age of consent, and you can do whatever you want, with whomever you want, but that's evidence. Don't be leaving proof of the ways you make money, besides tutoring some kid."

His eyes went large. "Leticia…"

"No, I won't snitch, but keep yourself clean. And if you want to hide that thing, then I'll give you my foundation."

He touched his neck. "Thanks."

Leticia turned to walk away, hoping he could see the outline of her tattoo beneath her nightshirt.

"¡Mijo! Congratulations."

Ramón's face glowed as he wolfed down his plate of brisket, potato salad, cornbread, and pinto beans.

"You better eat up," Leticia said, "because I bet they won't have barbecue that good at the Harvard cafeteria."

"Early admission. Full scholarship." Roseanna beamed. "That's amazing, Ramón."

"Once I'm done with undergrad I'm not stopping until I have my MBA." For once his face appeared devoid of tension. He didn't seem distracted at all as he sat with them. "They have an amazing, combined program."

"You have it all figured out, bro." Leticia tried hard to smile and be happy for him, but the piercing switchblade of self-doubt stabbed at her from the inside. "That's excellent."

"Yes, I do. I'm going to be everything past generations could not or *did* not have the fortitude to achieve."

"Be nice, Ramón." Roseanna gave him a stern look. "You'll see what it's like when you get there. Life is not black-and-white."

"Whatever it takes, tía." His gaze, the dark determination, was more dangerous than the tip of a blade. It had an inky blackness that swallowed instead of pierced. Leticia couldn't prevent herself from feeling anxious.

"I think I'm done eating," she said. "Going to go check on the chickens and take a walk."

"Okay, mija. There is dessert for later." Roseanna gave her a reassuring look and smile. She always knew when to let her go, and she knew not hearing from the Marines yet was bringing her lower as each day passed without a sniff of news.

Leticia wandered behind the house to the pond. She loved it there. The body of water was surrounded by large reeds and hundred-year-old oak trees. Lily pads and ducks floated without awareness of anything greater outside of the pond. What always struck her, though, was the symmetrical reflection of the sky above—clouds, sun, or moon. The heavens were brought to Earth.

However, that was just an illusion, a reflection of what could be. She wanted to *be* up there, soaring with her own accomplishments and exploration.

Leticia was happy for Ramón, she really was, but it also stung, like a light drizzle of fire falling on her bare skin. Everyone was receiving news, except her. It was like waiting for food while starving, and watching everyone's order coming up. Her body was tense, ready to grab the brown bag and devour its contents. The aroma filled the air, making it even worse.

The waiting.

Then there was the fact that this was it. She had no plan B, C, or D. She couldn't imagine living the life on a ranch with Avery. Sure, he would be devoted to her, but she didn't want children. She wanted the stars and wonder, to push the limitations of her own being. Maybe up there she would feel the presence of the parents she never knew.

She wasn't "better" than ranch life, but deep inside she knew a different destiny awaited her. From the moment she had pressed *submit*, she'd lit each seven-day candle until it was a smoking pool of drool with nothing left to burn. Nothing to show for the waiting but empty glass tarnished with soot.

There was nothing worse than waiting.

Unfortunately, the next part of her journey was completely out of her control. She knew her ship would come in. But when?

And how to keep the bitterness at bay?

Graduation came and went. She sat in the crowd watching her brother accept top honors, beaming with pride as he gave his Valedictorian speech. Leticia *was* proud, though not as proud as a cheering and crying Roseanna.

As her friends and other students walked the stage, she continued to hold on to hope that the message would arrive soon—otherwise they would run out of seven-day candles. Joslene and Nadia were both heading to the west coast. Avery and Lucinda going to A&M in College Station for their agriculture program. Leticia stood in the waiting line for her name to be called.

And it sucked.

There was one unread message.

It had been there when Leticia woke up. Her finger hovered over it. It would be a moment of celebration, or a moment of she didn't know what would happen next. All the drive and passion in her soul was consumed with achieving this dream that was bigger than her.

During her research she had seen the faces of the women who went missing during military training, or during their service. Their families given bullshit excuses when they pressed for answers. Cases of harassment, abuse, rape, real horrors. But nothing ever changed if there *was* no change. The cost was high for those trying to make it happen, and those trying to keep it. That was the struggle for power.

Her mother fought to take back her power, and to a certain extent she did so during her short career. Now was Leticia's time. Her chest became tight as she could feel tears welling in her eyes. She sat up in bed and tapped the message.

Scanned the screen.

Her entire body trembled as she burst into sobs. The building energy of fear, worry, resentment, jealousy, the toxins created by waiting and impatience all coming to the surface to be released.

"Mama!" she screamed into the room still dark.

Roseanna came bursting through the door.

"Leticia? Are you alright? What's wrong!"

She couldn't speak. All the wind, the howling storms of self-doubt finally lifting. She handed the tablet to Roseanna.

"Oh my God! Thank the spirits! You! You did it, mija!" Roseanna wrapped her arms around Leticia. "Let me make you the best breakfast. I'm so proud of you. But more importantly, be proud of yourself."

"Forget cooking. I want barbacoa, chorizo, and egg, and bean and cheese tacos from The Donut Shop! Extra tomatillo salsa."

"You got it. Let me go put on a pot of coffee."

Leticia sat in bed, feeling as light as a paper lantern or ash floating into the sky. However, it was real now. It was the beginning of a long journey filled with trials and tests. As a Marine she would be part of a greater cause, but there still would be competition. She had to prepare herself to lean on no one but herself. If her mother could do it, then she could.

As ecstatic as she was to start this new chapter, she couldn't help the clouds of sadness blowing inside. Roseanna had been a strong mother figure to her, the only mother she knew in the flesh. She had always been her rock. To get through basic training and survive becoming a Raider, she would have to be her own rock, all the pressure and time making her into a diamond.

Roseanna brought her breakfast on a tray and placed it on her desk.

"Here. I'll let you eat while you respond to the acceptance letter and fill out the rest of the forms."

Leticia gave Roseanna a tight hug, though to be honest she wanted to be alone. It was so overwhelming. After finishing her tacos down to the last piece of shredded beef, she made her way to the backyard. There she twisted and cut a fallen section of chicken wire in the fencing that surrounded the small vegetable patch. The work helped her untangle her emotions, and it would be something nice to do for her tía.

"Looks good. Thank you." Roseanna approached her while surveying the ground. One of her palms was closed. Leticia put the fencing down and wiped her sweaty neck with her T-shirt.

"It will be one less thing for you to worry about, or at least Robert," Leticia joked.

"I have something for you, mija. You weren't as excited as I thought you would be during breakfast. I know it's a big moment bringing up so many thoughts, fears, and emotions." Roseanna opened her palm.

There was a gold cross on a gold-linked chain. She placed it around Leticia's neck. "Your mother died with the one that belonged to your grandmother, but this one belonged to our father, and it was passed on from Seraphin. It belongs to you now."

"Are you sure?" Leticia touched the chain. "You always wear this."

"Yes. Let it remind you that we are each one of those links. Our memories, pain, hope, and blood. In the end it all comes full circle because we are connected. Unfinished business in this life or the next. Where one generation cannot, the other strives for more and is capable of more because we *demand* more from ourselves and others. Hold your head high, mujer."

Leticia threw her arms around Roseanna. "I love you so much."

Her aunt returned the embrace. "Before you leave I was hoping you would do the temazcal with me, and a shaman I know. Just a little something to deepen your journey. The temazcal has been used by the ancestors for centuries, even before boats landed on the shores of what is now Mexico. Every time I step into that little limestone hut, I find clarity."

Leticia took a step away, giving her a suspicious look.

"What will I see, you think?"

"I don't know. Whatever the spirit world or your subconscious is trying to tell you."

Leticia thought about it for a moment, then replied, "I'll do it. I want to *see*."

"Great. PJ has reserved an afternoon spot for us tomorrow."

Christopher Orozco lived half an hour away. He had been a curandero for fifteen years. Aside from his usual blessings, handmade candles, barridas, and advice, he had built a temazcal in his backyard. He brought lava stones back from Mexico and placed them inside the small, adobe hut to create the steam. His clients who tried it once always returned. It was better than any sauna. The guidance and re-centering they experienced was enough confirmation to reveal that they had to follow through.

Leticia and Roseanna sat cross-legged on a floor covered in sand, wearing their bathing suits and towels. PJ had to squat as he poured water on the stones.

"The best advice I can give you is focus on the moment you are in. If the mind is chattering, playing tricks on you, focus on your breath. Not just here in this place, but for any situation you find yourself in. You will be tested, Leticia. Be true to your breath because it comes from inside of you."

White clouds of hot vapor filled the small space. Leticia closed her eyes and could feel herself drifting as the heat of the steam took over her mind. Droplets of sweat landed on her folded legs, reminding her of the tears she had cried, not understanding why both her parents were gone.

"They say the ancestors are never far from us," the curandero said. "They act as guides to help us reach our full potential and correct broken generational paths, some predestined by the organization of the particles of dust that created everything. Each one a miniature dream that created a bigger one we lived in and on, and swam in."

Leticia's body lost all its weight as she was pulled through the darkness of space and back in time. High in the sky a cold disk, what looked like a planet, took shape. She could see the Aztec goddess Coyolxauhqui, her body in severed pieces slain by her brother, the god of war. It was a story she read about many times in the books Roseanna owned. The ancient tales of Mexico before it was called Mexico.

He shook a shaman's rattle, and the hypnotic rhythm bordered on a monstrous hiss as it carried her deeper into a lucid dream world.

Leticia shuddered, her joints ached. The hiss of the rattle and sizzling hot stones filled her head. The sweat falling from her body became viscous, no longer the tears of her mother but coming from the jaws of something waiting in the dark. In her mind she moved closer to the disk of the ancient goddess flung into the sky with veins, bone, and ligaments hanging from shredded flesh. Instinctively she brought her arms toward her face in protection as she crashed through a veil of blood and the thick atmosphere of whatever planet she approached.

Drums pounded, or was it her heartbeat thumping in her ribcage? Something wanted to emerge, to crack her wide open. She clutched her chest and opened her eyes. Lying on a stone altar below her was a large alabaster body split from the jugular notch to the bottom of the sternum. In her hand was a large blade. The open cavity of the body was a pool of black liquid. It wasn't human, even if the form vaguely resembled one.

Drums, the drums of war rang in her head.

Creatures cloaked in shadow and humanoids like the one in front of her fought at the foot of the pyramid where she stood. She watched the carnage of white flesh and creatures that resembled armored dragons moving with the speed of hungry locusts. Screams and shrieks rose above the fight to where she stood.

She looked into an obsidian pool of blood that resembled a scrying mirror. Within she could just see her reflection, but there was something else. The hiss. The hair on her body standing up and the shadow rising behind her in the reflection. Leticia slowly turned to face one of the creatures from the foot of the pyramid. It lunged toward her.

She screamed and lifted her blade to fight.

"Leticia! Leticia, it's okay. You're safe!" Roseanna wiped her neck and shook her out of her stupor. Leticia touched her chest, and then removed the bandana around her forehead. The cloth made her think of the Aztec warriors in their cotton armor. She wasn't the broken woman. She would survive, and do what others in her family could not do.

This meant something.

She could feel it growing inside of her, and only time would tell.

"What was any of that?" she asked.

"Facing your demon, yourself," the curandero replied. "All the parts no one sees, like the secret shame we all carry. Perhaps also signs of the future."

"I don't know if I can do it."

"You can," Roseanna said firmly. "Let me tell you a story. Before you were brought to me, I went out with a group of friends, ready to stay sober, but those old habits creeped up on me, the anxiety that sometimes wraps me up in a cocoon of death. I drank so much I fell asleep on my bedroom floor. I woke up in the middle of the night and vomited everywhere. Still drunk, I could feel myself choking on the undigested food.

"I sat there on the floor crying for help, beating myself up. All I could think of was if I died, where would that leave you and your brother when you arrived? Or myself? I wanted to live, and dedicated myself to change. That night I had let my fears get the best of me, so I drank until I couldn't see my reflection. I fucked up, and put the hard work in to not do that again."

"I'm so sorry, tía," Leticia said, her voice low. "You have to know you have been amazing all these years."

"I was so ashamed," Roseanna answered. "Been sober ever since. Don't ever underestimate the power of unfinished business."

PART 3

OBSTACLES

12

"She wants us to do *what*?" Dr. Moon shook her head, her mouth open wide as she stared at her companion. "They really don't give a damn…"

Dr. Patel stared back, her gaze devoid of expression. "I mean, aren't you a little curious? Plus, we don't pay ourselves. This is what we signed up for—and I rather *they* be in there than us."

"So the science project will be in charge of the science project… great." She glared. "Why was I not informed before? This is *my* gig."

Her expression turning sheepish, Patel looked off. "Most likely because of this reaction," she said. "Look, we have to go now. It's happening whether you like it or not."

The two scientists walked from Brenda's office to the elevator on the opposite side of the hallway. They remained silent as they descended to the facilities reserved for the research requiring the most security.

The viewing room for Lab 10 wasn't far from the elevator. It was the largest and most secure research room in the facility—and they would need it. The large rectangular one-way glass was the only barrier that separated Brenda from the thing she feared and hated the most, yet was the key to everything she ever wanted to accomplish.

She hated the Xenomorph.

And the heartless creature that was Weyland-Yutani even more.

Three synthetic technicians stood beneath bright lights, observing two human bodies—one male, the other female. None of the androids spoke a word. One of them, Natasha, typed on a tablet, her eyes shifting periodically to the bodies.

Moon studied her own tablet. At first glance, the inside of the male appeared as if the cardiovascular system had morphed into a black overgrown tangle of jungle vines. Viscous slime seeped from every orifice, including the incision from the top of the neck to the pelvis. Sticky pools of the stuff formed on the floor. They quivered as smaller larvae and eggs began hatching.

The parasites had eaten through every morsel of flesh until the skin and skeleton were the only things left intact. The hybrids that combined Xenomorphs with *Taenia solium*—the pork tapeworm—squirmed and violently whipped their tails. Miniature jaws snapped at other parasites, competing for scraps of sinew, tiny fangs scratching into bone.

The other body appeared somewhat normal. However, the female human was still alive, with her chest rising and falling as she breathed. One of the androids stepped toward the sleeping woman and took her temperature, then pulled down the sheet to uncover her distended belly. Her flesh rippled.

Though unconscious, she winced and one hand moved to her abdomen.

Brenda gasped. "What is inside of her?" She peered at her tablet.

Patel took a deep breath. "The synths suggested that the female body could carry the parasites for longer before expiring. We call them Xenosites. It also takes longer before any visible signs manifest."

Brenda clenched her jaw. She knew for certain she was going to pay for this and dreaded the moment that would arise, when she would be forced to make a decision between right and wrong. She glanced toward Gilda, who was staring at the mirrored window. The woman smiled, but it wasn't pleasant or friendly, and Brenda imagined it was sheer delight.

We are the experiment, and always will be, Brenda thought to herself.

2190

Ramón stood out of a crowd—especially here—and he knew it. Tall, with dark brown skin and thick black hair. His teeth were perfectly straight because Roseanna led an Alcoholics Anonymous group that included a dentist she knew well. He gave her a huge discount. In middle school it was an inconvenience, but now whenever he smiled and spoke, people looked and listened.

Being the smartest and best-looking was always a plus when in a place where everyone had out-earned you for generations. Sure, Roseanna never struggled to provide, but he had never seen so much concentrated wealth, saturating everything from the cars driven by the freshmen to the accommodation upgrades.

Whenever he passed a watch shop, he promised himself his first would be a Rolex. Then a sleek Porsche. He would never be caught driving some hooptie around like a vato out of the hood. The shoes and suits would be bespoke Italian. Eventually the right woman to give him children to inherit the empire he would run.

His tía often talked about the power of intention, and his was crystal clear.

The Vasquez name would carry weight.

Ramón sat in the third row of the small auditorium. Not too close, but not in the back where he might miss anything. He'd lost any desire to look cool back when he was a freshman in high school.

"Hey." A young man slid next to him. "Nice to see you again." Ramón recognized him from the dorms—he'd moved in across the hall the day Ramón had arrived. The memory stuck because he brought in three monitors of the latest design, explaining that they were meant for trading. It wasn't unusual for corporations to begin cherry picking early.

"I'm Luke Grant," he added. "Since we're neighbors, I might be asking you for notes once in a while."

"Sure thing. Ramón." He knew an opportunity when he saw one. "I specialize in providing notes, helping people get the grades… the ones they deserve, of course." Luke's dorm was filled with the newest tech and his watch a Patek Philippe.

"Whoa." He nudged Ramón's arm with his elbow and pointed toward the entrance. "That's Mary Anne Kramer. What a body—and she's insanely rich. Banking family." The woman Luke indicated scanned for a seat, and caught Ramón's gaze. As she climbed the short steps, Luke leaned closer. "Damn, she's heading this way. Might have to try my moves… later."

Mary Anne chose a desk two seats away from Ramón. He gave her a shy smile and looked away to avoid appearing as thirsty as Luke. She *was* pretty, though with features that were pleasant enough not to be distracting, and dressed well. Hazel eyes and wavy strawberry blond hair cut to just above her shoulders. From this distance he could smell her light fragrance of vanilla and maybe cherry blossom.

Luke probably had a million Mary Annes, and she was probably used to a million Lukes trying to get into her panties. Ramón looked straight ahead, determined not to give her any more obvious attention.

For the next hour the professor droned on about grades, attendance expectations, and the breakdown of the Philosophy course he would be teaching. Before it was done, Ramón decided he wanted to know more about this girl, and he wasn't going to leave anything to chance. Halfway through the class he took a sip from his water bottle and placed it on the empty desk between them.

At the end of the hour, he got up to leave.

"I think you're forgetting something."

Ramón turned around, giving her his full attention.

"Oh, thank you. I'm Ramón," he said coolly. "And you are?"

"Mary Anne. It's nice to meet you."

"It's nice to meet you," he replied. "I'll see you next week."

He turned and headed toward the stairs. Best to leave her wanting more. Luke's reaction was of pure disbelief.

The following week she took the seat next to Ramón and smiled as she sat down. He'd already decided to ask her out for coffee, but not for a couple of weeks. Until then, he would give her just enough attention to keep her coming to him.

She wore a lavender mohair sweater that showed only a hint of cleavage at the top opal button. Her lipstick was pale pink, and she wore minimal mascara to cover her light brown eyelashes.

He paid for the coffee, but showing an impressive amount of class, she offered to pay her portion. Although she came from a wealthy banking family, and ticked all his boxes for the perfect partner, she had a mild-mannered demeanor and didn't appear to be overly ambitious.

She didn't need to be. The Kramer family's wealth had been there for generations. Mary Anne could pursue any career she chose without worry of pay, as long as it fulfilled her, and expressed the hope to raise the next generation of Kramers. But he wasn't looking to be the husband of a Kramer. He wanted a woman who would be the wife of a Vasquez.

After their coffee date they walked back to the entrance of her dorm, and he kissed her on the cheek. With both hands she pulled his face to hers and kissed him on the lips.

"Next time let me cook dinner," she said. "Sorry, though—it will have to be in the communal kitchen."

"I would like that."

He left, feeling settled in pursuing Mary Anne, and confident that he would succeed.

With that decided, he had to turn his attention to other, more tangible concerns. Although he had a scholarship that covered his tuition, and had saved a substantial amount in high school, he relied heavily on credit to pay for the costs of living. At times, the rate he went through the cash alarmed him.

The day was approaching when he would need to find a job.

Julia Yutani entered the Modern History class late, and showed no concern over how much noise she made. He was fascinated from the start—she was the opposite of Mary Anne. Julia's sharp tongue and dark eyes captivated him, though he couldn't escape the fear that he might end up "that guy with the famous woman."

Even so, a relationship with her could be very... advantageous.

He knew she was interested, as well, when they received their grades for an essay that would account for a large portion of class credit. Julia leaned over to peer at his tablet.

"Smart and sexy," she said. "You'll be first pick on my team, any day."

He pulled the tablet away and leaned in close, focusing on her eyes.

"Do you make it a point to be nosy?"

She matched his gaze. "I make it a point to be just what I am, and just what I want to be," she replied. "Why hide or fight it?" Then she added, "I'd wager you feel the same way. I'll bet you want to know what everyone in this room got, so you can zero in on the ones you'll have to beat for the top spot."

That captivated him all the more—here was a woman who knew she wasn't a hundred percent good, but didn't care. She had teeth, and was willing to use them to get what she wanted out of the short experience called life.

Unlike the one with Mary Anne, his relationship with Julia wasn't entirely in his control, and it took months to move it to the next level—but he was determined to have them both. Each woman served a purpose in the grand plan he had for his life. A plan that included money and power.

Toward the end of the semester, a handful of students met at Julia's place—a nicely accustomed two-bedroom apartment near campus—for a group project.

"I have to throw you all out now," she announced. "It's ten, and I have to be up and out by six a.m. Believe me when I say I won't miss any of you after we graduate." With that Julia began to usher everyone out. Ramón gathered his things, but she motioned for him to stop.

"Ramón, I hate to ask, but do you mind hanging back and helping me clean up these bottles and delivery boxes?" She indicated the items that had piled up on her kitchen counter.

He could tell it was an excuse. They'd been exchanging glances all evening and she'd made a point of saying that she had someone coming the first thing in the morning, to clean the place top-to-bottom and pick up her laundry. It was an extravagance he couldn't afford.

"Of course," he said. "My first class is later in the day tomorrow, so there's no need to rush off."

"You don't need to run to… what's her name?"

He stopped in front of her, holding two Corona empties between the fingers of each hand. It shouldn't have shocked him that she knew about Mary Anne—he'd done his own research, and knew she currently was unattached.

"Where do you want these?"

She stepped closer, wrapping her arms around his waist. She was a full foot shorter than he, so she craned her neck to face him.

"I see. Come here, guapa." He dropped the bottles to the carpeted floor and grabbed her around the waist to pull her closer, kissing her mouth with a sexual aggressiveness she returned in kind. Both of his hands slipped into the back of her jeans to squeeze her ass beneath her panties. Her mouth released a sigh and a moan.

"Come to bed, Ramón," she purred between kisses.

Without a word he took his hands out of her jeans and lifted her up. She moved her arms to around his neck and wrapped her legs around his waist. Kicking the beer bottles and sending them spinning aside, he moved to the closed door of her bedroom, opening the way with one hand. When they reached the bed, he laid her down and she pulled off her thin, fitted jersey top. All night he had stolen glimpses of her body through the fabric.

Now he could devour all of her.

Their bodies fit perfectly together as they made love. Each thrust was a push and pull of will, chemistry, and desire. In perfect measure they took each other's breath away. Whatever it took, he decided he would never let go of this woman for the rest of his life.

Walking home the following morning, Ramón felt pangs of guilt like a cheap, skulking sancho. Checking his phone, he saw six messages from Mary Anne. Each message wanting to know where he was and letting him know how much she missed him. She had a good heart.

Which made him feel heartless.

Mary Anne wanted a Ken so she could play Barbie. Ramón could live with that, as long as she didn't get any ideas of stealing the show from him.

Julia, on the other hand, was every bit his equal. Before he had left her apartment, she invited him for two nights the following weekend on her family's yacht. There was someone she thought he should meet. Julia Yutani understood him—body, mind, and soul—and what a break that would be, getting a foothold in the Weyland-Yutani dynasty.

On a yacht.

He'd always wanted a boat.

A short stout man greeted Ramón and Julia as they boarded. He was wearing a white linen shirt with the long sleeves rolled to his elbows. It was unbuttoned too far for Ramón's taste, as he could see where the red sunburn ended and his pale chest began. The blue eyes behind round clear-framed glasses appeared slightly bloodshot.

He handed Ramón a beer, and extended his hand. Despite the fact that he probably was worth millions, the man had the smell of a borracho who had been drinking for days.

"Benjamin Ross." His grip was firm. "I hear you are the star of Harvard."

Ramón knew that even if he could match this caveman display of authority, it wasn't the time. Not yet. He had to play the school kid who needed to be "educated," so he gave Benjamin a friendly smile, and allowed his hand to go slightly limp.

"Who would tell you that?" Ramón replied, chuckling. Benjamin puffed out his chest slightly before retracting his hand and grabbing a leather cigar case from the wet bar to his right.

"Julia and I might have asked some of your professors," he said conspiratorially. "Checked your background." Ross held out the case. "Want one?"

Ramón had never smoked on a cigar in his life.

"I'd love one," he said. "It's been a while." It took a bullshitter to spot a bullshitter, he knew. Benjamin guided Ramón through the ritual until they both were smoking.

"As you know, Julia works for the company," Benjamin said, waving the cigar in her direction, "and I say 'work' very loosely."

"Careful, Benjamin. I know your boss," she joked. Or half joked.

"I know, and it won't be long before you *are* my boss."

Ramón suppressed a frown.

She would never be *his* boss.

Benjamin took his time with another puff. "As I was saying, there's a project I'm working on, and I need an extra pair of eyes, someone who would help with strategy. From what we hear, you're the best at anything you put your mind to, and—"

"And being a student, I'd come cheap and be easy to bury if I got a case of loose lips or blew the whistle."

Benjamin smiled, nodding his head. "True, true, but it won't come to that," he said. "This is a long-term thing, possibly your lifetime. It requires commitment, and loyalty. We need the best and brightest from the outset. People with vision. Truth to tell, I'm just a grunt who got here by kissing ass and doing whatever it took to get the job done.

"No," he continued, "we need someone who can take all the moving parts of a complex bioweaponry project, and put them together, make them sing—and in the process maintain strict confidentiality. Julia has been keeping an eye on certain students. You caught her attention, so I did a lot of digging. You might have fooled everyone in high school, but I found the sophisticated system you created to fleece rich kids out of their money for the grades they needed. You also rigged grades for teachers to get them their bonuses. From what I could find, you're doing the same now.

"People like you and trust you," Benjamin continued, a glint in his eyes, "even though you got ice running through your veins. And your class work is exceptional. I am confident that you can develop a program for the company that will take us to the next tier of weapons evolution—and the associated revenue stream. It won't be a cakewalk, though. Many have tried and failed. We have too many competitors to allow any of them to know what we're doing." He peered intently at Ramón, judging his response.

Ramón had to keep himself from shaking. It almost felt surreal. All his hard work, all his focus were on the verge of paying off. Everything he had sought, all his life, soon would be within his grasp. He just had to *take* it. Whatever it paid—even shit pay at Weyland-Yutani would be more than an entry-level gig where he'd have to slog to prove himself.

And the long-term payoff…

"You really don't care that I'm still just a kid in the midst of my education?" he asked, careful to sound sincere. "What is this project?"

"Sometimes, *kid*, the real education isn't in a book or in a classroom," Benjamin replied. "I can't talk about it—not here—but it's out there." He waved his cigar at the sky. "On an unnamed planet." Ramón couldn't keep from showing surprise. "Don't worry, no travel necessary… at least not yet. Tell you what, I'll send you some paperwork. Then come Monday morning, let's meet at the office and I'll show you what you need to know."

"Then we talk money," Ramón said.

Benjamin glanced at Julia with a smirk. "Now I know why you like this kid so much."

Julia looked away and blushed. "Enough for now—I need another drink. How about you, Ramón?"

He looked down at a full bottle of beer.

"You know, maybe I'll switch to scotch."

"Follow me." She took hold of one of his hands and led him to the bar. Collecting their drinks, they went to stand at the railing. The placid water reflected the setting sun, and it was the same color as bullion, Ramón noted.

"I could get used to this."

"I know." Julia touched his shoulder blade. "What would you say to being by my side?"

Ramón turned to her. There was a vulnerability in her gaze, and sincerity that made him want to reach out and kiss her, show her the same honesty.

"Is that an offer?" he said. "Second one today."

She giggled, something she rarely did in front of others. "Yes, it is, Mr. Vasquez. I'm looking for a partner. Not necessarily a husband, and I don't want children. Ever. The day-to-day rearing of small humans strikes me as tedious and unfulfilling. Most of the people I know who have kids regret it, or send them to boarding school. No thanks. There are worlds I want to explore, and build."

Ramón's smile flattened, at least inwardly. His heart ached. It had been on the top of his list to rebuild the family he'd lost, even if he had no real interest in the details of raising children. It was an open wound that never seemed to heal. Julia was perfect in so many ways, but he wanted a family, and he didn't want to be seen as Julia Yutani's lucky man.

It made him think of Mary Anne, the way she curled next to him feeling warm from sleep. *"All I want from you is to be my family, Ramón,"* she'd said. *"I have more than enough to live on… it will be wonderful, especially after the first little Ramón junior."*

He had turned to her. *"You know twins run in my family."*

"Even better."

He feared the demands Julia might have of him, whereas Mary Anne just craved his love and attention. She wanted babies, and a life outside of the one in which she had been raised.

Did he want to be a power couple, or a jefe of power in his own right?

He wasn't sure he had an answer.

13

Monday arrived and Ramón met with Benjamin Ross in the Manhattan offices of Weyland-Yutani. It was 6:45 a.m., well before anyone would be there except for the nightwatchman at the ground-floor reception. Having taken the first bullet train from Boston, he was exhausted as he exited the elevator on the twentieth floor, a backpack slung over his shoulder.

Ross was waiting for him.

"You ready?"

"Yes," Ramón answered. "Are you putting me to work already?"

"No, not today—not yet," Ross replied. "Later. First you need to know what's at stake. What you'll be committing to."

Ramón was confused, but refused to show it. Ross was talking in ciphers, still not letting on what they actually wanted of him. Julia probably knew, but no matter how he had pressed her, she just dodged the question while massaging his ego—and other things.

"Follow me," Ross said, turning to walk briskly through a long corridor of large executive offices. He carried a small valise. Gone was the jovial fellow with the white linen shirt, replaced by an expensive suit.

They continued along a windowless hallway until they reached what looked like a wall of dark expensive wood. The short man looked to the ceiling and centered himself beneath a small black globe. A portion of the wooden wall opened, but this was no ordinary door. It was a vault with large retractable locks, and the wall was at least two feet deep.

On the other side was a chamber with a wall full of monitors and a single rectangular table also made from expensive natural wood. The genuine stuff, not the synthetic materials most people had to use, and which never quite looked real. In the center a tray with six bottles of water, soda, an assortment of sandwiches, and a bowl of fruit. Ross walked to one of the monitors and flicked it on, his fingers tapping a tablet mounted to the wall.

"Since you've signed the NDA we sent," Ross said, "I can show this to you now. It's footage from the project you will live and breathe from this day forward," he said, "*if* you have the stomach—and the balls—for it." He stepped aside.

Ramón stepped closer to the monitor. His lips parted in disbelief as his mind tried to parse what he was seeing. Once again he could feel Ross staring at him, to gauge his reaction.

All those years of Leticia, so eager to leave the planet of their birth to follow their parents into the void. Of Roseanna, talking her mumbo jumbo about the universe and space and not being alone. If what he saw on the screen was real, then she had been right, but she couldn't have meant this… this *thing*.

Who could comprehend such a nightmare?

"What is this, Benjamin?" he said, finding his voice. "And more importantly, *where* is this? Where on Earth—?"

"They're called Xenomorphs," Ross said, "and they are the future. They call this one La Reina, and as for 'where,' this is a planet that takes about five years in cryo to reach. Meredith Vickers began the process of making the planet habitable, before she disappeared. She had enough influence to keep it under wraps and claim it for herself. No one had this on their radar—it wasn't even given an LV designation. As a result, there's a small facility, and nothing else. She never specified what she wanted it for.

"One of her descendants, Jacob Vickers, has taken an interest in the planet," Ross continued. "He is being groomed, quietly, by a small faction who seek to steer the company in a different direction. Julia Yutani is being groomed, as well, but not so subtly. You know her—she knows how to play ball in *our* world."

Ramón was mesmerized. The thing on the screen was black, with a shiny carapace that resembled that of an insect. It had four limbs that could have been arms and legs, but had been cut off, leaving sharp stumps. There was a long narrow head with a crown-like hood, ending in an eyeless face and wicked jaws. The chamber in which it was secured was featureless, and the creature remained almost motionless. Yet he was pretty sure it was aware.

Horrifying, and yet…

"What purpose could such a thing serve?" he asked. "For that matter, what purpose could *I* serve in a project involving such a creature? I'm no scientist."

He turned, and watched as Ross reached into his pocket and removed a small metal capsule large enough to fit into a nostril. He brought it to his nose and snorted, then noticed Ramón staring at him.

"You want a bump?"

"No," Ramón said. Then, "No thank you. I don't do llelo." His mind was his greatest asset, and he refused to do anything that might jeopardize the one thing that gave him an unassailable edge. Ross shrugged, threw his head back, and lifted an arm toward the monitor.

"Just as well you don't do the shit," he said. "We have too much work to do. Sometimes I just need a little edge. There was a party last night I didn't want to miss." He shook his head as if to organize his thoughts.

"As far as 'why you,' you're brilliant—you know that—and you're a hustler. Perfect grades, and you don't let anything get in your way. Since high school, probably before, you've used your brains combined with raw greed to get what you want. Competition is phlegm in your throat, something to be cleared away. We like that.

"And regarding the 'what purpose,' people don't mind seeing guns and missiles being made and traded, but the idea of biological weapons scares them in ways that are unnecessarily irrational. We need a long-term strategy. The scientists are good at creating and replicating, but we need it to fit into our business model. We're selling our weapons to the highest bidders, private or governments, and that's where you come in."

Ramón swallowed hard and turned back to the monitor displaying the hideous thing Ross had called a Xenomorph. Glancing to the side, he saw Ross wiping his nose. In that instant Ramón knew that taking the man's job would be easier than he might have anticipated. From the look of it, between the drugs and burning the candle at both ends, Ross would bury himself without any help.

On the monitor, the room in which the monstrosity was being held made it impossible to tell the creature's true size. It appeared big, however, and a translucent, slimy tube attached to the lower body wobbled and contracted like a serpent digesting a large prey. It was pushing something out.

An egg.

"What are you… *we* doing here? What's the value in this?" In response Ross cocked his head toward the wooden table. He took a seat, and Ramón joined him.

"I need you to read all the sciencey stuff and come up with a strategy," the older man said. "How can we make money off the things we're learning here, and use them to bury our competition?" He opened a bottle of water, took a swig, and continued. "You need to think *big*, because the better the idea, the fatter the budget. Focus on the biological weapons program. It needs a refresh. There's a lot of profit there—I'm sure of it—but greed is only as good as the marksman taking aim. Again, think big."

"What do I have access to?" Ramón asked. "How deep do I get to dive?"

"You have it all, Ramón."

"Really?" There had to be a catch. Ross had to have something up his sleeve. They didn't just hand a newcomer the keys to the kingdom.

"Julia Yutani made sure of it," Ross said, and he made a face as if he'd tasted something he didn't like. "What Julia wants, Julia gets—

even if she occasionally has to wait for it. Watch out when she gets tired of waiting."

Ramón thought of something.

"This might be a difficult find, but can you get me a whiteboard?" he asked. "My tía—my aunt—had an old one I used all the time to keep track of my, er, extra-curricular moneymaking ventures in high school. When faced with a particularly difficult challenge, I'd stare at it and come up with new ways to trick the school systems to access whoever I wanted, manipulate tests, find out dirt."

Ross looked as if he was about to jump over and dry hump him on the spot—exactly the reaction he was hoping for. He wanted this man to know *exactly* how valuable he was, and Ramón's confidence was growing stronger by the minute.

"I'll check the supplies list," Ross said. "No one uses those anymore, I don't think." He peered at Ramón, waiting for the next shoe to drop. "That's it?"

"I want a bonus," he said. "Think of it as a signing reward. Enough to cover the outstanding mortgage on my tía's house."

"Done."

"Paid by midnight tonight."

"Damn!" Ross slapped the tabletop. "You were born to work for us."

Ramón found himself beaming. "Benjamin... Ben, I'm really excited about this opportunity, but it's not the only thing I need to accomplish. I intend to complete my MBA, as well. It's not something I'm willing to leave unfinished. That will take time. I'll do what I can when I can."

"Ha!" Benjamin responded. "You won't need an MBA, doing this. Save your time and money. Stick with us, kid, and you'll get out of that dorm room. You'll have an apartment in a building owned by Weyland-Yutani."

That could present a problem.

"It can't be in the same place as Julia—"

"No, don't worry," Benjamin said. "You can still have both of them, in different places." Ramón opened his mouth to speak, but Benjamin raised a hand. "Don't," he said. "I've been there myself a few times."

He gave Ramón a cheeky wink, drank the rest of the water, and stood, picking up the valise and pulling out a tablet. "This is an overview of the program—study it. Stay here as long as you want, and help yourself to the food. You know the way out."

Ramón watched Benjamin leave. This would mean strange working conditions and stranger hours, but he didn't think that would be difficult. He'd always done things his own way.

He lifted his eyes back to the monitor.

La Reina.

The Queen.

The Xenomorph was moving now, rolling its head back and forth as another egg emerged. Largest fucking huevos he had ever seen in his life. It looked grotesque, with a large tongue hanging to its chest. Stumps where there should have been hands and feet and a tail with an abrupt, ragged end. Whatever had happened to this thing, it must have been pure agony. There was something in its stillness that made him go cold inside. It seemed impossible that a creature like this had evolved just to hang there as a docile surrogate.

No, he needed to know every last detail of its existence. This was a thing that should inspire fear—though he felt none, considering how far away it was. God willing, he would never encounter one in the flesh.

Hunger made his stomach rumble, so he poked through the fresh fruit and sandwiches. Fresh ingredients, the sort that were in increasingly short supply, especially to the general public. Yet piled high, here in this secret room.

Just for him.

"A bonus… my first and not my last. Good going, Ramón." He smiled before beginning to read a file detailing the first encounter with the Xenomorph.

The door opened again, startling Ramón, who was engrossed in reading. He looked at his phone to see an hour had already passed.

"Ask and ye shall receive," Benjamin said cheerily. "Just in time, before anyone arrives. Here's a whiteboard and a few pens. Had to look through the storage log, and this was the only one. It was kept as some sort of prop—don't ask me. Right. I'll leave this here and see you when we're done for the day."

Ramón liked whiteboards for the same reason he liked notepads—the kind with paper. There was a type of wizardry when an idea went from the mind to the hand to the page. The same person could type the same sentence on a tablet, but handwriting was unique. It was a stamp. He loved that concept.

With black marker in hand, he returned to his research.

The whiteboard was full by the time Benjamin came back early in the evening, carrying two lowball glasses filled with whiskey.

"How was the first day?"

"Good," Ramón answered, taking one of the drinks, "but I don't know how I'm going to manage my schoolwork, too. There's so much information here, so many applications to assess, and a political minefield to navigate. Do the right things and we're rich. Do the wrong things, and we're sunk. I haven't even begun to scrape the surface of the weapons program."

"Don't worry so much," Benjamin said, waving the glass in the air, careful not to spill any of the contents. "You think everyone at those fancy schools gets there by merit alone? You're smarter than all of 'em combined."

Ramón nodded, unconvinced. "Well, I need to go," he said. "I'm meeting Julia for a little birthday celebration. She took the train down to meet me here, and I don't want to disappoint her."

"Oh, yeah," Benjamin said, beginning to slur his words a bit. "Tell her I said happy birthday. By the way, one day you'll have to introduce me to that sister of yours." Ramón shot him a quizzical look. "I stumbled upon her when I was researching you. Marines—impressive and a little sexy, if I may say."

As if, Ramón thought as he threw his belongings into his backpack and zipped it closed, not wanting to respond. No way would Leticia ever go near him. She could be a brat, but she was a damned *smart* brat, and he loved her. She was out of Benjamin's league. *What a parasite.*

The thought caused him to stop fiddling with his backpack and flick his eyes to the screen that showed the Xenomorph. *Parasites*. He'd read they were developing some nasty shit.

Water Systems.

Silent Coercion.

Isolated Displays of Force.

Ramón had always been careful in life, with so many of his desires under control. This project would allow him to indulge in all those tendencies. Even if it meant destroying someone else without conscience. His imagination was a jet pack with that thought, but it would have to wait until he was mentally refreshed.

With his new access to records, he also planned on scanning the files for information on his mother. Roseanna had told them her last message concerned a mission to a Weyland-Yutani colony. She had died there. There had to be more details, and if he couldn't find them he would ask Julia to pull some strings.

He downed the last of his drink.

"I'll see you tomorrow."

Julia stood at the bar looking the picture of poised perfection, as she always did. Her heels were high enough to warrant a car service to and from the restaurant. Ramón knew he was hopelessly in love with her, despite his misgivings.

"Hi, gorgeous," she said. "The table is ready."

She leaned in and kissed him on the lips.

"Show me the way, guapa."

He loved the way he felt when she was close. They walked through the half-empty restaurant to a back corner table. A bottle in an ice bucket and two full glasses of champagne waited for them.

"I reserved this table so we could have privacy," she said. After they had both slid into their seats, she removed a box from her handbag and pushed it toward him.

"What's this?" he said. "It's your birthday, and you're giving *me* a gift?"

"I don't need anything," she replied, "and I wanted to celebrate your new position with the company. I'm so excited you've accepted."

"Thank you." He wasn't surprised that she already knew. "Benjamin wastes no time."

"Benjamin *can't*," she said, raising an eyebrow. "He's been a cat with nine lives over the years, and he doesn't have many left." He wondered what that meant, but decided not to press it.

Ramón untied the gold ribbon and opened the box.

"A Rolex?" He tried to hold his smile, but he couldn't hold back the slight anger welling up inside. "This is too much!"

"You have to look the part," she said. "It's nothing. We're the same, and we want the same things."

"Thank you." Being careful to hold back his emotions, he leaned over to kiss her on the cheek. "It's very generous. I'm afraid I didn't bring your gift with me, though. Didn't want to carry it on the train."

She waved him off. "You can pay for dinner. I'm starving. You must be, too, after your day. I want to hear all about it over a steak smothered in béarnaise sauce."

"Sounds like a plan." He picked up his champagne. "Where do I even start?"

"Start with *her*." Julia put down her glass. "I'm told she goes by La Reina. That's 'the queen,' isn't it?"

Ramón could feel himself tremble with the thought of the Xenomorph. *La Reina*. Usually he didn't drink, or kept it to a bare minimum, but tonight he would. He lifted the glass and took a fast gulp.

"What I'm thinking, I can't share it with just anyone," he said, his mind racing again. "You're the only one I can trust with what I *really* think."

Julia licked her lips and took another sip before sliding a hand up his thigh the way he liked.

"And what's that, my love?" she whispered as she stroked him through the fabric.

"I think La Reina is checkmate."

Julia's red lips curled into a smile.

"My thoughts exactly," she said, "but we have to get it right."

* * *

When he arrived back at his dorm the following day, the cold metal of the new watch on his wrist sent shivers down his entire body. Is this how their relationship would be? With Julia always one-upping him? He had wanted to buy that for himself. But goddamn, she beat him to it.

He thought about how he loved her touch, the way her mind followed his thought processes without judgment—or asking for anything in return. Fuck the Rolex. He would buy a boat.

His desire for her fought with his ambitions and ego.

It wasn't that way with Mary Anne. She had zero desire to challenge anything—including herself. She was entirely satisfied with the status quo, and he liked that most of the time. It helped him shut off his overworked brain.

The brain Julia set on fire, nonstop, along with his body. Her ambition rivaled his, which both excited and frightened him. He had to remind himself that it was all about the Vasquez empire, not Yutani. Julia would be a Yutani until the day she died, that bonfire on the beach with hot embers flying every which direction. It was mesmerizing because it touched something primal.

Mary Anne was the glowing tea lights on a long sleek bar with jazz playing in the background. Soothing and safe.

She was out that night with her mother Laurel and sister Henrietta, choosing bridesmaids dresses for Henrietta's upcoming wedding. Mary Anne never asked him where he was, where he had been, just if he was "coming home." He could never tell Mary Anne the truth about this new job. With both of her parents on boards for various charities, the simple fact that it was Weyland-Yutani would probably send them into apoplectic fits.

The less she knew, the better, and truth to tell, he didn't want to tell her about it. She would remain his oasis. Eating meals with small talk and gossip would enable him to rest from himself.

In a few days' time he would be going back home to see Roseanna… and Leticia. That, too, might be turned to his advantage. When the time was right he might need a connection to the Marines, and to military intel. Ironically, Leticia's decision might turn out for the best.

Stack the deck before you need your cards.

14

Ramón arrived looking pale, as if he hadn't seen the sun in months but had packed on a few pounds of muscle. Leticia grabbed his arm.

"I have some competition?" she said. "Looking buff, mi hermano. You never seemed the least bit interested in fitness. What changed your mind—or maybe I should ask, *who* changed your mind?"

"No way," he protested, pulling free. "You'll get no competition from me. I'm not the combat type. Let's just say I'm stuck most of the time with research and studying, and my dormitory has a gym on site. It's given me an outlet. Helps me think." He stepped back. "But enough about me, how's it going with special ops. How does it work, anyhow? What's your plan for getting in?"

Leticia was taken aback by his questioning. It had been so long since he expressed any interest in her hopes for the military, and when he did, it wasn't positive. Then she shrugged it off. Maybe he *had* changed.

"At this point, the only plan is to make it through," she admitted. "It's tough going. I suppose if I get into the Raiders, though, I'll be going on whatever missions they send me to. So I guess *that's* the plan—I won't stop until I get there."

Ramón nodded. "You'll get there—I'm sure of it," he said. "We haven't always been as close as we could have been, but we aren't kids anymore. Who knows what the future holds for us, and what opportunities might come and go."

That piqued Leticia's curiosity even more. All this talk of the future, and she hadn't even set foot on the training ground. Whatever Ramón was talking about, she couldn't tell what was going on in that complicated brain of his. Better to let it go... for now.

"Thanks, bro," she said. "I appreciate the vote of confidence. It's all so far off. If I *do* get into the Raiders, though, it'll all be hush-hush. I wouldn't be able to tell you about it, anyway."

"No, of course," he said. "Being away from home has made me appreciate our family a little more. I'm just trying to be a better brother.

We're familia. You never know what's going to happen—that's the way it's always been with us. If I can ever help... just say the word."

"We'll cross that bridge if we ever come to it. And thanks."

"Right, let's go find Roseanna." Ramón looked around. "I have a surprise for her."

"Really? What is it?"

"This place." Ramón gave her a sly smile that bordered on sinister, stretching his arms wide. "Who says generational wealth can't be ours?"

Generational what?

Before she could say a word, he dashed through the house. She knew something was up. Ramón had his hands into some cookie jar... just like in high school. There was no way a college student could be making serious money doing something legit. She just hoped whatever he had up his sleeve wouldn't come back to bite him.

Or any of them.

She heard a cry in the living room. Roseanna. Leticia took a deep breath and was determined to be happy. If it was good news, their tía might retire early, if she wanted to, or take a big trip without having to rely on Robert. She'd given them so much over the years, and never asked for anything in return.

Leticia found them in the living room.

"Did Ramón tell you what he did?" Roseanna said, excitement and pride in her voice. "He said the advance he got for a big freelance job covered the rest of the mortgage. The house will be paid off, and you two will always have this place to come home to."

"That's the best news," Leticia said, putting a big smile on her face. "You deserve it, and Ramón deserves everything he gets for all his hard work."

"You're next, Leticia." Roseanna took one of Leticia's hands in her own. "I promise. Your hard work will make your dreams come true." Then her smile went wide again. "Why don't we go celebrate?"

A couple of days passed, and on the last morning Leticia found Ramón in the kitchen. He had made a spread of fresh breakfast tacos from The Donut Shop, and fresh orange juice to go with them.

"I wanted to do something nice for you guys," he said, "because I don't know when we will all be together again. I always liked it when Robert did this."

"Thank you, mijo," Roseanna said, and she gave Ramón a tight hug. "He has always wanted to get to know you better, but didn't want to push."

"Well, I appreciated it, even if I didn't say anything."

They dug into the tacos, making small talk and unwilling to admit that the visit was going to come to an end. After breakfast, however, Ramón rose and said that he had to jet off for classes and work.

"I guess this is it, then, brother," Leticia said. "Thank you for taking time from your break to come see us." She gave him a meaningful look. "Can you be careful? Watch your back."

"Trust me," he answered. "I'm fine—and you're only a message away. Call me anytime you want. I really want to know how it goes in the Marines. And if you need money, with this side gig…"

"Or if I need an essay written?"

Ramón gave her a smile and chuckled. "Yes, something like that. Take care of yourself, and don't take any shit—not that you do, anyway."

"Wait, you can't go yet," Roseanna said. "One last photo for my altar!" Both Leticia and Ramón rolled their eyes.

"Go on, tía." Ramón beamed in his Harvard sweatshirt, and Leticia moved her body a little so the tattoo of their mother would be in the photo. Roseanna tapped her phone, then again, and a third time. "Right," Ramón said. "I'd better get to the airport—there's a lot to do before classes start again."

"And next time I want you to bring that girl you are seeing," Roseanna said. "I need to meet her, or maybe welcome her into our little family. Our home and land that I now own!"

"That sounds like a great idea." Ramón had a strange expression, Leticia thought, but he nodded. "You'll like her. She's very down to earth, wants a family of her own, *our* own, but doesn't need me to take care of her. Her name is Mary Anne. She comes from a great family, too."

"As long as she makes you happy and you feel at home with her," Roseanna said. "Really at peace."

Ramón paused before answering. "Of course. She is a very nice woman." A car horn made them all turn toward the open screen door. "That's me. Love you both."

"Hey, don't forget, *el riesgo siempre vive*," Leticia said, giving him a warm smile.

He nodded. "And good luck with you. If it doesn't work out the way you want, you'll find another way, Leticia, or another way will find you." He grabbed the real-leather duffel bag with his initials monogrammed on the side, and walked out the door.

15

The drive to the Marine Corps recruit depot was long, all the way to South Carolina. The original Parris Island facility had long since been swallowed by the rising ocean, and it was now situated just outside of Fairfax.

Every exit and stoplight released more excitement and trepidation in Leticia. Roseanna kept the music low on the radio to allow her niece to think or talk. They had waited so long for this fated moment, she didn't press her to speak.

Basic training and leaving home; two rites of passage in a single day. Leticia didn't know what to say. Then she began to see the road signs, and knew it was close. They turned off on a dusty unmarked road, and the only way they knew the destination was the GPS code given to them by the Marines. Then a large brick wall topped with barbed wire seemed to appear out of nowhere, along with the signs.

DANGER!

MILITARY

TRAINING AREA

RESTRICTED AREA

NO TRESPASSING

USCM GOVERNMENT PROPERTY

There was a sound from overhead, and helicopters cut through the humid atmosphere. They could hear unseen jets, as well. They were getting close.

At the entrance were two outdated, ancient tanks from previous wars. She thought of her family members who had served, and wondered what her mother felt when she passed through these very gates. The thumping of her pulse was a twenty-one-gun salute marking the end of her old life.

They pulled up to an entrance with a large metal gate. Leticia and Roseanna had to stick their heads out of the car windows to be verified with a facial scan. Roseanna was only allowed to pull into the visitor drop-off lot.

"You have everything?"

"I do, tía. Thank you."

"You made the right decision, and stuck out the time that was needed. You will succeed in everything you do."

"I love you, tía."

"I love you, too, mija, and I'm already proud of you. Your mother and all the ancestors before us would be proud. You have gone further than any of them could ever dream of. Jenette did the same."

"I'll call you with an update as soon as I can."

"Don't worry about me. This is your time."

They leaned in for a long, tight hug. Then Leticia got out of the car to follow the path that led where Roseanna could not accompany her, farther into the bustling training facility. If she lingered any longer, she thought, she might burst into tears. From that moment forward, she was the only one who would determine if she succeeded or not—or more accurately, how far she would go without quitting.

First get through basic, service for three years, then nine months of Raider training. That was the plan.

People passed her by, some in civilian clothes, others in fatigues. Seeing the strange faces made her think of something Lucinda had said before she left.

"I know you are set on doing this, you'll be great, but watch your back. Be careful. There are stories of young female recruits gone missing, or worse. The I Am Vanessa Guillain Act *did a lot of good. God bless her soul and those who lost their lives, or were never heard from again. You can take any harassment or complaint to authorities outside the military, but still…"*

Touched by her concern, Leticia had hugged her.

"I know. Believe me when I say I have researched it extensively. I know what I'm getting into. Keep in touch. This isn't the end."

Their final evening together had been wonderful, in front of a bonfire beneath the stars with a pot of pork tamales made by Lucinda's grandmother, and arroz con pollo courtesy of Robert and Avery.

Before she knew it, the intake building stood before her. There was a line, and she made her way to the back, not knowing anyone. Some of the others talked among themselves as if they had joined together straight out of school. When she finally made it to the front of the line a Black woman in uniform greeted her.

"Here are your fatigues," the woman said brusquely. "I highly suggest you remove all jewelry during training. Any feminine sanitary products are provided for free at sick bay." She peered at Leticia. "Looks like you've already had a haircut, so we can skip that. Any complaints about the food will go unnoticed, so don't waste anyone's time. If you have dietary requirements, those can be processed through the mess hall. Your assigned bunk is on this card. All the items you have can be stored in your trunk. Any questions?"

"No, ma'am."

Leticia headed off to find her new home. The people she would meet would have to be her new family as they pulled together, eventually to work as a unit. If she wanted to be a Raider, then she had to forget that anything existed outside of the mission that was basic training, and completing the Crucible.

* * *

"You aren't a Marine until I say so," the woman said. "My name may be Mercy, but you will get none from me. They pay me the big bucks to get you fighting fit—and if anyone dares to sing *Mercy Me*, it's an automatic fifty push-ups."

There was a hushed chuckle in the room.

"Thirteen weeks," she continued. "You are my little babies for thirteen weeks, and then I will kick your scrawny asses out of the nest. Fly or die. Now some of you indicated that you want to go deeper into the Corps. Rumor has it some of you think you are Raider material. I will also be determining if you get a pass for such an honor. You know who you are, and know that I am watching you."

A white woman with the name "Frida" printed on her green T-shirt leaned to whisper into Leticia's ear. "Who's she saying has a scrawny ass. Definitely not me—and look at that one… Damn I might be in love."

Leticia glanced toward the man Frida was admiring. "Mohammed" was printed on his shirt. He had two large crow tattoos, one on each forearm, and a close-cut beard on his face. Arabic lettering on the left side of his neck. She had to admit, his black eyes were impossibly beautiful.

Mercy, the drill sergeant, began to walk their way again. Leticia and Frida snapped back to attention.

"I will only say this once—only you determine if you make it to the Crucible. If you think what you have to offer isn't enough, then it probably isn't. Your new life starts today. Now, time for the first hump across the training ground. Move!"

Another drill sergeant waited outside the entrance of the barracks, ushering them out.

"You heard Mercy, move!" The recruits all complied. Leticia's feet started off as a shuffle, then turned into a jog. They passed a large wooden obstacle course some distance away, with other recruits fighting their way through in full gear and holding their weapons. There was a gigantic warehouse that housed the training facility to prep for space travel, and again she thought of her mother. Her heart pounded faster as she picked up her pace.

There was no turning back.

The only direction she cared about was forward and up.

When they arrived back at the barracks nearly everyone was exhausted and shaking their feet from running in combat boots. Every shirt was ringed with sweat beneath the arms, around the neck, and chests. A table had large water coolers and MREs for the recruits to help themselves. Leticia's entire body trembled. She had exhausted the glucose in her system, and the humidity had pulled every last drop of moisture from her body.

She trudged toward the table.

"I wasn't ready for that." The voice next to Leticia came from the woman who had stood next to her in the barracks, Frida.

"Same," Leticia admitted. "I spent time on a farm and my aunt's land, but it was mostly lifting and hauling. Did a lot of shooting. Endurance—like running at a steady pace—I totally skipped."

"At least you had a head start. I was working android sales."

"No shit? What brought you to the Marines?"

"I want to know more about androids beyond selling them. I like the idea of special ops and using the technology out in the field. In sales, all the boss cares about are the bottom line, making the quotas. Everything was on a need-to-know basis when it came to the technology. I mean, have you seen the new Narwhals? Those things are fast on the water and capable of doing real damage with the grenade launcher on the front. Genius."

"Respect," Leticia replied. "That's a great reason to enlist. Hope you get the chance to ride one." She held out her hand. "I'm Leticia."

"Frida... oh shit. There's that guy. He looks even better all sweaty. C'mon, I can't go by myself. I really want to say hi."

"You want to be the best of the best, but can't talk to one dude?" Leticia said. "One very *attractive* dude?"

"What can I say, I hang around androids most of the day."

Leticia chuckled. "Let's go."

As they approached, the man tossed water over his head and wiped it across his face. Frida grabbed an MRE and poured herself a cup of water.

"How about that run?" she said. "Where are you from?"

Leticia cringed inside.

"My dad warned me it was tough, but this will be something. I can feel it." He flashed a cheeky grin. "I'm Mohammed Faez." Another recruit joined them. Mohammed handed him an MRE. "This is my man Nathan Powell. We joined together because, what the hell is this world—or any of the worlds—coming to. The colonies fighting. So many damn wars. A lot of family and friends lost." He took a drink. "From Minnesota."

"I'm from Philly," Frida replied. "Go Flyers!"

While Nathan tore into his MRE, a Black woman from the barracks approached their corner of the table. She had been to her right before the run, and with the figure of a gymnast, appeared unaffected by the effort.

"Is this where the cool kids hang out?"

"Cool, not sure, but good-looking, yes." Nathan spoke up between bites. "And you are?"

"Desiree."

Frida brought her hand to her mouth. "Wait, I thought you looked familiar. Desiree Benson? The Olympian?"

Desiree nodded. "Retired and wanted to do something new. Got sick of the politics involved and wanted to make a difference, if I could. Sponsorships don't pay what they did back in the day, and this is a hell of a lot warmer than New York City in the winter."

She grabbed her cup and filled it with more water, before turning her attention back to Leticia.

"Cool tat on your arm. Relative?"

When she said this the others glanced at the tattoo. Leticia knew this wasn't a time to be shy or self-conscious. The Corps was all about teamwork, and honesty would be the best way to build trust.

"It's my mother. She was a Marine, and died during a mission to some colony. I'm from Texas, but *please* don't call me Tex!"

They all just nodded. Frida shifted the conversation.

"Is everyone planning on staying a grunt? Anyone want recon?"

Leticia spoke first, with confidence. "Raider all the way. For her." She tapped on her tattoo. Once again, all eyes were on her, until Nathan and Mohammed exchanged glances.

"What?" Leticia said. "You guys going for it, too?"

"Actually, we are." Mohammed placed a hand on Nathan's shoulder and squeezed.

"Been together since freshman year in high school. I'm the beauty and he's the beast."

"You two are a lucky pair…" Frida said, and Leticia detected a note of regret. She cocked her head and smiled. "I want to be more than a grunt, too. For sure."

"I guess this wasn't the spot for the cool kids, but budding Raiders," Desiree said. "We're all on the same page. Some coincidence."

"My tía doesn't believe in coincidences," Leticia said. "This is good—and Desiree, I'll be bothering you for training tips. An Olympian!"

"No bother, I started gymnastics when I could pretty much walk. If I know anything, it's the discipline required for training. I'll be glad to help."

Leticia lifted her cup of water. "To the Raiders. May we all have the ganas to do what must be done, in every situation. ¡Salud!"

"To the Raiders." They all followed her lead and lifted a salute to the stars.

The bond Leticia forged with her fellow recruits superseded any friendship she'd ever experienced in school, or even the one with her brother. When one dropped to their knees or wavered, another was waiting in the wings to show them back to the way of the warrior.

Mercy kept her eyes on them like the eagle on the Marines emblem, knowing they all wanted into Raider training. At the end of basic, her recommendations would be the difference between success and failure.

Leticia could shoot, but here she honed her skills and learned to take apart and put together any new weapon thrown her way. She studied harder than she ever had in school, learning everything there was to know about military strategy.

She watched Mohammed and Nathan with a secret envy. They had the kind of spark that was rare and undying. During training, their stolen glances of support radiated love and devotion. Their relationship was no secret, and Leticia would have no problem fucking up anyone who dared show they had a problem with it. Then again, both Nathan and Mohammed were built like sentinels—step up to them if you had a death wish. Mohammed was a boxer, with his father owning a string of gyms. He'd enlisted to see the world, and then space. Nathan had taught piano as a side hustle to his main job as a mechanic.

Though she hadn't wanted a commitment with Avery, she hoped there was someone out there for her. There were her dreams as a soldier, and those were her priority for now, but she still possessed those desires of a woman. Was there a man who would complement her life in ways that could only be described as a bright constellation to light her way for the times life went dark?

Maybe a distant star would bring them together.

In her footlocker she kept the photograph of her mother as a Marine. Desiree spotted it one morning.

"Your mom is… damn. A gorgeous machine. She would have been a Marine Raider."

"I know." Leticia instinctively smiled and ran her fingertips across the photo. "I want to get into that shape. What comes next is no joke."

"Where do you want to start?"

"The pull-up bar," Leticia said. "Running with a pulse rifle in hand, and all the rest of the gear, brings a special kind of pain."

"Sounds about right. Why don't we start fresh tomorrow?"

"Thanks, Desiree. You got it. Las lobas." When her companion gave her a look, she added, "The wolves."

If she wasn't practicing her marksmanship, Leticia was in the gym with Desiree, preparing her body for what would be the most grueling weeks of her life. Her goal was to fight the biggest motherfuckers and do so with her bare hands. Basic training was designed to create quitters, she knew. The more that dropped out, the easier it would be to find out who had the stuff to succeed, to become a part of the elite.

She would be one of them.

Their hard work—on the range, in the gym—began to pay off.

Combat water survival made her think of the first time she jumped into the pond back home, all her clothes on and without considering how deep it could be. There had been the biggest frog she had ever seen, and she wanted to touch it.

Water filled her mouth and ears. When she couldn't touch the bottom, her first instinct was to panic. She grasped at darkness with her hands and feet, and felt the bottom scrape her big toe. It wasn't far. Leticia allowed herself to sink a little farther to touch the bottom with her feet, then pushed toward the surface. Her arms propelled her through the water, pumping against the heaviness of her jeans and T-shirt that added weight to her frame.

She grabbed the roots of the reeds at the edge of the pond and pulled herself out.

Training required her to swim fifteen feet, wearing fatigues, and keeping her rifle out of the water. The main thing that was missing, though, was the panic. She swam with confidence, and tomorrow she would do a drop into the water blindfolded.

All of this with Mercy's eagle eyes still watching.

Every day, on the way out and on the way back, they passed by the gigantic warehouse. There were no windows—she couldn't see what was happening inside, but one day she would be in there, preparing for her destiny.

When the time came for the group to tackle the fifty-four-hour test called the Crucible, they were prepared for the lack of sleep, physical exhaustion, meager rations, and grueling demands. More importantly, they were working as a team.

Leticia held the two MREs that would have to last for the entire exercise, but food wasn't the only thing that would be in short supply. They would also only have eight hours of sleep for the entire time. She knew she would need all the ganas of her mother and all the Vasquez ancestors to make it through.

"How the hell are we supposed to wake up at three a.m. to march ten miles." Desiree playfully elbowed her as she packed her own backpack. "I'm wound up—how about you?"

"I think I'm more gassed for the leader stations once we get to the Crucible site." Leticia shoved the MREs into her backpack, happy she had eaten more than her fair share at breakfast and lunch.

"You're going to be great. And don't you mean 'warrior stations'?" Leticia smirked while securing a red bandana around her forehead. "Soldadera station for me. Ooh-rah!"

Getting to the Crucible site, they each carried fifty pounds of equipment and alternated between marching and running. Upon arrival, each squad went to a designated "warrior station" named for a hero from the history of the Corps. As she considered the bravery of their predecessors, Leticia thought of her mother.

Mi madre, Jenette Vasquez, should be here—but if she can't, then one day I will. That thought sharpened Leticia's focus and made her forget any hunger or physical exhaustion. This was so much bigger than her. This was the beginning of leaving bootprints for others to follow. Leticia completed her task as squad leader knowing the spirit of her mother, the ganas to persevere, would be her guide.

What followed was a series of complex problem-solving exercises, after which they moved to hand-to-hand combat, then an obstacle course. She and Frida had to squirm like larvae on their bellies in mud beneath the sharpened teeth of barbed wire while pulling a "wounded" Mohammed to safety. Leticia gritted her teeth and thought of her mother's photo glowing from the candlelight on Roseanna's altar.

When the obstacle course was complete, they marched and jogged back to the base. The Crucible ended when she stood before the Iwo Jima flag-raising statue. She wondered what wars lay ahead for her.

What was she willing to die for?

Setting aside those thoughts, she focused on the here-and-now. Her crew made it to the end, earning their Eagle, Anchor, and Globe. For the graduation ceremony, Leticia marched in her uniform feeling as if the ground didn't exist. She was already floating, that much closer to her mother.

Roseanna and Robert were somewhere in the watching crowd. Ramón had a deadline he couldn't miss, but he had sent her an email congratulating her. In formation she marched with her best friends toward what she hoped would become a pass into Raider training.

When the graduation ceremony was over, Mercy found them all standing together.

"Thought I might find you together," she said, an unusual warmth in her voice. "It's a good thing you built a tight crew and fought hard during your training. You've all received my recommendation for Raider training—after you finish your three years in the service. Don't go slacking or quitting, and make me look like a fool."

"Thank you, ma'am," Leticia said. She resisted the urge to jump up and down and kiss her friends.

Mercy gave them a short nod and turned to leave.

Frida and Desiree squeezed each other's hands as they squealed. Nathan and Mohammed shared an embrace. Leticia had never felt pride like this.

"Three years," she said. "We have three years to be on our shit, guys." As they were allowed to find their guests, Leticia found Roseanna and Robert at their agreed upon meeting place, a bench overlooking the space facility.

"I did it!" she said, breaking into a jog.

Roseanna nearly jumped out of her dress as Leticia approached.

"Of course you did!" she said. "Look how sharp that uniform is. Wow. I am so proud." She and Robert both gave her hugs.

"Lucinda and Avery both send their congratulations," he said. "You're welcome at the farm anytime. Roseanna has moved in, so my home is your home."

"Thank you, Robert. Congratulations to you both!"

Roseanna brought her hand to her mouth, and looked as if she might cry. "Remember when you were so worried. Everything worked out as was intended." She gathered herself, and added, "Do you know where you go next?"

"Not sure. Service is service, and you go where orders take you— but I also received a recommendation for Raider training!"

"Oh, that's wonderful! I knew it. See. You were always meant to fly." She glanced at Robert. "Well, you can always come home, whenever you want. We're keeping the house. Your room will always be yours, and Robert has space, too."

"Thank you. I know you will always keep a room for me, and that gives me the freedom to reach for more. I will carry the Vasquez name with pride wherever my boots take me.

"I promise you that."

16

Julia stood in her kitchen chopping vegetables. It was her favorite way of passing time as she organized her thoughts. Handcrafted in Kyoto, the Japanese knives were the best and the only ones she used. The handle was mother of pearl and wood.

"Are you feeding a vegetarian army?"

She glanced up long enough to take a sip of red wine and lean in for a kiss from Ramón.

"Looks like the Vickers school boy is gaining more support," he said, "after that media leak about one of the colonies going boom and killing a bunch of people, including kids. Then we have another story about weapons being smuggled to rebels in one of the colony wars. Of course, all Vickers can do is spout nonsense about philosophy, and what a reluctant leader he is."

"It used to be said that even bad press is good press," she said, returning her attention to the knife.

Her chopping became faster, but no less precise.

"I hear rumblings that he is also interested in Meredith's pet project, the planet we have been using."

"Exactly!" She lifted her knife in exasperation. "He wants to call it Olinka, or some such nonsense. What does he know?"

"So far, he has just been shown the small facility. He thinks it's a surveying outpost." Ramón leaned his back against the counter and crossed his arms as he tapped his foot. "What does he want to do? I'm a little behind on the politics, the weapons program has taken up all my time."

"He wants to build some mega facility for people to create... I don't know… art? Innovations that will bring peace? For people to live in harmony. In his idyllic world, there are no borders whatsoever."

"Then let him," Ramón suggested, and she shot him a look. "Rather, let me. I'll build his utopia—above the facility. Let him play for a bit, then we will take it back. And not just take it back; make sure Vickers is never in the game again."

She slowly stopped chopping.

"To make way for Vasquez."

"No, for us." He moved behind her to place his arms around her waist. "The Xenomorph, taken to the world stage in the hands of Weyland-Yutani, could be a game changer in all aspects of the business. If we have something no one else has or can control, the company will remain untouchable—even from governments, not that they matter anymore. Circus states run by clowns honking each other's noses in one big circle jerk as worlds including Earth continue to burn."

Julia placed her knife down and turned to face Ramón.

"This is why I love you," she said. "You're not just a big cock. That cunning brain of yours is such a turn on." She looked off, with her smile fading. "There's one issue, though. The scientist in charge is incredibly paranoid. I'm worried she might blow the entire project, if she can't keep her lunch down. Not literally, but she should be watched closely."

"Dr. Moon," he responded. "I know. At some point one of us, maybe both, will have to go out there. But I have a handle on her. Eyes everywhere."

Julia raised her eyes to Ramón. "I won't settle for anything less than the both of us." Her expression sent a shiver through him. "You either make a commitment to me, or it's over. You have to prove that you know when an investment just isn't good enough."

Ramón took both of her hands in his. "Leave it with me. You deserve a commitment, and I don't want to lose you. Ever. The idea of you with another man isn't something I can bear, let alone allowing it to become a reality—and I know you can have any man you want. I've had children to carry on the Vasquez name and my legacy. All Mary Anne wanted was to play house, and she had that opportunity. Can you handle being a stepmother?" He gave her a look. "They will always be in my life."

She wrapped her arms around his waist. "If that is the compromise then yes…" She raised an eyebrow. "What is that look, Ramón. Now?"

He broke away from her. "You know. Since this chopping is all for nothing you plan on cooking, how about you order dinner and come find me." Ramón left the kitchen to a smaller room.

All four walls were whiteboard, with nothing else in the room except a single chair on wheels. He sat down and stared straight ahead. He entered the space in his mind where all things of his creation came together. To his right a row of pens stood at attention on a magnetic square. Ramón rose and plucked one off. In the center of the wall he drew a large pyramid.

An hour later Julia entered. He sat on the chair with the whiteboard pen still in hand like a smoking gun. She began to rub Ramón's shoulders, and kissed his temple.

"I guess all our pillow talk has been recorded for posterity."

He craned his head to the left and kissed her hand.

"Benjamin Ross wanted all the fucked-up biological research pertaining to the Xenomorphs to have the same fear-inducing effect as a large planet-busting missile and to be as compact. The delivery of the weapons must be efficient. No waiting years and for the weapons to reach a location. No. They must be stored from day one on planets of interest, kept on ice. Either the Xenomorph eggs or humans carrying the engineered pathogens.

"They could be activated by the touch of a button," he continued. "Humans infected with the Xenomorph-spliced parasites could be sent anywhere undetected. We will hold the key—the bacteria used to neutralize the Xenomorphs and anything containing Xeno DNA. Unmanned ships could be sent to any location. Grim Reapers, I want to call them. They will have the ability to land and unleash silent hell without anyone knowing." He gave a wry grin. "My sister might put her faith in Santa Muerte, but I will be the Reaper."

Julia moved to Ramón's side, took the pen from his hand and walked to the whiteboard. She scribbled in her messy cursive.

Ramón's lips spread to a wide smile.

"Consider it done," he said.

"I want to see La Reina right now. In the flesh."

Dr. Patel screwed her face. "Usually you are so paranoid," she said. "Why? We can get up close with a drone."

Brenda didn't reply—she had slept just three hours the previous night, instead combing through correspondence from Weyland-Yutani for any clue as to why she had been kept from key information on the project. As she did, there seemed to be a precision to the requests from Weyland-Yutani beyond the scope she found acceptable.

She stared at her companion. The synths had seemed to be increasingly observant, taking more time with tasks assigned to them. Was someone using one to spy?

What Brenda wanted now was for La Reina to make the slightest move, provide the slightest provocation that would allow her to press the button. That would release the bacteria stored in the crown on her head, sending enough into her system to end her existence. She possessed a fob that would do the trick, created with the help of a human assistant she'd paid out of her own pocket to keep it a secret.

"Always keep watch," she said finally. "Make certain she doesn't move against any of the androids sent in there to retrieve the eggs."

"And if she does," Patel replied, "what are your orders?"

"I trust you will do the right thing." Brenda knew better, however. "Now let's go see our captive queen."

"Why are you doing this now?" Patel said. "We have the other project to oversee."

"The more we do here the less I understand," Brenda muttered. "Or sleep…"

They reached the chamber door, donned hazmat suits, and entered a complex series of security commands. The barrier slid open with a hiss, and Brenda stood in front of the huge, misshapen Xenomorph, feeling like an ant. Thanks to the amputations, and the scab-like growths that had formed where they had hacked off pieces of her body, she was the worst nightmare from the deepest parts of hell.

Normally only synths were allowed in here—she was the first human to face the monstrosity.

The upper part of the Xenomorph's jaw remained fixed with large, daggered teeth suspended in the air. Strings of mucus that might have been tears, had she possessed eyes, slid down to her glistening black body. Eddies of the humid atmosphere surrounded her, giving the lowest part of the facility an otherworldly sensation. Damnation according to Christianity, and while La Reina's scream might be silent, Brenda could imagine the hideous sound it made. No wonder humans had created the concept of hell.

Look what they were creating here.

Why did the queen remain so still? What was happening in this stasis? Brenda's thumb rubbed the fob as she looked at the slimy eggs strewn across the floor. They would be removed by remote-controlled machines to be cut into pieces, used in research, or frozen.

Brenda had prayed to Yemaya, the goddess of the sea, to send a mighty wave this way, or a storm that would destroy it all. The oceans here were as treacherous as they were beautiful.

"What are you planning?" she whispered as her eyes strained to take in every inch of the La Reina.

"*Planning?*" Patel said in the earpiece of the suit.

"Nothing. I…"

They stood in silence for what felt like an eternity.

"*We should go,*" Patel said. "*There's a lot to do in preparation.*"

Brenda nodded and turned to walk away. Keeping an eye on the Xenomorph, she reached out to touch one of the eggs. Then she stopped.

The long string of liquid dripping from the elongated inner mouth had begun to congeal, taking on a barbed aspect. Similarly, the scabs where her arms and legs were removed, had adopted much the same shape. Brenda moved her hand away from the egg to focus on La Reina. They needed to begin measuring these changes—which none of the androids had seen fit to report.

A scan would be sent to her every day.

She turned and left La Reina to the darkness of the Weyland-Yutani abyss.

"If we don't take preventative measures, one of these test subjects is going to make us all part of a sick experiment," Brenda said, free of the confining hazmat suit. "Yet we aren't permitted to destroy them—they're placed in cryo and shipped out—and why?"

Too much was being kept from her.

Several human technicians just nodded, but an android stopped what it was doing and addressed her.

"This is a research facility," he said, taking her words literally. "To destroy what we have produced would be counter-productive." The android's dead eyes and programmed smile sent a shiver down Brenda's spine.

Her own eyes went wide as more androids approached, wheeling bodies from Lab 10. As one of the gurneys came closer, a woman—perhaps the same one as before—moaned. A black viscous liquid leaked from one nostril.

"Stop!" Brenda shrieked. "Take her back *now*. We don't have enough of the antidote for everyone!" As she tried to control her panic, the other human techs moved to the exit, forming a clot in the doorway.

The woman on the gurney began to struggle against the straps across her chest and thighs. Her belly was still swollen, and more of the black liquid came out of her ears and one eye.

"I'm sorry, Dr. Moon." Patel appeared at Brenda's side. "I thought we had given her enough of the sedative to ameliorate the risk. It has always been enough."

The woman groaned and gnashed her teeth while her eyes rolled to the back of her head. An irrational part of Brenda feared an orisha, a deity of old, was about to speak through the snarling woman and tell her she had to answer for this.

"Do something!" she shouted at the android who had spoken before. When he made no move, she reached to her back and the small opening she had left in her lab coat—just enough for a pistol to fit through.

She aimed and fired.

The synth moved in front of the female subject, taking the bullet. He turned and lifted a taser to stun the test subject, who was still thrashing to free herself. Her body convulsed from the shock, then relaxed again onto the gurney.

"You shouldn't have done that, Brenda!" Patel said loudly.

"The fuck I shouldn't," Brenda responded. "We can't let any of the Xenosites get out. All we have is simulated data on the speed of infection, and not enough antidote for everyone in the facility." Her voice rose as her anger spiked. "What if one of the infected found their way onto a ship? We'd be—"

Something sharp bit into her back, where she'd pulled out the pistol. Patel held up a syringe.

"You have been overworked, doctor," she said. "Rest now." As she fell into a chair, Brenda wondered if any of this had been an accident.

PART 4

LETICIA

17

2195

The Rooster was quiet for a Thursday night. Leticia's core crew sat around eating a greasy dinner of burgers, curly fries, beers, and a pitcher of margaritas. They had just returned from a freezing-cold mission, and the heat of the south was a welcome change.

Before Peter Weyland's efforts to address climate change, the rising seas had swallowed entire shorelines, including some cities. Some called it the Great Rising. The United Americas had secretly used a small island just inside the Arctic Circle as a port for three submarines carrying nuclear weapons. When it was abandoned, the subs were thought to be secure, and were left behind.

Intelligence reports indicated that they had begun drifting, and were settling to impossible depths, but pirates had struck an agreement to claim them. If it was known which government was behind the scheme, Leticia wasn't privy to the intel.

She had been among the Marines sent to reclaim the submarines and guide them toward Alaska. As the systems were turned on remotely, it would pinpoint the location of their targets.

Their reinforced rib bounced on the arctic waters. Outfitted with an advanced propulsion system, it moved with an increased speed and remarkable maneuverability. A single sleek Narwhal jet ski was attached to the side. Droplets that hit their faces had the cold sting of rapidly falling hail. The only way they could communicate was through their helmets.

As a lance corporal, Leticia led a group that had managed to remain together through training and military service and hadn't lost a single member of her crew in all that time. Before every mission she instilled as much confidence as possible.

"Who are we?" she said over the comms.

They responded in unison, *"La Loba Pack! Ahhooooh!"* Mohammed gave three extra barks into the cold air. His breath releasing eddies of steam.

Nathan studied his handheld tablet.

"Right," he said. *"The sub's systems have been activated. We should be nearly above them."*

"Desiree, what do your eagle eyes say?"

"According to the drone, there's nothing on the approach. We just might get away with an easy peasy day."

Doubting they could be so lucky, Leticia still scanned the water and stark white snow along the shoreline. As more people had ventured into space, that left behind some of the less desirable elements, and piracy had become an epidemic.

Nathan gave a thumbs-up, and Frida slowed the rib.

"Don't let your guard down," Leticia warned them. "These guys are acquiring more and more sophisticated tech all the time."

Despite the hail, the water was relatively calm as they waited for the subs to rise far enough that they could be guided toward US waters. Mohammed leaned back against the railing. Without the sound of the engine, they could hear one another without needing the headphones.

"If this wasn't a job, I'd love to do some ice fishing out here. It's so—"

A large splash erupted to their left, accompanied by a *boom* that violently rocked the boat. Nathan had to grab the rail to keep from falling over the side. An engine roared to life and another rib approached, cleverly camouflaged to fool their drones. Three figures were inside the rib, and one had a rocket launcher.

Frida raised her rifle and sent a round in their direction, causing the trio to duck down below the edge of the inflatable hull. Tucking her rifle into a holster on her back, Leticia jumped onto the Narwhal and smacked a button on the side of the rib to detach it.

"You get those damn subs into friendly waters," she said. "Our aircraft carrier isn't far."

Desiree nodded. "We have firepower waiting in our airspace, as well. Be careful, Leticia."

"I will," she replied. "I'm getting tired of chasing these vermin, and we need to make sure our presence here stays off the books. I can buy you some time to get into friendly territory."

"We will wait for you," Mohammed said. "Wherever you find yourself, we will find you."

Leticia nodded and peeled off as their rib came to life again, to follow the subs toward the aircraft carrier that would be waiting. Tapping the control panel, she shot a grenade from the Narwhal at the pirate rib's engine. Behind her, Frida continued to fire to keep the pirates at a disadvantage.

As she approached, Leticia could see scuba gear on the deck of the enemy craft. These pirates didn't have a Narwhal, but they did have a jet ski attached to their rib. With one hand she pulled her rifle out of its holster, while controlling the Narwhal with the other. She wished this was one of the android models Frida had told her about, with its own AI.

A woman in white combat gear jumped onto the jet ski. Leticia fired, hitting the side of the rib, then with the butt of her rifle she hit the grenade launcher. She missed, and the grenade exploded uselessly off to the side, then one of the pirates popped up and aimed their rifle at her.

Veering to the right, she revved the Narwhal to move out of range. It was a minute late, though, as their shot hit the back of the propulsion system, nearly causing the Narwhal to topple over. Leticia veered left, and then right, conscious that if she fell into the frigid waters they could kill her within minutes. Ditching the rifle, she used both hands to maintain control of the jet ski.

Losing speed and with her maneuverability badly compromised, her plan would be to plow into the shoreline and run for the snow-covered forest until she could be extracted. Gripping tightly with both hands she braced for a bumpy impact. It wouldn't be long before whoever shot her would follow.

She amped up the speed as much as she could, with the smell of smoke filling her nostrils. The Narwhal, which had limited capabilities on land, skidded across the shore and, without missing a beat, she jumped off, rolled, and ran hard into the tree line.

Desiree's gymnastic instruction sure came in handy, she thought. From a short distance to one side, she could hear another vehicle approaching.

She ignored the branches hitting her face and body. Her only concern was the ground beneath her feet—and then she stopped.

Something growled. Something *large*.

The wolf's eyes seemed to glow in the shadows of the trees. It was all white except for a large strip of black fur on the top of its head, and a few smaller patches falling from the crown trailing down its neck. It was as if this creature had been anointed with some dark oil. It appeared to be a female, and judging from its protective stance, there must have been a litter somewhere near. Leticia knew she had to stay away, and keep calm.

"I don't want to hurt you, loba," she said, keeping her words steady. "I'm backing away. This is your turf. I respect that."

The crunching snow beneath her feet and the soft powder falling from the branches was the only thing that separated Leticia and a creature that could tear her to pieces, unless she shot it on the spot. She didn't want to do that. It wasn't the wolf's fault—she shouldn't be there, and neither should the nukes they were trying to retrieve.

The wolf stared intently and continued to growl but didn't attack her. She backed away until the animal seemed satisfied, and melted into the shadows of the forest.

She entered a clearing that was a cold haze. White crystals glittered on barren branches. Crouching in the trees she began to send her coordinates to Desiree, tapping them into a pad on the left arm of her all-white cold-weather camo fatigues. She still had a firearm strapped to her right leg, and a blade. Those should be enough.

Footfalls caused her to look up.

A woman dressed in a similar fashion to Leticia held a pistol in her hand. She hadn't yet spotted her target, but she had a scanner in the other hand. That would detect her—it was now or never. Leticia raised her weapon to shoot.

A crack in the snow caused her to shift her gaze to their right. A deer stopped, turning its head toward the woman and then in Leticia's direction before darting away again. The woman followed its gaze and swung her head toward Leticia.

"Fuck," Leticia muttered, and she ran toward the enemy to knock her off her feet. Hoping she wouldn't have to kill her. She always carried double flex cuffs to avoid going down that path if she could.

The woman fell backward. Her weapon flew into the air and sunk into the soft snow nearby. She gave Leticia a hard punch to the face, knocking off her reflective glasses. Leticia attempted to turn her face down.

"You don't want to do this!" the woman strained to say as Leticia put her in a head lock. "Instability creates opportunity. I don't expect you to understand, but you serve kings who keep you as a peasant. Soon governments will cease to exist. Take away that square patch with a skull, and you're just like me. Continue, and you'll piss a lot of important people off. The Weyl—"

"Tell them to file a complaint with the Marines, pendeja," Leticia spat as she grabbed the cuffs out of her left cargo pants pocket.

Then they both stopped struggling.

More growling was coming from the trees—more than one of them, this time. She slowly lifted her head, remembering what Lucinda had said, a lifetime ago.

"It doesn't understand anything but territory, hunger, and survival."

This wasn't a fight for her. She let go of the woman and silently backed away standing as tall as she could make herself. La loba— the wolf from before—was there. Leticia maintained eye contact. Her fingertips gently touched the pulse gun on her leg, just in case.

The other woman scrambled on the ground to look for the gun, her head moving violently toward the wolf pack that continued to growl. Then one howled, and another, and another.

Leticia continued to move back and away until she felt confident enough to turn away. Behind her, the sounds of snarls and barks turned to high-pitched shrieks from the woman who had been one of the pirates.

She sprinted through the trees, careful not to lose her footing. That would be the end of her. When she made it back to the shoreline, a

USCM team was already flying overhead. In the distance the pirates' rib floated in the icy waters, overturned and smoking. Two bodies bobbed with the waves.

"For a minute there I didn't think I would taste grease ever again," Leticia said. "You guys are the best."

"The pack is only as strong as each wolf," Mohammed said, "and every wolf is only as strong as their pack. You should know that more than ever now."

"To my lobas!" Leticia responded.

Frida raised her beer, looking slightly tipsy. "Don't forget yourself," she said. "An alpha with fangs! Gang, Gang, Gang, *jefa!*" She even pronounced it right this time, Leticia noticed.

"Don't worry, I haven't forgot myself," Leticia said, licking cheese from her hand. "That is why I want it."

"What? The promotion?" Nathan put his Corona down.

"You should." Desiree raised her glass. "Your marksmanship is hot, you're a decent leader, and judging from that last mission, the animals love you."

The table murmured in agreement as they continued to consume their meal. Leticia was proud of what she and her team had done, but she didn't want to be chasing pirates for the rest of her life. None of them did.

"Yep," she said. "We've been doing this, how long now?" She took a drink. "There's a way to get on the fast track, and I'm going to take it. Once I've completed the written test, according to the rules I'll need one other person to accompany me."

She left it there…

No one volunteered.

"I'd rather do the Crucible over again, than the twenty-four hours you're looking at," Mohammed said. "No sleep or rest. Even less food, if you eat at all. It's in the field and not in a simulated environment. Plus I need a break." He shook his head. "I hear Haas is interested…"

Leticia replied, "I don't trust her, or whoever she might take as her number one."

"Nothing against you, boss," he said, "but they should probably consider just handing her the promotion, considering her family. All military, all the way. Why go to the trouble, when you don't stand a chance?"

Desiree turned to Leticia. "Don't listen to Crow. He'll be eating his words. Give it a shot. If it doesn't work, then at least you'll know what your next move will be. I got you." She turned to their companions. "And the rest of you… you've all seen some shit up close and personal."

"Yeah, but I'm tired," Frida said. "The side gig is killing me."

"Yeah, same here." Nathan placed his hand on Mohammed's. "I'm tired of hearing about the pay and bonuses you get for going private, as long as you have the right military experience. You take your pick of a country, corporation, you name it, there's a job in the stars and your name on a big check. Desiree, can you say that you aren't tempted to go back to New York for some private sector job? Big city means big pay."

"It's tempting." Desiree hung her head. "If I do go back, you all have to come visit."

Leticia understood where they were coming from, and she shared the frustration. That was why she had to do this. She wanted more responsibility, *needed* more—and a bigger check. Maybe even get involved in policy.

The only way for her would be up.

"No hard feelings," she said. "I feel you, and thanks, Desiree. We can start on Monday. For now, let's just enjoy being alive."

Leticia stood next to Melissa Haas, who held the same rank as Leticia and wore a permanent haughty sneer on her face. Leticia wanted the satisfaction of wiping it right off when she was the one getting promoted.

Colonel Smith stood before them.

"You both know the rules. It was your responsibility to read the brief, and you got your one chance. Anything you can't remember, anything you do outside of what's been laid out, will count against you. Your number one will be taken to a pre-determined location, where there will be further instructions. You'll be taken to a different set of coordinates off the coast and dropped off.

"It will be dawn," he continued, "and you'll have twenty-four hours. Now go and get ready."

Haas turned to Leticia and offered her hand. "Good luck," she said, and she seemed to mean it. "We both have military in our blood, so may the best woman win."

A short time later they sat on the Narwhals, ready to drop into the water. From there they would make their way into a swamp that teemed with alligators, snakes, and who-knew-what other dangers. Clouds obscured the dawn, prolonging the darkness. By this time Desiree would already be waiting in an undisclosed place.

Leticia revved the engine on her vehicle. This exercise was all about speed and precision. There was a slight resistance on the controls, but there was no time to do a full diagnostic. Haas watched her from the corner of her eye.

Leticia didn't like that.

In their helmet earpiece they heard the CO.

"*It's time,*" he said. "*Go!*"

Both of them were propelled forward into the air. Using her right thumb Leticia pulled hard on the acceleration to get her onto the water smoothly. As the surface approached, the propulsion jets activated and she felt good about the distance she'd achieved.

She didn't bother looking to her side. All that mattered was the goal in front of her. The Narwhal glided with ease across the open water, and she pressed the acceleration again.

Nothing.

¡Pinche tu madre! Fuck!

Leticia tried again, and a sick panic formed in her gut. The Narwhal remained in neutral as it coasted and began to slow on its own. What the fuck was happening? Had it been sabotaged? Haas passed her by, leaving a large wake in the shape of a V.

Victory.

Dead in the water, she had to think. The shore was close, but so far away. The only option was to swim, and given the distance she would have to ditch everything. Leticia looked to the sky and screamed her frustration, until she remembered the shaman, Orozco.

Just this moment.

No time to blame Haas.

She removed her backpack and waterproof jacket. To make up time she had to be as light as possible. Reaching down, she made sure the switchblade was secure inside her boot. The helmet she kept on, to remain connected to the comms system. Her scanner and map were waterproof and would fit inside her cargo pocket on the side of her fatigues.

Jumping into the water, she swam hard. One arm at a time with her feet kicking. Forward, with each breath taking her closer. There was nothing else to do, and no point worrying.

After half an hour she made it. The sun was beginning to break through the clouds, which was good news. In this heat she would be dry in no time. Removing the water from her boots, she gave her T-shirt a quick wring. The scanner gave her the coordinates for the next rendezvous. As she began to jog, she could see Haas' footprints in the sand.

Anger gave her the fuel to pick up her pace.

Leticia's thighs burned with the increasing amounts of lactic acid building within the muscles, but she had to carry on through the mud. There had been heavy rains, so the water level in the swamp was higher than usual. The ground pulled on the soles of her boots with every step she took.

It had been hours, and hunger began to gnaw at her stomach. She had been forced to abandon her provisions, but there was enough in the swamp to keep her going if she needed to eat something. No sign that any people had been there, though, and nothing on her scanner to alert her to Desiree's presence. She continued on with eyes and ears on full alert, despite a niggling desire to crawl into a ball and sleep.

The sun was low in the sky, and nocturnal animals would be out soon. Her compass watch beeped, picking up Desiree's vitals, and Leticia stopped in her tracks. Sweat dripped from the bandana tied around her forehead. She was close, but the device didn't specify where.

The sunlight was filtered through the swampy canopy of trees, making it hard to see. Listening for sounds that couldn't be attributed to the environment, she scanned the area, taking in an inch at a time.

Then she saw it.

In the distance, the green wasn't the same as the other trees or foliage. It didn't move like it was of the swamp, either. Leticia moved forward cautiously, looking at the ground for footprints. No, they wouldn't have come this way. Too obvious.

As she got closer to the greenery that looked off, she saw that it was a camo canopy, and pulled it off. Nothing. A decoy?

A water snake slithered across her boot. She kicked it off. A chunk of mud flew into the air. That's when she saw a black wire that could have been mistaken for a vine or root. Following it, she tossed aside foliage and muck until her hands and fingernails were caked with dirt. The wire trailed into more water, murky so she couldn't see the bottom. Bright green scum floated on the surface.

With no visible signs of predators, she dipped both hands into the water and pulled on the cable. It wouldn't give, so she pulled as hard as she could, her shoulders flexing until they cramped. Still no release, and the water was getting deeper—she would have to go under. Holding on to the cable, she plunged her head beneath the surface, steadying both legs against the inner wall of a hole that was not natural.

With Haas' face in her mind, she pulled with both hands, giving it five hard yanks. It finally broke free. A loud hiss and beeping made her turn around.

"Amiga!"

It was Desiree. One of the wide swamp trees wasn't a tree after all. Leticia felt lightheaded from the hours of exertion.

"The instructions?" she said eagerly.

"What instructions?"

"They should be with you?"

Desiree frowned. "There was nothing inside, and no one told me anything. They blindfolded me during transport and I wasn't allowed to remove it until the door closed. I've literally been sitting in there, staring at darkness the entire time."

They searched the compartment in which Desiree had been kept, looking for a secret drawer or container, but the space was empty.

Leticia wanted to sink to the bottom of the swamp. She looked at her watch. Haas had a running start, and now this. She climbed out, not sure how to proceed.

She told Desiree what had happened with the Narwhal.

"I can't believe those motherfuckers sabotaged you," Desiree said. "Was there anything else in the initial brief?"

"There's a second marker," Leticia said. "According to my map, it's not far, and there should be a vehicle there. Haas will have it by now." Leticia shook her head. "It was all a set-up. They cheated—I *know* it. Haas pulled strings, and I'll bet you a bottle of whiskey they'll claim it was all a big joke, or just deny it."

"You're probably right," Desiree said. "But what do we do? Stay quiet?"

"No. Turn over every damn fact until there's enough proof piled up to climb to the top. That's what we do." She wiped away the sweat and peered around in the fading light. "Tell you what, though, I wouldn't mind being paired with one of them in another exercise, so I can knock them the fuck on their asses."

"How far are we from base?"

Leticia glanced at her comms control watch. "Not far. Fifteen short miles. I never realized how wild it was this close to the base, ever since the Great Rising. No wonder the base was relocated here. It's great for training."

Desiree kept her eyes on Leticia. "You have it in you for one big push?" she asked. "I know it's probably too late."

Leticia looked at her muddy boots and hands. She had to accept the "L"—everyone did at some point. Losses were a part of life.

Quitting didn't have to be.

"Fucking race you. I have unfinished business."

Desiree slapped her on the back and they began to jog. It quickly turned into a sprint.

They made it back to base looking as if they had run through every test of Mictlan. It felt like hell, too. She glanced at her compass watch. Everyone would be in the mess hall for supper.

"Where are you going, Leticia? Showers are this way."

Leticia ignored Desiree and headed toward the mess hall, marching with purpose. She burst through the doors, allowing mud to fly from her stomping feet. From the distance she could see Haas and Martinez. Her strides became longer, leaving muddy prints across the white floor.

With one swipe of her hand, she tossed Haas' tray across the table, then the Coke Martinez had in front of him.

"You have something to say to me, puta," Leticia screamed. "That little sabotage wasn't fun or fair. Both of you should be ashamed of yourselves and kicked the fuck out."

Haas stood to face Leticia. "I don't know what you're talking about."

Leticia continued to stand her ground with a snarl on her face.

"¡Mentirosa! Yeah, right."

"Haas and Vasquez! To the main office. Now."

A CO approached them.

"We will see, Haas," Leticia spat.

Leticia stood next to Haas in front of Colonel Smith.

"I realize you are disappointed, Lance Corporal Vasquez, but we have no proof that Lance Corporal Haas committed any wrongdoing. For all we know, you could have done it yourself. There are no cameras in the field, and for good reason. Candidates must perform without artificial distractions."

"Sir," she replied, careful to control her reactions. "It was clear someone had sabotaged my vehicle. And it clearly states in the rules that this is not permitted. 'No candidate is permitted to come into contact with the other candidate's equipment.'"

"But do you have proof?"

"With all due respect, sir, what proof do you need? I left the vehicle in the water. It should have been recovered."

"You could have done it yourself, to gain sympathy," Smith persisted, giving no ground. "This could be *your* way of sabotaging Haas." He looked at his tablet. "I see your mother is Jenette Vasquez. She died with dignity, but had a nasty track record."

Leticia stood there, trying to hold back the pounding waves of tears and anger hurling themselves just beneath her skin. She wouldn't cry. Not in front of them.

Colonel Smith shook his head.

"Just accept that you lost the promotion."

"Send someone to check the Narwhal."

"I have, and until then this matter is on hold. Haas will receive the promotion. I'm sorry. Maybe next time, but if you continue with this attitude, it will be highly unlikely." He tapped the screen and put the tablet on the desk.

Leticia stood there, feeling her cheeks go hot. Left out in the fucking cold, and for what? The part of her that resented Ramón for playing the game rose to the surface, whispering in her ear like a little devil.

Give up.

As much as she wanted to, she had to continue to hope. Hope for change. Hope could be buoyant, but carry it too long without anything in hand, and it could leave you exhausted.

"You both are dismissed."

Haas and Leticia saluted Colonel Smith, turned, and left his office.

Desiree was waiting outside of the building. "So? What happened?" She tried to keep up with Leticia who didn't slow her march.

"I have to let it go."

"That's bullshit, man. You know who her father is?"

Leticia stopped and looked at Desiree. "No, but I *want* to know," she growled. "They brought up my mother."

Desiree shook her head. "Her dad is an ex-major general who does private security for Weyland-Yutani. A big-time government contractor."

Leticia felt her entire body go slack. Every muscle losing the will to move. What was the point of all the stress, the striving to be better, to take a stand, when others had it all mapped out already? In that moment she understood the flares of anger she saw in Ramón's eyes, and how easy it was for determination to grow into something insatiable. The desire to win could make you do what you never thought you would.

Yet part of her couldn't sever that rope to the hope that she was on the right path, as much as it was a journey wading through tits-high muck.

"I'll catch up with you later tonight. I'm going to go for a walk."

"Yeah, I actually have a job interview," Desiree admitted. "Private security. Pay is great, and no threat to my life, except maybe falling in love. You better come see me."

"I hear you," Leticia said. "Good luck, Desiree." She gave an ironic smile. "So much for big dreams to change the world."

Feeling like a foolish, bitter idiot, she left her friend. The best remedy to resistance was not to resist it. If this was truly the way it was meant to be, then where the fuck was everything she hoped to accomplish?

Leticia remembered when that spineless pendeja in high school accused her of shoplifting. Then her mind raced to the long time it had taken to hear from the Marines, while watching everyone around her get their responses. Back then, all she could do was smile and keep the faith.

Where would she put her faith now? How could she have been so sure of traveling to space, and becoming an elite soldier?

Fuck this place and fuck waiting. Destiny didn't exist.

It was time to think about writing a resignation letter.

Find another way, Leticia, or another way will find you.

18

"This Dia de Los Muertos is extra special," Roseanna proclaimed. "Congratulations, Ramón. The youngest chief financial officer for the Weyland-Yutani Corporation!"

"Thank you, tía. I couldn't have done it without your support."

"And Mary Anne—she stopped working after the twins were born. You can't discount her contribution."

"Everyone is good. Lara Jenette and Lorenzo are growing up fast." Ramón turned toward Leticia slumped in a dining chair staring vacantly at a tray of condiments that went with dinner. "How about you, Leticia? Any good news? I was sorry to hear about the promotion."

Leticia rolled her eyes toward Roseanna, who turned the chicken flautas in a shallow pan of hot oil. Leticia could feel her temperature rising like sizzling grease. She didn't want to talk about the promotion. Any minute frustration would send her popping out of the frying pan.

"I'm taking night classes, and doing the Marine thing in the day—at least until my paperwork is processed," she said. "Who knows how long that will take. Not much else to report."

"I know we have not always been on the same page," he responded, "and this isn't charity, but I might have something for you."

"Like when you wanted to write my essay?"

"Nope. Not like that at all. I think you are being wasted, your *skills* are being wasted right now. Our mother left us letters, and mine said we had to look out for each other. Well, that is what I want to do."

Leticia played with a spoon, stirring it in a bowl of homemade salsa. She knew he wasn't lying because that was in her letter, as well.

"I'm listening."

"Thank you," he said, and he took a deep breath. "Weyland-Yutani has a new CEO who is trying to clean up past mistakes and create a new, ethical way of doing business. There's an opening for a prominent security job. It would be a big payday. You could buy your own home, or travel to another world. The point being that you would have the only kind of freedom that matters."

"I'm supposed to believe a company like that has grown a heart, like the Grinch? That's about as easy as making a U-turn in a vacuum." She shook her head. "Nah, I'm good. Our mother's last mission was for them."

"And why was she there in the first place?" he countered. "I'm talking real freedom, Leticia. I've accumulated more wealth than anyone in the family history, probably more than all of them combined. But not just money—what I'm *accomplishing*. Real wealth gives you a lifestyle to create more wealth and more opportunity. Real wealth spans across generations. My children will learn from me, and be bigger and better. Everyone will know the Vasquez name." When she didn't reply, he added, "Come on, don't be stupid."

Before she could respond, Roseanna spoke up. "Don't fight or be unfair with each other," she said. "It was bad enough when you were kids, but you are grown-ass adults now." She pointed tongs at them before turning back to the cooking.

"Will you at least give the executive a chance?" he persisted. "I'm talking one hour."

Roseanna stepped between them, placing a plate of flautas and rice on the table. She turned to Leticia. "It's just an hour," she echoed. "That's less time than it takes to get a tattoo, and maybe it's what you two need."

"Fine." Leticia grabbed a hot flauta and dipped it into the salsa, then the bowl of guacamole. "One meeting with Old Man Weyland."

"He's not a Weyland, or an old man."

"Whatever. Set it up. Let's eat, before the ancestors get pissed."

Ramón placed his hand over hers. "Thank you. After we eat, I will book a flight, hotel, and reserve a meeting in his calendar."

As usual, Ramón went above and beyond and chose a hotel in the tallest skyscraper in Manhattan. She craned her neck as she stared up at the enormous building, and wondered how many secrets those windows shielded the world from. Before this meeting she had dropped in on Desiree at her new job.

They met in a fancy coffee shop on the ground floor. Ramón ordered only the best for them, though it was too early for champagne, and he didn't drink much.

"Coffee?" the barista said.

Ramón took the paper cup. "Thanks."

The java came from a nearly extinct animal found in Indonesia that ate the coffee beans, then shit them out. That was what gave the joe its unique taste. It was the only brand Ramón would drink, he explained.

Rich folks.

"Don't worry," he said, "this is going to be super relaxed. Jacob is a little... different." Leticia decided not to press him. She would see what he meant, soon enough.

"Lead the way."

They walked through the lobby with the security team nodding in recognition. Ramón walked with confidence and importance, as well he should. He was a man with the good looks of the old film star Esai Morales, and the smarts beyond anyone he knew. Smart to the point that he was dangerous, which was precisely why he rose through the ranks. The company didn't want its *consigliere* floating around with its secrets, or worse, going to the competitors.

Ramón fiddled with the zip on his fleece as they stepped into the elevator that led directly to Jacob's personal office.

"Be cool, don't ask too many questions, and for God's sake smile," he said—the only words spoken on the ride to the penthouse. Leticia opted to give him a scowl. There was real worry on Ramón's face, though. He was always more concerned with appearances than she. The secretary sitting outside of Jacob's office greeted Ramón warmly, her smile a little *too* warm for Leticia's liking, but that was her brother.

"Go on in. He's waiting for you."

"Thank you, Sara. Your hair is lovely today."

Leticia ignored the comment. She could feel herself go tense, however, as if to put on invisible armor. She had one of her mother's bandanas in her back pocket.

The office overlooked the main hub of the MagnoRail train system. As busy as it was below, not a sound could be heard. There were windows from floor to ceiling, and it gave her a little vertigo, her mind and body tricked to thinking they were hovering above the real world. To her surprise, there was no old decrepit man speckled with age spots and trembling hands. The only occupant was a guy who looked of a similar age to her, dressed in head-to-toe Patagonia.

We're going into space, not Everest, she thought wryly.

As he stood to greet them, she wondered who this pencil-pushing chump was. Probably a lawyer with a million papers for her to sign, releasing the company from any knowledge, culpability, recourse, or anything that resembled responsibility. The world was built on this bullshit. She was ready, but truth be told, it was these kinds of people—men like her brother—who she feared the most.

"Hello, Jacob," Ramón said. "Please meet my sister Leticia."

Jacob? Her eyes slitted a bit, then she recovered.

"Hi, Leticia," Jacob Vickers said. "Your brother has told me a lot about you. I especially liked the stories about the frogs in his bed."

Leticia thought this guy might be okay, after all. That *was* a great story.

"Well, while he's been telling tales, he hasn't told me much about you," she replied. "I thought I was meeting 'Old Man Weyland.'" Then she remembered. *"He's not a Weyland, or an old man."*

Jacob smiled, extending his hand. "Old Man Vickers at your service. It's great to meet you. You're a Marine Raider, aren't you? That's very impressive."

Leticia felt slightly embarrassed. So sometimes she got it wrong. He moved closer to her without looking at her brother. She slipped her hand into his to shake it. Leticia didn't know if she imagined it, or if the weight of his hand possessed a gravitational force of its own.

He was anything but an "Old Man," and he wasn't just young— he was very attractive with blue eyes and light brown hair just long enough to tuck behind his ear. His gaze continued to hold her.

Avery was nice, sexy, and solid—a cowboy.

Vickers was electricity with a British accent.

"I don't know how much Ramón has told you about the job. You would go in as a contractor, to establish a basic security force for the colony. Nothing too 'military,' nor like we're trying to police the place. There should be some security presence to make people feel safe, but not to exert force."

"It sounds like more than a desk job, but without fighting or danger," she said, beginning to get her feet under her. "That should be no problem—the Raiders do a lot more than combat."

"Well, it was actually Ramón who suggested a specialized force," Vickers said. "He knows how much this project means to me, and made the point that if we ever faced an outside threat, we should be prepared. Special forces could remain low key if nothing overt is happening, yet react swiftly to anything unexpected. I agree with his thinking.

"Olinka isn't meant to be of any military value," he continued. "I want to gather the best and brightest to live there, to create wonders for humanity outside of the threat of war. With all of the conflicts currently flaring around the galaxy, I want to create a planet without borders or petty squabbles over resources. Everyone will have equal access to what they need to thrive.

"It's about bloody time humans learned how to govern and live a different way." His voice carried the strength of commitment. "It's time for us to evolve. You will be paid very well, and watch history as it's being made… I hope."

"I see." Leticia didn't hide her reticence.

Vickers must have recognized it. "Hey, I'm gambling, too, and doing my best to get people to take a chance on me. I can't make any promises how boring it might be, or not."

Leticia liked him, and found that strange, given his last name. Maybe he was the one in his family who *would* make a difference, and change the course of his industry. Hell, a Weyland had cured cancer. She supposed anything was possible.

"Send me more information," she said. "I want as many details as you can provide."

His eyes brightened with the light of a kid asked to play on someone's team.

"You'll have the essentials this afternoon," he promised. "And if you're available, there is a wine tasting tonight—an extracurricular activity sponsored by the company. You can meet the rest of the board. Will you join us? Your brother is invited."

Ramón spoke first. "You know I wouldn't miss it for the world. I'm not sure it's Leticia's thing, though."

She shot him a dirty look. "I'm available, and it *can* be my thing. I'll be there."

Ramón suppressed a frown, but Vickers didn't notice.

"Great," he said. "I will see you both at the Waldorf at eight."

Leticia didn't want to look away from him.

Once in the elevator Leticia felt comfortable to confront her brother.

"Why do you always have to try to speak for me?"

"You don't understand these people," he said. "They aren't simple. These are snakes, Leticia."

"I guess it takes one to know one?" she responded. "And are you calling *me* simple?"

Ramón rolled his eyes and forced a smile. "You're not simple, Leticia—you're just not devious. Your enemies tend to meet you head on."

"Only in combat do you see the whites of your enemy's eyes," she replied. "There's a hell of a lot to deal with before that." Once again, Haas' face appeared in her mind. It just made her angrier.

Ramón ignored her last comment, looking at a message on his phone.

"Hey, since you aren't booked into the hotel for another night, why don't you hang at my apartment. It can be like old times. It's not far. And go buy yourself something *nice* to wear tonight."

"When did you get a place in the city?" she asked. "I thought you worked from Boston. Everything okay at home?" She felt herself caught off guard. Was his mood related to something happening with his family? She'd always thought his good looks would get him in trouble one day.

"Yeah, as fine as it can be." Ramón blew air out of his mouth and looked to the top of the elevator until it stopped and the doors opened. "Look, I can't get into it now. Here are the keys, I'll text you the address." Then he dashed through the lobby. "Something nice!" he shouted over his shoulder.

Leticia smirked. She would wear something nice, all right, and he would pay for it. Mary Anne had told her they had an account at Saks where he got all of his suits tailor-made, and she bought her outfits for company events. Today Leticia would be a lady who lunched and shopped.

When she arrived at the apartment she was carrying an armful of bags. In addition to an outfit for the evening, she had bought a new pair of red-and-black sneakers and pretty underwear, just for fun. To avoid alarming Mary Anne, Leticia had texted her from the shop, sending photos of her haul.

Mary Anne texted her back a picture from the playground where she had taken the kids.

Next time I will join you!

Leticia thought she looked sad, but maybe it was just running after the twins. Her firm had made her redundant while on maternity leave, and she never bothered to go back. Neither she nor Ramón wanted a nanny.

"Our tía was the one person who pushed me, not a stranger she paid. No, our kids need a parent," Ramón had told her, making his feelings clear, and Mary Anne had complied.

The apartment was beautiful, with a view overlooking a small gated park kept exclusively for the tenants of the building. It struck Leticia as odd, though, that there were no family photos, not even of the children. It looked more like a bachelor pad, with nothing but sparkling water and beer in the fridge and a separate wine fridge that was fully stocked.

It had the feel of a show apartment.

Damn, I could get used to this, she thought.

Ramón rarely drank, and she wouldn't have been surprised if half the wine bottles were empty and only there to look good. Ramón's overriding vice was his ego. He couldn't resist indulging himself, and that left very little for others.

She tried to resist the urge to snoop, though it was in her nature. That had been how she found out Ramón was stealing tests for other high schoolers. When Roseanna wouldn't buy him a car, he bought one himself, saying the money came from odd jobs. Of course, she believed him, and Leticia hadn't wanted to snitch.

It would catch up with him one day.

The bedroom looked as unused as the kitchen. Her instinct got the better of her and she looked in both side tables and the bathroom cabinets to check for condoms. Nothing. There was plenty of time before she would have to be ready, so she propped her tablet on the coffee table, then sprawled out on the L-shaped green velvet sofa and slept until she needed to shower and dress.

In her gut Brenda always knew she couldn't trust Gilda Patel. The woman had literally stabbed her in the back, then insisted it was for her own good.

The incident reinforced the need to have the detonator fob, and for her to monitor the slightest physical changes in the three queens—who were only meant to produce eggs and Xenomorphs for further experimentation in the biological weapons program. There was still so much they had to learn before they could fully control them.

Especially La Reina.

While the queens remained in stasis, however, the other Xenomorphs were becoming more aggressive.

Now a poor soul appeared on a screen in her office that took up half of the wall behind her desk. He had been infected with the activated bacteria, and was to be sent into the holding pen with one of the monsters. Blinded, he would not see what he would face, and in its own way that was a mercy. His skin was streaked with black veins and his eyes were completely white. Sweat rolled down the side of his face.

The Xenomorphs were kept on a corridor one level above the queens, along one side of the pyramid. A steel acid-resistant door separated each from the rest. Along a corridor adjacent to the wing were the rooms where humans were kept. With the swift opening of a retractable door, the two would meet in a shared space.

Upon hearing the door open, the sightless man moved toward the sound. It shut just as quickly behind him, and he whipped his head around as it locked with the metallic *clang* of a death knell. He froze in place, until the silence was filled with a hiss.

"What are you doing to me?" He waved outstretched arms. "What have I done?"

The Xenomorph's head rolled left to right, but it did not move toward the intruder in its space. As the man slowly walked around the room in confusion, the Xenomorph kept its distance, yet snapped its jaws into the air. It let out a shriek, and Brenda felt every muscle in her body jerk.

The other Xenomorphs along the corridor screeched in unison, rearing their heads and pounding on the doors that separated them.

In the test chamber, true fear was displayed by both species. They only wanted to live, albeit for different reasons. She wondered how long this tango would last—they had seen what they needed to see. The bacteria did, indeed, fend off the monsters.

"That's enough," she growled. "Pipe the bacteria into the room at full strength." At least then the blind man would know peace.

"But we are not done." The android who had opposed her before flashed that same menacing smile. He swiped and clicked on a tablet. To Brenda's surprise, another door opened into the chamber, and another test subject—a woman—stepped through. This one had the same black streaks.

Wasting no time, the Xenomorph launched itself forward as the doors began to shut.

"No!" Brenda bellowed. "It can't get out!"

She tried to grab the tablet from the android.

The clang of metal hitting metal was as loud as the screams of the woman as her arms flew into the air. Her wailing stopped when the Xenomorph's tail arched like a javelin before tearing her head from her neck. Red and black spewed everywhere, covering the walls, and the blind man crumpled into a ball crying in the corner.

The Xenomorph ripped into the body, coating itself with her blood. Every sickening blow caused the blind man to jerk tighter into a ball.

"It knows the bacteria isn't active."

"A very smart pet indeed." Brenda would have sworn the synth was smiling smugly.

Caught up in a killing rage that must have overwhelmed its survival instincts, the Xenomorph used its tail to spear the crying man through the skull. Instantly blots of ash began to appear on its carapace, shrinking as they disappeared beneath the surface.

Brenda succeeded in jerking the tablet from the android and shoved him as hard as she could, sending him to the floor. His programming would prevent him from retaliating—at least she hoped as much.

Typing in commands, she gave the tablet a swipe and the entire screen became a black fog. The Xenomorph let out a guttural scream that sent the others into a renewed frenzy.

When the fog cleared, the man's flesh was disintegrating to crimson and obsidian ash. The Xenomorph appeared as if it were made of charred wood. Her hands trembled, despite a surge of power and relief. Certain she had headed off a disaster that could have consumed the entire facility, she handed the tablet back to the synth.

"Get that room sterilized and cleared out."

Brenda left her office to retire to her room and write a full report. She had to take a stand.

19

She arrived purposely looking out of place, mostly to stick it to Ramón. It would be a pleasure to see those corporate stiffs sweat, too. Just because she was a Marine didn't mean she didn't know how to hold her own in stilettos.

Anything could be used as a weapon in a pinch.

A backless dress made from shimmering black chainmail and held up by spaghetti straps revealed her tattoos and strong thighs that brushed each other when she walked. Bright red roses bloomed at the base of her spine, echoing her lipstick. The cowl-neck revealed just a hint of cleavage and the hem stopped mid-thigh. She carried a small purse—also a potential weapon.

Ramón waited by the coat check in the lobby of the Waldorf Astoria, which had only recently completed renovations.

"Wow," he whispered. "I said nice, not sexy." Then he added, "Saks called, thanking me for my continued support. Then Mary Anne messaged me saying she wants more time to go shopping with you."

"You can afford it."

"The attitude… I swear." She couldn't tell if he was being serious. "Never mind, anything for my sister. Why don't we go in."

She opened the door for Ramón. "After you, brother." He shook his head while walking past her.

The restaurant was filled with round tables and dark leather booths. The lights were low, even over the long bar. Jacob stood alone sipping on a lowball glass, dressed in what he had been wearing earlier in the day. He appeared relaxed as he watched the crowd, then he spotted Leticia and Ramón. Her eyes met his across the crowd of diners, and it felt like there was something there. Without giving Ramón a further thought, she walked straight over.

Jacob's eyes widened, accompanied by a smile. She could tell he was trying hard not to gawk.

"What happened to the black Nikes?"

"Well, Ramón told me to dress appropriately. I chose something fun."

He opened his mouth to speak then closed it again. Leticia cocked her head, knowing she looked good. Felt good, too. The flirtation was entirely inappropriate, but she had been lying low for a long time. She'd thought she might have imagined the tension between them in the office, yet it still lingered.

Ramón interrupted. "Guys, the tasting is in the private room." She shot him a look, but he continued. "We can hang out another time. We have business."

"Yes, you're right," Jacob said, and she caught a hint of disappointment. "By the way, Ramón, did you hear about Benjamin Ross? Terrible news. Isn't he the one who brought you in, while you were still at Harvard?"

Ramón looked off-balance.

"I heard," he said, "and I was shocked. I mean, to be found in a bathtub with llelo up his nose and on his chest? I've always kept it strictly professional with him, and it looks like that was for the best. He seemed to have a problem with the white stuff, but it was none of my business."

"Smart, Ramón," Jacob replied. "Alright, let's get this over with." Ramón led the way, and Jacob and Leticia trailed behind. As they did, Jacob leaned closer to Leticia's ear, close enough for her to smell the cologne he wore.

"I really don't like these things. Even though I went to good schools I grew up around pubs with sticky floors, pints, and packets of crisps. Football matches on the telly."

Goddamn, she loved a good accent.

They walked into a large room and found a long table topped with wine. There were spittoons, and well-dressed people wearing expensive clothing and even more expensive watches. Ramón did his best to talk to a variety of attendees, but he kept one eye on Leticia as she stood next to Jacob—who gave her all of his attention. Neither of them spat out the alcohol like they were supposed to when tasting fine wine.

She could feel the heaviness of her brother's watchful eye but ignored it. Jacob was captivating.

"So, you want me to get a team together," she said, trying to focus. "I got your email, and briefly looked over the details."

"Yes," he replied, "and the sooner the better."

"I'm not sure if Ramón told you, but I was passed up for a promotion—one that was important to me. It was a set-up, but it taught me something important. Maybe to change the game we're playing, even when we're made to think we've failed."

Jacob's gaze was one of understanding.

She thought it was sincere.

"That's exactly what I think," he said, "and it's what Olinka is about, and it's the way I choose to live, as well. I'm a Vickers. The politics that brought me to this position weren't pretty, and I have many opponents who would just as well like to see me strung up by the neck.

"Living life in England protected me in many ways," he continued, "and kept me sheltered from the business. Peter Weyland did many great things, but somewhere along the way the company became something else. He dealt with climate change. He saved the planet, and now we need to save the soul of humanity. I want to get back to his roots."

"Roots are important." Leticia looked around the room, at the crowd talking among themselves, and realized that she didn't belong here. Ramón was distracted for the moment, and she wanted to get to know Jacob better—without a chaperone. She touched his forearm.

"How about we leave this place and you come with me?"

He nodded. "Let me just say some—"

She interrupted him. "No goodbyes. Let's go before anyone"—*Ramón*, she thought but didn't say—"realizes we're gone." He shot her a strange look.

"Show me the way. I'm all yours."

Leticia gave the room one more glance then took Jacob by the hand. They took the elevator to the lobby, exited through revolving doors, and jumped into an automated taxi waiting in front of the hotel.

"Where are we going?"

"The bad side of town," she whispered in his ear.

Leticia scanned her watch and typed the location into the vehicle's keypad. Jacob laughed at her comment and watched the direction the taxi was moving. Traffic was steady, but not at a standstill.

They turned onto a block with very few streetlights and pulled up in front of a club that looked dark. No sign to indicate its name. There was a bouncer in the front who could have been a giant—he probably injected growth hormone.

"Leticia! Good to see you again."

"Hey, Jack." She gave him a wink. "I'm here to see Desiree."

"No problem. I know you, so I'll let you both in."

Jack opened the door to allow them to enter. Leticia held out her wrist for the cash band to be scanned by the receptionist. Jacob held out his wrist to swipe, but Leticia placed her hand on his arm.

"I got it." She turned to the receptionist. "Two please."

"You didn't have to pay," he protested.

"You paid for that fancy thing before," she said. "Now get ready for the best mozzarella sticks and wings. I'm starving!"

"So am I." Jacob followed Leticia down an aisle of half-naked women dancing behind slot tipping machines blinking with numbers. Leticia ran her wrist across every screen on the left side of the aisle as she walked. A whooping of cheers erupted in her wake, even above "Love Is Strong" by the Rolling Stones. They stopped in front of a woman who hung at the top of a pole, ten feet in the air. She had a robotic leg. One hand held on to the pole, and her metal thigh was magnetically attached. She circled down with her real leg splayed out. Clear platform heels glittered beneath the spotlight. A large grin spread across her face when she saw Leticia standing in front of her stage.

The number 100 blinked across her screen where Leticia had just tipped.

"Well, if it isn't my favorite bad bitch and Raider!" she shouted as she slapped her metal thigh to detach from the pole. "Come to see Desiree again? And who is this?" Leticia glanced at Jacob who must have been blushing—it was impossible to tell in the low purple lights of the room, punctuated by lights over each small stage.

"Hey, Taffy. Can you grab us a couch in the Champagne Room? I'm here to see Desiree."

"Sure, she was in the back office organizing the bouncer roster. I'll tell her you're here."

"Feel free to join us for food. Jacob here arranged for wine, and all they had were these little things that were supposed to pass for a meal." She turned. "Sorry, Jacob."

"I would have been happy for a Cornish pasty or ploughman's lunch," he replied. "The company arranges all that poncy stuff. Appearances…"

Taffy stepped off her small stage. "I'll be sure to reserve you a table and let Carl know to let you in to see Desiree. Your name will be a hologram above the table. New tech and it's getting fancy around here."

Leticia led Jacob through the rest of the darkened club until they reached a back office with another bouncer standing at the door.

"Here to see Desiree."

The bouncer just nodded and opened the door. As they entered, Desiree turned and gave Leticia a huge smile. In sharp contrast to the dancers, she was dressed in a black suit and white shirt unbuttoned to the top of her sternum. Her shoes were black-and-red Nike sneakers.

"This is unexpected." She looked Jacob up and down before giving him a nod, then went back to Leticia. "I guess I'm happy you brought your latest fling to meet me. Nice dress by the way. Your style expensive, now that you're a civilian."

"Actually, I'm here on business. Taffy was setting us up a private table in the Champagne Room. You free?"

"I'm always free for business. Let's go the back way."

Another door led to a narrow hallway, and they entered the Champagne Room from there. Each table was private, hidden behind silver drapes. The occupied spaces were drawn shut. Their table was open, with Leticia's name blinking above it. They ordered from a console in the table—two orders of mozzarella sticks, faux chicken wings, and a bottle of bourbon.

"You wouldn't be impressed with the wine they serve here," Leticia said. "No offense."

"None taken." Desiree made herself comfortable on a soft silver couch. "Right, so why are you here? Usually you call before."

"This came up kind of suddenly," Leticia said. "I'm not going to bullshit you, Desiree. The government didn't exactly take care of us like they promised, what with new cuts and a new administration. We don't owe them anything. Jacob here has a job, and yours truly might be the director of security. If I'm going to take it, I'm going to need a team—the best."

Jacob looked surprised, but kept silent. The bottle of bourbon and glasses arrived before the food.

"How much we talking?" Desiree asked.

Leticia flashed a persuasive smile. "Gimme your arm, bonita." Leticia pulled a pen out of her purse, and wrote a number.

Desiree looked at her arm, then Jacob, then back to Leticia. "You're shitting me." She frowned. "I don't do assassinations or overthrow governments."

"Nothing like that," Jacob interjected. "We're just securing a new settlement. As far as we know, there is no life there. Leticia's brother has built a grand facility over what was a small surveying outpost."

"Nice accent," Desiree said as she poured them drinks. "God knows I can't do this forever, and dashing into danger is getting to be old." She took a sip. "One last odyssey I suppose."

The food arrived. Leticia grabbed a mozzarella stick and greedily devoured it. Jacob couldn't help himself from chuckling.

"You seem to do everything with abandon," he said. "Unlike your brother. He has, how should we say, a more rigid personality."

Leticia took a sip of bourbon.

"You don't know the half of it."

"Tell me more." He grabbed a mozzarella stick and ate it as quickly as Leticia. "You have me all night."

Looking into his eyes, it felt like being caught in a pool of whiskey. Another glance was another shot of not giving a damn. It was always a risk to take attraction to the next level, but…

Taffy had slid next to Desiree and they spoke with their voices low. Desiree got up and left. Leticia moved closer to Jacob as he poured more bourbon for her.

"Can I ask you a personal question?"

"Sure," she said.

"Will you be leaving anyone behind?"

"Nope," she said, maybe a little too fast. "Don't think I have ever really been in love. And relationships... well when the time is right, I guess. You?"

He shook his head. "No one. I've yet to meet someone I connect with, who doesn't really want to connect with my name or money. And I want to build something. When I'm old can we sit on a boat and watch the sunset, knowing it could be our last. To me that would be a life well lived."

"Tell me about Olinka."

"Olinka is inspired by the real concept from the 1950s by a Mexican artist and philosopher, Gerardo Murillo—also called Doctor Atl. It was his idea of a utopian city for scientists, intellectuals, and artists. There would be vast resources that would be given to scientific and spiritual research, for humankind to reach their greatest potential. Philosophy was my minor in school."

He took a drink and continued. "In the summer between my junior and senior year I went to Peru. It got me thinking. The body count from company-sponsored secret missions was as great as the number of files on each misdeed and sin. Past generations made killing and murder a science, literally. I spent weeks poring over the files until I could read no more, feeling sick to my stomach.

"Yes, there is the money—billions," he said, "but I began my career in urban planning. Decided to join the Weyland-Yutani Corporation when politics got messy. Members of the board approached me, and it was the perfect opportunity. The planet was unnamed, but there is a close resemblance to Earth."

Leticia was... impressed.

"You know how Ramón made his first little fortune?" she said, maybe thanks to the bourbon. "He hacked the school and stole tests, as well as altering some grades."

Jacob frowned.

"Is that how he got to the top of his class?"

"Hell no! He's more psycho than that. He did it all himself, always had to prove he was the best. It was okay to help others cheat, but he needed to know he was intrinsically better than everyone else. No, he earned his place."

"I've never seen drive or dedication like his."

"I think we both got parts of our mother. We don't know much about our father, but she would definitely find some of her in us."

"For that I am grateful," he said, "and glad to have had the privilege of getting to know you, have you on my team."

Leticia fluttered inside. She wanted to kiss him. Feel his saliva on her mouth.

"What's the hardest lesson you've ever had to learn?"

Leticia drank the last of the bourbon in her glass. "To be alone."

He nodded. "Same."

"I guess we're both following our forebears' dreams, but attempting to do better than they did." Her mother's dream had been to get into the Marines and look where that got her, Leticia thought darkly. Where it got both of them.

"All we can do is try," he said, breaking her out of it. "I'm tired of war, greed, and destruction infecting generation after generation. On Meredith Vickers' final mission she encountered a place, and something ancient. There's little data available. Who knows what or who they were, but it scares me to think what course we have set for ourselves."

Desiree returned to the Champagne Room dressed casually in jeans, heeled timberlands, and a leather jacket.

"My shift is done. Let's head to The Rooster."

"Yes," Leticia shouted.

20

The Rooster was crowded. Heads turned as Leticia walked in, seriously over-dressed, but she didn't mind.

They grabbed a place at the bar and were waiting to order drinks when she noticed a guy with a robotic arm and robotic leg staring at them. His face was deeply grooved, likely from the sun, and there were blooms of purple spider veins across his cheeks and nose. Judging from his bloodshot eyes, he'd had one too many.

Leticia didn't say anything, but kept an eye on him. Desiree excused herself. Jacob and Leticia were alone when the man moved to approach.

"I recognize your face, you know," he said, his voice like gravel, "but you wouldn't recognize me. None of us grunts are given a second thought when we go up there, or have to survive down here."

Jacob looked baffled, and unsure how to react.

Leticia stepped in to defuse the situation.

"And how are you doing, sir? What can we do for you today?"

He pointed a fleshy middle finger toward Jacob. "That rich piece of shit can get the hell out of this bar. He's probably never worked a day in his life, or even paid taxes. No, he sat at home in a shitty diaper waiting to have his ass wiped while I had this done to me."

"Excuse me, but I am a qualified teacher and have spent years nurturing the minds of young people," Jacob said before Leticia could stop him. "Taxes were always deducted. Now, can I buy you and your friends a round?"

"Hey, Jerry!" the guy said, raising his voice. "This Weyland suit wants to buy us drinks. As if it can make up for all of it." Spittle from the man's mouth landed on Leticia's bare arms.

He was too damned close.

A large man with hair cut close to his scalp approached. The people at the bar began to move away from the escalating argument.

"The hell is *he* doing here?"

"He's with me," Leticia said, "and I lost both my parents up there. You don't see me acting like an asshole."

Both men looked her up and down. "You his hooker for the night? Must be, dressed like that." At that moment Desiree returned, standing at Leticia's back and watching the rest of the room.

Jacob started to speak again, but Leticia placed a hand on his chest without taking her eyes off of the two men.

"Could a hooker do this?" She grabbed a bottle of beer from a woman standing next to her, then a shot glass Desiree was holding. Leticia downed the shot in one gulp, then smashed the bottle into the chest of the larger man. She grabbed both of his shoulders then kneed him in the groin. As he bent over, groaning in pain, she put him in a head lock, digging the heel of her stiletto into one of his sneaker-wearing feet.

"You're lucky you're a woman," he moaned with spit falling from the side of his mouth.

"Tell me something I don't know, pendejo," she replied. "Now leave us the hell alone. You and your drunk-ass friend." Releasing her grip on his neck, she pushed him away and he stumbled before regaining his balance.

With a humiliated look, the two men skulked off.

Leticia turned to Jacob. "Now we can have fun. El riesgo siempre vive."

"Damn, bitch." Desiree stared at her friend. "Now I have to buy another shot. That took me ages!"

"Buy a bottle on me," Jacob suggested.

"I can do that."

Around 11:30 the lights lowered and the music turned louder. In the back of the bar Leticia ground her hips to the beat of the music. Desiree chatted to a woman who had caught her attention.

Jacob's hands found their way to Leticia's waist. He couldn't dance for shit, but the way he licked his lips and his hands touched her body told her he knew exactly what to do with his tongue and fingers.

"I have a confession."

Leticia tensed. If he had a girlfriend or wife, after he said he didn't, she would sock him in the mouth.

"I told your brother to join us."

Internally Leticia breathed a sigh of relief. Ramón was the ultimate cock block, but at least Jacob could still be hers for the taking. She brought her mouth closer to his as an invitation. He kissed her hard, with authority. She matched his power with her tongue, hands wandering to touch his chest.

"You still haven't given me an answer," he said breathlessly into her ear. "Say yes, Leticia. Be by my side."

She kissed his neck and dragged her lips across his flesh before giving his earlobe a little nibble.

"Yes, I'll take your job, and you will pay my crew a decent wage to set them up."

"Done," he replied, though she was pretty sure he would have promised her anything at that moment. "If the company can pay for bullshit that only ends in death, then let me spend some of their profits on real people."

"My own crew?" she said, pressing her advantage. "That includes Desiree, and a few others still in the Corps."

"If you can't trust the people with guns to have your back, then what the hell are you doing?" he said, looking painfully serious. "I will try. It might be an uphill battle. I won't promise you anything right now, but this... the politics..."

"Understood. I'll give you a list of names, and there's equipment we'll need."

"I already can't wait to hear from you again."

Their bodies were close—any closer and they should have been beneath sheets. Desiree tapped her on the shoulder.

"Attention, soldier. Your brother is here."

Ramón walked in with his usual air of confidence. He looked over the crowd until his gaze zeroed in on Leticia and Jacob. Everything about him looked tense, and *definitely* less than excited about the surroundings.

Leticia moved quickly away from Jacob. If Ramón stared any harder, smoke would be coming out of his ears. He was always the superstar, not her. Well, fuck him. She could hear his gripes before he even started.

"Leticia, you put me in a very awkward situation back there. Everyone wanted to know where Jacob went."

"I'm sure you're exaggerating, Ramón," Jacob said. "People pretend to like me, but I've called out too many of them on their shit. Half put up with me, and others want me out, one way or another. And Ramón, Leticia is... well I don't have to tell you."

Jacob gently touched the back of her arm.

She imagined what it would feel like for it to be her back, followed by her ass, instead of her arm. *Not now, not here.* But she wanted to know. She responded with a touch to his arm, and a small smile crossed his face. Ramón was too occupied with wanting to get out of the bar to notice. This would be something they would have to revisit another time even if it bordered on the unethical.

Then again, when did love or lust follow anything but the rules of biology? It was a creature that could only be satiated with flesh.

"Ramón, we need to talk Olinka," Jacob said. "Your sister is on board, but only if she can pick her own crew. I told her if there was one person who could get Satan into heaven, it would be you. You're the best with strategy. I will need your thoughts on Monday."

"She said yes to you." Ramón gave her a hard stare. "Then I guess, Leticia, you have work to do." Then he had a smile of his own, but it wasn't pleasant. "Don't stay up too late."

Leticia woke up the following morning alone with a dry mouth and pounding head, but no Jacob next to her. It was better that way. She would pop a couple of pain relievers before sending out messages explaining the proposal to Frida, Mohammed, and Nathan.

Desiree already knew the deal and wanted in.

The hope was they would all say yes because money talked, and none of them wanted to die young.

It didn't take long for her to hear back. Not a one of them could say no to the zeros on offer. Next she would contact Ramón with a figure, and let him work his sorcery to make it all happen. In the back of her mind, she wanted to contact Jacob again and see him. Camping out in Ramón's apartment was nice, but it didn't have the same rewards.

No, she had to keep it professional. Fought the urge to keep it strictly business, knowing Jacob could be at the front door in minutes.

Three days later her phone rang, and Leticia rolled over in her bed. The empty space with an unused pillow made her think of Jacob for the umpteenth time, and the sensation of his heartbeat beneath her hand as it had been slung across his bare chest.

The phone continued to ring.

It was him.

Even though it was probably business, a jolt of excitement pinched inside her belly.

"Good morning."

The sound of his voice increased the longing.

"Must be important for this early."

"I had an early night," he said. "Stayed in… alone. Anyway, your brother has one hell of a reputation. I don't know how he did it, but you got your team. He'll be joining us, too."

Leticia sat upright in bed. "Really? No wonder he's shot up the ranks." As usual, she didn't want the specifics of what Ramón had done. "Thank you. I'll get started on a plan—and travel, it seems."

"Contracts will be drawn up shortly, and we'll want to begin as soon as possible. Does everyone you want to include know that we leave on short notice?"

"They do," she said. "Leave the rest to me." There was a pause. Neither wanted to say goodbye. "Um, I guess we'll talk when there's an update."

"That would be great," he replied. "Feel free to drop by the office. If you need a space here to work, I can arrange it very easily."

Leticia smiled with that giddy schoolgirl rush of talking to a crush. She wanted to be close to him, too.

"I'll let you know. See you soon… I hope."

Leticia hopped out of bed, marveling at how it all had worked out. By not getting that promotion, something bigger had been reserved for her. *And* she had stumbled across Jacob. As she began to compile a checklist in her head, she pulled on a pair of jeans. Her soft brown belt with flowers and bees hung next to them, a gift from—

Roseanna.

She had to call Roseanna. Her tía would be sixty soon. Depending on what happened up there, she might never see her again. The price of travel throughout space, a place thought to be devoid of life, was time. Cryo bought you time, but it cost years for those left behind on Earth.

Leticia didn't know how long they would be up there, or what they might find themselves facing. The unknown wasn't just above their heads—it was also in her mind.

"Mija, it's so good to see your face. You look well."

"How are you, Roseanna?"

"The same. One day at a time. I have my plants and clients. Me and Robert have our horse shows. But you didn't call to talk about that."

"I said yes."

"I knew you would," Roseanna said. *"There was no way you wouldn't. You could have left a long time ago, both of you, but you stayed. I trust your decision. You have my blessing, and I will light a candle for you every day."* Leticia could tell that she was genuinely pleased, but also a little wistful. It hurt her heart.

"But I may not see... I don't know... We will be in cryo for five years, and after that who knows what awaits. It's not dangerous, at least." Leticia could feel her voice wanting to crack from the emotions of saying goodbye to her beloved Roseanna.

"You might not see me, but you will always feel me, just as I still feel your mother. I'm still fit and healthy." She took a deep breath, and continued. *"None of you know what lies ahead, but you can't live your life wondering. Don't go walking around like you're already in cryo. Go."*

"I love you, Roseanna. Thank you for... for everything. I wouldn't have made it this far without you."

"Yes, you would have. You're a Vasquez woman, a born soldadera. El riesgo siempre vive."

Leticia touched the tattoo of her mother on her arm.

"I'll send you a message as soon as I can. By the way, I don't know if you have spoken to Ramón, but he is going, too. Not sure what that is all about, with his kids and Mary Anne."

"I did speak to him. He just said they would move when the time was right. It's not my business. You can't tell him anything, anyway."

"Very true."

21

Departure day was unlike any she had experienced during her military career—or even before. All her life she had worked toward a goal, had objectives along the way. It felt strange signing on for a project that had no real directive. They would be reacting to the needs of the moment.

Leticia still requested a cache of weapons to be taken on board. It was her job to anticipate the worst, even in the best of conditions. One of the items had been a Narwhal. Jacob stood by the sleek vehicle, inspecting it intently. He motioned for Leticia to come over.

"It's not that I mind paying for it," he said, "but what is it?"

"I couldn't believe it when Ramón had that beast approved. It's a Narwhal. It's called that because it's small, like a jet ski, but lighter, and it has a long launcher attached to the nose. Inside there's a revolving chamber with a harpoon, a spear, grenades, and as a last resort you can blow the whole thing up to create a powerful explosion. It works best on the water, but the propulsion system can be used in short bursts for an air-to-water landing, or even to go a short distance on ground that isn't too rough."

"That's brilliant," he said, then he faced her. "How are you feeling?"

Leticia ran her hand across the amphibious craft, remembering the incident with Haas.

"If this job is as easy as the description then fine."

"If the job isn't, then I'm in trouble," Jacob countered, his gaze lingering on Leticia. There was an awkward moment caught between staying professional and wanting more.

"I better get back to work," she said. "I *am* on the clock."

"Sorry, yes," he said. "See you on board."

In addition to the soldiers directly under her command, there were people from the fields of science and anthropology—some at the top of their fields—and their assistants. Her crew seemed to be in good spirits as they prepared for a long sleep with no threat to face once their boots hit ground again.

Nathan and Frida showed each other pictures of family, bringing them up on their watches. Desiree and Mohammed inspected the weapons waiting to be loaded with their bags and other supplies. Leticia watched them, hoping this job would be good for them financially, and present opportunities not available to them otherwise. Not everyone had a hot-shot brother with good connections.

Speaking of Ramón, he was late. She looked at her watch. A missed message said he was nearly there.

Ramón arrived at the spaceport appearing sleep deprived, with dark circles beneath his eyes. He also seemed cagey and irritable as he snapped at peripheral staff, including a few of the scientists brought along by Jacob. His grumpy demeanor had to have been tied to his wife, and Leticia wondered what was going on with them.

"Hey, Ramón. What gives?"

He dropped his duffle. "Mary Anne isn't too pleased. She knew what she was getting into when she married me, but it's still been a long time coming."

"You don't have to go." Leticia patted her brother's bicep. "Why are you doing this, anyway?"

He looked at her as if he wanted to spit something out.

"Because I *want* to go."

That was all she was going to get out of him. Ramón was too deliberate. In the back of her mind, she wondered what or who waited on Olinka.

"Your call, bro, but please think of the twins."

"Oh, I am." He leaned in close to her ear. "And us, the Vasquez name." That left her bewildered, but a shout from Desiree broke her train of thought.

"We gotta go," Leticia said. "Get ready, and sweet dreams, hermano."

PART 5

OLINKA

22

Julia Yutani left her heart—and—scruples on Earth. Glory always required leaving something behind, she knew. Sometimes those things returned, and other times they only survived as rays of light reaching the Earth from a star long dead.

This project was her glory in the making.

Dr. Moon had perfected the bacteria, and it was time to introduce it in various scenarios. There was also promise in the engineered parasites spliced with Xenomorph DNA and the lowly pork tapeworm from Earth. Under the microscope the ugly things ate through tissue with a quiet viciousness. The hook on their tails cut with the sharpness of a razor's edge as they burrowed into tissue. They reproduced rapidly like the Xenomorphs, were easy to transport, and could invade an entire water system.

But no parasite would be complete without a cure. Dr. Moon's paranoia made her diligent in finding a neutralizing agent.

Julia had made this journey for another pressing reason. There had been an unexpected change in the three Xenomorph queens, and by Brenda's exacting protocols, nothing could be left to chance. For years the incapacitated queens had lain like sleeping giants, growing to their true size and reproducing with little overt movement except to generate eggs.

With the missing lower jaw, the inner mandible hung black and heavy like the tongue escaping from a drowned corpse's mouth. Saliva pooled directly beneath. Year after year it gathered and thickened. Ridges spiraled with bony thorns around the smaller inner mandible, the teeth lengthened across the top jaw—only by centimeters, but still a change—until they were longer than ever recorded.

Where the arms and legs had been amputated, barbs were beginning to sprout with the slowness of spring buds on a barren tree branch. Evolution. Given the environments in which they had been found, Xenomorphs were likely to experience hibernation, and Brenda postulated that their years of hibernation were a form of silent evolution. With these new, subtle changes, Brenda petitioned that they should be terminated as soon as possible.

No fucking way would Julia have any of that.

She had convinced the board to send her out to oversee the final decision. No hard feelings for the good doctor, but this was way above her pay grade.

As an unexpected bonus, the man who gave her everything and nothing at the same time would arrive on Olinka not far behind her. Ramón had promised a commitment, and with this relocation he had kept that promise. No more sneaking around or stolen moments. Now they would wake up and work side by side. Their story generated among the stars, because *they* were the corporate stars who would shape worlds.

Getting rid of Ross had made it all the easier. His use had run out, as did his ability to get things done the way Ramón could. Her body trembled when she thought of Ramón's hands on her waist again, the way he whispered that he wanted to make love to her before opening his eyes. It was always the subtle moments that created craters in the heart and soul.

She had been chasing him since college and meeting him in secret during the entirety of his sham of a marriage. His desire for a family was perfect as a Hallmark movie—something he couldn't let go of because of those old abandonment wounds. Part of her hated herself for always holding space for him. Year after year, her resolve had eroded away, knowing he was playing happy family with a woman who wasn't his true match, or the one he loved. Mary Anne had to know he wasn't faithful. Something in her roving eyes, when she accompanied him to corporate events, betrayed this truth.

"Who is it?" they said. *"Which one of these women am I sharing my husband with?"*

Julia did her best to give her a pleasant smile. Mary Anne ignored her as she clung to the crook of his arm with that pretty face, minimal makeup, modest dress, and kitten heels. The princess-cut diamond ring on her left hand blinding as it reflected the light in any room. And it was always, *"the twins this"* and *"the twins that"*… It was as if they married each other for nothing more than a photo opportunity.

Eventually his children would join them here. She didn't mind, because that was what staff was for, and there was something to be said about birthing your heirs as opposed to appointing them. Julia was an heir.

Ramón had been given an ultimatum, to confront what would he do, knowing he could lose her—or more importantly, lose a lifetime of wealth. Finally, he had come around and decided to leave his wife, under the convenient guise of work and an empty promise of sending for her once settled. His children would be placed in the best boarding school in the country, and he justified leaving them because in the end they would have it all. They would see it as training to be proper heirs.

It had happened to Julia.

When she had first relaxed into cryo for the journey, she smiled knowing that in five short years they would have their own empire. An instant, really, when spent in deep freeze. It would be easy to push out Jacob, who was unfit for his position.

Julia loathed Jacob and that the board had chosen a British-born Vickers to take the top spot. Weyland-Yutani had a long way to go before they could clean up their image. He was nothing like his great-grandmother, Meredith. His office was filled with photos of his trips with humanitarian projects, with students achieving high honors, and accolades from non-profits for his continued support to charities in the places with the most need.

God knew why he really took the position. She would have held more respect for him if he was hiding a secret agenda, and ended up poisoning the entire board who had voted him in. Altruism in its purest form only got you killed, or dying broke. Out here he would be isolated, though, chasing an illusion that was rays of light from a dead star. A half smile spread across her face.

Accidents happen all the time.

She stepped through the doorway of Brenda's office for the formal review.

"Julia, it's wonderful to finally meet you," Brenda said. "I know how busy you are, so I have everything already set up. Whatever we decide to do, it should be swift."

Leaning in closer to the screen on Brenda's wall, Julia played her fingertips across the screen and brought the image into closer focus. A queen Xenomorph sat upright with the stiffness of a sphynx. No riddle here.

"What's the problem?" she said brusquely. "You have her under control. You've managed to do what we need, tamed the bitch."

Brenda looked startled and pursed her lips. She pulled up another image.

"Look here and here." She pointed. "There is growth. It's as if they have matured into full-grown Xenomorphs while evolving or adapting to the… changes. The inner mandible is thicker. It doesn't move much, but it is changing. Here. Where we inserted our little bullets of insurance, they have grown out into sharp horns. Ironically it looks like a crown on their large hoods—and look at the tail and hands. See those barbs?"

Julia swung her head from one image to the other. "But has she moved an inch? Have any of them? All that matters is they continue to create more eggs for our research, and for the end results we need."

Brenda remained silent for a beat. "No. However, I still think we should terminate all the queens now. No waiting to see what happens next."

"You will do no such thing." Julia snapped her head away from the screen. "All the other Xenomorphs will be allowed to grow, as well. No more euthanizing them—*any* of them—while they're still small. What's the status of the eggs you're freezing? Have you figured out the optimal temperature for keeping them on ice, so they can be used as biological grenades?"

Brenda's mouth hung open as she struggled to regain her composure.

"We don't know enough about fully grown Xenomorphs," she said finally. "I don't trust this many queens changing in ways we can't predict and keeping full-grown Xenomorphs all in the same facility. What if they can communicate? What if these queens—"

"With all due respect," Julia said, "and I *do* respect everything you have done in your career, the sacrifices you have made; however, this is not up to you. You want to destroy something huge based only on a scientific hunch… or rather, on your own fear."

"Yes!" Brenda snapped. "You *should* fear these things, and respect them. They are hideous. She is a monstrosity." Brenda gestured toward the screen. "And another thing—we don't have a proper security team, or much of *anything* to defend ourselves in the event of an emergency."

"Is she hideous because of her latent power? Because you are afraid of how much we don't know about her yet, if we allow it to bloom?" Julia countered. "There could be so much more. You don't fear the bacteria or parasites you created. Those will be used in warfare, and against other humans. Where is your fear for those?"

Brenda stared, unable to answer. Julia could tell she had crushed the woman and her irrational arguments.

"As far as security is concerned," she continued, "that's being taken care of. The bacteria is all that should concern you. You've prepared safeguards, and the dosages have been calibrated. They're ready to go, should we need to wipe them all out.

"But it should *not* come to that," she said, making certain the scientist understood the implications. "If that happened, we start back at square one. Continue your work, or send me a letter of resignation. If you choose that route, however, you will forfeit the generous bonus you were given—or has that already been spent? Your sister is out on one of the colonies, isn't she, with her own business? It would be a shame for her to have to give it all back."

Brenda straightened her back.

"You're the boss, Ms. Yutani," she said. "But no matter what you decide, she is hideous." She looked at the abomination on the screen. "I know much of what they are capable of, and I fear everything we *don't* know they are capable of accomplishing—like these changes."

"Acknowledged," Julia said. "I'll expect a report about the frozen eggs, by the end of the day."

With that Julia walked out of the office, holding in the elation she felt. Spontaneous evolution. The queen would indeed be terminated, and then picked apart to find whatever was causing it. Imagine harnessing the power of evolution.

Her watch beeped. She had to move quickly for her next appointment, deeper in the facility.

The elevator doors opened to a wide research room from which all projects were monitored.

"Are we ready for the specimen?" Julia demanded as she stepped in front of a large screen showing a live feed.

"It's not fully grown, and should prove to be easy."

Human trials were always bogged down with red tape, money, and a little thing called ethics. Peter Weyland had changed the world and done what people labeled "good," but the path to it hadn't been paved with cobbles of altruism. Every human possessed an ego.

This round of trials would begin before any approval had been granted. The lab was far from anything or anyone who could get in the way. The participants had been recruited from floundering colonies, or people stranded in space who had been brought here with the promise of work, a fresh start.

The poor guy, Dylan, didn't even know he was part of an experiment, but this was how it had to be. There had to be that element of surprise. In times of war the chain of events couldn't be anticipated. If they were lucky, this thing would never have to be used—the threat of it might be enough. There also might be applications that hadn't yet appeared.

Xenomorphs proved that humans were not alone.

"Dylan, I'm Dr. Yutani." Julia maintained her cool, even tone as she gave the young man a reassuring smile. He still appeared to be filled with dread. "It's time for you to take the samples."

"*Is it safe?*" he said over the intercom, his eyes wide. "*I mean, what is the stuff. Th-this isn't what I was expecting. Could you use an android, instead?*"

He had no clue.

"You signed up for this," she said, "and we can't rely on androids for everything. As humans, that would make us obsolete. Do you want to be made obsolete?" Without giving him a chance to answer, she continued. "You're being paid well, and a lot of people wanted this opportunity, so you should be grateful." Her smile remained, but her eyes were a squeeze to his balls.

"*I'm sorry, Dr. Yutani,*" he said. "*I… I'll do it. I trust you.*" With that, he picked a vial off of the table in front of him and swallowed the contents.

"Good," Julia said, trying to sound reassuring. "That will offer you the protection you need as you collect the samples." It was a lie, of course, but the young man seemed to take it at face value and calm down a bit. He dressed hastily in a hazmat suit. An assistant behind him secured the back of the suit and latched the helmet.

"*All set.*"

Dylan approached the airlock carrying a tray holding the instruments he had been given, ostensibly to slice off pieces of the pulsating egg. When the door opened, they could see black weeping streaks shooting from the base to the top. Flakes of dead flesh lay on the floor. He glanced back at the camera where he knew Julia and the others would be watching.

Stretching out a shaky hand, he gathered pieces of curled dead flesh on the ground and placed them in a plastic vacuum bag. The egg continued to pulse, causing Julia's own heart rate to increase in pulsating beats. Her eyes widened. If only Ramón could be standing next to her for this. Afterward they could celebrate with champagne and sex.

As he hovered over the egg and reached out with the scalpel, the spider-like face-hugger came shooting out of the top, shattering the mask. In an instant Dylan lay on the ground mottled with black blooms spreading across his face. If all went as planned, the dosage would be just enough to transmit the bacteria. The assistant entered the room, lifting off Dylan's helmet.

"Looks good," he said. "Both the host and the *Manumala noxhydria* are still alive. Transmission appears to have been successful."

"Great," Julia replied. "We need to let the bacterium continue to do its work before the face-hugger falls off. Get him out of there."

Dylan was the last of five infected hosts. All of them would be kept in secure hatching rooms. Dr. Moon should have been there, watching with the same intensity she reserved for her objections. But she had made some bullshit excuse, and Julia would not forget.

Brenda's time was limited.

23

2201

The long sleep was over. A soothing voice greeted the crew while the sounds of chirping birds was piped into the cryopod. The light was bright to give the effect of curtains being drawn. They hadn't arrived at their destination, but they were close.

As Leticia's pod opened, Jacob was already up twisting his body in various yoga poses. Tennis and yoga. She chuckled to herself how different they were, despite the chemistry being so magnetic. After five years the thought of jumping his bones was also strong. The word that came to mind when she thought of Jacob Vickers was *caliente*. The scent of coffee filling the cabin distracted her from her fantasies.

This was a job.

Leticia tossed her legs to the side, feeling hungover without any of the fun. Hunger pangs pinched her awake, enough to move her feet to the floor. She'd kill for chorizo and egg breakfast tacos. Extra salsa, of course.

"When do we eat, I'm starving," she croaked.

Jacob answered her still doing his impromptu yoga session. "We meet in an hour for breakfast and debriefing."

She didn't want to wait an hour; patience was one of the virtues she'd never mastered. She looked around, but no Ramón. The rest of her crew were pulling on track suits or had wandered to use the hygiene facilities. The civilians on board were dressing in their own clothing while talking among themselves. Leticia quickly pulled on her own track suit and followed her nose to the mess cabin. She heard Ramón's voice as he spoke to a scientist.

"Good morning, director of security," he said cheerfully, turning as she entered. Five years must have done him good because the man who stood before her wasn't the man who lay down in his cryopod and immediately shut his eyes.

The spread was a lavish buffet, unlike the vacuum-sealed crap she was used to having dispensed by a machine or pulled from a backpack during a mission. Something was going on here. He was buttering them up for something. Fluffy pancakes with lashings of syrup, crispy bacon, fruit at its peak of ripeness, muffins, real coffee.

Man, this is mala, very, very bad.

But at least she could eat well, before he revealed whatever mission of death was in store. As her crew filtered in they showed the same astonishment as she. Not knowing Ramón so well, though, they didn't seem the least bit suspicious. Each one grabbed a plate, the others crowded in around. Jacob was the last one into the mess, and he joined her in the back as he watched the feast.

"Your brother really is generous," he said. "I wasn't sure about a celebration breakfast like this, but look at their faces." He turned to Leticia and smiled. "Why aren't you eating?"

"Why aren't *you* eating, Jacob?"

The smile left his face. "Nerves. Like being in love for the first time."

"C'mon, mi amigo. You have to eat something. I'll join you."

Leticia left it at that. This would be Jacob's moment to address them all. After a satisfying breakfast, the group of fifteen turned their attention to him as he stood in front of a white wall. Her stomach cramped from a mixture of overeating and excitement.

"I want to introduce you to planet E2," Jacob said. "We call it E2 because it has been terraformed to almost resemble Earth's long-lost sister, but its formal name will be Olinka. From our observations, it seems to be in a stage similar to what Earth was before humans. Anyone been to Iceland? Half of the planet resembles that country, with its vastly different landscapes, some dangerous. We lost a few rovers to geothermal activity, and at the very far reaches, the cold.

"There is also water, but not a place for wading or sunbathing. Until Ramón became involved, there was only one facility that had been established for Weyland-Yutani to stake their claim. Most of it existed beneath the ground. We will be going over virgin terrain because all prior work on Olinka One was completed on-site. No one was allowed to explore outward."

Jacob clicked on another photo. It was the pyramid Ramón had built.

"This will be our center of operations," Jacob said, "and these are the raw materials from which we will build our masterpiece." The enthusiasm built in his voice as he continued to run through drone photos taken from above. It was a beautiful, rugged, unspoiled version of Earth. Where other worlds were being terraformed by working-class families that had run out of options on Earth, people were going to pay big money for this place. Leticia could envision her brother living in some high-rise penthouse in the middle of unspoiled land, with an infinity pool overlooking his empire.

Her musings were interrupted when she heard her own name.

"... Leticia Vasquez, the director of security." All eyes turned toward her. Leticia smiled and lifted her hand to give a wave, and immediately felt self-conscious. Then she caught Ramón's eyes. If they hadn't been twins, she wouldn't have seen the shadow that lurked within.

"Whatever happens here—I don't care if you've found the one thing that will revolutionize mankind—if Leticia says move, you move," Jacob continued. "We don't expect anything dangerous to occur, but for the moment please stick together. No wandering, because while we have extensive footage of the planet, it's still a mystery of sorts. Some of you are here under Ramón's direction"—he nodded to a group standing with her brother—"and others are with me, but we *all* answer to Leticia if there is any sort of emergency." He paused and scanned the room, but all he got were nods and words of assent.

"Alright," he concluded, "let's get ready to land."

Jacob sought her out after his speech. Before she could get a word out, Ramón stepped in.

"Excuse me, Jacob, may I have a word with my sister?"

"Absolutely. We can catch up later, Leticia?"

"Whenever, you need me, come and find me." She watched him walk away without caring what her big brother might think of her wandering eye.

"Hey, sis, just watch it, okay?" Ramón said. "I see how you look at each other. It never hurts to have a little something on the side to keep you occupied, but he isn't some private you can hop on and off for fun. He's the company, and a little lip gloss isn't going to impress him."

"It's called trying to leave a good impression," she said, wondering why the hell he'd chosen this moment to bring it up. "And it's not lip gloss. It's Carmex."

"Just be professional, and keep your distance unless it's genuinely important. We have a lot to do when we arrive at the Olinka One facility. Neither of us needs the distraction. Maybe after some time passes, you can do whatever you want." When she didn't say a word, he added, "Just trust me and give him some space."

She still didn't know why he was bringing it up now—he had to have figured it out before. What, was he going to ask if she was on birth control? All she could guessed was that he didn't want competition.

Desiree arrived just in time, before her exchange with Ramón could become any more awkward.

"Looks like we're close enough to start heading down," Desiree said. "I'm thinking three dropships."

"Sounds good," Leticia replied. "You get the crew suited up and I'll tell Jacob to make the announcement. No more waiting."

The first team of scientists and assistants went down in two larger dropships, along with supplies to set up camp, including the rovers they would use to cross the terrain to the Olinka One facility. Jacob wanted to do it this way for everyone to see the planet with their own eyes and begin the surveying process for another facility.

Leticia, her crew, Jacob, and Ramón strapped themselves into their own ship loaded with what she had requested for their security detail. The ship disengaged and began its descent. As always, she began the mission with a little pep talk. This would be her first time formally leading her own team in space, a small band of soldiers, too restless for civilian life but too tired of and broke for service.

"Alright, my people. You know the drill. There's been no strange activity reported, so this should be a walk in the park—but when was that ever the case? Thanks to Ramón, we've had an amazing last meal that wasn't freeze-dried." They all smiled and sniggered, knowing exactly what she meant. This made her feel good. She wanted her crew to feel comfortable.

"We work as a team. Sounds like this is a nice payday for everyone, so we don't want any fuck-ups. Tell me everything. If a beetle shits the wrong way, I need to know. You know I will take everything you say under consideration.

"Let's do this."

It was an odd sensation, being the boss on the most unlikely of missions, like new boots on a marathon-long hike. Leticia attempted to read everyone's mood. Jacob had a permanent smile on his face, and the demeanor of a big kid about to have his first real visit to an amusement park.

Whereas Ramón looked straight ahead at a red sign reading **WARNING. ONLY PULL IF AN EMERGENCY.** Gone was the casual, even cheerful person who had woken—his grumpy and anxious demeanor had returned now that he didn't have to be on show for a large crowd. She couldn't help but feeling he wasn't being totally honest with her. When she looked his way, he avoided eye contact. His mind was elsewhere. But where?

Supposedly he knew everything there was to know about the Olinka One facility and this planet. Maybe the idea of leaving Mary Anne and the kids was hitting him again. Whatever it was, it would be revealed in its own time.

Leticia felt the dropship slowing down. They would land soon, and she found herself smiling with the same giddiness as Jacob.

Landing would be the easy part. Next they had to follow a drone through a hot and humid sulfur field that would eventually give way to lush meadows, an ocean, and a pleasant temperature. The cargo bay door opened, and Mohammed pulled a bandana over his nose and mouth. A skull with vampire teeth.

"Holy shit, that smell," he said. "There must be the biggest pile of manure under our feet."

Even so, Jacob and Ramón emerged from the dropship with the posture of kings. Jacob breathed in deeply and stretched his arms.

"Fascinating, isn't it?" he said, not seeming to notice the stench. "I can't wait to set up a research facility here. I wanted to see for myself the geothermal flats. The facility out here will expand the natural energy grid across the planet, making way for future habitation."

Mohammed patted him on the back before walking away. "Enjoy and good luck with that, buddy."

The sulfur yellow and burnt orange hardened fields of rock and dirt smelled like giant exploding rotten eggs. The breeze blew the stomach-churning scent from the smoking vents across the landscape. Ponds of bubbling mud of all sizes pockmarked the surface. Nothing grew here because the planet burned from beneath and belched out its contents for miles. There was no sign of animal life, either, though previous drone and satellite scans had shown it to be plentiful elsewhere.

"So Ramón, where you putting the casino?" Frida joked.

"Very funny," he said, but he didn't look amused. "Some respect would be nice. I *am* your superior."

"Sorry. I forgot—this is a super serious mission." Frida lifted her hands and eyebrows in surrender before walking off. Leticia joined Jacob, who scanned the area, taking it all in. The terrain had a sparse amount of foliage along the border of the hot mud springs.

"So this is it? Your big dream?"

"It is," he replied without a hint of irony. "If everything goes well on this trip, more scientists and civilians will follow."

The scientists had already organized themselves and their equipment and were exploring the area without concern for the smell or the dangers of the geothermal vents. They were too engrossed in this new world and its undiscovered secrets.

"Right," she said, "I have work to do. Have to make sure nobody gets sucked into one of those mud pots or steps into a sinkhole. I guess I will see you later." She jogged toward the civilians. "Yo! We don't have time for that now. Get into your rovers. You can eyeball the area from a safe and tracked path. In a rover."

She looked to the sky. So far so good. The fog was clearing as the heat from the sun sent its radiation into the atmosphere. This was good, because the vents emitted smoke that could disrupt their visibility. They would rely on the drones to safely guide them as they traversed the terrain.

They had a head start. It had been previously mapped via satellite, but with all of the geothermal activity, it was always changing. A tracker alerted them to unstable pockets that might lead to boiling ponds of mud. Jacob wasn't lying when he said this had been a work in progress.

Eventually their route would become a proper road. Their destination was located on the border of a forest with fresh water close by.

For two hours they sat in the rover with bandanas or other masks over their noses, looking out on virgin terrain. Halfway through the journey the wind changed direction and the air smelled less toxic. It felt light with the incoming breeze from the coast, not too far off.

As they approached Olinka One, Leticia stood in the open roof rover. She wondered what her mother had thought when she stepped on her first planet among the stars. She couldn't help but feel proud in this moment. Maybe it was the virgin air or feeling the ground beneath the vehicle's wheels, but out here was the best thing to happen to her.

Small tufts of grass cropped up before there were small shrubs, and the ground became stable. It seemed like the obvious place to set up camp, or possibly the first settlement. They would build the colony's power supply on the sulfur fields, and Jacob also wanted to be close to that point.

The rovers came to a stop and the technicians began surveying. The group looked like they had stepped off the island of misfit toys, with a tiny crew of soldiers and civilians. Jacob and Ramón were the only "suits."

Leticia walked the perimeter in absolute wonder at the sight of the outline of two moons. There was no sign of anyone, or anything, on this part of the planet, though it seemed likely there were some indigenous faunae hidden away. Its beauty made them all stop and stare at times, then sadness would appear on their faces at the grim reality they would face going back to Earth.

A short distance away there was a patch of large trees that appeared nothing like anything she had seen on Earth. The shape of something you might see in the Serengeti but the needles like those of a pine. From what she remembered from the photos, they extended all the way to the Olinka One facility and the cliffs overlooking the ocean. Leticia wandered closer. The faint hint of pine was refreshing, comforting.

At her feet lay a branch with a smooth surface. She reached down to feel it. It was heavy, roughly the size and weight of a baseball bat. It would be a souvenir to help her remember this first day of what could be the start of something exciting.

Her watch vibrated. It was time to get back to the business of securing the camp, setting up sensors and cameras, exploring the outlying area, then preparing for a night under the stars that would be brighter than on Earth. No flashing lights or pollution to dim their shine. Jacob and Ramón had gathered the civilians. Leticia needed to know their plan before she began hers.

"What are you thinking for today?"

For once Ramón didn't make a move to dominate. He took a physical step back to allow Jacob to speak.

"Surveying. I want the next facility to be between the sulfur fields and Olinka One. My architect will take notes to come up with a concept."

"Anyone going beyond the grass line needs to take a scanner with them," she asserted, "to alert them to hot spots and sinkholes. No one ventures alone. Tents are being set up where it's stable. As the light dims, all work beyond the perimeter stops."

Neither Ramón nor Jacob protested.

As much as Leticia appreciated the ease of this job she would reserve judgment until proof presented itself. She and her crew joined the staffers who had been brought in for labor to get the camp up and running—they would never be above getting their hands dirty. That was a quick way to lose the respect of people upon whom her life might depend.

The sun, roughly the size of Earth's own star, dipped toward the flaming horizon and the sky morphed from a pale blue to deep indigo.

She and her crew walked the perimeter to make sure all civilians came back to camp. There would be no stupid accidents that could have been prevented. The civilians moved to the mess tent, gathering in groups, keeping to themselves, discussing their findings and paying rapt attention to Ramón as he tapped away on his tablet.

He probably loved having that kind of control, she thought, then she shrugged it away. Whatever had bothered him before appeared to have been compartmentalized.

She and her four ex-Marines set up a small pop-up table as more and more stars appeared. Rather than starting a fire, they set a glowing globe on the table. That, combined with the glow from above, provided plenty of light. Frida was singing a Stevie Nicks song to herself, and on a small speaker "All Along the Watchtower" by Jimi Hendrix began to play. A light breeze blew in the air.

Nathan leaned back in his canvas chair and broke the silence.

"What I wouldn't give for a beer right now," he said, peering upward. "This place is really something. Look at that sky." Her Las Lobas crew gave a collective chuckle in agreement.

"Well, don't bother to ask for more, because we need to be on guard." Leticia pulled a small flask of Fireball out from the thigh pocket of her fatigues and handed it over with a mischievous smile.

"Hell, yes!" Frida said. "You get boss of the year award."

Leticia drank first and passed it around. Jacob joined the group and exchanged glances with Leticia before speaking to the crew.

"I want to know what brought all of you here."

Without missing a beat, they all said, "Dinero." The table erupted into collective laughter.

"I can't argue with that."

She thought he looked a little disappointed.

After an hour of Jacob getting to know the soldiers better, Leticia excused herself. Before leaving she flashed Jacob a smile. He also rose to leave.

The tents provided were spacious, made from the most advanced textiles. Compared with what she had endured in the military, the cot seemed as if it could easily fit two. Everything new. Then again, with

Ramón in charge of supplies, it would only be the best. That breakfast on the ship had been something else. Everyone ate until the food was ready to explode from their bellies and chests. In the field and on missions she had become accustomed to sleeping rough, managing hunger, braving the elements, and getting whatever supplies that were available. The only new tech had been the weaponry.

She looked forward to getting cozy in these new digs, and felt as if she could get used to it. By the looks on her team's faces as they set up camp, they could, too.

Peeling off her makeshift uniform, she opened her tablet. There were complete backgrounds on the civilians who were on board with them, plus files upon files of research on the planet. Concerning the already established facility, however, they didn't have much in the way of detail. She wanted to know why.

"Director of security," she whispered while smiling to herself. After what seemed like hours her eyes began to ache from reading. At least the sleeping bag on her cot was comfortable.

"Leticia, may I speak to you?"

Her heart fluttered. It was Jacob. She looked around the small space for something more appropriate than panties and a thin white tank top that she wore without a bra. He had already seen her like this in cryo but that was different, with others around and in the same state of undress.

"Uh… One second."

"I can go. This is probably—"

She stood up straight and alert. "No, no. Don't go!" She regretted sounding entirely too eager and tapped her forehead with her palm. From her peripheral vision she spotted the corner of a green towel robe sticking out of her backpack. It would have to do.

It's only business up here.

Be professional.

She couldn't help how irresistible she found him, and it wasn't some manufactured gravity between them. When their eyes met, it felt like a homecoming. Leticia took a deep breath before pulling back the canvas flap that served as a door. He held a pair of bottles, and looked good in the shadowy light of the two moons.

"You know, you need to stop impressing me," he said. "You're quickly making yourself indispensable." When she didn't answer, he continued. "I hope you don't mind me showing up like this. Do you want to join me under the stars for a drink?"

Leticia glanced at the bottles, and allowed her eyes to glide over his body. He was holding a bottle of Zacapa rum and Hibiki Japanese whiskey.

"What is this? Very nice stuff."

"This was already on board, as a gift from Julia Yutani wishing me well. Which is odd, because she hates me with a flaming passion. If you prefer wine or beer, though, I can go back and—"

"It's okay," she said. "I'm an equal opportunist with booze. Come in."

He paused before looking over his shoulder. "You sure? I don't…"

Leticia's heart pounded, but she didn't want to play this game any longer. Her resolve to keep a distance was gone with the night breeze. She felt like a nocturnal animal come to life. She licked her lips and flashed him a smile.

"I *want* you to come in."

"Whatever you say."

He looked around the tent and settled on a spot on the floor in front of her cot. Leticia grabbed two metal cups from a green canvas bag, then handed him one of them. He poured the rum first.

"I wanted to talk privately," he said, "about my plans for the colony, and your place in it. You chose a good group of solid people. I like them all. Despite their protests that they came here for the pay, it sounds like they want a place to settle down. That's what I'm looking for, individuals invested and valued in their community. I know I've told you bits and pieces, but we will need a permanent head of security. This has the potential for being more than a temporary job."

He handed her the rum with puppy dog eyes and an inviting mouth as he sipped on his own drink.

"Is that the only reason you stopped by?"

His gaze shifted to his hands, then back to her eyes.

"Why else would I?"

She leaned closer to him, taking the cup from his hand. "I'm about to do something really stupid."

He stretched out his legs and leaned his back against the cot. "Do it."

Now *that* was a surprise. She liked it. Direct. Not a bullshitter or a time waster. Get to the good stuff fast, because it was occupying too much space in her brain. Maybe the looks she'd been trying to hide hadn't been so hidden after all.

The sooner they fucked, the sooner she could forget wanting it to happen.

Leticia straddled him and pulled off his Patagonia water-wicking T-shirt. Would the fantasy live up to the reality? He slipped her signature bandana over her eyes while his mouth found its way to her neck.

Fuck that, she thought. She didn't want fifty shades of anything. Leticia liked to watch. He needed to know exactly what to do, just in case they didn't have this opportunity again. Their bodies connected and it felt like the most natural place to be.

His saliva trailed across her flesh like comets across the universe, bringing her closer to God and death. When it came to sex, she was an unapologetically greedy woman. Tonight, her hips were the drums, his thrust the guitar, and the pleasure he was giving her was every instrument in between. For a man in control, he let her take the lead, remaining still as she did whatever she wanted. She leaned in and kissed his lips while riding him, and he felt as good as the fantasies she had played in her mind, early in the mornings and late at night when her desire to be touched was at its peak.

The ripples of their lovemaking kept her wanting more, heated like the tall vents in the sulfur fields, steady and unrelenting.

After sex that didn't seem to end but ended too soon, they lay on her cot inside her sleeping bag, sipping on rich boy brown liquor. Leticia felt comfortable enough to press him for more information.

"You really haven't seen anything suspicious down there?" she asked. "When people aren't honest, that's when shit hits the fan. This place is amazing on paper, and from what I have seen, it definitely beats some of the places I've seen on Earth. It's almost too good to be true."

"I promise you, there is nothing that we know of," he said. "I trust

Ramón. This place means everything because, as we speak, there's a bidding war among the wealthiest for who gets first dibs at development. That was out of my hands, but I did manage to ban anything except geothermal energy, and there will be no formal borders—anywhere. This did little to dissuade anyone. Most of them just want clean air and a safe place to call their new home among people like themselves." He frowned. "Bunch of elitist assholes. I want this place to enjoy a new sense of freedom… for everyone."

Leticia looked at him, wondering if he knew who he was. Jacob must have read her mind or felt her body tense. He kissed her shoulder.

"I plan to live here to make sure this place isn't turned into a billionaire's playground. They don't know it—not even the board—but I've got a secret lottery going to bring everyday people here. Young families from the worst parts of the Earth, bright students needing a boost in life, even orphan kids, once it's safe. The ones who are paying will hate it, but what's the use of all this power if you can't wield it. Teaching opened my eyes to so many things. They all think I'm a little trust-fund professor playing tennis on the weekend, with my nose in a book, who knows nothing of real life."

Leticia ran her hand across his chest and burrowed her nose into his skin. He smelled good. She hoped the scent would linger on her flesh.

"I guess you've found your empire, Caesar," she said. "You're right, though. I don't think the other billionaires will like your plans. Watch your back."

He turned to his side, placing his hand on the inside of her thigh. "Well, my Cleopatra, they don't have to like it. If they want borders, mediocre air, and sandy beaches for vacations, they can stay on Earth or terraform their own planet. Don't get me wrong, I don't plan on running the place like a dictatorship. I believe in democracy."

She slid his hand farther up her thigh. "Baby, you're smart enough to know that utopias don't exist. Humans are incapable of such a thing. Believe me, I know."

Those perfect blue eyes wavered.

There it was.

A little tell that she was on to something. Her job, as a soldier in the trenches, seeing the gnarliest shit had had a way of giving her a sixth sense. Her second sight developed from experiencing the real Heart of Darkness, yet also seeing extraordinary acts of kindness in the most desperate of situations. Soldiers weren't welcome most places ravaged by war and corporate exploitation, but Leticia had been fed and sheltered when she didn't think she had a hope in the world. In turn she did whatever she could to bring her helpers whatever they might need in this village or that, even if it meant breaking the rules.

Bullshit archaic rules that were meant to be broken enough times until they exploded so the new way could be ushered in.

"I accept your challenge," he said while caressing her. "Did I not surprise you tonight?"

"Not there," she said, "here." Leticia liked him before—well, liked his body, his eyes, that geeky shy boy smile—but now she wanted to know more. She liked a rebel, and if his ability in the sack had anything to do with his yoga, maybe it wasn't so bad after all.

"You must know the feeling is mutual." She kissed hard. It was easy to ignore the blinking on her watch, lying on a small pop-up side table next to her cot. Ramón had been messaging Leticia.

His last one was direct.

Jacob is nowhere to be found.

Now you are not answering.

Be careful sister. Don't be getting too close to him.

Trust me on this. I don't want to warn you again.

24

Dylan imagined that he floated downstream on an inner tube, with the motion of being suspended. Bright lights that might be sunshine escaping through tree branches passed over his closed eyelids, causing them to flutter. Then his perceptions shifted.

A heated blanket covered him to mid-chest. He had the worst heartburn he'd ever experienced in his life. It had to be the thing that leapt out of the egg and crawled into his suit just before he blacked out.

They told him there was nothing inside.

Desperate to impress and despite his intuitive fear he gave them the benefit of the doubt. Julia Yutani did this to him. Her reputation wasn't just whispers among the low-level workers. Coming from a colony on the verge of war, he should have known that the offer extended to him was too good to be true. They always were.

He was tied to a gurney, and it was moving. Dylan flexed both hands to test his strength. Would it be enough to break free? He knew where the dropships were located, if he could somehow escape. First, though, he needed to discover where *he* was.

The motion stopped. The sound of a metal door opening, followed by more movement. He could feel the straps easing off his chest and legs. *Now.*

His eyes snapped open and he threw his entire body weight into knocking the assistant in the face and ripping the key fob off their wrist. It would be needed to open the myriad of doors in this maze of a facility that had felt like an emperor's tomb from the instant he saw it. The recruiter had said that Jacob Vickers—one of *them*—was establishing a place of peace and opportunity for everyone.

To his surprise, when he arrived in a group that disembarked from the same dropship, Julia Yutani herself had greeted them. He had a sense of relief when he saw the half-constructed building, thinking how it would mean steady work with good pay. Then when the facility was complete, he was given the opportunity for a new position.

Now here he was fighting for his life. It was a slim chance, but one he had to take. If he survived, everyone would know about this.

Dylan bolted out the door while the assistant scrambled to get to their feet. Before they could reach him, he secured it shut. Turning, he found another member of staff in the corridor, staring at him in shock, not knowing how to react. Dylan wasted no time in driving him into the wall and hitting him hard enough to knock him out.

Wrestling in high school came in handy.

Grabbing this person's fob, as well, he glanced through a round window in the top half of a door on the opposite side of the corridor. A man he didn't recognize sat upright on a cot rubbing his chest and neck. They got to him, too. Using one of the key fobs he opened the door.

"Let's go!" he shouted. There was another door in the corner, with a blinking disk. Dylan touched the fob to the keypad, then handed it to the fellow on the cot. "Open as many doors as you can."

The man's eyes went wide in bewilderment, but he eased off the cot and stood on shaky legs. Dashing out again, Dylan hit the corridor as the lights switched off, then went blue. A loud alarm blared, and he pivoted to run toward the elevator that would carry him through the residential space and to the dropships. Perhaps he could free more prisoners.

With the fury of vengeance, Dylan ran through to find more like him as alarms wailed throughout the facility. He spotted a row of sealed windowless doors, and swiped the fob. The heavy doors began to slowly lift, but he didn't wait to see who would emerge.

Julia sat in her office making last-minute preparations when the lights dimmed and turned blue. She spun around at her desk and pressed the keypad on her chair.

A feed from the research area lit up the wall. She jolted upright before slamming her palm against the desk, then scrolled until she found the office of Brenda Moon. The doctor appeared, already speaking to someone not visible in the frame.

"*Julia!*"

"Are you watching this?" Julia demanded. "Fuck! Get him—but do *not* under any circumstances unleash or activate the bacteria. And do not terminate *anything*." In spite of herself, Julia could feel the fear taking over.

"*I'm on it,*" Moon responded. "*We'll do what we can to neutralize any immediate threat of Xenos breaking free, and resecure the facility. The fob he's carrying shouldn't open any of the Xenomorph holdings… Wait. I think I hear him. Stay where you are.*"

Julia paced as she watched the chaos on the wall. The experiment was supposed to remain under control, as were the test subjects, *all* of them. The company was counting on her. All eyes in the family scrutinized what she did here, to prove her worthiness to take her place on the Weyland-Yutani throne. The Weyland name would be reduced to a prop, and Yutani would wield the power and influence. No matter how many people had to die, they were just numbers.

Dylan What's-His-Name, that low-level piece of shit, would not ruin it. No way in hell.

She was still pacing, trying to make sense of her limited point of view when the alarm indicated that sector XIXI—also called "the Pen"—had been opened. Red lights flashed in unison with the blue. She slowly turned her head toward the door to her office. A fear she had never known slithered down the length of her neck until pangs of disbelief stabbed her in the stomach and chest. The flashing lights added to her panic.

Julia pulled up a screen that would locate Brenda's watch.

Nothing—no indication of anything.

She tried again, and again with no luck. With one last scrap of hope she called Brenda's office through the video comms. The connection opened, but it wasn't Brenda. A sweating Dylan appeared, with black blooms on his skin.

"*Wrong number, Julia.*"

"Dylan, stop this. I have an antidote. Money. We can make this right. I was wrong."

"*Nope. Wrong, bitch. Your friend here had all her files open for you. You. Are. Lying.*"

"Dylan, what are you doing," she said. "Do you know what you just did?"

"*Yes, I do now.*" He laughed with a crazed look in his eye. "*Checkmate. You die.*" The video link went dead.

She threw herself into her chair and began to type as fast as her fingers would move on the surface of her desk. Her hands were shaking. The Throne Room was still secure, a small miracle at the very least. She took a deep breath to calm her thoughts long enough to follow protocol, perhaps salvage the situation. It was time to do what she had never wanted to do, following Ramón's ability to see an entire chess game being played out.

If the Xenomorphs got out, she knew what was coming.

Then she dropped to her knees and crawled beneath the desk to a hatch door in the floor. Her handprint in the center unlocked it. This panic space might be her only hope of survival. Once safely inside, she could send an alert and continue with the chain reaction she and Ramón had designed.

Before closing it above her head, she wondered if Ramón had anticipated, even *hoped* something like this might happen. Maybe not on this scale, but it was certainly enough to ruin Jacob for good. She pushed those thoughts away.

The panic room was scarcely a room, more like a pod. She looked around hoping there were enough supplies. She wouldn't be climbing out until she was met with boots and proper weapons.

Underground and at the corner of the pyramid was the space where two worlds met. Dylan Graves opened the gateway to hell with the swipe of a fob. A still-young Xenomorph cried out, then paused, surveying its surroundings before moving through the opening.

Behind it, a succession of locks clicked, and walls opened. A cacophony of shrieks filled the corridor with the power of an ancient steam engine traveling at full speed through a tunnel. Every human on the adjacent wing could hear.

The small Xenomorph skidded across the floor of the corridor. A synth was there, and her eyes were wide as she scanned the intruder. In one quick slice her torso went left and bottom half to the right. White liquid erupted from her body. Strings of cables flopped uselessly.

The humans that had been freed saw what happened and screamed, their cries echoing along the corridor. The hallway turned, then turned again until it met itself, a serpent eating its tail. Larger Xenomorphs emerged and charged ahead toward the running test subjects.

The synth stared at the ceiling, expressionless, and whispered a command.

"Send all files."

"Yutani."

"Vasquez."

Julia woke up to a wet tapping on her bare foot, and something sliding off. She jumped up and looked around in fear. A few hours of sleep had passed, filled with nightmares. Wet streaks like tears slowly crawled down one of the walls with another single drip where her foot previously rested.

"Fuck!" she said, and the sound echoed in the tiny space. "This is supposed to be air and watertight. Fuck!" She wiped her toes with her hand, not wanting to think what was happening out there, but needing to know if the Xenomorphs had unwittingly caused damage to the guts of the building.

Turning on the monitors she half expected to see chaos and their snarling faces. What she saw scared her even more. On every screen view it was deserted and silent. Not a single body or flickering light. There was no way of knowing where they could be, or who was still alive. How long could she stay down here? And what about this leak? The monitors only showed a fraction of the cavernous facility.

She turned the monitor off again. Someone had to come. She was too important to be left behind, and Ramón should have landed by now. The alert on her watch indicated that he was here.

It was ironic. All her life she had never had to rely on any knight in shining armor—she was both the knight and queen. For the first time she had zero control over a situation, a circumstance she had, in part, created. Brenda Moon had warned her, and she didn't listen.

If anyone could get a handle on this situation, it would be Ramón. She curled back onto the soft padding in the small space she had designed for herself with a few more comforts. For the moment she would wait, and dream.

25

The morning arrived with the warmth of the sun brightening the haze swept in from the sulfur fields, mixed with a descending fog. The wind direction had changed again. The slight smell of rotten eggs made most of the crew push their freeze-dried scramble to the side.

Leticia and Jacob kept a distance but could not prevent their gazes from finding each other again. She knew it had to be kept quiet, for now. However, whatever was happening between them felt part of the plan, whatever it was. Desiree slid in next to Leticia with her plate in one hand and a steaming cup of coffee in the other.

"So far so good, jefa," she said. "I could get used to this treatment—and what a planet."

"I agree," Leticia replied. "In fact, my exact words. Would you consider staying out here long-term, if the money was good?"

Desiree put her fork down. "We are a good team," she said. "I would go to the steps of hell with you to kick the devil's ass. This is practically paradise. After you left last evening, the rest of the crew couldn't stop talking about a future outside of the Corps."

Leticia started to speak, then stopped.

Her eyes shifted overhead. From a distance came the sound of an incoming air vehicle. Desiree picked it up as well. She looked around at the others, who were eating without care. Jacob approached.

"Did you send anyone out this morning?" he asked. "I thought we were leaving together?"

She shook her head, then scanned the mess tent again. "No, but Ramón isn't..." Her brother darted through the flaps of the tent, accompanied by Nathan, who was on watch.

"There's a dropship with an emergency beacon approaching us," he said. "We can't contact the crew, and no video link."

Ramón's eyes were wide with pure terror—she had never seen him look like this. After an awkward silence, he spoke again. "We have to get to Olinka One, and *now*. How quick can we move, and more than move, be prepared for combat?"

Everyone was watching them now, with their ears silently pricked. Whatever situation was developing, her crew could handle it, but she had to keep the rest of them calm to avoid dealing with more than one fire—if indeed a fire was approaching.

Leticia stood and grabbed Ramón by the elbow, then made eye contact with each one of her team. When her gaze met Desiree, she tapped her forefinger twice against her chest. The signal to get combat ready. The others would know to follow. Then she leaned close into Ramón's ear.

"Keep your voice down. Let's go outside." Before leaving the tent, she said in a firm voice, "Keep eating, everyone. Nobody leaves here until we come and get you." One or two might not listen, but she had to still say it. Otherwise they would all go in different directions. If a threat loomed, that would be bad. She couldn't spare one of hers to babysit the entrance of the tent.

Jacob, Leticia, and Ramón left the tent without meeting anyone's stare. Her crew followed behind.

The large dropship weaved back and forth as it approached in the distance. By the size, it was meant to carry quite a few people and cargo, but there was no way to tell if it was filled with many, or just one person. Whoever manned the ship didn't know what they were doing, or some sort of damage had occurred to the navigation system.

Ramón spoke first. "I can get into Olinka's system and manually control the dropship—there's nothing I can't access. We blow it up. We have no responsibility to answer that emergency call. Jacob, you have every right to get rid of it without any legal issue. You are Weyland-Yutani."

Leticia shot Ramón a look as swift as a switchblade to the jugular, even though fear fluttered in her bowels. Judging from his expression, however, he felt the same.

"How did we go from an emergency call to blowing it up?" she demanded. "That makes no sense, Ramón. Whoever is inside could be in real trouble."

He paced their surroundings, distracted as if he fought off multiple demons screaming in his head. Sweat ran down his temples and gathered above his stubbled lip. He was usually a man who found success by keeping his cool. This was not that man. Leticia walked in front of him, following his roving head, so he had to look at her, give her some sort of straight answer.

"What aren't you saying, Ramón? If you know something, any lost lives are on your head." He still retained the look of terror. His usual steely determination returned, however, when he stopped his imitation of a caged beast.

"Get combat ready. I'll explain later."

Leticia turned to Jacob. "Get into our dropship and seal it shut."

He looked confused and slightly hurt. "But I—"

"Now," she said in a stern voice. "This is what you hired me for. You can watch from inside. Ramón will secure you." There was a heavy silence between them, a tie that neither wanted severed.

He complied with his jaw clenched.

"If I see anything—"

"I know," she responded a little softer. "I feel the same. Stay safe, and just do as I say. Go."

Ramón placed his hand on Jacob's shoulder to lead him to the ship. Leticia ran toward her crew, who waited together for their next orders. Nathan was hefting a flamethrower. Frida already had Leticia's helmet, with a bandana tied to the chin strap. Leticia grabbed the red strip of cloth and placed it around her forehead before securing the helmet.

"¡Oye! You will be my medic," she said to Mohammed. "Frida, get everyone out of the mess tent and into the ships. We don't have much time. Then join Desiree and Nathan with me, and be ready for whatever is on that ship. It's coming in hot. *Vámanos.*"

"*Shitty eggs, and now an unannounced visitor,*" Mohammed growled. "*I thought this was going to be easy.*"

"Same, brother." Leticia grabbed his forearm before leaving. Then she spoke into the mouthpiece attached to her helmet. "I want a perimeter, the best we can do right now. Be ready as soon as the ship touches down." She raised her head to the sky. The fog was turning thicker and smoke was blowing from the sulfur fields in claw-like gossamer wisps. Visibility was poor at best.

Perfect fucking timing.

The ship arrived skidding and bumping before coming to a halt.

"¿Qué es esto, Ramón?" she said into the comms, shouting over the clatter of the landing. "What aren't you telling us?"

Then Ramón stepped up beside her, but remained silent as the ship powered down. Soon there wasn't a sound, except for their heartbeats. The back hatch began to open. Leticia's crew stood in wait with their weapons aimed and fingers on the triggers.

A barefoot man in a medical robe emerged from the ship, appearing ashen-faced with a tinge of jaundice and a black rash. His hair clung to his skull from sweat and dark circles tinged his eyes. He looked around in confusion before lifting his hands in the air.

"I need your help," he called out. "I didn't know there were others out here. I have valuable information." Mohammed wasted no time rushing toward him, but Ramón ran to block his way.

"Don't!"

Leticia didn't take her eyes off the man. Jacob's voice crackled in her earpiece.

"*I'm coming out,*" he said. "*I need to see this. Dammit, this project has my name on it.*" By the time he finished, he was standing with them.

"Jacob, get back into the ship," she shouted. "Ramón, stop him. People, expect the unexpected. This don't smell right."

"*No, I'm staying,*" Jacob protested. "*Ramón, what the hell is this?*"

"Nobody go near the ship, or him!" Ramón shouted as loud as he could without a helmet and mic. "Leticia, he's a dead man. You have to trust me on this."

The newcomer continued to stumble closer, coughing and clutching his chest until he fell to his knees as his body seized up. Every vein in his neck and forehead protruded, his fingernails were black, and there were bluish-black lesions on his skin. These were getting darker the more violently he convulsed. He pressed both hands against the middle of his chest as he shrieked in agony and terror.

Ignoring Leticia's instructions, a few of the scientists and crew had come to see what caused the commotion. She shot them a quick look before turning back to the man. There was no time to deal with the bystanders.

There was a *crack* with the *pop* of a busted piñata, and a slimy creature exploded from the dying man's sternum. Bone, blood, and viscera erupted from his body with the speed of an active volcano. He clawed at his chest, trying to hold the sharp-toothed monster biting at the air as it whipped around to escape the ruined chest.

Leticia pulled her trigger, shooting with perfect marksmanship and causing the small thing to let out a high-pitched screech as it took a bullet to the head. The man fell to the ground, dead before he landed.

His blood oozed into the dirt, an unusual shade of red—as dark as blood in the moonlight as it congealed into a tar-like substance.

A louder hiss and a screech echoed from the ship. Mohammed dropped his medic bag and pulled the pulse rifle from his back. He ran to Leticia's side.

"*What the fuck was that, and what's still in there?*" he demanded. "*I trust you, sister, but I don't trust whatever the hell they were doing here.*" He lifted his weapon to aim it at the hatch. "*Some fucking vacation.*"

"*Holy shit,*" Desiree shouted.

Two full-grown Xenomorphs crawled from the ship on all fours, with their barbed tails weaving in the air like cobras ready to strike. Recognizing them from the records, Leticia nevertheless couldn't believe what she was seeing. Her bandana, saturated with sweat, released a single drop, managing to sting the corner of her left eye. This was no time to flinch.

Their bodies were as dark as pure obsidian and their razor fangs as sharp as that black glass when it had been fashioned into a blade. Obsidian was used by their ancestors to see the future—they would stare at their reflections until the truth was revealed. It was also called Itzli, after the god of stone, human sacrifice, and rock blades.

One of the scientists who had disobeyed her orders let out a screech and tried to run off. Before he could, one of the monsters leapt into the air and punctured his back with its tail. Talons swiped across the scientist's skull. Fragments of bone and chunks of flesh burst into the air amid fireworks of blood. These beasts were killers of men and showed the only truth they could bring—certain death. Frightening enough for Leticia to believe that dark gods existed, to craft such perfect harbingers of destruction.

One of the hissing gargoyles opened its jaws to reveal another mouth that punched in and out like a battering ram.

That was the last straw.

"Now!" Leticia bellowed. They fired off a volley at both Xenomorphs. The one ripping into the scientist was hit multiple times and sent writhing to the ground. Pieces of its body blasted into the air, flinging chartreuse blood toward the soldiers. Frida cried out as a drop landed on her exposed left hand and forearm. The ground where the rest of the grotesque body lay began to smoke from the acidic blood scorching the earth.

The second monstrosity turned to flee.

"Don't let it get away!" Leticia shouted. "Blast this bitch now! Do whatever you have to do." She followed the second Xenomorph's path with her rifle and continued to shoot, but it gave new meaning to the old phrase "bat out of hell." Desiree and Mohammed followed her lead.

The other bystanders ran to wherever they thought would be safest cover, stumbling and scrabbling as they did so. Dropping his rifle in favor of the flamethrower, Nathan ran toward the Xenomorph, but too late. The creature leapt *through* the flames with slimy jaws open and the energy and terror of Satan himself. With one swipe of its hand it cut his body in half. Leticia could hear the rest of her Marines scream and meet the creature with everything they had. She didn't have the heart or time to look at Mohammed, who screamed into the comms.

Finally the Xenomorph fell to the ground, a smoking liquified corpse. The acid leaking from its body burning into the ground. Tears streaming from his eyes, Mohammed continued to shoot rounds into the creature. He didn't stop until his weapon ran out of ammunition.

Frida touched his shoulder.

"He needs you. This doesn't."

Mohammed's chest rose and fell along with the smoke coming from his expended rifle and searing acid. He turned to Nathan's remains, and fell to his knees.

"I can't," he said, his voice small. *"Someone... please."*

Jacob ran out with a foil heat sheet and placed it over Nathan's body while Frida led Mohammed to his tent. As he walked away, he spat at Ramón's feet. Leticia patrolled the scene of horror that was not meant to be. Part of her couldn't believe this was real, and not a nightmare. El Diablo had manifested before her eyes for a dance to the death. It had happened so fast and without warning. The sense of betrayal overwhelmed her, combining with the nauseating odor from the sulfur fields mingling with burned flesh.

Then the wind stopped—the air went still, leaving them surrounded by the aroma of death. She couldn't bear to look at Ramón, yet she knew she had business with him, and it wouldn't be pretty. She didn't care who heard or saw, or how high his pay grade. One of hers was dead. She approached Frida who was having her burns attended to by one of the scientists.

"What's the damage?"

"Not too bad," Frida replied. "Kinda like being splashed with a million-degree hot grease. It didn't get my throwing arm, though, and Jim here has this crazy numbing cream."

"Good," Leticia said. "And thanks, Jim. Please get back into the ship as soon as you are finished. We'll let you know if we need you." She turned back to her Marine. "Frida, after you're patched up, cover the corpses until we have a plan." She moved along to check on everyone else.

The dropships were open again, with the civilians wanting to get a look at what happened. She could hear gasps and hushed conversations as they craned their necks.

"Desiree, you make sure no one touches a thing. Not Nathan, or those things. Threaten them with a bullet to the knee if you have to. Get them back into the larger ships. And check on Mohammed, will ya?"

"On it, jefa."

Leticia pivoted to find her brother. "Ramón! Where the fuck are you?" she bellowed. No one dared look in her direction. Jacob stepped out of one of the smaller dropships.

"We're here."

She was ready to unleash hell, and could see that he was just as enraged, but more than ever she didn't know who she could trust—especially if they hadn't dragged themselves through the trenches of basic training back on Earth.

Leticia had to be sure.

"Start talking, man."

Jacob had a manic glint in his eye. "Leticia, I promise I didn't know... The entire planet could be at risk. I don't want another world destroyed because of the bullshit greed and politics of my own company. This isn't me."

Leticia had to feel this out. Every part of her wanted to believe Jacob, yet...

"He's telling the truth, Leticia."

Ramón appeared behind Jacob at the bay door of the dropship, looking like a sad sack. Hearing those words, Jacob's face sank into an abyss of betrayal.

"Let's talk inside." Leticia looked over her shoulder. Desiree and Frida had everything in control—of course. So they entered the ship and closed the bay door for absolute privacy.

"We have no time to waste," she said, struggling to control her words. "You waste any more of my time, or more of my people get killed… We have a big problem, brother. I don't give a fuck who you are, I will see to it that you get what's coming to you. Your types never see a day of time for the dirty shit they do, but there are ways. You better come clean, *hermano*." As she and Jacob faced him, Ramón stood as if he were on trial.

"I know this is bad," he said. "Very bad, but we have to stay calm. Think about the investment, and—"

"Fuck!" Jacob screamed as he ran his hands through his hair. Leticia jumped at the sound. "You *know* this is going to fall on my ass. Or was that your plan all along? An inside job to bring the Vickers boy down. How much did you get paid?"

Ramón paused a beat.

"Julia Yutani is at Olinka One," he said. "There are Colonial Marines two days away—she sent an alert before she messaged me. They may be too late—and if there is a Xenomorph infestation, they will need more muscle and firepower."

"The fuck, Ramón?" Leticia threw her hands up and began to pace, her boots echoing in the enclosed space. "Xenomorph infestation? Is that what you call it? These are not a nest of cucarachas we can squash with a boot! You better tell me everything. First, I need to know if that sick and dead man was contagious. He didn't look right."

"He wasn't… isn't. Not yet, but we should dispose of everything as quickly as possible. Jacob, those scalding hot fumaroles aren't just valuable because of the geothermal energy here. We've been using it as a biological waste disposal system."

Leticia saw Jacob's hands shaking. "I'm not a violent man, Ramón," he said, "but I could knock you the fuck out ten times over right now."

Leticia stepped between the two men.

"Both of you get the hell out of here—and Ramón, you're on clean-up duty. You want to shit chaos, then pick it up."

Ramón jerked his head toward Jacob who stepped back and put his hands up.

"Don't look at me," he said. "She's in charge now. You take orders from the director of security."

Ramón's lips tightened. "Where do you want me, *jefa*?"

Leticia felt guilty for the small satisfaction she got from watching Ramón heave and gag with a bandana around his nose and mouth as he assisted with the clean-up. They didn't have proper disposal gear, because none of this was meant to happen in the first place.

Ramón lowered the corpse of the man into one of the bubbling hot mud pots roughly the size of a small pond, to dissolve it quickly. The brown liquid hungrily dragged the figure below the surface. He then had the honor of lowering the Xenomorphs into the same vent, with help from Mohammed, who wore Nathan's dog tags around his neck.

He requested to lower Nathan's body alone in one of the fumaroles. Leticia allowed him to do what he needed to do.

Unlike the humans, parts of the Xenomorph skeletons remained intact, dissolving slower. Both skulls rose to the top.

"This could be the nastiest game of bobbing for apples," Frida said, shaking her head with a scowl of disgust on her face. "Where are these damn things from?"

"Yeah, not even the planet wants these things." Leticia couldn't help to throw Ramón another dirty glance. "My tía, Roseanna, would say it's a sign. Take them both out before they are gone for good."

"I was joking," Frida said, "but you're the boss."

"I want to inspect them."

"Me, too," Jacob said. "This is insane, and it's not like we can get close to a live one. Have you seen what their guts do? They're pure fire inside." He turned to Leticia, who had a vacant look in her eye as the Xenomorph skulls smoked on the barren dirt. "You alright? What are you thinking?"

"I had an experience with a shaman," she said. "Like what you may have seen when you went to Peru. It was almost a premonition, now that I see these things. I mean, Roseanna would say it was the ancestors or even my mom guiding me, but no way…"

"What's the plan, Leticia?" Jacob asked.

"What do you mean, what's the plan?" Ramón pulled down his bandana from over his nose and mouth. "We go get Julia now. The clean-up is done. We pack up and leave."

"No." Leticia turned. "Fuck no, Ramón. We are *not* going in unprepared, Yutani princesa or not. I will send in a drone first. Our parents died somewhere out here. I'm not risking the same fate, if I'm in charge. They didn't have a choice, but I do."

"I know this place better than anyone," he protested. "I'm telling you we need to move now. You said yourself we can't waste time."

"On lies," she said. "No more wasting time on lies." They stood face-to-face. She met his gaze in silence, without any giving in.

He broke away.

"Fine."

The Xenomorphs continued to run the perimeter of their level of the pyramid, crashing into every possible weak point, causing damage to the communications and electrical systems.

Four of them gathered, hissing and with their heads swaying toward the floor. Lights flashed in intermittent bursts like the Fourth of July fireworks of red and blue. Without warning the sprinkler system let out steam and water.

Tossing anything that might be heavy enough to break through to freedom, the humans also scrambled to find any way out, only to be eviscerated by the Xenomorphs. The youngest of the creatures managed to slip through a door Dylan had opened. Going its own way, it roamed and shrieked as it attacked any sudden movement. It did not care nor understand the damage it continued to cause.

A larger Xenomorph hissed above its head, and slinked into an open office.

26

Julia couldn't put it off any longer. The pool of water was growing larger, and the stack of sodden towels and blankets stored in the small pod were useless now, yet streams of water continued to flow. She looked at the monitors again.

Nothing. Not a soul. She hadn't seen a single human or Xenomorph. The feed appeared exactly the same as before. This room was soundproof, so maybe they were all dead and she hadn't been able to hear what was going on in the spaces not covered by the cameras.

Taking a deep breath, Julia tucked a flare gun into her lab coat pocket. Her quivering right hand reached for the center of the hatch to unlock it again, and the door rose in silence. She poked her head out to look at the entrance to the office. It was open, but she couldn't remember if it had been left when her colleague ran out. It should have shut automatically and locked.

Her eyes narrowed when she saw the source of the water. "Shitty contractors," she grumbled to herself. The water cooler in the corner of the room had fallen over. A stream from the external pump still drained into the square glass container on the floor. Barely visible to the eye was a small seam in the floor where the tiles met.

It must have been someone looking for a way out. She had conjured up all kinds of outrageous scenarios of those things burrowing closer to get to her. Surely if a Xenomorph had been inside of here, though, there would be more evidence of it. She exhaled a sigh of relief. It would be an easy and quick fix and she could return to her pod.

Her eyes darted around.

Nothing but sweet silence.

Twisting to exit the hatch, she stood upright and stretched, then stepped over to her console. She hit a control and the display lit up. A banner blinked.

LIVE FEED

At the sight of those words, her entire body shook. The images on the monitor she had been seeing all this time hadn't been live. It was a still. What she saw now defied what she thought the Xenomorph capable of accomplishing.

The bodies...

Brenda...

The rooms and passageways were unrecognizable, covered in a bizarre resin that was clear in places, opaque in others—transforming crisp, squared-off walls into rounded, uneven tunnels. Here and there she could see masses along the walls, each roughly the size of a human body. That sent shudders through her again. In a short amount of time they had managed to reshape the facility to create their own world. These mindless beasts wanted a home.

Well fuck them. As much as she hated to destroy valuable assets, they would all have to be terminated when backup arrived. For now, she would go into the system and terminate the queens remotely. *What a waste.*

Julia returned to the hatch and grabbed the door to close it. Her hand came away wet... and sticky. She brought it back to inspect it. Before she could, her eyes caught something else. A hole in the ceiling that hadn't been there before. She would have to open the door to her panic room completely to see the extent of the damage, and couldn't bring herself to do it.

Returning to her computer, she called up a list of the security breaches. Her eyes fixed on a specific one.

THRONE ROOM

The view was obscured—just a vague blur of light and darkness. Most likely the creatures had covered the camera in that weird organic material. But she knew what was in each of the holding chambers, and she knew what to do about them.

One click, and the crowns would explode.

She reached out to tap the command.

Black, bony fingers with long talons filled her vision. Her head was snapped back, and she lost consciousness.

* * *

Leticia, Jacob, and Ramón sat in Ramón's tent watching the live feed from the drone as it appeared on the control tablet. Desiree operated the brand-new machinery with skill and expertise—at least *this* part of the investment could be used to their advantage.

She slowed its approach as it arrived at the entrance to Olinka One. No one uttered a word. The dark, semi-transparent pyramid showed no damage to the outside, and no sign of life.

"Have you heard from Julia again?"

"No. Nothing." Ramón stared at the building without looking at Jacob. "But she made it into the panic pod." He spoke to Desiree. "Focus on the lower levels, where the labs are located. It wouldn't make sense for most of the inhabitants to be in the residential quarters, given when I received the alert."

She brought the drone close to the ziggurat. Due to the reflective energy-efficient glass, there was no visibility from the outside.

"I'm switching to scan for bio readings, movement, and heat."

The readings pulsed across the screen as the drone continued to whizz at speed around the perimeter. Every second was another breath none of them inhaled or exhaled too loudly. Abruptly words blinked yellow at the bottom of the screen.

HUMAN LIFE DETECTED

"See!" Ramón whipped his entire body toward Leticia. "Can we go in now? There are survivors. We *have* to go in."

Desiree shifted her eyes to Leticia, and nodded. "As much as I hate it, I have to agree with him," she said. "We don't leave anyone behind."

Leticia continued to watch as the drone circled the facility that was as still as a corpse. She didn't like the look or feel of the situation. Surely people with any ability to get out would have tried, or showed signs of trying.

"What if they're like that guy who was infected with one of those things?" she said. "Alive but *not* alive. Ramón, what kind of weapons do you have stashed inside?"

"Not much," he admitted. "Just enough to control the more dangerous projects like the Xenomorphs. If there are humans being used as hosts, then we have to put them out of their misery as we encounter them, find Julia, and shut it down."

Leticia nudged Ramón's shoulder. "Are you saying *there are more* like him?"

"Probably." He waited a beat before continuing. "But we can't be certain without knowing what has happened inside. The exterior was meant to withstand a lot, in the event of an attack. The interior is intricate. The upper floors store dropships, with a single exit. That's how that guy must have escaped, taking the Xenomorphs along without knowing it. Once he was out, an electromagnetic field sealed the exit even before the physical doors closed.

"The middle floors are residential units, leisure facilities, and communal spaces," he continued. "The lower floors and those located beneath the facility are where the research is conducted. We figured if anyone needed to escape, it would be out the top to leave by ship, rather than on foot out the front door.

"There's a ventilation system at the bottom that could be used for an escape, I suppose." Ramón pointed. "The bars couldn't be opened or penetrated by a Xenomorph—they don't have the intelligence or the strength. We coated them with PTFE—polytetrafluoroethylene, a synthetic polymer that's super strong. There is one lift from the basement that goes directly to the top. The basement and lower floors should be completely locked down, unless someone overrides the security system.

"Only the ones considered not expendable have access to that."

As opposed to the ones who are *expendable*, Leticia thought bitterly, but she didn't say it. There wasn't time.

Jacob turned to Leticia. "I don't like Julia, but we have to attempt to get her. Otherwise it will be very bad for the company… and she *is* a human being. If our competition gets wind of this…

"We have to try," he added. "This is bigger than her or me."

"Alright. Let's go." Leticia placed a hand on Desiree's shoulder. "Move to the dropship, but keep an eagle eye on every corner with the drone. Report the most insignificant thing you see, if it seems the least bit out of the ordinary. Keep the entire perimeter scanned."

"Got it, jefa."

Leticia turned to Ramón and Jacob. "You two, follow me. We have a lot to discuss before we crack open Olinka One. Ramón, are you sure reinforcements will be on the way?"

"I'm certain," he replied. "Julia would not leave herself in any position without an escape plan. Her family would not have allowed her to come here without one."

Leticia stepped outside. Ramón and Jacob followed. Soon it would be dusk, and the majority of their party was sticking close to the vessel in case another unexpected danger reared its ugly head. She spoke loudly enough for everyone to hear.

"I need everyone to gather around," she said. "If you know of anyone in their tents or the mess tent, then go get them. I'll give you five minutes."

"What are you doing, hermana?"

Leticia ignored Ramón. The small group of civilians and even smaller Raider crew found their way to her. She tried her best to not appear frightened or angry about the place in which they found themselves. It made her think of when she had been forced to swim to shore when her Narwhal was sabotaged.

She had to focus and move forward the best way she could.

"Okay, people—listen up," she said. "My crew are used to dealing with the unexpected. Well, not with blood-thirsty monsters from space, but it's still what we were trained to do. The rest of you are probably frightened and I understand." She paused, and added, "Reinforcements are on the way."

There was a murmur from the crowd. She could hear sighs of relief.

"But all of you—everyone except my crew—will remain here with the dropship until they arrive. We are leaving to make an extraction, and all of my team will go with me. I can't spare any of them to stay behind."

The civilians grumbled as they whispered among themselves.

Leticia raised both hands. "I know it's not ideal," she said. "Worse than that, it's shit. But we can't babysit. You will be safer near the two dropships, until you can be flown out and picked up by the Marines. Those of you who know how to use a weapon will be given one, until we run out. Frida will be waiting by the mess tent. Make your way to her. Absolutely *no* wandering beyond camp." She looked around to make sure they understood. "There are enough supplies to last until backup arrives. We leave as soon as you're all secured."

Leticia felt terrible, as if she was abandoning them, but this was the decision that had to be made. She just hoped it wasn't like a parent who said they were going out to get cigarettes and never coming back. This was the safest option for everyone.

She turned to Ramón. "Happy now?"

He didn't reply and couldn't meet her gaze.

The Raiders wasted no time preparing weapons, double-checking supplies, and securing the civilians they had to leave behind. They silently gave her the thumbs-up as she passed. This was why she loved her crew. They worked as a team, and without question. A true wolf pack, Las Lobas. When satisfied with their progress she called Ramón and Jacob over and climbed into the dropship. Frida and Mohammed followed soon after, and they all buckled into the passenger compartment. Desiree was already in the cockpit.

"*Ready?*" Desiree said over the comms.

Leticia took one more look at the screen on the tablet. Those they had to leave behind remained in their tents, and the hatches for the other two ships remained open in the event they needed a quick escape.

"Let's do this. Take her as fast as she will go."

As they lifted into the air Leticia noticed that Jacob kept his eyes on Ramón, one leg bouncing in place. He sat across from him without any of the passive or relaxed nature he always exuded.

"Before we get there," Jacob said finally, "you better talk fast. How the *hell* did the Xenomorphs get here? It was your job to make sure this colony followed my vision. A vision I thought we shared!"

"You really want to do this now? In front of others?"

"Yes," Jacob said. "These people are putting their lives on the line for something you and Julia did."

Ramón shook his head, vitriol in his eyes.

"You delusional trust-fund school boy. The perfect little niño," he said. "You have no clue how many people despise you. No matter which way you present yourself, the company used you to look good.

Fake and meaningless gestures to trick everyone into thinking they were changing direction, and get regulatory bodies and the press off their asses. You're nothing but a corporate tourist who needs to be running a charity on Earth."

He looked Jacob straight in the eye. Leticia had to give him credit—he had cojones.

"This has only been a success because of me," Ramón continued, not giving Jacob a chance to reply. "You are ruining the company with your stupid ideas of 'peace.' The math didn't make sense, and we had to generate revenues to keep your little project alive—all to satisfy those in the company who shared your views, and to justify it to the board of directors.

"Yes, we have been using Olinka to study the Xenomorph... and other things. They have been here since long before you became involved."

Jacob was silent for a moment.

"After the news breaks of what has happened here, are you hoping to save your skin by saving Julia?"

"You don't have a clue," Ramón said. "Julia was meant to be there all along. We need to salvage Olinka at all costs. The Yutani family is heavily invested in everything we are doing."

Leticia shifted her eyes to Jacob. Ramón's words were stinging. She could tell because she lived with him long enough. Part of her felt hurt for Jacob. No one wanted to be a puppet.

To her surprise, Jacob's demeanor remained calm.

"The difference between me and you, even me and the company, is that I know who I am without any of this. I want something greater than myself. I can survive stripped, and widdled down. Same with your sister. Her biggest concern in all of this was for her team. That's why she said yes to me." He leaned in. "Be hurtful all you want, but right now you have to give us every last detail concerning the shadow operations—this is a life-or-death situation.

"When we get through this crisis, I'll expect your resignation."

Leticia believed every word he said, and even felt bad for her brother—almost. He'd just got a taste of his own medicine.

"Whatever," Ramón spat out. "I don't care anymore."

"Of course you don't. You're probably already set for more than a lifetime."

"Niños, you've said your piece," Leticia said, cutting in. "We will arrive soon. If it won't help the mission, I don't want to hear it. Not now. This is the only moment that exists. We survive one minute, then survive the next."

Ramón cleared his throat. "Perhaps you should know that, like an Egyptian or Mesoamerican pyramid, the facility has been created with smaller chambers. It's not just the levels I mentioned before. There are the secure spaces where the team worked with the Xenomorphs—and other pathogens in development—but they're sealed tight. Julia's distress call would have ensured that.

"When I unlock any of those doors," he continued, "it will probably unlock the other large entrances or exits, including the dropship bay. I can't isolate the front entrance. And whatever damage has been done..."

Leticia slowly reared her head toward him. "This just gets better and better. We're walking into a tomb, then, and might let out the fucking mummy at the same time. Is that it?"

"I don't know, sis," he said. "I'll bring up the blueprints and see if I can find a hack." Ramón buried his head in his tablet, and Jacob turned to Leticia.

"Hey, can I ask you a favor—not that you owe me one."

"You can ask."

"I'm a bit embarrassed, but that won't matter if I'm dead." He scratched the back of his head. "You mind showing me how to use a weapon?"

Leticia could see the fear, and his desire to contribute in some way. She suspected that given the chance he would do anything to save Olinka. She had to give it to Jacob, he had heart and soul, even if he was naive. And she couldn't blame him for being taken in. Ramón had been a charmer all his life. He and Julia had created an elaborate plan with everyone else just bricks in their building.

Ironically, it was a pyramid they would enter. How many economic disasters had been built on such foundations?

"Alright, I will give you a crash course," she said. "It could save your life, or someone else's." She lifted her pulse rifle. "La Loba" was written in white across the body of the weapon.

"La Loba." He smiled as he said this. "The wolf?"

"Yeah, my roots are in Mexico." Leticia ran her fingers across the writing. "But if I were to be anything, it would probably be jaguar. In the Raiders we have our pack, and we fight like a pack, but the pack is only as strong as each wolf."

"That makes sense," he said. "So can we start that training now? Run through the basics. I don't give up easily on the things I want." A ray of hope glinted in his eyes as he said this. Part of her hoped she was included in the things he wanted.

Of course, if they were dead, romance didn't matter.

"Sure," she replied, and she showed him the basics of using the rifle. Mostly just made sure he could point and shoot. "When we land it will be dark. We'll need to create a perimeter of sensor mines, even if the building seems secure. Contain the threat as much as possible. And we need to stick together at all times." Remembering how well he'd obeyed orders before, she put extra emphasis on her words.

Then as the dropship got closer, they went silent. Leticia gave Mohammed and Frida a glance they would recognize as a sign to prepare for anything.

"*We have arrived,*" Desiree said from the cockpit. "*I'm landing us.*"

As soon as they touched ground, Leticia unbuckled herself from her seat. "Mohammed, get those sensor mines ready. Program them for anything bigger than you." She moved to the hatch to be the first out, rifle in hand.

A two-hundred-fifty-foot pyramid of reflective solar glass stood before her, utterly black in the approaching night. The main research facility, Olinka One. What different stories she heard from Jacob and Ramón. There were no visible lights, mayday signals, or *any* signs of human activity. Still not a trace of destruction to the outside.

Frida was next to her. "I don't know what's worse, a ruined war zone where you can guess what your opponent has in their pocket, or something like this. It's so silent, we could be entering another dimension." She nudged Leticia. "Good thing we aren't virgins—otherwise we would all be dead within minutes."

"No shit, and that's what worries me. The silence, I mean, and the dark. We're going in blind until we get the drone inside. Those Xenomorphs are big fuckers, they won't escape any radar, but they're predators, too, and will hunt like it. I'm not dealing with those things in the dark. We wait for daybreak." She looked up. "It won't be long—this ain't Earth, as much as it may feel like it.

"Seeing those things, it's made me feel farther from home," she added, "but closer to my mom. If Julia is in her 'panic room' then she can wait a little longer. To tell the truth, my gut says there are no survivors."

A voice from behind startled her. It was Ramón.

"I know whatever I say won't be heard," he said, "but we should act now, and pray it's enough."

"Go on in, be my guest, Ramón."

He could pout like a child, because it wasn't his show anymore. She scanned the area in the encroaching night. There was more vegetation here, and the cliffs backing into the ocean weren't far off. The faint scent of saltwater wafted in the breeze. The two moons in the shape of crescents glowed above the dusty indigo sky turning dark. The stars would be out soon, and in a few short hours the sun.

"Finish up prep and get a little shut-eye, Frida."

Jacob joined her, but didn't show any of the pride he'd held when they arrived on the planet.

"It's even more impressive than the photos," Leticia offered.

"I know," he said sadly. "Since I started this project, I had high hopes for how this first meeting would go."

"Let me go check on Desiree and Mohammed, and I'll come back to give you another short lesson with the pulse rifle."

"Anything I can do?"

She smiled and touched his cheek, remembering how good it felt to make love to him. Might have been the last time either of them experienced ecstasy.

"Pray."

Leticia left Jacob to check on their small band of lobas. Frida and Mohammed unloaded and took stock of the cache of weapons and ammunition. Desiree still scoured the perimeter with the drone. In covert operations they sometimes only had six, now they would have to make do with five.

The feeling of being diminished cut into her confidence, especially when she remembered how the Xenomorph towered over Nathan. It was her responsibility to keep him alive. To keep all of them alive.

Fuck the facility. Let it burn with the same acid fury as the blood of a Xenomorph. She turned the situation over in her mind, trying to see it from different directions, like trying to figure out the best place for a sniper to make the cleanest kill shot.

Desiree rushed toward her.

"We have incoming communication, and I think you'll want to take this." As they ran back to the dropship, she added, "They're already in orbit."

The fuck?

Leticia hit the comms. "This is Director Vasquez."

"Vasquez?" the voice said, sounding strange, and... *"Yeah, so we received a distress call. We're in orbit, but not over your position, so we can be ready to roll in a few hours. What's your plan?"*

"First, how long have you been in orbit?"

"Stand by," he responded. Then, *"Been here for a hot minute, on orders not revealed."*

"Well, that's damn good news for once," she said. "First light we head into Olinka One—I don't want to risk going in the dark with this one."

"Smart. We will be there as soon as we can. How hot is it? Our satellite shows things pretty quiet."

"Believe me when I say this threat isn't quiet. So far it's contained inside the facility. When we go in, that might open the door—no time to give you all of the details. There are civilians not far from us, with two dropships. They need a place to dock. Also be aware, we have created a perimeter of sensor mines for anything bigger than your largest soldier. Just be ready to use all the firepower you got. It's an alien species."

Leticia expected a snort, or silence. She received the latter.

"Gotcha," he said. *"See you soon. Stay alive."*

"Thanks. Desiree will connect you to our personnel comms, so we can stay connected once we go in. God speed."

"Roger that."

Leticia exhaled. The heaviness in the front of her skull lightened and the stinging that rimmed the inside of her eyes—where she held back her tears—burned less. She walked out of the dropship to let the group know the news.

"Everyone, try to get some sleep, or at least pretend. As soon as the sun rises, we move in." She jerked her thumb toward the cockpit. "That was backup. They're a few hours away, but they will be here soon."

Frida and Mohammed slapped hands—it was the closest she'd seen to a normal response from Mohammed. That was reassuring. Jacob sat on the ground, staring at Unalike One.

Leticia stood there, looking up at the burgeoning stars. In that instant she felt closer to her mother than she had ever before. Somewhere in the gases, meteors, icy comets, radiation, dark matter—all of it—Jenette Vasquez lived on. Leticia took a deep breath.

Keep us safe. Guide me, por favor.

She touched the gold cross around her neck and took the bandana out of her pocket, placing it across her forehead. It didn't matter much where her father was, because he hadn't faced the same battle as her mother—the battle that was Leticia's. Still his face flashed in her mind, and she said a prayer for him, too. Theirs had been a star-crossed brief affair that brought her and Ramón into existence, and ultimately to this moment in time for a destiny now out of their hands.

Leticia would never understand the machinations of humans, but she did understand herself and the desire to survive like the soldaderas during the Mexican Revolution, the pachucas in the 1950s LA riots, the migrant farmworkers, the boys who couldn't afford college and were drafted to fight in Vietnam. All the way back to her indigenous ancestor warriors suiting up in brightly painted cotton armor as they fought the conquistadors.

Their souls resided here and now she called on their power to survive this fight.

Ramón approached. "I have something I need to say, but in private."

"You have five minutes," she said, leading him a short distance away. "I'm teaching Jacob how to use a rifle. Is it more important than a man not wanting to die?"

"In my research, I uncovered all the files relating to the Xenomorphs and all previous encounters. Our mother died in one of them. They were there to neutralize the threat on a small colony. LV-426."

"And you brought them here," she said. "You're fucked up, Ramón."

"I suppose I wanted to know that I could change the course of destiny, and harness whatever destroyed her. That I was smarter and death could be… something I owned. It wouldn't hurt me because it was my possession."

"But instead, it's just doing what it does best," she said. "You can't cheat the stars, and death belongs to no one, but comes for us all."

"She was a hero," he said. "According to the files, she gave everything until the very end." He looked into her eyes. "I was wrong about all the things I said about her as a kid. She would have been proud of you."

Leticia wiped her eyes and touched her bandana. "You have a way with timing, but at least it gives me even more reason to fuck these things up. I hope you do what's right when we get in there. You need to make her—and yourself—proud."

Leticia walked away. She couldn't process this right now, but she could use the vengeance coursing through her veins. Those things would see who had acid for blood. She approached Jacob.

"You ready for a fight? Let's go over that weapon for you."

He rose from the ground then kissed her hard. She didn't care who saw.

"I'm ready," he said, "and I did that in case I never get the chance again. You're an extraordinary woman, Director Leticia Vasquez." She kissed him back.

"I have one helluva story, that's for sure."

27

The onyx pyramid reflected the morning light as it absorbed its radiation. The two moons were still present, remaining on watch until they would have to relinquish themselves to a mightier foe, a sun.

Leticia had planned to remain on watch, but Mohammed couldn't sleep and took her spot. "We need your leadership, which means you need rest," he said. "This is one job you can't sleep on. For Nathan."

"Mohammed, I'm sorry," she said. "This was not supposed to end up like this."

"I know." He closed his eyes and touched Nathan's dog tags. "I feel responsible, thinking there was anything more than war in the universe. Nathan and I saw the money, too. We get through this, the rest is a tale yet to be told. Now go sleep." Leticia reluctantly left, and drifted off quickly next to Jacob on top of a sleeping bag on the floor of the dropship.

Ramón could fuck off if he didn't like it.

It was the nightmare of her experience in the temazcal, years ago, that alerted her to the breaking day. The dark hands of the Xenomorph had her by the neck, and there was nothing she could do about it. Then she woke up. When Leticia emerged, Frida was already distributing energy bars to the rest of the group and pouring hot instant coffee.

"Last one for you, jefa."

"Thanks." Leticia took the coffee that went down hot and soothing. She raised one hand to get the group's attention as they prepped themselves and checked ammunition. "Las Lobas, are you ready?" They saluted in response, giving a *whoop*. "Desiree, do you still have the drone stationed on the dropship port at the top of Olinka One? I need eyes, in the event something wants to escape."

"It's already in place," Desiree replied. "Other than that, we are locked, loaded, and ready to fuck shit up. Still no update from the Eagles above, though."

So much for good news, Leticia thought darkly. "Mohammed, you're on party patrol. Keep the scanner looking for any movement that ain't us, and especially bigger than us."

"On it, jefa, but why do I feel like I'm living the song 'Hotel California'?"

"Ándale, then." Leticia finished her coffee in a gulp of heat that burned her mouth, then tossed the cup into the dropship. "We listen to the Eagles drunk as fuck when this shit is over." Mohammed nodded in agreement, and hefted a flamethrower—the one Nathan had carried.

Ramón had the tablet in his hand, ready to override the facility's main computer to open the doors.

"Open sesame..."

Leticia turned to Jacob, who now wore fatigues. He had stripped himself of his old life of the Eton boy, Oxford grad, and CEO. He held his pulse rifle, looking ready to fight and die. She admired him for that. He had no high horse, or if he did it wouldn't last long. The first time she saw a man die it looped through her brain with the same motion of an old movie in a projector. The silence in his eyes, with his brains splattered across a wall, made her aware of the illusion of time.

He had been talking to her one second and gone the next. The unknowing was the worst part of it. The inability to face an adversary head on was as close to death as she could get. When the anxiety built to an unbearable level, was life worth living?

You have to push through those illusions of shadow and imagination, past the difficulty of the moment to move forward.

The entrance that was as wide as three people, but felt like the mouth to hell the size of a pinhole. Leticia raised her arm and waved everyone to move forward. They all carried pulse rifles—all except Ramón. Just as well. She had no desire to die from friendly fire. He wore Raider-standard protective gear, though, and a helmet to stay connected.

Looking to the clear sky one more time she remembered sitting on Roseanna's back porch, barefoot with a book in her hands and the wind chimes serenading her. She hoped Santa Muerte was bringing their backup closer.

The inside of the facility no longer resembled anything created by a human hand. The simplicity of the interior—with clean lines, minimal decoration, and modern art seen in the photos taken when first built—

was nowhere to be seen. Viscous slime crawled down the walls. Some sort of hardened resin morphed the entire space to a level of an inferno only captured in fiction, from the writings of a wild imagination. But this was real.

The grooved walls resembled carved wet stone as they glistened beneath the pulsating emergency lights. This was no haunted attraction at Halloween. It was a temple garden for dark gods, the Xenomorphs. Those creatures had taken over.

Despite the heat and humidity of the interior, matching that of the towns close to what remained of the Gulf of Mexico or the re-established jungles on Earth, she felt her body go cold. The monsters had wasted no time creating a hive. If this happened in a confined space, in such a short amount of time, what would happen elsewhere? What might an entire world look like? Only a fool could think they could be tamed, made into bioweapons.

No one spoke, their breathing heavy in their helmets, shared with one another via earpieces. The farther they ventured, the hotter it became.

"This way."

His voice startling, Ramón guided them through the facility that could have been the guts of an organism. It was the anatomy of alien life taking hold doing what it did best, surviving. They continued on with slow deliberate steps, through an open thick vaulted door with triangle locks. The archway had been transformed to a trellis of onyx pumice dripping in precipitation and slime. The path spiraled deeper into the facility until it opened up again to what had been a large lab.

Cylinders contained small things, almost spider-like with legs that looked like the fingers of a bruja and a tail that could be the cousin of a rattlesnake. Four other containers held clear water that appeared harmless. The fourth had a powerful microscope attached to an extendable robotic arm, amplifying the contents. It showed what lurked invisible to the human eye.

"Híjole, Ramón," Leticia said. "What the hell?"

"We've linked Xenomorph DNA with the common pork tapeworm," he said, as if it was a perfectly natural thing. *"It's meant to contaminate water systems."* Writhing coiled parasites swam in unison. Mouths

snapped open and shut and were lined with jagged teeth. Barbs edged their bodies.

"*I want nothing to do with any of this,*" Jacob said, not disguising the disgust in his tone. "*We've fought so hard and long to bring clean water to humans everywhere, and here you are creating a weapon that will do the opposite.*" He growled. "*No wonder half of my family isolated me in England. The other half is pure poison. While I'm trying to spur human evolution to move ahead, they're finding more cunning ways to murder each other.*"

Clear chambers hung along a wall, tinged with frost that indicated refrigeration. In them were multiple Xenomorph corpses in various states of decay. Their bodies were deformed, the shiny carapace mottled.

Leticia's anger has risen above her fear. "I just need to know one thing," she demanded. "Why are you doing this? Why are you studying something like that? You can't bring it back to Earth, or take it to any world. These aren't dogs you can train, and they kill without mercy."

Ramón remained silent.

"*Answer, Ramón,*" Jacob said. "*I want to know, too.*" He gave her brother a look of disgust. Ramón shot him an equally acrimonious glare.

"*I'm doing what we do best,*" he said. "*We manufacture life and death, and sell it to the highest bidder. It's always been that way. You can't build better worlds if you are fighting over them. These will stop the fight once and for all, because no one will doubt our superiority.*"

Leticia could tell he was still holding back.

"Ramón, if we don't know what this is we can't fight it."

He stopped and pointed to a row of smaller tubes, a size that could be held in the hand. Something black shimmered inside.

"*We've been engineering our own weapon for use against the Xenomorphs,*" he explained. "*It's a type of necrotizing fasciitis—flesh-eating bacteria that passes quickly between the creatures. When activated, it can also be lethal to humans. With a high enough dosage, these samples can be used against the aliens. Their immune systems are tough, but we managed to crack them.*

"*The true test will be to infect a queen,*" he continued, "*then for her to pass the bacteria to her eggs. You should see the early footage of their reactions when the bacteria is introduced into their environment. With just the proximity, the Xenomorphs can sense the danger.*"

"*What does it do to humans?*" Desiree asked.

He didn't answer.

"*Burn this fucker down,*" she said.

"*Are you joking?*" he responded, his voice rising. "*We've worked too hard to lose all this valuable research, all this time, effort, and investment. None of our lives are that valuable.*"

"*Heads are going to roll.*"

"*Whatever, Jacob,*" Ramón spat. "*Yours has been on the chopping block for a long time now, you know.*"

"*You think I'm just a stupid boy scout? Of course I know. Hell, Julia Yutani is probably the chairman of that board.*"

"*Boys, callete!*" Leticia said. "Holster your balls." She turned to her brother. "Where are we going, Ramón?"

"*Here.*" He pointed to his tablet, then moved on.

Though she didn't want to show it, her skin was crawling. There was nothing secure about this place, and according to Ramón some bubonic plague-level bacteria just waiting to be let loose. Nothing about this was right. Leticia moved closer to Desiree.

"I want you to cover Jacob." Then she addressed Jacob. "You can expose all of this, but only if we manage to survive. If those things hate the bacteria, our only way may be to take it with us. So grab a vial. In fact, everyone grab one."

"*Say what?*" Frida said. She stared, but didn't move.

"There really is no other way," Leticia said. "We already have one foot in the grave. Better to take our chances where we find 'em. Once we get away from here, we can drop that bacteria shit into one of those steaming mud holes. Ramón, you said it had to be activated—how does that work, anyway?"

"*Um, aerosol, water supply, even a puncture wound, like the source fasciitis.*" He moved with the others to take a sample, stopping briefly at a desk. "*Now can we get out of here, and find Julia?*"

"Lead the way, Ramón. I want to get out of here as quickly as you do."

"*This way,*" he said, but he looked perplexed. "*We are… getting close… but it doesn't seem to be the panic room.*"

The path that had led them to the lab carried on spiraling down, with the heat intensifying. They turned on the lights that were attached to their rifles. The walls became thicker with the Xenomorph-made onyx insulation, and the floor a sodden mire of something she didn't want to know. Leticia looked behind them. It was as dark as the hand of the Xenomorph and the souls of the men who created them.

They moved into a larger space that could have been any place in the facility, with no discerning markers. Their lights strobed to illuminate bone and viscera. The open chests of the inhabitants resembled the remnants of a chorizo con huevos taco regurgitated by a drunk. It was an alien cathedral of gore, pain, and reproduction.

Some of the bodies were trapped in icicles of sludge and hardened mucus. Human waste covered the floors from the suspended bodies. The ammonia stung Leticia's eyes. Shards jutted in every direction, preventing any possible escape. The room breathed humidity, giving the facility its own atmosphere to help the Xenomorphs thrive in an inferno paradise.

To their horror, some of the poor souls attached to the walls were clinging to life. They wheezed and gasped for air, not realizing they no longer needed it—every life-form sought survival above all else. While it was as natural as breathing, now it only fed what grew inside of them. The sound was a hymn of desperate torture.

If Santa Muerte walked anywhere, it would be here. Her robes would bless this unholy ground and eat this torment.

"*We need to take their pain away,*" Mohammed said.

"I agree." Leticia turned toward Desiree, and her gaze was met with rows of gooey eggs pulsating with their own tempo of weeping slime. "Oh, shit," she breathed, "this is one cascarone fight I do not want to be in."

"*I can't believe…*" Ramón began. "*I knew they were dangerous, but this.*" His face showed nothing but terror now, as he continued to walk while trying to hold his vomit at the sight of the bodies. In the corner was the decomposing corpse of one of the queens. The hood on the roof of her had exploded from the inside.

"Ramón, what is that?" Leticia asked. "It doesn't look anything like the ones we encountered before." She shone her light directly on the dead creature.

"*That may be La Reina,*" he said, and she gave him a weird look. "*We raised more than one queen. See that metal halo above the fanned crown on her head? It shocked her with electricity that fried her from the inside out. It could have released the bacteria, if we chose, but we relied on her for eggs. It's good news that she's been killed—whoever did that must have got them all. We can't be sure, though, unless—*"

He stopped abruptly and turned his light toward the wall.

"*No,*" he said in a hoarse whisper.

Leticia froze.

28

Ramón couldn't help but feel his own ribcage throb and give way to the sharp-toothed bite of grief as he saw Julia's pale face. She moaned as her eyelids fluttered, and winced with the light on her face. Next to her was Brenda Moon, and the other people involved in the initial stages of the experiments. Some appeared to have been dead for some time, with decay setting in. Flesh flaked away in the natural cycle of things.

"Ramón..." she said, her voice a croak. "You came for me." To see her like this made him want to climb into the cocoon with her. It was a greater love than he even felt for his own children.

"Yes," he said. "I'm here. I love you. I left everything behind to be with you. We are going to get you down, right now." He frantically looked to Leticia. "Help me get her out of here. Please!"

Julia spoke again in a voice barely audible.

"Ramón, look at me. It's too late. Don't bullshit." She coughed, a dry, hacking sound. "I love you. It was always you... My files... Nothing. Don't let them get out. We only managed to destroy one. Destroy them all. Yutani has a plan... we talked about, already in motion. You'll have everything you need."

He darted his head toward Leticia, but Julia moaned in pain and he turned back as her head lolled. She looked toward Jacob.

"I'm sorry, Jacob, but this involves you. You'll be blamed for all of it, and Vickers will be forced out. Those who supported you… also discredited. Run. No other choice for you."

Her head slumped forward.

"Julia!" Tears flooded from Ramón's eyes. He had known death intimately all his life, but now it stared back at him for the first time. Coming here had been his way of course-correcting. This was his way of leaving Mary Anne and his children for Julia. This was supposed to be their own garden of Eden, a world they could build together with more money than could be spent in several lifetimes.

It was also his way to make it right with Leticia and give her a big payday. He didn't want her to fall into any of the traps of his aunt Roseanna, his mother, or Cutter's family. Leticia was his only true family, after all.

Julia's body began to convulse—the chestburster was trying to emerge. Pink foamy saliva oozed from her mouth. The unbuttoned portion of her blouse revealed the flesh between her breasts, and it was bubbling.

"*Ramón, look at me now!*" Leticia screamed.

He reared his head toward her. His eyes went wide as Leticia raised her gun, and she shot Julia in the chest four times. The chestburster shrieked a shrill cry before falling dead from the gaping hole. Ramón's entire body jerked at the sound of every bullet that echoed in the chamber of life and death, a birthing suite and cemetery at the same time.

"*I'm sorry, Ramón, but it had to be done, and you weren't going to do it,*" his sister said. "*I wouldn't want you to. If you want to make it right, then do as she requested. Get all of her information about these things—and we better move fast, because if they didn't know we were here before, then they know now.*"

Wordlessly Ramón nodded. "For Julia," he said, finding his voice. "We need to go to her office, adjacent to the lab. It isn't far."

Jacob squared off with Ramón again, holding his pulse rifle high to his chest. "*What the hell was she talking about when she said I had to run? What did you two do to get rid of me, and apparently any Vickers?*"

Without any emotion on his face or in his voice Ramón answered. "We were going to discredit you with these projects, and take over the entire planet but still keep the experiments going while you were the one being indicted. Or an accident would happen. Your death would uncover all the Vickers misdeeds, and anyone who supported a Vickers."

Jacob shook his head with a disgusted snarl.

"Lead the way. I'll deal with you later."

Ramón couldn't look at him. He refocused on his tablet.

"In here. Leticia, I don't know if you heard Julia, but we had a plan. A chain reaction of sorts in the event of any emergency. All her files would be transferred to me, then to you. You need to do the same. There's no time, in case we don't make it out." He said this while typing. "Right, who is your backup?"

She looked around. *"Jacob and Desiree of course. You think I'm going to let you and that bitch frame an innocent man? And make me part of it. Were you going to bribe me, or bump me and my team off eventually? We are done, brother. I fucking swear."*

"No," he said. "You would have believed it, too. And no offense, but Desiree? She has no power in the scheme of things. Jacob I can understand, but the files might not help him. It's all designed to point to his guilt."

"No offense taken," Desiree said sarcastically.

"Oh, she has power," Leticia said, *"and she's not part of the Weyland-Yutani gang. How can I trust you after all that has been said, all your lies from day one?"*

"You don't have a choice, and I'm trying to help you," he insisted, focusing on the moment. "I need both of you to press your thumb here. You will have a code for an electronic lock box."

Jacob and Desiree exchanged glances, but didn't move.

"Do it! I have nothing to lose or gain anymore. She's gone, and I don't want this anymore. There is a chance you might find a way to clear yourself. It's everything here. You see, humans aren't perfect, and our little scheme a failure. It's all you got."

Jacob pressed his thumb to the tablet, while maintaining eye contact with Ramón.

"We will see."

Desiree followed.

"*Is this episode of* Family Feud *over?*" Mohammed craned his neck as he scanned the space for movement. "*Fuck. Where the hell did they come from? We got company, wolves. There are a few of them. Everyone keep quiet, get your weapons ready.*"

Then the sounds began. A cacophony of monsters in the form of hissing like a valve of steam being released. It was the same as when the dropship opened with the dying man.

"*Eyes in all directions, people.*"

The small band put their backs to each other.

Ramón took a bag slung across his chest and handed it to Jacob without looking at him. "Consider this an apology. I snagged it from the lab with the bacteria. You can run, space is big, but maybe you need to clear your name, because this is only a small portion of what is going on."

"*What's this?*"

"Your lucky day and lottery ticket. Activated bacteria, and a chip with the formulas for activation and neutralization." He turned. "Leticia, go with Jacob and get him out of here."

"*Why aren't they attacking?*" Frida said.

It was exactly as she said. The Xenomorphs hissed and snapped at the group without attacking. Leticia maintained eye contact with a beast that had no visible eyes, but she damn well knew they saw everything.

"It's the bacteria," she said. "What Ramón was carrying. Fucking go! This is your chance. I'm not leaving—this is my mission. Backup should be here soon. Desiree, turn on your sensors and get Jacob out of here."

"*Leticia, we can all get out of here. Let's stay like this.*"

"No we can't. Look at them." Three Xenomorphs were gathering just beyond Jacob, who was holding the activated bacteria. "They will attack, even if we pass the bacteria around like a blunt at a party. No, they'll pick us off one-by-one and use the confusion to strike the rest. Desiree, go now with Jacob."

Desiree frowned, but then she braced herself.

"Will do, *jefa*," she said. "*As soon as we are clear I will try to find out where the fucking backup is.*" She squeezed Jacob's bicep to draw him away.

"*Leticia!*" he shouted.

Then they were gone. Laying down fire to cover them, Leticia ignored his desire to stay and fight these things head on. Now she had to get Ramón out. He knew weapons, had brokered arms deals, but didn't have any combat experience. Without her backing him up, he was as good as dead.

"It's time to use your good arm, Frida."

Frida grabbed a timed grenade from her waist band and aimed for pockets in the wall of human cocoons and open bodies. The more of the facility they could take down, the better. She made three perfect pitches. She had the fourth in hand when a black claw came from her right and grabbed her ankle.

"*Leticia!*"

Her scream made them turn. She hit the ground, and one of the monsters hovered over her. With the grenade still in her hand she grabbed the Xenomorph back. As it lifted her into the air, Mohammed took another one from his pocket. Frida looked back and gave them a thumbs-up.

The inner mandible pushed out between the hideous jaws.

Frida's body and the Xenomorph shattered together.

"Move!" Leticia bellowed. "Which way, Ramón!"

"*Back! We go back!*"

They ran up the spiral corridor. Leticia fired behind them, at times eliciting a shriek, until they were back into the lab.

"*It's a risk, but there's a ventilation system here,*" he said. "*Only one way out.*" Ramón typed fast. A square vent opened at the base of a wall at the far end of the lab. Behind them, Mohammed tossed a grenade toward the entrance. Leticia's watch vibrated.

Desiree and Jacob had made it out.

All the sensor mines were hot and ready to blast anything bigger than a human. She felt a small pinch of relief before slipping into the shaft with Mohammed and Ramón. The heat went from manageable to choking, and she blessed the bandana around her forehead. It was a source of comfort and protection, like Santa Muerte inked on her back.

"Ramón, lead the way as fast as you can. We're going to suffocate if we don't move." The bandana around her forehead leaked sweat as she hunched, wading through muck that smelled like the sewage system had been damaged. She did the best she could to calm herself and use as little oxygen as possible. No amount of training or physical strength would get her out of this trap if she couldn't be strong in mind.

The mind and soul are muscles. They were what determined success or failure. What propelled the soldaderas in war and got her mother through an unjust lockup. As the leader, the solution fell to her shoulders.

She closed her eyes and thought of her niece and nephew, toddling with their chubby legs in diapers, the aroma of Roseanna's borracho beans—without alcohol—cooking for hours.

Only Santa Muerte could save them, because some ruthless god had created these things in their image. Faith had fled Leticia the day she was arrested for assault. But now…

"Where's Vasquez?"

Leticia stopped. The voice was in her ear.

"Here—I'm here. What's good, backup?"

Something was familiar. It couldn't be…

"Who is this?"

"It's Major Haas."

"Listen to me," Leticia said. "We're practically in a fucking mine shaft. As hot as balls in a polyester suit on prom night. Can you register our location?"

"Depends how deep you are. Some of these facilities are built with tech to block scanners. They don't want their private business exposed."

Ramón shook his head.

"Good," Leticia said. "No tech. Give us some time to get out of here, and then blow it. This place has to be torched."

"Holy shit." Haas' voice broke with static.

"What? Talk to me!"

"I don't know what the hell is going on down there, but it looks like you got lice. There's an open escape hatch. The fuck is crawling out of there?"

"Blast them!" Leticia shook her head. Rolling sweat made her neck itch. "Kill them all! Don't let a single one off this building. Circle them like vultures!"

"*Roger, that. Get out of there, because blowing it all might be the only way. Holy shit! One just—*" The sound of grenades echoed through the building and in her earpiece, followed by the hideous shrieks.

The facility above them shook.

29

"*Jefa, I have a launcher at the base of the pyramid, below the hatch.*" Desiree's voice piped through her earpiece. "*It will do what it does until it runs out of grenades.*"

"*Fuck,*" Ramón said. "*You have to see this. This… wasn't supposed to happen. Not like this.*" He shoved his tablet in front of Leticia.

Two heavily weaponized dropships circled the top of the pyramid, blasting the Xenomorphs that were scaling the walls, trying to find a way out. Two of the monsters leapt and reached one of the ships, where they began tossing out soldiers. Then the entire thing was going down in flames like a paper plane.

Haas was having none of it. Her crew blasted the Xenomorphs and the ship that could not be saved. The sight gave Leticia some hope they just might make it out alive. Haas could be a cold-blooded bastard, if this was *the* Haas, but as long as she didn't do Leticia the dirty again, she was okay.

Leticia turned to Ramón and Mohammed. "We get out now. Move. We're not going to worry about the maternity ward back there. We have backup."

They picked up their pace with renewed vigor. Toward the end of the shaft blue and red lights flickered and it seemed to slope upward. Ramón tapped on the tablet.

"*I've opened the other side.*"

Mohammed forced his way to the front with his pulse rifle aimed. "*I want the first taste of whatever is there, for my Nathan.*" He touched the second pair of dog tags around his neck. Then they entered another space that could have been anywhere.

"Ramón, where…" His eyes moved above her head. She turned with her pulse rifle ready to be fired. Mohammed followed her actions.

The amorphous shadow against the wall stretched across with a menacing reach until she came into sight. The queen was a violated monstrosity. Her missing body parts had been replaced by a rage as she shrieked with only half of a mouth. The gaping hole poured saliva, with the long inner mandible swerving and striking at the air with a cobra's speed. It had grown to compensate for its changed anatomy.

La Reina had no hands or feet, but she used the thorned bony bayonets to move across the floor. She heaved and jolted forward, the umbilical-like cord quivered in her wake. With a sickening realization, Leticia saw that she was still producing eggs. Tarantula-like face-huggers followed in her wake and scrambled toward them on the floor. The ground was a carpet of the slimy creatures that possessed only one instinct before they gave their existence over to the perpetuation to their species. They were willing to sacrifice without knowing they were the sacrifice.

"Mohammed, now would be a good time to use that flamethrower."

"*This way!*" Ramón shouted.

Both Leticia and Mohammed unleashed fire on the face-huggers as they began to run in Ramón's direction. With a gurgle the Xenomorph queen regurgitated a greenish liquid. It fizzed and bubbled, and the onslaught of liquid flowed with the speed of magma. A river of acid. Mohammed unleashed a round on the cord containing the eggs.

"How far, Ramón?"

"*Keep going. Almost there.*"

Leticia turned to shoot more rounds at the queen. As Mohammed took aim to do the same, the monstrosity grabbed him by the waist and tossed him in the air as it coiled what remained of its tail around his body. Her inner mandible was a barbed vine that had unnatural dexterity. His weapon fired in the air as the barbs pierced his flesh to spew blood with the power of a sprinkler system. Leticia screamed and fired through a shower of blood.

The queen released his body as she convulsed from the shots. She collapsed to the ground in a pile of chartreuse-and-black pulp. Mohammed didn't move as his body smoked and sank into the acid.

"How the fuck is this happening, Ramón?"

"*I don't know,*" he shouted back. "*Dr. Moon is the one who named her La Reina. Said she was acting funny, that she would evolve to escape.*"

"Funny?" Behind them in the tunnel, she heard a scabbling on metal. "There isn't anything funny about this."

He pointed. "*Through there. We should be close to an exit.*" Ramón tapped the tablet and opened a metal door that would have been invisible to the casual passer-by. "*Get ready to jump.*"

They managed to make it through. Leticia pressed hard on the trigger on her rifle, and as more face-huggers leapt, the door slammed shut. They fell a short distance and landed with a splash in the semi-darkness of a larger chamber. Though a ruin, it didn't have the coating of resin. Instead they stood knee-deep in water thick with slime and blood.

The only sound was of trickling water. The reassuring blasts from Haas' crew had stopped, and there was no choice but to move forward. They dragged their legs through the muck.

"*It should take about ten minutes,*" he said, still gripping the tablet, "*then we can find our way out.*" She tried to pass him, to be the first out to secure the area, but Ramón matched her pace.

"Let me go first, hermano."

He ignored her and pushed ahead through the opening. She could see light from where artillery had blasted through the exterior.

Abruptly he stopped and looked up.

A Xenomorph rose from the water to spread its arms and legs wide enough to display its true size as it towered over Ramón. It whipped its tail in the air and darted it toward them with the anger of a threatened scorpion.

"Move, Ramón!"

But he was transfixed. "*So you are what we all chase, but can't seem to tame. Perfection…*"

"I said *mueves*, dammit!" she bellowed. "I need a shot and it's going to ricochet in here." As he turned, the tail speared him through the chest. His eyes widened and blood dribbled down his mouth. Ramón stretched both arms out toward Leticia.

"*Do it,*" he said. "*I deserve it. Don't leave unfinished business, sister.*"

Leticia brought her gun up. There were tears in her eyes that she refused to allow to fall until this was done. Before she could pull the trigger, however, a blast shot through his forehead. It also hit the Xenomorph. Flesh and blood mushroomed in her direction as they fell. She screamed in pain at the sight of losing Ramón and of her skin being seared, but she kept to her feet and looked to the blasted entrance.

Desiree stood with pulse rifle in hand.

"*I'm not losing you, too.*"

Her emotions released, Leticia screamed through tears. After what seemed like an eternity, but was only a few moments, she closed them off again.

"Gracias, mi amiga," she said. "Give me a report."

"*Haas is ready to land. Looks like we got 'em. I'll meet you in the front of the facility.*"

Leticia ran to Desiree and embraced her. "Thank you, hermana. Las Lobas."

"We ain't done." Tears fell from Desiree's eyes. "Fuck this joint. We need to turn it into a bonfire."

"Give me a minute."

"I'll cover you. Hurry."

Leticia turned to find Ramón's body. She used her pistol to shoot through the Xenomorph tail and release him from its spear. The backfire of Xenomorph blood still sizzled her skin to fajita meat, but the sight of her brother made her forget any physical pain she felt. He was not a good man. The worst, this had been his plan, with that cabrona Julia Yutani.

But he was still blood.

Her boots splashed through blood, water, and viscera. There would be no salvaging this facility. She would only take Ramón's body, and torch the rest. Mohammed was in too many pieces to be carried out, and it was too hot to go back in.

May Las Lobas rest in power.

When she emerged from the building pulling her brother's corpse by the arm, Jacob raced toward her, stopped short, and placed one hand on her hip.

"Leticia... I'm so—"

"I know you mean well," she said, switching off her comms as she laid him down, still holding his hand. She unhooked a chain from around his neck, and stowed it in a pocket. "He brought it upon himself. He knew he was dancing with the devil—Julia, too."

"What do you want me to do?" Desiree asked.

Leticia couldn't look her in the eye. Even though there was no way Leticia could have saved the crew, the guilt remained. That was the gig, though. She let go of Ramón's hand and let it fall, before raising her eyes to Jacob.

"We have to torch the entire premises. We have all the information we need." She looked back. "That place is not even a tomb, it's a slaughterhouse. I know it means a lot to you, but it has to be done. We won't get answers from those things, and we won't get them from the people who were trying to fuck with a beast built to not be controlled or studied."

"Smoke and mirrors," he said, following her gaze. "Everything we do is just smoke and mirrors. I feel like a fool. Maybe Julia and Ramón were right. All of this has left me questioning everything." He looked at her. "Do whatever you want."

"Smoke and mirrors, eh," she replied. "That is all we are, so it makes sense that it's what we build—but we can choose to be the light reflecting on that mirror. You can't give up. My mother blew herself up to keep these things from getting out. She took her own life for a world that had locked her up, made her abandon her children, and gave her no other choice but to be battle fodder. You have power, Jacob, and so do I.

"We will blow this facility up and bring down more boots to make sure none are left. Then you rebuild here from scratch and do it your way. So people like my mother can have a real chance."

There was the sound of engines and a fighter ship landed. The hatch opened and Leticia couldn't believe her eyes for the who-was-counting-fucking time. It *was* Haas, who had stolen her promotion.

"When I heard Vasquez I wasn't sure if it was you."

"Same. I want to say it's not a pleasure, but you showed up. That counts for a lot." She gave a grim smile. "By the way, you stole my promotion, and now it looks like you stole my hairstyle."

Haas didn't answer, and looked at the body beyond Leticia. She had heard everything on their connected communication link. Then she ran her hands over her scalp.

"Take it as a high form of flattery," she said. "I'm glad I could come through here."

"It would have been nice if you could have arrived a little sooner, but me, too." Leticia extended a hand. "Teamwork from here on out."

Haas took it, giving it a solid shake. "I'll give them the word to place explosives inside, to destroy everything."

"As long as there's nothing left to scavenge, including the Xenomorphs," Jacob said, and Haas looked as if she was noticing him for the first time.

"I agree," Leticia said. "Can we get as many of them as possible to the mud pots? That seems like the only guarantee."

Haas took a moment to think. "I got a net we can load them into, then drop them from the sky."

"What about the ocean?" Desiree said.

"No." Jacob shook his head. "We don't know what has evolved on the ocean floor, and I haven't seen all the files of what they were doing here. Keep this planet as clean as possible."

"We start with cremating Ramón, then scattering his ashes in the sea. He should remain here with the results of his work."

"You do what you need to do, Vasquez," Haas said. "You can count on us to start the clean-up. And for what it's worth, I'm sorry about your brother."

"I appreciate that, Haas. Thank you."

"And another thing," she said, and it was her turn to smile. "I'm an asshole. I got that job and had to grow up a bit by doing it day-in and day-out. It took me down a notch. Some of the shit I saw, had to do, humbled me in ways I wish I didn't have to experience. Glory for ego's sake is a bitch."

Leticia opened her palm to receive a light slap. "I appreciate that, too. I think we can call it even."

30

The waves were larger and more violent than any she had ever seen. The crests far from the shore looked powerful enough to obliterate a skyscraper. They were walls of water and beauty as they hit spires of basalt. The energy from the waves created a mist that hovered in the air. Leticia could smell and taste it when she licked her lips. But the sound… If her soul could scream it would sound like this. The water did what it did with little care of anything else. It was strange, though, to not see gulls in the air or any creatures leaping from the water.

She couldn't help but feel that everything came full circle, or was recycled if not resolved. Leticia had accomplished everything she had, as a young girl, set out to accomplish, but in the moment, she felt just as lost as she had before receiving the letter from her mother.

Once again, she needed to find her internal compass.

When she raised an upturned palm, fat drops of water splashed against her skin.

"It also rains here."

"It does indeed," Jacob said. "Didn't pack any umbrellas, though." The droplets became larger and fell more rapidly, soaking them both.

"This is pretty majestic… wow," she said. "You know if anything lives in those waters?" She could feel his hand on the small of her back.

"No, not from what I've been told. Then again, that seems unlikely, and there aren't many things I can trust anymore. To be honest, after all this I don't care to find out—but all that unbridled power…" He looked out to sea again. "We could harness that. At least that was the hope."

"I'll bet that's exactly what they said about the Xenomorphs, time and time again. It's in people's deceptions that you see their truths. Now you know the truth of Weyland-Yutani. I know the truth of my brother."

"It's not the same…" he began. "I guess you read the files."

"Yes, I did, and this I know—humans always want to control what they don't understand, in order to be less fearful of it. Then they are surprised their actions lead to chaos. It's like squeezing a lemon and expecting orange juice." She let out a sigh. "I guess part of me thought this would be an escape.

"I've seen razed villages, known people who lost their lives because of a choice I had to make on a moment's notice. I can't forget seeing bloated bodies torn by God-knows-what weapon. If the soul is made from anything, then I would say hope, or maybe love. See enough tragedy, and a piece of your own soul ignites, and sanity floats away as ash until nothing is left."

"Why did you want to scatter his ashes here?"

Leticia looked at the rum bottle acting as an urn, and chuckled. "He loved his damn boat, *Sail La Vie*. What a dumb name, but goddamn I loved some of the times we had on there with his kids, when I was on leave. Didn't mind that all he did was quiz me on my work. Now I understand why.

"What I wouldn't give to be listening to Christopher Cross's 'Sailing' and drinking a vodka and soda. Extra lime to go with the wind in my hair. A little sunburn on my cheeks. At least we had a few good memories. I figured this would be the best place to send him off. And his kids… Twins like us."

Leticia curled into Jacob's body as sobs began causing her chest to hitch. He squeezed her tighter, allowing his own tears to fall.

"They have their mother," he offered. "They are safe. I'm so sorry… If I had known—" He stopped, then added, "You have me."

Leticia broke away from him and wiped her eyes and nose with the back of her hand. She walked toward the steep cliff edge that filled her with dread. The grayish blue current churned with the ferocity of Neptune blue. There was no surviving these waters.

"Adios, hermano. See you next lifetime."

She took a few steps back, then dashed three steps forward to throw the rum bottle filled with Ramón's ashes into the gigantic waves. Leticia felt ready to die, because clearly death had plans for her and her bloodline. Might as well embrace it, and fuck it all the way to the afterlife.

Jacob stood behind her with another bottle.

"Tell me what to do." He placed a hand on her waist.

She grabbed the Hibiki from his hand and took a long swig. "Come to my bed in an hour, and don't leave."

He kissed her neck. "Whatever you need."

She looked back at him. "I need you to be a Vickers. You need to clear your name. Remove the deception and start your own company. Fight, Jacob. We *fight*, goddammit!"

"I'm not a warrior. I don't have what you have."

"Really? Because what I saw today says you are. We all are—we just have to have fucking guts to earn that title and claim it. I don't have any trust fund or a name in lights, but I *am* the motherfucking light. My mother was. My grandmother… my grandmother Francisca sacrificed her life so her daughter, my mother, could live."

"Then I'll follow you." Tears streamed again from Jacob's eyes. "Weyland-Yutani wants a war? They have it. I will clear my name even if I forfeit my fortune."

By the time Leticia returned to their position just outside of the Olinka One facility, Haas had left to find the civilians left near the sulfur fields and reassure them that help had arrived and to get them on the ship orbiting above.

"It's just the three of us now," Leticia said, looking around. "You think we're safe? What about weapons?"

"From what the scanners say… probably," Desiree said. "To be honest, that building is pretty complex. It's like a puzzle cube inside. Plus, those mines are still active. Haas will blow it all to hell when we move out at first light. Then this place will be empty again, except for the elements.

"As for weapons, there's nothing left," she added. "We took it all in with us. Jacob and I used all our rounds shooting at anything that moved, to keep our way clear. Flamethrowers, but you gotta get kinda close to hit one of those things. There's the Narwhal, but that would be tough to… Wait, I have a pistol!"

Leticia smirked. "Switchblade, and the launcher on the other side of the building, if it's still intact." She gestured back toward the ship. "Before you get any shut-eye, we need to bury the bacteria, insurance for a later date if we need evidence of what we witnessed. Ramón gave Jacob a live sample, plus the formulas for activation and neutralization. Those we keep on us." Another sigh. "Guess he developed a conscience, just a little too late."

"Got it, jefa."

Desiree wore a mask of grief. Her eyes red from crying on and off.

"Let's do it, and get some rest," Leticia said. "You fucking earned it."

"So did you, jefa." Desiree left to seek out the package with the bacteria, and to prepare a roll-out mat inside their dropship. Jacob was already on board, falling in and out of sleep as he read the files Ramón had given him. Leticia looked to the facility one last time before turning and walking away.

The first explosion rocked the dropship.

Leticia jumped from the floor and grabbed the flamethrower by the hatch. Desiree followed suit, but ran to switch on the flood lights attached to the ship. The rain had stopped and in the semidarkness two Xenomorphs lay twitching on the ground, blown to kibble from the sensor mines but leaving a space without protection. She and Leticia exchanged glances.

"We can get the bacteria," Desiree suggested.

"No. It stays buried."

"I'll call Haas and get the launcher."

"No time…"

Out from the bombed maw of the Olinka One facility, another Xenomorph emerged. It had a large hood that extended behind its head, and horns that were as sharp as its fangs protruding from its skull. This was her crown. The black mangled tail her scepter of death. She was larger than the other two.

This was La Reina.

Her missing jaw had only served to make her evolve into a more lethal creature. Her body had become a grand phoenix worthy of rising—she commanded respect. Where the ends of her legs and arms had been amputated, there were thick spikes lined with spirals of thorns. Free of the confining limitations of the tunnels, she walked on the spikes with the agility of a ballerina on her tiptoes.

The spikes on her arms helped to move her forward. The inner mandible had the same thick ridges and could now reach to the top of her hood. The mouth at the end snapped with a powerful crack to compensate for her missing lower jaw. Leticia had never before seen fangs the length of a human head.

La Reina screeched and hissed, then began to move toward them with determination. From the corner of her eye, Leticia noticed the Narwhal. It wasn't ideal, but...

"Go!" she commanded. "Take the ship and get out of here!"

"No!" Jacob said, standing at the hatch. "We stay."

"I agree with, Jacob. You need backup."

Without bothering to argue Leticia hopped onto the vehicle and switched on the launcher. The vehicle wouldn't be nearly as effective here on land, but she'd have to make it work. It was all they had.

"Adios, pendeja. Your reign is over."

She accelerated as hard as she could. With one hand she guided the Narwhal and the other she slapped the launcher. It blinked and as La Reina leapt forward, the grenade shot forward. Leticia swerved with both hands to a hard right. She could smell the flesh on her fingers sizzling. The Narwhal skidded into the ruins of Olinka One, and she looked back.

La Reina had barely been fazed.

And now she was *pissed*.

Desiree kneeled, firing a small pistol and doing minor damage to the large creature. La Reina charged again, but this time Leticia revved the Narwhal and released the harpoon into the leaping form. La Reina shrieked as it pierced her chest.

If only the Narwhal had enough power for what she was about to do next. Her thumb pushed the propulsion system to max, and she flew from Olinka One toward the sulfur fields not far off. She had to risk falling through the surface or flying into a fumarole. Either way, La Reina would be going, too.

The grotesque Xenomorph screeched as Leticia dragged her past the dropship. Jacob crouched in wait and blasted flames toward La Reina. Desiree had stopped shooting and held a tablet. Then Leticia was past them and couldn't look back as she raced toward the sulfur field at best speed.

It was just coming into view.

Smoke blocked her vision, and the Narwhal began to slow. La Reina must have dug her spiny arms and legs into the ground.

"Santa Muerte, ancestor soldaderas, Jenette Vasquez—see me through!" She revved the engine one last time as a large mud pot bubbled ahead. In an instant she felt herself jerk backward.

The Narwhal skidded left to right.

Leticia held on to the handlebars and looked back. As she dug with her arm and leg talons, La Reina's bulk had disturbed a sinkhole. Smoke rose from her body where the flames had licked her hardened exterior, but to no effect—that was what her mutation had accomplished. It hardened her exterior until it seemed able to survive anything.

The harpoon remained embedded, and it was dragging Leticia down with her foe. She scanned the unstable ground, not knowing what would happen if she jumped. Closer and closer she slid.

Her watch vibrated. Leticia glanced at it.

Santa Muerte still has my back!

Desiree had sent her a tracked map of the sulfur fields. She detached the harpoon and the cable snapped back as La Reina's head began bobbing up and down as she attempted to use her spikes to lift herself out of the hungry ground. The long, serpent-like mandible waved in the air, still snapping with the fury of survival.

The engine of the Narwhal finally died and Leticia jumped off, keeping an eye out on her watch. As she did, a large belch of gas exploded beneath the Xenomorph, piercing her carapace, charring every inch of her body, then dragging her once and for all into her sulfuric grave.

The perfect funeral for a demon that should not exist.

The sky began to lighten, with both moons and sun becoming visible. Jacob and Desiree stood in the distance.

Leticia looked up. "Thank you."

Her watch vibrated again. According to the map the ground beneath her feet was unstable, so she began to jog to make it to the edge. She raised her arm to keep an eye on the map as the ground rumbled behind her. Hot mud and water landed to her side as geysers began to spew their hot spittle from the depths of the planet.

Picking up her pace she began to run hard, pumping arms that wanted to fall off from exhaustion—but she couldn't call herself a Vasquez, soldadera, or Marine Raider if she didn't see this through to the bitter fucking end, even if it ended in blood and fire.

The other side was just there.

Desiree and Jacob had terror in their eyes, which was all she needed to know with the ground continuing to shake at her heels.

"Now!" Jacob bellowed. Leticia dove and tumbled onto solid ground. Instantly they were next to her and pulling her farther back. A large hole had opened. She made it with moments to spare.

"What you just did, jefa, it's fucking miraculous. One for the books."

"Get me the fuck out of here please." Leticia's chest heaved as she grabbed Jacob's arm. She needed to feel him close, otherwise she might think this was just a dream. "And get me some of that rich boy liquor, while you're at it."

Jacob chuckled. "You can have anything you want. There is only one La Reina now."

31

None of them wanted to stay there. As Haas flew in to bomb the facility to hell, Desiree, Jacob, and Leticia were picked up to be taken to the main ship that orbited overhead. There they would decide what the next move would be.

Still lost in the numbness of her twin being dead, Leticia stared at the burning wick of a white candle on the altar she had created using small wildflowers, Olinka soil, a photo of her mother, and some of Ramón's ashes not thrown into the sea. She had located two sheets of paper and a pencil. Technology was wonderful, but sometimes it wasn't enough. While she would send letters electronically, under these circumstances it felt right to write them down first for Ramón's children.

She still had a few of his personal items as well, including the dog tags she had made for him as a joke. When the opportunity arose she would send the letters and mementos back to Earth. They would get there when they were meant to, at the right time.

The handwritten words would be her vow to continue the work of her mother and their bloodline. The frigid emptiness of space expanded within her heart as she thought of her mother's letter and what she said about a switchblade not being enough out here. She was right. On the floor she had Xenomorph teeth she had taken from one of the skulls. She also had a large branch shaped like a club. With the switchblade she would whittle the wood to create what she needed it to be.

Like a jigsaw she arranged the teeth to surround the wood with which she would create a weapon. It was a weapon used by the Aztecs, a macuahuitl. Historically, it was a handheld club with obsidian points embedded in the wood along the sides, but this one would be embedded with the teeth of the very enemy she would use it to cut down.

Sorrow was a drowning man's acknowledgment of defeat, she knew, but rage could be a life raft until feet found dry ground again. Leticia was filled with new determination. At the foot of her altar was the other Xenomorph skull she had kept from the sulfur fields. The strange shape of the bone still didn't register as real. The universe was so very different from what she ever imagined.

At least she knew they were not indestructible. This was proof of it. They had fought like true warriors against this thing. On the top she carved "El riesgo siempre vive" and the names of her fallen crew, including Ramón. A token and reminder. Her mother would be proud. A life for a life.

Because in life we experience many deaths. There were the deaths of relationships, of dreams, of the illusions she held of herself and others. Life was full of many transformations, and there could be no beginning without a death. The Xenomorph egg gave way to the face-hugger, which died, but not until after it had found a host. The host only lived until the chestburster was ready to break free.

Embracing death was the only way to live without fear.

May our mother's spirit live on inside of me.

If she had her way, she would destroy an entire plane—or as many of them as she could find—to defeat the enemy. Then go after the men who sought to tame such things. Those creatures didn't end up out here on their own, and they would be taken somewhere else or unleashed. They took her mother, and now her brother.

Leticia remained still in the dim light of the candle.

Jacob entered their room. "I wanted to come check on you. If you still want to be alone, I can go."

"No," she said. "We should talk." He looked startled at that. "What are we doing?" she continued. "We blast a few, then what? I don't know how I can go back, knowing what I now know."

Jacob sat on the floor next to her. "I've been drinking and thinking the same thing. How can I set up a utopia, here or anywhere, and turn a blind eye to what others are doing out there with the Xenomorphs and the bacteria? Those parasites? Miniature Xenomorphs meant to be ingested? I thought we were fighting for clean water, a pure life. If these things are supposed to be some sort of weapon, eventually my vision won't matter because we will all be dead."

"Then we need to find where they are, or if they have some home world," she said. "We blow it."

"Genocide. Even if the Xenomorphs contribute nothing to the universe. And what about the people who will die in the process? You want to hand them that sentence? How will they be remembered in history? Or us?" He gave her a moment to think about that, then asked, "Have you read through the files?"

"A few, but I couldn't concentrate."

"Well, they seem to be everywhere. There are floating labs... Weird shit you only read about on conspiracy sites. This is far from isolated, and it's only a matter of time before something hits Earth. We like to posture about the apocalypse, yet we are actively engineering it. Messing with things we can't possibly understand, or control, is our own apocalypse." Anger filled his expression. "Fucking Weyland-Yutani."

"I hear you, but you of all people should know that history will repeat itself, and these monsters have no consciousness or values within their blind bloodlust. As well, there will always be men who will seek them out for gain."

Jacob took a swig of Hibiki before extending the bottle to Leticia.

"I needed that for what I am about to say. How about instead of making a grand—and high-profile—gesture by destroying an entire planet, we locate the monsters wherever they are, and infect them with the bacteria. We become the pest control."

"And Olinka? Your paradise?"

"Do we ever know what any of this is about, or where we stand? I can promise you one thing—those things don't. What an advantage. They are the epitome of 'ignorance is bliss.'"

"You're talking like a drunk philosophy student now."

"Student… More like fool."

"Aren't we all fools, looking for signs, misreading information, overthinking?"

"There's one thing I don't overthink or misread."

"What's that?"

Jacob scooted closer. "How I feel about you. The moment I laid eyes on you, I knew my world would never be the same. You would be mine or I would have to give you up forever. All I know is, I choose forever with you, and try to stop this. You are the most amazing woman I have ever met. Now we have the rest of whatever time we have left. If I'm going to die it might as well be next to you.

"I know without any doubt you are the one to do whatever it takes," he said. "You love hard and you fight hard. And you must know… in this short time we've spent together, I've fallen hard. Olinka can be my retirement. For now, I let it go and see what happens. No one will be allowed on the planet. It's mine."

"Letting go and allowing yourself to be carried by the whims of this universe," she said. "I've had to let go of my parents, Roseanna, and now Ramón. It ain't easy. Guess I'll have to trust what comes next."

Leticia leaned in and kissed Jacob tenderly. He gave her peace and a sense of home.

"I choose you, too, this mission whatever it turns out to be, and however far or long it takes. For now, let's go to bed. Forever begins tomorrow."

Jacob's hold on her body was tighter than before. The warmth of his hand on her hip was an anchor to what it meant to be human. This could be it for her, for both of them. They might be each other's last lovers. As much as she didn't want to know anything about romance, there was something poetic about their relationship. He made every other man's kiss and touch feel lukewarm. It made her think of when she asked Roseanna advice when it came to love.

"*I have had my fair share of lovers and fuckboys,*" her tía had said, "*and my best advice is don't give yourself away cheaply, and settle. You didn't stay with Avery. On the flip side, if a dude can't afford to give you all of his heart, then you are too damned expensive.*"

Here Jacob was, giving her his all.

Breaking away from his embrace she pressed the front of the drawer on the side of the bed. A small light illuminated. As she sat up she caught a reflection—in the full-length mirror on the closet door and the smaller mirror on the desk—of her Santa Muerte tattoo. The image writhed in the low light, and as she twisted and moved it took the form of a Xenomorph.

She snapped her eyes away.

That wasn't what she wanted, not right now.

One of the red bandanas that belonged to her mother always remained close, whenever she slept. She placed it on a plank jutting from the wall that served as a side table. Leticia kissed three fingertips and touched the faded cloth.

Looking at it made her think of "Dancing in the Dark" by Springsteen and her new relationship with Jacob. There were only so many strangers she could sleep with, or friends to meet for drinks, but here she was a hired gun. Dead or alive, she would be dancing in the dark for years to come.

ACKNOWLEDGEMENTS

I want to acknowledge Christopher Golden who sent an email on my behalf to Titan for an introduction. Steve Saffel is a shining star when it comes to editors. He has believed in me from day one and has never waned in his support. Working with him is fun! I will be forever grateful for this opportunity and the joy it has given me. I hope it will bring joy and entertainment to those who read it. For others, I hope it will inspire them to tell a story of their own even if it has never been told before.

From Titan: Nick Landau, Vivian Cheung, Laura Price, Michael Beale, Louise Pearce, Kevin Eddy, Katharine Carroll, and Julia Lloyd. At 20th Century Studios: Nicole Spiegel, Sarah Huck, and Kendrick Pejoro.

Beth Marshea from Ladderbird Lit. She has been a wonderful advocate of my work!

Clara Čarija who makes sure all the details are correct and in order.

ABOUT THE AUTHOR

V. Castro is a two-time Bram Stoker Award®-nominated author of *Immortal Pleasures, Aliens: Vasquez, The Haunting of Alejandra, The Queen of The Cicadas, Goddess of Filth, Hairspray and Switchblades,* and *Out of Atzlan.* She is a Mexican American expat living in the UK. As a full-time mother, she dedicates her time to her family and writing. Her official site is vcastrostories.com.

For more fantastic fiction, author events,
exclusive excerpts, competitions, limited editions and more

VISIT OUR WEBSITE
titanbooks.com

LIKE US ON FACEBOOK
facebook.com/titanbooks

FOLLOW US ON TWITTER AND INSTAGRAM
@TitanBooks

EMAIL US
readerfeedback@titanemail.com